More Praise For

TONY HILLERMAN AND THREE JIM CHEE MYSTERIES

PEOPLE OF DARKNESS

"Great suspense." —*The Chicago Tribune*

"Superb mystery.... A spine-tingling cat-and-mouse chase." —*The Washington Post*

"Fine action... and plenty of Hillerman's specialty, tribal legends and customs and wonderfully described New Mexican scenery." —*The San Francisco Examiner*

THE DARK WIND

"Hillerman's best book in an already strong series." —*The New Republic*

"A beauty of a thriller... exotic, compelling." —*The Philadelphia Inquirer*

"Background, characters, story—all first rate." —*Amarillo Texas News*

THE GHOSTWAY

"All the flavor and exoticism one associates with Mr. Hillerman... one of the best in the series." —*New York Times Book Review*

"Tony Hillerman's Jim Chee mysteries can't be recommended too highly." —*Dallas Morning News*

"A first-rate story of suspense and mystery." —*The New Yorker*

TONY HILLERMAN

THREE JIM CHEE MYSTERIES

TONY HILLERMAN

THREE JIM CHEE MYSTERIES

PEOPLE OF DARKNESS
THE DARK WIND
THE GHOSTWAY

WINGS BOOKS
NEW YORK • AVENEL, NEW JERSEY

This 1993 edition is published by Wings Books,
distributed by Random House Value Publishing, Inc.,
40 Engelhard Avenue, Avenel, New Jersey 07001
by arrangement with HarperCollins Publishers.

Random House
New York • Toronto • London • Sydney • Auckland

Printed and bound in the United States of America

Library of Congress Cataloging-in-Publication Data

Hillerman, Tony
Three Jim Chee mysteries / Tony Hillerman.
p. cm.
Contents: People of darkness—The dark wind—The ghostway.
ISBN 0-517-09281-6
1. Chee, Jim (Fictitious character)—Fiction. 2. Detective and mystery stories. American. 3. Police—Southwestern States—Fiction.
4. Navajo Indians—Fiction. I. Title.
PS3558.I45A6 1993
813′.54—dc20 93-3100
CIP

ISBN 0-517-09281-6

10 9 8 7 6 5 4 3

Contents

I

People of Darkness

1

IT WAS A JOB which required waiting for cultures to grow, for toxins to develop, for antibodies to form, for reagents to react. And while she waited, the bacteriologist would roll her wheelchair to the windows and look down upon the world. The world below was the parking lot of the Cancer Research and Treatment Center, the neighbor of the bacteriologist's Communicable Disease Laboratory on the University of New Mexico North Campus. It was a crowded lot, and a competitive one, and somewhere in the second year of watching it, the bacteriologist found herself familiar with its patterns. She knew when the meter maids made their rounds, and how long it usually took the tow truck to arrive, and what sort of violation provoked this ultimate punishment, and which vehicles tended to park illegally. She even knew of a romance which seemed to have flared between the female owner of a Datsun and the male owner of the blue Mercedes convertible that parked in the space reserved for one of the lofty administrators. Somewhere in that same second year she had started bringing her binoculars to the lab. She had finally left them there. They were in her hands now—focused upon a dirty green pickup truck which was nosing its way hesitatingly into a space guarded by a sign that read:

RESERVED FOR ASSOCIATE DIRECTOR
VIOLATORS WILL BE TOWED AT OWNERS EXPENSE

The bacteriologist had learned long ago that cancer patients tended to be scofflaws. They were dying and they knew it. In the face of that, other considerations became less important. But habits of civilized behavior still generally prevailed. It was rare to see such open defiance as the pickup was now demonstrating.

The defiant one was male, an Indian. Through the binoculars he didn't look defiant. He looked stolid and sick. He climbed laboriously from the cab. The bacteriologist noticed a suitcase on the passenger's seat and felt a sudden mild thrill of admiration. He was checking himself in, abandoning his truck forever to the mercies of the law. The nose thumbed at fate. But the Indian left the suitcase behind.

He was a large man, with the heavy torso and slender hips the bacteriologist had learned to identify with Navajos. He wore jeans and—despite the August heat—a denim jacket. He walked slowly toward the patients' entrance—a sick man's walk. He'll check himself in, the bacteriologist thought, and then he'll come back and get the suitcase, and move the truck.

Now there was another vehicle showing equally blatant illegality. It was a Chevrolet, silver-gray and new, which rolled past the green pickup and came to rest in the space reserved for the CRTC director. The driver's door opened and a slender man emerged, dressed in white, a straw hat pushed back on his head. The man stood for a moment, apparently looking at the pickup truck. Then he walked around his car and opened the door on the passenger's side. He leaned in, apparently working on something on the front seat. Finally he lifted out a grocery sack with its top folded down. He placed it on the bed of the pickup, among the boards and boxes against the cab. That done, he looked around him, studying the parking lot, the sidewalks, staring finally directly toward the bacteriologist. He was very blond, she saw. Almost an albino. Within a minute he was back in the gray Chevy, driving slowly away.

It was almost noon when the bacteriologist determined that the life form that had reproduced itself in her petri dish was not a food-poisoning salmonella but harmless nonpathogenic *Escherichia coli.* She made the required notes, completed the report, and pushed her chair back to the window. A tow truck had arrived. The bacteriologist focused her binoculars. The driver's helper was completing the attachment of the tow-ing bar to the rear of the green pickup. He waved his left hand and squatted beside the pickup wheel, watching something. The sound of the tow truck winch was lost to distance and insulated glass. But the bacteriologist could see the rear of the pickup begin to rise.

Abruptly, all vision was lost in a dazzle of light. The sound came a second later—a cannon-shot boom. The glass on the bacteriologist's window was pressed inward to its tolerance and just beyond; it cracked, then flexed violently outward, where its shards joined those of a hundred other windows raining down on the empty sidewalks below.

2

THE RAIN CONVERTED ITSELF abruptly into a flurry of popcorn snow. It rattled off Jim Chee's uniform hat, bounced down the collar of his uniform jacket, and made him shiver. It was the third day of November by the First National Bank of Grants calendar back on Chee's desk, and the very beginning of the Season When the Thunder Sleeps by the less rigid traditional calendar of the Dinee. By either calendar it was too early for this sort of weather—even at this mile-and-a-half altitude on the slope of Mount Taylor. Howard Morgan had predicted possible snow flurries on his Channel 7 weathercast, but Chee hadn't believed it. He'd left his winter coat back at the police station.

He glanced at his vehicle—a white Chevrolet with the seal of the Navajo Nation and the legend NAVAJO TRIBAL POLICE blazoned on its door. He could retire to the car and turn on the heater. He could seek shelter at the entryway of the residence of Benjamin J. Vines, and perhaps ring the bell a few more times in the hope of attracting someone. The bell made an odd singing sound which he could hear echoing pleasantly through the heavy door. While it had attracted no response at all, Chee was tempted to ring it again just to hear it. The third alternative was to turn up the collar of his jacket to ward off the sleet and continue satisfying his curiosity about this house. It had been designed, so he'd heard, by Frank Lloyd Wright, and was reputed to be the most expensive home in New Mexico. Chee's curiosity about it, as about all things in the white man's world, was intense. It was all the more intense at the moment because he might very soon enter that strange world. By December 10, less than five weeks away, he had to decide whether he would accept an appointment to the FBI, and a place in the world of singing doorbells.

He pulled his jacket collar around his neck, and folded down his hat brim, and continued his inspection. Chee was standing beside a semidetached triple garage. Like the house itself, it was built of native granite, linked to the structure by a low, curving wall of the same material. Just behind the wall, in a grassy plot no more than fifteen feet long, two small markers of black marble held Chee's attention. Gravestones. He leaned over the wall. The name chiseled into the one just to the right of where Chee stood was DILLON CHARLEY. Under it, the legend read:

He Didn't Remember When He Was Born
Died December 11, 1953
A Good Indian

Chee grinned. Was the sardonic double meaning intended? Was Vines, or whoever had ordered this legend carved, familiar with General Sheridan's dictum that the only good Indian was a dead Indian?

The stone to Chee's left read:

MRS. BENJAMIN J. VINES (ALICE)
Born April 13, 1909
Died June 4, 1949
A Faithful Woman

Faithful to B. J. Vines? It seemed an odd thing to put on a tombstone, but then everything about the white man's burial customs seemed odd to Chee. The Navajos lacked this sentimentality about corpses. Death robbed the body of its value. Even its identity was lost with the departing *chindi.* What the ghost left behind was something to be disposed of with a minimum risk of contamination to the living. The names of the dead were left unspoken, certainly not carved in stone.

Chee glanced again at the Charley tombstone. The name tugged at memory. There were no Charleys in Chee's clan—the Slow Talking Dinee—and none among the other clans that occupied the Rough Rock country of his family. But here on the east margin of the reservation—among the Salt Dinee, and the Many Goats Dinee, and the Mud Clan, and the Standing Rock Clan—the name seemed fairly common. And somebody named Charley had done something recently which he should be able to remember.

"Does it seem an unusual place for a graveyard?"

The voice came from behind him. A woman, perhaps in her mid fifties, with a thin, handsome, unsmiling face. She was wearing a coat of some expensive fur over jeans. A navy knit cap covered her ears. "It's one of B.J.'s little eccentricities, burying people by the garage. Are you Sergeant Chee?"

"Jim Chee," Chee said. The woman was looking at him, frowning critically, making no offer to shake his hand.

"You're younger than I expected," she said. "They told me you were an authority on your religion. Could that be right?"

"I'm learning to be a *yataalii,"* Chee said. He used the Navajo word because no English word really expressed it. The anthropologists called them shamans, and most people around the reservation called them singers, or medicine men, and none of these expressions really fit the role he would play for his people if he ever finished learning to play it. "Are you Mrs. Vines?" he asked.

"Of course," the woman said. "Rosemary Vines." She glanced at the tombstone. "The second Mrs. Vines. But let's get out of this sleet."

The house had puzzled Chee. Its front wall was a sweeping, virtually windowless curve, suggesting a natural formation of stone. But inside the massive entry doors and through the entry foyer the puzzle solved itself. The front was actually the back. The ceiling rose in a soaring curve toward a great wall of glass. Beyond the wall, the mountain slope fell away. Now the view was obscured by clouds and gusts of sleet, but on the usual day Chee knew the glass overlooked immense space—across the Laguna and Acoma Indian reservations to the south and east, southward across the forty-mile sea of cooled lava called the malpais toward the Zuni Mountains, and eastward across the Cañoncito Reservation to the great blue hump of the Sandia Mountains behind Albuquerque. The room was almost as spectacular as the view. A fireplace dominated the native-stone interior wall to Chee's left, with the pelt of a polar bear on the carpet by the hearth. On the wall to his right, a hundred glassy eyes stared from trophy heads. Chee stared back: water buffalo, impala, wildebeest, ibex, oryx, elk, mule deer, and a dozen species he couldn't name.

"It takes some getting used to," Mrs. Vines said. "But at least he keeps all the fierce-looking ones in his trophy room. These are the ones that couldn't bite back."

"I had heard he was a famous hunter," Chee said. "Didn't he win the Weatherby Trophy?"

"Twice," Rosemary Vines said. "In 1962 and 1971. Those were bad years for anything with fang, fur, or feathers." She draped the mink over the back of a sofa. Under it she wore a man's plaid shirt. She was a trim woman, one who took care of her body. But there was a tension about her. It showed in her face, in the way she held herself, in the taut muscles along her narrow jaw. Her hands twisted together at her belt line.

"I'll have a drink," Mrs. Vines said. "Join me?"

"No, thank you," Chee said.

"Coffee?"

"If it's no trouble."

Mrs. Vines spoke into the grillwork beside the fireplace. "Maria." The grille buzzed in response.

"Bring a Scotch and some coffee."

She turned back to Chee. "You're an experienced investigator. That's right, isn't it?" she asked. "And you're stationed at Crownpoint and you know everything about the Navajo religion."

"I was transferred to Crownpoint this year," Chee said, "and I know something about the customs of my people." This was not the time to tell this arrogant white woman that the Navajos had no religion in the white man's meaning of the term (in fact, had no word in their language for religion). First he would find out what she wanted with him.

"Sit down," Rosemary Vines said. She gestured toward a

huge blue sofa and seated herself in a chair of stainless-steel tubing and polished leather.

"Do you also understand witchcraft?" She perched at the edge of the chair, smiling, tense, her hands twisting now in her lap. "That business about Navajo Wolves, or skinwalkers, or whatever you call them. Do you know all about that?"

"Something," Chee said.

"I'll want to hire you, then," Rosemary Vines said. "You have some accrued annual leave coming. . . ." An elderly woman—a Pueblo Indian, but Chee wasn't sure which Pueblo—came in with a tray. Mrs. Vines took her glass—from its color, more Scotch than water—and Chee accepted his coffee. The Indian woman examined him from the corner of her eye with shy curiosity. "You have thirty days' leave time," Mrs. Vines continued. "That should be more than enough."

For what? Chee thought. But he didn't say it. His mother had taught him one learns through the ear and not the tongue.

"We had a burglary here," Mrs. Vines said. "Someone broke in, they got into B.J.'s quarters and stole a box of his keepsakes. I want to hire you to get it back. B.J.'s at a hospital in Houston. I want it back before he gets home. I'll pay you five hundred dollars now and twenty-five hundred dollars when you return the box. If you don't get it back, you don't get the twenty-five hundred dollars. That's fair enough."

"You can have the sheriff do it for you for free," Chee said. "What does the sheriff say about it?"

"Gordo Sena," Mrs. Vines said. "B.J. has no use for Sena. Nor do I. B.J. wouldn't want him involved in any way. Besides, what good would it do? They'd send out some ignorant deputy. He'd ask a lot of questions and look around and then he'd go away and that would be the end of it." She sipped Scotch. "There's absolutely nothing for the police to go on."

"I'm police," Chee said.

"It will be simple enough for you," Mrs. Vines said. "The People of Darkness stole the box. You find them and get it back."

Chee felt swallowed by the sofa, engulfed in velvety royal-blue comfort. He considered what Mrs. Vines had said, seeking some sense in it. Her eyes were studying him. One of her hands held the glass. The ice moved in the trembling liquid. The other hand fidgeted on the denim of her jean leg. Sleet rattled and scratched at the plate-glass window. Beyond the glass, night was coming.

"The People of Darkness," Chee said.

"Yes," said Rosemary Vines. "It must have been them. Did I tell you nothing was taken except the box? Look around you." She gestured at the room. "They didn't take the silver, or the paintings, or anything else. Just the box. They came to get it. And they took it."

The silver service was on the sideboard—a great urn and a dozen goblets on a massive tray. Worth a lot, Chee thought. And behind it, on the wall, a perfect little Navajo *yei* rug which on the reservation would bring two thousand dollars from the greediest of traders.

Chee resisted an impulse to ask Mrs. Vines what she meant by "People of Darkness." He'd never heard of them. But it would be smarter to simply let her talk.

She talked, perched on the edge of the chair, sipping occasionally. She said that when she had come to this place—the house then still under construction—the foreman of the B. J. Vines ranch had been a Navajo named Dillon Charley—the man now buried next to Vines' first wife by the garage. Vines and Charley had been friends, Rosemary Vines said. "The old man had organized himself some sort of church," Mrs. Vines said. "B.J. was interested in it. Or seemed to be. He claimed he wasn't; said he was just humoring the old man. But he was interested. I'd hear the two of them talking about it. And I know B.J. contributed money. And when you Navajo Police were arresting them, B.J. helped get them out of jail."

"Arresting them?" Chee asked. Understanding dawned. "Was it for using peyote?" If it was, Dillon Charley's cult was part of the Native American Church. It had flourished on the Checkerboard Reservation after World War II, and had been outlawed by the Tribal Council because of its use of the psychedelic drug in its ritual; but the federal court had thrown the tribal law out on grounds that it violated freedom of religion.

"Peyote. Yes. That was it," Rosemary Vines said. "Drug abuse." Her voice was scornful. "B.J. is never discriminating in his interests. Anyway, B.J. gave them some sort of thing out of that precious box of his. He and Dillon Charley had the box out several times. And whatever it was seemed to be very important to their religion. And now they've stolen it."

"What was in the box?" Chee asked.

Mrs. Vines took a drink. "Just keepsakes," she said.

"Like what?" Chee asked. "Anything valuable? What was it these people wanted?"

"I've never seen the inside of that goddamned box," Rosemary Vines said. She laughed. "B.J. has his little secrets. He has his private side, just as I have." Her tone said this was a source of an old resentment. "B.J. called it his keepsake box, and he said nothing in it was worth anything to anyone but him." She laughed again. "Obviously wrong about that."

"Do you have any idea what he gave Dillon Charley out of the box? Any idea at all?"

She looked over the glass at him, her expression wry. "Would moles make any sense?"

Now Chee laughed. This conversation, more and more, reminded him of his very favorite tale from the white culture: *Alice in Wonderland.*

"No," he said. "Moles wouldn't make any sense to me."

"What's your word for moles?"

"Dine'etse-tle," Chee said. He pronounced the series of gutturals.

She nodded. "That's what Dillon Charley called it," she said. "I asked him what B.J. had given him and that's what he said. We had a Navajo maid then—that was back when Navajos would work for B.J.—and I asked her what the word meant, and she said 'moles.' "

"That's right," Chee said. Technically, when broken into its parts, it meant more than that. *"Dinee"* was the word for "people." The expression literally meant "people of darkness."

"Why do you call Dillon Charley's church the 'People of Darkness'?" he asked her.

"That's what B.J. called them. Or something like that. It's been so many years, it's hard to remember."

But you do remember, Chee thought. He said, "There's another possible motive for taking that box. This is a legendary place." He motioned around the room. "B. J. Vines is a legendary person. So maybe there's a legend about his keepsake box. Maybe there's a rumor that he keeps it full of gold, or diamonds, or thousand-dollar bills. So somebody who came to take it wouldn't be interested in paintings, or silver, or Navajo rugs. Was it locked? Would they have to carry it out and break it open before they could find out what was in it?"

"It was always locked," Rosemary Vines said. "You'd have thought B.J. kept the crown jewels in it. But B.J. said it was just mementos, odds and ends to remember. I don't think he was lying." She smiled her taut, humorless smile. "B.J. is very big about saving keepsakes. He saves everything. If he can't frame it, he stuffs it." The humorless smile became a humorless chuckle. "You'd think he was afraid of losing his memory."

"But an outsider . . ."

"An outsider wouldn't have known where B.J. kept it," Mrs. Vines said. Her voice was impatient. "Dillon Charley knew. I can only presume that Dillon told his son." She rose, a graceful motion. "Come along and I'll show you."

Chee followed her. "One more point," he said. "Your husband knows all about this People of Darkness business. Wouldn't he rather go after the box himself?"

"I said he was at a hospital," Mrs. Vines said. "He had a stroke last summer. Away hunting in Alaska. They flew him back. He's partly paralyzed on his left side. They're fitting him with a device in Houston so he can get around better, but I don't want him chasing after burglars."

"No," Chee agreed.

She paused at an open doorway which led off the hall, motioning Chee past her. "He's the kind who would, crutches and all," she said. "He'd try to go after them in an iron lung. That's why I want the box back right away. I want it back when he gets home. I don't want him worrying about it."

The room that Rosemary Vines called "B.J.'s office" was down a carpeted hallway. It was large, with a beamed ceiling, a stone fireplace flanked by windows that looked across the mountain slope, and a great glass-surfaced desk. Three of the walls were covered with the heads of cats, each snarling in terminal rage. Chee's glance took in three lions, two lionesses, four tigers, and a variety of panthers, leopards, pumas, cheetahs, and predator cats which Chee could not identify. In all, forty or fifty, he guessed. The light reflected from hundreds of bared teeth.

"The burglar came through that window beside the fireplace and he went directly to the place where B.J. kept the box and he took it. He didn't disturb anything else," Rosemary Vines said. "He knew where it was." She looked at Chee. "Would you?"

Chee examined the room. Rosemary Vines had said her husband collected mementos. He did indeed. The room was cluttered with them. The west wall, the only one free of Vines' array of trophy predators, was a gallery of photographs and framed certificates. Vines beside a dead tiger. Vines at the controls of a speedboat. Vines holding a trophy. Vines dwarfed by the wheel of one of those immense ore trucks at the Red Deuce Mine. Vines' broad, gray-bearded face beaming under a pith helmet. His narrower, younger, black-bearded face peering out the cockpit window of a plane. Chee glanced away from the gallery of Vineses. Two glass-fronted cabinets, one crowded with trophies and cups, the other with carved and sculpted items of wood and stone. Shelves, a table, every flat surface carrying its burden of the artifacts of memory. Mrs. Vines was watching him, her face amused. "All those *objets d'art* are his sculpture," she said. She gestured toward the gallery of photographs. "And as you can see, my husband has a problem with his ego."

"Would it have been in the desk?" Chee asked.

"Wrong," Mrs. Vines said. She walked to the fireplace wall and lifted down the head of the smallest tiger. Behind it, a metal panel swung slightly open, one corner bent.

"They knew where to look, and they knew they had to bring something to pry this door open, and that's exactly what they did," Mrs. Vines said. "Didn't even bother to shut the panel, or hang the head back up."

Chee inspected the panel. It was mounted on heavy hinges and secured with a lock that looked expensive. Whoever had opened it had jammed something like a crowbar between panel and frame and pried until the lock gave. The door was thick and surprisingly heavy on its hinges, but it hadn't been strong enough to withstand the leverage. Chee was mildly surprised. The door looked stronger than it was.

"How big was the box?" Chee asked.

"Just about the size of that empty space," Mrs. Vines said. "B.J. had it made. It had the knob of a combination lock in the front of it. What I want you to do is find those people, and tell them unless they give it back—and everything that was inside of it—I'll make damn sure they go to prison for it." She moved to the doorway and motioned Chee out ahead of her. "You might also tell them B.J. will put a spell on them if he gets home and finds that box gone."

"What?" Chee said.

Mrs. Vines laughed. "The Navajos around here think he's a witch," she said.

"I had the impression that he got along well with the Dinee," Chee said.

"That was a long time ago. Dillon Charley died and that was the end of getting along with Navajos. Within a year or two nearly every one of them who was working here had quit. We haven't had one of your people on the payroll for years. Maria is an Acoma. Most of the hired hands are Lagunas or Acomas."

"What happened?"

"I honestly don't know," Mrs. Vines said. "I'm sure it was something B.J. did, but God knows what. I asked Maria, and she said the Navajos think B.J. is bad luck."

"And you haven't reported this burglary to the sheriff?"

"Gordo Sena would do absolutely nothing for us," Mrs. Vines said. "B.J. got him beaten for reelection once, many years ago, and tried it a couple of times since. Sena's not an honest man, and I don't want him involved with this in any way whatsoever."

"I'm going to have to report it," Chee said. "I have to get along with the sheriff. We're in the same line of work."

"Go ahead," Mrs. Vines said. "If he sends someone out, I'll tell him we're not signing a complaint and not pressing charges and it was all a mistake."

Chee retrieved his hat from the sofa. It was damp.

"The man you want to find is old Dillon Charley's son. He

took over the church. His name's Emerson Charley and he lives around Grants somewhere. He used to come around here some after his father died and get into arguments with B.J."

"About what?"

"I think he wanted whatever was in the box," Mrs. Vines said. "I heard him say something about having their luck locked up in it. Something like that. I remember hearing old Dillon saying about the same thing. He was laughing about it, but Emerson wasn't laughing."

Chee revolved his hat on his hands, looking thoughtful.

"Two more questions," he said. "How would Emerson Charley have known about the safe?"

"That's easy," Rosemary Vines said. "Dillon knew about it. Dillon was in here with B.J. a lot. I'm sure Dillon told his boy about it. After all, Emerson was going to keep Dillon's crazy cult going. What's the other question?"

"How did Dillon Charley die?"

"How?" Mrs. Vines looked puzzled. Then she laughed. "Oh," she said. "I see what you're thinking. Nothing mysterious. He died of cancer." She laughed again. "That's the reason for that strange line on the tombstone about him being a good Indian. He'd been sick and he came back from Albuquerque one day and told B.J. that the doctor told him he couldn't be cured. He told B.J. the doctor told him he was going to be a good Indian in a couple of months." Rosemary Vines grimaced. "Laughing at his own death—that's the sort of weird thing that impressed B.J. He put it on the tombstone." She handed him an envelope.

"I'm going to have to talk to my office about this," Chee said. "And give it some thought. I'll let you know in a couple of days. Maybe I'll return this."

"Your superiors will approve," Mrs. Vines said. "I already checked on that."

"I'll call you," Chee said.

The old woman from Acoma opened the front door for Chee and held it against the gusting wind. He nodded to her as he stepped into the darkness.

"Tenga cuidado," the old woman said.

It occurred to Chee as he started the cold engine that she

couldn't speak Navajo, and he wouldn't understand her Keresan language, and that it would have been more logical of her to say "Be careful" in English instead of Spanish, which he might not understand. Then it occurred to him that perhaps Mrs. Vines did not speak Spanish, and that the warning might not have anything to do with the weather.

3

BY THE TIME CHEE had made his cautious way down the mountain and into Grants, the storm had moved away to the east. It left behind an air mass which was windless, arid, and twenty degrees below freezing. It also left a half-inch layer of snow as light and dry as feathers. Chee detoured past the Valencia County Office Building on the chance that the tricky road conditions would have the Sheriff's Department working late. The light was on. He pulled into the parking lot.

Except for the east, the clouds were gone now and the night sky, swept clean of dust, was ablaze with starlight. Chee stood for a moment, enjoying it. He hunted out the autumn constellations—the formations that rose from the south as the earth tilted to end summer and begin the Season When the Thunder Sleeps. Chee knew them not by the names the Greeks and Romans had given them, but from his grandfather. Now he picked out the Spider Woman (named Aquarius by the Romans), low on the southern horizon, and the mischievous Blue Flint Boys, whom the Greeks called the Pleiades, just above the blackness of the storm against the northeast sky. Almost directly overhead was Born of Water, the philosophical member of the Hero Twins. Over his right shoulder, surrounded by stars of lesser magnitude, soared the Blue Heron. According to the Origin Myth as told in Chee's clan, it had been the Heron whom First Man had sent back into the flooding underworld to rescue the forgotten witchcraft bundle and thus bring evil into the surface world. Chee felt the cold seeping under his collar and through his pant legs. He hurried into the warmth of the county building.

The third door down the hall bore the legend LAWRENCE SENA, SHERIFF. VALENCIA COUNTY. WALK IN. The capitalized LAW, Chee had heard, represented Sena's effort to replace "Gordo" with a less insulting nickname. It hadn't worked. Chee turned the doorknob, hoping that Sena had left a deputy handling the overtime. He had met the sheriff only once, making a courtesy call after his transfer to Crownpoint. Sena had impressed him as being hard, smart, and abrasive—like Mrs. Vines, moved beyond the need for tact by access to power. Perhaps it was the product of having too much money, Chee thought. Uranium. Vines had found it, and had sold his leases for a fortune and an interest in the huge open pit mine called the Red Deuce. The Sena family's fortune was the accident of scratching a living on a worn-out ranch which happened to have radioactive ore twenty feet below the cactus roots. Ah, well, Chee thought, such a rich man would be at home on a night like this.

Sheriff Sena was standing in a glassed-in cubicle which insulated the department's radio operator from the world. He was listening while a middle-aged woman wearing headphones argued with someone about dispatching a wrecker somewhere. A long moment passed before he noticed Chee.

"Yeah," he said. "What can I do for you, Sergeant?"

"I want to report a burglary," Chee said.

Sheriff Sena registered the mildest form of surprise by lifting his heavy black eyebrows a fraction of a millimeter. His black eyes rested on Chee's face, bland and neutral, waiting for an explanation.

"Somebody got into B. J. Vines' house and stole his lockbox," Chee said. "Nothing very valuable. Just keepsakes."

Sena's eyes were watchful. "Well," he said finally. "That's interesting." He moved past Chee out of the cubicle. "Come on in to my desk and I'll get my pencil."

The sheriff's office was a room even smaller than the radio cubicle—barely large enough for a desk with a swivel chair on one side of it and a wooden kitchen chair on the other.

Sena eased his bulk into the swivel and looked up at Chee.

"I guess Vines broke his telephone," Sena said. "Is that why he didn't report it himself?"

"Vines is away," Chee said. "His wife told me she didn't report it because she didn't see how the police could solve it."

Sena pulled open the top desk drawer and extracted a pencil and a pad. "Couldn't solve it," he said. "She say why?"

"Nothing to go on," Chee said.

"Have a seat," Sena said, indicating the chair. The years and the weather had engraved Sena's round face with a thousand expressive lines. They expressed skepticism.

"She didn't say anything about old B.J. not having any use for me?"

Chee smiled. "I think she mentioned something about you two not being friendly. I don't remember exactly how she put it."

"How come she told you about the burglary? You a friend of the Vineses?"

"She wants to hire me to get the box back," Chee said.

"Oh," Sena said. The eyebrows rose again, asking why.

"She thinks an Indian did it. A Navajo. That it's got something to do with religion, or witchcraft. Something like that."

Sena thought about it. "Just the lockbox, that right? Nothing else missing?"

"That's what she told me."

"Most likely somebody figured he kept his money in it," Sena said.

"Probably," Chee said.

"But she don't think it's that simple," Sena said.

It was a statement, not a question, and Chee didn't answer it.

He was looking at a framed photograph on the wall behind the sheriff. It seemed to be a disaster scene, twisted steel wreckage in the foreground, a burned-out truck on its side, two men in khaki uniforms looking at something outside the frame, a police car and an ambulance of 1950 vintage. The scene of an explosion, apparently. A small white card stuck in the corner of the frame bore six typed names—all apparently Navajo. Victims, perhaps. The picture was grainy black-and-white, and glass and card were dusty. Sena inserted the pencil eraser between his teeth, leaned back in the swivel chair, and stared at Chee. The sheriff moved his jaw and the pencil waved slowly up and down, an antenna seeking logic. Sena removed it. "What else did she say?"

Chee described the hiding place for the box and how it had been pried open. "Nothing else was missing," he said. "Lots of valuable stuff in the house—right in plain view. Silver. Rugs. Paintings. Worth a lot of money."

"I imagine so," Sena said. "Vines has got more money than Saudi Arabia. What'd she say about religion?"

Chee told him, outlining briefly Mrs. Vines' account of her husband's interest in the church of Dillon Charley, her speculation that something in the box was important to the cult, and that only Charley had known where the box was kept.

"Dillon Charley's a long time dead," Sena said.

"Mrs. Vines said he had a son. She figured he'd told his son about it years ago, and the son decided to come and get it."

Sena sat immobile, studying Chee. "That what she figured?"

"That's what she told me."

"The son's name is Emerson Charley," Sena said. "That ring a bell?"

"Faintly," Chee said. "But I can't place him."

"Remember that killing they had in Albuquerque in August? Somebody put a bomb in a pickup and it killed a couple of fellows in a tow truck trying to haul the pickup away. That was Emerson Charley's pickup."

Chee recalled having read about it. It was a puzzling case. "I remember it," Chee said. "Understand they think the bomb was intended for one of the big shots at the hospital. Divorce settlement or argument or something, from what I heard."

"That's what the Albuquerque police seem to think," Sena said. His tone was skeptical.

"Anyway, Mrs. Vines figures Emerson got the box. She wants me to get it back from him."

"Emerson didn't get the box," Sena said. He reinserted the pencil and chewed on it. His eyes were on Chee, but his attention was far away. He sighed, shook his head, scratched his left sideburn with a thick forefinger. "Emerson's in the hospital,"

Sena said. "BCMC in Albuquerque. If he's not dead, that is. Last I heard, he was in bad shape."

"I thought he didn't get hurt," Chee said.

"He was already hurt," Sena said. "He'd gone to the hospital to check into that Cancer Research and Treatment Center the university has there. The son of a bitch is dying of cancer." He focused on Chee again, and emitted a snort of ironic laughter. "The APD and the FBI between 'em couldn't figure out why anyone would blow up a Navajo when he's already dying."

"Can you?" Chee asked.

The pencil waved, up and down, up and down. "No," said Sena, "I can't. Not a thing. Did Mrs. Vines say anything to you about some people they used to call the People of Darkness?"

Sena made the question sound casual.

"She mentioned it," Chee said.

"What did she say?" The sheriff's voice, despite his efforts, was tense.

"Not much," Chee said. He repeated what Rosemary Vines had told him about her husband's interest in Dillon Charley's church, about his contributing money, helping members when they were arrested, and giving Charley something "lucky" from the box—perhaps a talisman, Chee guessed. Halfway through it, Sena stifled a yawn. But his eyes weren't sleepy. "Like she said herself, it was all pretty vague," Chee concluded.

Sena yawned again. "Well, I'll send somebody out tomorrow or so and get all the details. No use wasting your time." Sena examined the pencil top. "You weren't figuring on taking that job, were you?"

"Hadn't really decided," Chee said. "Probably not."

"That'd be the best," Sena said. "It was like I was telling you that day you first came in here and introduced yourself—that first week you replaced old Henry Becenti. Like I was telling you then, this jurisdiction business can be a real problem if you ain't careful with it."

"I guess so," Chee said. As far as he could remember, jurisdiction hadn't been discussed during that brief meeting. He was sure it hadn't been.

"I don't know if you ever worked out here on the Checkerboard Reservation before," Sena said. "You're driving along and one minute you're on the Navajo reservation and the next minute you're in Valencia County jurisdiction and usually there's no way in God's world to know the difference. It can be a real problem."

"I bet," Chee said. The Navajo Police lived with jurisdiction problems. Even on the Big Reservation, which sprawled larger than all New England across the borders of New Mexico, Arizona, and Utah, jurisdiction was always a question. The serious felony brought in the FBI. If the suspect was non-Navajo, other questions were raised. Or the crime might lap into the territory of New Mexico State Police, Utah or Arizona Highway Patrol, or involve the Law and Order Division of the Bureau of Indian Affairs. Or even a Hopi constable, or Southern Ute Tribal Police, or an officer of the Jicarilla Apache tribe, or any of a dozen county sheriffs of the three states. But here on the southwestern fringe of the reservation, checkerboarding complicated the problem. In the 1880s, the government deeded every other square mile in a sixty-mile-wide strip to the Atlantic and Pacific Railroad to subsidize extension of its trunk line westward. The A&P had become the Santa Fe generations ago, and the Navajo Nation had gradually bought back part of this looted portion of its Dinetah, its homeland, but in many places this checkerboard pattern of ownership persisted.

"Tell you the truth, Becenti and I had us some trouble when he first took over the Crownpoint station. The Tribal Council had just passed itself a law outlawing peyote, and they were cracking down on the church. You old enough to remember that?"

"I knew about it," Chee said.

"Old Henry got pretty carried away with that," Sena said. "He got so interested in rounding up the peyoteheads that he'd forget where the reservation boundary was and he'd get over into my territory. So I had my boys arrest some of his boys and one thing and another, and finally we got together here and worked out a way so we wouldn't interfere in one another's business." Sena's eyes were intent on Chee's face, making sure he'd understood the lesson.

"I'd think enforcing that peyote ban would have been Lieutenant Becenti's business," Chee said.

"Normally," Sena said, "yes. This time, though, we were looking into another crime and Henry was messing us up." Sena wiped away the disagreement with a wave of his hand. "The point is we learned how to coordinate. Like I'd call Henry when something Navajo came up and find out where he was on it. And Henry'd call me when he had something that was crossing the Checkerboard lines and ask me if we was touchy about it. And if we was touchy, he'd stay over on the reservation and let it alone."

Sena replaced the pencil between his teeth and sat back in the chair. The pencil pointed directly at Chee's nose. Sena's eyes asked Chee if he had received the warning.

"Sounds sensible," Chee said.

"Yeah," Sena said. "It's sensible." He pushed back the swivel chair and pushed himself out of it. "Been a long day," he said. "Get a little dustin' of snow and the goddamn Texans coming through on I-40 ain't never seen it before and we got 'em slid off the road all the way from Gallup to Albuquerque." Sena moved around the desk, agile for such a bulky man, showing Chee out.

"I think you was smart deciding not to take that job," he said. "We'll just solve that little burglary for Mrs. Vines ourself. Just show her how to do it. She say anything about Dillon Charley? Anything at all?"

Again it seemed to Chee that the question was deliberately casual.

"Just what I told you," Chee said.

"You know, they got old Dillon Charley buried up there. Right by the house. That always seemed awful funny to me."

Chee said nothing. Sena's hand gripped his arm.

"She say anything about why they did that?"

"No," Chee said. "All she said was something about the old man joking about it when the doctor told him he was dying."

"About that burglary. You think she was telling all she knew?"

"People usually don't," Chee said.

Sena eyed him thoughtfully. "Yes," he said. "That's always been my experience." He released Chee's elbow. "You be careful, now," he said.

4

JIMMY CHEE SAT with his boot heels propped on the edge of his wastebasket and his fingers locked behind his head and his eyes on Officer Trixie Dodge. Officer Dodge was, as she had already told him, trying to get some work done.

"Come on, Trixie," Chee said. "Think about it. What could be in the box? Why is old lady Vines so hot to get it back? Why is old Gordo Sena so uptight about it?"

Officer Dodge was sorting through legal papers in her in-box, transferring them into a cardboard folder. The papers were to be delivered this morning to the Bureau of Indian Affairs office in Gallup. Officer Dodge was running late. "How the hell would I know?" Trixie said.

"And you never heard of anything called the People of Darkness?"

"Nope," Trixie said. "I've heard of moles. I've heard of the peyote church. In fact, I've got a cousin who's into that." Officer Dodge put the last of the papers into the folder and headed for the door. "And I've heard of people with moles, but I never heard of people who call themselves moles."

"Maybe it had something to do with an amulet, or a fetish—something like that," Chee said.

"Of a mole?" Officer Dodge's voice was incredulous. "What kind of a Navajo would use a mole for an amulet?" Officer Dodge left for Gallup without waiting for an answer.

What kind of a Navajo would use a mole for an amulet? It was a fair enough question. Chee sat, feet on wastebasket, hands locked behind head, thinking about it. It wouldn't be a traditional, old-fashioned Navajo, probably, except under unusual circumstances. More likely one of those Eastern Navajos whose clans had mixed more Pueblo Indian ritualism and Christianity into their culture. The Navajo used representations of the predator Holy People for his amulets. The mole was a predator in the Navajo mythology, but he was much less powerful and much less popular than his more glamorous cousins—the bear, the badger, the eagle, the mountain lion, and so forth. In Chee's own medicine pouch, suspended from a thong inside his trousers, was the figure of a badger. It was about the size of Chee's thumb and carved from soapstone, a gift from his father. In the mythology of the Slow Talking Dinee, Hosteen Badger was a formidable figure. Hosteen Mole played a trivial role. Why use the mole? He was the predator of the nadir, downward, one of the six sacred directions. He was the symbol of the dark underground, with access to those strange dark subsurface worlds through which the Dinee rose in their evolution toward human status. But compared to the bear, the eagle, or even the horned frog, he had little power and no prominence in ceremonials. Why pick the mole? The only explanation Chee could think of was the obvious one. The oil well drilled toward the nadir, into the mole's domain.

Chee unlocked his hands and put his feet squarely on the floor beneath his desk. He should get some reports finished. But halfway through the first one he found himself thinking of the nervous Rosemary Vines offering three thousand dollars for a box of keepsakes and the intense, probing questions of Gordo Sena. An arrogant woman presumed he could be bought, and an autocratic man presumed he could be bluffed. What was it that made this little burglary so important to them?

Chee picked up the Albuquerque telephone book. He found the number and placed a call to the Bernalillo County Medical Center. Two transfers later, he was talking to a nurse in the Cancer Research and Treatment Center.

"I'm sorry," she said. "The patient can't have any visitors."

"We're investigating a crime," Chee said. "Mr. Charley is the only one who can provide some information we need. It would be two or three quick questions."

"Mr. Charley is not conscious," she said. "He's under sedation. He's in very critical condition."

"It would only take a few seconds. I could come and wait for him to regain consciousness," Chee said.

"I'm afraid that won't happen," the nurse said. "He's dying."

Chee thought about that. It made the question he was going to ask sound absurd.

"Can the hospital confirm that Emerson Charley didn't leave the hospital last Tuesday?"

"We can confirm that Mr. Charley hasn't left his room for a month. He's being fed intravenously. He's too weak to move." The tone was disapproving.

"Well, then," Chee said, "I'll need the name of his next of kin."

He got it from the records office, and jotted it on his note pad. Tomas Charley, Rural Route 2, Grants. No telephone. A son, grandson of Dillon Charley. What would Tomas know of something that had happened about the time he was born? Probably not much. Perhaps nothing.

Then who would know?

One question, at least, Chee could find an answer for. What had caused the trouble between Sheriff Sena and Henry Becenti? He would locate Becenti and ask him. And then Chee would decide whether he would collect Mrs. Vines' three thousand dollars.

5

"SOME OF IT'S EASY to remember," Henry Becenti said. "Hard not to. Six people killed. But hell. It was way back in '47 or '48. That's a long time ago."

"I can just remember hearing somebody talking about it," Chee said. "But it was long before my time."

"It was a little independent outfit," Becenti recalled. "Trying to do some drilling back in there northeast of Mount Taylor, and they had an explosion that wiped out the whole crew. That's how old Gordo and I got in trouble with each other."

"Just an accident?"

"Yeah," Becenti said. "You know anything about oil drilling? Well, this one was a dry hole. No oil. So they was going to shoot it. Perforate the casing." Becenti glanced at Chee to see if he understood. "They lower a tube of nitroglycerin down the well to the level where it looks best and they shoot it off. Idea is to shatter the rocks down there and get the oil running into the hole. Anyway, this time the nitro went off on the floor of the rig. Wiped everybody out. Little pieces of 'em scattered all over."

A look of distaste crossed Becenti's face. He shook his head, shaking off the vividness of the memory. They were sitting on a shelf of stone that jutted from the slope above Henry Becenti's place. They were there because Chee's arrival had coincided with a visit from Becenti's mother-in-law to Becenti's wife. Changing Woman had taught the original Navajo clans that while the groom should join his bride's family, the mother-in-law and son-in-law should scrupulously avoid all contact. In forty years, Old Woman Nez and Henry Becenti had never broken that taboo. Becenti had built his house at his in-laws' place, but away from the hogan of his bride's parents. When Old Woman Nez came to call, Becenti arranged to be elsewhere. This high ridge, which looked across the great valley of Ambrosia Lakes, was a favored retreat.

"If it was an accident, what was bothering Sena?" Chee asked.

"Sena's older brother was one of them," Becenti said. "He was one of the drillers. I think he was what they call the 'tool pusher.' And Sena got sort of crazy about it."

Becenti shook a cigaret out of his pack, offered it to Chee, and then selected one for himself and struck a kitchen match to it. He sat smoking, looking at Mount Taylor, thirty miles to the east. The sun had dropped behind the horizon, but the top of the mountain, rising a mile above the valley floor, still caught the direct light. Tsoodzil, the Navajos called it, the Turquoise Mountain. It was one of the four sacred peaks which First Man had built to guard Dinetah. He had built it on a blue blanket of earth carried up from the underworld, and decorated it with turquoise and blue flint. And then he had pinned it to the earth with a magic knife, and assigned Turquoise Girl to live there and Big Snake to guard her until the Fourth World ended. Now it appeared the magic knife had slipped. The sacred mountain seemed to float in the sky, cut off from the solid earth by the ground haze.

Beautiful, Chee thought. And on the other side of the mountain was the home of B. J. Vines, who had a wife who decided the theft of a keepsake box was very, very important and probably involved witchcraft, or something akin to it. The smoke from Becenti's cigaret reached Chee's nostrils.

"The first couple of days we thought we had twelve people killed," Becenti said. "Wasn't no way of telling. Lot of people around there now, but then there wasn't nobody for miles. The only ones we could find that heard the explosion were a long ways off. They hadn't gone to see about it. Sometimes the crew stayed out on the rig for several days, so nobody got to wondering about it until the weekend. Somebody got nervous. Gordo was a deputy then. He went out to see about it."

Becenti inhaled a lungful of cigaret and exhaled slowly. The smoke made shapes in the motionless air. Seen in profile, his face was ageless. But his eyes had spent more than forty years looking at drunks, at knife fighters, at victims, at what happened when pickup trucks hit culverts at eighty. They were old eyes.

"The blast was on a Friday, I think it was. Gordo got out there Monday. The birds had been there, and the coyotes. Hauling bits and pieces off." He glanced at Chee, making sure he understood the implications. "Anyway, like I said, his brother worked out there. Gordo couldn't find him. Or couldn't find enough to know whether it was his brother or not. And then one of the men that we thought was killed showed up in Grants. It turned out there was a crew of six roustabouts working out there and we had 'em all down as dead and they was all alive."

Becenti's old eyes looked away from the mountain and made contact with Chee's. "They'd been warned not to go to work," he said.

"It was an accident," Chee said slowly. "Who knew it was going to happen?"

"Their foreman was a peyote chief. He'd had services the night before and he had a vision," Becenti said. "God talked to him and God told him something bad was going to happen out at the well."

"And he warned his crew?"

"That's right," Becenti said. "And when Sena found out about it he just about went crazy. Sena didn't believe in visions. He figured there was some funny business and somebody had killed his brother."

"Hard to blame him," Chee said.

"Anyway, Sena had three of the crew locked up at Grants and was looking for the peyote chief. I was, too—for illegal use of a narcotic on the reservation. One of our people found him first and we had him in custody when a deputy sheriff got there to arrest him." Becenti's wrinkled face folded itself into a grin. "Big damned argument over who was gonna get him. Whether it was reservation land or county jurisdiction where he lived, and where the oil well was. Looked like we was going to have another Indian war there for a while. But the well wasn't on Navajo land, so I let Sena have him."

Becenti inhaled a puff of cigaret smoke, breathed it out, and looked at the mountain. Its slopes were rosy now with the sunset. Chee said nothing. In Navajo fashion, when Becenti knew what he wanted to say next he would say it. There was no reason to hurry.

"Nothing ever came of it," Becenti said. "Not as far as Sena was concerned. The peyote preacher stuck to his story, and there wasn't any reason in the world to believe anyone would have blown up those men on purpose, and so finally Sena turned him loose. But something came of it for us. The Council wanted the peyote church stopped. So we was trying to arrest anyone with peyote. But word got around about the preacher saving those lives, and the congregation kept growing."

"And you kept arresting them?"

"Trying to," Becenti said. "They kept moving the services around. First one place and then another. Sort of went underground." Becenti laughed again. "Got real secret. The leaders took to wearing mole amulets and they called themselves the People of Darkness." Becenti used the same Navajo word that Mrs. Vines had remembered.

"The peyote chief was a Navajo named Dillon Charley?"

"That's right," Becenti said. "He was the peyote chief. He was the one who had the vision."

"Did B. J. Vines have anything to do with that oil well?"

"No," Becenti said. "He didn't come into this country until after all that happened." Becenti slammed his fist into his palm. "By God, though," he said, "Vines and Charley got connected later on. Charley worked for him. After that explosion Sena hated Charley and pretty soon Sena was hating Vines, too." He glanced at Chee. "How much you know about Vines?"

"Just what I've heard," Chee said. "Came in here a poor boy at the very beginning of the uranium discoveries. Made the big uranium find on Section 17 and sold his leases to Anaconda for ten million dollars and a percentage royalty on the ore, and now he gets a little richer every time they drive an ore truck out of the Red Deuce Mine. Got more money than the U.S. government, big-game hunter, flies an airplane, so forth."

"That's about it," Becenti said. "Except early on he and Sena had their troubles. Sena was sheriff by then, and Vines ran some Anglo against him and spent a lot of money and be damned if he didn't beat Sena. And Sena came back two years later and beat the Anglo. Sena's been sheriff of Valencia ever since, and he never did forgive Vines."

"How did Charley get involved with Vines?" Chee asked.

"Politics. He started working with Vines against Sena—getting out the Navajo vote, and the Lagunas and Acomas. On Vines' payroll, probably. Later on he worked out there at Vines' ranch. Died years ago."

"What happened to the People of Darkness?"

"Haven't heard of them for years," Becenti said. "But the church is still operating. You remember the courts ruled that peyote was a sacrament and they had a right to dope themselves up with it. Charley's son—I think his name was Emerson—he was the preacher after Dillon died. And Emerson's boy, he's a peyote chief since Emerson's sick."

"Tomas Charley?"

Becenti nodded. "He's a crazy little son of a bitch," Becenti said. "All them Charleys was crazy and this youngest one is the worst. His mother's a Laguna. From what I hear, he's into one of the Laguna kiva societies, and he's the peyote chief in the Native American Church around here, and he does some curing for the People on top of it all."

"How'd that happen?" Chee asked.

"One of the boy's paternal uncles is a *yataalii,"* Becenti said. "Pretty good old fellow. He taught Tomas the Blessing Way and the kid does it now and then. But most people would rather get someone else."

"Why do you say he's crazy?"

Becenti laughed and shrugged. "Chewed too goddamn many peyote buttons," he said. "Got his brains curdled. Sees visions. Thinks he's talking to God. Silly little bastard." Becenti paused, searching for an illustration. "He come in the office last year and said Jesus had told him there was going to be a terrible drought and we should warn everybody to stock up on food. And then this fall he was in telling us that some witch was making his daddy sick. His daddy, that's Emerson Charley."

"Well, it's been dry as hell," Chee said, "and his daddy is dying."

"It's always dry," Becenti said. "And his daddy's got cancer. That's what I heard. I didn't know he was dying." Becenti thought about it. "Anyway, he didn't get witched. I think cancer runs in that family, like craziness. I think that's what the grandfather died of, too."

"Dillon Charley? Yeah. That's what Mrs. Vines said."

Becenti looked uneasy. He was old enough to have the traditions of the People worn deep into the grain, and one of the traditions was not to speak the name of the dead. The ghost might overhear and be summoned to the speaker.

"Did you know Vines had Dillon Charley buried up at his house?" Chee asked.

"I heard that," Becenti said. "White men sure got some weird customs."

Especially their burial customs, Chee thought. He'd spent years among the whites, first at boarding school, then through enough years at the University of New Mexico to win a degree in anthropology, but he still couldn't fathom the attitude of whites toward the corpse.

"You have any idea why Vines would want to bury Dillon Charley?" Chee asked.

Becenti made a wry face. "Hell, no."

"This Tomas Charley," Chee said. "You said he was crazy. Would he be crazy enough to get into Vines' house and steal a lockbox with keepsakes in it?"

Becenti extracted the cigaret from between his lips and looked at Chee. "Did something like that happen?" he asked. "Why would he want to steal something like that? Vines and his woman are both big hunters. I understand either one of them would just as soon shoot somebody as not."

"I heard that Tomas' grandfather thought Vines kept the luck of the Darkness People in that box," Chee said. "Maybe Tomas heard about that."

Becenti nodded. "Okay, then. I'd say yes. That kid would be about crazy enough to break in to steal himself some luck."

6

THE SPIKE on his desk the next morning held three pink "While You Were Out" slips. One told him to call Captain Leaphorn at the Chinle substation. The other two, one left over from yesterday, and one received just before he'd got to work, told him to call B. J. Vines. He put those aside and called the Chinle station. Leaphorn's business involved identifying a middle-aged Navajo killed in a truck-pedestrian accident. The captain wanted him to send someone to Thoreau to check with a family there. Chee added it to the afternoon assignment of Officer Dodge. Then he picked up the "Call B. J. Vines" slips, leaned back in his chair and considered them. Both were initialed "T.D." Trixie Dodge was at her desk across the room. He glanced at her. She looked grim this morning. Trixie, he suspected, should have written "Call Mrs. B. J. Vines." Vines wouldn't be back for weeks.

"Hey, Trixie," he said. "You put down 'Call Vines' here. Wasn't the call from Mrs. Vines?"

Trixie didn't look up. "Vines," she said.

"*Mr.* Vines?" Chee insisted.

"It was a man. He said his name was B. J. Vines. He asked for you and then he asked you to call him at that number." Trixie's voice was patient.

Chee dialed the number. It rang once.

"Yes." The voice was male.

"This is Jim Chee of the Navajo Tribal Police. I have a note to call B. J. Vines."

"Oh, good," the voice said. "I'm Vines. I'd like to talk to you about that little theft we had. Could you come out?"

"When?"

"Well," the voice said, "the sooner the better. I understand my wife talked to you about it and . . ." The voice paused and interjected a nervous laugh. "Well, there's some misunderstandings that need to be cleared up." The tone was ironic now. "There tends to be when Rosemary gets involved."

"Okay," Chee said. "I'll be out there after lunch."

"Good," Vines said. "Thanks."

Chee marked the Thoreau assignment off Dodge's assignment sheet. It was on his way. He'd handle it himself.

7

THE PUEBLO WOMAN ANSWERED the doorbell and showed Chee into the predator room without a sign she'd ever seen him before. There was a man behind the glass-topped desk now—a small man with a round face made rounder by the great bush of iron-gray beard that surrounded it. The man pulled himself to his feet. "Ben Vines," he said, offering a small, hard hand. "Have a seat." Chee sat. So did Vines. The room was brighter now than it had been when he had seen it with Mrs. Vines. Autumn sunlight streamed in, reflecting from the glass eyeballs and ivory teeth of the cats. The sunlight made the room less hostile. The lioness above Vines' left shoulder seemed to be smiling. So did Vines.

"I understand my wife told you we had a break-in, and she hired you to solve the crime," Vines said.

"She asked me," Chee said.

"This is embarrassing," Vines said. What Chee could see of his face through its frame of hair didn't look embarrassed. His alert black eyes were studying Chee. "I have a feeling there really isn't a crime to be solved."

"No?"

"No," Vines said. He laughed. "My wife is not a very predictable woman at times. She's a very nervous woman. Sometimes things get confused."

"Having someone break into your wall safe can make you nervous," Chee said.

"How nervous it makes you depends on who broke into it,"

Vines said. He shifted his weight, glanced out the window and then back at Chee. "Do you know where the safe is?"

"It's behind that head," Chee said, nodding to the appropriate cat.

Vines got to his feet again and maneuvered himself laboriously to the wall. He balanced carefully and lifted the mounted head off its hook, dumping it on the carpet. The safe door eased itself open on well-oiled hinges. The space behind it was dark and empty. Vines looked at it, his expression thoughtful. He extracted a pack of cigarets from the side pocket of his jacket, shook one out and lit it. At his feet, the cat's head smiled benignly at the ceiling.

"Rosemary and I weren't young when we married," Vines said. "We'd enjoyed lives of our own and we were going to continue to be private persons as well as man and wife. We kept our old friends and our old memories. Both of us. Separate."

Vines had been talking to the safe. Now he glanced around at Chee. A trickle of tobacco smoke leaked through his lips. It made its way through his mustache like gray fog. Chee could see now that the left side of Vines' face was affected. The corner of his mouth and the muscles around his left eye drooped. "This safe operates with a key and a combination. Rosemary doesn't have either one of them. I have a toolbox in the stables. There's a prying bar in it." Vines pushed the safe door closed. "You'll notice that this wall safe is like a lot of wall safes. It has a limited purpose and it's not built like a bank vault. It's not designed to do more than slow down a safe-cracker. You can take a pry bar and jam it in the door fitting, and it gives you enough leverage to spring the lock. Take a look."

Chee looked. He noticed, as he'd noticed the first time he'd examined it, that the safe door did seem to have been pried open. Whatever had been used had left marks, and the door had been slightly bent. Once again, that seemed odd. The door was heavy. Unless it was poor metal, it would take tremendous strength to bend it even with the leverage of a wrecking bar. Chee looked for a trademark and found none.

"I think you should get your money back on that door," he said.

Vines laughed. "I'm afraid the warranty's run out. As a

matter of fact, I had the safe made and installed, and I guess they didn't use the most expensive material."

"Who did it for you?"

"I don't remember," Vines said. "Some outfit in Albuquerque. I had it done when I built this place, and that was thirty years ago." He pushed the door shut. "The point I was making was that Rosemary doesn't have a key to the wall safe, but she does have a key to the tool locker. The pry bar was gone. I found it in her closet."

"Oh," Chee said.

Vines shrugged. He produced a wry face. "So I want to apologize for all this. And I'd like to pay you for your trouble." He produced a check. "You made two trips out here. Would two hundred dollars be fair?"

Chee glanced from Vines to the sly smile of the tiger. He thought of the bent metal of the door and the empty space behind the door, and of what Mrs. Vines had told him. Among other things, she had told him that B. J. Vines was away at a hospital. But two hundred dollars was too much to be offered. Vines was watching him. Vines had told him, in effect, that the crime was family business, and thus no crime at all, and no concern of Chee's. To ask a question now would be impertinent.

"Did Mrs. Vines have the box?" Chee asked.

Vines considered this impertinence, his mild eyes on Chee's face. He sighed. "I don't know," he said. "Maybe she had it. Maybe she disposed of it. The point is it doesn't matter. I think she told you there wasn't much in it. There wasn't. Mementos. Things that reminded me of the past. Nothing of value. Not even to me any longer."

Vines held the check toward Chee, dangling it between his fingers.

"I understand you reported it to the sheriff," he said. "Of course you'd have to do that. Old Gordo came out yesterday to ask about it. I wondered how much you told him."

"Just what Mrs. Vines told me."

Vines took three careful steps toward Chee and put the check in Chee's shirt pocket.

"This isn't necessary," Chee said. "I'm not even sure it's allowed."

"Take it," Vines said. "Rosemary and I will both feel better. If it's against policy, tear it up. I wonder if you noticed that our sheriff is very interested in my business?" Vines made his laborious way back to his chair.

"I noticed," Chee said.

"Did he ask a lot of questions?"

"Yep," Chee said. Vines waited for more. He realized gradually that it wouldn't be forthcoming.

"Gordo asked me a lot of questions about the People of Darkness," Vines said. "I got the impression that you'd told him Rosemary thought one of the Charley boys had taken the box."

"That's right," Chee said.

Vines waited again. He sighed. "I've had a lot of trouble with Gordo Sena," he said. "Years ago. I thought it was over with." Vines put out his cigaret and walked to the window. Past him, Chee could see an expanse of Mount Taylor's east slope. At this altitude it was the zone of transition from ponderosa pine into fir, spruce, and aspen. The ground under the aspens was yellow with fallen leaves. The slanting sunlight created a golden glow a little like fire.

"It was early in the 1950s," Vines said. "I'd found that uranium deposit that the Red Deuce is mining now, and I was building this place, and I hired a Navajo named Dillon Charley as a sort of foreman to look after things. I didn't know it, but Gordo had a thing about Charley, and about a bunch of other Indians in a church old Dillon was running." Vines glanced back at Chee, the window light giving his gray beard a translucent frosting. "It was the peyote church. It was against tribal law in those days."

"I know about it," Chee said.

"Well, Sena was dogging them. He was picking them up, and beating them up. I got involved in it. Hired a lawyer over in Grants to take care of bonding them out and to bitch to the Justice Department about rights violations, and finally I put up some money behind a candidate and we got Sena beat for re-election for one term. For several years there, it was hairy between Sena and me. Things had settled down for the last few years. I'm wondering if he wants to stir it up again. That's why I wanted to know what kind of questions he was asking you."

"He asked why your wife wanted to hire me," Chee said. He gave Vines a quick résumé of Sena's questions.

"What do you think of that oil well business?" Vines asked. "Did Sena tell you about that? About why he hated old Dillon Charley?"

"He didn't talk about it," Chee said. "But I understand he thinks it's funny Dillon Charley got that advance warning."

"You don't believe in visions?" Through the bristling whiskers Vines' expression seemed to be amused. Chee couldn't be sure.

"It depends," Chee said. "But I don't believe in crimes without motives. No one can find one for this explosion, I guess."

"Well, there are some theories."

"Like what?"

"You know Sena's, I guess. He doesn't seem to have any ideas about a motive, but he appears to think that Dillon Charley was tied up in some sort of conspiracy. And then there's another theory that Gordo did it himself."

"Why?"

"The way the story goes, the older brother was the apple of everybody's eye—including his mother's. Gordo is supposed to have known that the old lady was leaving the ranch to Robert. So he blows up the oil well."

"How'd he handle it?"

Vines shrugged. "I don't know," he said. "I heard it was a nitroglycerin explosion, some sort of charge they lower down into the shaft of oil wells to shake things up, but it went off too early. I guess you could set that stuff off by shooting into it with a rifle. It was all before my time."

"How does the Sena-did-it theory explain Dillon Charley's vision?"

"That's easy," Vines said. "Dillon finds out somehow that Sena was planning something funny. So he arranges to have his peyote vision at the church service, and he tells his crew to stay away from the well. Sena blows the place up, but he finds out that Dillon must have known something. So he tries to drive him away with the harassment."

"Could be," Chee said.

"I think Gordo would like to know if Dillon Charley told me anything," Vines said. "Did his questions lead that way?"

"More or less," Chee said. "Did Dillon Charley tell you anything?"

Vines smiled. "Did Gordo tell you to ask me that?"

"You brought it up," Chee said. "I'll change the question. What do you think happened out at that oil well?"

"I understand nitro is touchy stuff. In those days those accidents happened. I think they had another case like that in the state a few years earlier."

"Do you think it was an accident? Do you think Dillon Charley was just nervous about having the nitro at the well?"

Vines swiveled his chair to give himself a view out the window. Chee could see only his profile.

"I think Gordo Sena murdered his brother," Vines said.

8

COLTON WOLF WAS RUNNING a little behind schedule. He had prepared *oeufs en gelée* for his breakfast. He meticulously followed the recipe in *Gourmet* and that took time. The aspic required twelve minutes at a rolling boil, and preparing the purée of peas for the garnish took longer still, and then another hour was required to allow the eggs to cool properly in their molds of aspic. It was mid-morning when he folded away the breakfast linen and cleared the silver and china from the Formica top of his trailer's eating surface. He had planned to work two hours on the model Baldwin steam engine he was building. Now he cut that to eighty minutes, working most of the time with his jeweler's glass in his eye and getting much of the fitting done on the piston assembly. The alarm dinged at 11:35 A.M. Colton pulled the covers over his lathe and drill and put his metal working tools carefully back in their proper places in his toolbox and the toolbox back in his lock cabinet. The cabinet also held his collection of steam engines, all of which actually operated—blowing whistles, driving belts, and turning wheels—and all of which had been made by Colton himself. The engines sat among the tools of his trade—two rifles, the chambers and trigger assembly sections of three pistols, an assortment of barrels to be screwed into these assemblies, an array of silencers, three small boxes trailing insulated wires, which were bomb detonators, a candy box which held plastic explosive (Colton kept eight sticks of dynamite and his dynamite caps safely cool in the refrigerator), and a row of cans of shaving cream and spray deodorant. Except for the rifles and their telescopic sights, he had manufactured much of this paraphernalia himself—partly because if it wasn't purchased it couldn't be traced and partly because some of it couldn't be bought. The shaving cream and deodorant cans were Colton's way of getting his tools through the x-ray stations at airport loading gates. One could fit the parts of one of Colton's pistols plus its silencer into two cans, screw the tops back on, and show an airport inspection nothing more questionable than Burma Shave. The bomb detonators were also the products of Colton's skill. He'd learned the principle from a former Special Services soldier he'd met in Idaho's Point-of-the-Mountain prison. It involved two batteries and a little ball of mercury which closed the electrical connection when the box moved.

Colton locked it all away, and went to make his mail check.

It wasn't that Colton Wolf expected any mail. It was part of the routine by which he lived. In whatever town he parked his trailer, Colton immediately rented a post office box. He rented it in the name of whatever commercial-sounding noun came to mind. Then he mailed a note to Boxholder at a post office box number in El Paso, Texas, in which he reported his new address. That was Colton's link to the man who provided him with his assignments. It was his only link with the world. In Colton Wolf's mind, and sometimes in his dreams, it was the flaw through which the world would someday catch him and kill him. Colton wished there were another way to do business. There wasn't. So he minimized the risk as much as he could. Minimizing risks was very much a part of Colton Wolf's life.

He drove his GMC pickup slowly past the branch post office, inspecting parked cars. Nothing looked suspicious. He parked at the Safeway lot and strolled the block and a half to the post office, taking inventory of what he saw. Two women and a man were in the lobby. The clerks behind the counter were familiar faces. Colton walked to the wall of post office boxes. Through the glass of box 1191 he could see an envelope. He ignored it and inspected box 960. It was empty. Colton walked out through the lobby, memorizing the customers. He went back to the Safeway, bought a small filet, a half pound of mushrooms, a pound of white grapes, a half pint of cream, and an ounce of black pepper. He put the groceries in the truck, climbed in himself, and tuned in a country western music station on the radio. He let twenty minutes pass while he listened. Then he walked back to the post office. Five customers were in the lobby now and none matched the previous three. Colton walked directly to box 1191 and removed the envelope. A smaller envelope lay under it. He slipped both into his jacket pocket and returned to the truck. No one followed him, and no one followed him a few minutes later as he drove back up the freeway ramp. Colton Wolf had survived another contact with the world.

The smaller envelope was addressed simply to his box number. It contained a slip of paper on which a series of numerals was penciled. Properly sorted out, they gave Colton a telephone number to call and the time of 2:10 P.M. to call it. He had put the slip in his shirt pocket. The second envelope bore the return address of Webster Investigations and a Los Angeles street number. Colton had known that it would, since no one else knew his box number, but even so he had felt his stomach tighten as he put the envelope on the seat beside him. When he got home he would open it. Meanwhile he would try not to think about it.

In the trailer, he put away the groceries and plugged in the coffeepot. Then he sat in his recliner, dried his palms on his trouser legs, slit open the envelope, and removed the contents. Two typewritten pages were folded around an expense statement. Wolf put the statement aside.

Dear Mr. Wolf:

First the bad news, which is that the lead I had run across in Anaheim didn't pay off. The woman was far too young to be your mother. I found her birth certificate in the county courthouse before I made arrangements with the detective in Anaheim, so I saved you that money.

The good news is that I located a truckdriver who worked at the Mayflower agency in Bakersfield in the early 1960s and he remembers working with Buddy Shaw. He found an address where Shaw lived in San Francisco. It's old, but it will give us a place to start tracking him down. . . .

Wolf finished the first page, laid it carefully on the arm of the recliner, and read through the second page. That done, he read both pages again, very slowly. Then he glanced at the itemized statement. It covered a month, charging Wolf for five days of time and an assortment of expenses which added up to a little more than eleven hundred dollars. He sat then with his slender, long-fingered hands resting in his lap, and thought.

His face, too, was slender, and his body and his bones, but a sinewy tension about him gave his thinness the look of a honed blade. His hair was thin, the shade of old straw, and his eyebrows and lashes were almost invisible against pale, freckled skin. His eyes were a faint blue-green—about the tint of old ice. Colton Wolf looked bleached, drained of pigment, antiseptic, neat, emotionless.

In fact, at the moment his emotions were mixed. At one level of his intelligence, Colton was encouraged. The detective would find Buddy Shaw. Shaw would still be living with Colton's mother. Or Shaw would know where to find her. And then there would be the reunion. At another level, Colton believed none of that. Webster was screwing him. The private detective had been screwing him for four expensive years. There were no trips, no hotel bills, no long-distance calls, no trace of Buddy Shaw. Webster had had no more success than the first private detective Colton had hired. Webster simply sat in his office in Encino and once a month dreamed up a letter and fabricated an itemized bill. The first detective had gone to the house Colton and his mother and Buddy Shaw had occupied in Bakersfield. He had found it occupied by transients who knew absolutely nothing helpful. Absolutely nothing about a man and a woman and a child who had lived there nineteen years before. Colton had destroyed that report, tearing it savagely into shreds. But he still remembered what it said. It said the house was now occupied by a Mexican woman. The realtor who handled the place kept records back only five years. During that time there had been three other occupants. None had left forwarding addresses. There was no record in the county courthouse of a marriage between a man named Buddy Shaw, or any other Shaw, and a woman named Linda Betty Fry. Mayflower Van Lines records showed that a Buddy Shaw had been employed at their warehouse for eleven months nineteen years earlier. He had been fired for drunkenness. Police records showed an E. W. Shaw, a.k.a. Buddy Shaw, three times. He had been booked once for drunk and disorderly, had done thirty days for aggravated assault, and had been arrested for assault with a deadly weapon. No disposition of that was recorded. Relative to the woman herself there was hardly a trace. Just the booking sheet on Shaw, showing a woman identified as Linda Betty Maddox, brought in with him on the disorderly charge.

Colton remembered the letter in detail. He especially remembered the final paragraph:

> Unless you can provide more information relative to this woman, there's no hope of finding her. Can you tell us her age, where she was born, something about her family, mother, father, brothers, sisters, where she was educated, where she was married, or any information about her past? Without such information to develop leads, there is simply no hope of finding her.

No hope of finding her. He had been living in Oklahoma City then, using the name Fry. He had driven to Bakersfield. Two hard days and nights on the highway. In Nevada, he'd decided his name probably wasn't Fry. Maybe it was Maddox, but it wasn't Fry. He remembered Fry faintly—a round, dark, pock-marked face, a round belly, a sullen, unhappy mouth. They had lived with him in San Jose and Colton had been Colton Fry in school there. He'd assumed Fry was his father. Perhaps it was someone named Maddox. Colton could remember no one by that name. Somewhere west of Las Vegas, he'd decided to choose a neutral name for himself. He'd use it only until he could find his mother. She'd tell him his real name. She'd tell him about his father, and his grandparents. And about the family home. It would be in a small town, Colton thought, and there'd be a graveyard with tombstones for the family. When he found her, she'd tell him who he was. Until then, he'd pick a last name. Something simple. He picked Wolf.

The coffee was perking now on the butane burner. Through the aluminum walls of the trailer came the sound of a truck's air horn blaring on the freeway. Colton was not conscious of either sound. He was remembering arriving in Bakersfield, the drive to the old neighborhood. The Mexican woman who came to the door spoke no English, but her daughter had talked to him. She knew nothing of a thin, blue-eyed blond woman named Linda Betty, nor of a burly man named Buddy Shaw. He could see the girl now, nervous at his questioning. And he could see the cracked concrete steps as he left the porch—no more broken now than they had been when he was eleven and had sat on them those nights when Buddy Shaw and his mother were drunk, had sat waiting for Shaw to go to sleep so that he could slip in.

Colton had stood beside his pickup, looking back at the house. The sparse grass he remembered was no longer there, the glass in one window was replaced by plywood. But otherwise it looked much the same. The last time he had seen it was the day after his twelfth birthday—the last time he had come home. The boy he knew at school had said he couldn't stay at his house any longer and he had walked home to see if Buddy Shaw had sobered up, and if Buddy Shaw would let him return. He had found the house empty. He had peered through the windows and seen the kitchen stripped of his mother's pans, and the bathroom stripped of her toiletries. But in the room where he slept, his things were still scattered. The bedclothing was gone from the cot, but the blue jacket his mother had got for him somewhere was still hanging on its peg. And his books were there. And his cap. He had broken a window and gone inside, cutting his hand in his panic. There had been nothing except the old furniture that had been there when they moved in and his own spare clothing.

Colton Wolf stirred uneasily in the recliner. All the desolation of that discovery came back to him again—the sense of loss and confusion and rejection, and with it the bleak, hopeless loneliness. Where could she be? How could he find her? Why had she gone? On the burner, the percolator gave a final cough and fell silent, its duty done. Colton Wolf ignored the sound, if he heard it. He was considering the same questions he'd considered for nineteen years.

A few minutes after one-thirty, he pushed himself out of the recliner and poured a cup of coffee. He took it to the truck, to sip as he drove. At a pay booth beside Central Avenue he made the call. He dialed the El Paso, Texas, area code, and the prefix number, and then waited while the second hand of his watch swept toward 2:10. Then he completed the dialing. He dropped in the coins and heard the number ring just a moment before the second hand swept past his deadline.

It was answered instantly. "This is Boxholder," the voice said. That address had become something of a joke between them. A joke and a code.

"Okay," Colton said. "Boxholder here, too."

"We have another opportunity in New Mexico," the voice said. "One thing led to another, I guess."

"Same client?" Colton asked.

Silence. "We never talk about clients," Boxholder said. "Remember?"

"Sorry," Colton said.

"Conditions are a lot the same, though. The subject won't be on guard. And there's a hurry."

"How much hurry?" Colton asked. Hurry bothered him. And his voice showed it.

"Nothing specific," Boxholder said. "Just the quicker the better. Every day increases the risk. So forth."

"I don't like to rush things," Colton said. "Things go wrong."

"You don't have to handle it," Boxholder said. "Maybe you'd better not. But I know you wanted to clean up that original business, and that kept you in Albuquerque anyway, and . . ."

"I think I'll have the other business finished in twenty-four hours or so," Colton said. "Maybe tonight."

"Well, that's all we're committed to. After that's done we've kept the original contract." Boxholder chuckled. "Took a little longer than anybody figured, but what the hell?" Silence.

"I thought maybe you'd like to show these folks how good you usually are."

Colton grimaced. Boxholder assumed the thought of a dissatisfied customer would bother him. That was correct. Boxholder assumed he took intense pride in his work. That was also correct. "Okay," he said. "Tell me about it."

Boxholder told him. Then, as they always did, they arranged the time and telephone number for Colton's report.

Colton used up three hours. He walked. He dropped the letter he had written to Webster Investigations into a mailbox. It contained his check for $1,087.50 and a note suggesting that Webster run personal ads in West Coast newspapers asking Linda Betty Shaw/Fry/Maddox to contact him. He walked some more. He sat on the bench at a bus stop. The bus stop was near a school crossing and he studied the homeward-bound students. They seemed to be junior-high age and younger, and most of them walked in little clusters and bunches, talking. Once a single kid came along, all by herself. Colton guessed the single was somebody who had just moved to the neighborhood. If you did that, you couldn't make friends, because everybody already had them. When he was eight they had lived in San Diego in this one apartment almost a year and he had made a friend there. And then when he was fourteen and had been in Taylorville long enough, he had made a friend or two. But that was different. In reform school nobody knew anybody at first and everybody was looking for connections. Taylorville had been a pretty good place, all in all, and he'd been glad enough to go back for his second stretch. They kept the gays off of you in Taylorville. Not like in Folsom, where he'd done his armed robbery time.

Finally it was late enough. He called the University of New Mexico Hospital and asked for Mrs. Myers on the terminal ward. As always, her voice was placid. "I'm afraid it's all over," she said. "He's been in a coma all day and his heart finally quit."

"Well, you just have to be philosophical about it."

"That's right," Mrs. Myers said. "But it's always a blow."

"Well," Colton said. He found himself searching for something else to say—a way to extend the conversation. But there was no reason for that. He was finished with Mrs. Myers. This would be the last of more than two months of intermittent conversations, all carefully planned, all carefully executed. First he had learned the name of the nurse who ran the middle shift on the cancer ward. He had got that from hospital information by pretending he wanted to send her a thank-you card. And then, on his first call to learn the patient's condition, he had said, "By the way, are you Mrs. Myers? He's told me how kind you've been to him. I want to thank you for that." That had set the tone. Colton rarely talked to anyone, but he knew how to do it well. He watched television, and he listened carefully to conversations in airports and restaurants and the waiting lines for movies—the places where people talked to each other. Once in a while he practiced, with cabdrivers or the call girls he took to motels twice a month. But he rarely talked to the same person more than once or twice, except for Boxholder. After all this time, he found himself imagining how Mrs. Myers looked and what she was like—just as he wondered about Boxholder. He had been tempted to go to the ward some evening and take a look at her. But that involved a risk. Colton did not take risks. "Well," he said again. "Thank you very much," and he hung up.

9

COLTON LEFT THE TRAILER just as the ten o'clock news was beginning on Channel 7. He was wearing charcoal slacks, a black pullover, and his crepe-soled shoes. He preferred going bareheaded, but tonight he pulled a navy-blue stocking cap over his straw-colored hair. He took with him a canvas flight bag in which he had put a folding shovel, a green blanket, a white cotton coat with the legend STRONG-THORNE MORTUARY printed on the back, and a New Mexico automobile license plate. He had driven past the Albuquerque airport after telephoning and had collected the plate from a car left in the low-rate parking lot where long-term travelers parked their cars. Then he'd replaced the plate he would use with one switched from another car. If the theft was reported, the police would have the wrong number.

He drove back to the airport now, left his pickup in the upper lot, and rented a Chevrolet station wagon from Hertz, using a driver's license and credit card that identified him as Charles Minton, with a Dallas post office box address. Then he took Interstate 25 south and turned the wagon westward at the Rio Bravo exit. He drove slowly, counting the tenths of miles on the odometer. Near the river, he turned off the pavement onto a narrow dirt road. He got out of the wagon there, taped down the switch to keep the courtesy light off when the door was opened, and replaced the Hertz license with the stolen plate. It was after 11:00 P.M. now, a cloudless night lit by a partial moon. The dirt road crossed a cattle guard, curved across a culvert, and branched. Colton angled left. The road became two tire tracks winding through the cottonwood of the Rio Grande's silted flood plain. The tracks crossed an irrigation drain on a rattling plank bridge and dropped abruptly downward. A hundred jolting yards beyond the drain levee, Colton stopped. His headlights illuminated the stripped body of an old Ford sedan, rusty and riddled with bullet holes. Beyond it was the ruins of another car, also the target of years of hunters. Trash was everywhere—a rotting mattress, the corpse of a refrigerator, cans, bottles, boxes, papers, rags, tattered roofing paper, brush. Colton flicked off headlights and engine and rolled down the windows on both sides of the car. He sat without moving for perhaps ten minutes. He heard the ticking of the cooling engine, and the occasional sound of diesels moving on the interstate far up the valley. It was a windless night and he heard nothing else. Satisfied, he removed the shovel from the bag and climbed out of the wagon.

He pulled the mattress aside and dug where it had been, piling the earth carefully. Even in the dark, it was easy going in the loamy soil. He wanted a hole about six feet long and at least four feet deep.

10

COLTON REACHED the University of New Mexico parking lot a little before 2 A.M. He had scouted it before, but two weeks had passed. If anything had changed, Colton wanted to know it early. He replaced his windbreaker with the mortuary coat. The woman at the desk didn't look up and the hall to the elevators was empty. The second-floor hall was also deserted. So far, fine. But down the hall Colton could see a paper sign taped to the door of the morphology laboratory. It read: MORPHOLOGY LABORATORY MOVED TO STATE LABORATORY BUILDING. He stared at the sign, dismayed. He moved quickly around the corner. The wide door that opened into the morgue was still shielded with a sheet of plywood to protect it from the bumps of metal body carts. He tried the knob. Locked. He had expected it to be locked. Would they have moved the morgue along with the autopsy laboratory? Even if they did, the hospital would need a place to hold bodies overnight. From his trouser cuff he extracted a thin steel blade which he had stitched into place. It proved as quick as a key. He swung the door shut behind him and found the switch in the darkness. Three body carts were lined against the wall. All were empty. Beyond them the stainless-steel door of the walk-in refrigerator stood closed. Colton swung it open. Two carts were parked inside, each bearing a sheet-shrouded figure. Colton read the tag on the nearest one. It identified the victim as Randy A. Johnson, 23 years old, Roswell, New Mexico. Dead on arrival. Head and neck injuries. Motorcycle accident. Colton checked the next tag. It said: EMER-

SON CHARLEY. AUTOPSY. HOLD FOR CRTC. "CRTC" would mean Cancer Research and Treatment Center. Colton folded back the sheet. He had seen the face before only at a distance. It was gaunt now, drawn with the effects of a lingering death. But he recognized it. This time nothing would go wrong. He replaced the sheet.

In the hall, he stood a moment, listening. A faint thumping came from the hospital laundry. All else was quiet. Colton glanced at his watch. Five after three. He decided not to wait. The odds, he decided, wouldn't improve.

It was fourteen after three when he parked the station wagon beside the loading dock. The dock door stood partly open, as he had left it, and he could still hear a thumping from the laundry. He left the station wagon's tailgate open. It was thirty-five steps from the doorway of the dock to the morgue door. He picked the lock again and slipped in.

There were two red plastic sacks of clothing on the floor beside the carts. He put the nearest one under the sheet beside the corpse and wheeled the cart out of the refrigerator. At the door of the morgue he paused again, listening. Thirty-five steps, and then perhaps sixty seconds on the dock while he lifted the body into the station wagon. The hall was absolutely silent. The cart rolled down it, trailing the slight sound of rubber tires on tile. On the dock, Colton pushed the cart out of sight of the doorway. He extracted the clothing sack and tossed it into the back of the wagon.

"Come on, friend," he said, and he tucked the sheet around the body and lifted it in his arms. It was stiff with rigor mortis. Surprisingly light. "Here we go now," Colton said. He slid the body into the station wagon and covered it with the green blanket.

The period of high risk was almost over now. He closed the tailgate, rolled the body cart back into the hallway. The station wagon's engine started instantly. As he did the left turn out of the service drive, he glanced in the rear-view mirror. The dock was deserted. No one had seen him. It had gone perfectly. Absolutely no tracks had been left.

Colton tuned in a country western station on his way back to the grave. He felt happier than he had for months. Happy for the first time since he had called Boxholder and told him of the failure. The memory was vivid. Two hours sitting in the airport, waiting for the time to call the El Paso number. Dreading it. He had never failed before. From the very first—torching the nightclub in Denver seven years before—he had always reported only success. Not just success but perfection. The job done. No witnesses. No evidence. No tracks. Perfection. And always Boxholder's voice, warm and friendly, congratulating him. This time there had been no congratulations. First there had been only silence, and then Boxholder's voice was cold.

"Give me the number you're calling from. Wait right there. I'll call the client and call you back. Be there."

"Tell him I won't accept the fee," Colton had said. "Tell him I'll finish the job."

"You just wait," Boxholder said.

Colton had waited. It was more than four hours before the telephone rang.

"Your man was checking into the hospital," Boxholder said. "He's in now. We're to just keep an eye on things and when he dies, you get rid of the body. Get it right away and get rid of it."

"My God," Colton said. "I baby-sit this guy until he dies?"

"Not long," Boxholder said. "He's got a kind of cancer that works fast."

"Then why . . ." Colton let the question trail off.

"Maybe it doesn't work fast enough," Boxholder said. "Do you care?"

"No," Colton said. "I guess not."

But it seemed curious then, and it seemed curious now, this business of getting rid of the body. Curious, but well done. The grave filled. The rotting mattress pulled across it and the trash scattered over the mattress. No one would ever find the body of Emerson Charley. Reporting time was noon tomorrow. Colton anticipated it happily. Boxholder would be pleased.

11

JIM CHEE HAD ROLLED the two-hundred-dollar check from Ben Vines and the five one-hundred-dollar bills from the envelope Mrs. Vines had handed him into a tight cylinder. It was not much larger than a cigaret. Each night he dropped the tube into one of the boots beside his bed. Each morning, after he'd said his brief prayer of greeting to the dawning day, he shook the tube out of the boot and considered what to do with it. And each morning he finally stuck the tube back into his shirt pocket, thereby signaling that the matter remained undecided. On the fourth morning, Chee noticed that the edge of the check was frayed. He unrolled the tube, put check and cash side by side on his table, and stared at them.

Two hundred dollars was too much to be offered for the little trouble he'd been involved in. Worse, why would Mrs. Vines offer him three thousand dollars to recover a box she had stolen herself? For those as inconceivably rich as the Vineses the money would be relatively meaningless. But his uncle had warned him against that kind of thinking.

"Don't think a man don't care about one goat because he's got a thousand of 'em," Hosteen Nakai would say. "He's got a thousand because he cares more about goats than he cares about his relatives." In other words, don't expect the rich to be generous.

And what would his uncle advise him to do about this particular money? Chee grinned, thinking about it. There'd be no advice—not directly. There'd be a hundred questions: Which one was lying? What motivated the large payments? Why did the Checkerboard Navajos think Vines was a witch? Or did they? How was the Charley outfit mixed into this affair? And when Chee could offer no answers, Hosteen Nakai would smile at him and remind him of what he had told Chee a long time ago. He'd told Chee he had to understand white people.

Chee used his two forefingers to tap the stack of currency into a neat pile. Mrs. Vines had lied to him, at least a little. He picked up the check and looked at B. J. Vines' bold signature. Vines' story had been almost purely lies. Chee folded the check and slid it into the credit card pocket of his billfold. He put the currency in the cash compartment. He would talk to Tomas Charley and see what he could learn.

Talking to Tomas Charley meant finding him. Becenti had remembered only that he lived somewhere beyond the eastern limits of the Checkerboard—somewhere near Mount Taylor. Chee made telephone calls. Shortly before noon he learned that Charley was employed by Kerrmac Nuclear Fuels. A quick call to the Kerrmac personnel office at Grants revealed that Charley was the driver of an ore loader, that he had the day off, that he had no telephone, the rural route address from the Grants post office matched the one the hospital had provided—a mailbox on the road between Grants and San Mateo village.

It was probably no more than thirty miles from Crownpoint as the raven flew, but for something with wheels it was around ninety. Chee told Officer Benny Yazzie, who was holding down the office, that he wouldn't be back until evening.

While he drove, Chee worked at memorizing the Night Chant. He switched on the tape recorder and ran the cassette forward to the place where the singer awakens the spirit of Talking God in the sacred mask. On Interstate 40, he drove in the slow lane, listening carefully. Truckers, wise to the ways of this stretch of highway, roared past him, safe in the knowledge that tribal police had no jurisdiction here. Passenger cars slowed to the legal fifty-five, eyeing him nervously. Chee ignored them all. He concentrated on the voice of his uncle, strong and sure, singing the words that Changing Woman had taught at the very creation of his people.

Above the hills of evening, he stirs, he stirs.
Covered with the pollen of evening, he stirs, he stirs.
The Talking God stirs, he stirs amid the sunset.
Along the trail of beauty, he stirs, he stirs.
With beauty all around him, he stirs, he stirs.

The recorder was on the seat beside him. Chee silenced Hosteen Nakai's voice with a touch of the off button, concentrated a moment, then repeated the five statements, trying to reproduce cadence and notes as well as meaning. By the time he reached the Grants interchange, he was confident he had the entire sequence of mask songs fixed in his mind.

Even among a people who placed high value on memory and who honed it in their children almost from birth, Chee's talent was unusually strong. It had caused his family to think of him from a very early age as one who might become a singer. The Slow Talking Dinee had produced more famous singers than any of the other more than sixty Navajo clans. And the family of his mother had produced far more than its share. His uncle, the brother of his mother, was among the most prominent of these. He was Hosteen Frank Sam Nakai, who performed the Night Chant and the Enemy Way and key parts of several other curing ceremonials, and who sometimes taught ceremonialism at the Navajo Community College at Rough Rock. It was Hosteen Nakai who had chosen Jimmy Chee's "war name," which was Long Thinker. Thus his uncle was one of the very few who knew his real and secret identity. His uncle had named him, but when he had asked his uncle to teach him to be a singer, his uncle had at first refused.

"There is a first step which must be taken," Hosteen Nakai had said. "Nothing important can happen before that." As a first step, Jimmy Chee must study the white man and the way of the white man. When he came to understand this white man's world which surrounded the People, he must make a decision. Would he follow the white man's way or would he be a Navajo?

His uncle had driven his truck into Gallup and parked it on Railroad Avenue, where they could see the bars and watch the Navajos and the Zunis going in and out of them. Jimmy Chee remembered it very well. He remembered the woman who came out of the Turquoise Tavern and the man in the black reservation hat who followed her. They had walked unsteadily, both drunk. The woman had lost her balance and sat heavily on the dirty sidewalk, and the man had bent to help her. His hat had fallen and rolled into the gutter. Hosteen Nakai's fierce eyes had watched all this.

"They cannot decide," he said. "The way Changing Woman taught us is too hard for them, and they have lost its beauty. But they do not know the white man's way. You have to decide. It is easy, now, to be a white man. You have gone to school and there are scholarships to go more, and jobs if you learn what the white man puts his value in."

Jimmy Chee had said that he had already decided. He wanted to walk in beauty as a Navajo.

"You can't decide until you understand the white man. They have much that we don't have. To be a Navajo is to have no money," Hosteen Nakai had said. "When you are older we will talk again. If you still wish it, I will begin teaching you something. But you must study the white man's way."

Chee had studied. After Shiprock High School, he had enrolled at the University of New Mexico. He'd studied anthropology, sociology, and American literature in class. Every waking moment he studied the way white men behaved. All four subjects fascinated him. When he came home during semester breaks to his mother's place in the Chuska Mountains, Hosteen Nakai taught him the wisdom of the Dinee. Finally his uncle began teaching him the ritual songs that brought the People back from their sicknesses to walk in beauty. And Chee's memory always served him well.

On the road that leads from Grants into the back side of Ambrosia Lakes uranium fields, Chee returned the recorder to its case and concentrated on finding the home of Tomas Charley. He found it some thirty feet west of the narrow asphalt pavement. It was a two-room adobe to which someone had connected a wooden frame lean-to with a roof of red composition shingles. A 1962 Chevrolet Impala squatted on cinderblock supports in the front yard, all four of its wheels missing. Chee pulled his patrol car to a stop beside it and sat waiting. If someone was home, willing to receive a visitor, he would appear at the door. If he didn't after a polite interval of waiting, Chee would knock.

The front door opened and Chee could see someone looking at him through the screen. A child. Chee waited. No one else appeared. Chee climbed out of the carryall.

"Ya-tah," he said. "Hello."

"Hello," the child said. It was a boy, about ten or twelve.

"I'm looking for Tomas Charley," Chee said.

"He went to get my mother," the boy said.

"Where's that?"

"They won't be there," the boy said. "She's a weaver. My uncle was taking her to the rug auction."

"At Crownpoint?" Chee asked.

"Yeah," the boy said. "She's going to sell a bunch of rugs."

Chee laughed. "I'm not very lucky today," he said. "That's where I came from and now I'll have to drive right back."

"You going to see my uncle there?"

"If I can find him," Chee said. "What's he driving?"

"A 1975 Ford pickup," the boy said. "An F-150. Blue. If you see him, tell him maybe somebody wants to buy our old Chevy. Tell him a man came by right after he left, looking for him," the boy said.

"Sure," Chee said. "Anything else?"

"Maybe the man will see him there at the rug auction," the boy said. "He's a blond guy, wearing a yellow jacket. He was going to look for him there."

"Okay," Chee said. He looked at the car with more interest now. The exposed brake drums were brown with rust and the upholstery in the back seat hung down in dusty festoons. Tomas Charley's nephew was overly optimistic. No one was going to drive all the way to Crownpoint to arrange to buy that junker.

12

IT WAS AFTER SUNDOWN when Chee drove past the Tribal Police office. It was dark. On the other side of the village, perhaps two hundred assorted vehicles were parked at the Crownpoint elementary school, suggesting a good turnout for the November rug auction. Chee found a blue Ford 150 pickup. Parked next to it was a green-and-white Plymouth, like the one Charley's nephew had said the would-be car buyer was driving. Chee checked it quickly. It was new, with less than three thousand miles on the odometer. A folder on the dashboard suggested it had been rented from the Albuquerque airport office of Hertz.

Inside the school, the air was rich with a mélange of aromas. Chee identified the smells of cooking fry bread, floor wax, blackboard chalk, stewing mutton and red chili, of raw wool, of horses, and of humans. In the auditorium, perhaps a hundred potential buyers were wandering among the stacks of rugs on the display tables, inspecting the offerings and noting item numbers. At this hour, most of the crowd would be in the cafeteria, eating the traditional auction dinner of Navajo tacos—tortillas topped with a lethal combination of stewed mutton and chili. Chee stood just inside the auditorium entrance, methodically examining its inhabitants. He had little idea what Charley would look like—just Becenti's sketchy description. His inspection was simply a matter of habit.

"Looking for someone?"

The voice came from beside him, from a young woman in

a blue turtleneck sweater. The woman was small, the sweater large, and the face atop the folds of bulky cloth was unsmiling.

"Trying to find a man named Tomas Charley," Chee said. "But I don't know what he looks like."

The woman's face was oval, framed by soft blond hair. Her eyes were large, and blue, and intent on Chee. A pretty lady, and Chee recognized the look. He had seen it often at the University of New Mexico—and most often among Anglo coeds enrolled in Native American Studies courses. The courses attracted Anglo students, largely female, enjoying racial/ethnic guilt trips. Chee had concluded early that their interest was more in Indian males than in Indian mythology. Their eyes asked if you were really any different from the blond boys they had grown up with. Chee looked now into the eyes of the woman in the bulky blue turtleneck and detected the same question. Or thought he did. There was also something else. He smiled at her. "Not knowing what he looks like makes it tougher to find him."

"Why not just go away and leave him alone?" she asked. "What are you hunting him for?"

Chee's smile evaporated. "I have a message from his nephew," he said. "Somebody wants to buy his old car and . . ."

"Oh," the young woman said. She looked embarrassed. "I guess I shouldn't jump to conclusions. I'm sorry. I don't know him."

"I'll just ask around," Chee said. Her distaste for police was another standard reaction Chee had learned to expect from the young Anglos the reservation seemed to attract. He suspected there was a federal agency somewhere assigned to teach social workers that all police were Cossacks and that Navajo police were the worst of all. "Are you with the Bureau of Indian Affairs?" he asked.

"No," she said. "I'm helping the weavers' cooperative." She gestured vaguely toward the check-in table, where two Navajo women were sorting through papers. "But I teach school here. Fifth grade. English and social studies." The hostility was gone from her eyes now. The curiosity remained.

"I'm Jim Chee." He extended his hand. "I've been assigned

to the police station here. Fairly new here."

"I noticed your uniform," she said. She took his extended hand. "Mary Landon," she said. "I'm new, too. From Wisconsin, but I taught last spring at Laguna Pueblo school."

"How do you do," Chee said. Her hand was small and cool in his, and very quickly withdrawn.

"I have to get back to work," Mary Landon said, and she was gone.

It took Chee about thirty minutes to establish that Tomas Charley was present at the auction and to get a description of the man. He might have done it faster had there been any sense of urgency. There wasn't. Chee was more involved in getting acquainted with the occupants of his territory. Then Mary Landon was at his elbow again.

"That's him," she said. "Right over there. The red-and-black mackinaw and the black felt hat."

"Thanks," Chee said. Mary Landon still wasn't smiling.

Tomas Charley was leaning against the wall alone. He seemed to be watching someone in the crowd. Mary Landon said something else, but Chee didn't hear it. He was studying Charley. He was a small man—not over five and a half feet—and skinny. His face was bony, with small, deep-set eyes and a narrow forehead under the brim of his tipped-back hat. There was an alertness about him, a tension. The eyes shifted to Chee now, quickly past him, and back again. Becenti had said he was half crazy, a fanatic. The small black eyes had the look of those who see visions. Getting Tomas Charley to talk, Chee thought, would take a lot of care and a lot of luck.

As it developed, it was no trouble at all. They talked a bit about the rug auction, and about the drought. Chee leaned against the wall beside the man, guiding the conversation. The auctioneer was on the stage now, a florid white man explaining the rules in a West Texas voice. Chee talked of Sheriff Gordo Sena, of jurisdiction problems between Navajo police and white sheriffs. The first rug was auctioned for $65. Bidding on the second one stuck at $110. The auctioneer put it aside and joked with the crowd about its stinginess. He moved the offer up to $155, and sold it.

Chee talked of Mrs. Vines' job offer, of what she'd said of

the burglary, of his decision not to get involved in it, and of Vines' withdrawing the offer. Tomas Charley said less and less.

"It's no business of mine," Chee said. "I don't care about the burglar." He grinned at Charley. "I know who went in Vines' house and got that box. You know who went in. And Gordo Sena never is going to know. What I'd like to know is what was in that box."

Charley said nothing. Chee waited. On the fifth rug, bidding was spirited. The auctioneer sold it for $240.

"I've got a curious mind," Chee said. "Lots of things funny about Vines. Lots of things funny about Gordo Sena. Mrs. Vines, too."

Tomas Charley glanced at him, then glanced away. He stood with his arms crossed in front of him. The fingers of his left hand, Chee noticed, tapped nervously against his right wrist.

"Why did Vines bury your grandfather there at his house?" Chee asked. "I wonder about that. And why did somebody try to kill your father? And why did Mrs. Vines want me to find Vines' old box? And then not want me to find it? And why did Gordo Sena warn me to mind my own business?"

Chee asked the last question directly to Charley. The drumming fingers stopped. Charley pursed his lips.

"I don't give a damn if you got into Vines' house and took something," Chee said. "None of my business. But what was in that box?"

"Rocks," Tomas Charley said. "Chunks of black rocks."

It occurred to Chee that he hadn't really thought about what the box might hold. But he hadn't expected this. He considered it. "No papers?" he asked. "Nothing with anything written on it?"

"Mostly rocks," Charley said.

"Nothing else?"

"Some medals," Charley said. "Stuff from the war. Stuff like that." He shrugged.

"Tell me everything that was in it."

Charley looked surprised. "Well," he said. "There's a little card glued inside the lid. Got Vines' name and address on it. Then there was three medals. One was the Purple Heart and the other two were like stars. One out of some kind of brown metal and the other one looked about the same, but it had a little silver star in the middle of it. And there was a set of wings like paratroopers wear, and a shoulder patch with an eagle head on it and silver bars like lieutenants wear in the army." Charley thought. "Photographs. A picture of a girl, and a picture of a man and woman standing by an old car, and then a whole bunch of black rocks." Charley stopped. The catalog was complete.

"Nothing else?" Chee asked. "What did you expect to find?"

Charley shrugged.

"Luck?" Chee asked.

Charley's face tightened. "Vines was a witch," he said. He didn't use the Navajo word, which meant witch, or skinwalker, or Navajo Wolf. He used a Keresan expression—the word the people of Laguna and Acoma used to mean sorcerer.

"I heard that, too," Chee said. "You think you'd find his medicine bundle?"

Charley glanced at Chee, then looked away. Time ticked past. The auctioneer began the rhythmic litany of another transaction.

"He was killing my father," Charley said. "I wanted to turn the witching around. I wanted to find something for that."

Chee didn't say any of the obvious things. He didn't say, "Your father is dying of cancer." He didn't say, "It's not witchcraft; it's something wrong with the way the cells grow." He said nothing at all. Tomas Charley was sure his father had been doomed by a witch. When that happened, the Navajo way was a ceremonial—usually the Enemy Way or the Prostitution Way. Each invoked a traditional formula which reversed the witchcraft and turned it against the witch. And each required something that the witch had used. But Tomas Charley was half Laguna. He saw Vines as the Lagunas saw sorcerers. Perhaps they had a different formula. The auctioneer completed his transaction, selling a small diamond-patterned rug to a woman using bidding card 72. Chee and Tomas Charley leaned against the wall, watching, their shoulders touching.

"Why was Vines witching your father?" Chee asked. "Do you know that?"

"Vines wasn't always a sorcerer," Charley said. "Once he was a good man, I think, and he helped my grandfather and he helped our church. He gave us our totem. He gave it to my grandfather. The mole. It is powerful, and it helps the Lord Peyote open the door for us. It helps bring us visions. Vines wanted to get it back. So he made my father sick. And then he stole my father's body."

On the stage, the auctioneer and his assistant held up a saddle blanket. "This un's a dandy," the Texan was saying. He leaned comically against its pretended weight. "Take a stout horse to carry this un. Wove so tight you couldn't get water through it. I'm starting at eighty. Yum at eighty. Eighty. Eighty. Yum at eighty. Eighty-five. Have eighty-five. Yum at eighty-five. Ninety. Yum at ninety."

"Stole your father's body?" Chee asked. He was thinking Emerson Charley had been alive last week. Very sick but alive. How long ago was it? Five days? Six? He glanced at Charley. The thin man was staring straight ahead, every line in his face rigid. He seemed to be remembering something.

"When did Vines steal your father's body?"

"Two, three days ago," Charley said. "Out of the hospital there at Albuquerque. And he got the mole back again."

"But how did he do it? Did he just walk in and walk out with it?"

Charley shrugged. "Vines is a witch," he said. "The hospital, they call me, and they tell me my father died and what to do with the body? When I get there, Vines had already got off with it. That's all I know."

"What was the hospital's explanation?"

"They didn't know what happened. Just the body was gone. One man told me that some of the kinfolks must have got a funeral home to get it. He said the body was put where they put the bodies, and the next day it was gone. He said it must have been a funeral home got it."

"You reported it to the police?"

"Yeah," Charley said. "They didn't do nothing."

They wouldn't, Chee thought. He imagined Charley showing up at the Albuquerque police building, trying to find somebody to take the report, telling a clerk (would the clerk have been incredulous, or merely bored?) of a missing body taken by a witch. What would the crime have been? At worst, transporting a cadaver without a permit from the medical examiner. And the police would have guessed it was merely a mix-up: the body claimed by another relative, a family feud perhaps. And Tomas Charley wouldn't have raised hell and pressed for answers. He already knew two answers. One was that nobody would pay much attention to a Navajo trying to raise hell. And the other was that a witch had flown away with the body. Still, Chee felt his anger rising at this indignity.

"Those sons-a-bitches," he said. "You want me to try to find him for you?"

Charley thought about it.

"Well," he said. "I'm half Acoma and half Navajo, and I guess I'm Navajo far as bodies go. When the old man died, he died. Body don't mean nothing but trouble. But my mother, she's Acoma. She'd like to know he's buried the right way. She wouldn't want a witch to have him."

"I'll see what I can do," Chee said. "Why do you think Vines got him?"

Charley hesitated. "It's got to do with our church," he said. "I got to go way back to explain it."

Tomas Charley went back to World War II, when his grandfather was working on the Santa Fe Railroad track crew, and had met an Indian from Oklahoma, and had been introduced to the Native American Church and Lord Peyote. His grandfather had founded a church in the Checkerboard country, and one day Lord Peyote had opened the door so his grandfather could see God. He was working then on an oil well, and God told him that something bad would happen the next day and to tell his crew not to go to work. The oil well had blown up just as God had warned and the word had spread among the Navajos and the Laguna-Acomas of this miracle, and the grandfather's congregation grew. By the next year more than two hundred people were coming to the Peyote Ways. Then one time a white man came. He was a uranium prospector named Benjamin Vines. Vines told everyone at the Peyote Way that the

Lord Peyote had given him a dream of where to find uranium ore.

"All this is the way my father told me," Charley said. "He said Vines came back about a month later and told my grandfather the uranium ore was where the Lord Peyote said it would be. They had another Peyote Way and Vines had another vision. This time Lord Peyote told Vines he had now done two miracles for my grandfather's church. He had saved the men from the explosion, and he had led Vines to the ore. He said Vines was blessed, and those men he had saved were blessed, and since the blessing had come from under the ground, from an oil well and uranium ore, their totem would be the mole and their name would be the name of the moles—the People of Darkness."

"And Vines gave your grandfather a mole fetish?"

"A little later," Charley said. "They didn't have a Way for a while because the Navajo Police and the BIA cops were arresting everybody and searching people for peyote buttons, and Gordo Sena was after everybody in the church. But then they had a Way at a secret place, and Vines gave these mole fetishes to my grandfather and to the other men who Lord Peyote had saved." Charley paused. "That was before Vines got to be a witch," he explained.

"How'd that happen?" Chee asked.

"First my grandfather got sick," Charley said. "They had a sing for him, but it didn't help very long. He went into the hospital. In and out a lot. Finally he died and Vines buried him up at his ranch. He was just building that big house then. The church sort of died out then for years. Then my father got it going again. After that, Vines came around. He tried to get my father to give him the medicine bundle, the box for Lord Peyote, the mole totem, all of the sacred things. My father wouldn't give them up. After that Vines didn't come to the Peyote Way again."

That seemed to be the end of the story. Charley slumped against the wall, looking across the crowded auditorium toward the stage. The Texan had just sold a small yellow *yei* rug to number 18 for forty-five dollars and was describing a black-and-gray diamond design from Two Gray Hills as "worth three hundred dollars in any trading post on the reservation."

"Then what?" Chee prodded.

Charley didn't say anything for a moment. "Then we started hearing things."

"Like what?"

"Hearing Vines was a witch."

There was another pause. The Navajo half of Charley seemed to be ascendant, Chee thought. Navajos did not like to talk about witches.

"Tell you what," Chee said. "You don't want that old box of Vines' with the rocks in it. You let me know where to look, and we'll get it back to the owner. If anybody asks how we found it, it was an anonymous telephone call."

"It's out in the malpais," Charley said. "It was locked. I took it to a place out there where I go and pried it open. It was heavy, so I just left it there." He explained to Chee how to find it. "I got to go now," he said. "I've got to work tomorrow."

"Did the man see you about buying that old Chevy?"

Charley looked surprised. "No," he said. "Somebody want to buy that?"

"That's what your nephew said. He said to tell you a man came looking for you, and he wanted to buy that old car, and he was going to look for you here."

"Must be crazy," Charley said. And he walked away.

And I must be crazy, too, Chee thought as he watched Charley move down the aisle toward the table where an association clerk was paying off rug weavers for their sales. Rocks in a keepsake box. B. J. Vines as mystic prophet. B. J. Vines as witch. A body lost out of a hospital morgue. And Chee wasting his time in an affair that made no sense at all.

He wasted more time watching the auction, moving among the spectators idly at first and then looking for Mary Landon. She was interested in him, of that he was sure. He was equally sure that it was nothing very personal. The interest was more generic than individual. Another Navajo male, adequately scrubbed and trimmed, would have been just as interesting to the blue-eyed woman. Fair enough. At the moment, he was particularly interested in whites, and white women. The Navajo women he knew—his mother, her two sisters, who were his "little mothers," the Navajo girls he'd been involved with—did nothing to explain Rosemary Vines. And he'd never really known the white girls. Their curiosity had put him off. But Mary Landon he would study. Unfortunately, Mary Landon was nowhere to be seen.

He walked into the parking lot, savoring the cold fresh air after the stuffy heat inside. Tomas Charley was standing beside his truck, talking to a white man in a yellow windbreaker. The white man was blond. The buyer of worthless rusty Chevrolets had found his man. Chee stared at him, curious. The white man seemed to feel the eyes on him. He stared back. The same man, Chee realized, had been watching him and Charley in their long conversation against the wall. Mary Landon was still invisible.

He found her, finally, in the cafeteria kitchen helping a half-dozen other women with cleanup operations.

"The message is delivered," Chee said. "Thanks."

It was the third time he had spoken to her, and Chee had a theory about third meetings between people. The third time you were no longer strangers.

"It must have been a long message," Mary said. "I think you found something to talk about besides someone wanting to buy a car." The words were skeptical, but after she said them she smiled.

Chee found himself trying to think of something to ask her, of a reason to be in this kitchen talking to her. His mind was blank. "How about having a cup of coffee?" he heard himself saying. "The coffee shop will be open late."

The first time she had looked at him she had been inspecting a Tribal Police sergeant. Now she was looking at a man asking her out for coffee. It was a different sort of inspection. "I have to finish with these pots," she said.

"I'll do it for you," Chee said.

Chee washed dishes each evening in his mobile home—a plate, cup, knife, and fork left over from breakfast, a second plate, a cup, and cutlery from dinner, and the frying pan used to cook both meals. But never since his university days had he washed dishes socially.

"You look like you enjoy that," Mary said. "Maybe you missed your calling."

Chee tried to think of something witty. He couldn't.

In the booth at the Crownpoint Café, Chee learned a little about Mary Landon, and she learned a little about him. She had come to Laguna the previous year to replace a teacher hurt in an automobile accident. Then she had landed the Crownpoint job. She was from a little place not far from Milwaukee. She had attended the University of Wisconsin. She liked canoeing and hiking, and the outdoors in general. She didn't like pretentious people. She liked teaching Navajo children, but wasn't sure what to do about their conditioning against competitiveness. She hoped to learn Navajo, but it was hard to pronounce and so far she could speak only a few phrases. She spoke them, and Chee pretended to understand, and Mary Landon was not fooled by the pretense but appreciated it and rewarded him with a genuinely friendly look. Chee asked her about her parents, and learned her father ran a sporting goods store. He decided not to ask her about her hostility to police. This wasn't the time for that, and the attitude was common enough.

Mary Landon learned Chee was one of the Slow Talking Dinee, the clan of his mother, and was "born to" the Bitter Water Dinee, the clan of his father. She learned that Chee's father was dead, that his maternal uncle was a noted *yataalii,* and she had been around Navajo country long enough to know about the role of these shamans in the ceremonial life of the People. She learned a good deal more about his family, ranging from his two older sisters through a galaxy of cousins, uncles, and aunts, one of whom represented the Greasy Water district on the Tribal Council.

"She's my mother's sister, which makes her my 'little mother,' " Chee said. "A real tiger."

"You're not playing the game," Mary Landon said. "I told you about me. You're just telling me about your family."

The statement surprised Chee. One defined himself by his family. How else? And then it occurred to him that white people didn't. They identified themselves by what they had done as individuals. He added sugar to his coffee, thinking about it.

"That's the way we play the game. If I was introducing you

to Navajos, I wouldn't say, 'This is Mary Landon, who teaches at Crownpoint,' and so forth. I'd say, 'This woman is a member of . . .'—your mother's family, and your father's family—and I'd tell about your uncles and aunts, so everyone would know just exactly where you fit in with the people around you."

" 'This woman'?" Mary Landon asked. "You wouldn't tell them my name?"

"That would be rude. Now more people have English names, but among traditional Navajos it's very impolite to say someone's name in their presence. Names are just reference words, when the person's not there."

Mary Landon looked incredulous. "I think that's . . ." She stopped.

"Silly?" Chee asked. "You have to understand the system. Our real names are secret. We call them war names. Somebody very close to you in the family names you when you're little. Something that fits your personality, if possible. Not more than a half-dozen people are ever going to know it. It's used for ceremonial purposes: if a girl is having her *kinaalda*—her puberty ceremony—or if you're having a sing done for you. Then, as you grow, people give you nicknames to refer to you. Like 'Cry Baby,' and 'Hard Runner,' or maybe 'Long Hands' or 'Ugly.' " Chee laughed. "I've got an uncle on my father's side everybody calls 'Liar.' "

"How about Jim Chee? Isn't that your real name?"

"Along came the trading posts," Chee said. "Along came the white man. He had to have a name to write down when one of us pawned our jewelry to him, or got credit for groceries. The traders started formalizing the nicknames, and before long we had to have names on birth certificates, so you got family names, like mine. I've had nicknames, too. Two or three. And I'm sure you do, too."

"Me?" Mary Landon looked surprised.

"How long you been at Crownpoint? Three months? Sure. The people have a name for you by now."

"Like what?"

"Something that fits. Maybe 'Pretty Teacher.' Or 'Stubborn Girl.' " Chee shrugged. " 'Blue Eyes.' 'Blond Woman.' 'Fast Talker.' Do you want me to find out for you?"

"Sure," she said. Then, "No, wait. Maybe just forget it. How about you? What do they call you?"

"Here? I don't know. When I was at Rough Rock they used to call me . . ." He paused, and then said the word carefully in Navajo. "It means 'One Who Studies to Be a Singer.' "

"Oh," Mary Landon said. "Are you?"

"I was," Chee said. "I guess I still am, in a way. It depends."

"On what?"

"I applied for admission to the FBI. More or less to see how I'd do. Took the tests. Got interviewed by the screening panel at Albuquerque. Last week I got a letter telling me I'd been accepted. I'm supposed to report to the academy in Virginia. December tenth."

She looked at him curiously. "So you're going to be an FBI agent."

"I don't know," Chee said.

"You haven't decided?"

"What's the rush? We work on Navajo time." Even as he said it, the flippancy sounded false. December 10 wasn't Navajo time. It was four weeks away. A specific, ironclad, unbendable deadline.

"But you can't be both a Navajo medicine man and an FBI agent?"

"Not really," Chee said. He wanted to change the subject, wanted not to talk about it. As a matter of fact, you couldn't be both a Navajo and an FBI agent. You couldn't be a Navajo away from the People. "By the way," he said, "thanks for helping with Tomas Charley. I learned what I needed to know. If he told me the truth, that is."

Mary Landon studied him. Chee remembered, belatedly, what he had told her about why he wanted to find Charley.

"Do people lie a lot in your business?"

The question sounded innocent. And if it was, the answer was yes, a lot of people lie to a policeman. But Chee sensed the barb. And the answer was different.

"I'm sorry about that," he said. "I did tell his nephew I'd pass on the message about the car. But I also wanted to see him about police business."

"And you couldn't tell me that." It was more a statement

than a question, and the proper answer, of course, was "No, I couldn't." But Chee sensed the hostility again (or perhaps it could now better be described as a mixture of caution and suspicion), and he was not in the mood to give the proper answer.

"I could tell you, but only if you don't mind complicated accounts of things that don't amount to much," Chee said. "Do you want to hear about it?"

She did. Chee told her about Vines, and Mrs. Vines, and the stolen keepsake box, and Sheriff Gordo Sena, and about the People of Darkness and the disappearing body, and finally about where Tomas Charley had left the box.

"And when you look at it all with a detached view," Chee said, "you see a Navajo cop simply exercising his curiosity. A crime of no particular importance. A total lack of jurisdiction."

"But it is curious," she said. "What do you think happened to Mr. Charley's father? And what are you going to do next?"

"I don't know about the body. Probably lost by the bureaucracy somehow and nobody cared enough to find it. As for me, next I'll go out in the malpais when I have some time and get the box and take a look at those rocks, and then I'll get the box back to Vines. He says he doesn't want his box back. But he must want those medals."

"What will you tell Vines?"

"I won't. I'll call the sheriff's office at Grants and tell them I got an anonymous tip on where the box had been left, and went out and found it, and for them to tell the Vineses to come and get it if they want it back."

Mary Landon raised her eyebrows and sipped her coffee.

"Okay," Chee said. "It's a lie. But how else does Vines get his box back without Charley getting in jail?"

"I can't think of a way," she said. "Something else puzzles me. How did Charley know he could trust you?"

Chee shrugged. "Because I look trustworthy?" he asked.

She laughed. "As a matter of fact, you don't," she said. "Could I go along when you go hunting the box?"

"Sure," Chee said. "We'll go tomorrow."

The apartments the Crownpoint school district provided for its teachers were a quarter mile beyond the school. The school was dark now, and the parking lot empty except for a single pickup truck. The pickup was a blue Ford 150. Charley's. Chee slowed his carryall, staring at it.

"Not here," Mary Landon said. "It's those apartments up ahead."

"I know," Chee said. "I'll get you home in just a minute."

He pulled into the parking lot, beside the pickup. "This is Charley's truck," he said. "Why would he leave it?"

The truck was locked. Frost was turning the windshield opaque. Chee walked around it, shone his flashlight into the cab, looking for anything that would answer that question. He didn't find it.

13

MALPAIS, TRANSLATED LITERALLY from the Spanish, means "bad country." In New Mexico, it signifies specifically those great expanses of lava flow which make black patches on the map of the state. The malpais of the Checkerboard country lies just below Mount Taylor, having been produced by the same volcanic fault that, a millennium earlier, had thrust the mountain fifteen thousand feet into the sky. Now the mountain has worn down to a less spectacular eleven thousand feet and relatively modern eruptions from cracks at its base have sent successive floods of melted basalt flowing southward for forty miles to fill the long valley between Cebolleta Mesa and the Zuni Mountains. Some of this malpais was ancient, long since softened by algae, moss, rain, wind, and durable desert grasses. Elsewhere it was only a few thousand years old, still raw, black, and relatively lifeless. The track Chee was following zigzagged its way across a smoother, more ancient flow. Nonetheless, it was rough going.

"I've never been out here before," Mary Landon said. "Not out in it. It's like someone was boiling a whole oceanful of black ink, and all of a sudden it froze solid."

"Even the rodents out here tend to be black," Chee said. "Protective coloration, I guess."

"It doesn't look like there'd be anything alive."

"Lots of reptiles," Chee said. "All kinds of snakes and lizards. And quite a few mammals. Rabbits, mice, kangaroo rats, so forth."

"What do they drink?" Mary asked.

"Some of them don't. They get their water from the plants they eat. But rain and snow melt and collect in potholes," Chee said. "And now and then there's a spring. That's where we're going. Charley has a spring out here. He collects herbs, datura, stuff like that. For his ceremonials. That's where he left the box."

"How do you find it?"

"Either by the powers of deduction," Chee said, "or by asking Charley. I asked Charley and he told me to follow this track until I came to the place where the new lava flow crosses the old." Chee pointed ahead. "Like right there. And then I'd see a place where the track forks. See? Right there ahead. And the spring was maybe a hundred yards down the right fork of the track. He said there was a bunch of tamarisk sticking up out of the lava flow to mark it. See? Over there."

"So why aren't you taking the right turn?" Mary asked.

"I want to show you that new lava up close," Chee said. "We'll park there and we can walk over."

The new lava was at least a thousand years old. It looked as if it had hardened yesterday. It was as black as coal, raw and rough, still marked with the froth of its white-hot bubbling as it boiled across the landscape. They climbed from the ancient lava onto the final wave of the new and stood looking across ten miles of tumbled, ragged blackness at the blue shape of Cebolleta Mesa.

"I'm impressed," Mary said finally. "It's like looking backward a hundred million years."

"Do you know any of our legends?" Chee asked.

"I know a few," Mary said. "A Laguna girl I know told me one about the Laguna migrations. And the Corn Maidens."

"Those are Pueblo," Chee said. "If you were Navajo you'd know that you are looking at the blood of the Horned Monster."

"Oh. Black blood." Mary grinned at Chee. "You Navajos have black-hearted monsters."

"Yes, indeed. A historic spot. Right around here is where the Hero Twins started making Dinetah safe for the Dinee to live in. The Horned Monster was the first one they bagged. Born of Water distracted him, and Monster Slayer shot him with an arrow."

"He certainly bled a lot," Mary said.

"And then they cleaned the rest of them out," Chee said. He helped her down from the lava crest. "The Winged Monster, and the Water Monster. We even had one they called One Who Kicks People Over the Cliff."

"How'd they do him in?"

"His hair grew out of the cliff, keeping him from falling," Chee said. "Monster Slayer gave him a haircut."

The ancient lava flow made fairly easy walking. Eons of time had rubbed away its roughness and turned its blackness gray. It was coated with lichens, and grass grew wherever dust had accumulated in its cracks. Chee talked of Navajo mythology. Mary Landon listened. He was carrying a grocery sack which contained a thermos of coffee, two apples, and two king-sized Lottaburgers picked up in Grants. Chee hadn't been on a picnic since school days. He was happy. To their right, the morning sun reflected off the snow on the high slopes of Mount Taylor, making it glitter against the dark-blue sky.

"We call it Turquoise Mountain," Chee said. "First Man built it out of earth he brought up from the Third World, and he pinned it to the world with a magic knife to keep it from flying away. He put Turquoise Girl on top of it, to keep the Navajos safe from monsters, and he assigned Big Snake to live on the mountain for eternity, to keep Turquoise Girl safe from whatever bothers Turquoise Girls."

"Speaking of big snakes," Mary Landon said. "Am I right in remembering that they hibernate in the winter, and I therefore have absolutely nothing to worry about? Or is that hibernation business just another of your myths?"

She was climbing a great hump of lava. Just beyond it were the tamarisks and the spring. "When are you going to tell me your war name?"

"It's a good rule to stay off those humps when you're walking on lava," Chee said. "They're the tops of old bubbles, and about one in twenty thousand is thin enough so that you can fall through and . . ."

Chee's voice trailed away. Mary had stopped atop the

hump and stood frozen, looking down.

"Jim," she said. "There's someone . . ."

Chee scrambled up beside her.

Just beyond the hump was a sinkhole, a circle of clear, dark water rimmed by cattails and a species of green reed. This was surrounded, in turn, by a small expanse of buffalo grass. The man wore a red-and-black mackinaw and his black hat lay beside his head. His hands were together behind his back, secured by what seemed to be an electric cord.

"I think he's dead," Mary Landon said in a very small voice.

"I'll see," Chee said. The left hand looked distorted, and coated with something dark. "I think you should wait in the truck."

"All right," Mary said.

The kneeling man was Tomas Charley. The black on his hand was blood, long dried. But when Chee placed his fingers on Charley's neck to confirm the certainty that he was dead, he found the flesh resilient and warm. He stepped quickly back from the body and studied the area around him. Tomas Charley had been dead only a matter of minutes. Chee became intensely aware that his pistol, inappropriate for a picnic with a girl, was locked in the glove box of the patrol car. Perhaps Tomas Charley had been left here hours ago and had been a long time dying. And perhaps he had been killed only moments ago, which would mean his killer must be nearby. Chee glanced at the body again. There was no sign of what had killed him. The only blood visible was from the hand. Chee grimaced. The hand had been methodically mutilated. He examined the mackinaw, looking in vain for a bullet hole. Then he noticed a place where the black hair on the back of Charley's head had been scorched. He knelt beside the body and gently parted the hair. Beneath it, the skin over the skull had been punctured, leaving a small round hole. A bullet hole, probably no larger than a .22. Turquoise Girl had not kept this half-Navajo safe from the monsters.

The sound of the car starting was close. It came from beyond the tamarisks. Chee trotted around the pool toward it, conscious that the driver was probably armed. The car, he saw when he reached the screen of brush, was a green-and-white Plymouth—the one that had been parked beside Charley's car. It was moving away from him down the track. He couldn't see the driver. Chee turned and scrambled up the lava formation. When the Plymouth reached the place where the tracks forked, it would angle left, back toward the highway and Grants. Then Chee could see the driver. And he would need only a glimpse to confirm what he already knew. It would be the blond man in the yellow jacket.

But the Plymouth didn't angle left. It turned right and jolted slowly toward Chee's patrol car.

He could see Mary at the passenger-side window, looking at the approaching car and then at him.

He cupped his hands and shouted: "Run. Mary. Run."

She emerged from the driver's-side door, running toward the new lava flow. She was carrying his 30-30 carbine. Chee raced toward the patrol car, doing what he could to keep out of sight behind the humps and hillocks of old lava. The Plymouth stopped and the driver got out. He was a blond man wearing a yellow jacket, and he raised his right arm and aimed the pistol he held at Mary Landon. It seemed to Chee to have a remarkably long and heavy barrel. The barrel smoked, or seemed to, but Chee heard nothing. Mary was in the new lava and out of sight. Chee's plan took no thought at all. He would circle around the patrol car, find Mary in the new lava, and get the rifle. The blond man would think he was armed and wouldn't come after him. The risks were relatively light. In the first place, the chances of being hit at one hundred yards by a pistol were small, unless the man was a hell of a lot better shot than most. And in the second place, a .22 bullet at that range wouldn't be lethal. Chee ran.

The pain was sudden and intense. Chee stumbled, lost his footing, and fell to his hands and knees. The pain was in his left chest. A heart attack, he thought for one illogical moment. And then he felt blood running down his side and made a quick inspection. A bullet seemed to have struck a rib. He inspected the place with cautious fingers and grimaced with the pain. The bullet had apparently broken the bone. But he didn't seem to be hurt in any critical way. No reason to change his plans, except for a more realistic view of the blond man's marksmanship. He raised himself cautiously. He'd locate his adversary exactly, and then he'd resume his run toward the new lava, on a wider, safer circle.

The blond man was trotting directly toward him across the worn waves of gray stone, the long-barreled pistol held in front of him. Chee ducked. The blond either didn't care if the Navajo policeman was armed, or knew that he wasn't. Perhaps he had seen that Chee wasn't wearing his holster. And now he came to finish the job, as he had finished it with Tomas Charley. Chee felt panic, choked it off, and started a scrambling zigzag run. He'd worry about reaching Mary Landon and his rifle later. Now the problem was to stay alive, to put some distance between himself and the blond, to find a place to hide. He vaulted over a ridge of stone and heard the sharp snap of a bullet whipping past him. He heard no gunshot. Behind the ridge, the lava had hardened into a wide trough perhaps five feet deep. Chee sprinted down it, the rib feeling like a knife in his chest. Then he heard the booming crack of a shot, and the whine of a ricocheting bullet. And then another, and another. Those were not the blond's silent .22. It was the muzzle blast of his 30-30. The trough ended at a grassy pothole catch basin. He was back at Emerson Charley's spring. Chee stopped and looked over the rim. The blond man was moving back toward his car, keeping low in a dodging run. From the escarpment of new lava, Chee saw a puff of blue smoke and heard again the cracking boom of the 30-30. Then the blond was behind Chee's patrol car. For a moment Chee lost sight of him. Then he was visible again, getting into the Plymouth. The Plymouth backed around the patrol car with a squeal of tires on rock and then was jolting down the track, far faster than was safe for tires or springs.

About then Chee realized that his patrol car was burning. The flames came from under the rear of it, apparently fed by fuel leaking out of the gas tank. The fire mushroomed abruptly, engulfing the rear half of the vehicle. Chee watched it grimly. The tank was about half full as he remembered it—perhaps twelve gallons. There was another twenty in the auxiliary tank. When that heated up, it would go off like a bomb.

What had been Tomas Charley still knelt, forehead to grass. Chee walked past the body and picked up the sack containing the thermos of coffee and the picnic lunch. They had a long walk ahead of them. He spent another few minutes making a methodical search of the spring area for the box. Charley had said he'd left it in plain view on the rock just beside the water. There was no box now. Behind him, he heard the muffled boom of the gas tank exploding.

"Boy," Mary Landon said when he walked up. "You Navajos give exciting picnics." She laughed, but it was a shaky laugh. The fire flared up again with a *whoosh* of flame as a front tire exploded, and she raised her hand to shade her face from the heat. Her sleeve was torn and her wrist was smeared with blood from a long scratch on her forearm.

"You all right?" he asked. "Thank God you took the rifle with you."

"I knew you'd say that." Suddenly Mary Landon was furious. "Why wouldn't I take it? Because I was stupid, that would be why. I'd just seen a tied-up dead body, and the man who must have killed him coming right toward me, and you yelling at me to run, and the rifle right there in the scabbard. Why wouldn't I take it?" Her voice was fierce. "Because I'm a half-wit woman? I wouldn't have said that if you'd taken the rifle. I'd take it for granted. But no. I'm a woman, so I'm stupid."

"Sorry," Chee said.

"What's wrong with this damned rifle anyway?" Mary said. She handed it to him, which reminded Chee that his spare ammunition was in the glove box and would be exploding any minute.

"Let's back away a little," he said. As he said it, the 30-30 rounds began exploding, no louder than firecrackers.

"I'm a pretty good shot, I thought," Mary said. "I was missing him a mile."

"Sorry about that, too," Chee said. "When I'm not using it I let the rear sight down." He showed her, pushing the leaf sight up with his thumb and sliding the calibrated wedge forward to the 200-yard mark.

Mary looked from Chee's thumb to Chee's face, her glance

asking: Is this man for real? She shook her head. "Why? Why would you do that?"

"Takes the strain off the spring," Chee said lamely.

Suddenly she leaned against him. He felt her shaking. "Sorry I've been so bitchy," she said, talking into his coat. "I'm not used to this."

"Me either," Chee said.

"That man back there. Was that Mr. Charley? The one you were looking for? He was dead, wasn't he? Did that blond man kill him? Do you know what's going on?"

"Yes," Chee said. "And no. It was Charley. He was dead. And I don't have any idea what the hell is going on."

While he was saying it, Mary became aware of the blood on his shirt. Childish as he knew it was, being wounded made him feel a little less foolish. If the rib hadn't hurt so much, and if he hadn't had a five-mile walk back to the highway ahead of him, it would have been almost worthwhile.

14

COLTON WOLF had left tracks. Two witnesses had seen him. Close and clearly. They could identify him. They could connect him with murder and with a rented car. The car-rental connection would provide other witnesses and uncover the false identity. He gunned the Plymouth down the access acceleration lane and onto Interstate 40 west. There was no time wasted deciding what to do. He'd decided that before he'd left his trailer. This was Plan B. Plan B was what he did if the operation created the sort of disturbance that made the routine withdrawal in some way risky. There had been a Plan B and variations of Plan B for each of his previous operations. But he'd never used one before because there had never been a disturbance. Previously, the targets had died unobserved, quietly and unobtrusively. The only exception had been the old CPA in Reno. The man had suspected something. Perhaps it had been the product of a guilty conscience, perhaps the product of age and wisdom. At any rate, part of the information provided to Colton had been the detail that the target would be alert and wary. And he had been. Colton had spent an extra day scouting because of that. And the set-up had seemed perfect. The accountant's office had been on the fifth floor of a downtown bank building. At midmorning for three consecutive days the old man had emerged from his office, crossed the corridor to the men's rest room, and relieved himself. Rest rooms were ideal. And this had been the best kind. A single-stall men's room. The jimmy blade flicking the latch open. The victim startled, embarrassed, refusing to credit what his eyes were telling him—that the intruder upon his privacy was pointing a pistol at his forehead. The victim starting to blurt some banality like "This booth is occupied." The voice being stopped by the *thud* of the silenced .22. The bullet fired into the hair, where it would go undetected for a time. The body propped on the stool. The unhurried departure. But this time it had been different. The old man had sensed something when Colton had come into the room. Through the gap beside the booth door, Colton had seen a single eye peering out at him, and the screaming had started the moment the jimmy touched the latch. The man was up from the stool, pants around ankles, trying to resist. It had taken three bullets and a little more time, and then, as he was propping up the body, the door had swung open and the old man's secretary had burst in. He had shot her twice, and wedged her body in with the old man's, and walked away. It had been tense for a moment, but when he emerged from the elevator, there had been absolutely no tracks left behind. He had dumped the pistol by opening the emergency hatch and putting it on top of the elevator car. When he stepped through the doors into the bank lobby, there was no chance of connecting him with the bodies in the men's room. He had hated to lose the pistol, but it couldn't be traced. There had been absolutely no tracks.

This time there were tracks everywhere. He drove west on Interstate 40 past the Grants interchange, thinking about them. Out here tracks were easy to follow. Too few people in too much space. Had all gone smoothly, Colton would have driven back to Albuquerque, checked in the car at the airport, picked up his truck, and returned to his trailer. That was Plan A, simple and quick. Then, after a few days, he would have hitched the trailer to the truck and moved along. Somewhere warmer. Maybe Houston, or maybe somewhere in California. It didn't matter where. Until he could find his mother. Then there would be a home place. A place to settle.

But now he had to use Plan B. That took him in the other direction—to Gallup. There he would check the car into a garage for a major tune-up, leaving a Gallup number to be called when repairs were completed and telling the mechanic that there wasn't any hurry. That would mean days before the car surfaced. He'd walk to the bus station, take the next bus to Phoenix, and fly back to Albuquerque.

He drove exactly five miles above the speed limit—the margin highway patrolmen allow. There was no serious hurry. He'd bought himself some hours by burning the policeman's car and radio. He'd wounded the man, probably in the abdomen. And it would take the woman at least three hours to walk out of the lava rock and turn in the alarm. By the time any serious search could be organized, he'd be well into Arizona. Outside the circle.

A semi-trailer rig breezed past him, going perhaps fifteen miles above the limit. That would mean the trucker's CB had assured him he was safe from the state police. But Colton held the rental Plymouth at a steady sixty. He was thinking how he would erase his tracks. Not since he was a boy had Colton felt so vulnerable. He knew the Indian policeman had seen him at the auction, clearly and close up. The policeman and the woman had seen him again on the lava. The policeman and the woman had to be killed just as quickly as Colton could manage it.

15

THE WAY JIMMY CHEE was propped against the pillows, he could shift his eyes to the left and look out the window of his fifth-floor room in the Bernalillo County Medical Center and see, across Lomas Avenue, the tan book tower of the University of New Mexico library and the modern-sculpture form of the Humanities Building. If he shifted his eyes to the right, he'd see on the TV screen the has-beens and never-would-bes of *Hollywood Squares* pretending to enjoy themselves. The TV screen was silent, the sound turned off. All Chee could hear was the voice of Sheriff Gordo Sena, whose face Chee could see when he turned his eyes straight ahead. Voice and face were angry. "What I want you to do," Sena was saying, "is drop all the bullshit. Just tell me some by-God truth for once. I want to know how you knew Tom Charley had that box. And what was in it. And what happened to it. And how come that feller in the Plymouth was after him."

And what I'd like to know, Chee was thinking, is how Gordo Sena got past the nurse. The FBI people had come earlier, while he was trying to eat his breakfast, and the nurse had peered in at him and said, "You're not ready to talk to police, are you," and that had been the end of the FBI. But thirty minutes later, Sena had simply pushed the door open, stalked in, turned off the TV volume, sat in the bedside chair, and said, "By God, we're going to get some things straightened out." It was now about thirty questions later.

"I didn't know Charley had the box," Chee said for the

third time. "It was an educated guess. I told you what Mrs. Vines told me. About thinking the burglary had a religious connection. Well, the religion is peyote, and Charley is the peyote chief. One plus one is two."

"Was," Sena corrected. *"Was* the peyote chief. So you just walk up to Charley and ask him if he's the burglar, and he admits it. That's what you're trying to get me to believe."

"That's what happened," Chee said. "Not quite, but just about." His ears were ringing, and his rib hurt, and the nausea that had come and gone all morning was coming again. He didn't feel like talking. He closed his eyes. Sena's glowering face went away, but not the voice. Question after question about why Charley had stolen the box, what Charley had said was in the box, what Charley had said about the Vineses. Questions that explored from every possible angle what Chee knew about the blond man in the green-and-white Plymouth.

"What kind of voice did he have?" Sena asked.

Chee opened his eyes. "Never talked to him." He'd told Sena that before. Twice, in fact.

"That's right, you didn't," Sena said. His alert eyes were studying Chee's face. Why did Sena think they had talked? Why was that so important to the sheriff?

More questions. Why had the blond man burned Chee's car? The answer seemed obvious to Chee, but he answered it. To prevent pursuit and the quick radio call that would have inevitably snared the Plymouth at a roadblock. Why did the blond man seem inclined to pursue Mary Landon? Obvious again. She and Chee had had a good look at the killer. He was trying to eliminate witnesses.

Sena hitched his chair closer to the bed. He leaned forward. "Did you find the box?"

"No," Chee said.

"Had Tomas Charley opened it? Did he tell you that?"

"He opened it," Chee said. They had already covered this.

"What was in it?"

Chee was dizzy. He wanted Sena to go away. The sheriff's avid face went slightly out of focus.

"Did he tell you that? What was in the box?"

"What I said; mostly just some rocks," Chee said. "A bunch

of black rocks, and some old military stuff—medals, a paratroop badge, a shoulder patch, and a few old photographs of people. Family, Charley thought they were."

"Rocks?" Sena said.

"Mostly full of black rocks," Chee said.

Sena was silent. His hard dark eyes stared at Chee. "You got any brothers?"

"No," Chee said. "Two sisters. No brothers." The question surprised him.

"I had one," Sena said. "Older brother. His name was Robert. He was smart. Smartest kid in Grants High School. Made the valedictorian speech. First time in years it hadn't been some Anglo girl. Got a scholarship to the university here, but he didn't go at first. Our old man had heart trouble. Robert worked in the onion fields, in the oil fields, things like that. He looked after us kids. Took care of us. Kept us out of trouble. The old man died and left some social security, so Robert finally went to the university. He was studying engineering."

Sena had delivered that information in a flat staccato. Now his voice trailed off. He looked down at his hands, drew in a long breath, held it and then let it go. When he looked up again, his eyes were no longer hard. "I'm going to ask you a favor," he told Chee. "I don't do that much."

Chee nodded.

"I want to tell you how Robert died," Sena said. He described the oil well explosion and how the chief of the Navajo roustabout crew had kept his men away that day. "For a while I thought he did it. Now I just think he was in on it somehow. Knew about the plan. Knew Robert was going to be killed. That fella was Dillon Charley, Tomas' granddaddy."

Sena looked down at his hands. The muscles in his jaw were working.

"What do you want me to do?" Chee asked.

Sena didn't look up. "I want to know who killed Robert," he said. "I want to nail the sons of bitches. You talked to Mrs. Vines. You talked to Dillon Charley's grandson. There's some secret here that's got to do with being Indian, and with that peyote religion. One of them told you something. You've figured something out. You know more than you're telling. Otherwise, you wouldn't have found Vines' box so quick."

"I don't know a damned thing," Chee said. "Not about that oil well explosion. You think the Vineses had something to do with it?"

Sena shook his head. "He didn't live here then. And she didn't get here until his first wife died. I think Dillon Charley told Vines something. Anyway, it's a damned cinch Mrs. Vines knows something. Why else would she connect stealing that box with that bunch of peyote freaks?"

"I don't know," Chee said.

The room fell silent. An ambulance turned off Lomas toward the BCMC emergency room entrance, its siren abruptly growling out.

"Nothing to tell me, then?" Sena asked.

"Not that I haven't already told you," Chee said.

Sena pursed his lips, glanced at his watch. "It's a hell of a way to kill a man," he said. "Blowing 'em to pieces like that. We didn't hardly find enough of Robert to bury. And part of what we buried might not have been him. Had one of his legs with the boot still on it. Part of the torso we could recognize because his belt buckle was in it. Never found a lot of him. The coyotes and the buzzards and things had had a couple of days to carry it away." Sena's eyes were hard and bright, staring into Chee's eyes. His jaw muscles were rigid. "My mother used to go out there and look. She'd walk around in the creosote bush looking for pieces of bone." Sena produced a series of sounds that might have been a laugh. "I think she wanted to put Robert all back together again. What do you think of that?"

Chee could think of nothing to say. White people's attitude toward their dead was beyond his understanding.

"Two things," Sena said. "One I'm asking you, and one I'm telling. If you can tell me anything about that peyote bunch, or the Vineses, or anything that will help me, well, I'd appreciate that. I'd remember it. I never forget a favor. And two, I'm telling you to stay out of my jurisdiction. This whole business is mine. The burglary and the killing and everything else. It's mine. It's been mine for most of my life, and I don't want you in it. I told you that once, and you didn't pay attention to me." Sena's voice was shaking. He stopped talking for a moment, gaining control.

"Now, I got a name for being hard," he continued. "I've killed a man or two in the line of duty, and there's some that says I've killed some that didn't need to be killed. However that is, I'll tell you this. You think you're unlucky that blond man run into you out there on the malpais. Fact is, you're lucky it wasn't me."

Sena got up and placed his chair neatly against the wall under the television set. He went through the door without a glance or a word.

On the television screen, a barrage of commercials replaced *Hollywood Squares* and gave way in turn to what seemed to be a soap opera. The screen was filled with the tear-wet face of a woman. Her lips moved soundlessly, and she dabbed at her eyes. Chee shifted his own eyes to the left, and stared out across the central campus of the University of New Mexico. He thought first about Gordo Sena's hatred. And then about the pattern of his questions. It had not been a debriefing—one officer collecting information from another. It had been an interrogation—the probing of a hostile witness, skillfully done. But exactly what had Sena wanted to learn?

Part of that was obvious. Part of it wasn't. Chee sorted it out in his mind. Three times, in three different ways, Sena had tried to learn if there had been any communication between him and the blond man. Why was that so important to Sena? Was the blond man working for the sheriff? Had Sena hired the man to get the box away from Tomas Charley? There was no way to answer that question. It would seem more logical that he had been hired by Vines.

The telephone rang. Chee groaned.

"I'm Sergeant Hunt," the voice said, "with the Albuquerque Police Department. You feel like having a visitor?"

It was a soft voice, very polite.

"Why not?" Chee said.

"You're going to have to tell that nurse, then," the voice said. "She wouldn't let me in."

"I'll tell her," Chee said.

"Be right up, then," Hunt said, and hung up.

Chee pushed the button to summon someone from the nursing station. Why would the APD send a man to talk to him? It was an FBI case, or, as Sena insisted, the Valencia County sheriff's. That would depend on whether you counted the abduction, which had happened in federal jurisdiction on the reservation, or the murder, which was probably in Sena's territory, depending on where the lines fell on the checkerboard. Either way, it would be of zero interest to the Albuquerque law.

Hunt was a small man, with pale-gray eyes and a narrow, bony face.

"Looks like you forgot to dodge," Hunt said. "In case you wondered, the bullet broke up, but it looks like a .22. Probably a hollow point."

"It looked like it might have been a .22 pistol with a silencer on the barrel," Chee said. "Felt like a cannonball."

"I've got the report you gave to the state police here," Hunt said. "Sounds like you got a pretty good look at him."

"Yeah," Chee said. "Close enough." He tried to remember what he had told the state policeman. It was all hazy. They had started to walk back to the highway, Mary Landon and he. It had quickly become slow and painful. Each step produced a stabbing pain in his chest. Soon he had been dizzy. He had sat beside the track. Mary had spread her coat on the ground and made him lie down, and she had gone, running, intending to flag down some driver and get help. He had dozed and awakened and dozed again. Finally, when the sun was almost directly overhead, he had awakened to see a man in the black uniform of the New Mexico State Police bending over him. He remembered talking to the policeman, and Mary's worried face, and driving to the interstate, and being transferred to an ambulance. He remembered Mary riding with him. But that was about all he remembered. Where was Mary now?

"We'd like to get another description," Hunt said. "Have you go over it again."

"Medium-sized," Chee said. "About thirty. Probably weighed about 150. Five ten, probably less. Looked to be in good shape. Hair was very blond, medium short. Sort of prominent bone structure, as I remember. Strong chin, blue eyes, light eyebrows. No mustache. No beard. Light complexion. Pale. Ears fairly large and laid close to his skull."

Hunt had been making notes. Chee closed his eyes, seeing the face again as he had seen it at the auction, the light-blue eyes watching him. "I can't think of any more details. He looked smart, if you know what I mean by that."

Hunt had opened a manila folder. "He look anything like this?" he asked. He handed Chee a sketch done in pencil on thin white cardboard. It looked like a sketch made by a police artist. It also looked a lot like the blond man.

Chee handed it back. "Could be him," he said. "Probably is. Who is he?"

"We don't know for sure," Hunt said.

Chee's rib throbbed. He felt a sudden wave of sickness. His ears were ringing. He was not in the mood for coyness. "God damn it," he said. "Let's not play games. Who was the sketch supposed to look like? And how come it's APD business? It's a hundred miles out of your territory."

"That takes a minute to explain," Hunt said. "We have a file on old unsolved homicides in the detective division, and I'm the one who keeps track of it. You know, review it every six months or so to see if anything new fits in. Anyway, last summer we had a funny double killing. Two guys on a wrecker were going to tow an old pickup out of a reserved parking zone, and the thing blew up and killed 'em both. We got lucky and found a witness who'd been sitting at a window watching the world go by. She had seen somebody who looked like this"—Hunt tapped the sketch—"put a package in the back of the pickup before it went boom."

"Ah," Chee said. He was no longer conscious of the ache in his left side, or of the nausea. Part of the pattern that had been trying to form in his mind for hours took firm, clear shape. Hunt was looking at him expectantly, waiting for a comment. "That's interesting," Chee said.

"It is," Hunt agreed. "We never could figure it out. Obviously the bomb wasn't intended for the wrecker crew—although we finally even checked on that. You'd figure if a guy puts a bomb in a pickup, he wants to waste the pickup driver. But the driver was a poor-boy Navajo who was already on his last legs with cancer. Already dying. No motive to hurry it along. Then we checked on the guy who had the parking space reserved. Big shot doctor. Money. Wife trouble. Maybe she wanted an instant divorce. No evidence, but we figured the doctor was the target. Now it looks like we got our bomber killing another Navajo, and he's got the same last name."

"They're father and son," Chee said.

Hunt slapped his leg. "That's exactly what I hoped you'd say. That, or maybe brothers. You know for sure?"

"I know it for sure," Chee said.

"Well, now," Hunt said. "That tells us a couple of things."

Yes, Chee was thinking. It should tell us a lot. But he couldn't think of what.

"Like what?" he asked.

"Like that bomb wasn't intended for the doctor. If that hit man was aiming for Charley Junior, he must have been aiming for Charley Senior."

"Yes," Chee said. His head ached. Who would hire a professional killer to murder a man who was already dying? Why would anyone want to hurry the death of Emerson Charley? There were no apparent answers. Hunt was watching Chee, waiting for more response.

"Did Emerson Charley's body ever turn up?"

Hunt frowned. "What do you mean?"

"Tomas Charley told me that the hospital lost his daddy's body. Emerson died one night, and Tomas came to get the body the next morning, and it was gone out of the morgue."

Hunt opened his mouth, and closed it again. "I didn't know that," he said. "Be damned. Why wasn't it reported?"

"Tomas reported it to APD," Chee said.

Hunt's embarrassment showed. "You know how that'd be," he said. "Probably told some clerk at the front desk, and filled in a form, and somebody did a little calling around, and that was about it. Nobody pushing it. By then the bombing case wasn't active. And nobody up front would have a way to know the detective division was interested in a sick Navajo."

"Guess not," Chee said.

"I'll check on it. Right away." He frowned again. "How can a hospital lose a body?"

"Tomas thinks it was stolen."

"Stolen? Why? Who'd steal it? This guy?" He tapped the drawing.

Chee didn't feel like talking about the Vineses. "Tomas

thinks a witch stole it," he said. "Why? Who knows?" But a reason was forming in his mind.

And, apparently, in the mind of Hunt.

"What did he die of?" Hunt asked. "They told us he had cancer."

"But maybe the guy who tried to hurry him along with the bomb found another way to hurry him along. That's what you're thinking?" Chee found himself respecting the way Hunt's mind worked, and liking the man.

"Exactly," Hunt said. "And if the body's gone, there's no autopsy. I'll check into that."

"Good," Chee said.

"I'll let you know," Hunt said. "And there's one other thing." He fished the sketch out of the folder again and looked at it. "If our man here is the same as your man, I think he's a biggie. I think the FBI's going to be very interested."

"They were here this morning," Chee said. "The nurse wouldn't let 'em in. What do they want?"

"Past several years they've had a run of professional killings done a lot the same. People shot in the head with a .22. Nobody hears a shot. And then there was a couple of cases where they had one person hit with a .22 and one bombed. A couple of hoods in the construction union in Houston and witnesses in an extortion case in Philadelphia. Anyway, mostly the little silenced pistol and a couple of times with the bomb. And both times the bombs seem to have been the kind that get set off by tilting the package. That's the kind of bomb he used here."

"Tilting the package?"

"Clever as hell," Hunt said. "It uses mercury to make the electrical connection. You just set the damn thing down and take off the safety gadget, and the next time the thing moves, or tilts, or shakes, the mercury slides and it goes off. No timer to screw you up, no wiring it up to the ignition. No fuss. No muss. If the driver doesn't see it, it goes off when the car moves. If he does see it, it goes off when he picks it up."

"Then what went wrong here?" Chee asked.

"Luck. Wrecker crew was going to haul off the truck," Hunt said. "They started to hoist the rear end. Tilt. Boom. But that was sheer bad luck. It's quite a gadget. Understand the CIA developed it."

The FBI arrived as Hunt was leaving. His name was Martin. He was young. He wore a brown suit with a vest. His mustache was trim, and his haircut would not have offended the late J. Edgar Hoover. Being second to an Albuquerque policeman did not please him.

"The nurse told me you were asleep," he said. It was more an accusation than a statement.

"No," Chee said. "I was watching *Hollywood Squares.* I guess she didn't want to interrupt. Ever watch 'em?"

Martin denied it. He wanted to talk about what the blond man looked like. And about why anyone would want Tomas Charley killed. And about the Vines burglary. It took Chee less than five minutes to exhaust all he knew about all three subjects and ten minutes more to go over it all twice more from slightly different angles.

"You find anything in the man's car?" Chee asked. "It was a rental car, wasn't it?"

"We haven't recovered it yet," Martin said. "We think it was rented from Hertz at the Albuquerque airport." He fished a folder from his briefcase and extracted a copy of Hunt's sketch.

"Your man look like this?"

"Pretty close," Chee said.

"The Hertz people identified him as the man who rented a green-and-white Plymouth sedan. Now the car's overdue. He gave his name as McRae and an Indiana address. It doesn't check out."

Chee didn't comment. Talking to Hunt had tired him. His chest hurt. His ears were ringing. He wanted Martin to go away.

"When you get out of here, we want you to come down to the office," Martin said. "We want you to look at mug shots and give us more details on the identification if you can."

"Mug shots? You think you have a record on him?"

"Not really," Martin said. "We think we have a ten-year accumulation of suspicions. We want you to look just in case. And we want you to spend a lot of time remembering everything you can about him. Everything."

Chee said nothing. He just closed his eyes.

"It's important," Martin said. "This guy's slick. That little pistol he used must be really silent. And he gets it in places where nobody sees anything. Apparently he scouts everything out very methodically, and then he likes to catch them alone for one quick close shot at the head. In the john is a favorite of his. We know of four found sitting on the john with the stall door closed. And a couple in telephone booths. Places like that. A quick shot and he just walks away. Never any witnesses. Not until the bombing. And now you and Miss Landon."

Chee opened his eyes. "We're the first witnesses?"

Martin was staring at him. "The first he knows about. He didn't know anyone saw him putting the bomb in Charley's truck. Medium-sized. Blond. So forth. You're the only two who actually got a look at him and who could pin him to a killing."

Chee's head ached. He closed his eyes again.

"You know," Martin said, "I think I'd be careful if I were you."

Chee had already had that thought.

16

WHEN MARTIN LEFT, Chee spent the next ten minutes on the telephone. He got Mary Landon's number from information, but no one answered when he called it. He remembered then that it was a school day and called the school. Miss Landon had taken the day off. He called his own office, explained the situation, and told Officer Dodge to see if she could find Mary and do what she could do to keep an eye on her. The doctor came in then—a young man with red hair and freckles. He inspected Chee's ribs, replaced the dressing, said, "Take it easy," and left. The nurse arrived, took his temperature, gave him two pills, watched while he took them, said, "This isn't a police station. You're supposed to be resting," and left. Chee rearranged himself on the pillow and gazed out across the university campus. He thought about Mary, and about the peyote religion, and B. J. Vines' keepsake box, and the ways of white men, and drifted off into an uneasy sleep. When he awoke it was late afternoon. The sun was slanting through his window and Mary sat in the bedside chair.

"Hello," she said. "How're you feeling?"

"Fine," Chee said. He did feel fine. Vastly relieved.

"Boy," she said. "You sure scared me. I thought you were dead. I waved down a truck, and he got that state policeman on his CB radio. And when we got back to you, you were just lying there." She grimaced at him. "Like dead."

Chee told her what he'd learned about the blond man. "You see the problem? There's a chance he's going to decide he needs to get rid of us."

Even as he was saying them, the words sounded melodramatic to him. In this quiet, antiseptic room, the idea of anyone wanting to kill Jim Chee and Mary Landon seemed foolish.

"Don't you think what he'd really do is just run?" Mary asked. "That's what I'd do."

"But you're not a professional gunman," Chee said.

"If that remark's a reflection on my shooting, I want to remind you that it was you who screwed up the rear sight."

"Be serious," Chee said. "This guy kills people."

The humor left Mary's face. "I know," she said. "But what can you do? It's sort of like being struck by lightning. You can't go around all the time hiding from clouds."

"But you don't stand under trees while it's raining, either," Chee said. "Why don't you take a leave and go off and visit some relatives somewhere for a while and don't tell anyone where you're going?"

Mary's expression shifted from somber to skeptical. "Is that what you're going to do?"

"I would if I could," Chee said. "But I'm a policeman. It's my business."

"No, it's not," Mary said. "You don't even have jurisdiction. That's what you told me. It's FBI business. Or maybe the sheriff's."

"Legally," Chee said. "But this sore rib sort of gives me a special interest. And besides, I'm a material witness."

"So am I," Mary said.

They argued about it, an uneasy, tentative sparring of two persons not yet sure of their relationship.

Mary changed the subject to his earlier visitors, to Sheriff Sena, to Sena's obsession with the death of his brother in the oil well explosion. The conversation was oddly strained and uncomfortable.

"When I get out of here," Chee said, "I'm going to dig into the newspaper files and learn everything I can about that oil well accident, and get some names, and see what I can find out."

"I'll go see about it," Mary said. "The university library keeps newspapers on microfilm." She got up and collected her purse. "I'll see if they have the right ones. If I hurry, I can get it done today."

17

IT WAS 3:11 A.M. when Chee looked at his watch. He had been awake perhaps fifteen minutes, lying motionless with his eyes closed in the vain hope that sleep would return. Now he gave it up. Sleeping away the afternoon had left him out of tune with time. The nurse had given him another sleeping pill at ten o'clock but he had let it lay. His policy was to take pills only when unavoidable. Having his sleeping habits dislocated was the price he was now paying for that pill at lunch. He sat on the edge of the bed and put on the hospital slippers. Much of the soreness had gone out of his side. Only when he moved was there still pain under the heavy bandages. Through the curtain that now partitioned the room he could hear the heavy breathing of a drugged sleep. They had wheeled a man in from the post-surgery recovery room about midnight—a young Chicano sewn up after some sort of accident earlier in the evening. Chee flicked on his bed light and began to reread the newspaper. Through the curtain he heard his roommate mumble in his sleep. The man shifted his position, groaned. Chee switched off the light. Let him sleep, he thought. This is the time of night for sleeping. But Chee had never felt more wide awake. He put on his robe and walked down to the nurse's station. The nurse was a woman in her middle forties, with a round, placid face and a complexion marred by those ten thousand wrinkles the desert sun inflicts upon white people. She glanced up from her paperwork through bifocal glasses.

"Can't sleep," Chee said.

"Let's see," Bifocals said. "You're Chee?" She found his folder and glanced at it. "You had a pill at ten, but I guess I could give you another one."

"I don't like 'em," Chee said. "They make me drowsy."

Bifocals gave him a double take, detected the irony, and grinned. "Yes," she said. "That's the trouble with sleeping pills."

"A while back this hospital lost a body," Chee said. "Fellow named Emerson Charley. You hear about that?"

"Not officially," Bifocals said. "But I heard." She grinned at the memory. "There was some hell raised over it."

"How could it happen? What do you do with bodies?"

"Well, first the attending physician comes, takes care of the certification," Bifocals said. She looked thoughtful. "Then the body is tagged for identification and moved to the morgue on the second floor. It's held there until relatives get a funeral home to claim it. Or, if there's an autopsy, it's tagged for that, and it's held until the morphology laboratory does the postmortem. The way I heard about this one, it was tagged for an autopsy, but somebody came and took it."

"Tell me about it," Chee said.

"Nothing to tell. He died late in the day. The body was taken down and put in the cooler. In the morning, morphology called for it and the body was gone." Bifocals grinned. "Lots of embarrassment. Lots of red faces."

"Did somebody steal the body?"

"Had to be that," Bifocals said. "Somebody in the family, probably. Indians usually don't want an autopsy made."

Chee didn't correct her. Charley was a Navajo and most Navajos had even less distaste for autopsies than do whites. It was the Pueblo Indians who tended to resist autopsies. Their dead needed to be buried in the same cycle of the sun as their death. They had to begin on time the tightly scheduled four-day journey of the soul into eternity. But for most of the Navajo clans, death produced only a short-lived and evil ghost, and everlasting oblivion for the human consciousness. They had little sentiment for corpses.

"Could somebody just walk in and walk out with a body?" Chee asked.

"I guess they did," Bifocals said. "And with clothing, too." She chuckled. "We had two flaps out of this one. First the body was missing, and then two days later it turned out we'd given this Emerson Charley's clothing to another corpse. Whoever took him took the other man's clothing."

"How could that happen?"

"Easy enough. When a patient comes in, his clothing goes into a red plastic bag—looks sort of like a shopping bag—and it goes to the morgue with the body. Whoever got the body just picked up the wrong bag."

"But don't they keep the place locked?"

"Supposed to be. But somebody probably left it open for some funeral home. That's what I think happened. And somebody from the man's family came, found it unlocked, and just walked out with the body. The morgue's right by the laundry dock. They could go out that way and nobody would see them. And you should be back in bed."

"Okay," Chee said. "Good night."

But Chee still wasn't sleepy. At his doorway, he glanced back. Bifocals was immersed in her paperwork. He walked down the hall, around the corner, and out the door to the elevator landing. He took the stairway down to second, and paused there to get his directions. From what Bifocals said, the morgue was near the laundry loading dock. That made sense in terms of logistics. The hospital was built on a slope, a hillside that angled downward from northeast to southwest. Thus if the laundry loading dock was on a second floor, it must be on the northeast side of the hospital. Chee took a hall that led north and made a right turn eastward. As he walked down this empty, echoing corridor he could hear thumping sounds ahead. The sounds, Chee guessed, a laundry would make. On the next door, a sheet of typing paper had been stuck. A legend printed on it with a marking pen declared that the morphology laboratory had been moved to the New Mexico State Laboratory. Just around the corner, Chee found the door to the morgue. It was a wide door, protected by a plywood bumper sheet. Three body-tables-on-wheels were parked beside it. The door was locked. Chee examined the lock. He guessed he could open it with a flexible blade, but there was no way to be sure. The ceiling offered another possibility. He glanced up and down the hallway and down the connecting hall that led to the laundry dock. All deserted. The only sound was the thumping of the laundry machinery. Chee pushed one of the carts against the door and climbed stiffly atop it. He lifted the acoustical ceiling tile and stuck his head through the opening. There was about four feet of crawl space between the false ceiling and the floor above. Chee tested the aluminum-alloy gridwork that supported the ceiling tiles. It seemed sturdy but probably not strong enough to support the full weight of a man. There were, however, other means of support—electrical-cable conduits, water pipes, and the heavily insulated sheet-metal tubes through which the hot and cold air of the heating-cooling system flowed. Chee could see well enough in the darkness now to tell that getting into the morgue wouldn't be difficult even if the door was locked. One could simply climb into the false ceiling, cross the partition, lift another of the acoustical tiles, and drop into the room. He withdrew his head, and sliding the ceiling section back into place, climbed gingerly down from the body cart. At the elevator he yawned. Suddenly he felt both tired and relaxed. He had answered a question that no one had asked, and that didn't matter anyway. But now he could sleep.

18

COLTON WOLF HAD LEFT the car parked in the darkness about fifty yards from the laundry loading dock. He tested the dock entrance door. It was unlocked. Then he circled the hospital, checking the parking lots. He found no police cars. His plan was simple. He would use the front entrance of the hospital. He would take the stairs to the fifth-floor post-surgical wing, find room 572, and kill the Indian policeman. The next steps would depend on the circumstances—whether there was any sort of disturbance. Colton expected none. The Indian policeman would be sleeping the heavy sleep that hospitals impose upon their patients. He should present no problem. If there was a nurse on duty, Colton would evade her if he could and kill her quietly if he couldn't. And then he would walk downstairs, take the hall past the morgue, go out the laundry loading dock exit, and drive away in a common, nondescript two-year-old Chevy. He had taken the Chevy from the low-rate, long-term parking lot at the airport; the ticket on the dashboard of the one he picked showed it had already been left overnight. It might not be missed for days. But in the event it was missed, he had stopped in the parking lot of an all-night grocery store and switched license plates.

It was cold. Colton hated cold. He felt exposed and vulnerable. Overhead, as he walked across the almost empty front-entrance parking lot, the sky was a dazzle of strange stars. Unlike the soft, warm protecting darkness of his California boyhood, the night here was hostile. He could hear the soft sound of his crepe-rubber soles on the asphalt, the sound of his trouser legs rubbing, cloth on cloth. Behind him a truck moved up Lomas Avenue. Except for that, the night was silent. Colton squeezed the pistol in his coat pocket. It had a solid, reassuring feel. It was a good piece. Long-barreled and unhandy to look at, but efficient. He had made most of it himself to exactly fit his needs. The grip was walnut, roughed to eliminate the possibility of fingerprints, as was every metal surface. The barrel was threaded at both ends so that a half turn removed the silencer from its muzzle and a turn and a half detached barrel from firing chamber. Only the barrel—with its telltale ballistic tracks left on the lethal bullet—was directly incriminating. Within minutes after a job, the barrel was disposed of and a new barrel screwed into place—apparent proof that the pistol Colton carried had never been fired.

The automatic door sighed open in front of him and closed behind him. Inside, the air was stuffy. The young woman at the reception desk was reading what looked like a textbook. She didn't glance at Colton. From somewhere out of sight down a hallway came the sound of a cart being pushed. No problems. Colton adjusted his plans. He walked past the stairwell door to the elevators. Entering a lift, he pushed the sixth-floor button. The elevator rose silently, a new machine in a new wing. Colton took out the pistol, quickly checked the round in the chamber and the cocking mechanism. Perfect. Some would have said the caliber was too small for killing humans. A .22, they would say, was for rabbits. But Colton believed in silence. With a silencer on, a .22 made no more sound than a finger makes thumping on a skull. Small but sufficient, and for Colton's purposes, it was perfect. He had studied the skull and the brain within it in the Baylor University library when he was living in Waco. He understood the skull's bone thickness, and the tissue forms behind the bone, and where a small lead pellet could be placed above the hairline so that it would kill instantly and inevitably.

Colton put his hand, with the pistol gripped in it, back into his coat pocket before the elevator stopped at the sixth floor. The door slid open. He listened. He moved to the front of the elevator, pushed the door hold button, and listened again. Nothing. No one was in the hall. He walked to the stairwell door and moved quietly downward.

The policeman's name was Jimmy Chee. The newspaper said he had suffered a bullet wound in the chest and had undergone surgery. The woman with him was named Mary Landon, a schoolteacher at Crownpoint elementary school. The woman could wait. She had not seen him as closely as had the policeman. The policeman had stared at him at the rug auction, and policemen were trained to remember faces. At the bottom of the stairs, Colton reviewed his plan.

Room 572 was a double room. At 6:00 P.M., when Colton had called to ask about Chee, the nurse had said he had no roommate. Probably he would still be alone. That would make it simpler. A roommate would probably not awaken. If he did awaken, his bed would doubtless be screened from the target's bed. Keep the killing to an absolute minimum, that was Colton's rule. The less killing, the shorter the manhunt it provoked.

Colton paused just inside the stairwell door, listening again. Here was a crucial point. With a policeman wounded under these circumstances, there was a chance a guard would be posted. This was why Colton hadn't risked arriving in an elevator. He peered through the glass panel of the stairwell door. No one visible. He slipped silently out of the stairwell to the ward door. He listened again. Nothing. Things had gone perfectly so far. Now the risk must be taken.

He pushed through the swinging doors. A nurse was walking directly toward him. She was a medium-sized woman, perhaps forty-five, with dark hair covered by a nursing cap. Behind horn-rimmed glasses, her face registered surprise. "Yes?" she said.

"I'm Dr. Duncan," Colton Wolf said. "You have a patient named Jimmy Chee. I think we have him down for the wrong medication." He said it without hesitation, walking directly toward the nursing station, where the charts would be kept. Dealing with the nurse was the sort of contingency Colton was always prepared for. There was no guard in sight. But one might be sitting in the room with Chee.

"I think it's just a broad-spectrum antibiotic and a painkiller," the nurse said.

"Let's take a look," Colton said. "I heard they were going to have a guard up here for one of the patients. What's the story?"

"Nobody told me anything about it," the nurse said. Behind the nursing station desk, she flipped quickly through the medication order slips. "I'm almost sure it was Achromycin and Empirin number three," she said, intent on the forms. "Who wanted it changed?"

"The surgeon," Colton said. He extracted the pistol, cocking it as it left his pocket. He raised it, muzzle a half inch from the tip of the white cap.

"Here it is," she said. "Let's see . . ."

Colton squeezed the trigger. The pistol thumped and produced a thin spurt of blue smoke. The nurse's head fell forward onto the desktop. Colton held her with his free left hand on her shoulder until he was sure she wouldn't slip from the chair. Then he felt under her ear. The pulse fluttered, and fluttered, and died. If anyone looked in, the nurse appeared to be asleep at her desk. Now he would find room 572, finish the policeman, and leave.

19

JIM CHEE HAD BEEN in the bathroom, getting himself a pre-bed drink. Then, from the doorway, he had watched the nurse get up from her desk and walk toward the swinging doors. He had seen them open, and the man enter. The man wore a blue cotton hospital coat. He was blond, with pale skin and pale-blue eyes, and Chee recognized him instantly. The recognition was a two-staged affair. First came the thought that he had seen the blond doctor now walking toward him at the Crownpoint rug auction; a millisecond later came the gut-wrenching realization that the blond doctor was the man who had killed Tomas Charley and was no doctor at all but had come here to kill him. Chee stepped back from the doorway. He felt a desperate panic. The window! It didn't open, and it led to nothing but a lethal drop. The man was between him and the only exit from the wing. Chee forced himself to think. A weapon? There was nothing that would work against this marksman's pistol. Could he hide?

He swung himself quickly onto the bed and stood pushing the acoustical tile overhead. The space here was like that on the second floor, and here, too, the space between the false ceiling and the floor above was crisscrossed with electrical wiring, pipes, and the rectangular sheet-metal conduits that carried hot and cold air. Chee had no time to check weight-carrying capacity. He pushed the tile aside, grasped the brace that held the air-return conduit, and pulled himself painfully into the ceiling space.

The conduit was perhaps two feet wide and wrapped in a white insulation material. Chee maneuvered himself on top of it, reached frantically back, and pushed the tile into place. He found he was panting, partly from the sudden violent exertion and partly, he guessed, from fear. He controlled his breathing. Even with the tiles pushed back into place, the darkness was not absolute. He lay face down on the conduit insulation, smelling dust. He could hear the sounds buildings make at night, a ticking from somewhere in the darkness to his left, the noise of the elevator motor, and a faint hiss which might be nothing more than air passing through the metal tube under his ear. There were no voices. The conversation between the blond man and the nurse had stopped. Chee raised his head and stared down the conduit into the darkness. If he crawled along it, it would take him over the elevator foyer. But could he reach it without noise? The conduit braces supported it about six inches above the ceiling tiles, which left about two feet of space above it—enough for crawling but not enough for any rapid hands-and-knees scrambling. Chee gripped the insulation and pulled himself cautiously forward. The movement was almost soundless, but it turned the throbbing pain in his ribs to a sharp dagger thrust of agony. He suppressed his gasp by holding his breath. As he released it, he heard a metallic noise just below him.

Chee recognized the sound. It was made when the curtain that surrounded the beds was pulled along its metal track. The man who had come to kill him was standing just below. Only a quarter inch of Celotex insulation and perhaps forty-eight inches of air separated him from the blond man and his pistol. Chee lay utterly still. What would the blond man do? Would he think of the hollow ceiling as a hiding place? Chee turned his thoughts away from that. What was that blond man doing now? Chee imagined him standing, pistol ready, staring with those patient, incurious eyes at Chee's empty bed. He would look behind the bed, and in the bathroom, and behind the curtain that surrounded the bed of Chee's roommate. With that thought another came. Would the blond man mistake the Chicano for a Navajo? He might. The realization brought two contradictory emotions. Pity for the man sleeping a drugged post-surgical sleep below him struggled with a desperate hunger to stay alive.

Something bumped against metal. Then silence. Then a creaking noise. Silence again. His rib stabbed him with pain, and his lungs cried out for air. The curtain rustled. What should he do? What could he do?

Then there was another sound. A thump. A knuckle whacked against wood? And then a sort of sigh and a rasping intake of breath. Silence again, followed finally by the whisper of soft soles on a polished floor. The room door clicked shut.

Chee took in some air as quietly as he could. Relief flooded through him. He felt himself shaking. The man had gone. Not far, perhaps. Perhaps only to check other rooms. Perhaps he would be back. But at least for the moment, death had walked away. Perhaps the blond man wouldn't come back. Perhaps Chee would live. He felt a kind of crazy joy. He would wait. He would lie there motionless forever—until morning came, until he heard the voice of a nurse below him, arriving with his morning medicine. He would take no chance at all that the blond man was waiting somewhere for him to move.

Chee waited, and listened. He heard absolutely nothing but the natural sounds of the night. Time ticked away. Perhaps three minutes. Chee became aware of an odor. It was acrid—faint but unmistakable. The smell of gun smoke. What could have caused it? He knew the answer almost instantly. The thumping sound had been a shot from the blond man's pistol.

Chee reached down from the conduit, carefully moved a ceiling tile aside, and looked down. To eyes adjusted to darkness above the ceiling, the room was comparatively bright. He could see only his bed and an expanse of floor beside it. He gripped the conduit braces and lowered himself. The blond man was gone. Chee pulled back the curtain by his roommate's bed. The man's dark head lay on the pillow, neatly, face toward the ceiling, eyes closed in the profound sleep that follows surgery. But behind the curtain the smell of smoke was stronger. Chee reached out a tentative hand. He touched the sleeping face. His forefinger rested just under the nose. His fingertip felt warm skin. But there was no breath. He moved his hand downward, letting the palm rest over the sheet against the chest, holding it there. The man's face, illuminated dimly by the city night through the window, was young and clean-shaven, a longish face with a slightly sardonic cast. Chee had been training himself away from seeing all non-Navajos as looking very much alike. This one looked mostly Spanish in blood, with a little Pueblo Indian. The chest under Chee's palm moved not at all. No lung stirred, no heartbeat. The mouth Chee saw was a dead mouth. He shifted his eyes away from it and looked for a moment out into the night. Then he walked quickly to the door and pulled it open. There was no fear now. He ran to the nurse's station and picked up the telephone beside the hand of the sleeping nurse, and dialed past the switchboard to the Albuquerque Police Department's number.

While he talked, quickly describing the deed, the man, and the pistol, and suggesting that the gunman was probably in a new green-and-white Plymouth sedan, his free hand touched the hair of the nurse, felt the cap, and found the small round hole burned in the crest of it.

"Make it two homicides," Chee said. "He also shot the fifth-floor nurse."

20

EVEN AS HE TROTTED down the stairs toward the laundry level something troubled Colton Wolf about the policeman's room. Why was the unused bed rumpled? Had a visitor sprawled on it? It seemed too unkempt for that. But there was something else out of tune. He had left the loading dock and was walking toward the car he was using when he realized what it was. The smell around the face of the man he had shot was an anesthetic. Natural enough. But it was too strong. It was still being exhaled. Chee had been out of surgery far too long to smell like that.

"Son of a bitch!" Colton said. He ran back to the loading dock and was through the door before his caution stopped him. How had Chee escaped? Where was he now? He would have called for help. Certainly he'd be alert. And Chee was a very smart cop—that was clear. A second try now would be too risky. There wasn't time.

He was out of the parking lot and heading westward on Lomas Avenue when he heard the first siren. But he wasn't worried. No one had seen the car. He left it three blocks from where he had stolen it, walked to his pickup, and drove slowly back to his trailer. By the time he had reached it, his new plan for killing Jimmy Chee was taking shape. It was a good plan. This time Chee wouldn't escape.

21

CHEE KEPT the control lever of the viewer pressed halfway to the right. Above his forehead, the microfilm reels hummed. The pages of the *Grants Daily Beacon* fled past his eyes like the boxcars of a freight passing a traffic signal. They moved too fast to be read, but not too fast to tell a front page from a grocery ad, or to spot the sort of black banner headline that would signal the kind of story he was looking for. Half of Chee's attention focused on the moving image under his eyes. But he was aware of the silence of this huge basement room in Zimmerman Library, of the new .38 caliber revolver that weighted his coat pocket, and of Hunt pretending to be studying beyond the glass pane of the carrel door behind him. He was also aware of the nearness of Mary Landon.

The page that flashed below his eyes had a heavy black streak across the top. He stopped the reel and pushed the lever to the left to back it up. The headline read:

POLLS PROJECT DEWEY LANDSLIDE

"Ha!" Mary Landon said. "Wrong disaster." She was sitting beside and a little behind him, saying nothing much. She brought to his sensitive nostrils the scent of clothing dried in sunlight, and of soap.

Chee pushed the lever to the right again and glanced up. A librarian moved down the aisle to his left, pushing a cart loaded with bound periodicals. A slender white girl with a fur-collared coat was hunting something in the microfilm files. Beyond her, movement caught Chee's eye. An elbow, covered with blue nylon, jutted out from behind one of the square white pillars. It retracted, jutted out again, retracted, jutted. Doing what? Someone scratching himself?

Chee wanted suddenly to look over his shoulder, to make sure that Hunt was still in the carrel, alert and ready. He resisted the urge. Theoretically, Hunt was tagging along as a guard. But while it hadn't exactly been spoken, it was understood that purpose number one was to get the blond man. Protecting Chee was a by-product. It sounded cold-blooded but it made sense. One protected Chee and Mary Landon by catching the blond man. There was no other way to do it. The law wanted very, very badly to catch the blond man. On the other hand, the world was full of tribal policemen.

Under his eyes, the record of June 1948 raced past and became July. The reels overhead hummed, paused, hummed again, paused again. On this pause the banner read:

WELL EXPLOSION KILLS CREW

"Here it is," Chee said.

The subhead added:

TWELVE FEARED DEAD
IN BLAST ON RIG FLOOR

"Scoot over a little," Mary said. She leaned over the projected page, pressed against him, reminding him again of sunshine and soap.

> All members of an oil well drilling crew were apparently killed instantly northwest of Grants several days ago in what authorities believe to have been the premature explosion of a nitroglycerin charge.
>
> Valencia County Sheriff Gilberto Garcia said the toll may be as high as twelve men, including ten working on the drilling crew on the east slope of Mount Taylor and two employees of the oil field

supply company, who had brought in the nitro charge.

Garcia said the death toll is uncertain because the force of the blast "blew everything apart and scattered bits and pieces of people for half a mile."

"It looks like they had the nitro on the floor of the well when it went off," Garcia said. "It didn't leave much." He said the explosion probably took place Friday, which was the day the crew from Petrolab, Inc., delivered the explosive to the site. The accident was not discovered until Monday, when a deputy sheriff went to the site to investigate why men working there had not been heard from.

Garcia said the well is about 25 miles north and west of Grants near the border of the Checkerboard district of the Navajo reservation. "We haven't found anyone who heard the explosion," the sheriff said. "No one lives for miles around out there."

The sheriff said coyotes, other predators, and scavenger birds had complicated the problem of identifications. "We think we have one identification positive now, and we expect we have enough to pin down a couple of others, but we're not too optimistic about the rest."

He said payroll records named the drilling crew as Nelson Kirby, about 40, of Sherman, Texas, the crew chief; Albert Novitski, age and address unknown; Carl Lebeck, age unknown, a geologist who was logging the well; Robert Sena, 24, of Grants, and six as yet unidentified Navajos working on the well as a roustabout crew.

Also feared killed were R. J. Mackensen, about 60, and Theo Roff, about 20, both employees of Petrolab, a Farmington company which supplied the explosive.

Chee scanned the remaining paragraphs.

"Pretty much what Sena told you?" Mary asked. "The names ring any bells?"

"Just Robert Sena," Chee said. "He was Gordo's big brother."

Mary was reading over his shoulder. "Carl Lebeck," she said. "My cousin used to date a boy named Carl Lebeck. Or maybe it was Le Bow. Something like that."

"Let's see what they said when they found the Navajos were alive," Chee said.

It was on the front page of the Wednesday edition, a brief item reporting that the crew of six Navajo laborers, originally believed killed in the explosion, hadn't gone to work that day. The story included their names, which Chee copied off in his notebook. It didn't mention why they had missed work. Chee found that in the following day's paper. Again the headline stretched black across the top of the page:

ARREST MADE IN WELL BLAST

SHERIFF REPORTS NAVAJOS
GIVEN ADVANCE TIP

One of the Navajo workers who escaped last week's fatal explosion at a Valencia County oil drilling site was being questioned today about reports that he had advance knowledge the explosion would occur.

Sheriff Gilberto Garcia identified the man as Dillon Charley. He said Charley has admitted warning five other Navajo co-workers at the well not to go to work last Friday "because something bad was going to happen."

"He claims he got the warning from God in some sort of religious vision," Garcia said. He said that Charley is the "peyote chief" in the Native American cult and that the five other Navajos on the work crew were also members of the religious organization.

Members of the cult chew seed buttons from the peyote cactus as part of their rites. A narcotic in the peyote reportedly affects the nervous system,

> causing hallucinations in some users. Possession of the substance is illegal, and the Navajo Tribal Council has passed specific legislation banning its use or possession on the reservation.
>
> The sheriff also revealed that Charley had been injured in what Garcia called "an attempt to resist arrest." He said Deputy Sheriff Lawrence Sena had been placed under suspension "until we can determine if undue force was used." Deputy Sena's brother, Robert Sena, was one of the men blown to bits when a nitroglycerin charge went off prematurely at the well last Friday.

"Notice that?" Chee asked. He poked his finger at the proper paragraph. "Gordo roughed up Dillon Charley. He must have *really* roughed him up to get suspended for it. Beating up a Navajo wasn't considered such a big deal in those days." He leaned back, away from the microfilm projector hood, and looked at Mary. Her expression was quizzical.

"What do you think?" he asked.

"I think you're strange," she said. "I think you're weird. You have this creepy murderer trying to shoot you, and you're down here all excited, reading about something that happened thirty years ago."

"You, too," Chee said. "How about you?"

"I'm not excited," she said.

"I mean he's trying to shoot you, too."

"I don't believe that," Mary said. "You're the one who got a good look at him. You're the one he came after." She looked away from him, leaning again into the microfilm reader. A nice profile, Chee thought. Nice. She was looking down, reading the projected type. Her eyes were very blue and the lashes curved away from them in a long, graceful sweep. Her hair fell across her cheek. Soft hair. Soft cheek.

"Another thing," Mary said without glancing up. "What's all this concern about a cop beating up a Navajo? From what I heard at Laguna, the worst cops for beating up Navajos were Navajo cops."

"We'd rather beat up Anglos," Chee said, "but we don't

have jurisdiction over you folks." He watched her profile as he said it, looking for the reaction that would tell him something about her. Her jibe about Navajo police was partly serious—probably mostly serious. Navajo police, like most police, had a reputation of being toughest on their own people. Her eyes were still on the projected page. "You haven't really told me what happened up in the hospital. How you got away. And you haven't told me your secret name."

The elbow had reappeared from behind the pillar. Motionless now. Its owner must be leaning on the pillar. Reading, perhaps.

"I hid," Chee said. "Like a rabbit."

She looked at him. "Why like a rabbit? You think you should have come on like Monster Slayer?" She grabbed his wrist and raised his hand. "Me mighty redskin. Me take on gun with bare hands. Me big hero. Me dead, but me hero." She dropped his hand. "If you didn't have time to do a little ghost dance to make your hospital gown bulletproof, I think the smart thing to do was get under the bed."

"The way it worked, I guess I was hiding behind another guy. My roommate." He gave her a quick sketch of what had happened, from the furtive trip downstairs to find out how the body had been stolen from the morgue. He told it quickly, without interpretation and without speculation. Just the facts, he thought. Just the facts. And while he told them, he watched her face.

She pursed her lips into a soundless whistle and shuddered. "I'd have been terrified." She looked at him a moment, her lower lip caught between her teeth. "How did you think to climb up into the ceiling?"

"That's not the point," Chee said. "The point is I got away because I left the blond man somebody to shoot. He came into the room to shoot himself an Indian. Nobody home but a Mexican. So the Chicano gets shot instead of me."

She was frowning at him again. "So?"

"So? What do you mean, so?"

"So what," she said. "You on some guilt trip? You think you should have stayed behind? Bared your chest and said, 'Here I am. Don't shoot this other guy.' Come *on.*" Her voice was scornful. "He shot the nurse, didn't he? The only difference would have been he'd have shot both of you."

"Maybe," Chee said.

"You really are weird," Mary Landon said. "Either that, or you want me to think you are."

"Well," Chee said. "No use talking about it now. Let's see what else we can find."

They found very little. There was a lengthy story about the Native American Church, the ceremony, and what the members said about Dillon Charley's vision of warning. There was a short item in which the sheriff reported that one of the victims had been definitely identified from dental work as an employee of Petrolab. But the story seemed quickly to die away for lack of new information.

If Sena, or any of the other victims, was identified, it wasn't mentioned in the *Beacon.* Nor was there any follow-up story on the arrest of Dillon Charley. His release, whenever it happened, went without notice in the paper.

They worked through the microfilm slowly now, page by page, looking for the remainders of a story that was no longer banner headline news. Halfway through the September editions, after an hour of finding nothing, Mary had an idea.

"Hey," she said. "Newspapers do anniversary stories. You know. They start, 'A year ago today . . .' and then they rehash it all. Why don't we skip ahead a year?"

Chee stood and stretched. He pushed the lever to the left. The reels hummed with the rewinding. The young woman had left the microfilm area. The elbow was missing from the pillar. Protruding now into Chee's line of vision was the tip of a nose and a shock of hair. The hair was blond. Very blond. Chee felt his stomach muscles tighten. He released the lever and moved his right hand into his coat pocket. The hand found the pistol grip. The thumb found the hammer.

"What?" Mary said. She was staring at him.

The man emerged from behind the pillar. He glanced at Mary. He was very blond, but he wasn't the blond man. Far too young. No resemblance at all. He moved to the microfilm file and began rummaging.

"Nothing," Chee said. "I'm just jumpy."

They found the anniversary story. It reported little new.

By the time the copying desk had made Xeroxes of the microfilmed stories for them, it was five o'clock.

"Now what?" Mary asked. "It occurs to me that Sergeant Chee of the Mounties has just wasted one afternoon, plus the afternoon of one Crownpoint schoolteacher, and isn't going to have the slightest idea of what to do next. This is a dead end. Right?"

"No," Chee said. They were climbing the stairway that spiraled upward through the four levels of the working end of the university library. An artist had used the stairwell walls to depict in paint and plaster the history of man's efforts to record his communication with his fellows. Here, below the ground floor, they climbed past pictographs and petroglyphs. The Phoenician alphabet was far overhead, and the symbolic language of computers even higher. "Maybe it doesn't lead anywhere, but I'd like to talk to some of those men who got warned away from that explosion. I'd like to find out what Dillon Charley told them."

They emerged on the ground-floor level. Through the glass south wall of the library, the Humanities Building loomed above the sycamores of the central mall, a monolithic sculpture against a dark-blue autumn sky. Usually Chee liked the building. Today it reminded him of tombstones.

"Why?" Mary said. "What can they possibly tell you that has anything to do with this?"

"Maybe nothing," Chee said. "But the killings grew out of the keepsake box, and stealing the keepsake box seems to have something to do somehow with Dillon Charley's peyote religion, and everything seems to lead back to what happened at the oil well."

"Or maybe you're just curious," Mary said. "Anyway, you won't be able to find them. It's been thirty years."

"It won't be so hard," Chee said. "They'll probably all be kinfolks of Dillon Charley. He hired them, so they'll be kinfolks. Cousins, or uncles, or in-laws at least. The Navajos not only invented nepotism. We perfected it."

"But thirty years," Mary said. "They'll be dead. Or half of them will be."

"One or two, probably," Chee said. "We know Dillon Charley is. But the odds are about four of them are still around." They were outside now, walking across the bricked mall south of the library with the brittle sycamore leaves underfoot and the heatless light of the setting sun throwing their shadows a hundred yards ahead and turning the craggy east face of the Sandia Mountains the color of diluted blood. Chee thought of that, and of Hunt walking fifty feet behind them, and of the target they would make for someone standing at any of the walkways or balconies that overlooked the mall.

"And what can they remember about thirty years ago? Probably not much."

"Who knows?" Chee said. He thought. Probably nothing with any real accuracy. But there was no other lead to follow. And if nothing else, hunting survivors of the People of Darkness would take him out on the reservation. He would take Mary with him. On the reservation, the blond man would never know where to look for them.

22

A DAY LATER, Chee had taken a fruitless shot in the dark and added a few details to his list of names of Dillon Charley's People of Darkness.

The shot in the dark had taken him to the university's Geology Department library. With some help from a cooperative graduate student, he had found a copy of the geologist's log of the oil well. "It looks fairly typical of that area," the student told him. "There's been some shallow production from the Galisteo formation." He checked through it quickly. "Looks like they found the formation but not the oil."

"You see anything unusual about it?" Chee asked. The log was totally incomprehensible to him. He stared at the sheet of symbols and notations, feeling foolish.

"I'm no authority on Valencia County petroleum geology," the young man said. "But it looks like what I'd expect. What are you looking for?"

"That's the trouble," Chee said. "I don't know."

His luck in hunting Charley's roustabout crew had been only a little better. He and Mary had driven to the reservation and spent the remaining hours of daylight jolting over the washboard back roads and wagon trails of the Checkerboard, hunting information to go with the names extracted from the *Grants Beacon.* By nightfall the list had looked like this:

> Roscoe Sam, Ojo Encino or Standing Rock. Mud Clan. Dead. Confirmed.

Joseph Sam, Ojo Encino or maybe Pueblo Pintado area. Mud Clan and married into Salt Clan. One report he died in the 1950s. Others say no.

Windy Tsossie. Mud Clan. Married into Standing Rock Clan. Used to live around Heart Butte? May be dead?

Rudolph Becenti. Mud Clan. Coyote Canyon? Married?

Woody Begay. Mud Clan. Sister lives at Borrego Pass?

It had been generally frustrating, except for Roscoe Sam who had got sick at Tuba City and died in the BIA hospital there, and was remembered as being dead. Joseph Sam was another matter. A distant cousin on the paternal side of the family thought, rather vaguely, that he, too, was dead. Another even more distant paternal-side cousin said he'd moved his wife's sheep and his own belongings over to the Cañoncito Reservation and probably still lived there. Dead or alive, no one had seen Joseph Sam for years. It was the same for the rest of them. An in-law remembered that Rudolph Becenti had moved to Los Angeles but had heard he'd come back again. Windy Tsossie was recalled dimly and unfavorably by a few of his contemporaries around Ambrosia Lakes as one of the Tsossie "outfit" which had lived at Coyote Canyon but had moved away a long time ago. Except for Roscoe Sam, definitely and specifically dead and buried, the day had produced nothing concrete. As for Woody Begay, there was only an old woman's memory that his sister lived north of the Borrego Pass chapter house, and his sister's name was Fannie Kinlicheenie.

The vagueness of it had puzzled Chee. It was almost as if these People of Darkness existed only in shadowy rumors and not as flesh and blood. Even the site of the oil well explosion eluded them. The hunt for Roscoe Sam had taken them near the place where Chee's notes said it had been. They found only the immense dusty hole that was the Red Deuce—a dozen gigantic power shovels eating the earth in a pit that was already two hundred yards deep and a half mile across. The oil well site, too, seemed part of a memory of something that never was.

But Fannie Kinlicheenie was definitely flesh and blood.

She had looked out the doorway of her house at them when they drove up. Chee parked his patrol car a polite thirty yards from the residence, thereby respecting a modest people's tradition of privacy. When Fannie Kinlicheenie was ready to receive guests she would let them know. Meanwhile they would wait. Chee offered a cigaret to Mary, and she took it.

"I shouldn't smoke these things," she said, as he lit it for her.

"Neither should I," Chee said.

"This guy's going to be dead, too," Mary said. "Either that or moved way off somewhere."

Chee had a feeling she was right. Otherwise, someone would have remembered him.

"You're too pessimistic," Chee said.

"No. I'm a realist. There's four of them left. After thirty years, you'd have a mortality rate of about twenty-five percent. I think Woody Begay's the one."

Chee considered this logic. He exhaled a cloud of cigaret smoke.

"You started with six," he said. "We got Dillon Charley dead, and Roscoe Sam dead. That's already a thirty-three percent mortality."

Mary didn't comment for a moment.

Then she said, "If you think like that you should avoid poker games. What happened in the past doesn't affect the mathematics. It doesn't affect the probabilities. Forget the other two. Now we have the names of four men who were alive thirty years ago. Chances are one of the four is dead now and three of them are alive."

"Okay," Chee said. "I'll buy that. Now tell me how you figure the dead one will be Woody Begay."

"That's intuition," Mary said. "Women have intuition."

Chee reached for the key in the ignition. "Any use sticking around, you think? Wasting Fannie's time."

Mary grinned at him. "As long as we've come this far, maybe we might as well confirm the hunch."

"I'd like to," Chee said. "Sure you won't be insulted?"

"Naw," she said. "I was wrong once."

"But not recently," Chee said.

"I think I was four." She paused. "No, as a matter of fact, make that twice I was wrong. The second time was being dumb enough to go along on this Great Jimmy Chee Manhunt. Boy, am I tired. How far did we drive today?"

"I don't know," Chee said. "Maybe two hundred and fifty miles. It just seems longer because a lot of it was dirt roads."

"It seems like a thousand," Mary said. "This thing rides like a truck. I think you have too much air in the tires."

"We put in the specified amount," Chee said. "It's intended to jar us around enough so we don't doze off while driving."

"Come to think of it, there was another time I was wrong." She glanced at him and looked quickly away. "That was at the auction, when I got the impression you were interested in me."

"I am," Chee said.

"I mean romantically. You're interested in me because I'm an Anglo. Questions all day long. I feel like I'm being interviewed by a sociologist."

"Anthropologist," Chee said. "And that's the same reason you came along with me. 'What's this Navajo Indian really like?' You just won't admit it."

Mary laughed. "I admit it," she said. "Now I know what you're really like. You're weird."

"But who knows," Chee said. "Maybe something great will grow out of it. We had a Shakespeare teacher at UNM who said that Romeo was doing a paper on the Capulets for his social studies class. He just wanted to pick Juliet's mind."

"I think he was the Capulet," Mary said. "She was a Montague."

" 'What's in a name?' " Chee recited. " 'A rose by any other name . . .' "

"So what's your secret name?" Mary asked.

"Rose," Chee said. "Something like that."

The Kinlicheenie house was of wood-frame construction, insulated with black tar paper. It sat on an expanse of sandstone elevated enough to offer a fine view of a rolling, eroded landscape—gray-silver sage and black creosote brush.

On the horizon Mount Taylor dominated, as it dominated everything in the Checkerboard. Its top was white, but its slopes were blue and serene. Behind the house was a circular stone hogan, its doorway facing properly eastward. And behind that stood a small Montgomery Ward steel storage shed and the humped roof of the dugout where the family took its sweat baths. "Ever notice how Navajos always build their houses where they have a view?" Chee asked.

"I've noticed that Navajos build their houses as far as they can possibly get from other Navajos," Mary said. "Any significance to that?"

"We don't like Indians," Chee said.

Mrs. Kinlicheenie was at the door now. Her hair was neatly tied in a bun, and she was wearing a heavy silver squash-blossom necklace and a wide silver-and-turquoise bracelet. Mrs. Kinlicheenie was ready to receive guests.

23

"MY BROTHER?" Fannie Kinlicheenie's expression was puzzled. "You want to find him?"

They were in the front room of the house. The chair in which Jim Chee sat was covered with a stiff green plastic. He felt the chill of it through his uniform shirt. The house was the "summer hogan" of the Kinlicheenies. There was no heating stove in it. In a while, when the high country frost arrived full force, the family would shift its belongings into the old earth-and-stone "winter hogan" and abandon this poorly insulated structure to the cold. Until then, the problem of the chilly margin between the seasons was solved by wearing more layers of clothing. Fannie Kinlicheenie looked about eight layers deep. Chee wished he had worn his jacket in from the patrol car.

"We heard this man was your brother," Chee said. "We need some information from him."

"But he's dead," Fannie Kinlicheenie said. "He's been dead for . . ." She paused, trying to put a date on it. "Why, he was dead when I got married, and that was 1953."

Chee glanced at Mary. "I didn't know that," he said.

Fannie Kinlicheenie was frowning at him.

"Why did you want to talk to him?"

"He used to be a member of the peyote church. The one over by Grants. We wanted to ask him about that."

"Those sons-a-bitches," Fannie Kinlicheenie said in English. "What you want to know about them?"

"About something that happened way back. Your brother

and some of them were working on an oil well. The peyote chief warned them not to go one day, and the well blew up while they were away."

"I know about that," Fannie said. "I was a girl then and I was in that peyote church, too. I was the water carrier. You know about that?"

"Yes," Chee said. He didn't know everything about the Native American Church, but he knew the water carrier, usually a woman, played a minor role in the ritual.

"Those sons-a-bitches," she repeated. "There was . . ." She paused, glanced at Mary, and back at Chee. They had been speaking in English, the language shared by all three. Now Fannie Kinlicheenie shifted languages. "There was witches in that church," she said in Navajo. One talked cautiously of witches. One discussed them with strangers reluctantly. One talked of them not at all in front of those who were not members of the People. Mary was not Dinetah—not of the People.

"How do you know they were witches?" Chee asked. He stuck to English. "Sometimes people get blamed for being skinwalkers when they're not."

Fannie Kinlicheenie answered in Navajo. "They gave my brother corpse sickness," she said.

"Maybe he ran into a witch somewhere else."

"It was them," she said. "There were other things. There was that oil well that blew up that year. They pretended the Lord Peyote told them it was going to happen. They told everybody that the Lord sent a vision to tell them not to go to work that day. But the witches blew up that oil well. That's how they knew it was going to happen."

"How do you know that?" Chee asked. He had forgotten to speak English. In fact, he had forgotten Mary, who sat there listening and looking puzzled.

"I just know it," Fannie Kinlicheenie said.

Chee considered this. An irrelevant thought intruded. In a white man's home there would not be this complete silence. There would be the ticking of a clock, the sounds refrigerators make, the noise of a TV coming from somewhere. Here there was no sound at all. No traffic noise. No sirens. Outside it was sunset now; even the breeze was still.

"My aunt," Chee said, using a young man's title of respect for an older woman, "I have come a long way to talk with you here because what you know may be very important. I think that something very bad happened at that oil well and that people may still die because of it. If Navajo Wolves did it, then I think we are still dealing with the same bunch of witches. Can you tell me how you knew Navajo Wolves blew up that oil well? Did somebody tell you?"

"Nobody told me. Just my own head."

"How was that?"

Fannie Kinlicheenie thought about how to answer.

"My brother got sick. He had pains in his middle here." Fannie indicated her stomach. "Where the spirit is. And pains in his legs. We got a hand trembler to come in and find out what was wrong. The hand trembler said a witch had done it to him. He found a little bump on the back of Woody's head where the witch had put the corpse powder in. Then another one of them got sick, and they got the hand trembler for him. And he'd been witched, too. And the hand trembler said to have an Enemy Way for both of them." Fannie Kinlicheenie paused, organizing what she wanted to say.

"What's going on?" Mary asked.

Chee held up his hand. "Just a minute," he said. And then to the Kinlicheenie woman: "Another one got sick, you said. You mean another member of the church?"

"It was Roscoe Sam," Fannie said. "One of the bunch that worked at the oil well with Woody. One of them that called themselves the People of Darkness."

"Ah," Chee said. He was speaking in English again, conscious of Mary's curiosity. "And the hand trembler said to have an Enemy Way? To do that right, you have to know who the witch is. Who . . ."

"That's right," Fannie Kinlicheenie said. "They did the Enemy Way for both of them, and it was done right. Both of them got better for a while, but then they had to take Woody off to the hospital at Gallup and he died."

"They don't much believe in Navajo Wolves at the hospital," Chee said. "What did they think he died of?"

"They said it was cancer," Fannie said. "Leukemia got in his blood."

"Does Joseph Sam still live around here?"

"He died too," Fannie Kinlicheenie said. "I heard it was the same thing. Leukemia."

"I'd say that the Enemy Way didn't work too well," Chee said.

"I think they waited too long. But part of it worked. It turned the evil around and pointed it at the Navajo Wolf." Fannie Kinlicheenie's smile was full of malice. "He died, too."

"Do you know who it was?" Chee knew he'd have to wait for an answer and that he might not get one. The Dinee didn't like to talk of the dead, or of witches. Speaking the name of a dead witch was doubly dangerous.

Fannie Kinlicheenie licked her lips.

"It was the peyote chief," she said.

And thus she avoided pronouncing the name of Dillon Charley.

24

THEY JOLTED DOWN THE DIRT TRACK toward the graded road that would take them to the asphalt pavement and back to Crownpoint. The sun was down now. High overhead a strip of feathery cirrus clouds glowed salmon pink in the afterglow. But all around them the landscape was dark. Mary had been saying almost nothing.

"Are you going to tell me what all that was about?" She asked it without looking at him.

Chee glanced at her profile. "The part where she started talking Navajo?"

"And you started talking Navajo. Yes. That part."

"She said some people in the Native American Church were witches, and they gave Woody Begay and Roscoe Sam corpse poisoning, and they both died. And before they died, they held an Enemy Way for them, and that turned the witching around against the witch. And the witch was Dillon Charley, and that's what killed Dillon."

Mary was looking at him now. "What do you think of all that?"

"And she said the witches made the oil well blow up," Chee added. "And that Joseph Sam is dead, too."

"Did she say why they wanted to do that?"

"No," Chee said.

"Did she know? Did you ask her?"

"No," Chee said. "You have to understand about our witches. They wouldn't need a motive in the normal sense. Do you know about Navajo Wolves?"

"I thought I did," Mary said. "Aren't they like the white man's witches, and witches in general, and our Laguna-Acoma witches?" She laughed. "Hyphenated witches," she said. "Only with the U.S. Bureau of Indian Affairs would you get hyphenated witches."

"The way it works with Navajos, witchcraft is the reversal of the Navajo Way. The way the Holy People taught us, the goal of life was *yo'zho'.* No word for it in English. Sort of a combination of beauty/harmony, being in tune, going with the flow, feeling peaceful, all wrapped up in a single concept. Witchcraft is the reverse of this concept, basically. There's a mythology built up around it, of course. You get to be a witch by violating the basic taboos—killing a relative, incest, so forth. And you get certain powers. You can turn yourself into a dog or a wolf. You can fly. And you have power to make people sick. That's the opposite of the good power the Holy People gave us—to cure people by getting them back into *yo'zho'.* Back into beauty. So, to make a long story short, a witch wouldn't have a motive for blowing up an oil well. It's a bad thing to do, blowing people up. That's all the motive a skinwalker needs."

"And she said Dillon Charley was a witch?"

"That's what she said. The families had an Enemy Way and turned the witching spell around, and Dillon Charley died."

"That proves he was the witch?"

"Well, sort of," Chee said. "They'd have to already have him spotted as the witch. Then someone has to get something that belonged to a witch—hair, pair of socks, a hat, something personal. That represents the scalp in the Enemy Way ceremonial. On the last day of the ceremonial, the scalp is shot with an arrow. If everything has been properly done, and they have the right witch, this causes the witch to get sick and die from his own spell."

"And the patient gets well?"

"That's the way it works. But it didn't work for our friend Woody. And it didn't work for Roscoe Sam."

The patrol car jolted into a shallow wash and out again. The cloud overhead had changed from pink to a deep glowing red. "Two more dead," Mary Landon said. "Or three."

"You predicted Woody," Chee said.

"There were six of them to begin with," she said. "Six People of Darkness. Six men who didn't go to work at the oil well. Now Roscoe Sam is dead, and Joseph Sam and Begay, and Dillon Charley."

"Leaves Windy Tsossie and Rudolph Becenti," Chee said. "And so far nobody knows where to find them."

"That's too many dead," Mary Landon said. "They wouldn't be all that old. Probably late middle age if they were alive now. But they died a long, long time ago. When they were pretty young. Just a few years after the oil well. That's too many to be dead." She looked at him thoughtfully. "You think somebody poisoned them all? Something like that? Maybe revenge?"

"As far as we know, Begay died of leukemia," Chee said. "Same thing with Roscoe Sam. Dillon Charley died in the hospital. Vines says he told him he had some sort of cancer. Anyway, in a hospital they'd have detected poison if it was that."

"With an autopsy?" Mary asked.

Chee drove a little while. "I think you're thinking the same thing I'm thinking," he said. "You're thinking about Emerson Charley."

"Yes," Mary said. "I'm thinking about how Emerson Charley didn't have an autopsy."

"Because somebody stole his body out of the cold room at BCMC," Chee said.

"Which seems a funny thing to steal."

"Right," Chee said.

"Unless you don't want an autopsy performed."

"Right," Chee said.

"Which is also what you'd get if you blow the guy into little pieces by bombing his truck. No autopsy. Right?"

"Yeah," Chee said.

"Yeah," Mary said. "Yeah, or maybe baloney. Why would anyone want to poison Emerson Charley? Or Dillon Charley? Or Woody Begay, or any of those guys?"

"No reason," Chee said. "But you know what? Let's go to Albuquerque and see what we can find out at the hospital."

"I don't know," Mary Landon said. "When I go places with

you, it's no picnic." She hesitated. "Do you think he'll be there?" She didn't have to say the blond man. Chee knew what she meant.

"I've thought about that," Chee said. "If I was him, I wouldn't go near that hospital. And if I was looking for you and me, that would be the last place I'd look."

25

THE DOCTOR'S NAME was Edith Vassa. The midmorning sun slanted through the window behind her desk and flashed through her short reddish hair. She was a young woman with that pink complexion which made Jimmy Chee wonder why the white men called Indians redskins. Dr. Vassa was the physician who had treated Emerson Charley at the University of New Mexico Cancer Research and Treatment Center. Thus she had been stuck with the job of trying to find out what had happened to the Charley corpse. It had been a frustrating, embarrassing dead end. Edith Vassa was sick of it. Her expression showed it.

"I can tell you everything I know in a very few words. Emerson Charley's vital signs ceased at approximately 5:13 P.M. The physician on duty made the usual examination and certified death. The body was tagged for autopsy and moved to the morgue cold room. The next morning, the morgue attendant noticed he had only one body instead of two. He guessed the body had gone to the morphology laboratory without being properly checked out." Dr. Vassa made an impatient gesture with her hands. "To skip the unnecessary details, it was finally learned that the body had disappeared."

"You presume it was stolen?"

"I presume his relatives collected him," Dr. Vassa said. "The Albuquerque police thought we might have just misplaced it somewhere." She laughed, but she didn't think it was funny.

"All we actually know is that one of the morgue carts was found the next morning in the hallway near the loading dock. Presumably it was used to move the body. And we found that the bag of personal effects that belonged to a second body in the morgue was also missing. It seems safe to presume that someone got into the morgue, picked up the wrong bag of personal effects, put the bag on the cart with the body, rolled it down the hallway to the loading dock, and loaded everything into a car or something."

"It was being held for an autopsy?"

"It was supposed to be held for an autopsy."

"Why the autopsy?"

"It's the routine. We're studying cancer. How it affects cells. How treatment affects tumors. Effect of treatment on blood platelets. On bone marrow. Metastasis. So forth."

"Metastasis?"

"Spreading. How cancer spreads from one part of the body to another."

"You didn't suspect foul play?" Chee asked.

Dr. Vassa smiled, very faintly. "You don't get leukemia through foul play. It's not like a poison. And it's not like an infectious disease, which you could cause by inserting a bacteria. It's caused by . . ." Dr. Vassa hesitated.

Jimmy Chee waited, curious. How would this woman describe the origins of leukemia to a Navajo?

"We don't know exactly what causes it. Perhaps some sort of virus. Perhaps some malfunction in the bone marrow, where blood cells are produced."

Fair enough, Chee thought. He couldn't have done better himself.

"And it's rare, especially among adults?"

"Relatively," Dr. Vassa said. "I think the current case rate for all sorts of malignancies this year is less than three per thousand. Leukemic diseases are about one percent of that. Say three in a hundred thousand."

"Three per thousand?" Mary Landon said. "What would you think of a situation in which you had six men, friends, members of the same church, sort of distant relatives, and three of them die of cancer?"

"I'd be surprised," Dr. Vassa said.

"How surprised?" Mary Landon asked. "Three out of six instead of three out of a thousand."

"It would be quite a coincidence," Dr. Vassa said, "but things like that can happen. Mathematical probabilities work in odd ways. Was Emerson one of the three?"

"He was the son of one of the three," Chee said.

"His father died of cancer?"

"That's what we're told," Mary said.

"But you don't know for sure?" Dr. Vassa asked. "Did they all live in the same area? Work at the same jobs? I think if they really did all die of cancer our epidemiology people would be interested." Dr. Vassa smiled. "Especially if it happened to be cancer of the gall bladder. They're fascinated by that." She reached for the phone. "I'll make you an appointment with Sherman Huff."

Sherman Huff's office was in the basement. Dr. Huff asked questions and took notes, and picked up the telephone. "Three out of six is unusual," he said. "So first we try to find out if the tumor registry has them." He spoke into the telephone, identifying himself and reading the names of Dillon Charley, Roscoe Sam, and Woody Begay off his notes. He kept the receiver pinned to his ear with a raised shoulder and turned back to Chee and Mary Landon.

"Just be a minute or two," he said. "It's a matter of checking the names with the computer. The registry tries to keep a file on every cancer case diagnosed in the state, but these were way back when they were first setting it up. And it could be they were out on the reservation, where they weren't diagnosed."

"In other words, if you don't have the names registered, it won't necessarily mean they didn't have cancer?"

"Not from the early 1950s it won't," Huff said. "And not from the Navajo reservation. However, even in those days, they were getting most of them. They had a pretty good . . ."

The telephone said something into Huff's ear. "Just a second," he said.

He made a note. "Okay," he said. He wrote again. "Thanks. Pull the folders for me. I'll want to look at them." He hung up and glanced at Chee.

"Dillon Charley, leukemia. Roscoe Sam, malignancy affecting liver and other vital organs. Woody Begay, leukemia." Huff's face was thoughtful. "That's a hell of a lot of cancer," he said. "And a lot of leukemia for men their ages."

"And Emerson Charley," Mary Landon added. "He also died of leukemia."

"That's what Vassa told me," Huff said. "Let's make sure. Let's get that folder, too." He dialed the phone again.

"While you have them, give them some more names," Chee said. "Give them Rudolph Becenti, Joseph Sam, and Windy Tsossie."

"Those the other three of the six? You hear they had cancer, too?"

"All we know is that Joseph Sam probably died back in the 1950s, and we couldn't find Becenti or Tsossie," Chee said.

"Tumor registry data is confidential," Huff said. "I can confirm a cancer death for law enforcement. I'm not sure I can just go on a fishing expedition for you."

"I'm only trying to confirm that their cause of death was cancer. It saves me time. Otherwise, I'd have to go hunting for death certificates in county courthouses."

Huff talked into the telephone again. He asked for the Emerson Charley file and a check on Tsossie, Becenti, and Joseph Sam. Then he waited, phone to ear. He was a burly man, with a gray mustache merging into a bushy gray beard, sun-weathered skin, and bright blue eyes. Behind him, the wall was covered with posters: "Smoke Can Make Your Doctor Rich." "Little Orphan Annie's Parents Smoked." "Stamp Out Old Age: Smoke!" "To Kill a Mockingbird: Blow Smoke on It." In the silence, Chee became conscious of a tapping. Mary's little finger was drumming against the arm of her chair. The telephone receiver made a sound.

"Go ahead," Huff said. He wrote on his note pad. "Okay," he said. "I'd like to see them all." He hung up and sat for a moment looking silently at what he had written. "Well," he said.

"Another one?" Mary asked.

"Rudolph Becenti," Dr. Huff said. "Another form of leukemia."

"That's four out of six," Mary Landon said.

"That sure is," Dr. Huff said. "That's a hell of a high percentage."

"How about the other two?" Chee asked. "Tsossie and Joseph Sam?"

"Neither name showed up," Huff said. He was frowning. "Four out of six," he said. "What in the world could account for that? What were they doing?"

"In 1948 they were the members of a roustabout crew on an oil well out near Grants," Chee said. "The common labor. Beyond that they were all members of the same little cult in the Native American Church."

"They ever work in the uranium mines out there? We think we had a little increase from that. But that was lung cancer."

"Not as far as we know. And the mining was just getting well started in Ambrosia Lakes when these guys were dying," Chee said.

"How about asbestos? Were they installing insulation?" He shook his head. "No. Inhaled asbestos fiber is a carcinogen, but nothing like this. Nothing like four out of six. And not that quickly. And it's the wrong kind of cancer. You know anything else about them?"

"Damn little," Chee said.

"Did they ever work up at the Nevada test site? Did they work up there when we were doing that atmospheric testing of the bombs?"

"I don't know," Chee said. "It's not likely."

"That could explain it," Huff said. "We just found out this fall that we had a whole rash of leukemia fatalities downwind from the test site in the middle of the 1950s. We've pinned down twelve cases in one tiny little community. Blood cell formation is particularly sensitive to some forms of radiation."

"I know Dillon Charley didn't work anywhere near Nevada," Chee said. "He was working at Mount Taylor until just before he died."

"As for Emerson Charley," Mary said, "they stopped atmospheric testing years ago, and he just died."

Huff looked disappointed. "Yes," he said, "but sometimes

it takes years to develop. And the cases might not all be connected." He produced a wry smile. "And also, of course, maybe none of them have been within a thousand miles of the test site. Do you think you could find the other two of the six?"

"We can keep trying on Tsossie," Chee said. "But Joseph Sam's dead. He won't do you any good."

"Actually, he might do us some good," Huff said. "Some kinds of cancers affect bone tissue. Some other kinds leave their traces in bone when they metastasize. You can often find the damage in ribs, or vertebrae, or sometimes large marrow bones. Do you know where he's buried?"

"We can try to find out," Chee said.

"And we'll try to find some sort of common denominator among them," Huff said. "How about this church they all belong to?"

"Native American Church," Chee said. "The peyote church."

Huff grinned through his beard. "If we suspected peyote of being carcinogenic, we'd have our mystery solved. But it isn't. Anything else? Anything that ties them all together?"

Chee told him of Dillon Charley's peyote vision, which had saved them all from the oil well explosion, and of the survivors being joined, or so it seemed, in their own cult—the People of Darkness.

"With a mole as their amulet figure? Isn't the fetish usually a predator? A mountain lion, or a bear, or something like that?" Huff asked.

"The mole's the predator of darkness," Chee said. "But it *is* unusual to use him for an amulet."

"So why did they pick the mole?" Huff asked.

"I've wondered," Chee said. And as he said it, he had a thought. "Whoever took Emerson Charley's body left his personal effects. Could we take a look at them?"

"Why not?" Huff said. "If we haven't lost them, too."

26

THE RED PLASTIC BAG was in a storage room on the second floor among scores of identical plastic bags, all arranged in alphabetical order.

"Bracken," the attendant said. "Caldwell. Charley. Here it is. Emerson Charley. You can take a look at it there on that table."

Chee removed a crushed black felt hat, a pair of cowboy boots which needed half soles, a denim jacket, a Timex watch with a steel band, a plaid cotton shirt, a T-shirt, a pair of jockey shorts, a pair of worn denim jeans, socks, a set of car keys, a pocket knife, a small leather pouch attached to a long leather thong, two blue shoestrings, a package of paper matches, and a billfold. He put the leather pouch and the billfold aside and quickly explored all the pockets. They were empty. Then he inspected the billfold. It contained a five, two ones, a driver's license, a social security card, and a card identifying the agent who had written the liability policy on Charley's pickup truck.

Then he picked up the leather pouch.

"What's that?" Mary asked. "What are you looking for?"

"It's where you carry your ceremonial stuff," Chee said. "Supposed to be made of the hide of a deer killed in the ritual fashion. It holds your gall medicine. What you use against witchcraft. A little pollen. Maybe a little ceremonial corn meal. . . ." He pulled open the draw cord and fished into the pouch with his fingers. "And it's where you carry your amulet, if you carry one."

The amulet he extracted was black, and dull, and shaped into the eyeless, sharp-nosed form of a mole. He held it up for Mary's inspection. It was heavy, formed from a soft stone. Some sort of shale, Chee guessed. "Here we have Dine'etse-tle," Chee said. "The predator of the nadir. The hunting spirit of the underworld. One of the People of Darkness."

He stared at it, heavy on his palm, hoping for some information. It was well formed—better than most amulets. Chee remembered the amateur sculpture in B. J. Vines' huge office. Had Vines made this? Was this formed from one of those fragments of black rock Emerson Charley had found in Vines' keepsake box? Perhaps. But what did that mean? He slipped the mole back into the pouch.

"Did it tell you anything?"

Chee recited two lines of Navajo. "That's from one of the blessing chants," he said.

The mole, his hunting place is darkness.
The mole, his hunting song is silence.

27

THE SECRETARY from Dr. Huff's office met them as they left the storage room. The message was from Chee's Crownpoint office. It told him to call Martin at Albuquerque FBI headquarters.

"I thought nobody knew where we are," Mary said. She was frowning. "Wasn't that how we were going to stay safe?"

"Nobody but my office," Chee said.

"But if your office knows, can't somebody else . . . ?"

"How?" Chee asked.

Mary thought about it, still frowning. She shrugged. "I guess you're right," she said. "But you know how people are."

Martin wanted to remind Chee that he was supposed to come in and look at photographs.

"Maybe in a day or two," Chee said. "To tell the truth, I'm going to stay away from places where this guy might be waiting around for me."

"I think you can relax a little now. He's gone."

"How do you know?"

"We made a clean sweep," Martin said. "Checked every motel, every hotel, every place he could be staying. We even checked new apartment rentals."

"Lot of work," Chee said.

"He's no place around here," Martin said. "And we found the green-and-white Plymouth. It was in a little garage in Gallup. The son of a bitch drove it in and told the mechanic it needed a valve job and he was in no hurry for it. That's why we didn't find it abandoned anywhere."

"That was smart," Chee said. "You know how he got out of Albuquerque this time?"

"We're pretty sure he stole a car. Just drove it somewhere. Maybe El Paso or Denver. Somewhere far enough to miss our stakeouts. And then he took a plane for wherever he goes."

"So he's not in Albuquerque?"

"Not unless he's staying with relatives," Martin said.

28

AT THE COST OF HOURS of driving from here to there in search of older members of the Mud Clan, Jimmy Chee learned a little about Windy Tsossie. He learned that not long after the oil well explosion, Tsossie had married a daughter of Grace Yazzie of the Standing Rock Clan. He had moved northwestward to the Bisti country to join his new family. He had been seen around Ambrosia Lakes no more. Chee learned that Tsossie's wife was dead. He learned other things as well. Among the important ones was that Tsossie's sister-in-law, a woman named Romana Musket, was alive and well and living between Thoreau and Crownpoint in the log house with the tin roof and the sheep pens behind it that was visible on the slope above the highway. Mrs. Musket seemed likely to know where Tsossie could be found, alive or dead. Chee had also learned that no one seemed to know for sure which one it would be. No one had heard Tsossie had died. On the other hand, Chee had found no one who had actually seen him for years. And finally Chee had accumulated a general impression of Windy Tsossie. It was a negative impression. His kinsmen and his clansmen, when they admitted remembering him at all, remembered him without fondness or respect. They talked of him reluctantly, vaguely, uneasily. No one put it in words. Since Chee was Navajo, no one needed to. Windy Tsossie did not "go in beauty." Windy Tsossie was not a good man. He did not follow those rules which Changing Woman had given the People. In a word, Windy Tsossie was believed by his kinsmen to be a witch.

"I don't see how you can say that," Mary said. "You told me what they said. Nobody even hinted at anything like that."

"They wouldn't," Chee said, "not to a stranger. I might be a witch myself. Or you might be. And witches don't like people talking about witches."

Mary yawned. "You're stretching things," she said.

"Did you notice that talking about Tsossie made them nervous? That's the tip-off."

"The thing that interests me is I think we're finally going to find one of them alive," she said. "What's he going to tell us? I really think now he's going to remember something."

"If he's alive."

"He will be."

"I have the same sort of hunch," Chee said.

They were driving the subagency's pickup truck, having traded the relative comfort of the patrol car for the ability to follow wagon tracks. They drove northeastward, mostly in second gear, over a rutted road which now tilted downward. Chee flicked his lights to bright. The beams lit the broad, sandy bottom of an arroyo below. When they reached it, he stopped.

"Chaco Wash," he said. He switched on the dome light, unfolded his map, and examined it. The map was one entitled "Indian Country," produced by the Auto Club of Southern California; Chee had found it both accurate and detailed. It rated routes of travel in nine categories, ranging from Divided Limited Access Highways, down through Gravel, Graded Dirt, and Ungraded Dirt to Doubtful Dirt. For the last fifteen miles, they had been driving on Doubtful Dirt. According to the map, the Doubtful Dirt ended at Chaco Wash.

Chee folded the Indian Country map and extracted from his shirt pocket a lined sheet of notebook paper. It had come from a red-covered Big Chief notebook at the home of Mrs. Musket. On it, a grandson of Ramona Musket had drawn another map to show how to reach the hogan where Rudolph Charley was conducting a Peyote Way. His grandmother was attending the services. The grandson was about twelve. He wore a T-shirt with the S symbol of Superman decorating its front, and he drew the map carefully with a ballpoint pen, and while he drew he explained that Rudolph Charley was the new peyote chief because somebody had shot the old peyote chief, who was Rudolph Charley's older brother.

"Right at Chaco Wash the regular road got washed out," Supergrandson said. "You turn right there, and you drive up the sand if you want to, because it's smoother. You got to pay attention or you'll miss the turns. I'll put down some landmarks to look for." He glanced up and grinned at Mary, and switched politely to English. "If you're not careful out there you can get lost," he assured her.

On the Big Chief map, Supergrandson had penned in "salt cedars" at the point where the Doubtful Dirt road petered out at the wash bottom. Now, in the beam of his headlights, Chee could see a cluster of winter-bare salt cedar below. Chee let the truck roll forward again, past the trees and onto the smoothness of the arroyo floor.

"Here's where we get to the place where if we're not careful we can get lost," Mary said. "Is that right?"

"Right," Chee said.

"Let's not," Mary said. "I'm too tired. I'm flat out exhausted. It seems like we've been in this truck about seventeen days."

"Just since about sunrise," Chee said.

Mary turned suddenly and stared back out the rear window. "I get a feeling I'll look back there and see somebody following us," she said. "Not somebody. That blond man."

"How could he?" Chee asked. "There's no way he could know where we're going."

She shivered, and hugged herself. "Let's say he's smart," she said. "Or let's say he has some reason himself to go to this peyote ceremony."

"I can't think why he would."

"It's a memorial service for Tomas Charley, isn't it? Or something like that. Maybe he's looking for people, just as we are. Maybe we'll just run into him there."

"I doubt it," Chee said.

"I think you're like me. Too tired to care. You're so tired you're going to tell me your war name."

"It won't be much longer now," Chee said. "We want to be at Charley's place at midnight, and then Mrs. Musket will tell us that Windy is living in Grants and give us his address and telephone number. Then we go get some sleep and tomorrow we'll call Tsossie, and he'll tell us who blew up the oil well and why, and where to find the evidence to give to the grand jury, and who to arrest and why Emerson Charley's body was taken out of the hospital, and who hired the blond man to shoot Tomas Charley, and . . ."

"Oh, stop," Mary said. She yawned hugely behind her hand. "With the luck you and I have," she said through the end of the yawn, "that kid gave us the wrong address or the wrong night, or Mrs. Musket won't be there, or she never heard of Windy Tsossie, or she won't like your looks and won't talk to you, or she'll tell you Tsossie moved to Tanzania and didn't leave an address, or it's the wrong Tsossie, or the blond will be there and he'll shoot you. Or even worse, he'll shoot me."

Chee smiled. "Well," he said, "we'll soon know."

At seven minutes to midnight the track they were following skirted a rocky outcrop covered with stunted juniper. The truck's headlights reflected from a windshield, and then from the corrugated metal roof of a shack and the glass of the window below the roof. Chee slowed the truck to a crawl and examined what the headlights showed him. Three pickup trucks, an old white Chevy, and a wagon on which bales of hay served as seats. Twenty yards behind the shack was the round stone shape of a hogan, with a thin wisp of blue smoke emerging from the smoke hole in the center of its conical dirt-insulated roof. No one was in sight.

Chee parked the truck beside the newest of the pickups, flicked off the headlights, and stepped out into the darkness. The moon was down and the black sky was brilliant with a billion stars. He stood with face raised, drinking it in—the great fluorescent sweep of the Milky Way, the pattern of the winter constellations, the incredible silent brightness of the universe.

Mary was standing beside him now. "My God," she said in a hushed voice. "I never saw the sky like that."

"Altitude," Chee said. "We're almost at the Continental Divide here. Mile and a half above sea level; air's thin. And partly it's because there's no ground lights. Look," he said, pointing to the southeast. "See that little glow on the horizon?

That's Albuquerque. Hundred miles away, but you can see what it does."

"It makes you forget for a minute how cold you are," Mary said. She shuddered. "The minute's up. I'm cold."

From the hogan came the sound of song and the tapping of a pot drum. Distance and the hogan walls muted it, and the singing was not much more than a rising and falling rhythm, part of the background of the windless night. Chee glanced at his watch. The followers of Lord Peyote wouldn't recess their ceremonial until midnight. They began at sunset after a prayer to inform the setting sun that their intentions were holy, and the ritual would not end until sunrise. But at midnight there was a break. And that meant another five minutes to wait.

"When I was a boy," Chee said, "sometimes my mother would wake me up in the darkest part of the night, and we'd go out away from the hogan, and she'd teach me star lore. How the constellations move and how you can tell the direction and the time of night if you know the time of year. And how it all began."

"How did it all begin?" Mary asked.

"There weren't any Navajos yet. Just Holy People. First Man, First Woman, Talking God, Gila Monster, Corn Beetle, all the various *yei* figures. At night, the sky was black and blank except for the moon. So First Man decided to hang out the stars. And he put up the Blue Flint Boys"—Chee pointed to Cepheus—"and the Bear, and the Stalking God, and all the rest. And along came Coyote, and he grabbed the blanket where First Man had the stars waiting to be hung, and he gave it a toss and threw all that were left out in one great swinging motion. That's what made the Milky Way."

"Quite a coyote," Mary said. She shivered again and hugged herself.

The hogan was silent now, and suddenly there was light at the doorway as the blankets hung across the opening were pulled back.

Chee reached into the cab of the truck and turned on the dome light. It was polite to let people know who was calling on them.

Contrary to Mary's pessimism, Mrs. Musket was there. She

was a gray-haired, sturdy woman with a red-and-green mackinaw over the voluminous velveteen blouse and skirt of traditional Navajo womanhood. She wasn't sure she wanted to talk about Windy Tsossie.

Rudolph Charley invited them into the hogan out of the cold, and stood beside them listening. Rudolph Charley looked a lot like Tomas Charley. Just a little younger and even thinner.

"It all happened a long time ago," Chee was saying. "Before he married your sister. There was an explosion at an oil well where he worked. We want to see if he remembers what happened."

Mrs. Musket stared at Chee, glanced nervously at Mary, at Charley, and then back at Chee.

"He won't remember anything," Mrs. Musket said.

"It seems like just about everybody else who was working with Tsossie is dead," Chee said. "We can't talk to them. We want to talk to him."

"I think Windy is dead, too," Rudolph Charley said. "I think the witch got them all."

"Yes," Mrs. Musket said. "He's dead."

"When did he die?" Chee asked. He suspected Mrs. Musket was lying. Experience taught one to watch the face of a person being questioned. Lying made almost everyone nervous. Mrs. Musket was nervous. But then she would be nervous anyway, at being questioned by strangers who appeared out of the darkness to talk of death. And there was more to it than nervousness. Something vague and hard to define. And he thought that he knew what was causing it. Mrs. Musket had eaten peyote and drunk of the "black drink" of the ceremonial—peyote tea. She was in that dreamy world of the psychedelic. He glanced at Rudolph Charley. The road chief of his ceremonial, too, looked at Chee as if he wasn't sure that Chee existed.

"When did he die, then?" Chee repeated. "And where did they put the body?"

"Long time ago," Mrs. Musket said. She stood looking at Chee and through Chee. The seconds ticked away. "They lived out behind Bisti in the badlands. I wasn't with them. But my sister's husband was a witch, and somebody turned the witching around against him. He got corpse sickness and he died."

"You weren't there, but you heard about it? Is that right? From your sister?" Chee asked.

"From my sister," Mrs. Musket agreed.

"He died of a sickness?"

"Corpse sickness," Mrs. Musket said.

"Where?"

"In my sister's hogan."

"And they buried him there?"

"They got a white man who worked there at Bisti to come and put the body out in the rocks. They told me that he put it in a little blowhole in the side of a cliff and covered it over with rocks."

"It's all starting up again," Rudolph Charley said suddenly. "More witching."

Chee looked at him. Charley's eyes were focused somewhere a long way off.

"The first time it killed my grandfather, and all the people who the Lord Peyote let see through the doorway. The witching killed all six of them. And now it has started up again. First it killed my grandfather. Now it has killed my father, and it killed my brother. Tonight we are asking the Lord Peyote to let us see what will happen next. . . ." His voice trailed off.

Mary began a word and bit it off. The four of them stood there, silently, waiting for the road chief to continue. Beyond Charley, Chee could see the room. The packed earthen floor had been cleared of furnishings. The peyote altar had been built across the back of it—a low crescent shape of hard-packed sand. The peyote moon, they called it. At its center, where the sand was perhaps six inches high, a cup-sized bed of cedar twigs had been built. In this nest the gnarled, hairy shape of a peyote button rested. On the sand beside it was a small silver box, lid open. Behind the peyote moon two zigzag lines were inscribed in the earth, representing the footprints of Christ. The Native American Church as it came to the Checkerboard was more or less Christian. Christ taught the white man only through the Bible, because the white man had crucified him. But the Navajo, who had not harmed Christ, God instructed directly through visions. And Lord Peyote was the instrument, the key to the door which led to reality.

Rudolph Charley still stood motionless, caught in some odd drug-induced expansion of time.

"Did he let you see?" Chee asked.

"I saw the mole," Rudolph Charley said. "The amulet that was my father's and my grandfather's."

"Nothing else?" Chee asked.

The door opened and two men ducked through—both young. They glanced at Chee and at Mary. One added sticks to the piñon fire which had burned to a bed of coals in the hogan fire pit. The other went to the back wall and squatted by the pot drum, watching and waiting. Rudolph Charley's mood changed.

"Nothing you would understand," he said. "We have to start again now. We have to finish the service."

"The man you want to talk to is dead," Mrs. Musket said.

"All right," Chee said. "Then tell me where to find the blowhole where they put his body."

29

FINALLY COLTON WOLF was ready. He'd had both a CB radio and a radiotelephone installed in the cab of the pickup. He had driven up an arroyo east of the Sandia Mountains and refreshed his marksmanship with both his rifle and his .22 caliber pistol. The rifle was an expensive .30 caliber Ruger equipped with a scope. He'd fired off half the shells from a 100-round carton, adjusting the open sights for ranges up to 250 yards and the scope up to 800. Then he'd established with a telephone call to the hospital that Western Union couldn't deliver a telegram to Jim Chee because Jim Chee had checked out. That confirmed what Colton had expected. Next he called the city desk at the *Albuquerque Journal,* identified himself as a professor at the university, and got permission to do some research in the newspaper's library. An hour of reading through clippings of crime reports provided him with the names of FBI agents and sheriff's officers who worked on or around the Navajo reservation. He jotted the names and pertinent information into his notebook and then asked if there was a file on B. J. Vines. There was. The oldest clipping reported a transfer of uranium leases from Vines to a consortium of mining companies headed by Kennecott Copper and Kerrmac Nuclear Fuels. Another, a wire service story originating in New York, reported that Vines had won the Weatherby Trophy, the world championship of big-game hunting. The only substantial story was a feature, with photographs, of the construction of Vines' home on the slope of Mount Taylor. The residence was described as "probably the most expensive ever built in New Mexico." The man whose name Colton had found in the box he'd been hired to recover was obviously rich enough to pay the cost of recovering it. There was a good chance, then, that Vines was the client. Not a certainty, because someone else seemed to have wanted the box. But Vines seemed most likely. Colton added to his notes a description of the house and its location. If all else failed, that might be useful.

Colton's last stop was at the municipal library, where he checked through the file of telephone books and noted the numbers he might need. And then he drove westward from Albuquerque, climbing out of the Rio Grande valley, crossing the Rio Puerco breaks, and rolling at a steady fifty-five miles an hour across the empty mesa-butte landscape of west central New Mexico. As he drove, he tested his radio reception on the federal and law-enforcement channels. Reception was excellent. The technique and terminology of the radio dispatchers was no different from what he'd heard in other states. Then he tested the telephone connection by calling the U.S. Weather Service for the forecast. For the west central plateau of New Mexico, the forecast was for increasing afternoon cloudiness, periodic gusty winds, and colder temperatures through the afternoon, with a 60 percent chance of snow before midnight. The green interstate information sign told Colton that the Grants interchange was ahead. To his right, Mount Taylor rose against an unnaturally blue sky, its highest slopes white with snowbanks. He let the camper roll to a stop on the shoulder of the highway, picked up the phone, checked his notebook for the names he wanted, and placed a call to the Navajo Tribal Police subagency office at Crownpoint.

The voice that answered was a woman's.

"This is the Federal Bureau of Investigation," Colton said, "Albuquerque. Agent Martin. Is Captain Largo there?"

"He works out of Tuba City," the voice said. "That number . . ."

"I know that," Colton said, "but Largo told me he might stop in there today. How about Jim Chee, then?"

"Chee's not here, either," the voice said. "He's taking some time off."

"How's he feeling? Hope those ribs are healing up."

"Okay, I guess."

"I was calling about Chee," Colton said. "We got some things we want him to look at. About that shooting. How can I get hold of him?"

"Just a minute," the voice said. There was a pause.

Colton waited. This was the crucial moment. He would allow the delay to stretch four minutes. More than that would risk a successful trace. He couldn't chance the police learning that this was a radiotelephone call. The second hand on his watch dial swept into the second minute.

"We'll have to get him on the radio." It was a man's voice now. "What's the message?"

"Tell him Martin has some information for him, and I need to show him some pictures. Tell him I'm coming out to the reservation and have him call me on my car telephone." He provided a wrong number that sounded reasonable. "Is he near a telephone?"

"I doubt it," the voice said.

"Look," Colton said. "This is urgent. See if you can find him, and if he's a long ways from a telephone, can I get you to call me back and let me know how long it will be?"

"Sure," the voice said.

"Okay. Thanks," Colton said. He hung up, switched on the radio receiver, and pulled the truck back onto Interstate 25. He hadn't gone a mile before he monitored the first call from the Crownpoint dispatcher trying to reach Jimmy Chee.

Colton drove steadily westward, past Grants, past the uranium-processing mills of Ambrosia Lakes, into the rougher country which climbed toward the Continental Divide. Crownpoint was trying to reach Chee at ten-minute intervals. At the Thoreau interchange, Colton pulled off the highway and parked. It was here he had decided to wait. He had never thought there was a serious chance that Chee would run far after the fiasco in the hospital. There was no need to run. Where better to hide an Indian than on an Indian reservation?

He sat with his knees propped against the dash and put together a sandwich of the materials he had brought from the trailer. As always, he ate slowly. The mountain was miles to the east now, but it still dominated the landscape, cold and ominous. When this was over, when he had caught Jim Chee and killed him, and killed the woman; when his tracks were erased and he was once again secure, then he would find a better way to trace his mother. Perhaps a hypnotist could help him remember something he had forgotten. Something useful. There was that old woman in one of his earliest memories. She had put him on her lap and her breath had smelled of tobacco. He had always guessed she might be a grandmother. If he could remember that—or even the place where they had lived when he was very small—it might be helpful. He could remember so little of that. Only a sense of days of cold fog, days of rain, days in an upstairs apartment with his meals left in a refrigerator, his mother coming home in the mornings, his mother's hair damp against his face, his mother's hands cold against his skin. There were men then, too, but no particular man he could remember.

He was staring outward at the blank blue sky, but his thoughts were on that room. He could remember the cracks in the gray linoleum. He'd had two marbles then and the marbles would chase one another down the cracks. He could remember playing that game endlessly, day after day, and the grimy windows, but not the name of the town. Surely he had heard it. Surely, even at four or five, it had meant something to him. His mother had not talked to him often. She wouldn't have been likely to tell a child they were living in Seattle, or Portland, or wherever it was. But he must have heard it. He would find himself a hypnotist and maybe then he could remember something. Colton was aware that things were wrong with his memory. Gaps in it. He ran his thumb down his sweater, feeling the bump under the skin where the rib had healed crookedly. He could remember when he didn't have the bump—when they lived in San Diego. He could remember having it, already healed, in Bakersfield. But he couldn't remember the beating that produced it. It was the same with the ridge of thick white scar tissue under the hair above his left ear. That also had grown from some blank spot in his childhood. The last time he had tried to remember about that was in Taylorville, but trying had made him sick and he had stopped.

His radio spoke again, the voice of the Crownpoint dispatcher called for Jim Chee.

This time, Chee answered. Colton put down his sandwich and picked up his notebook. Crownpoint relayed the message he had left.

"Well, hell," Chee's voice said. "We're way over here by the old Bisti trading post."

Colton jotted "We're by Bisti" on his pad. He underlined "We're."

"If you're away from the telephone, he wanted me to call him and let him know where he could meet you. He said he'd be coming to the reservation," the dispatcher said.

There was a pause. "Well," the voice of Chee said. "I guess he's going to have to wait, then. We're trying to find a hogan northwest of the old trading post. It's about nine miles back in there, and it'll take me a while to find it. Tell him I'll meet him at our office in Crownpoint tonight. Tell him I'll try to be there by nine, but I might be a little late."

"Ten-four," the dispatcher said. "You paying attention to the weather? It's supposed to snow."

"Right," Chee said. "We'll watch it."

Colton jotted "We" on his note pad. He also wrote "nine miles back in there." He didn't make a note of the nine o'clock meeting time at Crownpoint. By nine o'clock Jimmy Chee would be dead.

30

THE BISTI TRADING POST had burned years ago, with the thoroughness with which buildings burn when there is no fire department to interfere. The fire had left only the blackened stone foundation and odds and ends of melted glass and twisted metal. Years of casual Navajo scavengers had sorted through the ashes, and years of weather had piled tumbleweeds and dust against the ruins. The great cypresses imported to protect the post from the sun had long since starved for water, like town dogs abandoned in the desert. The row of bare dead trunks now served as an incongruous landmark for a ruin that had otherwise almost returned to nature.

Chee turned the pickup truck left beyond the dead trees, leaving a road marked "Graded Dirt" for a track his map did not show. It ran, fairly straight and fairly smooth, across an expanse of creosote brush.

"You sure this is the right way?" Mary asked.

"No," Chee said, "but I'm sure it's the right direction."

"And you still think we can find the hogan? After all these years?"

"Probably," Chee said. "She said nine miles northwest by north of the trading post, at the south side of an isolated butte. And she described the butte." He pointed ahead. "That must be it. And out here they'd have had to build the hogan of stone, so it's still there. It's just a matter of hunting it. And I'm pretty good at hunting." Chee paused, thinking about that statement. "Or I used to think I was."

The land sloped downward now, into an immensity of erosion. What once had been a sandstone plain had been carved into a grotesquerie of shapes—tables, heads, layer cakes, twisted spires, exposed ribs, serrations, and weird forms that suggested things to which Chee's imagination could not attach names. Wind and water had cut through the overlay into the blackness of coal deposits, into crimson clay, into the streaky blue of shale. Every color showed except green. This was the Bisti badlands. It stretched away for fifty miles under a sky in which clouds had been steadily building.

"I have a hunch he's not dead," Mary said. "I sort of sensed she was hiding something."

"She was nervous," Chee said. "Maybe she was lying and maybe there was another reason. But if the bones are there, we'll find them. And if they're not, we'll find Tsossie."

As he said it, his confidence surprised him. But he *was* confident. Finding Tsossie, skeletal or breathing, involved things purely Navajo—a pattern of thinking and behavior with which Chee was in intimate harmony. He felt no such harmony with the thinking of the whites who must be involved in this affair. For all enterprises, such harmony was essential. Especially for the hunter. And this was from the very start a hunt.

One of the prayers from the Stalking Way ran through his mind, and the voice of his uncle chanting:

I am the Black God as I sing this,
Black God I am. I come and I stand
beneath the East, beneath the Turquoise Mountain.
The crystal doe walks toward me,
as I call it, as I pray to it,
toward me it comes walking, understanding me
it walks this day into my right hand.
Pleasant, it comes to join me,
in its death it obeys the voice of my singing.
In its beauty I obey the crystal doe.

Perfect understanding, Chee thought. Harmony between deer and man. Harmony between Jim Chee and Tsossie, or the bones of Tsossie, and the thinking of those who had placed

Tsossie's corpse among the rocks. But Jim Chee didn't understand the thinking of whites. Neither Changing Woman nor Talking God had given him a song to produce that understanding. What would his uncle say to that? Chee knew exactly what the old man would say. He could almost hear him, because he had heard him so often:

"Boy, when you understand the big, you understand the little. First understand the big."

And that would mean, in this case, that if Chee learned to understand all men (the big), he could understand white men (the little). His uncle would add that if a Navajo could find harmony with a deer, he could find equal harmony with a white man. Chee grimaced at the windshield. And then his uncle, who never failed to belabor a point, would add some wisdom about deer and men. He would say that the deer is much like the Navajo in fundamental ways. It loves its offspring and its mate, food, water, and its rest. And it hates cold, hunger, pain, and death. But the deer is also different. Its life is short. It builds no hogans. The Navajo is more like a white man than like a deer.

That's about what his uncle would say, Chee thought sourly. But his uncle had no dealings with the whites when he could avoid them. And how would his uncle explain the thinking of a white man who filled his home with mementos of his achievements but kept his greatest honors hidden away in a keepsake box? The medals Tomas Charley had described were a Bronze Star and a Silver Star, which—as the military encyclopedia in the university library had informed him—are awarded for deeds of courage in combat; and the Purple Heart, awarded to those wounded in action. You would expect to find them framed in places of prominence on Vines' wall, along with his other trophies. Why did he hide them away with a package of old boyhood photographs and a double handful of rock fragments? A Navajo might either advertise his exploits or modestly conceal them. Why would anyone hide some and advertise others?

The sky was darker now and the wind blew from the northwest. It gusted around the pickup, kicking up a flurry of sand and tumbleweeds.

"That has to be our butte," Chee said. He pointed through the right side of the windshield. "It's the only one within nine miles of the trading post. And it's in the right direction."

The track emerged on a great sheet of barren granite and skirted an island of overlaid sandstone. The island was capped by a slab of white limestone, which left a wide overhang where the softer rock had worn away. It suggested to Chee a table where giants dined. Suddenly, just beyond this landmark, he took his foot from the gas pedal and let the truck roll to a stop.

"What?" Mary asked.

Chee looked at her. "Boy," he said. "Am I stupid." He slammed his fist against the steering wheel. Two sets of keepsakes, he was thinking. One on the walls. One hidden in the safe. What was the difference between them? The difference was in time.

Mary was staring at him. "Come on," she said. "Cut it out. Let me in on it."

"I'm still getting it sorted out," Chee said. "But what it boils down to is why a man who's very much into keeping mementos and showing them off would hide the best of them in his wall safe."

"Like those medals," Mary said.

"Like those and his high school football team picture, and a couple of athletic awards."

"And black rocks," Mary said.

"Let's get to those later. Stick to the easy stuff now."

"Easy if you've thought of the answer," Mary said. "Quit showing off, damn it. What have you thought of?"

"The only difference I can see is the ones in the safe were all from Vines' early life. Boyhood and young man in the military. The stuff on the wall is after he struck it rich."

Mary had her lower lip caught between her teeth. Her expression said she was looking for significance in this. "Before the oil well explosion and after the explosion. Is that it? And how about the rocks?"

"We better get moving," Chee said. "It's going to get dark." He put the pickup in gear.

"In other words, you don't know about the rocks."

"Somehow they had to be important. A memento of something important," Chee said. "And from his early life."

"I'll buy that," Mary said. Moments ticked away as the pickup jolted over the rocky surface. "Hey," Mary said. "I know what. The rocks are from when he found the uranium deposit. They're his first ore samples. Don't you think?"

"That would fit," Chee said. "Sure. Why didn't you think of that earlier?"

"You didn't ask me," Mary said. "All you had to do was ask."

"Okay, then. Explain why he keeps those medals in the safe."

"Maybe he's keeping them for somebody else," Mary said.

The wind rocked the pickup again, buffeting it with a barrage of driven sand. Chee down-shifted to pull the truck up a steep incline.

"Mary," he said, "you're a genius." He switched on the transmitter and raised the dispatcher at Crownpoint. His instructions were specific. Call Martin at the FBI. Tell him to have the Veterans Administration make a high-priority emergency check on the military record of Benjamin J. Vines. Was he a first lieutenant in the 101st Airborne Division? Had he won the Silver Star, Bronze Star, and Purple Heart? What kind of discharge? Any criminal record in the service?

The dispatcher read the instructions back. "Anything else?"

"Tell Martin I'll explain it to him when I see him tonight. Tell him I'll be late. And . . . wait a minute." Chee fished out his notebook. "Give him these names, too." He read off the names of those killed in the oil well explosion. At the name of Carl Lebeck, he paused. Lebeck the geologist. Lebeck the well-logger. For a geologist, black rocks might be a memento. "Put the name of Lebeck first," Chee said. "Tell Martin that if Vines didn't win those decorations, to have the VA go down that list of names and see if Lebeck or any of the others won them."

"Got it," the dispatcher said. "You still at Bisti?"

"Northwest of the burned-out trading post," Chee said. "We'll be out here until after dark, the way it looks."

"Better watch the weather," the dispatcher said. "It's snowing some over on the west side. Inch on the ground at

Ganado. Not supposed to amount to much, but you know how that is."

"We'll watch it," Chee said. He flicked the radio switch and put the pickup back into gear.

"What are you thinking?" Mary asked.

Chee frowned at the windshield. "Mostly, I'm just taking a shot in the dark."

"But just mostly," Mary said. "Have you figured a way that Vines and the oil well connect?"

"They must," Chee said. "They have to connect. If not Vines, then Gordo Sena. One or the other has to connect."

Mary laughed. "Sure," she said. "Now all you have to do is figure out how."

"I think I have," Chee said. "At least part of it."

The track angled to the right and up the slope of dark-blue shale marbled with reddish impurities. Above it, the top of the butte loomed, now no more than a thousand yards away. Chee shifted down. Mary was watching him impatiently.

"I'm waiting," she said.

"Okay," Chee said. "First we agree there has to be a reason. White man or Navajo, you do things for a reason. With a Navajo, something this bad—blowing up people wholesale—would have to be witch business. Irrational. Evil for the sake of evil. No other motive would make sense. For the white man, I think it would be greed." He glanced at her. "All right so far?"

Mary looked puzzled. "I guess so," she said.

"If we're dealing with witchcraft, what's happened since doesn't connect. Maybe a Navajo would want to kill the Charleys if he knew they were witches who'd done him harm. That's happened. But he would do it in the heat of rage, not years later. So let's set that aside."

Mary shrugged.

"So we're dealing with a white man's crime," Chee continued. "The motive's greed. Who gains by blowing up an oil well? You have to remember where that well was. We couldn't find the remains because the Red Deuce has swallowed up the site. So the oil company drilling the well had a mineral rights lease on that piece of land. If the well produces oil, the lease is extended as long as production lasts. That's the standard oil lease form. So let's say somebody knows there's a uranium deposit under the well. Who'd benefit?"

"You mean the Senas? Because it was on their ranch?"

"Maybe the Senas," Chee said. "When it finally did happen, uranium made Gordo Sena rich. But something doesn't fit with thinking Gordo did it."

"You mean like killing his own brother?" Mary asked. "Maybe Robert Sena planned it himself and then something went wrong and he killed himself, too."

"I didn't mean that," Chee said. "I meant the Sena ranch is like most ranches out here. It's a little bit of privately owned land connected to a big spread of federal Bureau of Land Management land. Most of what you own is a permit to graze your cattle on BLM land. That's where the well was drilling. On federal land. The Senas had the grazing lease, but it was about a quarter of a mile from the boundary of their own land. So they wouldn't benefit directly from either an oil strike or a uranium find. Sena got rich because the uranium deposit spread over onto his family property."

"So you rule out Sena," Mary said. "Who then?"

"I don't quite rule out the Senas," Chee said. "There's a piece missing somewhere. I can't think it through."

The pickup tilted abruptly downward into a narrow wash. Chee shifted into his lowest gear, braked to a stop, and inspected the arroyo. The problem would be pulling the truck up the other side. The arroyo carried very little water even after downpours, and a tall growth of mesquite and rabbit brush on both sides of the track had limited erosion. But still, years of cutting away had made the opposite bank steep enough so that getting traction to the pickup out of it looked chancy.

"Looks like the end of the line," Mary said. "But aren't we close enough to walk?"

"We'll try the pickup," Chee said. "If we don't make it, there's plenty of room down there to turn it around."

The vehicle produced a great shower of flying gravel, lost traction briefly, and skidded sideways. But it made the brief, steep climb. Ahead now, no more than four hundred yards away, they could see three gnarled cottonwoods. In a desert climate they signaled either a spring or a very shallow water sand that could be tapped by a well. And that in turn explained why this track led across the badlands and why the Tsossies had picked the site for their hogan. Chee and Mary could see the hogan now about twenty feet beyond the trees. It was a hexagon of stacked sandstone slabs, roofed with poles which radiated outward from a central smoke hole. The earth that once insulated the roof against cold and heat had long since washed away.

Chee pulled the pickup to a stop against an outcrop of cliff. He clipped on his holster and hung his binocular case around his neck. "Be prepared," he said, and stepped out into the wind.

The doorway of the hogan was closed with planks nailed across the lintel logs. The only opening now was on the north side—a hole knocked through the stone wall to provide an exit for the ghost and to warn strangers that this was a death hogan. Chee stood looking into the hole. The evening light that filtered through the latticework of roof showed nothing but odds and ends of junk too worthless to carry away even by an impoverished family. Dirt had blown in and tumbleweeds had bounced through the ghost hole, but the danger posed by the *chindi* had made the place secure from scavengers.

"If Tsossie didn't die here, someone did," Chee said. "Let's find the place the old lady said they put him."

Mary was staring at the hogan. "I've heard about this," she said, "about Navajos not using buildings after somebody dies in them. It seems awfully wasteful."

"Unless maybe they died of something contagious," Chee said. "When the custom started, I guess that was the purpose."

"They carry the body out the hole? Is that right? Always on the north side?"

Chee didn't want to talk about it now. The wind gusted again, carrying around a light load of dry, feathery snowflakes. "North is the direction of evil," he said.

Mrs. Musket had told them the blowhole was in the mesa wall, west of the hogan. The butte was formed of layers of geological formations, capped with a gray erosion-resistant granite. Below that was a stratum of red sandstone perhaps thirty feet deep, which covered porous, whitish volcanic tuft that had been riddled with wind pockets and seepage holes.

Only two of these near the hogan were large enough for a burial. Chee examined both through the binoculars and saw nothing conclusive. They climbed the talus slope toward the nearest one. Against the perpendicular walls of the butte, sections of the soft perlite had been worn away, undermining the sandstone. A section of it had fallen in a clutter of blocks, each as large as a freight car. Chee scrambled up the sloping side of one of the blocks and looked into the blowhole. Rocks had been piled on its floor. From beneath one of them a ragged fragment of blue cloth protruded. The wind eddied into the hole. The cloth fluttered.

"Come on up," Chee said. "I guess we found Windy Tsossie."

Sometimes the dry cold of a desert winter will protect a corpse from decay and turn it into a desiccated mummy. Since the placement in the cliff and the covering of rocks had protected Tsossie from both animal predators and scavenger birds, this might have happened to him. But Tsossie, apparently, had died in the summer, and thirty years of insects had reduced what he had been to a clean white skeleton.

With the last rocks removed, Chee squatted in the low opening and looked at what remained. The skeleton was still wearing moccasins, put on the wrong feet to confuse any *chindi* that might follow the spirit into the darkness of the afterworld. The denim trousers Tsossie had worn had been reduced to scraps of decayed rags, but for some reason the shirt was about half intact. Two buttons still held it across the empty cage of ribs. Chee checked the skeleton's left hand. A finger was missing. Mrs. Musket had said Tsossie had lost a finger. The wind caught the shirttail and blew it against the ribs, revealing the dull silver of leather-strung conchas. The heavy belt that had once encircled a waistline now encircled only a row of whitened vertebrae. Under the concha buckle Chee saw a leather string, the thong of a medicine pouch. Pouch and belt lay just above the socket where the ball joint of Tsossie's thigh bone connected to the pelvic socket. The thigh bone was distorted by a heavy, unnatural growth of scar tissue, an ugly lesion which ran from the joint almost halfway down the heavy bone. It looked very much like the illustration Dr. Huff had pointed out to them in his medical text. Bone cancer. The sort of crazy growth that happens in bone tissue with the metastasis of cell malignancy.

Chee picked up the pouch and pried open the brittle leather.

"It's snowing again," Mary Landon said. She was sitting on the slab outside the cave entrance inspecting the landscape through the binoculars. "And it's getting dark."

"Just another minute or two," Chee said.

The leather broke apart under his fingernail. Inside there was a coating of yellow dust—what once had been sacred pollen. The pollen coated four small fragments of abalone shell, a gallstone taken from some small animal, two feathers, a withered bit of root, and the small stone shape of a mole.

Chee held the mole delicately and polished away the pollen dust. It looked just like the one he had found in Emerson Charley's medicine pouch. Almost identical.

"Jimmy. Somebody's coming."

It was as if they were the same mole. The same amulet. The feel under his fingers was the same. The same blunt legs, the same sloping, pointed snout.

The tone of Mary's voice cut through his concentration more than the meaning of the words. The tone was fear.

"What?" he asked. "Where?"

"There." She pointed over the open hogan roof, past the almost bare cottonwoods, down the track they had followed.

At first he saw nothing. Then a man wearing a navy-blue stocking cap and a heavy black windbreaker trotted into sight. He carried a rifle in his right hand and ran easily, in a low crouch. Chee could see just enough of his face to confirm what he instinctively knew. It was the blond man. In his crouching, careful trot, he was skirting Chee's pickup truck.

"Climb in here," Chee whispered. He helped pull Mary into the blowhole. "It's him," Chee said. "But I don't think he's seen us. He's looking for us around the truck."

"How could he have found us here?" Mary whispered.

"God knows," Chee said. The blond man was kneeling behind a growth of rabbit brush, apparently watching the truck. Chee lifted the binoculars and surveyed the landscape down the track. The man must have driven here and left his vehicle parked somewhere. Chee could see no sign of it. It was probably parked out of sight in the bottom of the arroyo they'd crossed.

Mary found a place behind the bones and the rocks that had covered them. She sat pressed against the sloping wall, looking first at Chee and then at the skeleton. The blowhole was an elongated circle perhaps six feet along its longest diameter and flattened at the bottom by fallen debris and accumulated dust. The wind had cut into the soft ash no more than four feet. If the man with the rifle learned they were there, the blowhole offered no safety.

Chee spoke in a very low voice. "We stay absolutely still until it gets dark. No motion. No sound. Nothing to attract attention. I want you to ease yourself down as flat as you can get. You're out of sight from where he is now, but do it slowly and carefully. I'm going to lay flat, too. Then he won't be able to see anything in here, even if he tries. Not without climbing up on the slab."

"And we can't see him, either," Mary said in a very faint voice. "We won't know where he is. We won't be able to do anything to defend ourselves."

"He has the rifle," Chee said. "We don't have any defense against that. Not until it gets dark."

Chee lay on his stomach, his left hand pressed against the tuft beneath him, his right hand gripping the butt of his revolver. Ready to move. There was the smell of dust and ashes in his nostrils. The wind picked up again and hooted through the blowhole opening. Grains of perlite fell against his cheek. The blowhole had become infinitesimally deeper. There was a sound outside. The blond man? The wind? A brushy branch scratching against stone?

Chee struggled against an overwhelming urge to run.

The sound came again. A creaking.

"What was that?" Mary asked. The question had a frantic sound. Panic had come to her a little later than it had to him.

He reached across the bones for her, gripping her leg with his left hand. "The wind," he whispered. "Mary, listen. The way the owl hunts, he sits in a piñon and he hoots. He can't see the rabbits, and they can't see him. And that's the problem for the rabbits. He hoots. And he waits a little to let them think about it, and he hoots again. And the rabbits think. And one of them will think too much. He thinks the owl is getting closer and closer. He thinks the owl has found him. So he makes a run for it, and the owl has her meal for the night."

Mary moved his hand from her leg. "Okay, wise guy," she whispered. "I get your point."

A flurry of snow blew into the hole, the flakes cold against his face. Noises came again and with them a return of panic. He found himself imagining the blond man's face appearing suddenly over the rim of the hole behind the silenced .22 pistol. Chee found his muscles rigid with tension. He forced himself to think of other things. In three weeks he would go to Albuquerque and buy his ticket and report to the FBI Academy. Or he would drive out to the place of Hosteen Nakai and tell his uncle that he was ready to work with him—that Hosteen Nakai could count on him this winter when the calls came to conduct his sings. Which one would it be? He couldn't concentrate on the question. Instead he planned what he would do when darkness came. He would move when there was still a little light. He would find the blond man's car. If the blond man was in it, he would kill him. If he wasn't, then Chee would wait. He waited now, hearing the sound of the wind when it gusted and the sound of Mary breathing when it was silent. He had time now to add what Tsossie's bones and Tsossie's mole had told him to what he had already surmised. The People of Darkness had been murdered. Tsossie had been an unpleasant man, perhaps even a witch. But he had been reduced to bone for a motive that had nothing to do with the anger his unpleasantness had provoked. The motive was mathematical, not emotional. A simple matter of improving the odds against the future. A white man's crime.

Chee felt an impatience to move, to begin the contest. It was much darker, but not quite dark enough. Words from the Stalking Way ran through his memory, his uncle's husky voice singing them, his uncle's stubby fingers tapping rhythm on the pot drum.

I am the Black God, arising with twilight, a part
of the twilight.
Out from the West, out from the Darkness

Mountain, a buck of dark flint stands out before me.
The best male game of darkness, it calls to me, it hears my voice calling.
Our calls become one in beauty. Our prayers become one in beauty.
As I, the Black God, go toward it. As the male game of darkness comes toward me.
With beauty before us, we come together. With beauty behind us, we come together.
That my arrow may free its sacred breath. That my arrow may bring its death in beauty.

The song ran on and on in Chee's mind, a pattern of repetitions, of slightly varied sounds and slightly varied meanings, exorcising the primal dread of death and preparing man and animal for the sacred hunt.

Jimmy Chee was ready. The wind gusted again, sucking into the blowhole, eroding away another thousand infinitesimal grains of ash and moving icy air up Chee's pant leg.

"I'm going now," Chee said. "Stay quiet for a few more minutes, until it's darker, and then slip out and find a sheltered place. But stay within shouting range. When it's safe, I'll call you."

He raised himself to a crouch, surprised at how stiff his muscles had already become.

"I've got a better idea," Mary whispered. "Give me the pistol, and I'll go out and see what I can do. I don't like this being the only one out here who can't shoot back."

Chee grinned. "No; it's my gun. I bought it with my own money."

And with that, he slipped quickly out of the hole, dropped to the slab, and from the slab to the brushy ground behind it. If the blond man had seen the motion, he hadn't seen it quickly enough to react.

Chee moved as fast as caution allowed. He made a wide circle away from the butte, angling on a course that would cross the little arroyo they'd had trouble traversing. That's where the blond man's vehicle would be and that's where Chee would find the blond man. Somehow, God knew how, he must have guessed the trail ended at the butte and that Chee would be there, and he hadn't risked the noise of trying to grind up the steep arroyo slope. He had parked and come for Chee on foot.

Chee had thought it through very carefully. The blond man had found Chee's pickup truck, but he hadn't found Chee. Hunting him in the brush and boulders around the butte would have been like searching the white man's proverbial haystack for a dangerous needle. So the blond man would opt for another solution. He'd return to his own vehicle and simply wait. When he heard the engine on Chee's pickup start and saw the reflection from Chee's headlights, he would have plenty of time to set up his ambush. The arroyo would be a perfect place for it. Chee's truck creeping down the steep arroyo bank. The blond man shooting Chee through the truck door. Shooting at point-blank range and with plenty of time for as many more shots as were needed if the first one didn't get the job done.

Where Chee reached the arroyo it was much shallower and broader. He hurried up it, moving silently on the sand. Wind and snow had almost stopped, but now the wind rose again, blowing in icy gusts against his face. The right direction for the hunter. Blowing scent and sound away from the prey. Even so, when the arroyo deepened, and when the dim light told him he was within a hundred yards of the point where the track dipped into it, he left the open bottom and moved slowly through the brush.

The vehicle was almost exactly where he'd thought it would be. The blond man had simply nosed it down the arroyo and left it far enough off the track to be out of sight. Chee moved carefully along the extreme edge of the arroyo bottom, slipping from one bit of brush cover to the next. He held the pistol in his right hand at full cock, so that a touch of his thumb to the safety would make it ready to fire.

The eastern sky was totally black now, but the west still filtered a dim twilight through the cloud cover. The blond man's vehicle was a dark-blue GMC pickup truck. From halfway up the arroyo bank where he was crouched, Chee could see the right front and side and look slightly downward into the cab. The cab seemed to be empty. It was empty unless the blond man was prone on the front seat or sitting on the floor. That seemed unlikely. A long willowy wand jutted upward from the back bumper—the antenna of a two-way radio. That was how the blond man had known he could find Chee at Bisti. He had monitored the Navajo Police radio calls.

With that thought came another. What had Chee said when he talked to Crownpoint? Had he mentioned Mary Landon in that call? Had he even said "we"? Had he said anything that would have told the blond man that Mary was with him? Chee squeezed his eyes shut, concentrating, trying to remember. As always, his memory served. He had said "we." "We're going nine miles northwest of the old trading post. We'll be there until after dark." Those had been his words. So the blond man knew Mary was with him.

Chee slouched back on his heels, his eyes still on the truck, and thought. He considered that the blond man—apparently, at least—was not waiting where Chee's good sense told him the blond man should be waiting. So where was the blond man? He was back at the butte, hunting Chee and Landon. Or he was back at the butte, staked out, watching for them to return to their pickup. Either way he might find Mary, or she might, cold and confused, walk into his trap.

Chee put the pistol carefully on a rock beside his boot. He extracted his billfold, and from the billfold the check Vines had given him. It was perfect for the message. The check itself would tell the blond man that Vines had been in contact with the police. He wrote carefully, trying for legibility in the darkness.

Killing us won't help. Vines is
dealing with FBI. He gets off light.

Chee pushed his hand back into his warm glove, picked up the pistol, and moved cautiously to the truck. The door on the driver's side was locked. Chee pulled out the wiper blade and wrapped the check around it securely. If the blond man got back to the truck, he couldn't miss seeing it. It appealed to Chee's Navajo sense of balance, order, and harmony—this business of using the check, the witch's own poison, to turn the evil back against its source. It was the way Changing Woman had taught. Chee trotted off in the darkness toward the butte.

An hour later there was no light at all left in the west. The snow was falling again, still dry, feathery flakes, now drifting almost vertically downward, now whipped by gusts which whistled and moaned around the cliffs of the butte and sent the snow stinging against the skin. Chee had scouted the ground carefully, using his pickup truck as a center and making cautious, time-consuming circles widening around it. He'd moved when the wind blew and crouched motionless, listening, when it dropped into calm. He'd checked every bit of cover that a man in ambush might use to watch the pickup. He'd found nothing. Now he squatted beside a scrubby juniper, thinking. He could see the shape of the pickup against the dark stone of the outcrop. Where could the blond man be? What was he doing? Chee reexamined everything he had been told of the man and everything he had observed himself. He considered the way the man had behaved on the malpais and in the hospital and what Martin had told him of his assassinations. Always meticulous care. Always caution. Never a chance taken. That was the key. No unnecessary chances. No overlooked possibilities. That was why Chee hadn't found him in the two places where the man might logically have been. Because the man had thought it through, had realized that he might have been seen, had realized that Chee might be smart enough to expect a trap or an ambush. Chee frowned into the darkness. The blond man would hardly be floundering around the butte in darkness. He had to be hiding somewhere, waiting. Waiting for what? Waiting for Mary and Chee to get into the pickup and drive into an ambush somewhere? Not if he suspected he had been seen. Then Chee would simply slip into the pickup and radio Crownpoint for assistance. The minute such a call was made, the blond man would be hopelessly trapped. Therefore, the blond man must keep him from his radio. Why isn't he doing that? Chee asked himself. What is to keep me from slipping into the front seat and calling for help? Perhaps he doesn't know that police disconnect the switch that turns on the courtesy light when the door opens. Perhaps he is somewhere, waiting for that flash of light. But no, Chee thought. The blond man would know that. Perhaps he is waiting inside the pickup? No. Chee had left the truck locked. Even if the man picked the lock, hiding inside would be risky.

So how was the blond man protecting himself against the radio call? Chee went over what he knew of the blond man again, incident by incident, from the hospital to the very beginning and the bombing of Emerson Charley's truck in the parking lot. When he reached that, he knew exactly what the blond man had done and what he was waiting for.

He had put a bomb in Chee's pickup. Now he was off somewhere in the darkness, out of the wind and totally unfindable, waiting patiently for Jim Chee and Mary Landon to blow themselves to pieces.

It took Chee only a few minutes to climb the outcrop. From atop that table of stone, he could look directly down into the bed of the truck thirty feet below. It was too dark to be sure, but he could see nothing in the pickup bed that hadn't been there before. If the blond man had placed a bomb, it wasn't likely he had put it in the same place he had used in his effort to kill Emerson Charley. Here, most likely, he would have placed it on the truck frame under the body. If the FBI knew what it was talking about, his bombs detonated when they were moved. Driving over the first bump would do the job. Under the cab, the effects would be certain.

The point where the outcrop jutted from the face of the butte was littered with chunks of fallen stone. Chee picked up one that weighed perhaps twenty pounds and carried it to the edge. He placed himself carefully, over the center of the truck bed. In the same motion he tossed the boulder and jumped backward away from the edge.

The crash of the boulder striking metal was engulfed a minisecond later by a great flash of light and sound. Chee, already off balance, found himself sprawling on hands and knees, his ears ringing and his eyes seeing only the red and white circles imprinted on his retinas by the flash. He lowered himself on the surface of the stone, waiting for sight and hearing to recover.

Soon he could hear a second sound through the receding ringing and see a flickering light through the flash blindness.

The truck was burning. At first the flames from the burning gasoline flared above the rim of the outcrop, but they quickly lost their force. Now Chee lay in the darkness looking out across a landscape illuminated by the fire. It was the ideal place to be. When the blond man came to make sure of his victims, Chee would shoot him. Chee lay on his stomach, the cocked pistol held in front of him, waiting.

The wind rose, fanned the flames into a roar, and then died away. The snow drifted straight down again, still dry and feathery. The rock around Chee, blown clear by the most recent gusts, collected another thin layer of snowflakes. Gasoline and oil were almost exhausted now, and the fire fed itself on rubber and upholstery. Chee could smell the rancid black smoke of burning tires and plastic. The landscape the blond man would be crossing was white now. He would be easy to see in the firelight. But the blond man did not come. Through the sound of the fire below him, Chee heard the sound of a starter, and then of a motor, grinding in low gear. Across the ridge where the blond man's pickup had been parked, there appeared a fan of light reflecting in the falling snow. Chee jumped to his feet. The light tilted upward, two visible beams jutting into the snowy sky. The truck was climbing out of the arroyo bottom. But the headlights were pointed away from the butte. The blond man was driving away.

31

THEY BUILT THE FIRE in the crevasse between two of the great fallen slabs in a sheltered cul-de-sac protected from the wind. Chee had picked the spot carefully and then had made a walking circuit, assuring himself that no light, even dimly reflected, was visible. The blond man had driven away toward the Bisti road. Chee had watched the truck lights moving eastward until finally they no longer reappeared through the falling snow. The blond man probably wouldn't return. There was no reason for him to do so. But he might.

Now, finally, they were out of the wind. Mary Landon sat across from him, back against the vertical stone, her denimed legs stretched straight in front of her. Above them the wind gusted past the butte top with a hooting noise. Between these walls of fallen stone, it only caused the fire to flicker. But Mary shivered and hugged herself.

"I think it was a mistake," she said, "leaving that note about Mr. Vines."

"Why?"

"Because," Mary said. "Because maybe he'll go and shoot Vines—and you don't know for sure Vines killed anyone. You don't have any proof."

"I know for sure," Chee said.

"You don't have anything to prove it with. You're not a judge."

Chee thought about that. The firelight was red, burning the rosin of dead piñon. It reflected on Mary Landon's face, casting deep shadows where her hair fell across her forehead.

"Yes," Chee said, "I am a judge. If the blond man kills Vines, then that's justice. But he's not going to kill Vines. He won't have time. He can't get there tonight because of the weather. If we get three inches of snow down here, there'll be two feet of it up on Mount Taylor. The road won't be open until they get a snowplow on it—and that won't be until tomorrow morning. They'll be using the snowplows where there's more traffic."

"Still, you don't have any right to . . ."

"We don't have much violence, we Navajos. What there is is mostly associated with witchcraft. Changing Woman taught us how to cope with the Navajo Wolves. We turn the evil around so it works against the witch."

"But first you have to know for sure he's the witch," Mary said.

The snow started again, larger flakes now. The wind moaned around the butte top and the snowflakes eddied and swirled above them, lit by the redness of the fire. Some settled into the cul-de-sac. They landed on Chee's knee, on Mary's hair, on stone surfaces. Some drifted into the fire and vanished—cold touched by the magic of heat.

It was going to be a long, frigid night, and there was nothing that could be done until there was a little light. When it was light, the pipeline companies would be scouting their collection systems to make sure the abrupt drop in temperature had cracked no exposed metal, separated no joints, jammed no valves. The little slow-flying planes would be up looking for signs of gas leaks. Whatever those signs were. Spurts of blowing dust, Chee guessed. He remembered they had crossed the El Paso Natural Gas trunk line between Bisti and the butte. When dawn came, they would walk to it and build a smoky fire and wait to be spotted. Until then there was nothing to be done, except help time pass, avoid freezing, and think.

"I am born a Slow Talking People," Chee said. "I'm also a member of the Red Forehead Clan because my father was one. And I'm connected with the Mud Clan, because my uncle—the one teaching me to be a singer—he's married into the Muds. All of those clans have the same tradition. To become a witch, to cross over from Navajo to Navajo Wolf, you have to break at least one of the most serious taboos. You have to commit incest, or you have to kill a close relative. But there's another story, very old, pretty much lost, which explains how First Man became a witch. Because he was first, he didn't have relatives to destroy. So he figured out a magic way to violate the strongest taboo of all. He destroyed himself and recreated himself, and that's the way he got the powers of evil."

"I never heard about that," Mary said. "I thought for a minute you were changing the subject. But you're not, are you?"

"I'm not," Chee said. "Lebeck decided to be a witch. He destroyed himself. And he came back."

Mary was frowning at him. "Lebeck? The geologist at the oil well?"

"Yes; the geologist," Chee said. "Think about what we know. We know the oil well was drilled through uranium, because the Red Deuce is now mining that deposit where the oil well stood. Lebeck was what they call the 'well logger'—the one who inspects samples of the rock they're drilling through and maps the deposits. Very shallow, maybe down just fifty feet or so, the bit goes through pitchblende, a thick layer of the very richest uranium ore. So Lebeck suddenly knows something that's worth hundreds of millions of dollars. How can he cash it in? He can cash it in only if this oil lease is allowed to expire. Then he can file his own mineral lease claim. So he falsifies the log."

Mary was leaning forward, intent. "Hey," she said. "You looked at the log. Did he? Why didn't you tell me? How could you tell?"

Chee made a wry face. "I couldn't tell," he said. "I checked out that log and a couple of other ones from other wells drilled in Valencia County, and they all looked about alike. The oil companies were all looking for a shallow oil sand, just down about two thousand feet. I was looking for God knows what down at the bottom of the well, down at the end where they were deciding to shoot the tubing with the nitro. I didn't know what I was looking for, and I didn't see anything."

"But you should have seen something," Mary said slowly.

"You should have seen they'd drilled through the uranium ore."

"Exactly!" Chee said. "I've heard that Red Deuce deposit is a couple of hundred feet deep. It should have been noted on the log." Chee felt an overpowering urge to smoke. He hadn't had a possibility of lighting a cigaret since the blond man's arrival at the butte. He fished out a Pall Mall, offered it to Mary. She shook her head. He lit it.

"Those things will kill you," Mary said.

"Actually, I think now he must have falsified the log twice. Once when they drilled through the ore and again at the end. I think they found the oil sand they were looking for, and Lebeck put it down as something else and had them drill right through it. Or maybe he had the log show they were drilling into a geological formation which should be below the oil sand—which would mean the sand didn't exist at this particular place. Anyway, he wanted them to shut down the well and let the lease lapse, so he could get a lease on it himself. If they struck oil, the lease would be renewed by the oil company and he would never get the uranium. So when the company decided to shoot the well, Lebeck must have known there was a good chance that would start the oil flowing. He couldn't risk that." Chee inhaled a lungful of smoke and let it trickle from between his lips. It made blue swirls in the slowly moving air, drifting upward while the white flakes drifted down. Far above at the butte top, the north wind, the evil wind, began hooting again. Chee puffed out the last of the smoke, destroying the pattern with his breath. "And so Lebeck decided to blow everything, and everyone, sky high. Lebeck decided to become a witch."

He glanced at Mary.

"To die, or seem to die, and to come back as B. J. Vines," she said.

"Yes," Chee said. "But when the nitro truck arrived, something went wrong. Dillon Charley's crew didn't show up for work."

"How did Dillon Charley know?"

"The Lord Peyote told him in a vision," Chee said. "Or perhaps Lebeck warned him—which I doubt. Or perhaps Dillon Charley saw things that made him nervous. I think Charley was a very perceptive man. Mrs. Vines told me that her husband and Dillon Charley were friends—had a sort of rapport. Perhaps that was already true when Vines was Lebeck." Chee shrugged. "Who knows? Lord Peyote, or nervousness about nitroglycerin, or what? Anyway, he didn't show up that day, and he warned his crew away. I think Lebeck wanted them all there. No one else around here knew him. No one else would recognize him as Vines. But he didn't have any choice. The nitro truck came. He had to act then or never."

"How did he do it?" Mary asked.

"I have to guess. Obviously he left the rig. I'd say he probably got far enough away to be safe, and he had a rifle and fired a shot into the nitro bottle at the proper moment."

Mary Landon shivered again and hugged herself. "And then he just walked away, so he'd be counted among the dead. Didn't he have a family? A mother and father? People who loved him?"

"I don't know anything about Lebeck," Chee said.

"And then to come back here. Wouldn't he be afraid someone would recognize him?"

"Probably nobody knew him, or had even seen him much. Just the well crew. It was an isolated place. Hardly a road then, and the crew would have lived out at the well, where nobody saw them. And then he stayed away two years. Maybe a little more. Long enough for the mineral lease to expire. Long enough to grow a heavy beard. Who knows—maybe he did something else to change his looks. I said we didn't know anything about Lebeck, but we do know a little. You get into the paratroops by volunteering. And once he was in, he won two top decorations for courage. So I guess he wasn't afraid of taking chances. Or of killing, either. He must have done a lot of it." Chee paused, thinking about it. "I guess he knew he'd have some more to do."

"The People of Darkness," Mary said.

"Yeah. He couldn't count on Dillon Charley forgetting him."

"You think Dillon Charley saw Vines and recognized him as Lebeck?"

"Maybe. But I'll bet Lebeck didn't wait for that to happen.

I'll bet he went looking for him. Maybe he told Charley the Lord Peyote had given him a vision, too. Or maybe he just offered him a job, money, so forth. He'd know Charley wouldn't tell the sheriff anything—not with the way Gordo was harassing him and his church. And besides, Charley wasn't going to live very long."

"Lebeck knew Dillon Charley had cancer?"

"Lebeck knew Charley was going to have cancer," Chee corrected. "That black rock, it must be pitchblende. When the oil well bit drilled through it, Lebeck recognized pitchblende, and that's the hottest kind of natural uranium deposit. He didn't put it on the log, but he saved a piece of the core to test and make sure. And then he kept it because he saved mementos, and this one was going to change his life. Maybe he already knew it was going to be useful to him."

"You're losing me," Mary said. "How do you know it's pitchblende? I never heard of it. How do you know so much about it?"

"Out here everybody is prospecting half the time," Chee said. "You learn about minerals, and mostly you learn about uranium-bearing minerals. I should have thought of it before. I think if we get a mineralogist to check those rock samples and those mole amulets, we're going to find they're radioactive. Vines gave Charley the mole knowing he would carry it in his medicine pouch—hanging from his waist under his clothing right against the groin."

"Dillon Charley, and Tsossie, and Begay, and Sam, and all of them," Mary said. She shivered again.

"He didn't overlook much," Chee said. "I think Dillon Charley must have been the first to die, and Vines got the body and buried it, just in case an autopsy would show something. But Navajos don't have much interest in bodies, and the authorities don't have much interest in dead Navajos, and people got scattered out, so after Dillon Charley it wasn't worth the trouble, I guess. It looked like he could quit worrying. Everybody on that work crew who had ever seen him as Lebeck was dead, or soon would be. Nothing to worry about for years."

"Not until Emerson Charley gets cancer," Mary Landon said.

"I think that's right," Chee said. "Old Dillon was a pretty important religious leader, and people like that sometimes try to pass it along to their children. I guess he gave Emerson his medicine bundle, hoping he'd become the peyote chief, and one day, years later, Emerson decides to revive the cult. He starts wearing old Dillon's mole, and of course he gets sick. . . ."

Mary was leaning forward now. "And Vines gets nervous," she said. "Now it's 1980, and Vines doesn't want Emerson checking into a modern cancer research center, where he's sure to undergo an autopsy, and so he hires somebody to kill him."

"And to steal the body," Chee said.

"And probably to get the mole back. But the blond man missed the mole."

"And Tomas Charley was too suspicious. The Navajos around Mount Taylor may not know a lot about radioactive pathology, but they could count up the fact that people who associated with Vines seemed to die. They knew he was a witch. When Emerson Charley's truck was bombed, Tomas was suspicious. He wanted to prove Vines was a witch. He broke in and stole the box, and all Mrs. Vines knew was that the box was extremely important to Vines, so she asked me to get it back. I think she wanted to know Vines' secret."

The snow was falling more heavily now, drifting almost straight down out of an abruptly windless sky.

"Can't we build that fire a little higher?" Mary asked.

"A little," Chee said. He moved two chunks of piñon trunk into the blaze.

"You can't prove any of this, can you?" Mary said. It wasn't a question.

"I won't have to," Chee said. "I told the blond man. Tomorrow we'll tell Gordo Sena. Sena won't need proof either."

32

CHEE PASSED THE WORD to Sheriff Sena via the radio in an El Paso Natural Gas Company helicopter. The copter had found them where the EPNG collector pipe bridges Nagasi Wash. They had built a fire in the brush that flourishes there, and not ten minutes after the greasy smoke spiraled into the sky, the little Bell had puttered over the rise. The pilot was a young man with a scarred nose, a walrus mustache, and the emblem of a First Cavalry Division gunship unit sewed on his greasy flying jacket. He had already spotted their bombed pickup truck, and circled it curiously, and he was ready to believe Chee's story of a police emergency.

Chee told the sheriff's dispatcher at Grants no more than Gordo Sena would need to know.

"Tell him the man who killed Tomas Charley is headed for B. J. Vines' house. Tell him that Vines hired the man, and tell him that Vines' real name is Carl Lebeck."

"Lee what?" the dispatcher asked.

"Lebeck," Chee said. "Be sure to get that right. Carl Lebeck." Except for describing the truck, and the blond man, Chee offered no more details. They would be redundant. Gordo Sena had lived for thirty years with the details of that oil well explosion burning in his mind. He'd know instantly who Lebeck was, and he was smart enough to put it all together. The dispatcher had said Sena had left for the Anaconda Mine. The same road led through the fringes of the Laguna reservation toward the high slopes of Mount Taylor and Vines' place. About fifteen miles, Chee guessed, compared to the sixty they had to cover in the helicopter. But that last mile or two would be impassable to something on wheels. Sena would have to walk in. Chee would get there first.

The thought excited him. At one level he was afraid of the blond man. At another, he longed to find him. His broken rib ached, as it had ached all morning. But it was more than vengeance. The man had shot him once. He had twice hunted Chee down to kill him. The memory still rankled—of the interminable minutes spent on the metal duct above the hospital ceiling, of the helpless panic in the blowhole. Now he was the stalker. He tried to analyze the feeling. Expectant? Exultant? Something between, and something more. There was a mixture of fear and of the remembered childhood feeling of the hunt. The smell of smoke, of boiling coffee, the forest scents carried on the predawn dew. His uncle greeting the sun with the dawn chant and blessing them all with the sacred pollen and singing the final song to call the spirits of the deer. Through the scarred, oil-smeared Plexiglas he could see the Turquoise Mountain rushing toward them, its upper slopes a virginal white, glittering in the sunlight against a sky swept clean by the night's storm. The thump of the copter blades covered the words as he repeated the Stalking Song. Perhaps Mary heard them, jammed as she was between him and the pilot. She glanced at him curiously.

They found the blond man's pickup truck about three twisting miles below the Vines house. Chee examined it through his binoculars, and the tracks told a story that was easy to read. The truck had slid off the narrow forest service road, losing traction on an upslope, where its spinning rear wheels moved sideways into the ditch. The driver had emerged, walked uphill several hundred yards, and then returned to the truck. He'd done this while the snow was still falling heavily, and his tracks were half-filled depressions. Later, when the snow was no longer falling, he had emerged again, walking uphill through snow that now was perhaps two feet deep. The new tracks were easy to follow, but there was no reason to follow them. They would lead to Vines' house.

The only question was whether they had yet reached the

house. How fast could the blond man struggle uphill through deep snow? A mile an hour? At the butte the snowfall had stopped about 4:00 A.M. On the mountain, it would have lasted longer. Perhaps until 5:00 or 6:00.

"Let's take the shortest way to Vines'," Chee said. "When we're there, get close to the ground and try to keep behind the trees. They'll hear us, but I don't want them to know where you're letting me off."

"Letting you off?" Mary said. "You're out of your mind. We'll wait for the sheriff. He can't get away now."

"No," Chee said. "There's something I have to do."

The copter settled in a great cloud of feathery snow behind a cluster of blue spruce which screened off the garage. Chee dropped into a snowbank deeper than his knees and stood blinded for a moment while the copter pulled up and away. Then he ran, floundering, to the stone wall of the garage. The blond man, and Vines, and Mrs. Vines, anyone in the house, would have heard the copter, but they couldn't have seen it, and they wouldn't know it had dropped him. Still, he'd be careful. He stood against the wall, remembering the layout of the house. It sat with its back into the mountain slope, looking outward across the great panorama below. But the view was limited. Behind the house, the wall was low and windowless, and in many places one could step from the mountainside to the tile roof. Chee trotted around the garage. The tombstones of Dillon Charley and the first and faithful Mrs. Vines wore high white hats of snow. Behind the house, he stopped to listen. The stillness was almost total—the silence of a windless morning on a mountain buried under new white insulation. From somewhere back in the forest, a fir limb bent and gave up its bushels of snow with a sibilant sound. From the house, only silence.

Thirty feet ahead there was a doorway. Perhaps a laundry room, or some other sort of utility entrance. Chee moved toward it cautiously, keeping close to the wall, with the pistol, cocked, in his right hand. He tried the knob. Unlocked.

Over the roof he heard the sound of the copter. It was approaching fast. The sound peaked, receded, and returned. First Cavalry was creating a distraction for him, Chee realized.

Mary's idea, probably. He pulled the door open and slipped inside.

The room seemed almost totally dark. He stood, back to the door, giving his eyes a chance to make the adjustment from the brilliance of sunlight off snow to the interior gloom. He was in a sort of washroom/supply room. Down a short, narrow hall he could see into the kitchen. His ears told him absolutely nothing. The house was as silent as the snow outside. But something reached his nose. Acrid. The smell of blue smoke produced by gunpowder. Chee leaned against the edge of the clothes drier, unlaced his wet boots and removed them. He moved silently down the hall, placing his stockinged feet noiselessly. The kitchen was empty. It was lighter. The room was lit by a row of small high windows and more light came in from the broad doorway, which opened into what seemed to be a game room. Chee moved through the kitchen, back to the wall, trying to see into the adjoining room without being seen himself. He edged past the door of what was probably a pantry. Then he froze.

From behind him came a quick gasping sound, a quick release of breath, a quick intake of breath. Someone was standing behind the door, inches away from his back.

Chee slid away from the door. He stood beside it. Listening. His pistol was cocked. The safety off. He squatted just to the left of the door, facing it. He reached across his body with his left hand and gripped the knob. Then he thought. This was not where he would find the blond man—not hiding in a closet. He heard the clamor of the helicopter again from the front of the house, and he jerked the door open.

The Acoma woman stood there. She looked startled, but she made no sound.

Chee put a finger to his lips, signaling silence. "Where is everyone?" he whispered in English.

The Acoma woman stared at his pistol. It was pointed at her stomach. Chee lowered it.

"A blond man came here," Chee said. "Is he here?"

She seemed not to understand. She appeared to be stunned. "Where is everyone?" Chee repeated.

The woman released another gasp of breath. *"El brujo está muerto,"* she said. That was all she would say. She said it twice, and then she turned abruptly and walked silently down the hallway and disappeared into the laundry room. Chee heard the outside door open. And then close.

"The witch is dead." Did she mean the blond man? Did she mean Vines? Not Mrs. Vines. She had used the masculine noun. The dead witch was male.

Chee found him in Vines' study. He sat behind the great desk, still upright because the swivel chair had been tilted slightly backward, and the impact of the bullet had pushed his head against the leather cushion. The light from the sunny snow outside streamed through the shutters and lit his face and showed a spot low on the forehead just above the bridge of his nose. It hadn't bled much, but a trickle had run down across his cheek and into his white beard. B. J. Vines' eyes were still open, but the witch was forever dead.

Where was the blond man? Chee stood just inside the door, back to the wall, listening. He heard nothing. The copter had gone now. Had it landed? Vines' dead face wore a look of shocked surprise. He had seen death coming. A tigress looked over his shoulder, her glittering glass eyes staring at Chee. Where was the blond man? Chee found himself thinking instead of B. J. Vines' head mounted among those of the other predators, the blue eyes glittering. The blond man might have left. He would hardly stay after he had accomplished his purpose. Chee moved quickly around the desk. He put his finger against Vines' throat. The skin was still soft and warm. He touched the bloody streak that ran down the side of the nose. Not even sticky yet. Vines had been dead only minutes. No more than five or ten. The blond man was close. Then where was Rosemary Vines? Perhaps she was away from home.

Chee stood beside the desk, watching the door, listening. What would the blond man do? The copter thudded close again, hovering in front of the house. Mary trying to help. He remembered the blond man's rifle. Stay away, Mary. Stay out of range. She was a woman among women. She made him happy. She was a friend. She made him feel like singing. She deserved nothing but beauty all around her. But now, stay away. The blond man must be in the house. Close. Doing what? Looking for servants? Making sure he'd leave no one alive to report this visit? Chee's eyes rested on the telephone. The line would be cut. He picked up the receiver, expecting deadness. Instead he heard the buzzing dial tone. He dialed 0. It rang, and a woman's voice said, "Operator. Can I help you?"

"Sorry," Chee whispered. He hung up. Why had the blond man left the telephone intact? He hadn't got to it yet. Then he heard the sound. Someone coughed. And coughed again.

The blond man was sitting on the floor of the entrance foyer, his shoulder against the massive door. Blood was everywhere. It splashed across the polished wood, it soaked the blond man's trousers, it spread in a still-growing stain across the patterned ceramic tiles of the floor. A pistol lay in the blood, black, with the long cylinder of a silencer on its barrel. The blond man coughed again. He glanced at Chee, then focused his eyes on him. He moved his lips, tentatively. Then he said:

"It's cold."

Chee could see what had happened. The shot had hit the blond man as he reached the door. One of Vines' hunting rifles, probably. Something big. The slug had torn through him from the back, splashing the door with blood. It had broken the blond man as a stick is broken.

"Is there someplace warm?" the blond man asked.

"Maybe the fireplace," Chee said. He put his pistol in its holster, walked through the blood, and squatted beside the blond man. He put an arm under his legs and an arm behind his shoulders and lifted him—carefully because the blood was slippery under his socks, carefully because the man was dying.

In the big room, a log fire had burned itself down to flickering coals in the fireplace. Chee knelt in front of it and put the blond man on the skin of the polar bear. The man's back was broken somewhere between the shoulder blades. The blond man's head rolled toward the fire. His voice was small.

"There's this detective agency," he said. "Webster. In Encino. He's going to find my mother. She'll know about the cemetery. She'll come and get me."

"All right," Chee said. "Don't worry."

"I thought I killed him," Rosemary Vines said. She was standing in the doorway, holding a long-barreled rifle. It was pointed roughly in Chee's direction.

"You did," Chee said. "It takes a few minutes."

Mrs. Vines' face was bloodless. The lipstick she wore made a grotesque contrast against chalky skin.

"Did you know who your husband was?" Chee asked.

Rosemary Vines stared past him, her eyes on the blond man. She's in shock, Chee thought. She didn't even hear me.

"I knew he'd had another life somewhere," she said slowly. "I suspected that even before we were married. He loved to talk about himself, but not back before a certain time. Earlier than that—when he was a boy, when he was in college, any of that time before he'd come out here and found his mine—any time before that it was all very vague. So he had to be hiding something. And finally he admitted he had his secrets. But he'd never tell me what. I told him it had to be criminal or he wouldn't be ashamed of it. But he'd just laugh."

On the pelt of the dead polar bear, the blond man was now quite motionless. Rosemary Vines still stared at his body, the rifle still ready.

"I knew it was in his safe. In his box. It had to be. That's the way B.J. was. Everything he did, he had to keep the evidence. Heads. Pelts. Photographs. He was compulsive about it. Like he had to have proof it had happened. He wouldn't take twenty-five years of his life and just throw it away. If I could get the box before he got back, there'd be things in there to tell me who B.J. had been when he was young. And there'd be something to tell me what it was he was so ashamed of."

The thought brought something like animation to her face—a look of triumph anticipated. It was a sort of smile. "Ashamed of, or afraid of," Mrs. Vines said, still smiling.

Jim Chee looked away from her, away from the body, and the white fur stained with red. Through the great soaring expanse of glass that lit the room he could see only sky and snow. Blue and white purity. Such beauty should have aroused in Jim Chee an exultation. Now he felt nothing. Only numb fatigue and a kind of sickness.

But he knew the cause, and the cure. Changing Woman had taught them about it when she formed the first clans of the Dinee from her own skin. The strange ways of strange people hurt the spirit, turned the Navajo away from beauty. Returning to beauty required a cure. He would go tomorrow to Hosteen Nakai and ask him to arrange an Enemy Way, to gather family, the interlinked relatives of the Slow Talking Dinee and the Red Forehead Dinee—the brothers and sisters of his blood, his friends, his supporters. Then there would be another eight days for the songs and the poetry and the sand paintings to recreate the past and restore the spirit.

He would persuade Hosteen Nakai that Mary, too, should undergo the blessing even though she was not born Dinee. The arrangements would take weeks—picking the site, spreading the word, getting the proper singer, arranging the food. But when it was over, he would go again with beauty all around him.

II

The Dark Wind

This book is dedicated to the good people of Coyote Canyon, Navajo Mountain, Littlewater, Two Gray Hills, Heart Butte, and Borrego Pass, and most of all to those who are being uprooted from their ancestral homes in the Navajo-Hopi Joint Use country.

AUTHOR'S NOTES

The reader should be aware that I make no claims to being an authority on Hopi theology. Like Jim Chee of the Navajo Tribal Police, I am an outsider on the Hopi Mesas. I know only what one learns from long and respectful interest, and suggest that any of you who wish to learn more of the complex Hopi metaphysics turn to more knowledgeable writers. I particularly recommend *The Book of the Hopi* by my good friend Frank Waters.

The liturgical year of the Hopi religion is divided into seasonal halves which are more or less mirror images and which involve an elaborate calendar of ritual observances. These include the events which provide some of the background for this novel, but the calendar I use is not accurate.

Time has been even crueler to the village of Sityatki than is suggested herein. It was abandoned long ago and sand has drifted over what remains of its ruins.

All characters in this book are products of my imagination. None is based in any way on any living person.

1

THE FLUTE CLAN BOY was the first to see it. He stopped and stared.

"Somebody lost a boot," he said.

Even from where he stood, at least fifteen yards farther down the trail, Albert Lomatewa could see that nobody had lost the boot. The boot had been placed, not dropped. It rested upright, squarely in the middle of the path, its pointed toe aimed toward them. Obviously someone had put it there. And now, just beyond a dead growth of rabbit brush which crowded the trail, Lomatewa saw the top of a second boot. Yesterday when they had come this way no boots had been here.

Albert Lomatewa was the Messenger. He was in charge. Eddie Tuvi and the Flute Clan boy would do exactly what he told them.

"Stay away from it," Lomatewa said. "Stay right here."

He lifted the heavy pack of spruce boughs from his back and placed it reverently beside the path. Then he walked to the boot. It was fairly new, made of brown leather, with a flower pattern stitched into it and a curved cowboy heel. Lomatewa glanced past the rabbit brush at the second boot. It matched. Beyond the second boot, the path curved sharply around a weathered granite boulder. Lomatewa sucked in his breath. Jutting from behind the boulder he could see the bottom of a foot. The foot was bare and even from where Lomatewa stood he could see there was something terribly wrong with it.

Lomatewa looked back at the two his kiva had sent to

guard him on this pilgrimage for spruce. They stood where he had told them to stand—Tuvi's face impassive, the boy's betraying his excited curiosity.

"Stay there," he ordered. "There is someone here and I must see about it."

The man was on his side, legs bent stiffly, left arm stretched rigidly forward, right arm flexed upward with the palm resting beside his ear. He wore blue jeans, a jean jacket, and a blue-and-white-checked shirt, its sleeves rolled to the elbows. But it was a little while before Lomatewa noticed what the man was wearing. He was staring at his feet. The soles of both of them had been cut away. The bottom of the socks had been cut and the socks pushed up around the ankles, where they formed ragged white cuffs. Then the heel pads, and the pads at the balls of the feet, and the undertips of the toes had been sliced away. Lomatewa had nine grandchildren, and one great-grandchild, and had lived long enough to see many things, but he had never seen this before. He sucked in his breath, exhaled it, and glanced up at the hands. He expected to find them flayed, too. And he did. The skin had been sliced from them just as it had been from the feet. Only then did Lomatewa look at the man's face.

He had been young. Not a Hopi. A Navajo. At least part Navajo. There was a small, black-rimmed hole above his right eye.

Lomatewa stood looking down at the man, thinking how this would have to be handled. It had to be handled so that it would not interfere with the Niman Kachina. The sun was hot on him here, even though it was still early morning, and the smell of dust was in his nostrils. Dust, always dust. Reminding him of why nothing must interfere with the ceremonial. For almost a year the blessing of rain had been withdrawn. He had thinned his corn three times, and still what little was left was stunted and withering in the endless drought. The springs were drying. There was no grass left for the horses. The Niman Kachina must be properly done. He turned and walked back to where his guardians were waiting.

"A dead Tavasuh," he said. Literally the word meant "head-pounder." It was a term of contempt which Hopis sometimes used for Navajos and Lomatewa chose it deliberately to set the tone for what he must do.

"What happened to his foot?" the Flute Clan boy asked. "The bottom was cut off his foot."

"Put down the spruce," Lomatewa said. "Sit down. We must talk about this." He wasn't worried about Tuvi. Tuvi was a valuable man in the Antelope Kiva and a member of the One Horn Society—a prayerful man. But the Flute Clan boy was still a boy. He said nothing more, though, simply sitting on the path beside his spruce bundle. The questions remained in his eyes. Let him wait, Lomatewa thought. Let him learn patience.

"Three times Sotuknang has destroyed the world," Lomatewa began. "He destroyed the First World with fire. He destroyed the Second World with ice. He destroyed the Third World with flood. Each time he destroyed the world because his people failed to do what he told them to do." Lomatewa kept his eyes on the Flute Clan boy as he talked. The boy was his only worry. The boy had gone to school at Flagstaff and he had a job with the post office. There was talk that he did not plant his corn patches properly, that he did not properly know his role in the Kachina Society. Tuvi could be counted on but the boy must be taught. Lomatewa spoke directly to him, and the boy listened as if he had not heard the old story a thousand times before.

"Sotuknang destroyed the world because the Hopis forgot to do their duty. They forgot the songs that must be sung, the *pahos* that must be offered, the ceremonials that must be danced. Each time the world became infected with evil, people quarreled all the time. People became *powaqas,* and practiced witchcraft against one another. The Hopis left the proper Road of Life and only a few were left doing their duty in the kivas. And each time, Sotuknang gave the Hopis warning. He held back the rain so his people would know his displeasure. But everybody ignored the rainless seasons. They kept going after money, and quarreling, and gossiping, and forgetting the way of the Road of Life. And each time Sotuknang decided that the world had used up its string, and he saved a few of the best Hopis, and then he destroyed all the rest."

Lomatewa stared into the eyes of the Flute Clan boy. "You understand all this?"

"I understand," the boy said.

"We must do the Niman Kachina right this summer," Lomatewa said. "Sotuknang has warned us. Our corn dies in the fields. There is no grass. The wells are drying out. When we call the clouds, they no longer hear us. If we do the Niman Kachina wrong, Sotuknang will have no more patience. He will destroy the Fourth World."

Lomatewa glanced at Tuvi. His face was inscrutable. Then he spoke directly to the boy again. "Very soon it will be time for the kachinas to leave this Earth Surface World and go back to their home in the San Francisco Peaks. When we deliver this spruce back to our kivas, it will be used to prepare for the Going Home Dances to honor them. For days it will be very busy in the kivas. The prayers to be planned. The *pahos* to be made. Everything to be done exactly in the proper way." Lomatewa paused, allowing silence to make the effect he wanted. "Everybody thinking in the proper way," he added. "But if we report this body, this dead Navajo, to the police, nothing can be done right. The police will come, the *bahana* police, to ask us questions. They will call us ousm Sothe kivas. Everything will be interrupted. Everybody will be thinking about the wrong things. They will be thinking of death and anger when they would be thinking only holy thoughts. The Niman Kachina will be messed up. The Going Home Dances would not be done right. Nobody would be praying."

He stopped again, staring at the Flute Clan boy.

"If you were the Messenger, what would you do?"

"I would not tell the police," the boy said.

"Would you talk of this in the kiva?"

"I would not talk of it."

"You saw the feet of the Navajo," Lomatewa said. "Do you know what that means?"

"The skin being cut away?"

"Yes. Do you know what it means?"

The Flute Clan boy looked down at his hands. "I know," he said.

"If you talk about that, it would be the worst thing of all.

People would be thinking of evil just when they should be thinking of good."

"I won't talk about it," the boy said.

"Not until after the Niman dances," Lomatewa said. "Not until after the ceremonial is over and the kachinas are gone. After that you can tell about it."

Lomatewa picked up his bundle of spruce and settled the straps over his shoulders, flinching at the soreness in his joints. He felt every one of his seventy-three years, and he still had almost thirty miles to walk across Wepo Wash and then the long climb up the cliffs of Third Mesa. He led his guardians down the path past the body. Why not? They had already seen the mutilated feet and knew the meaning of that. And this death had nothing to do with the Hopis. This particular piece of evil was Navajo and the Navajos would have to pay for it.

2

JUST AS HE REACHED THE RIM of Balakai Mesa, Pauling checked the chronometer. It was 3:20:15. On time and on course. He held the Cessna about two hundred feet above the ground and the same distance below the top of the rimrock. Ahead, the moon hung yellow and slightly lopsided just above the horizon. It lit the face of the man who sat in the passenger's seat, giving his skin a waxy look. The man was staring straight ahead, lower lip caught between his teeth, studying the moon. To Pauling's right, not a hundred yards off the wingtip, the mesa wall rushed past—a pattern of black shadows alternating with reflected moonlight. It gave Pauling a sense of speed, oddly unusual in flight, and he savored it.

On the desert floor below, the sound of the engine would be echoing off the cliffs. But there was no one to hear it. No one for miles. He had chosen the route himself, flown it twice by daylight and once by night, memorized the landmarks and the terrain. There was no genuine safety in this business, but this was as safe as Pauling could make it. Here, for example, Balakai Mesa protected him from the radar scanners at Albuquerque and Salt Lake. Ahead, just to the left of the setting moon, Low Mountain rose to 6,700 feet and beyond that Little Black Spot Mesa was even higher. Southward, blocking radar from Phoenix, the high mass of Black Mesa extended for a hundred miles or more. All the way from the landing strip in Chihuahua there was less than a hundred miles where radar could follow him. It was a good route. He'd enjoyed finding it, and he loved flying it low, with its landmarks rising into the dying moon out of an infinity of darkness. Pauling savored the danger, the competition, as much as he delighted in the speed and the sense of being the controlling brain of a fine machine.

Balakai Mesa was behind him now and the black shape of Low Mountain slid across the yellow disk of the moon. In the darkness he could see a single sharp diamond of light—the single bulb which lit the gasoline pump at Low Mountain Trading Post. He banked the Cessna slightly to the left, following the course of Tse Chizzi Wash, skirting away from the place where the sound of his engine might awaken a sleeper.

"About there?" the passenger asked.

"Just about," Pauling said. "Over this ridge ahead there's Oraibi Wash, and then another bunch of ridges, and then you get to Wepo Wash. That's where we're landing. Maybe another six or seven minutes."

"Lonely country," the passenger said. He looked down upon it out of the side window, and shook his head. "Nobody. Like there was nobody else on the planet."

"Not many. Just a few Indians here and there. That's why it was picked."

The passenger was staring at the moon again. "This is the part that makes you nervous," he said.

"Yeah," Pauling agreed. But what part of "this part" did the man mean? Landing in the dark? Or what was waiting when they landed? For once Pauling found himself wishing he knew a little more about what was going on. He thought he could guess most of it. Obviously they weren't flying pot. Whatever was in the suitcases would have to be immensely valuable to warrant all the time and the special care. Picking this special landing place, for example, and having a passenger along. He hadn't had anyone riding shotgun with him for years. And when he had, when he'd first moved into this business—cut off from flying for Eastern by the bad reading on his heart—the passenger had been just one of the other hired hands sent along to make sure he didn't steal the load. This time the passenger was a stranger. He'd driven up to the motel at Sabinas Hidalgo with the boss just before it was time to go to the landing strip. Pauling guessed he must represent whoever was buying the shipment. The boss had said that Jansen would be at the other end, at the landing point with the buyers. "Two flashes, then a pause, and then two flashes," the boss had said. "If you don't see it, you don't land." Jansen representing the boss, and this stranger representing the buyers. Both trusted. It occurred to Pauling that the passenger, like Jansen, was probably a relative. Son or brother, or something like that. Family. Who else could you trust in this business, or in anything else?

Oraibi Wash flashed under them, a crooked streak of shadowed blackness in the slanting moonlight. Pauling eased the wheel slightly backward to move the aircraft up the desert slope, and then forward as the land fell away again. Broken ground under him now, a landscape cut by scores of little watercourses draining Black Mesa's flash floods into Wepo Wash. He had the engine throttled down to just above stalling speed now. To his left front he saw the black upthrust of basalt which was the right landmark shape in the right place. And then, just under his wingtip, there was the windmill, with the shadowed bottom of the wash curving just ahead. He should see the lights now. He should see Jansen blinking his . . . Then he saw them. A line of a dozen points of yellow light—the lenses of battery lanterns pointing toward him. And almost instantly, two flashes of white light, and two more flashes. Jansen's signal that all was well.

He made a slow pass over the lights and began a slow circle, remembering exactly how the wash bottom looked as his wheels approached it, concentrating on making his memory replace the darkness with daylight.

Pauling became conscious that the passenger was staring at him. "Is that all you have?" the passenger asked. "You land by that goddamn row of flashlights?"

"The idea is not to attract any attention," Pauling said. Even in the dim light, he could see the passenger's expression was startled.

"You've done this before?" the man asked. His voice squeaked a little. "Just put it down blind in the dark like this?"

"Just a time or two," Pauling said. "Just when you have to." But he wanted to reassure the man. "Used to be in the Tactical Air Force. We had to practice landing those transport planes in the dark. But we're not really landing blind here. We have those lights."

They were lined up on the lights now. Pauling trimmed the plane. Wheels down. Flaps down. His memory gave him the arroyo bottom now. Nose up. He felt the lift going mushy under the wings, the passenger bracing himself in the seat beside him, that brief moment before touchdown when the plane was falling rather than flying.

"You do this on trust," the passenger said. "Jesus. Jesus." It was a prayer.

They were below the level of the wash banks now, the lights rushing toward them. The wheels touched with a jounce and a squeal as Pauling touched the brakes. Perfect, he thought. You have to learn to trust. And in the very split second that he had the thought, he saw that trust was a terrible mistake.

3

AT FIRST JIM CHEE ignored the sound of the plane. Something had moved beyond Windmill Number 6. Moved, and moved again, making a small furtive sound which carried much farther than it should have in the predawn stillness. A half hour earlier he'd heard a car purring up the sandy bottom of Wepo Wash, stopping perhaps a mile downstream. This new sound suggested that whoever had driven it might now be approaching the windmill. Chee felt the excitement of the hunt rising in him. His mind rejected the intrusive hum of the aircraft engine. But the engine sound became impossible to ignore. The plane was low, barely a hundred feet off the ground, and moving on a path that would take it just west of the nest Chee had made for himself in a growth of stunted mesquite. It passed between Chee and the windmill, flying without navigation lights but so close that Chee could see reflections from the illumination inside the cabin. He memorized its shape—the high wing, the tall, straight rudder; the nose sloping down from the cabin windshield. The only reason he could think of for such a flight at such an hour would be smuggling. Narcotics probably. What else? The plane purred away toward Wepo Wash and the sinking moon, quickly vanishing in the night.

Chee turned his eyes, and his thoughts, back toward the windmill. The plane was none of his business. Navajo Tribal Policemen had absolutely no jurisdiction in a smuggling case, or in a narcotics case, or in anything involving the U.S. Drug Enforcement Agency or the white man's war against white man's crime. His business was the vandalism of Windmill Subunit 6, the steel frame of which loomed awkward and ugly against the stars about one hundred yards west of him and which, on the rare occasions when the breeze picked up on this still summer night, made metallic creaking sounds as its blades moved. The windmill was only about a year old, having been installed by the Office of Hopi Partitioned Land to provide water for Hopi families being resettled along Wepo Wash to replace evicted Navajo families. Two months after it was erected, someone had removed the bolts that secured it to its concrete footings and used a long rope and at least two horses to pull it over. Repairs took two months, and three days after they were completed—with the bolts now securely welded into place—it had been vandalized again. This time, a jack handle had been jammed down into the gearbox during a heavy breeze. This had provoked a complaint from the Office of Hopi Partitioned Land to the Joint Use Administration Office at Keams Canyon, which produced a telephone call to the FBI office at Flagstaff, which called the Bureau of Indian Affairs Law and Order Division, which called the Navajo Tribal Police Headquarters at Window Rock, which sent a letter to the Tuba City subagency office of the Navajo Tribal Police. The letter resulted in a memo, which landed on the desk of Jim Chee. The memo said: "See Largo."

Captain Largo had been behind his desk, sorting through a manila folder.

"Let's see now," Largo had said. "Where do you stand on identifying that John Doe body up on Black Mesa?"

"We don't have anything new," Chee had said. And that, as Chee knew Captain Largo already knew, meant they had absolutely nothing at all.

"I mean the fellow somebody shot in the head, the one with no billfold, no identification," Largo said, exactly as if the Tuba City subagency was dealing in wholesale numbers of unidentified victims, and not this single exasperating one.

"No progress," Chee said. "He doesn't match anyone reported missing. His clothing told us exactly zero. Nothing to go on. Nothing."

"Ah," Largo said. He shuffled through the folder again.

"How about the burglary at the Burnt Water Trading Post? You doing any good on that one?"

"No, sir," Chee said. He kept the irritation out of his voice.

"The employee stole the pawn jewelry, but we can't get a trace on him? Is that the way it stands?"

"Yes, sir," Chee said.

"Musket, wasn't it? " Largo asked. "Joseph Musket. On parole from the New Mexico State Penitentiary at Santa Fe. Right? But the silver hasn't turned up sold anywhere. And nobody's seen anything of Musket?" Largo was eyeing him curiously. "That's right, isn't it? You staying on top of that one?"

"I am," Chee had said. That had been midsummer, maybe six weeks after Chee's transfer from the Crownpoint subagency, and he didn't know how to read Captain Largo. Now summer was ending and he still didn't know.

"That's a funny one," Largo had said. He had frowned. "What the hell did he do with all the pawn goods? Why doesn't he try to sell it? And where'd he go? You think he's dead?"

The same questions had been nagging Chee ever since he'd gotten the case. He didn't have any answers.

Largo noticed that. He sighed; peered back into the folder. "How about bootlegging?" he asked without looking up. "Any luck nailing Priscilla Bisti?"

"Just one near miss," Chee said. "But she and her boys got all the wine out of the pickup before we got there. No way to prove it was theirs."

Largo was looking at him, lips pursed. Largo's hands were folded across his ample stomach. The thumbs waved up and down, patiently. "You going to have to be smart to catch old Priscilla." Largo nodded, agreeing with himself. "Smart," he repeated.

Chee said nothing.

"How about all that witchcraft gossip out around Black Mesa?" Largo asked. "Doing any good with that?"

"Nothing I can pin down," Chee said. "Seems to be more of it than's natural, and maybe it's because so many people are going to be uprooted and moved out to make room for the Hopis. Trouble is I'm still too new around here for anybody to be telling me anything about witches." He wanted to remind Largo of that. It wasn't fair of the captain to expect him, still a stranger, to learn anything about witches. The clans of the northwestern reservation didn't know him yet. As far as they knew, he might be a skinwalker himself.

Largo didn't comment on the explanation. He fished out another manila folder. "Maybe you'll have some luck on this one," he said. "Somebody doesn't like a windmill." He slipped a letter out of the folder and handed it to Chee.

Chee read what Window Rock reported, with half of his mind trying to analyze Largo. The way the Navajos calculate kinship, the captain was a relative through clan linkage. Chee's crucial "born to" clan was the Slow Talking Dinee of his mother, but his "born for" clan—the clan of his father—was the Bitter Water People. Largo was born to the Standing Rock Dinee, but was "born for" the Red Forehead Dinee, which was also the secondary "born for" clan of Chee's father. That made kinsmen. Distant kinsmen, true enough, but kinsmen in a culture that made family of first importance and responsibility to relatives the highest value. Chee read the letter and thought about kinship. But he was remembering how a paternal uncle had once cheated him on a used-refrigerator sale, and that the worst whipping he'd ever taken in the Two Gray Hills Boarding School was from a maternal cousin. He handed the letter back to Largo without any comment.

"Whenever there's any trouble out there in the Joint Use Reservation it's usually the Gishis," Largo said. "Them and maybe the Yazzie outfit." He paused, thinking about it. "Or the Begays," he added. "They're into a lot of trouble." He folded the letter back into the file and handed the file to Chee. "Could be just about anybody," he concluded. "Anyway, get it cleared up."

Chee took the folder. "Get it cleared up," he said.

Largo looked at him, his expression mild. "That's right," he said. "Can't have somebody screwing up that Hopi windmill. When the Hopis move onto our land, they got to have water for their cows."

"Got any other suggestions about suspects?"

Largo pursed his lips. "We have to move about nine thousand Navajos off that Joint Use land," he said. "I'd say you could cut it down to about nine thousand suspects."

"Thanks," Chee said.

"Glad to help," Largo said. "You take it from there and get it narrowed down to one." He grinned, showing crooked white teeth. "That'll be your job. Narrow it down to one and catch him."

Which was exactly what Chee had been spending this long night trying to do. The plane was gone now, and if anything stirred around the windmill, Chee could neither see nor hear it. He yawned, unholstered his pistol, and used its barrel to scratch an otherwise unreachable place between his shoulder blades. The moon was down and the stars blazed without competition in a black sky. It was suddenly colder. Chee picked up the blanket, untangled it from the mesquite, and draped it around his shoulders. He thought about the windmill, and the sort of malice involved in vandalizing it, and why the vandal didn't spread his attentions among windmills 1 through 8, and then he thought about the perplexing affair of Joseph Musket, who had stolen maybe seventy-five pounds of silver concha belts, squash blossom necklaces, bracelets, and assorted pawn silver, and then done absolutely nothing with the loot. Chee had already worked the puzzle of Joseph Musket over in his mind so often that all the corners were worn smooth. He worked it over again, looking for something overlooked.

Why had Jake West hired Musket? Because he was a friend of West's son. Why had West fired him? Because he had suspected Musket of stealing. That made sense. And then Musket came back to the Burnt Water Trading Post the night after he was fired and looted its storeroom of pawned jewelry. That, too, made sense. But stolen jewelry always turned up. It was given to girl friends. It was sold. It was pawned at other trading posts, or in Albuquerque, or Phoenix, or Durango, or Farmington, or any of those places surrounding the reservation which traded in jewelry. It was so logical, inevitable, predictable, that police all through the Southwest had a standard procedure for working such cases. They posted descriptions, and waited. And when the jewelry started turning up, they worked back from that. Why hadn't the inevitable happened this time? What was different about Musket? Chee considered what little Musket's parole officer had been able to tell him about the man. Even his nickname was an enigma. Ironfingers. Navajos tended to match such labels with personal characteristics, calling a slim girl Slim Girl or a man with a thin mustache Little Whiskers. What would cause a young man to be called Ironfingers? More important, was he still alive? Largo had asked that, too. If he was dead, that would explain everything.

Except why he was dead.

Chee sighed, and wrapped the blanket around his shoulders, and found himself thinking of another of his unresolved cases. John Doe: cause of death, gunshot wound in the temple. Size of bullet, .38 caliber. Size of John Doe, five feet, seven inches. Weight of John Doe, probably 155 pounds, based on what was left of him when Chee and Cowboy Dashee brought him in. Identity of John Doe? Who the hell knows? Probably Navajo. Probably mature young adult. Certainly male. He had been Chee's introduction to duty in the Tuba City district. His first day after his transfer from Crownpoint. "Go out and learn the territory," Largo had said, but a few miles west of Moenkopi the dispatcher had turned him around and sent him into Joint Use country. "Subject at Burnt Water Trading Post has information about a body," the dispatcher said. "See Deputy Sheriff Dashee. He'll meet you there."

"What's the deal?" Chee had asked. "Isn't that outside our territory now?"

The dispatcher hadn't known the answer to that, but when he got to the Burnt Water Trading Post and met Deputy Sheriff Albert (Cowboy) Dashee, the deputy had the answer.

"The stiff's a Navajo," he explained. "That's what we hear. Somebody's supposed to have shot him, so somebody figured one of you guys ought to go along." When they had finally got to the body it was hard to imagine how anyone had guessed his tribe, or even his sex. Decay was advanced. Scavengers had found the body—animal, bird, and insect. What was left was mostly a tattered ragbag of bare bone, sinew, gristle, and a little hard muscle. They had looked at it awhile, and wondered why the boots had been removed and left on the path, and made a fruitless search for anything that would identify the man, or explain the bullet hole in his skull. And then Cowboy Dashee had done something friendly.

He'd unrolled the body bag they'd carried along and when Chee had bent to help him, he'd waved Chee away.

"We Hopis have our hang-ups," he said, "but we don't have the trouble you Navajos got with handling dead bodies." And so Dashee had tucked John Doe into the body bag while Chee watched. That left nothing to do but discover who he'd been, and who had killed him, and why he took off his boots before they did it.

A sound from a long way off brought Chee back to the present. It came from about where the car had stopped down in the wash—the sound of metal striking metal, perhaps, but too dim and distant to identify. And then he heard the plane again. This time it was south of him, moving eastward. Apparently it had circled. The moonset had left a bright orange glow outlining the ridge of Big Mountain. For a moment the plane was high enough to reflect moonlight from a wing. It was turning. Completing a circle. Once again it came almost directly toward him, sinking out of the moonlight and down into the darkness. Chee heard a clanking sound over the low purr of the engine. The wheels being lowered? It was too dark to tell. The plane passed within two hundred yards of him, downhill and not much above eye level. It flew just above Wepo Wash and then it disappeared.

Abruptly the purr of the engine stopped. Chee frowned. Had the pilot cut the engine? No. He heard it again, muted now.

It takes about five seconds for sound to travel a mile. Even after a mile, after five seconds of dilution by distance, the sound reached Chee's ear like a thunderclap. Like an explosion. Like tons of metal striking stone.

There was silence again for a second or two, perhaps even three. And then a single sharp snapping sound, from a mile away but instantly identifiable. The sound of a gunshot.

4

THE RAW SMELL of gasoline reached Jimmy Chee's nostrils. He stopped, aiming the flashlight down the arroyo ahead of him, looking for the source and regaining his breath. He'd covered the distance from his clump of mesquite in less than fifteen minutes, running when the terrain permitted it, scrambling up and down the dry watercourses, dodging through the brush and cactus, keeping the glow of the setting moon to his left front. Once, just before he had reached the cliff edge of Wepo Wash, he had heard the grind of a starter, an engine springing to life, and the receding sound of a vehicle moving down the dry watercourse away from him. He had seen a glow where the vehicle's lights had reflected briefly off the arroyo wall. He'd seen nothing else. Now the flashlight beam reflected from metal, and beyond the metal, more metal in a tangled mass. Chee stood inspecting what the light showed him. Over the sound of his labored breathing, he heard something. Falling dirt. Someone had scrambled up the cliff and out of the wash. He flicked the light beam toward the noise. It picked up a residue of dust, but no movement. Whatever had dislodged the earth was out of sight.

Cautiously now, Chee walked to the wreckage.

The plane's left wing had apparently struck first, slamming into a great outcrop of rock which had forced the wash into an abrupt northward detour. Part of the wing had torn off, and the force had pivoted the plane, slamming its fuselage into the rock at about a forty-five degree angle. Chee's flash reflected from an unbroken cabin window. He peered through it. His light struck the side of the head of a man with curly blond hair. The head was bowed forward as if the man were sleeping. No sign of blood. But lower, the front of the cabin had been crushed backward. Where the man's chest had been, there was metal. Beyond this, Chee could see a second man, in the pilot's seat. Dark hair with gray in it. Blood on the face. Movement!

Chee ducked through the torn gap in the aluminum where the cabin door had been, forced a bent passenger seat out of the way, and reached the pilot. The man was still breathing, or seemed to be. Chee, squatting awkwardly amid the torn metal, reached forward and unfastened the pilot's safety belt. It was wet and warm with blood. He eased himself between the seats, far enough forward to examine the pilot in the light of his flash. The man had bled copiously from a tear on the right side of his neck—a ragged gash which now barely seeped. It was too late for a tourniquet. The heart had run out of anything to pump.

Chee sat back on his heels and assessed the situation. The pilot was dying. If this cramped space were an operating room with a surgeon at work and blood being pumped back into the pilot, the man might have a chance. But Chee was helpless to save him.

Yet there's the human urge to do something. Chee eased the man out of the pilot's seat and slid the limp form between the seats and out of the torn cabin. He laid the pilot carefully, face up, on the packed sand. He took the pilot's wrist and felt for a pulse. There was none. Chee switched off his flashlight.

With the moon down, at the bottom of Wepo Wash the darkness was total. Overhead, freed now from competition with the moon, a billion stars blazed against black space. The pilot no longer existed. His *chindi* had slipped away to wander in the darkness—one more ghost to infect the People with sickness and make the nights dangerous. But Chee had come to terms with ghosts long ago when he was a teenager in boarding school.

He gave his eyes time to adjust to the darkness. At first there was only the line of the clifftop, which separated the starscape from the black. Gradually forms took shape. The upthrust surviving wing of the plane, the shape of the basalt outcrop which had destroyed it. Chee felt cold against the skin of his hands. He put them into his jacket pockets. He walked to the outcrop and around it, thinking. He thought of the car he had heard driving away and of the person, or persons, who must be in it. Persons who had walked away from the pilot and left the man to die alone in the dark. Now the starlight gave the canyon shape, defining a difference between its sandy bottom and its walls, even suggesting brush at the base of its cliffs. It was absolutely windless now, utterly silent. Chee leaned his hip against the basalt, fished out a cigaret and a kitchen match.

He struck the match against the stone. It made a great flare of yellow light which illuminated the gray-yellow sand around his feet, the slick black of the basalt, and the white shirtfront of a man. The man sat on the sand, legs outthrust, and the quick flare of the sulfur flame reflected from the lenses of his eyeglasses.

Chee dropped the match, stepped back, and fumbled out his flashlight. The man was wearing a dark-gray business suit with a vest and a neatly knotted blue necktie. His feet had slid from under him, leaving heel tracks in the sand and pulling up his trouser legs, so that white skin was bared above the top of black socks. In the yellow beam of Chee's flash he looked perhaps forty-five or fifty, but death and yellow light ages the face. His hands hung at his sides, resting on the sand. Between thumb and forefinger of his right hand he held a small white card. Chee knelt by the hand and focused his light on it. It was a card from the Hopi Cultural Center. Holding it by the edges, Chee slipped it out and turned it over. On the reverse side someone had written:

"If you want it back, check into here."

Chee slipped the card back between the fingers. This would be a federal case. Very much a federal case. None of this would be any of his business.

5

CAPTAIN LARGO WAS STANDING at the wall map, making calculations.

"The plane's here," he said, punching a stubby finger against the paper. "And your car was parked here?" He touched the paper again. "Maybe two miles. Maybe less."

Chee said nothing. It had occurred to him about three questions back that something unusual was happening.

"And you called your first report in at twenty minutes after five," the man named Johnson said. "Say it takes forty minutes to walk to your car, that would leave another fifty minutes from the time you said the plane crashed." Johnson was a tall, lean, red-haired man, his face a mass of freckles. He wore black cowboy boots of some exotic leather, and denims. His pale mustache was well trimmed and his pale-blue eyes watched Chee. They had watched Chee since the moment he'd entered the office, with the impersonal unblinking stare policemen tend to develop. Chee reminded himself that it was one of several professional habits that he must try to avoid.

"Fifty minutes," Chee said. "Yeah. That sounds about right."

Silence. Largo studied the map. Johnson was sitting with his chair tilted back against the wall, his hands locked behind his head, staring at Chee. He shifted his weight, causing the chair to creak.

"Fifty minutes is a lot of time," Johnson said.

A lot of time for what? Chee thought. But he said nothing.

"You say before you got to the wreck you heard a car engine starting, or maybe it was a pickup truck, and somebody driving away. And then when you got there, you heard somebody climbing out of the wash behind the plane." Johnson's tone made the statement into a question.

"That's what I say," Chee said. He caught Largo glancing at him. Largo's face was full of thought.

"Our people turned in a report a lot like yours," Johnson said. "You don't count your own tracks, of course, so you were looking at four sets and they were looking at five. Someone climbing out of the wash, like you said." Johnson held up one finger. "And the smooth-soled, pointy-toed shoes of the stiff." Johnson held up a second finger. "And a set of waffle soles, and a set of cowboy boots." Two more fingers went up. "And the boot soles we now know were yours." Johnson added his thumb to complete the count at five. He stared at Chee, waiting for agreement.

"Right," Chee said, looking into Johnson's cold blue stare.

"It looked to our people—that's the FBI—that the cowboy boot tracks stepped on your tracks some places, and in some places you stepped on them," Johnson said. "Same with the waffle soles."

Chee considered what Johnson had said for about five seconds.

"Which would mean that the three of us were there at the same time," Chee said.

"All together," Johnson said. "In a bunch."

Chee was thinking he'd just been accused of a crime. And then he thought that someone had once said a little knowledge is a dangerous thing, and how well that axiom applied to reading tracks. Trackers tend to forget that people step on their own footprints. It was something his uncle had taught him to watch for—and to read.

"Any comments on that?" Johnson asked.

"No," Chee said.

"You saying you weren't there at the same time as the other fellows?"

"Are you saying I was?" Chee said. "What you seem to be

saying is that the FBI hasn't had much luck finding somebody who can read tracks."

Johnson's stare was totally unselfconscious. Chee looked into it, curious about the man. The face was hard, intelligent, grim—a confident face. Chee had seen the look often enough to recognize it. He'd seen it in the Hopi boy who'd set the Arizona High School cross-country track record at the Flagstaff marathons, and on the face of the rodeo cowboy who won the big belt at Window Rock, and elsewhere in people who were very, very good at what they were doing, and knew it, and let a sort of arrogant confidence show in the careless way they used their eyes. Chee's experience with federal cops had not left him with any illusions of their competence. But Johnson would be another matter altogether. If Chee were a criminal, he would not want Johnson hunting him.

"You're sticking to your report, then," Johnson said finally. "Anything you can add that would help us?"

"Help you what?" Chee asked. "Maybe I could help your man learn something about tracking."

Johnson let the chair legs hit the floor, unlocked his hands, and stood.

"Nice to meet you folks," he said. "And, Mr. Chee, I'll probably be talking to you again. You going to be around?"

"Most likely," Chee said.

The door closed behind Johnson. Largo was still examining the map.

"I can't tell you much about that," Largo said. "Just a little."

"You don't need to tell me much," Chee said. "I would say that the narcs don't think it was a coincidence that I was out there by the wash when the plane landed. They think I was really out there to meet the plane and that me and waffle soles and cowboy boots hauled off the drug shipment—or whatever it was. Spent the missing fifty minutes loading the stuff. That about it?"

"Just about," Largo said mildly.

"There's more?"

"Nothing much," Largo said. "Nothing they exactly told me."

"But something that makes them suspicious of me?"

"Makes 'em suspicious of somebody local," Largo said. "I get an impression that the Drug Enforcement Agency don't think that shipment got hauled very far. They think it's hidden around there someplace close."

Chee frowned. "How would they know that?"

"How does the DEA know anything?" Largo asked. "I think they got about half of the drug smuggling industry on their payroll. Ratting for them."

"Seems like it," Chee said.

"And then they do a hell of a lot of guessing," Largo added.

"I noticed that, too," Chee said.

"Like about you helping haul away the shipment."

"You think that was a bad guess?"

"Most likely," Largo said.

"Thanks," Chee said. "Johnson tell you who was in the plane?"

"I gather the pilot was somebody they know. One of the regulars who flies stuff in from Mexico for one of the big outfits. Fellow named Pauling. I don't think they have an identification on the passenger yet. The guy on the ground, the guy who got shot, his name was Jerry Jansen. Lawyer from Houston. Supposed to be in the narcotics business."

"I didn't move him," Chee said. "Shot, was he?"

"In the back," Largo said.

"It looks simple enough," Chee said. "A plane's hauling in dope. Somebody comes in a vehicle to accept the delivery, right? Only the plane crashes. Two of the guys receiving the shipment decide to steal it. They shoot their partner in the back, leave a note to the owners, or maybe the buyers, to tell them how to make contact to buy their stuff back. Then they haul it away. Right? But the DEA doesn't seem to think the shipment got hauled out. They think it's hidden out there somewhere. Right?"

"That's what Johnson seemed to be thinking," Largo said.

"Now why would they think that?" Chee asked.

Largo was looking out his window. He seemed not to have heard the question. But finally he said, "I'd guess the DEA had this shipment wired. I think they had themselves an informer in the right place."

Chee nodded. "Yeah," he said. "But for some reason beyond the understanding of this poor Indian, the DEA didn't want to move in and grab the plane and arrest everyone."

Largo was still looking out the window. He glanced back at Chee. "Hell," he said. "Who knows. The feds work in strange and mysterious ways and they don't explain things to the Navajo Tribal Police." He grinned. "Especially they don't when they think maybe a Navajo Tribal Policeman got off with the evidence."

"Makes you curious," Chee said.

"It does," Largo said. "I think I'll do some asking around."

"I'm thinking about that card," Chee said. "That could be why the feds think the shipment's still around here. Why else would the hijacker do his dealing through the Hopi motel? Why not contact 'em in Houston, or wherever they operate?"

"I wondered when that was going to occur to you," Largo said. "If Jim Chee stole the shipment, he wouldn't know how to get in touch with the owners. So Jim Chee would leave a note telling them how to contact him."

"Thinking the press would report the note? Is that what I'd think? Wouldn't it occur to me that maybe the DEA would keep the note secret?"

"It might," Largo said. "But if you thought of that, you'd be smart enough to know they'd have lawyers nosing around. Whoever owned that plane has a legal, legitimate interest in that crash. They'd ask to see the investigating officer's report, and we'd show it to them. So Jim Chee would be sure to put what it said on the card in his report. Like you did."

Jim Chee, who actually hadn't thought of that at all, nodded. "Pretty slick of Jim Chee," he said.

"Got a call about forty-five minutes ago," Largo said. "From Window Rock. Your buddy did it again. To the windmill."

"Last night?" Chee's tone was incredulous. "After the crash?"

Largo shrugged. "Joint Use Office called Window Rock. All

I know is somebody screwed up the machinery again and Window Rock wants it stopped."

Chee was speechless. He started for the door, then stopped. Largo was standing behind his desk, reading something in Chee's folder. He was a short man with the barrel-chested, hipless shape common among western Navajos, and his round face was placid as he read. Chee felt respect for him. He wasn't sure he would like him. Probably he wouldn't.

"Captain," he said.

Largo looked up.

"Johnson had trouble with that lost fifty minutes at the airplane. Do you?"

"I don't think so," Largo said. His expression was totally neutral. "I know something Johnson doesn't." He held up the folder. "I know how slow you work."

6

JAKE WEST WAS BEHIND the counter explaining the ramifications of money orders to a teenaged Navajo girl who seemed to want to buy something out of the Sears catalog. West had acknowledged Chee's presence with a nod and a grin but had done nothing to hurry his dealings with his customer. Nor did Chee expect him to. He leaned against the metal of the frozen foods cabinet, and waited for West, and thought his thoughts, and listened to the three gossips who were talking about witches on the porch just outside the open door. The three were a middle-aged Navajo woman (a Gishi, Chee had deduced), an elderly Navajo woman, and an even older Navajo man, whom the younger woman had called Hosteen Yazzie. She was doing most of the talking, loudly for the benefit of a hard-of-hearing audience. The subject was witchcraft in the Black Mesa-Wepo Wash country. The witchcraft gossip sounded typical of what one expected to hear in a season of drought or hard times—and for the Joint Use Reservation Navajos this was indeed a season of hard times. The usual pattern. Somebody had been out at dusk hunting a ram and had seen a man lurking around, and the man had turned into an owl and flown away. One of the Gishi girls had heard her horses all excited and had gone out to see about it, and a dog had been bothering them, and she shot at the dog with her .22, and the dog had turned into a man and disappeared in the darkness. An old man back on the mesa had heard sounds on the roof of his hogan during the night, and had seen something coming down through the smoke hole. Maybe it was dislodged dirt. Maybe it was corpse powder dropped by the witch. Chee's attention wandered. He heard Hosteen Yazzie say, "I guess the witch got the corpse powder from that man he killed," and then Chee was listening again, intently now. The Gishi woman said, "I guess so," and the conversation drifted away, to another day and another subject. Chee shifted his weight against the refrigerator case and considered the witch who had killed a man. If he walked through the door and asked Hosteen Yazzie to explain himself, he would meet only blank silence. These Navajos didn't know him. They'd never talk of witchcraft to a person who might be the very witch who was worrying them.

From across the store, West's laugh boomed out. He was leaning over the teenager now, his bulk making her seem a scaled-down model of a girl. He'd weigh 275 pounds, Chee guessed, maybe 300—some of it fat and some of it muscle, built on a barrel-like frame which made him seem short until he stood close to you. The laughter showed a great row of teeth through a curly beard. Where the beard and mustache didn't hide it, Jake West's face was a moonscape of pits and pockmarks. Only his forehead, revealed by a central baldness, was smooth—a placid lake of pink skin surrounded by a mass of graying curls.

Jim Chee had first met West when Chee was brand new in the district—the day they'd recovered John Doe's body. And the day after they'd brought the body in, the dispatcher had relayed a message to drop in at the Burnt Water store because West had something to tell him. The something hadn't been much—a little information which suggested the location one of the area's bootleggers might be using to deliver to his customers. But it was that day that Chee had seen, actually seen, Joseph Musket. It isn't often that a cop gets to see the burglar the day before the burglary.

Chee had parked in front, come in, seen West in his office in conversation with a young man wearing a red shirt. West had shouted something like "Be with you in a minute," and in a minute the young man had walked out of West's office and past Chee and out the front door. West stood at the office door, glaring after him.

"That son of a bitch," West had said. "I fired him."

"He didn't look like he cared much," Chee had said.

"I guess he didn't," West said. "I give him a job so he can qualify for parole and the bastard shows up for work whenever it damn well pleases him. And that ain't often. And I think he was stealing from me."

"Want to file a complaint?"

"Let it go," West said. "He used to be a friend of my son's. My boy wasn't ever good at picking friends."

And the very next morning, there'd been another call. Somebody had unlocked the storage room where West kept jewelry pawned by his customers, and walked out with about forty of the best pieces. Only West and Joseph Musket had access to the key. Since then Chee had learned a little about West. He'd operated the Burnt Water store for twenty years. He'd come from Phoenix, or Los Angeles, depending on your source, and he'd once been married to a Hopi woman, but no longer was. He'd had a son, maybe two, by a previous marriage, and had established a fairly good reputation, as reputations go among trading post operators. He was not on Captain Largo's list of known bootleggers, had never been nailed fencing stolen property, paid relatively fair prices for the jewelry he took in pawn and charged relatively fair interest rates, and seemed to get along well with both Navajo and Hopi customers. The Hopis, Chee had been told, considered him a *powaqa*—a "two-heart"—one of those persons in whom dwelled the soul of an animal as well as the soul of a human. This was the sophisticated Hopi's version of a witch. Chee had asked two Hopis he'd met about this rumor. One said it was nonsense—that only descendants of the Fog Clan could be two-hearts and that the Fog Clan was almost extinct among the Hopi villages. The other, an elderly woman, thought West might be a two-heart, but not much of one. Now West had collected his money from the Navajo girl and given her the money order.

He loomed down the counter toward Chee, teeth showing white through the beard in a huge grin.

"Officer Chee," he said, offering his hand. It engulfed Chee's hand, but the handshake, like the voice, was surprisingly gentle. "You're just a little bit late. I expected you five minutes ago." The grin had been converted to sternness.

Chee had seen West's playfulness before. He wasn't fooled. But he played along.

"How'd you know when I was coming?"

"Mind power," West said. "And because you Navajos won't believe in powers like that, I planted a thought in your mind so I could prove it to you." West stared down at Chee, his eyes fierce. "You are thinking of a card."

"Nope," Chee said.

"Yes you are," West insisted. "It's subconscious. You don't even know it yourself, but I planted the thought. Now quit wasting our time and tell me the card."

Chee found himself thinking of cards. A deck of cards spilled across a table. A bunch of spades. No particular card.

"Come on," West said. "Out with it."

"Three of diamonds," Chee said.

West's fierceness modified itself into smiling self-satisfaction. "Exactly right," he said. West wore blue-and-white-striped coveralls, large even for his bulk. He fished into one of their pockets. "And since you Navajos are such skeptical people, I arranged some proof for you." He handed Chee a small envelope of the sort used to mail notes and invitations.

"The three of diamonds," West said.

"Wonderful," Chee said. He noticed the envelope was sealed and put it in his shirt pocket.

"Aren't you going to open it?"

"I trust you," Chee said, "and I really came in to see if you can help me."

West's eyebrows rose. "You working on that plane crash? The drug business?"

"That's a federal case," Chee said. "FBI, Drug Enforcement Agency. We don't handle such things. I'm working on a vandalism case."

"That windmill," West said. He looked thoughtful. "Yes. That's a funny business."

"You been hearing anything?"

West laughed. "Naturally. Or I was. Now everybody's talking about the plane crash, and drug smuggling, and killing that guy—a lot more interesting than a vandalized windmill."

"But maybe not as important," Chee said.

West looked at him, thinking about that.

"Well, yes," he said. "From our point of view, yes. Depends on who gets killed, doesn't it?" He motioned Chee around behind the counter and led him through the doorway from store into living quarters. "They ought to kill them all," West said to the hallway in front of him. "Scum."

The West living room was long, narrow, cool, dark. Its thick stone walls were cut by four windows, but vines had grown so thickly over them that they let in only a green dimness. "Sit down," West said, and he lowered himself into a heavy plastic recliner. "We'll talk about windmills, and airplanes, and men who get themselves shot in the back."

Chee sat on the sofa. It was too soft for him and he sank into its lumpy upholstery. Such furniture always made him uneasy. "First we need to settle something," Chee said. "That fellow wrecking that windmill might be a friend of yours; or it could be that you think wrecking that windmill isn't such a bad idea under the circumstances. If that's the way it is, I'll go away and no hard feelings."

West was grinning. "Ah," he said. "I like the way your mind works. Why waste the talk? But the way it is, I don't know who's doing it, and I don't like vandalism, and worse than that, maybe it's going to lead to worse trouble and God knows we don't need any of that."

"Good," Chee said.

"Trouble is, the thing has me puzzled." West put his elbows on the armrests of the chair, made a tent of his fingers. "Common sense says one of your Navajo families is doing it. Who'd blame 'em? I guess the Gishi family has been living along that wash for four generations, or five, and the Yazzies something like that, and some others maybe as long. Toughing it out, hauling water in, and as soon as the federal court turns it over to the Hopis, the feds drill 'em a bunch of wells." West had been studying his fingers. Now he looked at Chee. "Sort of adds insult to the injury."

Chee said nothing. West was an old hand at communicating with Navajos. He would talk at his own pace until he said what he had to say, without expecting the social feedback of a white conversation.

"You got a few mean sons-a-bitches out there," West went on. "That's a fact. Get too much to drink in Eddie Gishi and he's a violent man. Couple of others as bad or worse. So maybe one of them would pull down a windmill." West examined his tented fingers while he considered the idea. "But I don't much think they did."

Chee waited. West would explain himself when he had his thoughts sorted out. On the mantel of the stone fireplace behind West's chair a clutter of photographs stood in an uneven row: a good-natured-looking boy in Marine blues, the same boy in what Chee guessed was a blowup of a high school yearbook photograph, a picture of West himself in a tuxedo and a top hat, looking a great deal younger. All the other photographs included more than one person: West with a pretty young Hopi woman who was probably West's second wife, West and the same woman with the boy, the same trio with assorted persons whom Chee couldn't identify. None of the pictures looked new. They had collected dust—a sort of gallery out of a dead period from the past.

"I don't think they did," West continued finally, "because of the way they're acting. Lot of gossip about it, of course. Lots of talk." He looked up at Chee, wanting to explain. "You come from Crownpoint. Over in New Mexico. It's more settled around there. More people. More things to do. Out here, the nearest movie show's a hundred miles away in Flagstaff. Television reception's poor and most people don't have electricity anyway. Nothing much happens and nothing much to do. So if somebody pulls down a windmill, it breaks the monotony."

Chee nodded.

"You hear a lot of speculation. You know—guessing about who's doing it. The Hopis, they're sure they know. It's the Yazzies, or it's the Gishi bunch, or somebody. They're mad about it. And nervous. Wondering what will happen next. And the Navajos, they think it's sort of funny, some of them anyway, and they're guessing about who's doing it. Old Hosteen Nez, he'll say something speculative about a Yazzie boy, or Shirley

Yazzie will make a remark about the Nezes being in the windmill-fixing business. So forth."

West took down his tent of fingers and leaned forward. "You hear a little of that from *everybody.*" He stressed the word. "If one of the Navajos was doing it, I think they wouldn't be speculating. I think they'd be keeping quiet about it. That's the way I've got these Wepo Wash Navajos figured." West glanced at Chee, looking slightly embarrassed. "I've been living with these people twenty years," he said. "You get to know 'em."

"So who's breaking the windmill?" Chee asked. "Rule out us Navajos and that doesn't leave anybody but the Hopis, and you."

"It's not me," West said, grinning his great, irregular grin. "I got nothing against windmills. When all the Navajos get moved out of here, most of my customers are going to be Hopis. I'm in favor of them having all their windmills in good working order."

"Always the same mill," Chee said. "And over on the Gishi grazing permit. You'd think that would narrow it down to the Gishis."

"The *former* Gishi grazing permit," West corrected. "Now it's Hopi territory." He shook his head. "I don't think it's the Gishis. Old Emma Gishi runs that bunch. She's tough and you don't push her. But she's practical. Knocking down a windmill don't do her no good. She wouldn't do it out of meanness, and if Emma says don't do it, none of the Gishis does it. She runs that bunch like a railroad. You want a drink of something? I heard you don't drink whiskey."

"I don't," Chee said.

"How about coffee?"

"Always," Chee said.

"I'll mix up some instant," West said. "What I meant was she runs that bunch like they used to run railroads. Not like they run 'em now."

West disappeared through the doorway into what Chee presumed was the kitchen. Something clattered. Chee pulled the envelope out of his pocket and inspected it. A perfectly plain white envelope without a mark on it. Inside he could see the shape of a playing card. He was absolutely certain it would be the three of diamonds. How had West done that? Chee felt faintly guilty. He shouldn't have denied West the pleasure of seeing the finale of the trick. He slipped the card back into the pocket of his uniform shirt and examined the room. Three Navajo rugs, two of them fine examples of collector-quality Two Gray Hills weaving. An old dark-stained bookcase along the wall away from the windows held a few books and a gallery of kachina figures. Chee recognized Masaw, the guardian spirit of this Fourth World of the Hopis, and the god of fire and death, and the lord of Hell. It was a beautiful job, almost a foot tall and probably worth a thousand dollars. Most of the other kachinas were also Hopi, but the Zuni Shalako figures were there, and the Zuni Longhorn spirit, and two grotesque members of the Mudhead fraternity. All good, but Masaw was clearly the feature of the collection. It held a torch and its face was the traditional blood-spotted mask.

West reappeared in the doorway, bearing mugs. "Hope it's hot enough. I didn't let the water boil."

Chee sipped. The coffee was one stage past lukewarm and tasted muddy. "Fine," he said.

"Now," West said, easing himself back into the recliner. "We have talked about windmills. Now we talk a little about airplane crashes and dead gangsters."

Chee took another sip.

"From what was in the paper, and on TV last night, and what dribbles in from here and there, I get the impression that somebody got off with the shipment."

"That seems to be what the feds are thinking," Chee said.

"Two men killed in the plane crash," West said. "A third man shot and left sitting there with a message in his hand. So the DEA figures the dope got hijacked. Right?"

"I'll bet you know as much about it as I do," Chee said. "Maybe more. It's not our jurisdiction."

West ignored that. "From what I hear, you fellows figure the dope is hidden back in there someplace. That whoever got off with it didn't haul it away with him?"

Chee shrugged. West waited expectantly. "Well," Chee said finally, "I do get that kind of impression. Don't ask me why."

"Why wouldn't it be hauled out?" West asked. "They came in there to haul it off. Why not haul it off? Where would they hide it? How big is it?"

"I don't know," Chee said. "You thinking about finding it?"

West's huge grin split his beard. "Wouldn't that be fine? To find something like that. It'd be worth a fortune. They say it's cocaine, and that stuff sells for thousands of dollars an ounce. I heard the pure stuff would bring five hundred thousand dollars a pound, time you dilute it down and sell it to the customer."

"Where you going to find a buyer?"

"There's a will, there's a way," West said. He finished his coffee, put down the cup, grimaced. "Terrible-tasting stuff," he said. "How about the pilot? Somebody said he was still alive when you got there."

"Just barely," Chee said. "Who is this somebody that's telling you all this?"

West laughed. "You're forgetting the first rule of collecting gossip. You never tell anybody who told you, or they stop telling."

Probably Cowboy Dashee, Chee thought. Cowboy was a talker, and it was the sort of information he'd have. But a half-dozen various kinds of cops would have been through the trading post since the crash. It could have been any of them, or it could have been second or third hand, or it could just be an educated guess.

West changed the subject. Had any of his stolen pawn silver turned up? Had any trace been found of Joseph Musket? Had Chee heard the latest witchcraft gossip, which concerned one of the Gishi girls seeing a big dog bothering her horses, and shooting at it with her .22, and the dog turning into a man and running away. Chee said he'd heard it. Then West switched the conversation back to Musket.

"Reckon he had anything to do with any of this?"

"With the dope business or the witch business?"

"Dope," West said. "You know he was a con. Maybe he got wind of it some way. Jailhouse telegraph. I've heard of that. Maybe he's into it. You think of that?"

"Yes," Chee said. "I've thought of that. Something else I've thought of. If you're serious about trying to find whatever it is we're looking for, I think I'd forget it. Whoever has that stuff is going to have the worst kind of trouble. If the feds don't get him, the owner will."

"You're right," West said.

Chee got up. He took the envelope out of his pocket.

"Is this really the three of diamonds in here?"

"Whatever you said it was. Three of diamonds, I think you said."

Chee opened the envelope. He pulled out the three of diamonds.

"How do you do that?"

"Magic," West said, grinning.

"I can't figure out the angle."

West spread his great hands. "I'm a magician," he said. "For years, a professional. With the circus in the good days and then many years with the carnivals."

"But you're not going to tell me how it works?"

"Takes the fun out of it," West said. "Just think about it as mind over matter."

"Thanks for the coffee," Chee said. He put on his hat. "Fine-looking boy you've got there." Chee nodded toward the photographs. "Is he still in the Marines?"

All the easy mobility left West's big face. It froze. "He was killed," he said.

"I'm sorry," Chee said. "In the Marines?"

He wished he hadn't asked the question. West wasn't going to answer it. But he did.

"After he got out," West said. "He made some bad friends in El Paso. They killed him."

7

AT DAWN, Chee parked the pickup at the windmill. He slammed the door behind him and stood facing the glow on the eastern horizon. He yawned and stretched and inhaled deeply of the cold early air. He felt absolutely fine. This was *hozro.* This was the beauty that Changing Woman taught them to attain. This was the feeling of harmony, of being in tune. The orange glow in the east turned to a hot yellow as Chee sang his dawn chant. There was no one in miles to hear him. He shouted it, greeting Dawn Boy, greeting the sun, blessing the new day. "Let beauty walk before me," Chee sang. "Let beauty walk behind me. Let beauty walk all around me." He opened his shirt, extracted his medicine pouch, took out a pinch of pollen, and offered it to the moving air. "In beauty it is finished," Chee sang.

The mood continued through breakfast—hot coffee from his stainless-steel thermos and two sandwiches of bologna and thin, hard Hopi *piki* bread. As he chewed he reviewed. Did Joseph Musket disappear to set up a narcotics hijacking? Was the burglary done simply to provide a cover motive for his disappearance? That would explain why none of the missing jewelry had turned up. Or had Joseph Musket's disappearance some connection with the murder of John Doe? The burglary had been two nights after they'd brought in Doe's body. Could Musket have intentionally provoked West into firing him because—once the body was found—there was some reason he had to run and he wanted to run without causing suspicion? For a moment that seemed to make some sense. But only for a moment. Then Chee remembered that there hadn't been any genuine effort to hide the body. It had been left along the path to Kisigi Spring. Isolated and not often used, but the only route to an important Hopi shrine, if Dashee knew what he was talking about. That provoked another thought. If you could learn from the Hopis when the shrine was visited, you could get a closer estimation—or maybe you could—of when the man had been killed there. All they had now was the medical examiner's casual estimate of "dead not more than a month, not less than two weeks." Would knowing when the body appeared on the trail help?

Chee took another bite, chewed, and thought about it. He couldn't see how. But who knows? At the moment he felt supremely optimistic. A brace of horned larks were singing their morning song beyond the windmill and the air was cool against his face and the crusty *piki* bread was tasting of wheat and bacon fat in his mouth. Someday he would unravel John Doe. Someday he would find Joseph Musket. (Why do they call you Ironfingers?) Someday, perhaps even today, he would catch the man who was vandalizing this windmill. He felt in harmony with all such things this morning—capable even of persuading these strange Black Mesa Navajos to confide in him about their witch. In a moment the sun would be high enough to give him the slanting light he needed to read even the faintest tracks. Then he would see what he could learn about this latest vandalism. Probably he would learn nothing very much. But even if the hard-packed, drought-baked earth told him nothing at all, that, too, would be right and proper, in tune with his relationship with this ugly windmill and the vandal who so hated it. Sooner or later he would understand this business. He'd find the cause. Senseless as it seemed, there'd be a reason behind it. The wind did not move, the leaf did not fall, the bird did not cry, nor did the windmill provoke such violent anger without a reason. All was part of the universal pattern, as Changing Woman had taught them when she formed the first four Navajo clans. Jim Chee had ingested that fact with his mother's milk, and from the endless lessons his uncle taught him. "All is order," Hosteen Nakai taught him. "Look for the pattern."

Chee left half the coffee in the thermos and wrapped a

towel around the bottle. That, with two more bologna sandwiches still in his sack, would serve for lunch. A covey of Gambel's quail, their long topknot feathers bobbing, paraded single file along the slope below the windmill, heading for the arroyo a hundred yards to the north. The quail would be after an early-morning drink. Far down the arroyo three cottonwoods stood—two alive and one a long-dead skeleton. They were the only such trees in miles and must mark a shallow water table. Perhaps a spring. Without some source of water, the drought would force all birds away from here.

Chee found scuff marks on the earth, left by the vandal and by the Hopi who had discovered the vandalism. They told him nothing useful. Then he examined the mill itself. This time the vandal had used some sort of lever to kink the long connecting rod that tied the gear mechanism overhead to the pump cylinder in the well casing. It was an efficient means of destruction which left the force of the turning blades and the pumping action to strip the gears. But the vandal was exhausting such opportunities. Now the footing bolts were securely brazed into place, and the gearbox was secured. The custodians of the windmill could easily prevent a repetition of this new outrage by using a two-inch pipe to provide a protective sleeve for the pump rod. Chee scrutinized the mill thoughtfully, looking for weak points. He found nothing that could be damaged without some sort of special equipment. A portable cutting torch, for example, could take a slice out of one of the metal legs and topple the whole affair again, or make hash out of the gearbox once more. But the vandal so far hadn't used anything sophisticated. Horses, a rope, a steel bar—nothing complicated. What could a man without equipment do now to cause serious damage? The best he could find involved putting the mill in neutral to stop pump action, then pouring cement down the pump shaft. That would require only a small plastic funnel, a sack of cement, some sand, and a bucket. Maybe a ten-dollar investment. And the solution would be permanent.

The sun was higher now and Chee broadened his search, covering the ground in widening circles. He found hoofprints and human tracks, but nothing interesting. Then he dropped into the arroyo and scouted it—first upstream and then down.

Someone who wore moccasins had used its sandy bottom often as a pathway. The moccasins were surprising. Navajos—even old people—almost never wore them, and as far as Chee knew, Hopis used them only when ceremonial occasions demanded.

The path ended at the cottonwoods. As Chee had guessed, there was water seepage here in wetter seasons and the moisture had produced a robust growth of tamarisk bushes, chamiso, Russian olives, and assorted arid country weeds. The path disappeared into this cover and Chee followed it. He found the origin of the seep. Here the arroyo had cut its way past an outcropping of hard gray shale. Seeping water had eaten away at this formation, leaving a cavity perhaps four feet high, three times as wide, and as deep as Chee's vision would go into the shaded darkness. The rock here was stained green with now-dead algae and covered with a heavy growth of lichen. Chee squatted, studying the shale. The morning breeze moved through the brush around him, died away, and rose again. Chee's eye caught movement back in the shadowy cavity. He saw a feather flutter and two tiny yellow eyes.

"Ah," Chee said. He moved forward on hands and knees. The eyes were painted on a stick—a tiny semi-face framed by two downy feathers. Behind this stick in an irregular row were others, scores of them—a little forest of feathered plumes.

Chee touched nothing. He perched on hands and knees and studied the shrine and the prayer plumes which decorated it. The Hopis called them *pahos,* he remembered, and offered them as gifts to the spirits. Those that Chee could see well from his position seemed to have been made by one man. The carved shapes were similar and the mix of colors was the same. One, he noticed, had toppled. Chee examined it. One of the feathers was bent but the paint was fresh. It seemed to be the newest of the *pahos.* An unhappy kachina rejecting this season's gift? Or had some clumsy intruder knocked the *pahos* over?

Back at his pickup at noon, Chee fished his lunch out of the glove box. He sat with his feet out the open door and ate slowly, sorting the odds and ends of information he had accumulated during the morning. Nothing much. But not a total waste. The spring, for example, provided a good view of the windmill. Whoever tended it might have seen the vandal. He washed down the sandwich with a sip of coffee. How had West done the card trick? Name a card. Chee had named the three of diamonds. West had handed him the three sealed in a little envelope. There seemed no way it could be done. He went over it again, in his memory. He'd said, "Three of diamonds," and West's hand had dipped into the left-hand pocket of his coveralls and extracted the envelope. What would West have done if Chee had said jack of clubs? He thought about it. Then he chuckled. He knew how the trick was done. He glanced at his watch. A little after noon. A flock of red-winged blackbirds had been foraging along the arroyo. They moved from one growth of Russian olive toward another, veered suddenly, and settled in another growth, farther up the arroyo. Chee was chewing the first bite of his second sandwich. His jaws stopped. His eyes examined the area. They saw nothing. The chewing began again. Chee finished the sandwich, drained the thermos. A dove flew down the gully. It banked abruptly away from the same growth of olives. Chee drank. The only thing that would arouse such caution in birds would be a human. Someone was watching him. Was there a way he could approach the olive brush without alerting the watcher? Chee could see none.

He put the thermos on the seat. Who would the watcher be? Perhaps Johnson, or one of Johnson's people from the DEA, hoping Chee would lead them to the stolen stuff. Perhaps the windmill vandal. Perhaps the Hopi who tended the shrine. Or perhaps God knows who. The air was almost motionless here, but a swirl of breeze started a dust devil across Wepo Wash. It moved into the wash, and across it, coming obliquely toward Chee. Over his head, the windmill groaned as its blades began turning. But the pump rod was motionless. The gearing mechanism which connected the rod to the fan was gone now—away to have its vandalism repaired—and the mill pumped nothing. Chee tried again to calculate who the vandal might be. Not enough information. He tried again to calculate who might be watching him. No luck. He reexamined his solution to the card trick and found it correct. Why had the pilot flown into the rocks? Chee locked the truck and began walking toward Wepo Wash.

He walked parallel to the arroyo, watching the blackbirds.

If the birds were startled out of the olive grove where they were now feeding, it would signal that his watcher was following him—moving down the arroyo toward the wash. If not, he'd guess the watcher was more interested in the windmill than in a Navajo cop. The birds rose with a clatter of sound and flew back up the arroyo to the trees they had been avoiding. Chee had expected them to do exactly that.

8

THE ONLY REASONS Jimmy Chee would have admitted for climbing down into Wepo Wash was to give himself a chance to identify—and perhaps even confront—whoever was watching him. He'd give the watcher time to follow. Then he would drop out of sight—probably by moving into a side arroyo somewhere up the wash. Once Chee was out of sight, the watcher would have to make a decision: to follow or not. However he made it, Chee would be able to reverse the roles. He'd become the stalker.

That was the plan. But now he was in the wash, and just a hundred yards up the hard-packed sandy bottom from where he stood, the sun glinted from the remains of the aircraft. The wreckage was FBI and DEA business. A Navajo Tribal Policeman would not be welcome here without a specific invitation. But Chee was curious. And to his watcher, a visit to the wreckage would seem a logical reason for this walk.

The ground around the site was thoroughly trampled now and the plane itself had been ransacked. Wing and stabilizer panels had been peeled open, a gas tank removed, and holes punched in the thin aluminum skin of the rudder, in what must have been a search for the cargo it had carried. Chee stared up the wash, up the plane's landing path, frowning. As he remembered, it had struck an upthrust of basalt which jutted from the floor of the wash. The wash had flowed around the extrusion on both sides, eroding the earth and leaving a black stone island in a sea of sand. If there wasn't room to land upwash from this wall of stone, and there seemed to be plenty of space, there was obviously room enough to miss it to the right or left. Why hadn't the pilot avoided it? Surely he hadn't simply landed blindly in the dark. Chee walked upwash, out of the trampled area. He kept his eyes on the sand, looking for the answer. The watcher could wait.

A little more than an hour later, he heard the sound of a car engine. By then he knew why the plane had crashed. But he had new questions.

The car was a dark-blue Ford Bronco. It pulled to a stop beside the wreckage. Two persons emerged. A man and a woman. They stood a moment, looking upwash toward Chee, and then walked to the aircraft. Chee walked toward them. The man was tall, hatless, gray-haired, wearing jeans and a white shirt. The woman was hatless, too. She was rather small, with short dark hair that curled around her face. Not FBI. Probably not DEA, although anybody could be DEA. They stood beside the wreckage, looking at the plane but waiting for him. Chee saw the man was older than he had looked from a distance—perhaps in his early fifties. One of those men who take care of themselves, join racquet clubs, jog, lift weights. His face was long, with deep lines along the nose, and eyes which, because of large black pupils, looked somewhat moist and luminous. The woman glanced at Chee and then stared at the wreckage. Her oval face, drained of color, looked shocked. She was in her fifties, Chee guessed, but at the moment she looked as old as time. Something about her tugged at Chee's memory. The man's expression was defensive, the look of someone caught trespassing, who expects to be asked who he is and what he's doing. Chee nodded to him.

"We came out to see the aircraft," the man said. "I was his attorney and this is Gail Pauling."

"Jim Chee," Chee said. He shook the man's hand and nodded to the woman.

"Jim Chee," the woman said. "You're the one who found my brother."

Chee knew now what she reminded him of. Her brother was the pilot. "I don't think he had any suffering," Chee said.

"It must have happened in an instant. Too quick to know what happened."

"And what did happen?" Miss Pauling asked. She gestured toward the outcrop. "I can't believe he would just fly right into this."

"He didn't, exactly," Chee said. "His wheels touched down about fifty yards up there. He was on the ground."

She was staring at the wreckage, her face still stunned. Chee wasn't sure she had heard him. "Something must have happened to him," she said, as if to herself. "He would never have flown right into this."

"It was in the dark," Chee said. "Didn't they tell you that?"

"They didn't tell me anything," Miss Pauling said. She seemed to really see Chee for the first time. "Just that he crashed, and he was dead, and the police think he was flying in some contraband, and that a policeman named Jim Chee was the one who saw it all."

"I didn't see it," Chee said. "I heard it. It was a couple of hours before dawn. The moon was down." Chee described what had happened. The lawyer listened intently, his moist eyes studying Chee's face. Chee didn't mention hearing the shot, or the other sounds.

The woman's face was incredulous. "He landed in the pitch dark?" she asked. "He used to be in the Tactical Air Force. But on an airfield. And with radar. I worried about it. But I can't believe he'd just land blind."

"He didn't," Chee said. He gestured up the bed of the wash. "He'd landed at least three times before. Just a day or two earlier, the way the tracks look. Probably in the daylight. Practicing, I'd guess. And then when he made this landing, he had lights."

"Lights?" the lawyer asked.

"It looks like battery lanterns," Chee said. "A row of them on the ground."

Miss Pauling was staring up the wash, looking baffled.

"They left their marks," Chee explained. "I'll show you."

He led them down the side of the wash. Was the watcher still out there somewhere? If he was, what would he think of all this? If the watcher was Johnson, or one of Johnson's DEA people assigned to follow Chee, he'd never believe this meeting was not prearranged. Chee considered that. It didn't bother him.

They walked along the narrow strip of shade cast by the almost vertical wall of the wash. Beyond this shadow, the sunlight glittered from the gray-yellow surface of the arroyo bottom. Heat waves shimmered from the flatness and the only sound was boot soles on the sand.

Behind him the lawyer cleared his throat. "Mr. Chee," he said. "That car you mentioned in your report, driving away—did you get a look at it?"

"You read the report?" Chee asked. He was surprised, but he didn't look around. It was exactly what Largo had predicted.

"We stopped at your police station at Tuba City," the attorney said. "They showed it to me."

Of course, Chee thought. Why not? The man was the attorney of the accident victim. The attorney and the next of kin.

"It was gone," Chee said. "I heard the engine starting. A car or maybe a pickup truck."

"The shot," the attorney asked. "Rifle? Shotgun? Pistol?"

That's an interesting question, Chee thought. "Not a shotgun. Probably a pistol," he said. The memory of the sound echoed in his mind. Probably a large pistol.

"Would you say a twenty-two, or something larger? A thirty-two? A thirty-eight?"

Another interesting question. "I'd be guessing," Chee said.

"Would you mind?"

"I'd guess a thirty-eight, or larger," Chee said. What would the next question be? Chee's guess at who pulled the trigger, maybe.

"I've always been interested in guns," the lawyer said.

And then they were opposite the place where the plane had first touched down. Chee moved out of the shade and walked into the glittering heat. He squatted beside the marks.

"Here," he said. "See? Here's where the right wheel first touched." He pointed. "And there the left wheel. He had the plane almost exactly level."

Near this touchdown point, a line about two inches deep had been drawn across the sand. Chee rose and took a dozen steps down the track. "Here the nose wheel touched," he said. "I think Pauling drew that line to mark the place. And over there . . . See the tracks?" Chee pointed toward the center of the wash. "That's where he took off both times."

"Or maybe he landed over there and took off here," the lawyer said in his soft voice. He laughed a mild, soft sound. "But what difference is it?"

"Not much," Chee said. "But he did land here. Deeper impression at the impact point, and the bounce marks. And if you go over there and take a close look, you notice the sand is blown back more on the tracks where he lifted off. Engine really revving up then, you know, and idling when he landed."

The attorney's soft eyes were examining Chee. "Yes," he said. "Of course. Can you still read that in the sand?"

"If you look," Chee said.

Miss Pauling was staring down the wash toward the wreckage. "But if he touched down here, he had plenty of time to stop. He had more room than he needed."

"The night he crashed, he didn't touch down here," Chee said. He walked toward the wreckage. A hundred yards, two hundred yards. Finally he stopped. He squatted again, touched a faint indentation in the sand with a fingertip. "Here was the first lantern," he said. He glanced over his shoulder. "And his wheels touched right there. See? Just a few feet past the lantern."

Miss Pauling looked at the wheel tracks and then past them at the wreckage, looming just ahead of them. "My God," she said. "He didn't have a chance, did he?"

"Somebody put out five lanterns in a straight line between here and the rock." Chee pointed. "There were five more lanterns on the other side of the rock."

The lawyer was staring at Chee, lips slightly parted. He read the implications of the lantern placement instantly. Miss Pauling was thinking of something else. "Did he have his landing lights on? Your report didn't mention that."

"I didn't see any light," Chee said. "I think I would have seen the glow."

"So he was depending on whoever put the lanterns out," Miss Pauling said. Then what Chee had said about the lanterns beyond the rock finally reached her. She looked at him, her face startled. "Five more lanterns beyond the rock? Behind it?"

"Yes," Chee said. He felt a pity for the woman. To lose your brother is bad. To learn someone killed him is worse.

"But why . . . ?"

Chee shook his head. "Maybe somebody wanted him to land but not to take off," he said. "I don't know. Maybe I'm wrong about the lanterns. All I found was the little depressions. Like this one."

She stared at him wordlessly. Studying him. "You don't think you're wrong."

"Well, no," Chee said. "This little oval shape, with these sharp indentations around the edge—it looks just the size and shape for those dry-cell batteries you attach the lantern bulb to. I'll measure it and check, but I don't know what else it would be."

"No," Miss Pauling said. She released a long breath, and with it her shoulders slumped. A little life seemed to leave her. "I don't know what else it would be, either." Miss Pauling's face had changed. It had hardened. "Somebody killed him."

"These lanterns," the lawyer said. "They were gone when you got here? They weren't mentioned in your report."

"They were gone," Chee said. "I found the trace of them just before you drove up. When I was here before, it was dark."

"But they weren't in the follow-up report either. The one that was made after the airplane was searched and all that. That was done in the daytime."

"That was federal cops," Chee said. "I guess they didn't notice the marks."

The lawyer looked at Chee thoughtfully. "I wouldn't have," he said finally. He smiled. "I've always heard that Indians were good trackers."

A long time ago, in his senior year at the University of New Mexico, Chee had resolved never to let such generalizations irritate him. It was a resolution he rarely managed to keep.

"I am a Navajo," Chee said. "We don't have a word in our language for 'Indians.' Just specific words. For Utes, and Hopis, and Apaches. A white is a *belacani,* a Mexican is a *nakai.* So forth. Some Navajos are good at tracking. Some aren't. You learn it by studying it. Like law."

"Of course," the lawyer said. He was still observing Chee. "But how do you learn it?"

"I had a teacher," Chee said. "My mother's brother. He showed me what to look for." Chee stopped. He was not in the mood to discuss tracking with this odd stranger.

"Like what?" the lawyer said.

Chee tried to think of examples. He shrugged. "You see a man walk by. You go look at the tracks he made. You see him walk by, carrying something heavy in one hand. You look at the tracks. You go again tomorrow to look at the tracks after a day. And after two days. You see a fat man and a thin man squatting in the shade, talking. When they leave, you go and look at the marks a fat man makes when he squats on his heels, and the marks a thin man makes." Chee stopped again. He was thinking of his uncle, in the Chuska high country tracking the mule deer. Showing how the bucks dragged their hooves when rutting, how to estimate the age of a doe by reading the splaying of its cloven toes in its tracks. Of his uncle kneeling beside the track left in the drying mud by a pickup truck, testing the moisture in a ridge of dirt, showing him how to estimate how many hours had passed since the tire had left that print. Much more than that, of course. But he had said enough to satisfy courtesy.

The lawyer had taken out his billfold. He extracted a business card and handed it to Chee.

"I'm Ben Gaines," he said. "I'll be representing Mr. Pauling's estate. Could I hire you? In your spare time?"

"For what?"

"For pretty much what you'd do anyway," Ben Gaines gestured toward the wreck. "Putting together just exactly what happened here."

"I won't be doing that," Chee said. "This isn't my case. This is a first-degree felony. It involves non-Navajos. This was part of the Navajo-Hopi Joint Use Reservation, but now it's Hopi. Outside my territory. Outside my jurisdiction. I'm here working on something else. Came down here because I was curious."

"All the better," Gaines said. "There won't be any question of conflict of interest."

"I'm not sure the rules would allow it," Chee said. "I'd have to check with the captain." It occurred to Chee that one way or another he'd be doing what the lawyer wanted. His curiosity would demand it.

Gaines was chuckling. "I was just thinking that it might be just as well if your boss didn't know about this arrangement. Nothing wrong with it. But if you ask a bureaucrat if there's a rule against something, he'll always tell you there is."

"Yeah," Chee said. "What do you want me to do?"

"I want to know what happened to Pauling here," Gaines said. "The report sounded like there were three people here when it happened. I want to know for sure. You heard a shot. Then you heard a car, or maybe a truck, driving away. I want to know what went on." Gaines waved around him. "Maybe you can find some tracks that'll tell."

"Plenty of tracks now," Chee said. "About a dozen federal cops, Arizona State Police, county law, so forth, trampling all around. And yours and mine and hers." Chee nodded to Miss Pauling. She had walked back to the wreckage and stood staring at the cabin.

"My law firm pays forty dollars an hour for work like this," Gaines said. "Find out what you can."

"I'll let you know," Chee said, making the answer deliberately ambiguous. "What else you want to know?"

"I get the impression," Gaines said slowly, "that the police aren't sure what happened to the car you heard driving away. They don't seem to think it ever left this part of the country. I'd like to know what you can find out about that."

"Find out what happened to the car?"

"If you can," Gaines said.

"It would help if I knew what I was looking for," Chee said.

Gaines hesitated a long moment. "Yes," he said. "It would. Just tell me what you find out."

"Where?"

"We'll be staying at that motel the Hopis run. Up on Second Mesa," Gaines said.

Chee nodded.

Gaines hesitated again. "One other thing," he said. "I've heard there was a cargo on that plane. If you happened to turn that up, there'd be a reward for that. I'm sure some pay-out would be available from the owners if that turned up." Gaines smiled at Chee, his eyes friendly and moist. "A big one. If you happen onto that, let me know about it. Quietly. Then I'll get to work and find out a way to get into contact with whoever owned whatever it was. You find the stuff. I find the owners. Sort of a partnership between the two of us. You know what I mean?"

"Yes," Chee said. "I know."

9

THE LATE-AFTERNOON SUN slanted through the windows of the Burnt Water Trading Post, breaking the cavernous interior into a patchwork of harsh contrasts. Dazzling reflected sunlight alternated with cool darkness. And in the sunlight, dust motes danced. They reminded Chee of drought.

"Shrine?" Jake West said. "Hell, between you people and the Hopi, this country is covered up with shrines." West was sitting in a patch of darkness, his heavy bearded head silhouetted against an oblong of sunlight on the wall.

"This one is in the arroyo just east of the windmill," Chee said. "By a dried-up spring. It's full of prayer plumes. Some of 'em fresh, so somebody's been taking care of it."

"Pahos," West said. "You call 'em prayer plumes, but for the Hopis they're *pahos*."

"Whatever," Chee said. "You know anything about it?"

Through the open front door came the sound of a car, moving fast, jolting into the trading post yard. Over the noise, West said he didn't know anything about the shrine. "Never heard of that one," he said. There was the sound of a car door slamming. The smell of aroused dust drifted to their nostrils.

"That Cowboy?" Chee asked.

"Hope so," West said. "Hope there's not somebody else that parks like that. You'd think they'd teach the sons-a-bitches how to park without raising a cloud of dust. Ought to teach that before they let 'em into a car."

At the door a bulky young man in a khaki uniform paused

to exchange remarks with a cluster of old men passing the afternoon in the shade. Whatever he said provoked an elderly chuckle.

"Come on in, Cowboy," West said. "Chee here needs some information."

"As usual," Cowboy said. He grinned at Chee. "You caught your windmill vandal yet?"

"Our windmill vandal," Chee corrected. "You solved the great airplane mystery?"

"Not quite," Cowboy said. "But progress has been made." He extracted an eight-by-ten glossy photograph from a folder he was carrying and displayed it. "Here's the dude we're looking for. You guys see him, promptly inform either Deputy Sheriff Albert Dashee or call your friendly Coconino County Sheriff's Department."

"Who is he?" West said. The photograph obviously had been blown up from a standard police mug identification shot. It showed a man in his middle forties, with gray hair, close-set eyes, and a high, narrow forehead dominating a long, narrow face.

"Name's Richard Palanzer, also known as Dick Palanzer. What the feds call a 'known associate of the narcotics traffic.' All they told me is he was indicted a couple of years ago in Los Angeles County for conspiracy, narcotics. They want us looking for him around here."

"Where'd the picture come from?" Chee asked. He turned it over and looked at the back, which turned out to be bare.

"Sheriff," Cowboy said. "He got it from the DEA people. This is the bird they think drove off with the dope after the plane crash." Cowboy accepted the photograph back from Chee. "That is if Chee didn't do the driving. I understand the feds can't decide whether Chee rode shotgun or drove."

West looked puzzled. He raised his eyebrows, looked from Dashee to Chee and back.

Dashee laughed. "Just a joke," he said. "Chee was out there when it happened, so the DEA was suspicious. They're suspicious of everybody. Including me, and you, and that fellow over there." Dashee indicated a geriatric Hopi who was easing himself out of the front door with the help of an aluminum walker and a solicitous middle-aged woman. "What was it Chee wanted to know?"

"There's a little shrine in that arroyo by the windmill," Chee said. "By a dried-up spring. Lots of *pahos* in it. Looks like somebody's taking care of it. You know anything about it?"

At the word "shrine," Cowboy's expression changed from joviality to neutrality. Cowboy was listed on the payroll of the Coconino County, Arizona, Sheriff's Department as Albert Dashee, Jr. He'd accumulated sixty hours credit at Northern Arizona University before saying to hell with it. But he was Angushtiyo, or "Crow Boy," to his family, a member of the Side Corn Clan, and a valuable man in the Kachina Society of his village of Shipaulovi. Chee was becoming a friend, but Crow Boy was Hopi and Chee Navajo, and shrines, any shrines, involved the Hopi religion.

"What do you want to know?" Cowboy asked.

"From where it is, you can see the windmill," Chee said. "Whoever tends it might have seen something." He shrugged. "Long shot. But I've got nothing else."

"The *pahos*," Cowboy said. "Some of them new? Like somebody is taking care of it now?"

"I didn't look at them real close," Chee said. "I didn't want to touch anything." He wanted Cowboy to know that. "But I'd say some were old and some were new and somebody is taking care of it."

Cowboy thought. "It wouldn't be one of ours. I mean not Shipaulovi village. That's not our village land. I think that land down there belongs either to Walpi or to one of the kiva societies. I'll have to see what I can find out."

As the Navajos saw it, the land down there was Navajo land, allotted to the family of Patricia Gishi. But this wasn't the time for renewing the old Joint Use arguments.

"Just a long shot," Chee said. "But who knows?"

"I'll ask around," Cowboy repeated. "Did you know they're fixing that windmill again today?" He grinned. "You ready for that?"

Chee was not ready for that. It depressed him. The windmill would be vandalized again—as certain as fate. Chee knew it in his bones, and he knew there was nothing he could do to stop it from happening. Not until he understood what was happening. When the new vandalism happened it would be Cowboy's fault as much as his own, but Cowboy didn't seem to mind. Cowboy wouldn't have to stand in Captain Largo's office, and hear Captain Largo reading the indignant memo from the pertinent bureaucrat in the Bureau of Indian Affairs, and have Largo's mild eyes examining him, with the unspoken question in them relative to his competence to keep a windmill safe.

"With the BIA doing it, I thought it would be Christmas before they got it done," Chee said. "What the hell happened?"

"Something must have gone wrong," West said.

"The BIA got efficient. It happens every eight or ten years," Cowboy said. "Anyway, I saw a truck going in there. They said they had all the parts and they was fixing it today."

"I think you can relax," West said. "They probably got the wrong parts."

"You going to stake it out again?" Cowboy asked.

"I don't think that will work now," Chee said. "The plane crash screwed that up. Whoever it was learned I was out there. They'll make damn sure next time nobody's watching."

"The vandal was out there the night the plane crashed?" West asked.

"Somebody was," Chee said. "I heard somebody climbing out of the wash. And then while I was busy with the crash, somebody screwed up the windmill again."

"I didn't know that," West said. "You mean the vandal was right down there by the wreck? After it happened?"

"That's right," Chee said. "I'm surprised everybody didn't know that by now. They're handing the report around for everybody to read." Chee told West and Cowboy about the lawyer and the sister of the pilot.

"They was in here yesterday morning, asking for directions," West said. "They wanted to find the airplane, and they wanted to find you." West was frowning. "You mean to tell me that fellow had read the police report?"

"That's not so unusual," Cowboy said. "Not if he is the lawyer for somebody involved. Lawyers do that all the time if there's something they want to know."

"So he said he was the pilot's lawyer," West said. "What was his name?"

"Gaines," Chee said.

"What did he want to know?" West asked.

"He wanted to know what happened."

"Hell," West said. "Easy enough to see what happened. Fellow ran his airplane into a rock."

Chee shrugged.

"He wanted to know more than that?" West persisted.

"He wanted to find the car. The one that drove away after the crash."

"He figured it was still out there somewhere, then?"

"Seemed to," Chee said. He wanted to change the subject. "Either one of you heard any gossip about a witch killing a man out in Black Mesa somewhere?"

Cowboy laughed. "Sure," he said. "You remember that body was picked up last July—the one that was far gone?" Cowboy wrinkled his nose at the unpleasant memory.

"John Doe?" Chee asked. "A witch killed him? Where'd that come from?"

"And it was one of your Navajo witches," Dashee said. "Not one of our *powaqa.*"

10

COWBOY DASHEE DIDN'T KNOW MUCH about why the gossipers believed John Doe had been killed by a witch. But once he got over his surprise that Chee was sincerely interested, that Chee would attach importance to such a tale, he was willing to run the rumor to earth. They took Dashee's patrol car up Third Mesa to Bacobi. There Cowboy talked to the man who had passed the tale along to him. The man sent them over to Second Mesa to see a woman at Mishongovi. Dashee spent a long fifteen minutes in her house and came out smiling.

"Struck gold," Cowboy said. "We go to Shipaulovi."

"Find where the report started?" Chee asked.

"Better than that," Cowboy said. "We found the man who found the body."

Albert Lomatewa brought three straight-backed chairs out of the kitchen, and set them in a curved row just outside the door of his house. He invited them both to sit, and sat himself. He extracted a pack of cigarets, offered each of them a smoke, and smoked himself. The children who had been playing there (Lomatewa's great-grandchildren, Chee guessed) moved a respectful distance away and muted their raucous game. Lomatewa smoked, and listened while Deputy Sheriff Dashee talked. Dashee told him who Chee was, and that it was their job to identify the man who had been found on Black Mesa, and to find out who had shot him, and to learn everything they could about it. "There's been a lot of gossip about this man," Dashee said, speaking in English, "but we were told that if we came to Shipaulovi and talked to you about it, you would tell us the facts."

Lomatewa listened. He smoked his cigaret. He tapped the ash off on the ground beside his chair. He said, "It is true that there's nothing but gossip now. Nobody has any respect for anything anymore." Lomatewa reached behind him, his hand groped against the wall, found a walking cane which had been leaning there, and laid it across his legs. Last week he'd gone to Flagstaff with his granddaughter's husband, he told them, and visited another granddaughter there. "They all acted just like *bahanas*," Lomatewa said. "Drinking beer around the house. Laying in bed in the morning. Just like white people." Lomatewa's fingers played with the stick as he talked of the modernism he had found in his family at Flagstaff, but he was watching Jim Chee, watching Cowboy Dashee. Watching them skeptically. The performance, the attitude, were familiar. Chee had noticed it before, in his own paternal grandfather and in others. It had nothing to do with a Hopi talking of sensitive matters in front of a Navajo. It involved being on the downslope of your years, disappointed, and a little bitter. Lomatewa obviously knew who Cowboy was. Chee knew the deputy well enough to doubt he was a solidly orthodox Hopi. Lomatewa's statement had drifted into a complaint against the Hopi Tribal Council.

"We weren't told to do it that way," Lomatewa said. "The way it was supposed to be, the villages did their own business. The *kikmongwi,* and the societies, and the kiva. There wasn't any tribal council. That's a *bahana* idea."

Chee allowed the pause to stretch a respectful few moments. Cowboy leaned forward, raised a hand, opened his mouth.

Chee cut him off. "That's like what my uncle taught me," Chee said. "He said we must always respect the old ways. That we must stay with them."

Lomatewa looked at him. He smiled his skeptical smile. "You're a policeman for the *bahanas*," he said. "Have you listened to your uncle?"

"I am a policeman for my own people," Chee said. "And I am studying with my uncle to be a *yataalii*." He saw the Navajo word meant nothing to Lomatewa. "I am studying to be a singer, a medicine man. I know the Blessing Way, and the Night Chant, and someday I will know some of the other ceremonials."

Lomatewa examined Chee, and Cowboy Dashee, and Chee again. He took the cane in his right hand and made a mark with its tip in the dust. "This place is the spruce shrine," he said. He glanced at Cowboy. "Do you know where that is?"

"It is Kisigi Spring, Grandfather," said Cowboy, passing the test.

Lomatewa nodded. He drew a crooked line in the dust. "We came down from the spring at the dawn," he said. "Everything was right. But about midmorning we saw this boot standing there in the path. This boy who was with us said somebody had lost a boot, but you could see it wasn't that. If the boot had just fallen there, it would fall over on its side." He looked at Chee for agreement. Chee nodded.

Lomatewa shrugged. "Behind the boot was the body of the Navajo." He pursed his lips and shrugged again. The recitation was ended.

"What day was that, Grandfather?" Chee asked.

"It was the fourth day before the Niman Kachina," Lomatewa said.

"This Navajo," Chee said. "When we got the body, there wasn't much left. But the doctors said it was a man about thirty. A man who must have weighed about one hundred sixty pounds. Is that about right?"

Lomatewa thought about it. "Maybe a little older," he said. "Maybe thirty-two or so."

"Was it anyone you had seen before?" Cowboy asked.

"All Navajos—" Lomatewa began. He stopped, glanced at Chee. "I don't think so," he said.

"Grandfather," Cowboy said. "When you go for the sacred spruce, you use the same trail coming and going. That is what I have been taught. Could the body have been there under that brush the day before, when you went up to the spring?"

"No," Lomatewa said. "It wasn't there. The witch put it there during the night."

"Witch?" Cowboy Dashee asked. "Would it have been a Hopi *powaqa* or a Navajo witch?"

Lomatewa looked at Chee, frowning. "You said that you and this Navajo policeman got the body. Didn't he see what had been done?"

"When we got the body, Grandfather, the ravens had been there for days, and the coyotes, and the vultures," Cowboy said. "You could only tell it had been a man and that he had been dead a long time in the heat."

"Ah," Lomatewa said. "Well, his hands had been skinned." Lomatewa threw out his hands, palms up, demonstrating. "Fingers, palms, all. And the bottoms of his feet." He noticed Cowboy's puzzled surprise and nodded toward Chee. "If this Navajo respects his people's old ways, he will understand."

Chee understood, perfectly. "That's what the witch uses to make corpse powder," Chee explained to Cowboy. "They call it *anti'l.* You make it out of the skin that has the individual's soul stamped into it." Chee pointed to the fingerprint whorls on his fingertips and the pads of his hands. "Like on your palms, and fingers, and the soles of your feet, and the glans of your penis." As he explained, it occurred to Jim Chee that he could finally answer one of Captain Largo's questions. There was more than the usual witchcraft gossip on Black Mesa because there was a witch at work.

11

BY THE TIME CHEE DROVE BACK to Tuba City, typed up his report, and left it on Captain Largo's desk, it was after 9:00 P.M. By the time he let himself into his trailer house and lowered himself on the edge of his bunk, he felt totally used up. He yawned, scrubbed his forearm against his face, and slumped, elbows on knees, reviewing the day and waiting for the energy to get himself ready for bed. He had tomorrow off, and the day after. He would go to Two Gray Hills, to the country of his relatives in the Chuska Mountains, far from the world of police, and narcotics, and murder. He would heat rocks and take a sweat bath with his uncle, and get back to the job of mastering the sand paintings for the Night Chant. Chee yawned again and bent to untie his boot laces, and found himself thinking of John Doe's hands as the old Hopi had described them. Bloody. Flayed. In his own mind the only memory he could recall was of bones, sinew, and bits of muscle ends which had resisted decay and the scavengers. Something about what the Hopi had said bothered him. He thought about it and couldn't place the incongruity, and yawned again, and removed his boots. John Doe had died on the fourth day before the Niman Kachina, and this year the ceremonial had been held on July 14. He'd confirmed that with Dashee. So John Doe's body had been dumped onto the path on July 10. Chee lay back on the bunk, reached out, and fished the Navajo-Hopi telephone book off the table. It was a thin book, much bent from being carried in Chee's hip pocket, and it contained all telephone numbers in a territory a little larger than New England. Chee found the Burnt Water

Trading Post listed along with a dozen or so telephones on Second Mesa. He pushed himself up on one elbow and dialed it. It rang twice.

"Hello."

"Is Jake West there?"

"This is West."

"Jim Chee," Chee said. "How good is your memory?"

"Fair."

"Any chance you remembering if Musket was at work last July eleventh? That would have been four days before the Home Dances up on Second Mesa."

"July eleventh," West said. "What's up?"

"Probably nothing," Chee said. "Just running down dead ends on your burglary."

"Just a minute. I don't remember, but I'll have it written down in my payroll book."

Chee waited. He yawned again. This was wasting his time. He unbuckled his belt and slid out of his uniform pants and tossed them to the foot of the bed. He unbuttoned his shirt. Then West was back on the line.

"July eleventh. Let's see. He didn't show up for work July tenth or the eleventh. He showed up on the twelfth."

Chee felt slightly less sleepy.

"Okay," he said. "Thanks."

"That mean anything?"

"Probably not," Chee said.

It meant, he thought after he had removed the shirt and pulled the sheet over him, that Musket might have been the man who killed John Doe. It didn't mean he was the one—only that the possibility existed. Drowsily, Chee considered it. Musket possibly was a witch. The killing of John Doe possibly was the reason Musket had departed from the Burnt Water Trading Post. But Chee was too exhausted to pursue such a demanding exercise. He thought instead of Frank Sam Nakai, who was his maternal uncle and the most respected singer along the New Mexico–Arizona border. And thinking of this great shaman, this wise and kindly man, Jim Chee fell asleep.

When he awakened, there was Johnson standing beside his bunk, looking down at him.

"Time to wake up," Johnson said.

Chee sat up. Behind Johnson another man was standing, his back to Chee, sorting through the things Chee kept stored in one of the trailer's overhead compartments. The light of the rising sun was streaming through the open door.

"What the hell?" Chee said. "What are you doing to my trailer?"

"Some checking," Johnson said.

"Nothing here either," the man said.

"This is Officer Larry Collins," Johnson said, still looking at Chee. "He's my partner on this case." Officer Collins turned and looked at Chee. He grinned. He was perhaps twenty-five. Big. Unkempt blond hair dangled from under a dirty cowboy hat. His face was a mass of freckles, his eyes reckless. "Howdy," he said. "If you got any dope hidden around here, I haven't come up with it. Not yet."

Chee couldn't think of anything to say. Disbelief mixed with anger. This was incredible. He reached for his shirt, put it on, stood up in his shorts.

"Get the hell out of here," he said to Johnson.

"Not yet," Johnson said. "We're here on business."

"We'll do any business we have over at the office," Chee said. "Get out."

Collins was behind him now and it happened too quickly for Chee to ever know exactly how he did it. He found himself face down on the bunk, with his wrists twisted high behind his shoulders. He felt Johnson's hand pinning him while Collins snapped handcuffs on his wrists. It must have been something the two of them practiced, Chee thought.

They released him. Chee sat up on the bunk. His hands were cuffed behind him.

"We need to get something straight," Johnson said. "I'm the cop and you're the suspect. That Indian badge don't mean a damn thing to me."

Chee said nothing.

"Keep on looking," Johnson said to Collins. "It's got to be bulky and there can't be many places it could hide in here. Make sure you don't miss any of them."

"I haven't," Collins said. But he moved into the kitchen area and began opening drawers.

"You had a little meeting yesterday with Gaines," Johnson said. "I want to know all about that."

"Go screw yourself," Chee said.

"You and Gaines arranged a little deal, I guess. He told you what they'd be willing to pay to buy their coke back. And he told you what would happen to you if you didn't cough it up. That about right?"

Chee said nothing. Collins was looking in the oven, checking under the sink. He poured a little detergent into his palm, examined it, and rinsed it off under the tap. "I already looked everyplace once," Collins said.

"Maybe we're not going to find that coke stashed here," Johnson said. "Maybe we're not going to find the money here either. It don't look like you were that stupid. But by God you're going to tell me where to find it."

Johnson struck Chee across the face, a stinging, backhanded blow.

"The best way to do it would be unofficial," Johnson said. "You just tell me right now, and I forget where I heard it, and you can just go on being a Navajo cop. No going to jail. No nothing. We do a lot of unofficial business." He grinned at Chee, a wolfish show of big, even white teeth in a sunburned red face. "Get more work done that way."

Chee's nose hurt. He felt a trickle of blood start from it, moving down his lip. His face stung and his eyes were watering. But the real effect of the blow was psychological. His mind seemed detached from all this, working at several levels. At one, it was trying to remember the last time anyone had struck him. He had been a boy when that happened, fighting with a cousin. At another level his intelligence considered what he should do, what he should say, why this was happening. And at still another, he felt simple animal rage—an instinct to kill.

He and Johnson stared at each other, neither blinking. Collins finished in the kitchen and disappeared in the tiny bath. There was the noise of him taking something apart.

"Where is it?" Johnson asked. "The plane had the stuff on it, and the people who came to get it haven't got it. We know that. We know who took it, and we know he had to have some help, and we know you were it. Where'd you take it?"

Chee tested the handcuffs behind him, hurting his wrists. The muscles in his left shoulder were cramping where Collins had strained it. "You son of a bitch," Chee said. "You're crazy."

Johnson slapped him again. Same backhand. Same place.

"You were out there," Johnson said. "We don't know how you got onto the deal, but that doesn't matter. We just want the stuff."

Chee said nothing at all.

Johnson removed his pistol from its shoulder holster. It was a revolver with a short barrel. He jammed the barrel against Chee's forehead.

"You're going to tell me," Johnson said. He cocked the pistol. "Now."

The metal of the gun barrel pressed into the skin, hard against the bone. "If I knew where that stuff was, I'd tell you," Chee said. He was ashamed of it, but it was the truth. Johnson seemed to read it in his face. He grunted, removed the pistol, lowered the hammer, and stuck the gun back in the holster.

"You know something," Johnson said, as if to himself. He looked around at Collins, who had stopped his hunt to watch, and then stared at Chee again, thinking. "When you know a little more, there's a smart way for you to handle it. Just see to it that I get the word. An anonymous note would do it. Or call me. That way, if you don't trust the DEA not to hammer you, you'd know we couldn't prove you tried to steal the stuff. And I couldn't turn you in for killing Jerry Jansen."

Chee had his mind working again. He remembered Jansen was the body left at the plane. But how much would Johnson tell him?

"Who's Jansen?" he asked.

Johnson laughed. "Little late to ask," he said. "He's the brother of the big man himself, the one who put this all together. And the one killed on the airplane, he was big medicine, too. Relative of the people buying the shipment."

"Pauling?"

"Pauling was nothing," Johnson said. "The taxi driver. You worry about the other one."

There was the sound of breaking glass in the shower. Collins had dropped something.

"So you see, I haven't got much time to work with you," Johnson said. He was smiling. "You've got two sets of hard people stirred up. They're going to make the connection right away and they're going to be coming after you. They're going to twist that dope out of you and if you can't deliver it, they'll just keep twisting."

Chee could think of nothing helpful to say to that.

"The only way to go is the easy way," Johnson said. "You tell me where you and Palanzer put it. I find it. Nobody is any wiser. Any other way we handle it, you're dead. Or if you're lucky you get ten to twenty in the federal pen. And with those two people killed, you wouldn't last long in federal pen."

"I don't know where it is," Chee said. "I'm not even sure what it is."

Johnson looked at him, mildly and without comment. A smell of cologne seeped into Chee's nostrils. Collins had broken his aftershave lotion. "What did Gaines want?" Johnson said. He pulled Gaines's card out of his shirt pocket and looked at it. It had been in Chee's billfold.

"He wanted to know what happened to the car. The one I heard driving off."

"How'd he know about that?"

"He read my report. At the station. He told 'em he was the pilot's lawyer."

"Why'd he give you the card?"

"He wanted me to find the car for him. I said I'd let him know."

"Can you find it?"

"I don't see how," Chee said. "Hell, it's probably in Chicago by now, or Denver, or God knows where. Why would it stay around? From what I hear, you're circulating the picture of the guy that's supposed to be driving it. This Palanzer. Why would he stick around?"

"I'll ask the questions," Johnson said.

"But don't you think Palanzer got off with the stuff? Why else are you looking for him?"

"Maybe Palanzer got it and maybe he didn't, and maybe he had a lot of help if he did. Like a Navajo tribal cop who knows this country and knows a hole they can hide it in until things cool off some."

"But—"

"Shut up," Johnson said. "This is wasting time. I'll tell you what we're going to do. We're going to wait just a little while. Give you some time to think it over. I figure you've got a day or two before the people who own that dope decide to come after you. You give some thought to what they'll do to you and then you get in touch with me and we'll deal."

"One thing," Collins said from just behind Chee. "It damn sure ain't hid in here."

"But don't wait too long," Johnson said. "You haven't got much time."

12

WHEN CAPTAIN LARGO WORRIED, his round, bland face resolved itself into a pattern of little wrinkles—something like a brown honeydew melon too long off the vine. Largo was worried now. He sat ramrod straight behind his desk, an unusual position for the captain's plump body, and listened intently to what Jim Chee was saying. What Chee was saying was angry and directly to the point, and when he finished saying it, Largo got up from his chair and walked over to the window and looked out at the sunny morning.

"They pull a gun on you?" he asked.

"Right."

"Hit you? That right?"

"Right," Chee said.

"When they took off the cuffs, they told you that if you filed a complaint, their story would be you invited them in, invited them to search, they didn't lay a hand on you. That right?"

"That's it," Chee said.

Largo looked out the window some more. Chee waited. From where he stood he could see through the glass past the captain's broad back. He could see the expanse of bunch grass, bare earth, rocks, scattered cactus, which separated the police building from the straggling row of old buildings called Tuba City. The sky had the dusty look of a droughty summer. Far across the field a cloud of blue smoke emerged from the sheet-metal garage of the Navajo Road Department—a diesel engine being test run. Largo seemed to be watching the smoke.

"Two days, they said, before the people who owned the dope figured you had it. Right?"

"That's what Johnson said," Chee agreed.

"He sound like he was guessing, or like he knew?" Largo was still looking out the window, his face away from Chee.

"Of course he was guessing," Chee said. "How would he know?"

Largo came back and sat at the desk again. He fiddled with whatever odds and ends he kept in the top drawer.

"Here's what I want you to do," he said. "Write all this down and sign it, and date it, and give it to me. Then you take some time off. You got two days coming. Take a whole week. Get the hell away from here for a while."

"Write it down? What good will that do?"

"Good to have it," Largo said. "Just in case."

"Shit," Chee said.

"These white men got you screwed," Largo said. "Face it. You file a complaint. What happens? Two *belacani* cops. One Navajo. The judge is *belacani,* too. And the Navajo cop is already under suspicion of getting off with the dope. What good does it do you? Go back in the Chuskas. Visit your folks. Get away from here."

"Yeah," Chee said. He was remembering Johnson's hand stinging across his face. He would take time off, but he wouldn't go to the Chuskas. Not yet.

"These drug police, they're hard people," Largo said. "Don't work by the rules. Do what they want to do. I don't know what they're going to do next. Neither do you. Take your time off. This isn't our business. Get out of the way. Don't tell anybody where you're going. Good idea not to."

"Okay," Chee said. "I won't." He walked to the door. "One other thing, Captain. Joseph Musket didn't show up for work at Burnt Water the day John Doe was killed and dumped up on the mesa. Not that day or the day before. I want to go to Santa Fe—to the state pen—and see what I can find out about Musket. Will you set it up?"

"I read your report this morning," Largo said. "You didn't mention that."

"I called Jake West later. After it was written."

"You think Musket is a witch?"

Largo might have smiled very faintly when he asked it. Chee wasn't sure.

"I just don't understand Musket," Chee said. He shrugged.

"I'll get a letter off today," Largo said. "Meanwhile you're on vacation. Get away from here. And remember this drug case is none of our business. It's a federal felony. Where it happened, it's Hopi reservation now, not joint jurisdiction. It doesn't concern Navajo Tribal Police. It doesn't concern Jim Chee." Largo paused and looked directly at Chee. "You hear me?"

"I hear you," Chee said.

13

IT SEEMED TO CHEE, under the circumstances, that the wise and courteous thing to do was to make the telephone call from somewhere where there was no risk of Captain Largo's learning of it. He stopped at the Chevron station on the corner where the Tuba City road intersects with Arizona 160. He called the Hopi Cultural Center on Second Mesa.

Yes, Ben Gaines was registered at the motel. Chee let the telephone ring eight or nine times. Then placed the call again. Did they have a woman named Pauling registered? They did. She answered on the second ring.

"This is Officer Chee," Chee said. "You remember. The Navajo Tribal . . ."

"I remember you," Miss Pauling said.

"I'm trying to get hold of Ben Gaines," Chee said.

"I don't think he's in his room. The car he rented has been gone all day and I haven't seen him."

"When I talked to you, he wanted me to find a vehicle for him," Chee said. "Do you know if that's turned up yet?"

"Not that I've heard about. I don't think so."

"Would you tell Gaines I'm looking into it?"

"Okay," the woman said. "Sure."

Chee hesitated. "Miss Pauling?"

"Yes."

"Have you known Gaines a long time?"

There was a pause. "Three days," Miss Pauling said.

"Did your brother ever mention him?"

Another long pause.

"Look," Miss Pauling said. "I don't know what you're getting at. But no. That wasn't the sort of thing we talked about. I didn't know he had a lawyer."

"You think you should trust Gaines?"

In Chee's ear the telephone made a sound which might have passed for laughter. "You really are a policeman, aren't you," Miss Pauling said. "How do they teach you not to trust anybody?"

"Well," Chee said, "I was . . ."

"I know he knew my brother," Miss Pauling said. "And he called me and offered to help with everything. And then he came, and arranged to get the body brought back for the funeral, and told me what to do about getting a grave site in a national cemetery, and everything like that. Why shouldn't I trust him?"

"Maybe you should," Chee said.

Chee went home then. He put on his walking boots, got a fresh plastic gallon jug of ice out of the freezer and put it in his old canvas pack with a can of corned beef and a box of crackers. He stowed the bag and his bedroll behind the seat in his pickup and drove back down to the Chevron station. But instead of turning east toward New Mexico, the Chuska Mountains, and his family, he turned west and then southward on Navajo Route 3. Route 3 led past the cluster of Hopi stone huts which are Moenkopi village, into the Hopi Reservation, to Burnt Water Trading Post, and Wepo Wash, and that immensity of empty canyon country where a plane had crashed and a car might, or might not, have been hidden by a thin-faced man named Richard Palanzer.

14

THE FIRST THING CHEE LEARNED about the missing vehicle was that someone—and Chee guessed it was the Drug Enforcement Agency—had already searched for it. Chee had worked his way methodically down from the crash site, checking every point where a wheeled vehicle could have left the wash bottom. Since the walls of the wash were virtually vertical and rarely rose less than eighteen to twenty feet, these possible exit points were limited to arroyos which fed the wash. Chee had checked each of them carefully for tire tracks. He found none, but at every arroyo there were signs that he wasn't the first to have looked. Two men had done it, two or three days earlier. They had worked together, not separately—a fact taught by noticing that sometimes the man wearing the almost new boots stepped on the other's tracks, and sometimes it worked the other way. From the nature of this hunt, Chee surmised that if the truck, or car, or whatever it was, was hidden out here anywhere, it had to be someplace where it couldn't be found from the air. Whoever was looking this hard would certainly have used an airplane. That narrowed things down.

When it became too dark to work, Chee rolled out his bedroll, dined on canned meat, crackers, and cold water. He got his book of U.S. Geological Survey Quadrangle Maps of Arizona out of his truck and turned to page 34, the Burnt Water Quadrangle. The thirty-two-mile-square section was reduced to a twenty-four-inch square, but provided a map scale at least twenty times larger than a road map, and the federal surveyors had marked in every detail of terrain, elevation, and drainage.

Chee sat on the sand with his back against the bumper, using the truck headlights for illumination. He checked each arroyo carefully, coordinating what the map showed him with his memory of the landscape. Behind him, there was a sudden pinging sound—the sound of the pickup engine cooling. From beyond the splash of yellow light formed by the truck lights, an owl screeched out its hunting call, again, and again, and then lapsed into silence. All quiet. And now, faint and far away, somewhere south toward the Hopi Mesas, the purr of an aircraft engine. From Chee's own knowledge, only three of the arroyos that fed Wepo Wash drained areas where a car might easily be hidden. He had already checked the mouth of one and found no tracks. The other two were downstream, both draining into the wash from the northwest, off the slopes of the great eroded hump with the misleading name Big Mountain. Both would lead high enough to get into the big brush and timber country and into the steeper slopes where you could expect to find undercuts and overhangs. In other words, where something as large as a car might be hidden. Tomorrow he would skip down the wash and check them both.

And, he thought, find absolutely nothing. He would find that whoever the DEA was using as a tracker had been there first and had also found nothing. There would be nothing to find. A plane had flown in with a load of dope and a car had come to meet it. The dope had been taken out of the plane and the car had driven away with it. Why keep it out here in the Painted Desert? The only answer Chee could think of to that question led him to Joseph Musket. If Musket was making the decisions, keeping it here would make sense. But Musket was a third-level, minor-league police character involved in a very big piece of business. Richard Palanzer would be the man making the decisions—or at least giving the orders. Why wouldn't Palanzer simply haul the lead away to some familiar urban setting?

Or was he underestimating Joseph Musket? Was the young man they called Ironfingers more than he seemed to be? Was there a dimension in this which Chee hadn't guessed at? Chee considered the shooting of John Doe. Was this dead Navajo a loose end to something that Musket had taken the day off to tie up with a bullet? And if so, why leave the body out to be found? And why remove the parts a witch would use to make his corpse powder?

From the darkness beyond the range of the headlights he heard the sound of a dislodged pebble rolling down the wall of the wash. Then the sound of something scurrying. The desert was a nocturnal place—dead in the blinding light of sun but swarming with life in the darkness. Rodents came out of their burrows to feed on seeds, and the reptiles and other predators came out to hunt the rodents and each other. Chee yawned. From somewhere far back on Black Mesa he heard a coyote barking and from the opposite direction the faint purr of an aircraft engine. Chee reexamined the map, looking for anything he might have missed. His vandalized windmill was too new to have been marked, but the arroyo of the shrine was there. As Chee had guessed, it drained the slope of Second Mesa.

The plane was nearer now, its engine much louder. Chee saw its navigation lights low and apparently coming directly toward him. Why? Perhaps simple curiosity about why a car's lights would be burning out here. Chee scrambled to his feet, reached through the driver-side window, and flicked off the lights. A moment later the plane roared over, not a hundred yards off the ground. Chee stood for a moment, looking after it. Then he rerolled his blanket, and picked up his water jug, and walked up the arroyo. He found a place perhaps two hundred yards from the truck, where a cul-de-sac of smooth sand was screened from sight by a heavy growth of chamiso. He scooped out a depression for his hips, built a little mound of sand for his head, and rolled his blanket around this bed. Then he lay looking up at the stars. His uncle would tell him that wherever the car was driven, it was driven there for a reason. If it had been hidden out here, the act was a product of motivation. Chee could not think of what that motivation might be, but it must be there. If Palanzer had done this deed, as it seemed, he surely wouldn't have done it casually, without forethought and planning. He would have run for the city, for familiar territory, for a place where he could become quickly invisible, for a hideaway which he surely would have prepared. He'd want a safe place where he could keep the cargo until he could dispose of it. Hiding the car and the cargo out here made sense only if Musket was heavily involved. Musket must be involved. He would be the logical link between this isolated desert place and the narcotics business. Musket had been in the New Mexico prison on a narcotics conviction. He was a friend of West's son, probably he had visited here, probably he had seen Wepo Wash and remembered its possibilities as a very secret, utterly isolated landing strip. Musket had suggested it. Musket had used his old friendship to get a parolee job at Burnt Water so he could be on the site and complete the arrangements. That's where he had been when he was missing work at the trading post—up the wash, doing whatever had to be done to pave the way. But what in the world would there have been to do? Setting out the lanterns would have taken only a few minutes. Chee was worrying about that question when he drifted off to sleep.

He wasn't sure what awakened him. He was still on his back. Sometime during the night, without being aware of doing it, he had pulled the blanket partly over him. The air was chilly now. The stars overhead had changed. Mars and Jupiter had moved far down toward the western horizon and a late-rising slice of moon hung in the east. The darkness just before the dawn. He lay still, not breathing, straining to hear. He heard nothing. But a sort of memory of sound—a residue of whatever had awakened him—hung in his mind. Whatever it had been, it provoked fear.

He heard the sound of insects somewhere up the arroyo and down in Wepo Wash. Nothing at all nearby. That told him something. Something had quieted the insects. He could see nothing but the gray-green foliage of the chamiso bush, made almost black by the darkness. Then he heard the sighing sound of a breath exhaled. Someone was standing just beyond the bush, not eight feet away from him. Someone? Or something? A horse, perhaps? He'd noticed hoof marks in the wash bottom. And earlier he'd seen horses near the windmill. Horses tend to be noisy breathers. He strained to hear, and heard nothing. A man, most likely, just standing there on the other side of the bush. Why? Someone in the plane obviously had seen his truck.

Had they come, or sent someone, to check on him?

Click. From just beyond the bush. Click. Click. Click. Click. A small metallic sound. Chee couldn't identify it. Metal against metal? And then another exhalation of breath, and the sound of feet moving on the sand. Footsteps moving down the arroyo toward its intersection with the wash. Toward Chee's truck.

Chee rolled off the bedroll, careful not to make a sound. His rifle was on the rack across the back window of the truck. His pistol was in its holster, locked in the glove box. He raised his head cautiously above the bush.

The man was walking slowly away from him. He could only presume it was a man. A large shape, a little darker than the darkness surrounding it, a sense of slow movement. Then the movement stopped. A light flashed on—a yellow beam probing the boulders along the wall of the arroyo. The moving light silhouetted first the legs of whoever held the flashlight, then the right arm and shoulder and the shape of a pistol held, muzzle down, in the right hand. Then the light flicked off again. In the renewed darkness Chee could see only the shape of the yellow light imprinted on his iris. The shape of the man was lost to him. He ducked behind the chamiso again, waiting for vision to return.

When it did, the arroyo was empty.

Chee waited for the first dim light before he made his move for his truck. His first impulse was to abandon it. To slip away in the darkness and make the long walk back to the Burnt Water Trading Post and thereby avoid the risk that the man who had hunted him in the darkness was waiting for him at the truck. But as time ticked away, the urgency and reality of the danger diminished with it. Within an hour, what his instincts had told him of danger had faded along with the adrenaline it had pumped into his blood. What had happened was easy enough to read. Someone interested in recovering the drugs had rented a plane to keep an eye on the area. Chee's lights had been seen. Someone had been sent to find him and learn what he was doing. The pistol in hand was easily explained. The hunter was seeking the unknown in a strange and lonely darkness. He was nervous. He would have seen Chee's rifle on its rear-window rack but he'd have had no way of knowing Chee's pistol was locked away.

Even so, Chee was cautious. He moved along the arroyo rim to a point where he could look down at the truck. He spent a quarter of an hour sitting in the shelter of the rocks there, watching for any sign of movement. All he saw was a burrowing owl returning from its nocturnal hunt to its hole in the bank across from him. The owl scouted the truck and the area around it. If it saw anything dangerous, it showed no sign of it until it saw Chee. Then it shied violently away. That was enough for Jim Chee. He got up and walked to the truck.

With his pistol back on his belt, Chee checked the area around the arroyo mouth to confirm what the burrowing owl had told him. Nothing human was watching the area. Then he took a look at the tracks his hunter had left. The man wore boots with worn waffle soles, the same soles he'd noticed at the site of the crash. Someone in these same boots had placed the fatal lanterns. He'd approached the truck from downwash, left tracks all around it, and then walked almost a half mile up the arroyo and back again. Finally he'd left the way he had come.

Chee spent the rest of the morning examining the two downwash arroyos which the map suggested might have offered hiding places for a car. Nothing that left tire tracks had gone up either of them. He sat in the truck cab, finished the last of his crackers with the last of his water, and thought it all through again. Then he went back to both arroyos, walked a half mile up from their mouths, and made an intensive hands-and-knees spot check of likely places. Nothing. That eliminated the possibility that Palanzer, or Musket, or whoever was driving, had done a thorough and meticulous job of wiping out tracks at the turn-in point. With that out of the way, he drove back up to the arroyo where he'd spent the night.

Once it had been his favorite prospect. But he'd written it off, just as he had first written off the downstream arroyos when he'd found no trace of tracks at the mouth. Now he intended to be absolutely sure, and when he was finished, he would be equally sure that no car was hidden up Wepo Wash. Chee skipped the first hundred yards, which he'd already studied fruitlessly. Upstream the arroyo had cut through an extensive bed of hard-packed caliche. Here there were only occasional pockets of sand and Chee inspected those which couldn't have been avoided by a wheeled vehicle. He took his time. He found lizard tracks, and the trail left by a rattlesnake, the tiny paw marks of kangaroo rats, the marks left by birds and a variety of rodents. No tire marks. At a broad expanse of packed sand another hundred yards upstream, he made the same sort of check. Here he found a scratch curving across the sandy surface. Parallel with it were other lines, almost invisible. Chee squatted on his heels, looking. What had caused this? A porcupine might have dragged his tail across here. But this wasn't porcupine country. It would starve a porcupine.

Chee reached behind him, broke a limb off a growth of rabbit bush. He swept it across the sand. It produced a half-dozen scratches and a pattern of tiny parallel furrows. Chee examined them. Given a week for wind and gravity to soften their edges, these furrows would look much like what he had found. The sand had been swept.

Chee walked rapidly up-arroyo with hardly a glance at its bed. Sooner or later whoever had done the sweeping would have run out of time, or of patience, and decided enough had been done. About a thousand yards later, he found where that had happened.

He noticed the broom first. It was dried now, its color changed from its normal gray-green to gray-white, which made it instantly visible in the growth of healthy brush where it had been thrown. Chee salvaged it, inspected it, and confirmed that it had been used as a broom, then he tossed it away.

He found tire tracks at the next stretch of sand. They were faint, but they were unmistakable. Chee dropped to his hands and knees and studied the pattern of marks. He matched them in his memory with the tracks he had seen at the site of the wreckage. They were the same tread pattern.

Chee rocked back on his heels, pushed his hat off his forehead, and wiped away the sweat. He had found the invisible car. Unless it could fly, it was somewhere up this arroyo.

15

AFTER THAT there was no need for tracking. Chee paused only to check the few places where small gullies drained into the arroyo, places which might conceivably provide an exit route. He walked steadily up-arroyo toward the Black Mesa. The arroyo wound through increasingly rough country, its bed narrowing, becoming increasingly rocky and brush-choked. At places now the vehicle had left a trail of broken branches. Late in the afternoon, Chee heard the airplane again, droning miles away over the place where he had left his truck parked. When it approached up the arroyo he stood out of sight under an overhang of brush until it disappeared.

It was just sundown when he found the vehicle, and then he almost walked past it. He was tired. He was thirsty. He was thinking that within another hour it would be too dark to see. He saw not the vehicle itself but the broken brush it had left in its wake. Its driver had turned it up a narrow gully that fed the arroyo, forced it into a tangle of mountain mahogany and salt brush, and closed the growth as well as possible behind it.

It was a dark-green GMC carryall, apparently new. In a little while Chee would find out if it was loaded with cocaine, or perhaps with bales of currency intended to pay for cocaine. But there was no hurry. He took a moment to think. Then he scouted the area carefully, looking for tracks. If he could find the tracks of waffle soles and of cowboy boots, it would confirm what he already knew—that those men had driven away in the car he'd heard leaving. The area around the carryall was a mat of leaves and twigs, and the gully bottom was granular decomposed granite where it wasn't solid rock. Impossible for tracking. Chee found scuff marks but nothing he could identify.

The carryall was locked, its windows rolled all the way up, and totally fogged with interior moisture. With a sealed vehicle, some such fogging was usual, even in this arid climate, but these windows were opaque. There must be some source of moisture locked inside. Chee sat on a boulder and considered what to do.

Not only wasn't this his case; he'd been specifically warned away from it by the people whose case it was. Not only had he been warned off by the feds; Captain Largo had personally and specifically ordered him to keep clear of it. If he broke into the carryall, he'd be tampering with evidence.

Chee took out a cigaret, lit it, and exhaled a plume of smoke. The sun was down now, reflecting from a cloud formation over the desert to the south. It added a reddish tint to the light. To the northwest, a thundercloud that had been building over the Coconino Rim had reached the extreme altitude where its boiling upcurrents could no longer overcome the bitter cold and the thinness of the air. Its top had flattened and been spread by stratospheric winds into a vast fan of ice crystals. The sunset striped the cloud in three color zones. The top several thousand feet were dazzling white—still reflecting the direct sunlight and forming a blinding contrast against the dark-blue sky. Lower, the cloud mass was illuminated by reflected light. It was a thousand shades of pink, rose, even salmon. And below that, where not even reflected light could reach, the color ranged from dirty gray to blue-black. There, lightning flickered. In the Hopi villages the people were calling the clouds. It was already raining on the Coconino Rim. And the storm was moving eastward, as summer storms always did. With any luck, rain would be falling here within two hours. Just a little rain—just a shower—would wipe out tracks in this sandy country. But Chee was desert-bred. He never really believed rain would fall.

He took a long drag off the cigaret, savored the taste of the smoke, exhaled it slowly through his nostrils, watched the blue haze dissipate. He was thinking of Chee in the grand jury room, under oath, the Assistant U.S. District Attorney staring at him. "Officer Chee, I want to remind you of the penalty for perjury; for lying under oath. Now I want to ask you directly: Did you, or did you not, locate the GMC carryall in which . . ." Chee switched from that thought to another. The memory of Johnson smiling at him, Johnson's hand stinging across his face, Johnson's voice, threatening. Anger returned, and shame. He inhaled another lungful of smoke, putting anger aside. Anger was beside the point. The point was the puzzle. Here before his eyes was another piece of it. Chee stubbed out the cigaret. He put the remains carefully in his pocket.

Jimmying the wing window would have been easy with a screwdriver. With Chee's knife it took longer. Even shaded as the vehicle was, the day's heat had built up inside, and when the leverage of the steel blade broke the seal, pressurized air escaped with a sighing sound. The odor surprised him. It was a strong chemical smell. The heavy, sickish smell of disinfectant. Chee slid his hand through the wing, flicked up the lock, and opened the door.

Richard Palanzer was sitting on the back seat. Chee recognized him instantly from the photograph Cowboy had shown him. He was a smallish white man, with rumpled iron-gray hair, close-set eyes, and a narrow bony face over which death and desiccation had drawn the skin tight. He was wearing a gray nylon jacket, a white shirt, and cowboy boots. He leaned stiffly against the corner of the back seat, staring blindly at the side window.

Chee looked at him through the open door, engulfed by the escaping stench of disinfectant. The smell was Lysol, Chee guessed. Lysol fog and death. Chee's stomach felt queasy. He controlled it. There was something funny about the man's left eye, an odd sort of distortion. Chee eased himself into the front seat, careful of what he touched. At close range he could see the man's left contact lens had slipped down below the pupil. Apparently he had been shot where he sat. On the left side, from just above the waist, both jacket and trousers were black with dried blood, and the same blackness caked the seat and the floor mat.

Chee searched the carryall, careful not to smudge old fingerprints or to leave new ones. The glove box was unlocked. It contained an operating manual and the rental papers from the Hertz office at Phoenix International Airport. The vehicle had been rented to Jansen. Cigaret butts in the ashtray. Nothing else. No bundles of hundred-dollar bills. No great canvas sacks filled with dope. Nothing except the corpse of Richard Palanzer.

Chee rolled the side vent shut as tightly as he could, reset the door lock and slammed it shut. The vehicle was left exactly as he had found it. A careful cop would notice the vent had been forced, but maybe there wouldn't be a careful cop on the job. Maybe there wouldn't be any reason for suspicion. Or maybe there would be. Either way, there was nothing he could do about it. And if the pattern continued, he could count on the feds screwing things up.

He walked back down the arroyo in the thickening darkness. He was tired. He was nauseated. He was sick of death. He wished he knew a lot more than he did about Joseph Musket. Now he was all there was left. Ironfingers alive, and four men dead, and a fortune in narcotics missing.

"Ironfingers, where are you?" Chee said.

16

THE MAN WHO ANSWERED the telephone at the Coconino County Sheriff's Office in Flagstaff said wait a minute and he'd check. The minute stretched into three or four. And then the man reported that Deputy Sheriff Albert Dashee was supposed to be en route to Moenkopi—which was good news for Jim Chee since Moenkopi was only a couple of miles from the telephone booth he was calling from, at the Tuba City Chevron station. He climbed into his pickup truck, and rolled down U.S. 160 to the intersection of Navajo 3. He pulled off at a place from which he could look down into the patchy Hopi cornfields along the bottom of Moenkopi Wash and onto the little red stone villages, and at every possible route Cowboy Dashee could take if he was going anywhere near Moenkopi. Chee turned off the ignition, and waited. While he waited he rehearsed what he would say to Cowboy, and how he would say it.

Cowboy's white patrol car drove by, stopped, backed up, stopped again beside Chee's truck.

"Hey, man," Cowboy said. "I thought you were on vacation."

"That was yesterday," Chee said. "Today I'm wondering if you've caught your windmill vandal yet."

"One of the Gishis," Cowboy said. "I know it. You know it. Everybody knows it. Trouble is, all Navajos look alike, so we don't know who to arrest."

"In other words, no luck. No progress," Chee said.

Cowboy turned off his ignition, lit a cigaret, relaxed. "Tell you the truth," he said, "I been sort of laying back on that one. Wanted to see how you could do with not much help."

"Or maybe not any help?"

Cowboy laughed. He shook his head. "Nobody's ever going to catch that son of a bitch," he said. "How you going to catch him? No way."

"How about your big drug business?" Chee said. "Doing any good?"

"Nothing," Cowboy said. "Not that I know of, anyway. But that's a biggy. The sheriff and the undersheriff, they're handling that one themselves. Too big a deal for just a deputy."

"They take you off of it?"

"Oh, no," Cowboy said. "Sheriff had me in yesterday, wanting me to tell him where they had the stuff hid. He figured I'm Hopi, and it happened on the Hopi Reservation, so I gotta know."

"If it happened in Alaska, he'd ask an Eskimo," Chee said.

"Yeah," Cowboy said. "I just told him you probably got off with it. Reminded him you were out there when it happened, had your truck and all. They ought to look in the back of your truck."

The conversation was going approximately in the direction Chee wanted to take it. He adjusted it slightly.

"I think they already have," he said. "I didn't tell you about the DEA people talking to me. They had about the same idea."

Cowboy looked startled. "Hell they did," he said. "Seriously?"

"Sounded serious," Chee said. "Serious enough so Largo reminded me about Navajo Police not having jurisdiction. Warned me to stay completely away from it."

"He don't want you distracted from our windmill," Cowboy said. "The crime of the century."

"Trouble is, I think I can guess where they put that car the feds are looking for."

Cowboy looked at him. "Oh, yeah?"

"It's up one of those arroyos. If it's out there at all, that's where it is."

"No it ain't," Cowboy said. "The sheriff was talking about

that. The DEA and the FBI had that idea, too. They checked them all."

Chee laughed.

"I know what you mean," Cowboy said. "But I think they did a pretty good job this time. Looked on the ground, and flew up and down 'em in an airplane."

"If you were hiding a car, you'd hide it where an airplane couldn't see it. Under an overhang. Under a tree. Cover it up with brush."

"Sure," Cowboy said. He was looking at Chee thoughtfully, his elbow propped on the sill of the car window, chin resting on the heel of his hand. "What makes you think you could find it?"

"Look here," he said, motioning to Cowboy. He dug his Geological Survey map book out from beneath the seat.

Cowboy climbed out of his patrol car and climbed into Chee's truck. "I need me a book of those," he said. "But the sheriff would be too tight to pay for 'em."

"You're hiding a car," Chee said. "Okay. God knows why, but you're hiding it. And you know the law's going to be looking for it. The law has airplanes, helicopters, all that. So you've got to get it someplace where it can't be seen from the air."

Cowboy nodded.

"So what do you have?" Chee ran his finger down the crooked blue line which marked Wepo Wash on the map. "He drove down the wash. No tracks going up. Personally, I'd bet he drove right down here to where it goes under the highway bridge, and then drove off to Los Angeles. But the feds don't think so, and the feds have got some way of knowing things they aren't telling us Indians about. So maybe he did hide his car. So where did he hide it? It's not in the wash. I'd have seen it. Maybe you'd have seen it." Chee made a doubtful face. "Maybe even the feds would have seen it. So it's not in the wash. And it's somewhere between where the plane crashed and the highway. Gives you twenty-five miles or so. And it gives you three arroyos which are cut back into country where you've got enough brush and trees and overhang so you could hide a car." He pointed out the three, and glanced at Cowboy.

Cowboy was interested. He leaned over the map, studying it.

"You agree?"

"Yeah," Cowboy said slowly. "Those other ones don't go anywhere."

"These two lead back into the Big Mountain Mesa," Chee said. "This one leads into Black Mesa. In fact, it leads back up toward Kisigi Spring. Back up toward where we found John Doe's body dumped."

Cowboy was studying the map. "Yeah," he said.

"So if Largo hadn't promised to break my arm and fire me if I didn't stay away from this, that's where I'd be looking."

"Trouble is, they already looked," Cowboy said. But he didn't sound convinced.

"I can see it. They drive along the wash and when they get to an arroyo, somebody gets out and looks around for tire tracks. They don't find any, so he climbs back in and drives along to the next one. Right?"

"Yeah," Cowboy said.

"So if you're going to hide the car, what do you do? You think that if you leave tracks they're going to just follow them and find you. So you turn up the arroyo, and you get out, and you take your shirttail or something, and you brush out your tracks for a little ways."

Cowboy was looking at Chee.

"I don't know how hard the feds looked," Cowboy said. "Sometimes they're not the smartest bastards in the world."

"Look," Chee said. "If by chance that car does happen to be hidden out in one of those arroyos, you damn sure better keep quiet about this. Largo'd fire my ass. He was sore. He said I wasn't going to get a second warning."

"Hell," Cowboy said. "He wouldn't fire you."

"I mean it," Chee said. "Leave me out of it."

"Hell," Cowboy said. "I'm like you. That car's long gone by now."

It was time to change the subject. "You got any windmill ideas for me?" Chee asked.

"Nothing new," Cowboy said. "What you've got to do is convince Largo that there's no way to protect that windmill short of putting three shifts of guards on it." He laughed. "That, or getting a transfer back to Crownpoint."

Chee turned on the ignition. "Well, I better get moving."

Cowboy opened the door, started to get out, stopped. "Jim," he said. "You already found that car?"

Chee produced a chuckle. "You heard what I said. Largo said keep away from that case."

Cowboy climbed out and closed the door behind him. He leaned on the sill, looking in at Chee. "And you wouldn't do nothing that the captain told you not to?"

"I'm serious, Cowboy. The DEA climbed all over Largo. They think I was out there that night to meet the plane. They think I know where that dope shipment is. I'm not kidding you. It's absolutely goddamn none of my business. I'm staying away from it."

Cowboy climbed into his patrol car, started the engine. He looked back at Chee. "What size boots you wear?"

Chee frowned. "Tens."

"Tell you what I'll do," Cowboy said. "If I see any size ten footprints up that arroyo, I'll just brush 'em out!"

17

BLACK MESA IS NEITHER BLACK nor a mesa. It is far too large for that definition—a vast, broken plateau about the size and shape of Connecticut. It is virtually roadless, almost waterless, and uninhabited except for an isolated scattering of summer herding camps. It rises out of the Painted Desert more than seven thousand feet. A dozen major dry washes and a thousand nameless arroyos drain away runoff from its bitter winters and the brief but torrential "male rains" of the summer thunderstorm season. It takes its name from the seams of coal exposed in its towering cliffs, but its colors are the grays and greens of sage, rabbit brush, juniper, cactus, grama and bunch grass, and the dark green of creosote brush, mesquite, piñon, and (in the few places where springs flow) pine and spruce. It is a lonely place even in grazing season and has always been territory favored by the Holy People of the Navajo and the kachinas and guarding spirits of the Hopis. Masaw, the bloody-faced custodian of the Fourth World of the Hopis, specifically instructed various clans of the Peaceful People to return there when they completed their epic migrations and to live on the three mesas which extend like great gnarled fingers from Black Mesa's southern ramparts. Its craggy cliffs are the eagle-collection grounds of the Hopi Flute, Side Corn, Drift Sand, Snake, and Water clans. It is dotted with shrines and holy places. For Chee's people it was an integral part of Dinetah, where Changing Woman taught the Dinee they must live in the beauty of the Way she and the Holy People taught them.

Chee was familiar with only a little of the eastern rim of this sprawling highland. As a boy, he had been taken westward by Hosteen Nakai from Many Farms into the Blue Gap country to collect herbs and minerals at the sacred places for the Mountain Way ceremony. Once they had gone all the way into Dzilidushzhinih Peaks, the home of Talking God himself, to collect materials for Hosteen Nakai's *jish,* the bundle of holy things a shaman must have to perfect his curing rituals. But Dzilidushzhinih was far to the east. The camp of Fannie Musket, the mother of Joseph Musket, was near the southern edge of the plateau, somewhere beyond the end of the trail that wandered southward from the Cottonwood day school toward Balakai Point. It was new country to Chee, without landmarks that meant anything to him, and he'd stopped at the trading post at Cottonwood to make sure the directions he'd gotten earlier made sense. The skinny white woman running the place had penciled him a map on the page of a Big Chief writing tablet. "If you stay on that track that leads past Balakai arroyo you can't miss it," the woman said. "And you can't get off the track or you'll tear the bottom outa your truck." She laughed. "Matter of fact, if you're not careful you tear it out even if you stay on the track." On his way out Chee noticed "Fannie Musket" scrawled in chalk on the red paint of a new fifty-gallon oil drum which sat on the porch beside the front door. He went back in.

"This barrel belong to the Muskets?"

"Hey," the woman said. "That's a good idea. You want to haul that out for them? They're dried up out there and they're hauling water and they had me get 'em another drum."

"Sure," Chee said. He loaded it into the back of his pickup, rolled the truck to the overhead tank that held the post's water supply, rinsed out the drum, and filled it.

"Tell Fannie I put the barrel on her pawn ticket," the woman said. "I'll put the water on there, too."

"I'll get the water," Chee said.

"Two dollars," the woman said. She shook her head. "If it don't rain we ain't going to have any to sell."

Fannie Musket was glad to get the water. She helped Chee rig the block and tackle to lift the barrel onto a plank platform where two other such barrels sat. One was empty and when

Chee tapped his knuckles against the other, the sound suggested no more than ten gallons left.

"Getting hard to live out here," Mrs. Musket said. "Seems like it don't rain anymore." She glanced up at the sky, which was a dark, clear blue with late summer's usual scattering of puffy clouds building up here and there. By midafternoon they would have built up to a vain hope of a thundershower. By dark, both clouds and hope would have dissipated.

Chee and Mrs. Musket had introduced themselves, by family, by kinship, and by clan. (She was Standing Rock, born for the Mud Clan.) He had told Mrs. Musket that he hoped she would talk to him about her son.

"You are hunting for him," she said. Navajo is a language which loads its meanings into its verbs. She used the word which means "to stalk," as a hunted animal, and not the form which means "to search for," as for someone lost. The tone was as accusing as the word.

Chee changed the verb. "I search for him," Chee said. "But I know I will not find him here. I am told he is a smart man. He would not come here while we search for him, and even if he had, I would not ask his mother to tell me where to find him. I just want to learn what kind of a man he is."

"He is my son," Mrs. Musket said.

"Did he come home after they let him out of the prison? Before he went to work at Burnt Water?"

"He came home. He wanted to have an Enemy Way done for him. He went to see Tallman Begay and hired Hosteen Begay to be the singer for it. And then after the sing, he went to Burnt Water."

"It was the right thing to do," Chee said. It was exactly what he would have done himself. Purified himself from prison, and all the hostile, alien ways the prison represented. The character of Joseph Musket took on a new dimension.

"Why do you come to ask me questions this time? Before, another policeman came."

"That's because the police station at Chinle is closer," Chee explained. "A policeman came from there to save money and time."

"Then why do you come now?"

"Because there are many odd things about that burglary," Chee said. "Many questions I can't answer. I am curious."

"Do you know my son did not steal that pawn?"

"I don't know who stole it," Chee said.

"I know he didn't. Do you know why? Because he had money!" Mrs. Musket said it triumphantly. The ultimate proof.

"There are people among the *belacani* who steal even when they don't need to steal," Chee said.

Mrs. Musket's expression was skeptical. The concept was totally foreign to her.

"He had hundred-dollar bills," she said. "Many of them." She held up six fingers. "And other money in his purse. Twenty-dollar bills." She looked at Chee quizzically, waiting for him to concede that no one with hundred-dollar bills could be suspected of stealing. Certainly no Navajo would be likely to.

"He had this money when he first got here?"

Mrs. Musket nodded. "He wrote us that he was coming and my husband took the pickup truck on the day and drove out to Window Rock to meet the bus. He had all that money then."

Chee was trying to remember what prisoners were given when they left the penitentiary. Twenty dollars, he thought. That and whatever they might have in the canteen fund. A maximum of another fifty dollars, he suspected.

"It doesn't sound like he would steal the jewelry if he had all that money," Chee said. "But where did he go? Why doesn't he talk to us and tell us he didn't steal it?"

Mrs. Musket wasn't going to answer that question. Not directly at least. Finally she said, "They put him in prison once."

"Why was that?"

"He made bad friends," Mrs. Musket said.

Chee asked for a drink of water, got it, drank it, changed the subject. They talked of desperate difficulties of sheepherding in a drought. All her sons-in-law were out with their herds, as was her husband, and now they had to drive them so far for grass and water that they could not return to their hogans at night. The women took them food. And already they had lost eleven lambs and even some of the ewes were dying. With Chee guiding it, the conversation gradually edged back to Joseph

Musket. He had always been good with sheep. A careful hand with the shears, adept at castration. Reliable. A good boy. Even when he had been thrown from his horse and smashed his fingers and had to wear metal splints for so long, he could still shear faster than most young men. And he had told her that when he finished working at Burnt Water—by the end of summer—he would have plenty of money to buy his own herd. A big herd. He planned to buy two hundred ewes. But first he would go to all the squaw dances, find himself a young woman to marry. Someone whose family had plenty of grazing rights.

"He said that after he worked for the trading post a little while he didn't want to have anything else to do with the white men after that," Mrs. Musket said. "He said he only had one white man who had ever been a friend, and that all the others just got you in trouble."

"Did he say who the friend was?"

"It was a boy he knew when he went to the Cottonwood school," Mrs. Musket said. "I can't remember what he called him."

"Was it West?" Chee asked.

"West," Mrs. Musket said. "I think so."

"Does he have any other friends? Navajo friends?"

Mrs. Musket examined Chee thoughtfully. "Just some young men around here," she said vaguely. "Maybe some friends he made when he was away with the white people. I don't think so."

Chee could think of nothing more to ask. Not with any hope of getting an answer. He gave Mrs. Musket the message about the cost of the water barrel being added to her pawn ticket and climbed back in the truck.

Mrs. Musket stood in the yard of the hogan, watching him. Her hands clasped together at her waist, twisting nervously.

"If you find him," she said, "tell him to come home."

18

CHEE SPENT THE NEXT DAY as Largo had arranged, a long way from Tuba City and Wepo Wash. He drove fifty miles north toward the Utah border to see a woman named Mary Joe Natonabah about her complaint that her grazing right on Twenty-nine Mile Wash was being trespassed by somebody else's sheep. She identified the trespasser as an old man called Largewhiskers Begay, who had his camp in the Yondots Mountains. That took Chee to Cedar Ridge Trading Post and down the horrible dirt road which leads westward toward the Colorado River gorge. He found the Begay camp, but not Largewhiskers, who had gone to Cameron to see about something or other. The only person at the camp was a surly young man with his arm in a cast, who identified himself as the son-in-law of Largewhiskers Begay. Chee told this young man of the Natonabah complaint, warned him of the consequences of violating another person's grazing right, and told him to tell Largewhiskers he'd be back one day to check it all out. By then it was noon. Chee's next job took him to Nipple Butte, where a man named Ashie McDonald had reportedly beaten up his cousin. Chee found the camp but not Ashie McDonald. McDonald's mother-in-law reported that he'd got a ride down to Interstate 40 and was hitchhiking into Gallup to visit some relatives. The mother-in-law claimed to know nothing of any beating, any fight, any cousin. By then it was a little after 4:40 P.M. Chee was now sixty miles as the raven flew, ninety miles by unpaved back roads, or 130 miles via the paved highway from his trailer at Tuba City. He took the more direct dirt route. It wandered northeast across the Painted Desert, past Newberry Mesa, and Garces Mesa, and Blue Point, and Padilla Mesa. The country was dead with drought, no sign of sheep, no trace of green. He was off duty now, and he drove slowly, thinking what he would do. This route would take him through the Hopi villages of Oraibi, Hotevilla, and Bacobi, and near the Hopi Cultural Center. He would stop at the café there for his supper. He would learn if Ben Gaines was still in the motel, or the Pauling woman. If Gaines was there, Chee would see what he could learn from him. Maybe he would tell Gaines where to find the car. Most likely he wouldn't. Cowboy had two days to get there and find it, but maybe something had interfered. Most likely he wouldn't risk telling Gaines yet. He'd tell him only enough to determine if he could learn anything from the lawyer.

The parking area at the Hopi Cultural Center held about a dozen vehicles—more than usual, Chee guessed, because the upcoming ceremonials were beginning to draw tourists. Or was it that a missing cocaine shipment was beginning to draw in the hunters? Before he parked, Chee circled the motel, looking for the car Gaines had been driving. He didn't find it.

In the restaurant he took a table beside one of the west windows, ordered a bowl of what the menu called Hopi Stew, and coffee. The Hopi girl who served it was maybe twenty, and pretty, with her hair cut in the short bangs that old-fashioned Hopis wore. She had dazzled the group of tourists at the next table with her smile. With Chee, she was strictly business. The Hopi dealing with the Navajo. Chee sipped his coffee, and studied the other dining room patrons, and thought of the nature of the drought, and where Ironfingers Musket might be, and of ethnic antagonisms. This one was part abstraction, built into the Hopi legends of warfare: The enemy killed by the Hopi Twin War Gods were Navajo, as the enemy killed by the Navajo Holy People were Utes, or Kiowas, or Taos Indians. But the long struggle over the Joint Use Reservation lands lent a sort of reality to the abstraction in the minds of some. Now, at last, the U.S. Supreme Court had ruled, and the Hopis had won, and 9,000 Navajos were losing the only homes their families could remember. And the anger lingered, even among the winners.

The windowpane beside him reflected red. The sun had gone down behind the San Francisco Peaks and turned the bottom of the clouds that hung over it a luminous salmon-pink. The mountain, too, was contested territory. For the Hopis, it was Mount Sinai itself—the home of the kachina spirits from August until February, when they left this world and returned underground where the spirits live. For Chee's people it was also sacred. It was Evening Twilight Mountain, one of the four mountains First Man had built to mark the corners of Dinetah. It was the Mountain of the West, the home of the great *yei* spirit, Abalone Girl, and the place where the Sacred Bear of Navajo legend had been so critically wounded by the Bow People that the ritual songs described him as being "fuzzy with arrows"—verbal imagery which had caused Chee as a child to think of the spirit as looking like a gigantic porcupine. The mountain now was outlined blue-black against a gaudy red horizon and the beauty of it lifted Chee's mood.

"Mr. Chee."

Miss Pauling was standing beside his table.

Chee stood.

"No. Don't get up. I wanted to talk to you."

"Why don't you join me?" Chee said.

"Thank you," she said. She looked tired and worried. It would be better, Chee thought, if she looked frightened. She shouldn't be here. She should have gone home. He signaled for the waitress. "I can recommend the stew," he said.

"Have you seen Mr. Gaines?" she asked.

"No," Chee said. "I haven't tried his room, but I didn't see his car."

"He's not here," she said. "He's been gone since yesterday morning."

"Did he say where he was going?" Chee asked. "Or when he'd be back?"

"Nothing," Miss Pauling said.

The waitress came. Miss Pauling ordered stew. The reflection from the fiery sunset turned her face red, but it looked lined and old.

"You should go home," Chee said. "Nothing you can do here."

"I want to find out who killed him," she said.

"You'll find out. Sooner or later the DEA, or the FBI, they'll catch them."

"Do you think so?" Miss Pauling asked. The tone suggested she doubted it.

So did Chee. "Well, probably not," he said.

"I want you to help me find out," she said. "Just whatever you can tell me. Like things that the police know that don't get into the newspapers. Do they have any suspects? Surely they must. Who do they suspect?"

Chee shrugged. "At one time they suspected a man named Palanzer. Richard Palanzer. I think he was one of the people the dope was being delivered to."

"Richard Palanzer," Miss Pauling said, as if she was memorizing it.

"However," Chee said. He stopped. He'd been out of touch all day. Had Cowboy found the car? Was it known that Palanzer was no longer a suspect? Almost certainly.

"He was flying in narcotics, then," Miss Pauling said. "Is that what they think?"

"Seems to be," Chee said.

"And Palanzer was supposed to pay for it, and instead he killed him. Was that the way it went? Who is this Palanzer? Where does he live? I know there are times when the police know who did something but they can't find the evidence to prove it. I'd just like to know who did it."

"Why?" Chee asked. He wanted to know, too, because he was curious. But that wasn't her reason.

"Because I loved him," she said. "That's the trouble. I really loved him."

The stew arrived. Miss Pauling stirred it absently. "There was no reason for killing him," she said, watching the spoon. "They could have just pointed a gun at him and he would have given it to them with no trouble at all. He would have just thought it was funny."

"I guess they didn't know that," Chee said.

"He was always such a happy boy," she said. "Everything was fun for him. I'm five years older and when our mother left . . . You know how it is—I sort of took care of him until Dad remarried."

Chee said nothing. He was wondering why it was so important for her to know who was to blame. There was a puzzle here to be solved, but after that, what did it matter?

"There was no reason to kill him," she said. "And whoever did it is going to suffer for it." She said it with no particular emphasis, still moving the spoon mechanically through the well-stirred stew. "They're not going to kill him and just walk away from it."

"But sometimes they do," Chee said. "That's the way it is."

"No," she said. The tone was suddenly vehement. "They won't get away with it. You understand that?"

"Not exactly," Chee said.

"Do you understand 'An eye for an eye, a tooth for a tooth'?"

"I've heard it," Chee said.

"Don't you believe in justice? Don't you believe that things need to be evened up?"

Chee shrugged. "Why not?" he said. As a matter of fact, the concept seemed as strange to him as the idea that someone with money would steal had seemed to Mrs. Musket. Someone who violated basic rules of behavior and harmed you was, by Navajo definition, "out of control." The "dark wind" had entered him and destroyed his judgment. One avoided such persons, and worried about them, and was pleased if they were cured of this temporary insanity and returned again to *hozro.* But to Chee's Navajo mind, the idea of punishing them would be as insane as the original act. He understood it was a common attitude in the white culture, but he'd never before encountered it so directly.

"That's really what I want to talk to you about," Miss Pauling said. "If this Palanzer did it, I want to know it and I want to know where to find him. If somebody else was responsible, I want to know that." She paused. "I can pay you."

Chee looked doubtful.

"I know you say you're not working on this. But you're the one who found out how he was killed. And you're the only one I know."

"I tell you what I'll do," Chee said. "You go home. If I can find out whether Palanzer is the one, I'll call you and tell you. And then if I can find out where you could look for Palanzer, I'll let you know that, too."

"That's all I can ask," she said.

"Then you'll go home?"

"Gaines has the tickets," she said. "It was all so sudden. He called me at work, and told me about the crash and arranged to meet me. And he said he was Robert's lawyer and we should fly right out and see about it. So he took me home and I put some things in a bag and we went right out to the airport and all the money I have is just what was in my purse."

"You have a credit card?" Chee asked. She nodded. "Use that. I'll get you a ride to Flagstaff."

Two men at a table near the cash register had been watching them. One was about thirty—a big man with long blond hair and small eyes under bushy blond eyebrows. The other, much older, had thin white hair and a suntanned face. His pin-striped three-piece suit looked out of place on Second Mesa.

"Do you know who Gaines is?" Chee asked.

"You mean besides being my brother's attorney? Well, I guess from what I hear that he must be somebody involved in this drug business. I guess that's the real reason he wanted me along." She chuckled, without humor. "To make him legitimate in dealing with people. Is that right?"

"So it would seem," Chee said.

Cowboy Dashee came through the walkway, paused a moment by the cash register, spotted Chee, and came over.

"Saw you parked out there," he said.

"This is Deputy Sheriff Albert Dashee," Chee said. "Miss Pauling is the sister of the pilot of that plane."

Cowboy nodded. "Everybody calls me Cowboy," he said. He pulled a chair over from an adjoining table and sat down.

"Why don't you pull up a chair and join us?" Chee asked.

"You know this guy's a Navajo?" he asked Miss Pauling. "Sometimes he tries to pass himself off as one of us."

Miss Pauling managed a smile.

"What's new?" Chee asked.

"You talked to your office this afternoon?"

"No," Chee said.

"You haven't heard about finding the car, or turning up the necklace?"

"Necklace?"

"From the Burnt Water burglary. Big squash blossom job. Girl over at Mexican Water pawned it."

"Where'd she get it?"

"Who else?" Cowboy said. "Joseph Musket. Old Ironfingers playing Romeo." Cowboy turned to Miss Pauling. "Shop talk," he said. "Mr. Chee and I have been worrying about this burglary and now a piece of the loot finally turned up."

"When?" Chee asked. "How'd it happen?"

"She just pawned it yesterday," Cowboy said. "Said she met this guy at a squaw dance over there somewhere, and he wanted to . . ." Cowboy flushed slightly, glanced at Miss Pauling. "Anyway, he got romantic and he gave her the necklace."

"And it was Ironfingers."

"That's what she said his name was." Cowboy grinned at Chee. "I notice with intense surprise that you're not interested in the car."

"You said you found it?"

"That's right," Cowboy said. "Just followed a sort of hunch I had. Followed up an arroyo out there and believe it or not, there it was—hidden up under some bushes."

"Good for you," Chee said.

"I'll tell you what's good for me," Cowboy said. "I jimmied my way into it through the vent on the right front window, pried it right open."

"That's the best way to get in," Chee said.

"I thought you'd say that," Cowboy said.

Miss Pauling was watching them curiously.

Chee turned to her.

"You remember me telling you that the plane crash and the narcotics case wasn't my business? Well, it's in the jurisdiction of Mr. Dashee's sheriff's department. Coconino County. And now Cowboy has found that car that everyone's been wondering about. The one that drove away from the plane crash."

"Oh," she said. "Can you tell us about it?"

Cowboy looked slightly doubtful. He glanced at Chee

again. "Well," he said. "I guess so. Not much to tell, really. Green GMC carryall. Somebody drove it way up that arroyo and jammed it under the brush where it couldn't be seen. Been rented at Phoenix to that guy Jansen—the one that was found out there by the plane crash. Bloodstains on the back seat. Nothing in it. I think the FBI's out there now, checking it for fingerprints and so forth."

"Nothing in it?" Chee said. He hoped he'd kept the surprise out of his voice. Cowboy looked at him.

"Few butts in the ashtray. Rental papers in the glove box. Owner's manual. No big bundles labeled cocaine. Nothing like that. I guess we'll be hunting around there tomorrow."

Chee became aware that Miss Pauling was staring at him.

"You all right?" she asked.

"I'm fine," Chee said.

"Funny thing," Cowboy said. "The inside had a funny smell. Like disinfectant. I wonder why that would be."

"Beats me," Chee said.

Chee considered it as he drove back to Tuba City. Obviously the body had been gone when Cowboy found the vehicle. Obviously someone had come and taken it. Why? Perhaps because whoever had seen him parked at the arroyo mouth had become nervous and decided the body might be found. But why preserve it in the first place? And who had moved it? Joseph Musket, it would seem. But tonight he felt very disappointed in Ironfingers. Disillusioned. Musket should be smarter than the run-of-the-mill thief. In his mind Chee had built him up to be much too clever to do the same thing that always trips up small-time thieves. And the facts as Chee knew them seemed to make him too smart to give a girl that stolen necklace. Someone seemed to have thought so. Someone had given him something close to seven hundred dollars—probably, Chee guessed, an even thousand—to do something when he left the prison at Santa Fe. And whatever it was, it involved working until the end of summer at Burnt Water. Doing what? Setting up and watching the landing strip for a multimillion-dollar narcotics delivery. That seemed to be the answer. But if he had seven hundred dollars in his pocket, if he had coming a payoff big enough to buy a wealth in sheep, why would he steal the pawn jewelry? Chee had been over all of that before, and the only motive he could think of was to provide what would seem to be a logical reason for disappearing from the trading post. Something which might put off the hunters if he intended to steal the shipment. And that meant he was too damn smart to give an instantly identifiable piece of squash blossom jewelry to some girl he'd picked up.

"Ironfingers, where are you?" Chee asked the night.

And oddly, just as he said it, aloud, to himself, another little mystery solved itself in his mind. He knew suddenly what had caused the clicking sound he'd heard in the darkness on the other side of the chamiso bushes. To make certain, he slid his .38 out of its holster. With his thumb he moved the hammer back and forth—off safety, to full cock, and back to safety. Click. Click. Click. He glanced at the pistol and back at the highway again. It was the kind of nervous thing a man might do if he was tensely ready to shoot something. Or someone.

The thought of Musket, pistol cocked, hunting him in the dark aroused a surprising anger in Chee. It made the abstraction intensely personal. Well, Largo wanted him away from Tuba City. He'd quit postponing that trip to the prison in New Mexico. He'd take another step down the trail of Ironfingers.

19

THE DRIVE FROM TUBA CITY to the New Mexico State Penitentiary on the Santa Fe plateau is about four hundred miles. Chee, who had risen even earlier than usual and cheated a little on the speed limit, got there in the early afternoon. He identified himself through the microphone at the entrance tower and waited while the tower checked with someone in the administration building. Then the exterior gate slid open. When it had closed behind him, and locked itself, another motor purred and the inside gate rolled down its track. Jim Chee was inside the fence, walking up the long, straight concrete walk through the great flat emptiness of the entrance yard. Nothing living was visible except for a flight of crows high to the north, between the prison and the mountains. But the long rows of cell block windows stared at him. Chee looked back, conscious of being watched. Above the second-floor windows of the second block to his right, the gray concrete was smudged with black. That would be cell block 3, Chee guessed, where more than thirty convicts were butchered and burned by their fellow prisoners in the ghastly riot of 1980. Had Joseph Musket been here then? If he'd been among the rioters, he'd concealed his role well enough to justify parole.

Another electronic lock let Chee through the door of the administration building, into the presence of a thin, middle-aged Chicano guard who manned the entrance desk. "Navajo Tribal Police," the guard said, eyeing Chee curiously. He glanced down at his clipboard. "Mr. Armijo will handle you."

Another guard, also gray, also Chicano, led him wordlessly to Mr. Armijo's office.

Mr. Armijo was not wordless. He was plump, and perhaps forty, with coarse black hair razor-cut and blow-dried into this year's popular shape. His teeth were very, very white and he displayed them in a smile. "Mr. Chee. You're not going to believe this, but I know this Joseph Musket personally." Armijo's smile became a half inch broader. "He was a trusty. Worked right here in our records section for a while. Have a seat. I guess we'll be getting him back now." Armijo indicated a gray steel chair with a gray plastic cushion. "Violated his parole, is that it?"

"Looks like it," Chee said. "I guess you could say he's a suspect in a burglary. Anyway, we need to know more about him."

"Here he is." Armijo handed Chee a brown cardboard accordion file. "All about Joseph Musket."

Chee put the file on his lap. He'd read through such files before. He knew what was in them, and what wasn't. "You said you knew him," Chee said. "What was he like?"

"Like?" The question surprised Armijo. He looked puzzled. He shrugged. "Well, you know. Quiet. Didn't say much. Did his work." Armijo frowned. "What do you mean, what was he like?"

A good question, Chee thought. What did he mean? What was he looking for? "Did he tell jokes?" Chee asked. "Was he the kind of guy who sort of takes over a job, or did you have to tell him everything? Have any friends? That sort of thing."

"I don't know," Armijo said. His expression said he wished he hadn't started the conversation. "I'd tell him what to do and he'd do it. Didn't ever say much. Quiet. He was an Indian." Armijo glanced at Chee to see if that explained it. Then he went on, explaining the job—how Musket would come in each afternoon, how he'd set up the files on the new prisoners received that day and then sort through the File basket and add whatever new material might have developed to the folders of other inmates. "Not a very demanding job," Armijo said. "But he did it well enough. Didn't make mistakes. Got good reports."

"How about friends?" Chee asked.

"Oh, he had friends," Armijo said. "In here, you got money, you got friends."

"Musket had money?" That surprised Chee.

"In his canteen account," Armijo said. "That's all you can have. No cash, of course. Just credit for smokes, candy, and stuff like that. All the little extras."

"You mean more money than he could earn in here? Outside money?"

"He had connections," Armijo said. "Lots of narcotics dealers have connections. Some lawyer depositing money into their account."

And that seemed to be all Armijo knew. He showed Chee into an adjoining room and left him with the file.

In the file there were first the photographs.

Joseph Musket stared out at Chee: an oval face, clean shaven, a line extending down the center of the forehead, the expression blank—the face a man puts on when he has cleared everything out of his mind except the need to endure. He hadn't changed a lot, Chee thought, beyond the change caused by the thin mustache, a few added pounds, and a few added years. But then maybe he had changed. Chee turned his eyes away from the stolid eyes of Musket and looked at his profile. That was all he had seen of Joseph Musket—a quick disinterested glance at a stranger walking past. The profile showed Chee a high, straight forehead—the look of intelligence. Nothing more.

He looked away from the face and noted the vital statistics. Musket today would be in his early thirties, he noticed, which was about what he had guessed. The rest checked out with what he had already learned from Musket's probation officer: born near Mexican Water, son of Simon Musket and Fannie Tsossie, educated at Teec Nos Pos boarding school and the high school at Cottonwood. As he'd remembered from what the probation officer had shown him at Flagstaff, Musket was doing three-to-five for possession of narcotics with intent to sell.

Chee read more carefully. Musket's police record was unremarkable. His first rap had been at eighteen in Gallup, drunk and disorderly. Then had come an arrest in Albuquerque for grand theft, dismissed, and another Albuquerque arrest for burglary, which had led to a two-year sentence and referral to a drug treatment program, suspended. Another burglary charge, this one in El Paso, had led to a one-to-three sentence in Huntsville; and then came what Chee had been (at least subconsciously) looking for—Joe Musket's graduation into the more lethal level of crime. It had been an armed robbery of a Seven-Eleven Store at Las Cruces, New Mexico. On this one, the grand jury hadn't indicted, and the charge had been dismissed. Chee sorted through the pages, looking for the investigating officer's report. It sounded typical. Two men, one outside in a car, the other inside looking at the magazines until the last customer leaves, then the gun shown to the clerk, money from the register stuffed into a grocery bag, the clerk locked in the storeroom, and two suspects arrested after abandoning the getaway car. Musket had been found hiding between garbage containers in an alley, but the clerk wasn't ready to swear he was the man he'd seen waiting in the car outside. At the bottom of the page, a Xerox out of the Las Cruces police files, was a handwritten note. It said:

"True bill on West—no bill on Musket."

Chee glanced quickly back up the page, found the suspect-identification line. The man who'd gone into the store with the gun while Joseph Musket waited in the car was identified as Thomas Rodney West, age 30, address, Ideal Motel, 2929 Railroad Avenue, El Paso.

It didn't really surprise Chee. West had said Musket was a friend of his son's. That was the reason he'd given Musket the job. And West had said his son had bad friends and had been in trouble, and had been killed. But how had he been killed? Chee hurried now. He found Thomas Rodney West once again in the investigation report which covered the drug bust that had sent Musket to the Santa Fe prison. He had been nailed along with Musket in the pickup truck carrying eight hundred pounds of marijuana. The pot had been unloaded off a light aircraft in the desert south of Alamogordo, New Mexico. The plane had eluded the DEA trap, the pickup hadn't. Chee put down the Musket file and stared for a long moment at the gray concrete wall. Then he went into Armijo's office. Armijo looked up from his paperwork, teeth white.

"Do you keep files on inmates after they're dead?"

"Sure." Armijo's smile widened. "In the dead file."

"I'm not sure he was here," Chee said. "Fellow named Thomas Rodney West."

Armijo's smile lost its luster. "He was here," he said. "Got killed."

"In here?"

"This year," Armijo said. "In the recreation yard." He got up and was stooping to pull open the bottom drawer of a filing cabinet. "Things like that happen now and then," he said.

"Somebody?" Chee said. "It wasn't solved?"

"No," Armijo said. "Five hundred men all around him and nobody saw a thing. That's the way it works, usually."

The accordion file of Thomas Rodney West was identical to that of Joseph Musket (a.k.a. Ironfingers Musket), except that the string which secured its flap was tied with a knot, giving it the finality of death, instead of a bow, which suggested the impermanence of parole. Chee carried it back into the waiting room, put it beside the Musket file, and worked the knot loose with his fingernails.

Here there was no question of recognizing the mug shots that looked glumly out from the identification sheet. Thomas Rodney West, convict, looked just like Tom West, schoolboy, and Tom West, Marine, whose face Chee had studied in the photographs in the Burnt Water Trading Post. He also looked a lot like his father. The expression had the suffering blankness that police photographers and the circumstances impose on such shots. But behind that, there was the heavy strength and the same forcefulness that marked the face of the older West. Chee noticed that West had been born the same month as Musket. West was nine days younger. Chee corrected the thought. The knife in the recreation yard had changed that, sparing young West the aging process. Now Musket was a month or so older.

Chee worked through the pages, wondering what he was looking for. He noticed that West had come out of the armed robbery with a plea bargain deal: Guilty with a four-year sentence, suspended into probation. He'd still been on probation when the narcotics arrest happened. And he was carrying a gun when arrested. (Musket hadn't been, Chee recalled. Had he been smart enough to ditch it when he saw what was happening?) Those two factors had netted West a stiffer, five-to-seven-year rap.

It was warm in the room, and airless. Chee flipped to the last page and read the data on the death of Thomas Rodney West. It was as Armijo had reported. At 11:17 A.M., July 6, the guard in tower 7 had noticed a body in the dust of the recreation yard. No inmate was near it. He called down to the guard in the yard. West was found to be unconscious, dying from three deep puncture wounds. Subsequent interrogation of inmates revealed no one who had seen what had happened. Subsequent search of the yard had produced a sharpened screwdriver and a wood rasp which had been converted into makeshift daggers. Both were stained with blood that matched West's blood type. Next of kin, Jacob West, Burnt Water, Arizona, had been notified and had claimed the body on July 8. The carbon copy of an autopsy report was the final page in the file. It showed that Thomas Rodney West, his first name mutilated by a typographical error, had died of a slashed aortal artery and two wounds to his abdominal cavity.

Chee flipped back a page and looked at the date. A busy month. July. West had been stabbed to death July 6. John Doe had been killed July 10, almost certainly, since his body was found early on the morning of July 11. On July 28 Joseph Musket disappeared after burglarizing the Burnt Water store. Any connection? Chee could think of none. But there might be, if he could identify Doe. He yawned. Up early this morning, and little sleep during the night. He lit a cigaret. He'd read quickly again through everything in the West file, and then return to the Musket file and finish it, and get out of there. The place oppressed him. Made him uneasy. Made him feel an odd, unusual sense of sorrow.

There was nothing unusual in West's commissary credit account, or in his health check reports, or in his correspondence log, which included only his father, a woman in El Paso, and an El Paso attorney. Then Chee turned to the log of visitors.

On July 2, four days before he'd been stabbed to death, Thomas Rodney West had been visited by T. L. Johnson, agent, U.S. Drug Enforcement Agency. Purpose: Official business.

Chee stared at the entry, and then at the ones which preceded it. West had been visited five times since his arrival at the prison. By his father, and once by the woman from El Paso, and twice by someone who had identified himself as Jerald R. Jansen, attorney at law, Petroleum Towers Bldg., Houston, Texas.

"Ah." Chee said it aloud. He sat back in the chair and stared at the ceiling. Jansen. Attorney. Houston. He'd met Jansen. Jansen dead. Sitting cold and silent beside the basalt, holding the Hopi Cultural Center message between thumb and finger. Chee blew a plume of smoke at the ceiling, rocked the chair forward, and checked the dates. Jansen had visited West on February 17, and again on May 2. Long before the parole of Joseph Musket, and then after it. Then West had been visited by the DEA's freckled, red-haired T. L. Johnson four days before he'd been stabbed. Chee thought about that for a moment, looking for meaning. He found nothing but a take-your-choice set of contradictory possibilities.

Then he checked Joseph Musket's log of visitors. He'd had none. Not one visitor in more than two years in prison. He checked Musket's log of correspondence. None. No letters in. No letters out. The isolated man. Chee closed the Musket file and put it atop the West file.

Armijo was no longer alone. Two convicts were at work in his office now—a burr-haired young blond who glanced up from his typewriter as Chee brought the files in and then looked quickly back at his work, and a middle-aged black man with a gauze bandage on the back of his neck. The black man seemed to be Musket's replacement as file clerk. He was sifting papers into files, eyeing Chee curiously.

"If West had any close friends in here, I'd sure like to talk to one of them," Chee said. "What do you think?"

"I don't know," Armijo said. "I don't know anything about friends."

How would he know? Chee thought. Such things as friendships were not the stuff that filled accordion files.

"Any way of finding out?" Chee asked. "Down the grapevine, or whatever you do?"

Armijo looked doubtful.

"Who's in charge of inside security?" Chee asked.

"That would be the deputy warden," Armijo said. "I'll call him."

While Armijo dialed, the sound of the burr head's typewriter resumed. Typing makes it hard for him to listen, Chee thought.

The deputy warden for security wanted to talk to Chee directly, and then he wanted to know what Chee was doing in the prison, and why, specifically, he wanted to talk to a friend of West.

"Nothing to do with anything in here," Chee assured him. "We've got an unsolved burglary on the reservation, and we're looking for a parole violator named Musket. Musket got sent up with West. They were friends from way back. Did an armed robbery or so together before going into drugs. I just need to know if West and Musket stayed friendly in prison. Things like that."

The deputy warden said nothing for several seconds. Then he told Chee to wait, he'd call back.

Chee waited almost an hour. Burr head typed, eyeing him now and then. The black man with the bandaged neck finished emptying the Out basket into the proper accordion files and left. Armijo had explained that he was working on his annual report, which was late. He used a pocket calculator, comparing figures and compiling some sort of list. Chee sat in his gray metal chair, thinking now and then, and now and then listening to the sounds that came through the door beside his right ear. Footsteps, approaching and receding, an occasional distant metallic sound, once an echoing clang, once a whistle, shrill and brief. Never a voice, never a spoken word. Why did Johnson visit Thomas Rodney West? Had West heard of the impending drug delivery near Burnt Water and summoned the agent to trade information for a parole recommendation? West must have been connected to the group involved in the transfer. Why else had Jansen visited him twice? Johnson could have known that. Probably would have. Almost certainly did. Obviously did. Had he visited, hoping to pry out of West some information about the impending shipment? That seemed the best bet.

The sound now was the telephone shrilling. Armijo spoke

into it, listened. Handed it to Chee.

"Fellow will talk to you," the deputy warden said. "Name's Archer. Good friend of West. Very good." The deputy warden laughed. "If you know what I mean."

"Girl friend?" Chee asked.

"I think it was boy friend," the D.W. said.

The same middle-aged Chicano appeared, to guide Chee, taking him down a long, blank corridor. The two convicts they met on the journey walked against the walls, giving them the middle of the aisle. The interview room was windowless and the fluorescent tubes which lit it gave its dirty white paint a grayish tinge. The man named Archer was big, perhaps forty years old, with the body of a man who worked on the weights. His nose had been broken a long time ago and broken again more recently and the scars from one of the breaks glistened white against the pallor of his skin. Archer was sitting behind the counter that split the small room, looking curiously at Chee through a pane of glass. A guard leaned against the wall behind him, smoking.

"My name's Jim Chee," Chee said to Archer. "I know Tom West's father. I need a little information. Just a little."

"This can be a short conversation," Archer said. "I wasn't in the yard when it happened. I don't know a damned thing."

"That's not what I'm asking about," Chee said. "I want to know why he wanted to talk to T. L. Johnson."

Archer looked blank.

"Why he wanted to talk to Johnson the narcotics agent."

Archer's face flushed. "T. L. Johnson," he said slowly, memorizing the name. "Was that who it was? Tom didn't want to talk to that son of a bitch. He didn't know nothing to tell him. He was scared to death of it." Archer snorted. "For a damn good reason. The son of a bitch set him up."

"It wasn't West's idea, then?"

"Hell, no, it wasn't. Nobody in here is going to volunteer to talk to a narc. Not in here, they're not. The bastard set him up. You know what he did? He arranged to take him out of here. Right down the front walk, right out the front gate, right into his car, and drive away. Just drove down toward Cerrillos, out of sight of the prison, and sat there. No way for West to prove he hadn't snitched." Archer glared at Chee, his pallid face still flushed. "Dirty son of a bitch," he said.

"How do you know about this?" Chee asked.

"When they brought him back, Tom told me." Archer shook his head. "He was mad and he was scared. He said the narc wanted to know about when a shipment was going to come in, and where, and all about it, and when Tom told him he didn't know nothing, Johnson laughed at him and just parked out there and said he was going to stay parked until all the cons figured he had time to spill his guts."

"Scared," Chee asked. "Was he? He didn't ask to get put in segregation, where he'd be safe. Or if he did ask, it wasn't in the files."

"He talked about it," Archer said. "But once you go in there you got to stay. That's rat country. Everybody in there is a snitch. You go in there you can't come out."

"So he decided to risk it?"

"Yeah," Archer said. "He had a lot of respect in here. So do I." He looked at Chee, his expression strained. "It seemed like we could risk it," he said. "It seemed like a good gamble."

Archer had argued for the gamble, Chee guessed. Now he wanted Chee to understand it.

"Can you tell me anything about who killed him, or why, or anything?"

Archer's face assumed the same expression Chee had always noticed in official police identification photographs.

"I don't have no ideas about that," he said. "Look, I've got to get out of here. Work to do."

"One more thing," Chee said. "He got sent up here with a man named Joseph Musket. Friends from way back. Did they stay friends?"

"Musket's out," Archer said. "Paroled."

"But were they friends up until then?"

Archer looked thoughtful. Chee guessed he was looking for traps. Apparently he found none.

"They were friends," Archer said. He shook his head, and his face relaxed. "Really," he said, "Tom was a great guy. He had a lot of respect in here. People didn't screw with him. The bad ones, you know, they'd walk around him. He looked after

Musket some, I think." Then Archer's expression changed. "Maybe I said that wrong. Tom was Musket's friend, but I don't know if it really worked both ways. I didn't never trust Musket. He was one of them guys, you know, who you never know about." Archer got up. "Just too damn smart. Just too damn clever. You know what I mean?"

On his way out, Chee stopped at Armijo's office a final time to use the telephone. He dialed the deputy warden's number.

"I wonder if I could get you to check and see if a DEA agent named T. L. Johnson asked permission to take Thomas West out of the prison," Chee asked. "Was that arranged?"

The deputy warden didn't have to look it up. "Yeah," he said. "He did that. Sometimes we let that happen when there's a good reason for privacy."

20

CHEE TOOK THE ROUNDABOUT WAY HOME—circling north through Santa Fe and Chama instead of southward down the Rio Grande valley through Albuquerque. He took the northern route because it led through beautiful country. He planned to play the tapes he had made of Frank Sam Nakai singing the Night Chant and thereby memorize another section of that complicated eight-day ritual. Beauty helped put him in the mood for the sort of concentration required. Now it didn't work. His mind kept turning to the distraction of unresolved questions. Ironfingers? "Too damn clever," Archer had called him, but not too smart to give stolen jewelry to a girl. Had Johnson, as it seemed, deliberately set up Thomas Rodney West for a prison yard killing? And if he had, why? Who had taken the body of Palanzer from the carryall? And why had the body been left there, in its cocoon of Lysol mist, in the first place? The moon rose over the jagged ridge of the Sangre de Cristo range as he drove up the Chama valley. It hung in the clear, dark sky like a great luminous rock, flooding the landscape with light. When he reached Abiquiu village, he pulled off at the Standard station, bought gas, and used the pay phone. He called Cowboy Dashee's home number. The phone rang six times before Cowboy answered. Dashee had been asleep.

"I didn't think bachelors went to bed so early," Chee said. "Sorry about that. But I need to know something. Did they find the dope?"

"Hell," Dashee said. "We didn't find nothing. That's why

I'm trying to get some sleep. The sheriff wanted us out there at daylight. Everybody figured they'd hauled that stuff up the arroyo in that carryall and then hid it someplace around there. If they did, we sure as hell couldn't find it."

"Does anybody really know what you're looking for?" Chee asked. "Any idea how big it is, or what it weighs, or how big a hole it would take to bury it?"

"Seem to," Cowboy said. "They were talking about a hundred pounds or so and something as bulky as maybe three forty-pound sacks of flour. Or maybe a bunch of smaller packages."

"So they do know what they're after," Chee said. "The DEA was there?"

"Johnson was. And a couple of FBI agents from Flagstaff."

"And you didn't find anything interesting? No dope, no machine guns, no tape-recorded messages on how to ransom the cargo, no dead bodies, no maps. Absolutely nothing?"

"Found a few tracks," Cowboy said. "Nothing useful. There just flat wasn't any big cache of dope hidden up there. If they hauled it up there in that GMC in the first place, then they just hauled it off again, and we didn't see any sign of that. Wouldn't make sense anyway. Think about it. No sense to it."

Chee did think about it. He thought about it intermittently all the way north to Chama and then on the long westward drive across the sprawling Jicarilla Apache reservation. As Cowboy said, there was no sense to it. Another apparently irrational knot to be unraveled. Chee could think of only one possible place to find an end to the string. Whoever was vandalizing Windmill Subunit 6 had been a hidden witness at the crash. He must have seen something. It was merely a matter of finding him.

It was afternoon when Chee returned to the windmill. He stood looking at it, realizing that any sensible, sensitive human could come to detest it. It was an awkward discordant shape. It clashed with the gentle slope on which it stood. The sun reflected painfully bright from the zinc coating which armored it against softening rust. It made ugly clanking, groaning noises in the breeze. The last time he'd been here his mood had been cheerful as the morning, and then the mill had seemed merely neutral—a harmless object. But today heat shimmered off the drought-stricken landscape and dust moved in the arid wind, and his mood was as negative as the weather. This ugly object represented injustice to thousands of Navajos. Any one of them might be vandalizing it, or all of them, or any member of their multitudinous families. Or maybe they were taking turns vandalizing it. Whatever, he didn't blame them and he'd never solve the mystery. Maybe it wasn't a Navajo at all. Maybe it was some artistic Hopi whose sense of aesthetics was offended.

Chee walked past the steel storage tank and peered into it. Bone dry. A reservoir for dust. Leaning against the hot metal, Chee took inventory of what he knew. It was all negative. The vandal always used some simple means—no dynamite, cutting torches, or machinery. In other words, nothing to trace down. He apparently arrived on foot or by horse, since Chee had never found any wheel tracks which he couldn't account for. And Jake West had guessed it wasn't a local Navajo, for what that was worth. West could be misleading him deliberately to protect a friend, or West could be wrong. West had not, however, been wrong about BIA efficiency. The BIA crew had apparently brought the wrong parts, or done something wrong. The gearbox was still not operating and the mill's creaks and groans were as impotent as they'd been for most of the summer.

Chee repeated his methodical examination of the grounds, working in widening circles. He found no off-brand cigarets smeared with odd-colored lipstick, no discarded screwdrivers with handles which still might retain fingerprints, no lost billfolds containing driver's licenses with color photographs of the windmill vandal, no footprints, no tire tracks, nothing. He hadn't expected to. He sat down on the slope, cupped his hand against the dusty wind, and managed to get a cigaret lit. He stared down toward the mill, frowning. He hadn't found anything specific, but something in his subconscious was teasing him. Had he found something without realizing it? Exactly what had he found? Almost nothing. Even the rabbit droppings and the trails of the kangaroo rats were old. The little desert rodents which congregate wherever there is water had moved away. Last year the inevitable leakage around the windmill had provided for them. But now the thick growth of sunflowers, tumbleweeds, and desert asters which had flourished around the storage tank were just dead stalks. The plants were dead and the rodents were gone because the vandal had dried up their chance of living here. Desert ecology had clicked back into balance on this hillside. The rodents would have returned to the arroyo with its seeping spring, with its *pahos* and its guardian spirit, Chee guessed, but the spring, too, was virtually dry. The victim of drought. Or was it?

Chee jumped to his feet, snubbed out his cigaret, and hurried down the slope toward the arroyo. He trotted along the sandy bottom, following the path the moccasins of the shrine's guardian had made. The shrine looked just as he had left it. He crouched under the shale overhang, careful not to disturb the *pahos.* When he had been here before, there had been a film of water on the granite under the shale, so shallow that it was not much more than a pattern of wetness. Chee studied the rock surface. The dampness had spread. Not much, but it had spread. The spring had been barely alive when he had seen it before. It was still barely alive. But the spring was no longer dying.

Chee walked back to his pickup truck, climbed in, and drove away without a backward glance. He was finished with the windmill. It offered no more mysteries. He'd stop at the Burnt Water store and call Cowboy Dashee. He'd tell Cowboy he had to talk to the keeper of the shrine. Cowboy wouldn't like it. But Cowboy would find him.

21

COWBOY HAD ARRANGED TO MEET HIM at the junction of Arizona Highway 87 and Navajo Route 3. "We're going to have to go to Piutki," Cowboy had told him. "That's where he lives. But I don't want to have you floundering around up there by yourself, getting lost. So meet me, and I'll take you up."

"About when?"

"About seven," Cowboy said.

So Chee had arrived about seven. Five minutes before, to be exact. He stood beside his pickup truck, stretching his muscles. The early evening sun lit the slopes of Second Mesa behind him, making a glittering reflection off the hot asphalt of Navajo 3 where it zigzagged upward. Just to the north, the cliff of First Mesa was dappled with shadow. Chee himself stood in the shadow. A cloud which had been building slowly all afternoon over the San Francisco Peaks had broken free of the mountain's updrafts and was drifting eastward. It was still at least twenty miles to the west, but its crest had built high enough now to block out the slanting light of sun. The heat of the day had produced other such thunderheads. Three, in an irregular row, were sailing across the Painted Desert between Chee and Winslow. One, Chee noticed with pleasure, was actually dragging a small tail of rain across Tovar Mesa. But none of the smaller clouds promised much. With sundown they would quickly evaporate in the arid sky. The cloud spawned by the San Francisco Peaks was another matter. It was huge, its top pushed up into the stratospheric cold by its internal winds, and its lower levels blue-black with the promise of rain. As Chee appraised it, he heard the mutter of thunder. The clouds would be visible for a hundred miles in every direction, from Navajo Mountain across the Utah border, as far east as the Chuska Range in New Mexico. One cloud wouldn't break a drought, but it takes one cloud to start the process. For a thousand Navajo sheepmen across this immense dry tableland the cloud meant hope that rain, running arroyos, and new grass would again be part of the *hozro* of their lives. To the Hopis, rain would mean more than that. It would mean the endorsement of the supernatural. The Hopis had called for the clouds, and the clouds had come. It would mean that after a year of blighted dust, things were right again between the Peaceful People of the Hopi Mesas and their kachina spirits.

Chee leaned against the truck, enjoying the cool, damp breeze which the cloud was now producing, enjoying the contrast between the dappled browns and tans of the First Mesa cliffs and the dark-blue sky over them. Above him the rim of the cliff was not cliff at all, but the stone walls of the houses of Walpi. From here it was hard to believe that. The tiny windows seemed to be holes in the living rock of the mesa.

Chee glanced at his watch. Cowboy was late. He retrieved his notebook from the front seat, and turned to a clean page. Across the top he wrote: "Questions and Answers." Then he wrote: "Where is J. Musket? Did Musket kill John Doe? Witch? Crazy? Tied up with the narcotics heist?" He drew a line down the center of the page, separating the Answers section. Here he wrote: "Evidence he was away from work day Doe killed. Musket connected with narcotics. Likely came to Burnt Water to set up delivery. How else? Would have known the country well enough to hide the GMC." Chee studied the entries. He tapped a front tooth with the butt of the ballpoint pen. He wrote under Questions: "Why the burglary? To provide a logical reason for disappearing from the trading post?" Chee frowned at that, and wrote: "What happened to the stolen jewelry?" He drew a line under that all the way across the page. Under it he wrote:

"Who is John Doe? Somebody from the narcotics business? Working with Musket? Did Musket kill him because Doe smelled the double cross? Did Musket make it look like a witch killing to confuse things?" No answers here. Just questions. He drew another horizontal line and wrote under it:

"Where's Palanzer's body? Why hide it in the GMC? To confuse those looking for dope? Why take it out of the GMC? Because someone knew I'd found it? Who knew? The man who walked up the arroyo in the dark? Musket? Dashee?" He stared at the name, feeling disloyal. But Dashee knew. He'd told Dashee where to find the truck. And Dashee could have been at the windmill site when the crash happened. He wondered if he could learn where Dashee had been the night John Doe's body had been hidden. And then he shook his head and drew a line through "Dashee," and then another line. Under that he wrote a single word: "Witch."

Under that he wrote: "Any reason to connect witch killing with dope?" He stared at the question, worrying his lower lip between his teeth. Then he wrote: "Coincidence of time and place." He paused a moment, then jotted beside it: "Doe died July 10, West died July 6." He was still thinking about that when Dashee drove up.

"Right on the money," Cowboy said.

"You're late," Chee said.

"Operating on Navajo time," Cowboy said. "Seven means sometime tonight. Let's take my car."

Chee got in.

"You ever been to Piutki?"

"I don't think so," Chee said. "Where is it?"

"Up on First Mesa," Cowboy said. "Back behind Hano on the ridge." Cowboy was driving more sedately than usual. He rolled the patrol car down Navajo Route 3 and did a left turn onto the narrower asphalt which made the steep, winding climb up the face of the mesa. His face was still, thoughtful.

Worried, Chee thought. We're getting involved in something religious.

"There's not much left of Piutki," Cowboy said. "It's pretty well abandoned. Used to be the village of the Fog Clan with some Bow Clan, and the Fog Clan is just about extinct. Not many Bow left either."

Fog Clan touched a memory. Chee tried to recall what he'd learned about Hopi ethnology in his anthro classes at the University of New Mexico, and what he'd read since, and what he'd picked up from gossip. The Fog Clan had brought to the Hopis the gift of sorcery. That had been its ceremonial contribution to Hopi society. And of course, the sorcerers were the *powaqas,* the "two-hearts," the Hopi culture's peculiar version of what witches were like. There was something about the Bow Clan, too. What? Chee's reliable memory served up the answer. He'd read it in some treatise on Hopi clan history. When the Bow Clan had completed its great migrations and arrived at the Hopi Mesas, it had accumulated such a reputation for creating trouble that the Bear Clan elders had repeatedly refused its request for lands and a village home. And after it had finally been allowed to join the other clans, the Bows had been involved in the single bloody incident in the history of the Peaceful People. When the Arrowshaft Clan at Awatovi had allowed Spanish priests to move into the village, the Bows had suggested a punitive attack. The Arrowshaft males had been slaughtered in their kivas, and the women and children had been scattered among the other villages. The Arrowshaft clan had not survived.

"This man we're going to see," Chee said. "What's his clan?"

Cowboy eyed him. "Why you ask that?"

"You said it was the Fog Clan village. I heard somewhere that the Fog Clan had died out."

"More or less," Cowboy said. "But the Hopis use a sort of linked clan system, and the Fog is linked to the Cloud Clan and the Water Clan and . . ." Cowboy let it trail away. He shifted into second gear for the steep climb along the mesa cliff.

The road reached the saddle of the narrow ridge. It climbed straight ahead to Walpi. Cowboy jerked the patrol car into the narrow turn up the other side of the saddle toward Sichomovi and Hano. The rear wheels skidded. Cowboy muttered something under his breath.

Chee had been watching him. "Had a bad day?"

Cowboy said nothing. Clearly Cowboy had had a bad day.

"What's bothering you?" Chee asked.

Cowboy laughed. But he didn't sound amused. "Nothing," he said.

"You'd just as soon not be doing this?"

Cowboy shrugged.

The patrol car edged past the ancient stone walls of Sichomovi . . . or was it Hano now? Chee wasn't sure yet where one of the villages ended and the other began. It seemed inconceivable to Chee that the Hopis had chosen to live like this—collecting right on top of each other in these tight little towns without privacy or breathing room. His own people had done exactly the opposite. Laws of nature, he thought. Hopis collect, Navajos scatter. But what was bothering Cowboy? He thought about it.

"Who is this guy we're going to see?"

"His name is Taylor Sawkatewa," Cowboy said. "And I think we're wasting our time."

"Don't think he'll tell us anything?"

"Why should he?" Cowboy said. The tone was curt, and Cowboy seemed to realize it. When he continued, there was a hint of apology in his tone. "He's about a million years old. More traditional than the worst traditional. On top of that, I hear he's sort of crazy."

And, Chee thought, you hear he's a *powaqa.* And that's what's making you a little edgy. Chee thought about what he'd heard about *powaqas.* It made him a little edgy, too.

"Not much use appealing to his duty as a law-abiding citizen, I guess," Chee said.

Cowboy laughed. "I don't think so. Be like trying to explain to a Brahma bull why he should hold still while you're putting a surcingle around him."

They were clear of Hano now, jolting down a stony track which followed the mesa rim. The cloud loomed in the southwest. The sun on the horizon lit the underface of its great anvil top a glittering white, but at its lower level its color varied. A thousand gradations of gray from almost white to almost black, and—from the dying sun—shades of rose and pink and red. To Cowboy Dashee's people such a cloud would have sacred symbolism. To Chee's people, it was simply beautiful, and thus valuable just for itself.

"Another thing," Cowboy said. "Old Sawkatewa don't

speak English. That's what they tell me anyway. So I'll have to interpret."

"Anything else I need to know about him?"

Cowboy shrugged.

"You didn't tell me what his clan is."

Cowboy slowed the patrol car, eased it past a jagged rock and over a rut. "He's Fog," he said.

"So the Fog Clan isn't extinct?"

"Really, it is," Cowboy said. "Hardly any left. All their ceremonial duties—what's left—they're owned by the Water Clan now, or Cloud Clan. It was that way even when I was a boy. Long before that, I guess. My daddy said the last time the Ya Ya Society did anything was when he was a little boy—and I don't think that was a full ceremony. Walpi kicked them out a long time ago."

"Kicked them out?"

"The Ya Ya Society," Cowboy said. He didn't offer to expand. From what Chee could remember hearing about the society, it controlled initiation into the various levels of sorcery. In other words, it was a sensitive subject and Cowboy didn't want to talk about it to a non-Hopi.

"Why did they kick 'em out?" Chee asked.

"Caused trouble," Cowboy said.

"Isn't that the society that used to initiate people who wanted to become two-hearts?"

"Yeah," Cowboy said.

"I remember somebody telling me something about it," Chee said. "Somebody told me the deal where they saw a pine tree trunk on the ground and the sorcerer caused it to move up and down in the air."

Cowboy said nothing.

"That's right?" Chee asked. "A lot of magic at a Ya Ya ceremony."

"But if you have power, and you use it for the wrong reasons, then you lose the power," Cowboy said. "That's what we're told."

"This man we're going to see," Chee said. "He was a member of the Ya Ya Society. That right?"

Cowboy eased the patrol car over another rough spot. The

sun was down now, the horizon a streak of fire. The cloud was closer and beginning to drop a screen of rain. It evaporated at least a thousand feet above ground level, but it provided a translucent screen which filtered the reddish light.

"I heard he was a member of the Ya Ya," Cowboy said. "You can hear just about anything."

The village of Piutki had never had the size or importance of such places as Oraibi, or Walpi, or even Shongopovi. At its peak it had housed only part of the small Bow Clan, and the even smaller Fog Clan. That peak had passed long ago, probably in the eighteenth or nineteenth century. Now many of its houses had been abandoned. Their roofs had fallen in and their walls had been quarried for stone to maintain houses still occupied. The great cloud now dominated the sky, and illuminated the old place with a red twilight. The breeze followed the patrol car with outriders of dust. Cowboy flicked on the headlights.

"Place looks empty," Chee said.

"It almost is," Cowboy agreed.

The plaza was small, houses on two sides of it in ruins. Chee noticed that the kiva, too, was in disrepair. The steps that led to its roof were rotted and broken, and the ladder that should have protruded from its rooftop entrance was missing. It was a small kiva, and low, its walls rising only some five feet above the dusty plaza earth. It seemed as dead as the men who had built it so long ago.

"Well," Cowboy said. "Here we are." He stopped the car beside the kiva. Beyond it, one of the houses that still walled two sides of the plaza was occupied. The breeze blew smoke from its chimney toward them, and a small pile of coal stood beside its doorway. The door opened. A boy—perhaps ten or twelve—looked out at them. The boy was an albino.

Cowboy left the car unlocked and walked through the blowing dust without waiting for Chee. He spoke to the boy at the door in Hopi, listened to his answer, thought about it, and spoke again. The boy disappeared inside.

"He said Sawkatewa is working. He'd tell him he had visitors," Cowboy said.

Chee nodded. He heard a thumping of thunder and glanced up at the cloud. Only its upper levels were red with sunset now. Below that, its color shaded from blue to almost black. While he looked at it, the black flashed with yellow, and flashed again. Internal lightning was illuminating it. They waited. Dust eddied in the plaza. The air was much cooler now. It smelled of rain. The sound of thunder reached them. This time it boomed, and boomed again.

The boy reappeared. He looked at Chee through thick-lensed glasses and then at Cowboy, and spoke in Hopi.

"In we go," Cowboy said.

Taylor Sawkatewa was sitting on a small metal chair, winding yarn onto a spindle. He was looking at them, his bright black eyes curious. But his hands never stopped their quick, agile work. He spoke to Cowboy, and motioned toward a green plastic sofa which stood against the entrance wall, and then he examined Chee. He smiled and nodded.

"He says sit down," Cowboy said.

They sat on the green plastic. It was a small room, a little off square, the walls flaking whitewash. A kerosene lamp, its glass chimney sooty, cast a wavering yellow light.

Sawkatewa spoke to both of them, smiling at Chee again. Chee smiled back.

Then Cowboy spoke at length. The old man listened. His hands worked steadily, moving the gray-white wool from a skein in a cardboard beer carton beside his chair onto the long wooden spindle. His eyes left Cowboy and settled on Chee's face. He was a very old man, far beyond the point where curiosity can be interpreted as rudeness. Navajos, too, sometimes live to be very old and Chee's Slow Talking Dinee had its share of them.

Cowboy completed his statement, paused, added a brief postscript, then turned to Chee.

"I told him I would now tell you what I'd told him," Cowboy said. "And what I told him was who you are and that we are here because we are trying to find out something about the plane crash out in Wepo Wash."

"I think you should tell him what happened in a lot of detail," Chee said. "Tell him that two men were killed in the airplane, and that two other men have been killed because of what the airplane carried. And tell him that it would help us a lot if someone had been there and had seen what happened and could tell us what he saw." Chee kept his eyes on Sawkatewa as he said this. The old man was listening intently, smiling slightly. He understands a little English, Chee decided. Maybe he understands more than a little.

Cowboy spoke in Hopi. Sawkatewa listened. He had the round head and the broad fine nose of many Hopis, and a long jaw, made longer by his toothlessness. His cheeks and his chin wrinkled around his sunken mouth, but his skin, like his eyes, looked ageless and his hair, cut in the bangs of the traditional Hopi male, was still mostly black. While he listened, his fingers worked the yarn, limber as eels.

Cowboy finished his translation. The old man waited a polite moment, and then he spoke to Cowboy in rapid Hopi, finished speaking, and laughed.

Cowboy made a gesture of denial. Sawkatewa spoke again, laughed again. Cowboy responded at length in Hopi. Then he looked at Chee.

"He says you must think that he is old and foolish. He says that he has heard that somebody is breaking the windmill out there and that we are looking for the one who broke it to put him in jail. He says that you wish to trick him into saying that he was by the windmill on that night."

"What did you tell him?" Chee asked.

"I denied it."

"But how?" Chee asked. "Tell me everything you told him."

Cowboy frowned. "I told him we didn't think he broke the windmill. I said we thought some Navajos broke it because they were angry at having to leave Hopi land."

"Please tell Taylor Sawkatewa that we wish to withdraw that denial," Chee said, looking directly into Sawkatewa's eyes as he said it. "Tell him that we do not deny that we think he might be the man who broke the windmill."

"Man," Cowboy said. "You're crazy. What are you driving at?"

"Tell him," Chee said.

Cowboy shrugged. He spoke to Sawkatewa in Hopi. Sawkatewa looked surprised, and interested. For the first time his fingers left off their nimble work. Sawkatewa folded his hands in his lap. He turned and spoke into the darkness of the adjoining room, where the albino boy was standing.

"What did he say?" Chee asked.

"He told the boy to make us some coffee," Cowboy said.

"Now tell him that I am studying to be a *yataalii* among my people and that I study under an old man, a man who like himself is a hosteen much respected by his people. Tell him that this old uncle of mine has taught me respect for the power of the Hopis and for all that they have been taught by their Holy People about bringing the rain and keeping the world from being destroyed. Tell him that when I was a child I would come with my uncle to First Mesa so that our prayers could be joined with those of the Hopis at the ceremonials. Tell him that."

Cowboy put it into Hopi. Sawkatewa listened, his eyes shifting from Cowboy to Chee. He sat motionless. Then he nodded.

"Tell him that my uncle taught me that in many ways the Dinee and the Hopi are very, very different. We are taught by our Holy People, by Changing Woman, and by the Talking God how we must live and the things we must do to keep ourselves in beauty with the world around us. But we were not taught how to call the rain clouds. We cannot draw the blessing of water out of the sky as the Hopis have been taught to do. We do not have this great power that the Hopis were given and we respect the Hopis for it and honor them."

Cowboy repeated it. The sound of thunder came through the roof, close now. A sharp, cracking explosion followed by rumbling echoes. Good timing, Chee thought. The old man nodded again.

"My uncle told me that the Hopis have power because they were taught a way to do things, but they will lose that power if they do them wrong." Chee continued: "That is why we say we do not know whether a Hopi or a Navajo is breaking the windmill. A Navajo might do it because he was angry." Chee paused, raised a hand slightly, palm forward, making sure that the old man noticed the emphasis. "But a Hopi might do it because that windmill is *kahopi.*" It was one of perhaps a dozen Hopi words Chee had picked up so far. It meant something like "anti-Hopi," or the reverse-positive of Hopi values.

Cowboy translated. This time Sawkatewa responded at some length, his eyes shifting from Cowboy to Chee and back again.

"What are you leading up to with all this?" Cowboy asked. "You think this old man sabotaged the windmill?"

"What'd he say?" Chee asked.

"He said that the Hopis are a prayerful people. He said many of them have gone the wrong way, and follow the ways the white men teach, and try to let the Tribal Council run things instead of the way we were taught when we emerged from the underworld. But he said that the prayers are working again tonight. He said the cloud will bring water blessings to the Hopis tonight."

"Tell him I said that we Navajos share in this blessing, and are thankful."

Cowboy repeated it. The boy came in and put a white coffee mug on the floor beside the old man. He handed Cowboy a Styrofoam cup and Chee a Ronald McDonald softdrink glass. The light of the kerosene lamp gave his waxy white skin a yellow cast and reflected off the thick lenses of his wire-rimmed glasses. He disappeared through the doorway without speaking.

The old man was speaking again.

Cowboy looked into his cup, cleared his throat. "He said that even if he had been there, he was told that the plane crashed at night. He asks how could anyone see anything?"

"Maybe he couldn't," Chee said.

"But you think he was there?"

"I know he was there," Chee said. "I'd bet my life on it."

Cowboy looked at Chee, waiting. The boy returned with a steaming aluminum pan. He poured coffee from it into the old man's mug, and Cowboy's Styrofoam cup, and Chee's McDonald's glass.

"Tell him," Chee said, looking directly at Sawkatewa, "that my uncle taught me that certain things are forbidden. He taught me that the Navajos and the Hopis agree on certain things and that one of those is that we must respect our mother earth. Like the Hopis, we have places which bring us blessings and are sacred. Places where we collect the things we need for our medicine bundles."

Chee turned to Cowboy. "Tell him that. Then I will go on."

Cowboy translated. The old man sipped his coffee, listening. Chee sipped his. It was instant coffee, boiled in water which tasted a little of gypsum and a little of rust from the barrel in which it was stored. Cowboy finished. Again there was a rumble of thunder and suddenly the pounding of hail on the roof over their heads. The old man smiled. The albino, leaning in the doorway now, smiled too. The hail converted itself quickly into rain—heavy, hard-falling drops, but not quite as noisy. Chee raised his voice slightly. "There is a place near the windmill where the earth has blessed the Hopis with water. And the Hopis have repaid the blessing by giving the spirit of the earth there *pahos.* That has been done for a long, long time. But then people did a *kahopi* thing. They drilled a well in the earth and drained away the water from the sacred place. And the spirit of the spring stopped providing water. And then he refused the offering of the *pahos.* When it was offered, the spirit knocked it down. Now, we Navajos, too, are peaceful people. Not as peaceful as the Hopis, perhaps, but peaceful. But even so, my uncle taught me that we must protect our sacred places. If this had been a shrine of the Navajos, if this had been a shrine left for me to protect, then I would protect it." Chee nodded. Cowboy translated. Sawkatewa sipped his coffee again.

"There are higher laws than the white man's law," Chee said.

Sawkatewa nodded, without waiting for Cowboy to translate. He spoke to the boy, who disappeared into the darkness and returned in a moment with three cigarets. He handed one to each of them, took the chimney off the lamp and passed it around to give each of them a light from the wick. Sawkatewa inhaled hugely and let a plume of smoke emerge from the corner of his mouth. Chee puffed lightly. He didn't want a cigaret. The dampness of the rain had flooded into the room, filling it with the smell of water, the ozone of the lightning, the aroma of dampened dust, sage, and the thousand other desert things which release perfume when raindrops strike them. But this smoke had ceremonial meaning somehow. Chee would not alienate the old man. He would smoke skunk cabbage rather than break this mood.

Finally Sawkatewa stood up. He put the cigaret aside. He held his hands before him, palms down, about waist level, and he began speaking. He spoke for almost five minutes.

"I won't translate all of it now," Cowboy said. "He went all the way back to the time when the Hopi emerged into this world through the *sipapuni* and found that Masaw had been appointed guardian of this world. And he tells how Masaw let each of the kinds of peoples pick their way of life, and how the Navajo picked the long ear of soft corn for the easy life and the Hopi picked the short, hard ear so that they would always have hard times but would always endure. And then he tells about how Masaw formed each of the clans, and how the Water Clan was formed, and how the Fog Clan split off from the Water, and all that. I'm not going to translate all that. His point is—"

"If you don't translate for about three or four minutes, he's going to know you're cheating," Chee said. "Go ahead and translate. What's the rush?"

So Cowboy translated. Chee heard of the migrations to the end of the continent in the west, and the end of the continent to the east, and the frozen door of the earth to the north, and the other end of the earth to the south. He told how the Fog Clan had left its footprints in the form of abandoned stone villages and cliff dwellings in all directions, and how it had come to make its alliance with the animal people, and how the animal people had joined the clan, and taught them the ceremony to perform so that people could keep their animal hearts as well as their human hearts and change back and forth by passing through the magic hoop. He told how the Fog Clan had finally completed its great cycle of migrations and come to Oraibi and asked the Bear Clan for a village site, and land to grow its corn, and hunting grounds where it could collect the eagles it needed for its ceremonials. He told how the *kikmongwi* at Oraibi had at first refused, but had agreed when the clan had offered to add its Ya Ya ceremonial to the religion of the Hopis. Cowboy stopped finally, and sipped the last of his coffee.

"I'm getting hoarse," he said. "And that's about it anyway. At the end he said, yes, there are higher laws than the white man's. He said the law of the white man is of no concern to a Hopi. He said for a Hopi, or a Navajo, to involve himself in the affairs of white men is not good. He said that even if he did not believe this, it was dark when the plane crashed. He said he cannot see in the dark."

"Did he say exactly that? That he can't see in the dark?"

Cowboy looked surprised. "Well," he said. "Let's see. He said why do you think he could see in the dark?"

Chee thought about it. The gusting wind drove the rain against the windowpane and whined around the roof corners.

"Tell him that what he says is good. It is not good for a Navajo or a Hopi to involve himself in white affairs. But tell him that this time there is no choice for us. Navajos and Hopis have been involved. You and I. And tell him that if he will tell us what he saw, we will tell him something that will be useful for keeping the shrine."

"We will?" Cowboy said. "What?"

"Go ahead and translate," Chee said. "And also say this. Say I think he can see in the dark because my uncle taught me that it is one of the gifts you receive when you step through the hoop of the Ya Ya. Like the animals, your eyes know no darkness."

Cowboy looked doubtful. "I'm not sure I want to tell him that."

"Tell him," Chee said.

Cowboy translated. Chee noticed the albino listening at the doorway. The albino looked nervous. But Sawkatewa smiled.

He spoke.

"He says what can you tell him? He's calling your bluff."

He'd won! Chee felt exultance. There'd been no bargaining now. The agreement had been reached.

"Tell him I said that I know it is very hard to break the windmill. The first time was easy. The bolts come loose and the windmill is pulled over and it takes a long time to undo the damage. The second time it was easy again. An iron bar stuck into the gearbox. The third time it was not so bad. The pump rod is bent and it destroys itself. But now the bolts cannot be removed, and the gearbox is protected, and soon the pump rod will be protected, too. Next time it will be very hard to damage the windmill. Ask him if that is not true."

Cowboy translated. Taylor Sawkatewa simply stared at Chee, waiting.

"If I were the guardian of the shrine," Chee said, "or if I owed a favor to the guardian of the shrine, as I will when he tells me what he saw when the plane crashed, I would buy a sack of cement. I would haul the sack of cement to the windmill and I would leave it there along with a sack full of sand and a tub full of water and a little plastic funnel. If I was the man who owed the favor, I would leave all that there and drive away. And if I was the guardian of the shrine, I would mix up the cement and sand and water into a paste a little thinner than the dough one makes for *piki* bread and I would pour a little through the funnel down into the windmill shaft, and I would then wait a few minutes for it to dry, and then I would pour a little more, and I would do that until all the cement was in the well, and the well was sealed up solid as a rock."

Cowboy's face was incredulous. "I'm not going to tell him that," he said.

"Why not?" Chee asked.

Sawkatewa said something in Hopi. Cowboy responded tersely.

"He got some of it," Cowboy said. "Why not? Because, God damn it, just think about it a minute."

"Who's going to know but us?" Chee asked. "You like that windmill?"

Cowboy shrugged.

"Then tell him."

Cowboy translated. Sawkatewa listened intently, his eyes on Chee.

Then he spoke three words.

"He wants to know when."

"Tell him I want to buy the cement away from the reservation—maybe in Cameron or Flagstaff. Tell him it will be at the windmill two nights from now."

Cowboy told him. The old man's hands rediscovered the wool and the spindle in the beer carton and resumed their work. Cowboy and Chee waited. The old man didn't speak until he had filled the spindle. Then he spoke for a long time.

"He said it is true he can see pretty good in the dark, but

not as good as when he was a boy. He said he heard someone driving up Wepo Wash and he went down there to see what was happening. When he got there a man was putting out a row of lanterns on the sand, with another man holding a gun on him. When this was finished, the man who had put out the lanterns sat beside the car and the other man stood there, still pointing the gun." Cowboy stopped abruptly, asked a question, and got an answer.

"It was a little gun, he says. A pistol. In a little while an airplane came over very low to the ground and the man on the ground got up and flashed a flashlight off and on. Little later, the plane came back again. Fellow flashes his light again, and then—just after the airplane crashes—the man with the pistol shoots the man with the flashlight. The airplane hit the rock. The man with the gun takes the flashlight and looks around the airplane some. Then he goes and collects all the lanterns and puts them in the car, except for one. That one he leaves on the rock so he can see something. Then he starts taking things out of the airplane. Then he puts the body of the man he shot up against the rock and gets into the car and drives away. Then Sawkatewa says he went to the plane to see, and he hears you running up, so he goes away."

"What did the man unload out of the airplane?"

Cowboy relayed the question. Sawkatewa made a shape with his hands, perhaps thirty inches long, perhaps eighteen inches high, and provided a description in Hopi with a few English words thrown in. Chee recognized "aluminum" and "suitcase."

"He said there were two things that looked like aluminum suitcases. About so"—Cowboy demonstrated an aluminum suitcase with his hands—"by so."

"He didn't say what he did with them," Chee said. "Put them in the car, I guess."

Cowboy asked.

Sawkatewa shook his head. Spoke. Cowboy looked surprised.

"He said he didn't think he put them in the car."

"Didn't put the suitcases in the car? What the hell did he do with them?"

Sawkatewa spoke again without awaiting a translation.

"He said he disappeared in the dark with them. Just gone a little while. Off in the darkness where he couldn't see anything."

"How long is a little while? Three minutes? Five? It couldn't have been very long. I got there about twenty minutes after the plane hit."

Cowboy relayed the question. Sawkatewa shrugged. Thought. Said something.

"About as long as it takes to boil an egg hard. That's what he says."

"What did the man look like?"

Sawkatewa had not been close enough to see him well in the bad light. He saw only shape and movement.

Outside, the rain had gone now. Drifted off to the east. They could hear it muttering its threats and promises back over Black Mesa. But the village stones dripped with water, and muddy rivulets ran here and there over the stone track, and the rocks reflected wet in the headlights of Cowboy's car. Maybe a quarter inch, Chee thought. A heavy shower, but not a real rain. Enough to dampen the dust, and wash things off, and help a little. Most important, there had to be a first rain before the rainy season could get going.

"You think he knows what he's talking about?" Cowboy asked. "You think that guy didn't load the dope into the car?"

"I think he told us what he saw," Chee said.

"Doesn't make sense," Cowboy said. He pulled the patrol car out of a skid on the slick track. "You really going to haul that cement out there for him to plug up the well?"

"I refuse to answer on grounds that it might tend to incriminate me," Chee said.

"Hell," Cowboy said. "That won't do me any good. You got me in so deep now, I'm just going to pretend I never heard any of that."

"I'll pretend, too," Chee said.

"If he didn't haul those suitcases off in that car, how the devil did he haul them out?"

"I don't know," Chee said. "Maybe he didn't."

22

CHEE HAD NOTICED THE TRACKS when he first turned off the asphalt onto the graded dirt road which passed the Burnt Water Trading Post and wandered northeastward up Wepo Wash. The tracks meant only that someone was up even earlier than he was. They meant a vehicle had come this way since last night's shower. It was only when he noticed the tread marks on the damp sand on the wash bottom that he became interested. He stopped his pickup and got out for a closer look. The tires were almost new, the tread common to heavy passenger cars and pickup trucks. Chee memorized them, more from habit than intention, the reflex of a life way in which memory is important. Deputy Sheriff Dashee might be making this trip this morning, but Dashee's tires were Goodyears and this tread Firestone. Who would be driving up Wepo Wash at dawn? Where would they be going, except to the site of the plane crash? Ironfingers returning to the scene of his crime? Chee drove slowly, keeping his engine noise down and his eyes open. As soon as the early light permitted, he flicked off his headlights. Twice he stopped and listened. He heard nothing except the sound of morning birds, busy with their first post-rain day. He stopped again, at the place where a side arroyo provided the exit route to the track that led to his windmill. The fresh tire tracks continued upwash. Chee pulled his pickup to the right, up the arroyo. He had a good official reason to visit the windmill. He'd been warned to stay away from the airplane.

A flock of crows had occupied the windmill area and the

sentinel, perched atop the stationary directional vane, cawed out a raucous alarm as Chee drove up. He parked, more or less out of sight, behind the water tank, and walked directly to the shrine. The parched earth had soaked in most of the rain, but the fall had been abrupt enough to produce runoff an inch or so deep down the arroyo bottom, sweeping it clean. There were no fresh tracks.

Chee took his time, making frequent stops to listen. He was near the point where the arroyo drained into Wepo Wash when he first saw footprints. He inspected them. Someone had walked about one hundred fifty yards up the arroyo, and then down again. The arroyo mouth was a bit less than a quarter mile upwash from the crash site. Chee stood behind the heavy brush which had flourished there. A white Chevy Blazer was parked by the wreckage. Two men were in view. He recognized Collins, the blond who'd handcuffed him in his trailer, but the other man was only vaguely familiar. He was heavyset, a little short of middle age and beginning to show it, dressed in khaki pants and shirt and wearing a long-billed cap. He and Collins were about fifty yards apart. They were searching along the opposite bank of the wash, poking into the brush and examining crevices. Collins was working downwash, away from where Chee stood. The other man moved upwash toward Chee. Where had he seen him before? It seemed to have been recently, or fairly so. Probably another federal cop from somewhere. While he thought about it, he heard footsteps on the sand.

Chee ducked back into the brush, squatting to make himself less visible. From that position, he could see only part of the man who walked just past the mouth of the arroyo. But he saw enough to recognize Johnson, walking slowly, carrying a driftwood stick.

Johnson stopped. Chee couldn't see his upper torso, but the way his hips pivoted, the man seemed to be looking up the arroyo. Chee tensed. Held his breath. Then Johnson turned away.

"Finding anything?"

Chee heard only one answer. A voice, which might have been Collins's, shouting, "Nothing."

Johnson's legs moved quickly out of view down the wash.

Chee moved back to the mouth of the arroyo, cautious. Until he could locate Johnson, the man might be anywhere. He heard the DEA agent's voice near the crash site and breathed easier. He could see all three men now, standing under the uptilted wing, apparently discussing things. Then they climbed into the vehicle, Johnson driving. With a spinning of wheels on the damp sand, it made a sweeping turn and roared off down the wash. If they'd found any aluminum suitcases, they hadn't loaded them into the Blazer.

Chee spent a quarter of an hour making sure he knew where and how Johnson and friends had searched. Last night's runoff down Wepo Wash had been shallow but it had swept the sand clean. Every mark made this morning was as easy to see as a chalk mark on a clean blackboard. Johnson and friends had made a careful search up and down the cliffs of the wash and around the basalt upthrust. Brush had been poked under, driftwood moved, crevices examined. No place in which a medium-sized suitcase might have been hidden was overlooked.

Chee sat under the wing and thought his thoughts. In the wake of the shower the morning was humid, with patches of fog still being burned off the upper slopes of Big Mountain. A few wispy white clouds already were signaling that it might be another afternoon of thunderheads. He took his notebook out of his pocket and reread the notes he'd made yesterday. On the section where he'd written "Dashee" he added another remark: "Johnson learns immediately what old Hopi told us. How?"

He looked at the question. When Cowboy had returned to Flagstaff he'd typed up a report, just as Chee had done at Tuba City. Johnson obviously had learned about the suitcases during the night. From Dashee? From whoever was on night duty at the sheriff's office?

Chee closed the notebook and muttered a Navajo imprecation. What difference did it make? He wasn't really suspicious of Cowboy. His thinking was going in all the wrong directions. "Everything has a right direction to it," his uncle would have told him. "You need to do it *sunwise.* From the east, toward the south, to the west, and finally around to the north. That's the way the sun goes, that's the way you turn when you walk into a hogan, that's the way everything works. That's the way you should think." And what the devil did his uncle's abstract Navajo generality mean in this case? It meant, Chee thought, that you should start in the beginning, and work your way around to the end.

So where was the beginning? People with cocaine in Mexico. People in the United States who wanted to buy it. And someone who worked for one group or the other, who knew of a good, secret place to land an airplane. Joseph Musket or young West, or maybe even both of them plus the elder West. Musket is released from prison, and comes to Burnt Water, and sets up the landing.

Chee paused, sorting it out.

Then the DEA gets wind of something. Johnson visits West at the prison, threatens him, sets him up to be killed.

Chee paused again, fished out the notebook, turned to the proper place, and scribbled in: "Johnson sets up West to be killed? If so, why?"

Then, a couple of days later, John Doe is killed on Black Mesa, maybe by Ironfingers Musket. Maybe by a witch. Or maybe Ironfingers is a witch. Or maybe there was absolutely no connection between Doe and anything else. Maybe he was simply a stray, an accidental victim of evil. Maybe. Chee doubted it. Nothing in his Navajo conditioning prepared him to accept happily the fact that coincidences sometimes happen.

He skipped past Doe, leaving everything about him unresolved, and came to the night of the crash. Three men must have been in the GMC when it arrived. One of them must have been already dead. A corpse already seated in the back seat and the other man a prisoner held at pistol point. Held by Ironfingers? Two outsiders coming in to oversee the delivery of the cocaine. Meeting Musket to be guided to the landing site. Musket killing one, keeping the other one alive. Why? Because only this man knew how to signal a safe landing to the pilot. That would be why. And after the signal had been flashed, killing the man. Why would Ironfingers leave one body and hide the other? To give the owners of the dope a misleading impression about who had stolen it? Possibly. Chee thought about it. The business about the body had bothered Chee from the first and it bothered him now. Musket, or whoever had been the driver, must have planned to bury it eventually. Why else the shovel? But why bury it when it would be easier to carry it back into some arroyo and leave it for the scavengers?

Chee got up, took out his pocket knife, and opened its longest blade. With that, he probed into the bed of the wash near where he had sat. The blade sank easily into the damp sand. But two inches below the surface, the earth was compact. He looked around him. The basalt upthrust was a barrier around which runoff water swirled. There the bottom would be irregular. In some places the current would cut deeply after hard rains, only to have the holes filled in by the slower drainage after lesser storms. Chee climbed out of the wash and hurried back to his pickup at the windmill. From behind the front seat he extracted the jack handle—a long steel bar bent at one end to provide leverage for a lug wrench socket and flattened into a narrow blade at the other to facilitate prying off hub caps. Chee took it back to the wash.

It took just a few minutes to find what he was looking for. The place had to be behind the basalt, because old Taylor Sawkatewa had said the man who unloaded the suitcases had taken them out of sight in the darkness. Chee probed into the damp sand no more than twenty times before he struck aluminum.

There was the thunk of steel on the thin metal of the case. Chee probed again, and again, and found the second case. He knelt and dug back the sand with his hand. The cases were buried upright, side by side, with their handles no more than six inches below the surface.

Chee carefully refilled the little holes his jack handle had made, replaced the sand he had dug away with his hands, patted it to the proper firmness, and then took out his handkerchief and brushed away the traces he'd left on the surface. Then he walked over the cache. It felt no different from the undisturbed sand. Finally he spent almost an hour making himself a little broom of rabbit brush and carefully erasing the tracks of Jimmy Chee from the bottom of Wepo Wash. If anyone ever tracked him, they'd find only that he had come down the arroyo to the wash, and then gone back up it again to the windmill. And driven away.

23

THE DISPATCHER REACHED CHEE just as he turned off the Burnt Water–Wepo Wash road onto the pavement of Navajo Route 3. She had a tip from the Arizona Highway Patrol. One of their units had watched Priscilla Bisti and her boys loading six cases of wine into her pickup truck at Winslow that morning. Mrs. Bisti had been observed driving northward toward the Navajo Reservation on Arizona 58.

"What time?"

"About ten-fourteen," the dispatcher said.

"Anything else?"

"No."

"Can you check my desk and see if I got any telephone messages?"

"I'm not supposed to," the dispatcher said. The dispatcher was Shirley Topaha. Shirley Topaha was just two years out of Tuba City High School, where she had been a cheerleader for the Tuba City Tigers. She had pretty eyes, and very white teeth, and perfect skin, and a plump figure. Chee had noticed all this, along with her tendency to flirt with all officers, visitors, prisoners, etc., requiring only that they be male.

"The captain won't notice it," Chee said. "It might save me a lot of time. It would really be nice if you did."

"I'll call you back," the dispatcher said.

That came about five minutes later. It came about two minutes after Chee had turned his patrol car westward toward Moenkopi and Tuba City. Which was too bad, because it meant he had to stop and turn around.

"Two calls," Shirley said. "One says call Johnson, Drug Enforcement Agency, and there's this number in Flagstaff." She gave him the number. "And the other says please call Miss Pauling at the Hopi motel."

"Thanks, Shirley," Chee said.

"Ten-four," said Shirley.

The man at the desk of the Hopi Cultural Center motel rang Miss Pauling's telephone five times and declared that she wasn't in. Chee checked the motel dining room. She was sitting at a corner table, a cup of coffee in front of her, immersed in a Phoenix *Gazette*.

"You left a call for me," Chee said. "Did Gaines come back?"

"Yes," Miss Pauling said. "Sit down. Do you know how to tap a telephone?" She looked intense, excited.

"Tap a telephone?" Chee sat down. "What's going on?"

"There was a message for Gaines," Miss Pauling said. "Someone called and left it. They'd call back at four, and if he wanted me to make an arrangement, to be in his room to take the call."

"The clerk showed you the message?"

"Sure," she said. "He checked us in together, and we got adjoining rooms. But we don't have much time." She glanced at her watch. "Less than half an hour. Can we get the telephone tapped?"

"Miss Pauling," Chee said. "This is Second Mesa, Arizona. I don't know how to tap a telephone."

"I think it's easy," she said.

"It looks easy on television," Chee said. "But you have to have some sort of equipment. And you have to know how."

"You could call somebody?"

"Not and get a telephone tapped in anything less than about three days," Chee said. "In the Navajo Police, it's out of our line of work. If you call the FBI in Phoenix, they'd know how, but they'd have to get a court order." And then, Chee thought, there's Johnson of the DEA, who wouldn't worry about a court order, and would probably have the equipment in his hip pocket. He wondered why Johnson wanted him to call.

Whatever, it was a call he didn't intend to make.

Miss Pauling looked stricken. She worried her lower lip with her teeth.

"How about just listening at the wall?" Chee asked. "Where do they put the telephones? Could you hear from one room to the next?"

Miss Pauling thought about it. "I doubt it," she said. "Not even if he talked loud."

Chee glanced at his watch. It was 3:33 P.M. In twenty-seven minutes, more or less, Ironfingers would be calling Ben Gaines, making arrangements to trade two aluminum suitcases full of cocaine for . . . for what? Probably for a huge amount of money. Whatever he exchanged it for, Musket would have to name a time and a place. Chee wished fervently that he had the clips and the earphones, or whatever it took to eavesdrop on a telephone call.

"Could we tell the guy at the switchboard that when the call came, Gaines would be in your room? Have him put it through your telephone?"

"Wouldn't work," Miss Pauling said.

Chee had seen it wouldn't work as soon as he'd said it. "Not unless I could imitate Gaines's voice."

Miss Pauling shook her head. "You couldn't," she said.

"I guess not," Chee said. He thought.

"What are you thinking about? Anything helpful?"

"No," Chee said. "I was thinking it would be good if we could get in the back of that telephone switchboard and somehow do some splicing with the wires." He shrugged, dismissing the thought.

"No," Miss Pauling said. "I think it's a GTE board. It takes tools."

Chee looked at her, surprised. "GTE board?"

"I think so. It looked like the one we had at the high school."

"You know something about switchboards?"

"I used to operate one. For about a year. Along with filing, a lot of other things."

"You could operate this one?"

"Anybody can operate a switchboard," she said. "If you're

smart enough to dress yourself." She laughed. "It's certainly not skilled labor. Three minutes of instructions and . . ." She let it trail off.

"And the switchboard operator can listen in on the calls?"

"Sure," she said, frowning at him. "But they're not going to let . . ."

"How much time do we have?" Chee said. "I'll cause some sort of distraction to get that Hopi away from there, and you handle the call."

Later, several possibilities occurred to Chee that were much better than starting a fire. Less flamboyant, less risky, and the same effect. But at the moment he only had about twenty minutes. The only creative thought he had was fire.

He handed Miss Pauling a ten-dollar bill. "Pay the check," he said. "Be near the switchboard. Two or three minutes before four, I come running in and get the clerk out of there."

The raw material he needed was just where he remembered seeing it. A great pile of tumbleweeds had drifted into a corner behind the cultural center museum. Chee inspected the pile apprehensively. It was still a little damp from the previous night's shower but—being tumbleweed—it would burn with a furious red heat, damp or not. And the pile was slightly bigger than he remembered. Chee glanced around nervously. The weeds were piled into the junction of two of the cement-block walls which formed the back of the museum, conveniently out of sight. He hoped no one had seen him. He imagined the headline. NAVAJO COP NAILED FOR HOPI ARSON. OFFICER CHARGED WITH TORCHING CULTURAL CENTER. He imagined trying to explain this to Captain Largo. But there wasn't time to think of it. A quick look around, and he struck a match. He held it low under the prickly gray mass of weed stems. The tumbleweed, which always burned at a flash, merely caught, winked out, smoldered, caught again, smoldered, caught again, smoldered. Chee lit another match, tried a drier spot, looked nervously at his watch. Less than six minutes. The tumbleweed caught; flame flared through it, producing a sudden heat and smoggy white smoke. Chee stepped back and fanned it furiously with his uniform hat. (If anyone is watching this, he thought, I'll never get out of jail.) The fire was crackling now, producing the chain reaction of heat. Hat in hand, Chee sprinted for the motel office.

He ran through the door, up to the desk. The clerk, a young man, was talking to an older Hopi woman.

"Hate to interrupt," he said, "but something's burning out there!"

The Hopis looked at him politely.

"Burning?" the clerk said.

"Burning," Chee said loudly. "There's smoke coming over the roof. I think the building's burning."

"Burning!" the Hopi shouted. He came around the desk at a run. Miss Pauling was standing at the coffee shop entrance, watching tensely.

The fire was eating furiously into the tumbleweeds when they rounded the corner. The clerk took it in at a glance.

"Try to pull it away from the wall," he shouted at Chee. "I'll get water."

Chee looked at his watch. Three minutes to four. Had he started it too early? He stomped at the weeds with his boots, kicking a section of the unburned pile aside to retard the spread. And then the Hopi was back, bringing two buckets of water and two other men. The tumbleweeds now were burning with the furious resinous heat common of desert plants. Chee fought fire with a will now, inhaling a lungful of acrid smoke, coughing, eyes watering. In what seemed like just a minute, it was over. The clerk was throwing a last bucketful of water over the last smoking holdout. One of the helpers was examining places where embers had produced burn holes in his jeans. Chee rubbed watering eyes.

"I wonder what could have started it," Chee said. "You wouldn't think that stuff would burn like that after that rain."

"Goddamn tumbleweeds," the Hopi said. "I wonder what did start it." He was looking at Chee. Chee thought he detected a trace of suspicion.

"Maybe a cigaret," he said. He started poking through the blackened remains with his foot. The fire had lasted a little longer than it seemed. It was four minutes after four.

"Blackened up the wall," the Hopi said, inspecting it. "Have to be repainted." He turned to walk back to the motel office.

"Somebody ought to check the roof," Chee said. "The flames were going up over the parapet."

The Hopi stopped and looked toward the flat roof. His expression was skeptical.

"No smoke," he said. "It's all right. That roof would still be damp."

"I thought I saw smoke," Chee said. "Be hell if that tarred roof caught on fire. Is there a way to get up there?"

"I guess I better check," the clerk said. He headed off in the other direction at a fast walk. To get a ladder, Chee guessed. He hoped the ladder was a long ways off.

Miss Pauling was coming, hurried and nervous, from behind the counter when Chee pushed through the door. Her face was white. She looked flustered.

Chee rushed her outside to his patrol car. The clerk was hurrying across the patio, carrying an aluminum ladder.

"Call come?"

She nodded, still speechless.

"Anybody see you?"

"Just a couple of customers," she said. "They wanted to pay their lunch tickets. I told them to just leave the money on the counter. Was that all right?"

"All right with me," Chee said. He held the car door for her, let himself in on the driver's side. Neither of them said anything until he pulled out of the parking lot and was on the highway.

Then Miss Pauling laughed. "Isn't that funny," she said. "I haven't been so terrified since I was a girl."

"It is funny," Chee said. "I'm still nervous."

Miss Pauling laughed again. "I think you're terrified of how embarrassed you're going to be. What are you going to say if that man comes back and there you are behind his counter playing switchboard operator?"

"Exactly," Chee said. "What are you going to say if he says, 'Hey, there, what are you doing burning down my cultural center?' "

Miss Pauling got her nerves under control. "But the call did come through," she said.

"It must have been short," Chee said.

"Thank God," she said fervently.

"What'd you learn?"

"It was a man," Miss Pauling said. "He asked for Gaines, and Gaines answered the phone on the first ring, and the man asked him if he wanted the suitcases back, and—"

"He said suitcases?"

"Suitcases," Miss Pauling confirmed. "And Gaines said yes, they did, and the man said that could be arranged. And then he said it would cost five hundred thousand dollars, and they would have to be in tens and twenties and not in consecutive order, in two briefcases, and he said they would have to be delivered by The Boss himself. And Gaines said that would be a problem, and the man said either The Boss or no deal, and Gaines said it would take some time. He said it would take at least twenty-four hours. And the man said they would have more than that. He said the trade would be made at nine P.M. two nights after tonight."

"Friday night," Chee said.

"Friday night," Miss Pauling agreed. "Then the man said to be ready for nine P.M. Friday night, and he hung up."

"That's all of it?"

"Oh, the man said he'd be back in touch to tell Gaines where they'd meet. And *then* he hung up."

"But he didn't name the place?"

"He didn't."

"Say anything else?"

"That's the substance of it."

"He explain why the boss had to deliver the money?"

"He said he didn't trust anybody else. He said if the boss was there himself, nobody would risk trying anything funny."

"Any names mentioned?"

"Oh, yes," Miss Pauling said. "The man called Gaines Gaines and once Gaines said something like 'Palanzer.' He said something like: 'I don't see why you're doing this, Palanzer. You would have made almost that much.' That was after the man—Palanzer, I guess—said he wanted the five hundred thousand."

"What did the man say to that?"

"He just laughed. Or it sounded like a laugh. His voice sounded muffled all through the conversation—like he was talking with something in his mouth."

"Or with something over his mouth." Chee paused. "He specified nine P.M.?"

Miss Pauling nodded. "He said, 'Exactly nine P.M.' "

Chee pulled off the asphalt, made a backing turn, and headed back toward the motel. He smelled of smoke.

"Well," Miss Pauling said. "Now we know who has it, and when they're going to make the switch."

"But not where," Chee said. Why the muffled voice, he was asking himself. Because the caller would have been good old Ironfingers, and because Ironfingers would want Gaines to believe the caller was Palanzer. Joseph Musket, despite his years of living among whites, would not have lost his breathy Navajo pronunciation.

"How do we find out where?"

"That's going to take some thinking," Chee said.

24

THINKING DIDN'T SEEM TO HELP. Chee went to sleep that night thinking. He got up the next morning and went over to his office, still deep in thought. His only conclusion was that he must be thinking the wrong way. There was nothing much in his In basket except a note that Johnson of the DEA was trying to reach him and a carbon of the report on the Burnt Water necklace turning up. It simply repeated what Dashee had told him, with the details filled in.

Subject named Edna Nezzie, twenty-three, unmarried, of the Graywoman Nezzie camp, north of Teec Nos Pos, had pawned the necklace at Mexican Water. It had been recognized from the description left with the post manager by Tribal Police. Subsequently, subject Nezzie had told investigating officer Eddie Begay that she had been given the necklace by a male subject she had met two nights earlier at a squaw dance next to Mexican Water. She identified the subject as a Navajo male about thirty, who had identified himself as Joseph Musket. The two had gone to a white Ford pickup Musket was driving. There they had engaged in sexual intercourse. Musket then had given the subject the necklace and they had returned to the dance. She had seen no more of him.

Chee frowned at the paper, trying to identify why something was wrong about it. Still staring at the report, he fumbled for the telephone, and dialed the operator, and asked for the number of the trading post at Teec Nos Pos. It rang five times before he got an answer.

Chee identified himself. "Just need some information. What clan is Graywoman Nezzie?"

"Nezzie," the voice said. "She's born to Standing Rock and born for Bitter Water."

"You're sure?"

"I'm one of the old lady's sons-in-law," the voice said. "Married into 'em. The father is Water Runs Together and Many Poles."

"Thanks," Chee said, and hung up. He remembered Mrs. Musket identifying herself. Born to Standing Rock Dinee, she had said, and born for the Mud Clan. So the man who had identified himself as Joseph Musket at the Mexican Water squaw dance could not possibly have been Joseph Musket. For a Navajo male to dance with a Navajo female of the same maternal clan violated the most stringent of taboos. And the intraclan intercourse that followed was the most heinous form of incest—sure to cause sickness, sure to cause insanity, likely to bring death. If it was Musket, it could only mean that he had lied to the girl about his clan. Otherwise she would never have danced with him, gone to the truck with him, even talked to him except in the most formal fashion. And no Navajo male would engage in such a ghastly deception.

Unless, Chee thought, he was a witch.

Chee left a note to tell Largo where to find him and headed for Cameron. En route he remembered what Mrs. Musket had told him about the homecoming of Ironfingers, his urgent need for the traditional Navajo purification ceremonial, his stated intentions to rejoin the People as a herder of sheep. Such behavior was incongruous with deliberate incest—an act which any traditional Navajo knew endangered the health of the entire clan. Chee narrowed it down to two choices. Either someone had imitated Ironfingers at the squaw dance, or Ironfingers was a madman. Or in other words, a witch.

In Cameron he bought a sack of cement at the lumberyard, and a tub at the hardware store, and a flexible plastic funnel at the drugstore. Then he made the long, lonely drive back to the Hopi Reservation, still thinking. At the windmill he left the sack of cement beside the well shaft, put the funnel beside it, and covered both with the tub, just in case the rain clouds building up again in the west produced some moisture.

He drove back down Wepo Wash to Burnt Water Trading Post and parked in the shade of the cottonwood beside West's battered and rusty jeep. By then he had come up with only a single idea. He could stake out the cache of suitcases and nail Musket when he came to dig them up. It wasn't a very good idea. Chee didn't think he could count on Musket coming for the suitcases. More likely, Ironfingers would collect his money and tell the buyers where to pick up the goods. Chee was not interested in the buyers. He was officially, formally, and by explicit orders not interested. But Ironfingers was his business. He had been told to solve the burglary at Burnt Water. He had been told to unravel the business of witchcraft on Black Mesa. Ironfingers was the answer to the first. Ironfingers might have some answers to the second.

Chee sat. He watched the thunderheads boiling up in the west. He went through it all again. The conclusion was the same. Musket would have to come to whatever meeting place he established to get his money. He would not be likely to go dig up the suitcases. The crash scene must seem dangerous to him. Musket couldn't tell Gaines where to meet him until the last moment—to do so could give the buyers a chance to set up a trap. Chee could think of no possible way he could intercept the information. He had thought of digging up the suitcases himself, rehiding them somewhere, and leaving a note to force Musket to come to him. But more likely it would be the buyers who would find the note and come to him. That was the sort of trouble Chee didn't intend to invite. In fact, it was the sort of trouble that had been at the back of his mind ever since Johnson had warned him that the drug dealers would be looking for him. Johnson's prediction hadn't proved true—but still might. The people for whom Gaines worked might well guess that Palanzer would have needed a local helper. There was no way for Chee to know for sure that they knew about Ironfingers.

Chee fished out his notebook and reexamined what he had written while waiting for Cowboy Dashee. "Where is J. Musket?" He stared at the question. And then at another. "Why the burglary?" And then at "Who is John Doe?" He thought about the dates. Doe had died July 10, young West had died July 6.

Musket had walked out of this trading post two weeks later and vanished—apparently after coming back the same night to haul off a load of pawn jewelry. Then, weeks later, he carelessly gives away a single piece. Or someone gives it away in Musket's name.

Chee climbed out of his truck and walked into the trading post. If West wasn't occupied, he'd go over the whole burglary business with him again.

West was putting an order of groceries and odds and ends into a box for a middle-aged Navajo woman. The purchase included a coil of that light, flexible rope which Navajos used to tie sheep, horses, loads on pickup trucks, and all those thousands of things which must be tied. West had left the coil for last. Now he dropped it into the box, said something to the woman, and took it out again. He measured out fifteen or twenty feet of it with quick outthrusts of his arms, and then collected this in a tangle of loops in his right hand, talking to the woman all the time. Still standing at the doorway, Chee couldn't overhear what he was saying. Whatever it was, it attracted two men who had been standing down the counter. West handed the woman the rope. All three Navajos inspected it. They were grinning. West the sorcerer was about to perform. He took the rope back, folded it into a half-dozen dangling loops in his huge right hand. His left hand extracted a knife from his coveralls pocket. He slashed through the loops, and held up eight cut ends. Then he disposed of the knife, extracted a bandanna from his pocket, covered the severed ends with the handkerchief. He was talking steadily. Chee guessed he was explaining the curing quality of his magic handkerchief. A moment later West pulled the bandanna away and with the same motion dropped the rope. It fell to the floor, a single piece again. West whipped it up, snapped it between his outstretched hands. He handed it to the woman. She inspected it, and was impressed. The two male watchers were grinning appreciatively. Chee grinned, too. A good trick, well done. He'd seen it before—a magic show done for donations on the Union Mall at the University of New Mexico. It had taken him most of the day to narrow down the only possible way the trick could be done. And that night he'd gone to the library, and found a book of magic tricks in the stacks, and confirmed that he'd been right. The trick was in creating the illusion with the gathered loops that the cord had been cut into fragments when actually only short bits had been sliced from one end—and those disposed of in a pocket when the bandanna was whipped away.

Chee stood by the doorway, remembering the three of diamonds trick, which also depended on creating an illusion—the distracting thought that it mattered which card the victim named. West was a master of this business of controlling how one thought. A master of illusion.

Chee's smile faded. His face fell into that slack, mindless appearance of totally concentrated thought. Slowly the smile appeared again, and broadened, and converted itself into a great, exultant laugh. It was loud enough to attract West's attention. He was looking at Chee, surprised. His audience was also staring.

"You want to see me?" West asked.

"Later," Chee said. He hurried out, the grin fading as his thoughts took better shape, and climbed into his pickup truck. The notebook was on the seat. He opened it, flipped to the proper page.

Across from "Why the burglary?" he wrote: "Was there a burglary?" Then he studied the other questions. Across from "Did Musket kill John Doe?" he wrote: "Was John Doe Ironfingers?" Then he closed the notebook, started the engine, and pulled the truck out of the trading post parking lot. He would talk to West later. First, he wanted time to think this through. Had West, the magician, the sorcerer, used Jim Chee to create one of his illusions? He wanted time to answer that. But now, as he drove down the bumpy road beside Wepo Wash, toward the reddish sunset, and the towering thunderclouds which promised rain and delivered nothing, he was fairly sure that when he had thought it through he would know the answer. The answer would be yes. Yes, for all these weeks Ironfingers had been hidden behind Jim Chee's stupidity.

25

IN FACT, THE ANSWER WAS not a definite yes. It was "probably."

With sundown, the thunderheads lost their will to grow. With the cool darkness, they lost their will to live. Chee drove slowly, arm rested on the sill of the open truck window, enjoying the breeze. Lightning still flashed yellow and white in the cloud west of him, and the dark north also produced an occasional jagged bolt. But the clouds were dying. Overhead, the stars were out. The Colorado Plateau and the Painted Desert would live with drought through another cycle of sun. But Chee was aware of this only on a secondary level. He was reaching conclusions.

The man he'd seen coming from West's office; the man West had said he'd just fired; the man West said was Joseph Musket, might not have been Musket at all. Probably wasn't, Chee thought. West had simply used Jim Chee, a brand-new policeman who'd never seen Musket, to establish on the official record that Musket was alive, and well, and being fired by West, the day after John Doe's remains had been collected on Black Mesa. He'd done it neatly, asking Chee to come in when he knew some appropriate Navajo would be available, then arousing Chee's interest in the man when it was too late to get a good look at him. The pseudo Musket, Chee guessed, would be someone from somewhere else—whom Chee wouldn't be seeing around Burnt Water.

That was the first conclusion. The second revolved around

another illusion. West had probably performed his Musket deception, and then staged the pretended burglary, because Joseph Musket was already dead. Killed by whom? Probably by West himself. Why? Chee would leave that for later. There'd be a reason. There always was. Now he concentrated on the faded white line illuminated by his headlights, and on recreating what must have happened.

The cool air smelled of wet sage, and creosote bush, and ozone. For the first time in days, Chee felt in harmony with his thoughts. *Hozro* again. His mind was working as it should, on the natural path. West had found himself with the body of Musket on his hands. He had killed Musket, or someone else had done it, or Musket had simply died. And West didn't want it known. Not yet. Perhaps he'd gotten wind of the impending drug shipment. Perhaps his son had told him. Perhaps he'd learned it from Musket. And West wanted to steal it. And if shippers knew their man at Burnt Water was dead, they might move the landing point, or call everything off. So the death and the body had been concealed.

Chee found himself appreciating the cleverness. West knew he was dealing with very dangerous men. He knew they'd come after the thief. He wanted someone besides West for them to hunt. Ironfingers got the job. Which meant he could never, ever, afford the risk of having the corpse, or even the skeleton, of anyone who met Musket's description turning up to be identified. A skeleton, even a bit of jawbone, would be enough to match against the name of a missing person who'd been in prison—whose dental charts and fingerprints and all other vital statistics would be easily available. Therefore West had put the body out along the traditional pathway of the spruce Messenger's party, where it would be found exactly when he wanted it found. He'd faked the witchcraft mutilation—the hands and feet and probably the penis, too—to eliminate the automatic fingerprinting an unidentified corpse would undergo. It was his only wrong guess—not calculating that the Hopis wouldn't report the corpse before their Niman Kachina ceremonials—and it hadn't mattered. And then—Chee grinned again, savoring the cleverness of it—West had made certain that the official record would show Musket alive and well in

Burnt Water after the corpse was found. That would kill any chance of matching dental charts. He would have done that, somehow, even if the body had been reported immediately.

Chee had this sorted out by the time his pickup made the long climb up the cliff of Moenkopi Wash, passed the Hopi village, and reached the Tuba City junction. By the time he'd reached Tuba City he reached another conclusion. West was hiding the body of Palanzer for the same reason he'd made Musket forever invisible. Palanzer-plus-Musket gave the owners of the cocaine an even more logical target for their rage.

Puddles from a rain do not long survive in a desert climate. The puddles in the track to Chee's mobile home had disappeared long ago. But the ruts were still soft and driving through them would cut them deeper. Chee parked the pickup, climbed out, and began walking the last fifty yards toward his home. There was still an occasional mutter of thunder from the north, but the sky now was a blaze of stars. Chee walked on the bunch grass, thinking that much of his problem still remained. There was absolutely nothing he could prove. All he would have for Captain Largo would be speculation. No. That wasn't true. Now the remains of John Doe could be identified—unless, of course, Musket had never been to a dentist. That wasn't likely. Chee enjoyed the night, the washed-clean smell of the air. The smell, suddenly, of brewing coffee.

Chee stopped in his tracks. Coffee! From where? He stared at his trailer. Dark and silent. It was the only possible source of that rich aroma. He had placed the trailer here under this lonely cottonwood for privacy and isolation. The site gave him that. The nearest other possible coffeepot was a quarter mile away. Someone was waiting in his dark trailer. They'd grown impatient. In the darkness, they'd brewed coffee. Chee turned and walked rapidly back toward his truck. The trailer produced a sudden clatter of sound. They'd been watching since he'd driven up and parked. They'd seen him turn away. Chee's walk became a run. He had his ignition key in his hand by the time he jerked the pickup door open. He heard the trailer door bang open, the sound of running feet. Then he had the key in the ignition. The still-warm motor roared into life. Chee slammed the gears into reverse, flicked on the headlights.

The lights illuminated two running men. One of them was the younger of the two men Chee had noticed watching him in the Hopi Cultural Center dining room. The other man Chee had seen hunting at the crash site, helping Johnson in his search for the suitcases. The younger man had a pistol in his hand. Chee switched off the lights and sent the pickup truck roaring backward down the track. He didn't turn on the headlights again until he was back on the asphalt.

26

CHEE SPENT THE NIGHT beside his pickup truck in a sand-bottomed cul-de-sac off Moenkopi Wash. He'd stopped twice to make absolutely sure he hadn't been followed. Even so, he was nervous. He shaped the sand to fit hips and shoulders, rolled out his blanket, and lay looking up at a star-lit sky. Nothing remained of the afternoon's empty promise of rain except an occasional distant thunder from somewhere up around the Utah border. Why had the two men waited for him in his trailer? Obviously it hadn't been a friendly visit. Could he have been wrong about one of the men having been with Johnson in Wepo Wash? It would have made more sense for them to be members of the narcotics company. As Johnson had warned him, they might logically come looking for him. But why now? They would have learned by now that the dope was being sold back to them. Did they think that he was one of the hijackers doing the selling? He, and Musket, and Palanzer? But if the man had been the one he'd seen with Johnson in the wash, that meant something different. What would the DEA want with Chee? And why would the DEA wait for him in the dark, instead of calling him into Largo's office for a talk? Was it because, once again, the DEA's intentions were not wholly orthodox? Because he hadn't returned Johnson's call? That line of speculation led Chee nowhere. He turned his thoughts to the telephone call to Gaines. Tomorrow night the exchange would be made—five hundred thousand dollars in currency for two suitcases filled with cocaine. But where? All he knew now, that he hadn't known, was that the caller might have been West, and that Musket might be dead. That didn't seem to help. Then, as he thought it through all the way, through from the east, the south, the west, and the north, and back to the east again, just as his uncle had taught him, he saw that it might help. Everything must have a reason. Nothing was done without a cause. Why delay the payoff more than necessary—as the caller had done? How would tomorrow night be different from tonight? Different for West? Probably, somehow or other, the nights would be different on the Hopi ceremonial calendar. And West would be aware of the difference. He had been married to a Hopi. In the Hopi tradition, he had moved into the matriarchy of his wife—into her village and into her home. Three or four years, Dashee had said. Certainly long enough to know something of the Hopi religious calendar.

Chee shifted into a more comfortable position. The nervous tension was draining away now, the sense of being hunted. He felt relaxed and drowsy. Tomorrow he would get in touch with Dashee and find out what would be going on tomorrow night in the Hopi world of kachina spirits and men who wore sacred masks to impersonate them.

Chee was thinking of kachinas when he drifted off into sleep, and he dreamed of them. He awoke feeling stiff and sore. Shaking the sand out of his blanket, he folded it behind the pickup seat. Whoever had been waiting in his trailer had probably long since left Tuba City, but Chee decided not to take any chances. He drove southward instead, to Cameron. He got to the roadside diner just at sunrise, ordered pancakes and sausage for breakfast, and called Dashee from the pay telephone booth.

"What time is it?" Dashee said.

"It's late," Chee said. "I need some information. What's going on tonight at Hopi?"

"My God," Dashee shouted. "It's only a little after six. I just got to bed. I'm on the night shift for the next week."

"Sorry," Chee said. "But tell me about tonight."

"Tonight?" Dashee said. "There's nothing tonight. The Chu'tiwa—the Snake Dance ceremony—that's at Walpi day after tomorrow. Nothing tonight."

"Nowhere?" Chee asked. "Not in Walpi, or Ilotevilla, or

Bacobi, or anywhere?" He was disappointed and his voice showed it.

"Nothing much," Dashee said. "Just mostly stuff in the kivas. Getting ready for the Snake ceremonials. Private stuff."

"How about that village where West lived? His wife's village. Which one was it?"

"Sityatki," Dashee said.

"Anything going on there?"

There was a long pause.

"Cowboy? You still there?"

"Yeah," Cowboy said.

"Anything at Sityatki tonight?"

"Nothing much," Cowboy said.

"But something?"

"Nothing for tourists," Dashee said.

"What is it?"

"Well, it's something we call Astotokaya. It means Washing of the Hair. It's private. Sort of an initiation ceremony into the religious societies of the village."

It didn't sound to Chee like the sort of thing that would be useful to West.

"Does it draw a big crowd? I think that's what we're looking for."

Dashee laughed. "Just the opposite—they close the roads. Nobody is supposed to come in. Everybody is supposed to stay indoors, not even look out the windows. People who live in houses that look out on the kivas, they move out. Nobody stirs except the people working on the initiation in the kivas and the young people getting initiated. And they don't come out until dawn."

"Tell me about it," Chee said. The disappointment was gone. He thought he knew, now, where West would set up his rendezvous.

Cowboy was reluctant. "It's confidential," he said. "Some of that stuff we're not really supposed to talk about."

"I think it might be important," Chee said. "A funny thing happened yesterday. I was at the cultural center, and the clerk got called away from the desk, and the telephone was ringing, so Miss Pauling went over there and worked the switchboard and—"

"I heard about that fire," Dashee said. "You start that fire?"

"Why would I start a fire?" Chee asked. "What I'm trying to tell you is Miss Pauling overheard this guy telling Gaines that the people who owned the cocaine could buy it back for five hundred thousand dollars. He said they should have the money available in two briefcases by nine o'clock Friday night. And he said he'd be back in touch to say where the trade-off would be made."

"How'd you know when to start the fire?" Dashee said. "How'd you know when that call was coming? You son of a bitch, you almost burned down the cultural center."

"The point is why hold off until nine o'clock Friday night? That's the question; and I think the answer is because they want to make the switch in a place where the buyers will figure there's going to be a bunch of curious people standing around watching, when actually it will be private."

"Sityatki," Cowboy said.

"Right. It makes sense."

Long pause, while Cowboy thought about it. "Not much," he said. "Why go to all that trouble if they're just going to swap money for cocaine?"

"Safety," Chee said. "They need to be someplace where the guys buying the dope back won't just shoot them and keep the money and everything."

"No safer there than anyplace else," Dashee argued.

Maybe it wasn't, Chee thought. But why else wait until nine Friday night? "Well," he said, "I think the swap's going to be made in Sityatki, and if you'd tell me more about what goes on, maybe I'll know why."

So Cowboy told him, reluctantly and haltingly enough so that Chee's pancakes and sausages were cold by the time he had prodded it all out, and it added nothing much. The crux of the matter was the village was sealed from darkness until dawn, people were supposed to remain indoors and not be looking out to spy on the spirits who visited the kivas during the night, and the place was periodically patrolled by priests of the kiva—but more ceremonially than seriously, Cowboy thought.

Chee took his time over breakfast, killing some of the minutes that had to pass before he could call Captain Largo at his office. Largo would be just a little bit late, and Chee wanted his call to be hanging there waiting for the captain when he walked in. Sometimes little psychological edges like that helped, and Chee was sure he'd need some.

"He's not in yet," the girl on the switchboard reported.

"You're sure?" Chee asked. "Usually he gets in about eight-oh-five."

"Just a minute," she amended. "He's driving into the parking lot."

Which was exactly how Chee had planned it.

"Largo," Largo said.

"This is Chee. There's a couple of things I have to report."

"On the telephone?"

"When I came in last night, there were two men waiting for me in my trailer. With the lights off. With a gun. One of them, anyway."

"Last night?" Largo said.

"About ten, maybe."

"And now you're reporting it?"

"I think one of them was Drug Enforcement. At least, I think I've seen him with Johnson. And if one was, I guess they both were. Anyway, I wasn't sure what to do, so I took off."

"Any violence?"

"No. I figured they were in there, so I headed back to my truck. They heard me and came running out. One of them had a gun, but no shooting."

"How'd you know they were there?"

"Smelled coffee," Chee said.

Largo didn't comment on that. "Those sons-a-bitches," he said.

"The other thing is that Miss Pauling told me she overheard a telephone call from some man to Gaines. He told Gaines he could have the cocaine back for five hundred thousand dollars and to be ready with the money at nine P.M. Friday and—"

"Where?"

"He didn't say. This isn't our case, so I didn't ask too many questions. I told Cowboy Dashee and I guess they'll go out and talk to her."

"Heard they had a little fire out there," Largo said. "You know anything about that?"

"I'm the one who reported it," Chee said. "Bunch of tumbleweeds caught on fire."

"Listen," Largo said. "I'm going to do some seeing about the way the DEA is behaving. We're not going to put up with any more of that. And when I talk to people I'm going to tell them that I gave you strict orders to stay away from this drug case. I'm going to tell people I'm going to kick your ass right out of the Navajo Police if I hear just one little hint that you're screwing around in federal territory. I'm going to tell people you understand that perfectly. That you know I'll do it. No question about it. You know that if you get anywhere near that drug case, or anybody involved with it, you are instantly and permanently suspended. Fired. Out of work."

Largo paused, allowing time for the speech to penetrate. "Now," he continued. "You do understand that, don't you? You understand that when I hang up this telephone I am going to write a memo for the files which will show that for the third and final time Jim Chee was officially and formally notified that any involvement on his part in this investigation would result in his immediate termination, said memo also showing that Chee did understand and agree to these instructions. Now, you got all that?"

"I got it," Chee said. "Just one thing, though. Would you put in the memo what I'm supposed to be doing? Put down that you've assigned me to working on that windmill, and solving the Burnt Water burglary, and finding Joseph Musket, and identifying that John Doe case up on Black Mesa. Would you put all that down, too?"

Another long pause. Chee guessed that Largo had never intended to write any memo for the record. Now he was examining Chee's motives.

"Why?" Largo asked.

"Just to get it all in, all in one place on the record."

"Okay," Largo said.

"And I think we should ask the medical examiner's office

in Flagstaff to check the New Mexico State Penitentiary and see if they can come up with any dental x-rays on Joseph Musket, and then check them against the x-rays they took of John Doe's teeth."

"Wait a minute," Largo said. "You saw Musket alive after Doe's body was found."

"I saw somebody," Chee said. "West said it was Musket."

Another silence. "Ah," Largo said. "Yes, indeed."

"And about the windmill. I think I know who has been doing it, but it's nothing we're ever going to prove." He told Largo about the spring, and the shrine, and about how old Taylor Sawkatewa had tacitly admitted being there the night the plane had crashed, when Deputy Sheriff Dashee and Chee had talked to him.

"Wait a minute," Largo said. "When was this visit? It was after I ordered you to stay away from that drug case."

"I was working on the windmill," Chee said. "Sometimes you get more than you go after."

"I notice you do," Largo said grimly. "I've got to have the paperwork done on all this."

"Is tomorrow soon enough?"

"Just barely," Largo said. "What's wrong with coming in to work and doing it now?"

"I'm way down at Cameron," Chee said. "And I thought I'd spend the day seeing if I can catch us that Burnt Water burglar."

27

THE FIRST STEP toward what Chee called catching the Burnt Water burglar was ceremonial. In effect, Chee was going hunting. From their very beginnings, the Navajos had been a society of hunters. Like all hunting cultures, they approached the bloody, dangerous, and psychologically wounding business of killing one's fellow beings with elaborate care. Everything was done to minimize damage. The system had been devised in the dim, cold past, when the Dinees preyed with the wolves on the moose and caribou of the Arctic. And the first step of this system was the purification of the hunter.

There was no place anywhere near his trailer lot where Chee could build a sweat house. So he had found a place on the ridge behind Tuba City. He'd built it in a little arroyo, using one of the banks for a wall and erecting a sort of lean-to of rocks and juniper limbs. There was plenty of dead wood all around to fuel its fire pit. The necessary water Chee carried in from his truck in two collapsible plastic containers. By midmorning, the rocks were hot enough. Chee stripped to his Jockey shorts. He stood, facing east, and sang the first of the four sweat lodge songs:

I am come from Graystreak Mountain;
I am standing nearby.
I am the Talking God,
A son of Female Wind. I stand near you
With a black bow in my right hand,
With a yellow-feathered arrow in my left hand.
I am the Talking God, standing ready. . . .

He sang all the verses, dropped to his hands and knees, and ducked through the sweat house entrance into the hot darkness inside. He poured water from one of the plastic containers onto the sizzling boulders and pulled the heavy canvas cover down over the entrance. In the steamy blackness he sang three other songs, recounting how Talking God and the other *yei* figures of this legend had caught Black God in his guise as a crow, and how Black God had removed his suit of black feathers, and how Black God had been tricked, finally, into releasing all the game animals which he had held captive.

With that ritual finished, Chee was not certain how he should proceed. It was not the sort of question he would have ever thought to ask Frank Sam Nakai. "How, Uncle, does one prepare himself for a hunt which will take him into a Hopi village on a Holy Night when the kachina spirits are out? How does one prepare himself to trap another man?" Had he ever asked, he knew Frank Sam Nakai would have had an answer. He would have lit a cigaret, and smoked it, and finally he would have had an answer. Chee, his sweat bath songs finished, sat in the choking wet heat and thought about it in the Navajo Way—from east through north. The purpose of the hunting ceremony—the Stalking Way—was to put hunter and prey in harmony. If one was to hunt deer, the Stalking Way repeated the ancient formula by which man regained his ability to be one with the deer. One changed the formula only slightly to fit the animal. The animal, now, was man. An Anglo-American, ex-husband of a Hopi woman, trader with the Navajos, magician, wise, shrewd, dangerous. Chee felt the sweat pouring out of him, dripping from his chin and eyebrows and arms, and thought how to change the song to fit it to West. He sang:

I am the Talking God. The Talking God.
I am going after him.
Below the east, I am going after him.
To that place in Wepo Wash, I am going after him.
I, being the Talking God, go in pursuit of him.
To Black Mesa, to the Hopi villages,
The chase will take me.

I am the Talking God. His luck will be with me.
His thoughts will be my thoughts as I go after him.

Verse after verse he sang, adopting the ancient ceremonial songs to meet this new need. The songs invoked Talking God, and Begochidi, and Calling God, and Black God himself, and the Predator People: First Wolf, First Puma, First Badger; recounting the role of Game Maker, and all the other Holy People of the Great Navajo myth of how hunting began and how man became himself a predator. Through it all, verse by verse, the purpose was the same as it had been since his ancestors hunted along the glaciers: to cross the prehuman flux and once again be as one with the hunted animal, sharing his spirit, his ways, thoughts, his very being.

Chee simply substituted "the man West" for "the fine buck" and sang on.

In the evening twilight, the man West is calling to
me.
Out of the darkness, the man West comes toward
me.
Our minds are one mind, the man West and I, the
Talking God.
Our Spirits are one spirit, the man West and I, the
Talking God.
Toward my feathered arrow, the man West walks
directly.
Toward my feathered arrow, the man West turns
his side.
That my black bow will bless him with its beauty.
That my feathered arrow will make him like the
Talking God.
That he may walk, and I may walk, forever in
Beauty.
That we may walk with beauty all around us.
That my feathered arrow may end it all in Beauty.

There should be a final ceremony, and a final verse. In the old, traditional days, the bow of the hunter would have been blessed. These days, sometimes it was done to the rifle before a deer hunt. Chee unsnapped his holster and extracted his pistol. It was a medium-barrel Ruger .38. He was not particularly good with it, making his qualifying score each year with very little to spare. He had never shot at any living thing with it, and had never really decided what he would do if the situation demanded that some fellow human be fired upon. Given proper need, or proper provocation, Chee presumed he would shoot, but it wasn't the sort of decision to be made in the abstract. Now Chee stared at the pistol, trying to imagine himself shooting West. It didn't work. He put the pistol back in the holster. As he did, it occurred to him that the final verse of the usual sweat bath ceremonial could not be done now. The prescribed verse was the Blessing Song from the Blessing Way. But Jim Chee, a shaman of the Slow Talking People, could sing no blessing songs now. Not until this hunt was finished and he had returned to this sweat bath to purify himself again. Until then, Jim Chee had turned himself into a predator, dedicated by the Stalking Way songs to the hunt. The Blessing Song would have to wait. It put one in harmony with beauty. The Stalking Way put one in harmony with death.

28

JIM CHEE WAITED for West, or for Ironfingers, or for whoever would come, just as a mountain lion waits for game at a watering place. He picked a place which gave him a good view of the burial place of the suitcases and from which he could move quickly to make an arrest. He had checked the area and found no sign that West's jeep, or any other vehicle, had been here since Johnson's futile search. He poked his jack handle into the sand until he felt the steel tapping against aluminum. The bait was still in place. Then he sat behind a screen of junipers on the bank of the wash and waited. He didn't expect West to come. But if West did come, Chee would be waiting.

It was midafternoon now, a little less than six hours before the 9:00 P.M. deadline the caller had announced for the transfer of drugs for money. It was humid—a rare circumstance for the Colorado plateau—and the thunderheads were boiling up northward toward Utah and over the Mogollon Rim to the West. Chee still felt the effects of the heat and dehydration of the sweat bath. He'd taken two huge drinks of water to replace the lost fluids and was, in fact, sweating again now. Still, he felt a kind of clear, clean sharpness in his vision and in his mind. Hosteen Nakai had taught him of the time when all intelligent things were still in flux, when what-would-be-animal and that-which-would-be-human could still talk together, and change forms. In a ceremonial way, the Stalking Way was intended to restore that ancient power on some much-limited intellectual level. Chee wondered about it as he waited. Was he seeing and thinking a little more like a wolf or a puma?

There was no way to answer that. So he reviewed all he knew of this affair, from the very beginning, concentrating on West. West the magician, causing him to think of mental telepathy instead of the mathematics of how a deck of cards can be divided. West misdirecting the attention of the Navajo buying the rope, misdirecting Chee's attention away from the easy solution of the three of diamonds, misdirecting attention away from why Joseph Musket's hands were flayed. Always distorting reality with illusion. And now, why was West asking only five hundred thousand dollars for a cocaine shipment that the DEA said was worth many millions of dollars? Why so little? Because he wanted it fast? Because he wanted to minimize any risk that the owners wouldn't be willing to buy it back? Because West was not a greedy man? That was his reputation. And it seemed to be justified. He had no expensive tastes. No drinking. No women. As trading posts went, Burnt Water seemed to be moderately profitable, and West's prices, and his interest rate on pawn, showed no tendency to gouge. He was, in fact, known to be generous on occasion. Cowboy had told him once of West giving a drunk twenty dollars for bus fare to Flagstaff. Not the act of a man who valued money for money's sake.

So what would he do with five hundred thousand dollars? How would he use it, a lonely man with no one to spend it on, no one to spend it with? There must be a reason for demanding it, for setting up the steal, for the killing and the danger. A West reason. A white man's reason.

Chee stared out across the sandy bottom of Wepo Wash. Slowly, the white man's reason emerged. Chee checked it against everything he knew, everything that had happened. Everywhere it fit. Now he was sure West wouldn't come for the suitcases.

Chee left his hiding place, and walked back to the arroyo where he had left his patrol car. He drove it, with no effort at all at concealment, up the wash to the crash location. He parked it beside the basalt upthrust. His shovel was in his pickup truck but he didn't really need it. He dug with his hands, exposing the two suitcases, and pulled them out. They were surprisingly heavy—each sixty to seventy pounds, he guessed.

He loaded them into the trunk of his patrol car, slammed the trunk shut, then reached in through the window and got his clipboard.

If he was right, this work was wasted. But if he was wrong, someone would come today—or someday—to dig up the cache and vanish with it. Questions would be left unanswered then, and Chee would no longer have a way to find the answers. Chee hated unanswered questions.

On the notepad on the clipboard, he wrote in block print: I HAVE THE SUITCASES. HANG AROUND BURNT WATER AND REMEMBER THE NUMBER OF LETTERS IN THIS MESSAGE. Then he counted the letters. Seventy-nine.

He fished through the glove box, found an empty aspirin bottle he used to keep matches in, removed the matches, and folded in the note. He wiped off his fingerprints and dropped the bottle in the hole where the suitcases had been.

29

THE VILLAGE OF SITYATKI, like many of the Southwest's pueblo villages, had been split by the human lust for running water. The original village still perched atop the east cliff of Third Mesa, from which it stared four hundred feet straight down into the sandy bottom of Polacca Wash. But along the wash itself, the Bureau of Indian Affairs had built a scattering of those brown frame-and-plaster bungalows which are standard government housing, equipped them with refrigerators and a pressure-tank water system, and thereby lured perhaps three-fourths of the younger residents of Sityatki down from the cliffs. The deserters, for the most part, remained loyal to village traditions, to their duties to the Fox, Coyote, and Fire clans which had founded it in the fourteenth century, and to the religious society into which they had been initiated. But they were usually present in the village only in spirit, and when ceremonial occasions required. Tonight, the presence of most of them was not required—was in fact discouraged—and the little stone houses which were theirs by right through the wombs of their mothers and grandmothers and great-grandmothers for twenty or so generations now stood empty. Tonight was the night of the Washing of the Hair, when the four great religious fraternities of the village—the Wuchim, the Flute, the One Horn, the Two Horn—initiate young people. For more than a week, the *na'chi* of the Wuchim Society had been planted atop the Wuchim kiva at the east edge of the Sityatki plaza, its sparrow-hawk feathers ruffled by the August breezes—a sort of flag notifying the Hopis that the priests of Wuchim were preparing for the ritual. The kivas of the three other societies were also marked by their distinctive standards. And this afternoon the few families who still lived on the east side of the village had moved from their houses and hung blankets over windows and doorways. When darkness came, no profane eyes would be looking out to witness the kachinas coming from the spirit world to visit the kivas and bless their new brothers.

Jim Chee knew this—or thought he knew it—because he had taken a course in Southwestern ethnology at UNM, which had taught him enough to pry a little more out of a reluctant and uneasy Cowboy Dashee.

Chee had never been to Sityatki, but he'd had Cowboy describe it in wearisome (for Cowboy) detail—from the layout of its streets to the ins and outs of its single dead-ended access road. Now he reached one of the few "outs" the road offered, a side track which zigzagged downward to provide risky access to the bottom of Polacca Wash. His plan was to leave the car here, out of sight from the access road. If what Dashee had told him was accurate, a little after dark a priest of the One Horn Society would emerge from the society's kiva and "close" the road by sprinkling a line of corn meal and pollen across it. He would then draw similar sacred lines across the footpaths leading into the village from the other directions, barring entry except by the "spirit path" used by the kachinas. Chee's intentions were to reach the village when it was dark enough to avoid being seen by West, or anyone else who might know him, but before Sityatki was ceremonially closed against intruders. Chee parked the car behind a growth of junipers near the wash, transferred the flashlight from the glove box to the hip pocket of his jeans, and locked the door. About a mile to walk, he guessed, including the steep climb back up to the mesa rim. But he'd left himself at least an hour of daylight. Plenty of time.

He hadn't covered a hundred yards when he saw West's jeep. Like Chee's patrol car, it had been driven behind a screen of brush. Chee checked it quickly, saw nothing interesting, and hurried up the hill. He felt a sense of urgency. Why had West come so early? Probably for the same reason that had motivated Chee. He had probably called in the location of the meeting place at the last possible moment and then rushed to make sure he'd be here first and that no trap could be set for him. On the mesa top, Chee kept away from the road but near enough to watch it. An old pickup passed, driving a little faster than the bumpy road made wise or comfortable. Hopis, Chee guessed, hurrying to some ceremonial duty, or perhaps just anxious to get to their homes before the village was sealed. Then came a car, dark blue and new, a Lincoln edging cautiously over the stony surface. Chee stopped and watched it, feeling excitement rising. It wouldn't be a local car. It might be a sightseer, but the usually hospitable Hopis did not advertise this event, nor encourage tourists to come to it. More likely, the blue Lincoln confirmed his guess about where West had arranged the buy-back. This was The Boss coming to ransom his cocaine shipment. The car eased into a depression, moving at no more than walking speed. At the bottom of the dip, the rear door opened, and a crouching man stepped out, clicked the door shut behind him, and was out of sight behind the junipers along the cliff. Too much distance, too little light, too short a moment for Chee to register whether the man looked familiar. He could see only that he was blond, and wore a blue-and-gray shirt. The Boss apparently had not followed orders to come alone; he'd brought along a bodyguard. Like Chee, the bodyguard intended to slip into the village unnoticed.

Chee waited; he wanted to give this man time to get well ahead. But when he thought of it, it didn't matter whether this fellow saw him or not. Out of uniform, in his off-day jeans and work shirt, Chee conceded that he would be seen by this white man as just another Hopi walking home from wherever he'd been. Chee conceded this reluctantly. To Chee, Navajos and Hopis, or Navajos and anyone else for that matter, looked no more alike than apples and oranges. It wasn't until Hosteen Nakai pointed out to him that after three years at the University of New Mexico, Chee still couldn't sort out Swedes from Englishmen, or Jews from Lebanese, that Chee was willing to admit that this "all Indians look alike" business with white men was genuine, something to be added to his growing store of data about the Anglo-American culture.

Chee hurried again, not worrying about being seen. Like

himself, the man who had slipped out of the car was keeping away from the road. And like Chee, he was skirting along the rim of the mesa. Chee kept him periodically in sight for a while, and then lost him as the twilight deepened. He didn't think it would matter. Sityatki was a small place—a cluster of no more than fifty residences crowded around two small plazas, each with two small kivas. It shouldn't be hard to find the blue Lincoln.

He reached the edge of the village a little earlier than he'd planned. The sun was well below the horizon now, but the clouds which had been building up all afternoon gave the dying light a sort of glum grayness. Far to the west, back over the Mogollon Rim and Grand Canyon country, the sky was black with storm. Chee stopped beside a plank outhouse, glanced at his watch, and decided to wait for a little more darkness. No breeze moved the air. It was motionless and, rarity of rarities in this climate, damp with a warm, smothering humidity. Maybe it would rain. Really rain—a soaking, drought-breaking deluge. Chee hoped it would, but he didn't expect it. Even when the storm is breaking, the desert dweller maintains his inbred skepticism about clouds. He finds it hard to believe in rain even when it's falling on him. He's seen too many showers evaporate between thunderclap and the parched earth.

There was thunder now, a distant boom, which echoed from somewhere back over Black Mesa. And when it died away, Chee heard a faint, rhythmic sound. Ceremonial drumming, he guessed, from the depth of one of the village kivas. It would be time to move.

A path from the outhouse led along the rim of the cliff, skirting past the outermost wall of the outermost residence, threading through a narrow gap between the uneven stones and open space. Chee took it. Far below, at the bottom of the wash, the darkness was almost total. Lights were on in the BIA housing—rectangles of bright yellow—and the headlights of a vehicle were moving slowly down the road which followed the dry watercourse. Normally Chee had no particular trouble with heights. But now he felt an uneasy, shaky nervousness. He moved along the wall, turned into the walkway between two of the crowded buildings, and found himself looking out into the plaza.

No one was in sight. Neither was the blue Lincoln. An old Plymouth, a flatbed truck, and a half-dozen pickups were parked here and there beside buildings on the north and west sides of the plaza, and an old Ford with its rear wheels removed squatted unevenly just beside where Chee stood.

The black belly of the cloud beyond the village lit itself with internal lightning, flashed again, and then faded back into black. From the kiva to his left, Chee heard the sound of drumming again and muffled voices raised in rhythmic chanting. The cloud responded to the call with a bumping roll of thunder. Where could the Lincoln be?

Chee skirted the plaza, keeping close to the buildings and making himself as unobtrusive as possible, remembering what Dashee had told him of the layout of this village. He found the alley which led to the lower plaza, a dark tunnel between rough stone walls. Across the lower plaza, the blue Lincoln was parked.

The oldest part of the village surrounded this small open space, and much of it had been deserted generations ago. From where Chee stood in the blackness of the alley mouth, it appeared that only two of the houses might still be in use. The windows of one glowed with a dim yellow light and the other, two doorways down, was producing smoke from its stovepipe chimney. Otherwise there was no sign of life. The window frames had been removed from the house against which Chee leaned and part of its roof had fallen in. Chee peered into the dark interior and then stepped over the windowsill onto the packed-earth floor inside. As he did so, he heard a rattling sound. It approached, suddenly louder. Rattle. Rattle. Rattle. The sounds were spaced as if someone, walking slowly, shook a rattle with each step. The sound was in the alley which Chee had just left. And then Chee saw a shape move past the window he had just stepped through.

A booming rumble of thunder drowned out the sound. Under cover of the noise Chee moved cautiously to the front of the building, ducking under fallen roof beams. Through the hole where the front door had been, he could see the walking man slowly circling the little plaza. He wore a ceremonial kirtle, which came to about his knees. Rattles made of tortoise shells were tied just below his knees. On his head he wore a sort of helmet, dominated by two great horns, curved like the horns of a ram. In his hand he carried what looked like a staff. As Chee watched, the walker stopped.

He turned, and faced Chee.

"Haquimi?" The walker shouted the question directly toward him.

Chee froze, held his breath. The man couldn't possibly see him. There was still a residue of twilight in the plaza, but the darkness under this fallen roof was complete. The walker pivoted, with a flourish of his rattles, and faced a quarter turn away from Chee's hiding place. *"Haquimi?"* he shouted again, and again he stood motionless, waiting for an answer that didn't come. Another quarter turn, and again the question was shouted. Chee relaxed. This would be part of the patrol Cowboy had told him about—members of the One Horn and Two Horn societies giving their kivas the ceremonial assurance that they were safe from intruders. They shout "Who are you?" Cowboy had said, and of course nobody answers because nobody is supposed to be out except Masaw and certain of the kachinas, coming into the village over the spirit path. If there's a kachina coming, then he answers, "I am I."

The patrol was facing to Chee's left now. He shouted his question again. This time, instantly, it was answered. *"Pin u-u-u."* A hooting sound, more birdlike than human. It came from somewhere just off the little plaza, out of the darkness, and it made the hair bristle on Chee's neck. The voice of a kachina answering his human brother? Chee stared through the doorway, trying to place the sound. He heard the mutter of thunder and the cadenced rattles of the patrol, walking slowly away from the source of the response. A flare of lightning lit the plaza. It was empty.

Chee glanced at the luminous dial of his watch. The caller had said 9:00 P.M. for the transfer. Still almost an hour to wait. Why so long? West (or should he still be thinking of Ironfingers?) must have told the man in the blue Lincoln to arrive by twilight, before the road was closed. Must have told the man where to park, and to sit in his car and wait. But why so long? Why not get it over with? Lightning again—a great jagged bolt which struck somewhere back on Black Mesa. It lit the empty plaza with a brief white light, bright enough to show Chee that the man in the blue Lincoln was wearing a straw hat.

Chee was aware he was sweating. Unusual in desert country—especially unusual after dark, when temperatures tended to drop. Tonight the humidity held the day's heat like a damp blanket. Surely it would rain. Another flash of lightning, repeated and repeated. Chee saw that the house to the left of the alley he'd used was also empty and abandoned. It would give him a better view of the Lincoln. Under the cover of the booming thunder, he slipped from his hiding place, crossed the narrow passageway, and stepped through the empty window.

He stood a moment, giving his eyes a chance to adjust to the deeper darkness here. Something teased his nostrils. A sweetish smell. Faint. Somehow chemical. Like a bad perfume. Lightning. Far away, but producing enough brightness through the open doorway to show him he stood on the earth floor of an empty room. A room littered with scattered debris, fallen plaster, wind-blown trash. To his left, a gaping doorway into what must be a back room. The smell might come from there. But the smell could wait. He moved to the doorway. It gave him a good view of the Lincoln and he stood staring at the dark shape, waiting for lightning to show him more.

Suddenly there was a breeze, surprisingly cool, wet, and carrying the rich and joyful perfume of rain. The breeze died as abruptly as it had risen and Chee heard the rattle, rattle, rattle, of the ceremonial patrolman's tortoise shells. The sound was very close and Chee shrank back from the doorway. As he did, the patrolman walked slowly past. A different patrolman. Chee could see only a dark shape, but this man was larger. Lightning lit the plaza briefly and Chee saw the man was peering into the empty doorway of the adjoining house.

Chee moved as quickly as caution and the darkness would allow toward where his memory told him he'd seen the entrance to the back room. He'd be out of sight there, even if the patrolman checked this house. He moved his fingertips along the rough plaster, found the wooden doorframe, and moved through the opening, placing his feet cautiously in the darkness. The smell now was strong. A distinctly chemical smell. Chee frowned, trying to identify it. He moved carefully, back into the blackness. Then stopped. Within a few feet of him, someone breathed.

It was a low sound, the simple exhalation of a deep breath. Chee froze. A long way over the mesa, thunder thumped and rumbled and died away. Silence. And into the silence the faint sound of breath taken, breath exhaled. Easy, steady breathing. It seemed to come from the floor. Someone asleep? Chee took the flashlight from his back pocket, wrapped several thicknesses of his shirttail over the lens, squatted, pointed the light toward the sound. He flicked it on, and off again.

The dim light showed a small, elderly man sprawled on his back on the floor. The man wore only boxer shorts, a blue shirt, and moccasins. He seemed to be asleep. Still squatting, Chee edged two steps closer and flicked on the light again. The man wore his hair in the short bangs of old-fashioned Hopi traditionalists, and seemed to have some sort of ceremonial decoration painted on his forehead and cheeks. Where were his trousers? Chee risked the flashlight again. The room was bare. No sign of clothing. What was the man doing here? Drunk, most likely. In here to sleep it off.

Chee put the flashlight back in his pocket. From outside he heard the ceremonial question being called by the patrolman. He returned to the outer room. Still forty minutes to wait. It would be safe again to resume his watch of the Lincoln.

Chee stood just inside the exterior doorway. It was full night now, but the open plaza, even on this cloudy night, was much lighter than the interior from which Chee watched. He could see fairly well, and he saw the patrolman-priest of the Two Horn Society walking slowly toward the Lincoln. The priest stopped beside the car, standing next to the door where the man in the straw hat sat, leaning toward him. In the silence, Chee heard a voice, low and indistinct. Then another voice. The watchman asking straw hat what he was doing there? Or telling him to move? What would straw hat do? And why hadn't West, or whoever had set this up, foreseen this snag in their plans?

As that question occurred to him, Chee thought of the answer to an earlier question. Several earlier questions. The man in the back room wasn't drunk. He wouldn't be drunk on such a ceremonial occasion. The sweet chemical smell was chloroform. The man hadn't been wearing trousers. He'd been wearing a ceremonial kirtle. And tortoise shell rattles. He'd been knocked out, and stripped of his Two Horn costume.

At the blue Lincoln, the Two Horn priest was moving away from the car window now, moving fast. No longer did he rattle as he walked.

There was a blinding flash of blue-white light, followed almost instantly by an explosive crash of thunder. The flash illuminated the Two Horn priest. He was hurrying past the kiva toward a gap in the buildings which led to the upper plaza. He must be West. But he should have been carrying two briefcases. He should have been carrying five hundred thousand dollars. He was carrying nothing. Chee hesitated a moment and then sprinted to the Lincoln. The first drops struck him as he ran across the plaza. Huge, icy blobs of water, scattered at first, and then a cold, thunderous torrent.

Again there was lightning. A tall blond man emerged from a ruined building just beyond where the Lincoln was parked. He had something in his hand, perhaps a pistol. He was moving fast, like Chee, toward the car. The flash told Chee little more than that—just the blond man in the blue and gray shirt and a glimpse of the Lincoln, where the hat was no longer visible.

The blond got to the car perhaps three seconds before Chee did. Chee didn't intend to stop—didn't have time to stop. The blue Lincoln, the straw hat, didn't concern Chee now. But the blond man stopped him.

He put up his left hand. "Help him," the blond man said. The rain was a downpour now. Chee extracted his flashlight, turned it on. The rain beat against the back of his head, streamed down the face of the blond man, who stood motionless, looking stunned. A pistol hung from his right hand, water dripping from it.

"Put away your gun," Chee said. He pulled open the front door of the Lincoln. The straw hat had fallen on the floorboards under the steering wheel and the middle-aged man who had worn it had fallen too, sideways, his head toward the passenger's side. In the yellow light of the flash, the blood that was pouring from his throat across the pale-blue upholstery looked black. Chee leaned into the car for a closer look. The damage seemed to have been done with something like a hunting knife. Mostly the throat, and the neck—at least a dozen savage slashing blows.

Chee backed out of the front seat.

"Help him," the blond man said.

"I can't help him," Chee said. "Nobody can help him. He killed him."

"That goddamned Indian," the blond man said. "Why did he?"

There were two briefcases on the floorboards on the passenger side. Blood was dripping off the front seat onto one of them. West could have taken them by simply reaching in and picking them up. He'd asked for five hundred thousand dollars. Why hadn't he taken it?

"It wasn't an Indian," Chee said. "And I don't know why."

But as he said it, he did know why. West wanted vengeance, not money. That's what all this had been about. The dark wind ruled Jake West. Chee left the blond man standing by the Lincoln and ran across the plaza. West would head for his jeep. He wouldn't know anyone knew where he'd parked it.

30

THE FIRST LEG of the trip to the place where West had left his jeep Chee covered at a run. That phase ended when he ran into a piñon limb, which knocked him off his feet and inscribed a bloody scratch across the side of his forehead. After that he alternated a fast walk, where visibility was bad, with a cautious trot, where it wasn't. The rain squall passed away to the east, the sky lightened a little, and Chee found himself doing more running than walking. He wanted to reach the jeep before West got there. He wanted to be waiting for West. But when he found the thickets where the jeep was parked, and pushed his way through them as quietly as he could, West was already climbing into the driver's seat.

Chee pulled out his pistol and flicked on the flash.

"Mr. West," he said. "Hold your hands up where I can see them."

"Who's that?" West said. He squinted into the brightness. "Is that you, Chee?"

Chee was remembering the bloody throat of the man in the Lincoln. "Get your hands up," he said. "That sound you hear is me cocking this pistol."

West raised his hands, slowly.

"Get out," Chee said.

West climbed out of the jeep.

"Put your hands on the hood. Spread your legs apart." Chee searched him, removed a snub-nosed revolver from his hip pocket. He found nothing else. "Where's the knife?" he asked.

West said nothing.

"Why didn't you take the money?" Chee asked him.

"I wasn't after money," West said. "I wanted the man. And I got the son of a bitch."

"Because your son was killed?"

"That's right," West said.

"I think maybe you killed the wrong one," Chee said.

"No," West said. "I got the right one. The one who gave the orders."

"Put your hands behind your back," Chee said. He handcuffed West.

Chee was suddenly dazzled by a beam of light.

"Drop the gun," a voice ordered. "Now! Drop it!"

Chee dropped his pistol.

"And the flashlight!"

Chee dropped the flashlight. It produced a pool of light at his feet.

"You're a persistent bastard," the voice said. "I told you to stay away from this."

It was Johnson's voice. And it was Johnson's face Chee could see now in the reflected light. "Hands behind your back," he said, and cuffed Chee's hands behind him.

He picked up Chee's pistol, and West's, and tossed them into the back of West's jeep.

"Okey dokey," Johnson said. "Let's get this over with and get out of the rain. Let's go get the coke." He gestured with the pistol toward West. "Where've you got it?"

"I guess I'll get me a lawyer and talk to him first," West said.

Chee laughed, but he didn't feel like laughing. He felt stupid. He should have expected Johnson. Johnson would have found a way to intercept West's instructions about the meeting. Certainly if another telephone call was involved, tapping a line would be no problem for the DEA agent. "I don't think Johnson is going to read your rights to you," Chee said.

"No, I'm not," Johnson said. "I'm going to leave him with the same deal he made the organization. He keeps the five hundred thousand dollars. I get the coke."

"How do you know he hasn't already delivered it?" Chee asked.

"Because I've been watching him," Johnson said. "He hasn't picked the stuff up."

"But maybe he had it stashed out in the village up there," Chee said.

Johnson ignored him. "Come on," he said to West. "We'll take my car. We'll go get the stuff."

West didn't move. He stared through the flashlight beam at Johnson. Johnson hit him with the pistol—a smashing blow across the face. West staggered backward, lost his balance, fell against the jeep.

Johnson chuckled. There was lightning again, a series of flashes. The rain came down harder. "That surprised him," Johnson said to Chee. "He still thinks I'm your regular-type cop. You don't think that, do you?"

"No," Chee said. "I haven't thought that for a while."

West was trying to get to his feet, awkwardly because of his arms cuffed behind him. "Not since when?" Johnson asked. "I'm curious."

"Well," Chee said, "when you were hunting for the shipment down by the crash site, down in Wepo Wash, one of those guys hunting with you was one of the hoods. Or at least I thought he might be. But I was already suspicious."

"Because I knocked you around?"

West was on his feet now, blood running down his cheek. Chee delayed his answer a moment. He wanted to make sure West was listening to it.

"Because of the way you set up West's boy in the penitentiary. You take him away from the prison, and somehow or other you get him to talk, and then you put him back with the regular population. If you'd have put him in a segregation cell to keep him safe, then the organization would have known he'd talked. They'd have called off the delivery."

"That's fairly clear thinking," Johnson said. He laughed again. "You know for sure the son of a bitch is going to have to absolutely guarantee everybody that he didn't say one damn word."

In the yellow light of the flash, West's face was an immobile mask staring at Johnson.

"And you know for sure they're not going to let him stay

alive, not with you maybe coming back to talk to him again," Chee said.

"I can't think of any reason to keep you around," Johnson said. "Can you think of one?"

Chee couldn't. He could only guess that Johnson was stalling just a little so that the shot that killed Chee would be covered by thunder. When the next flash of lightning came, Johnson would wait a moment until the thunderclap started, and then he would shoot Chee.

"I can think of a reason to kill you," Johnson said. "West, here, he'll see me do it and then he'll know for sure that I won't hesitate to do it to him if he don't cooperate."

"I can think of one reason not to kill me," Chee said. "I've got the cocaine."

Johnson grinned.

There was a flicker of lightning. Chee found himself hurrying.

"It's in two suitcases. Aluminum suitcases."

Johnson's grin faded.

"Now, how would I know that?" Chee asked him.

"You were out there when the plane crashed," Johnson said. "Maybe you saw West and Palanzer and that goddamn crooked Musket unloading it and hauling it away."

"They didn't haul it away," Chee said. "West dug a hole in the sand behind that outcrop and put in the two suitcases and covered them over with sand and patted the sand down hard, and the next morning you federals walked all over the place and patted it down some more."

"Well, now," Johnson said.

"So I went out and took the jack handle out of my truck and did some poking around in the sand until I hit metal and then dug. Two aluminum suitcases. Big ones. Maybe thirty inches long. Heavy. Weight maybe seventy pounds each. And inside them, all these plastic packages. Pound or so each. How much would that much cocaine be worth?"

Johnson was grinning again, wolfishly. "You saw it," he said. "It's absolutely pure. Best in the world. White as snow. Fifteen million dollars. Maybe twenty, scarce like it is this year."

Lightning flashed. In a second it would thunder.

"So you've got a fifteen-million-dollar reason to keep me alive," Chee said.

"Where is it?" Johnson asked. Thunder almost drowned out the question.

"I think we better talk business first," Chee said.

"A little bit of larceny in everybody's heart," Johnson said. "Well, there's enough for everybody this time." He grinned again. "We'll take your car. Police radio might come in handy. If Mr. West here stirred up any trouble back there in the village, it'd be nice to know about it."

"My car?" Chee said.

"Don't get cute," Johnson said. "I saw it. Parked right down the slope in all those bushes. Let's go."

The rain was a downpour again now. The Navajos have terms for rain. The brief, noisy, violent thunderstorm is "male rain." The slower, enduring, soaking shower is "female rain." But they had no word for this kind of storm. They walked through a deafening wall of falling water, breathing water, almost blinded by water. Johnson walked behind him, West stumbling dazedly in front, the beam of Johnson's flash illuminating only sheets of rain.

They stopped beside Chee's car.

"Get out your keys," Johnson said.

"Can't," Chee said. He had to shout over the pounding of rain on the car roof.

"Try," Johnson said. He had the pistol pointed at Chee's chest. "Try hard. Strain yourself. Otherwise I whack you on the head and get 'em out myself."

Chee strained. Twisting hips and shoulders, he managed to hook his trigger finger into his pants pocket. Then he pulled his trousers around an inch or two. He managed to fish out the key ring.

"Drop it and back off," Johnson said. He picked up the keys.

Chee became aware of a second sound, even louder than the pounding of the rain. Polacca Wash had turned into a torrent. This cloudburst had been developing over Black Mesa for an hour, moving slowly. Behind it and under it, millions of tons of water were draining off the mesa down dozens of smaller washes, scores of arroyos, ten thousand little drainage ways—all converging on Polacca, and Wepo, sending walls of water roaring southwestward to pour into the Little Colorado River. The roaring Chee could hear was the sound of brushwood and dislodged boulders rumbling down Polacca under the force of the flood. In two hours, there wouldn't be a bridge, or a culvert, or an uncut vehicle crossing between the Hopi Mesa and the river canyon.

Johnson was tossing the keys in his palm, staring thoughtfully at Chee and West. The flashlight beam bobbed up and down. In the light, Chee could see how much the flood had already risen. The turbulent water was tearing at the junipers no more than twenty-five feet down the slope from where he'd parked.

"I've just been having some interesting thoughts," Johnson said. "I think I know where you've got that cocaine."

"I doubt it," Chee said.

"I've been asking myself why you two guys didn't come together. You know, save gasoline, wear and tear on the tires. And I tell myself that West, he wanted to come early and scout things out to make sure nobody's got you set up. So he don't bring the cocaine. Where do you hide it in a jeep?"

As Johnson talked, he let the beam of the flash drift to the windows of Chee's patrol car. He looked inside.

"Then after West has everything scouted out and it's safe—and if anybody grabs him they gotta just turn him loose because he doesn't have the stuff and they want it—after all that, along comes Mr. Chee here in his police car. And what could be a safer place to hide cocaine than in a police car?"

Johnson shone the flash into Chee's eyes.

"Where's safer than that?" he insisted.

"Sounds great," Chee said. He was trying desperately to make some sort of plan. Johnson would open the trunk and look. Then there would be no reason at all to keep Chee alive. Or West alive. The flash left Chee's face and moved to West. Bloody water was streaming down from the cut across West's cheekbone, running into his beard. Chee thought he'd never seen so much hate in a face. West understood now why his son had died. West understood he'd knifed the wrong man.

"Sounds like a good little theory," Johnson said. "Let's see how it works out in real life."

He put the flash under his armpit and kept the pistol pointed at Chee while he fumbled with getting the key into the lock. The trunk lid sprang open. The trunk lights lit the scene.

Johnson laughed, a joyful chortle of a laugh.

"One little problem remains," Chee said. "What if what you see there are two suitcases containing Pillsbury's Best wheat flour. It doesn't weigh as much as the cocaine, but if you don't know how heavy those things are supposed to be, you could never tell the difference by looking."

"We'll just take a look, then," Johnson said. "I can tell the difference and I'm getting a little tired of you."

He put the flash in the trunk, kept the pistol aimed at Chee. He didn't look at the suitcases, but Chee could hear him fumbling with a catch.

"Where's the key?" he asked.

"I don't think they sent one along," Chee said. "Maybe they mailed the key to the buyers. Who knows?"

"Keep back," Johnson said. He pulled both suitcases upright, unfastened the tire tool, and jammed the screwdriver end into a joint. He pried. The lock snapped. The suitcase fell open. Johnson stared.

"Looky there," he chortled.

Chee moved, but West moved faster. Even so, Johnson had time to swing the pistol around and fire twice before West reached him. West was screaming—an incoherent animal shriek. Johnson tried to step away, slipped on the wet surface. West's shoulder slammed him against the open trunk. There was the sound of something breaking. Chee moved as fast as he could, off balance because of his pinned arms. The collision had knocked Johnson off his feet and West, too, had fallen. Chee stood with his hands in the trunk, fumbling for the tire tool, for anything his hands could grasp that he could use—hands behind him—to kill a man.

The unopened aluminum suitcase had been knocked on its side. His hands found its handle. He pulled it out of the trunk, staggering momentarily as the weight swung free. Johnson was regaining his feet now, feeling around him in the darkness for the fallen pistol.

Chee spun, swinging the suitcase behind him, guessing, releasing it at the point where he hoped it would hit Johnson. It missed.

The suitcase bounced just past Johnson's legs, and tumbled down the slope toward the roaring water of Polacca Wash.

"My God," Johnson screamed. He scrambled after it.

West was on his feet again now, running clumsily after Johnson. The rain pounded down. Lightning flashed, illuminating falling water with a blue-white glare.

The suitcase had stopped just above the water's edge, held by a juniper. Johnson had reached it and was pulling it to safety when he realized what West was doing. He turned and was struck by West's body, and went sprawling backward downhill into what was now Polacca River.

West was lying, head down, feet high, beside the suitcase. Chee struggled down the slope, slipping and sliding.

He sat beside West. "You all right?"

West was breathing hard. "Did I knock him in?"

"You got the right man this time," Chee said. "Nobody could swim in that water. He's drowning. Or by now, maybe he's drowned."

West said nothing. He simply breathed.

"Can you get up?"

"I can try," West said. He tried. A brief struggle. Then he lay still again. His breathing now had a bubble in it.

"You're going to have to get up," Chee said. "The water's rising and I can't help you much."

West struggled again. Chee managed to catch his arm and pull him upward. They got him on his knees, on his feet. Finally, after two falls, they got him to the car, and into it. They sat, side by side, under the overhead light, on the front seat, simply breathing. The rain pounded thunderously against the roof.

"I've got a problem," Chee said. "The key to the handcuffs I'm wearing is in Johnson's pocket and there's no way we're going to get that. But the key to the handcuffs on you is on my key ring. If I take off your cuffs, can you drive?"

West's breath bubbled in his chest. "Maybe," he said, very faintly.

"They're checking on Joseph Musket's dental charts," Chee said. "Comparing them with the John Doe the witch is supposed to have killed. They're going to match, so they're going to nail you for killing Musket."

"Worked pretty well, though," West said. He made a sound that might have started as a chuckle but became a cough. Clearly, West was bleeding in his lungs.

"I'm telling you this because I want you to know they've got you nailed. If I take off your cuffs, it's no good trying to kill me and get away. You understand that."

Chee still had the keys in his right hand. He had held them there since extracting the ring from the trunk lock and unlocking the front door of the car.

"Lean the other way, toward the other door, and hold out your hands."

West breathed, bubbling, gasping.

"Lean," Chee said. "Hold 'em out."

West leaned, laboriously. Chee leaned the other way, fumbling behind him, finding West's strong hands, finding the lock. Fumbling the key into it, getting—finally—the handcuffs opened and West's hands out of them.

But West had fallen against the passenger-side door now.

"Come on, West," Chee said. "You're loose now. You got to start the engine, and drive us to get help. If you don't you're going to bleed to death."

West said nothing.

Chee reached behind his back, pulled West straight. West fell against the door again, coughed feebly.

Chee gave up. "West," he said. "How did you manage the business with the squash blossom necklace turning up at Mexican Water? That was a mistake."

"Friend of mine did it for me. Navajo. Owed me some favors." West coughed again. "Why not? Looked like it could confirm Musket was still alive."

"Your friend picked a girl out of the wrong clan," Chee said. He wasn't sure West was hearing him now. "West," he said. "I'm going to have to leave you here and see if I can get help."

West breathed. "Okay," he said.

"One thing. Where'd you hide the rest of the jewelry?"

West breathed.

"From your burglary. When you faked the burglary. Where'd you hide the jewelry that's missing? Lots of good people would like to have their stuff back."

"Kitchen," West said faintly. "Under the sink. Place there where you can crawl under to fix things."

"Thanks," Chee said. He pushed the car door open and swung his legs out, and leaned far enough forward to get his weight on his feet. He lost his balance and sat down again. He was aware that he was used up, exhausted. And then he was aware that West, leaning against the door behind him, was no longer breathing.

After that there was no hurry. Chee rested. Then he reached clumsily behind him and felt the pocket of West's jacket. He worked his fingers into it and extracted a soggy mass of little envelopes. His fingers separated them. Thirteen. One for each card in a suit of cards. Arranged, Chee was sure, so that West's nimble fingers could quickly count inward to the three of diamonds. Or if the seven of clubs was called for, perform the same magic in whichever pocket stored the clubs. But West's illusions were all ended now. Chee had another problem. He remembered Captain Largo, grim and angry, ordering him to stay away from this narcotics case. He imagined himself opening the trunk of his patrol car and confronting Largo with a suitcase full of cocaine—seventy pounds of evidence of his disobedience. A scene worth avoiding. Chee listened to the rain and decided how this avoidance could be accomplished. Then he let his thoughts drift to Miss Pauling. She, too, had gotten her revenge. West had killed her brother to make it possible to revenge himself. And now her brother, too, was revenged. At least, Chee thought he was. It wasn't a value taught, or recognized, in the Navajo system and Chee wasn't sure he understood how it was supposed to work.

Finally he pushed himself to his feet again, and walked to the car trunk, and managed, with his cuffed hands, to get the second aluminum suitcase shut again, with the broken catch holding. He eased it out of the trunk and down the slippery, rain-washed rocks toward Polacca Wash. The water was higher now, lapping against the first suitcase. Chee gave that one a hard shove with his foot. It floated briefly and then was sucked down into the boiling current. He spun around then, and sent the second case spinning after it. When he turned to look, it had already been lost in the darkness.

III

The Ghostway

For Margaret Mary

With special thanks to Sam Bingham and those students at Rock Point Community School who took time to help me understand how Navajos deal with the chindis *of Dine' Bike'yah in 1984.*

1

HOSTEEN JOSEPH JOE remembered it like this.

He'd noticed the green car just as he came out of the Shiprock Economy Wash-O-Mat. The red light of sundown reflected from its windshield. Above the line of yellow cottonwoods along the San Juan River the shape of Shiprock was blue-black and ragged against the glow. The car looked brand new and it was rolling slowly across the gravel, the driver leaning out the window just a little. The driver had yelled at Joseph Joe.

"Hey!" he'd yelled. "Come here a minute."

Joseph Joe remembered that very clearly. The driver looked like a Navajo, but yelling at him like that was not a Navajo thing to do because Joseph Joe was eighty-one years old, and the people around Shiprock and up in the Chuska Mountains called him Hosteen, which means "old man" and is a term of great respect.

Joseph Joe had put his laundry sack into the back of his daughter's pickup truck and walked over to the car. He noticed its plates weren't yellow, like New Mexico's, or white, like Arizona's. They were blue.

"I'm looking for a man named Gorman," the driver had said. "Leroy Gorman. A Navajo. Moved here little while ago."

"I don't know him," Joseph Joe had said. He had said it in Navajo, because when he got close he saw he had been right. The man was a Navajo. But the driver just frowned at him.

"You speak English?" the driver asked.

"I don't know Leroy Gorman." Hosteen Joe said it in English this time.

"He's been around here several weeks," the driver said. "Young fellow. Little older than me. Medium-sized. Hell, small as this place is, I'd think you'd have seen him."

"I don't know him," Joseph Joe repeated. "I don't live in this town. I live at my daughter's place. Out there near the Shiprock." Joseph Joe had gestured toward the Arizona border and the old volcano core outlined by the sunset. "Don't live in here with all these people," he explained.

"I'll bet you've seen him," the driver said. He took out his billfold and fished a photograph out of it. "This is him," the driver said and handed the photograph to Hosteen Joe.

Joseph Joe looked at it carefully, as courtesy demanded. It was a Polaroid photograph, like the ones his granddaughter took. There was something written on the back of it, and an address. The front was a picture of a man standing by the door of a house trailer, which was partly shaded by a cottonwood tree. Hosteen Joe took off his glasses and wiped them off carefully on his sleeve and looked a long time at the young man's face. He didn't recognize him, and that's what he said when he handed the driver his photograph. After that, he didn't remember the rest of it quite as clearly because just then it all began to happen.

The driver was saying something to him about the trailer, maybe about Gorman living in it or trying to sell it or something, and then there was the sound of a car braking on the highway, tires squealing a little, and the car backing up and whipping around and driving into the Wash-O-Mat parking lot. This car was new too. A Ford sedan.

It stopped just in front of the driver's car. A man wearing a plaid coat got out of it and walked toward them and then stopped suddenly, apparently noticing Joseph Joe for the first time. Plaid Coat said something to the driver. As Joseph Joe remembered, it was "Hello, Albert," but the driver didn't say anything. Then Plaid Coat said, "You forgot to do what you were told. You've got to come along with me. You're not supposed to be here." Or something like that. And then he had looked at Joseph Joe and said, "We've got business, old man. You go away now."

Hosteen Joe had turned then and walked back toward his

daughter's truck. Behind him he heard the sound of a car door opening. Then closing. A yell. The sharp clap of a pistol shot. And then another shot, and another, and another. When he turned he saw Plaid Coat on the gravel and the driver holding himself up by clinging to the door of his car. Then the driver got in and drove away. When the car got to the asphalt, it turned toward the river and toward the junction, which would either take it west toward Teec Nos Pos or south toward Gallup.

People were running out of the Wash-O-Mat by then, yelling questions. But Hosteen Joe just looked at Plaid Coat, sprawled on his side on the gravel with a pistol on the ground beside him and blood running out his mouth. Then he got into his daughter's truck.

The driver was Navajo, but this was white man's business.

2

"FUNNY HOW a premonition works," the deputy said. "I been in this business almost thirty years, and I never had one before."

Jim Chee said nothing. He was trying to re-create precisely and exactly the moment when he had known everything was going wrong with Mary Landon. He didn't want to think about the deputy's premonitions. He'd said something to Mary about his house trailer being too small for both of them, and she'd said, "Hey, wait a minute, Jim Chee, what have you done about that application with the FBI?" and he'd told her that he'd decided not to mail it. And Mary had just sat there in the Crownpoint Café, not looking at him or saying anything, and finally she'd sighed and shook her head and said, "Why should you be any different from everybody else?" and laughed a laugh with absolutely no humor in it. He was remembering all this and concentrating on his driving, following the rocky track which led along this high hump of the Chuska Mountains. The moon was down and the night was in that period of implacable cold darkness that comes just before the first gray light of dawn. Chee was driving with only his parking lights—just as Sharkey had told him to drive. That meant going slowly and risking a wrong turn at any of the places where the trail divided itself to go wandering off toward a spring, or someone's hogan, or a sheep dip, or who knows what. Chee wasn't worried about the slowness. Sharkey's plan was to get to the hogan of Hosteen Begay long enough before daylight to let them get into position.

There was plenty of time. But he was worried about a wrong turn. And his mind was full of Mary Landon. Besides, the deputy had said it all before.

Now the deputy was saying it all again.

"Had a funny feeling from the very first," the deputy said. "When Sharkey was telling us about it back there in Captain Largo's office. Felt the skin tightening on the back of my neck. Kind of a coldness. And prickling on the arms. Somebody's going to get hurt, I thought. Somebody's going to get their butt shot off."

Chee sensed the deputy was looking at him, waiting for him to say something. "Um," Chee said.

"Yes," the deputy agreed. "I got a feeling that Gorman fella's laying up there with his pistol cocked, and when we walk in somebody's going to get killed."

Chee eased the Navajo Tribal Police carryall around a washout. In his rearview mirror he could see the parking lights of Sharkey's pickup truck. The FBI agent was staying about a hundred yards behind him. The deputy now interrupted his monologue to light a cigaret. In the flare of the kitchen match, the man's face looked yellow—an old and sinister face. The deputy's name was Bales and he was old enough, with even more years weathered into his skin by the high-country sun of San Juan County. But not sinister. His reputation was for easygoing, overtalkative mildness. Now he exhaled smoke.

"It's not a feeling that I'm going to get shot," Bales said. "It's a sort of general feeling that somebody will."

Chee was conscious again that Bales was waiting for him to say something. This white man's custom of expecting a listener to do more than listen was contrary to Chee's courteous Navajo conditioning. He'd first become aware of it his freshman year at the University of New Mexico. He'd dated a girl in his sociology class and she'd accused him of not listening to her, and it had taken two or three misunderstandings before he'd finally fathomed that while his people presume that if they're talking, you are listening, white people require periodic reassurance. Deputy Sheriff Bales was requiring such reassurance now, and Chee tried to think of something to say.

"Somebody already got shot," he said. "Couple of people got shot, including Gorman."

"I meant somebody new," Bales said.

"If it's not you," Chee said, "that leaves me, or Sharkey, or that other FBI agent he brought along. Or maybe Old Man Begay."

"I don't think so," Bales said. "I think it would need to be one of us, the way this premonition feels." Satisfied now that Chee was listening, Bales inhaled deeply and allowed a moment of silence while he savored the taste of the tobacco.

Mary Landon had stirred her coffee, looking at it and not at him. "You've made up your mind to stay," she'd said. "Haven't you. When were you going to tell me?" And he'd said what? Something stupid or insensitive, probably. He couldn't remember exactly what he'd said. But he remembered her words—vividly, clearly, exactly.

"Whatever you say about it, it just has one meaning. It means I come second. What comes first is Jim Chee, being Navajo. I'm to be sort of an appendage to his life. Mrs. Chee and the Navajo children." He'd interrupted her, denying that accusation, and she had said the Navajo Way was important to him only when it reinforced what he already wanted to do. She'd said that before, and he knew exactly what was coming. The Navajos, she'd reminded him, married into the wife's clan. The husband joined the wife's family. "How about that, Jim Chee?" she'd asked. There was nothing he could say to her.

The deputy exhaled again and rolled down the window a bit to let the cold air suck out the smoke. "Always chaps my butt the way the FBI won't ever tell you anything," he said. " 'The subject is Albert Gorman.' " Bales raised the pitch of his voice a notch in a weak attempt to mimic the West Texas sound of Agent Sharkey. " 'Gorman is believed armed with a thirty-eight-caliber pistol.' " Bales switched back to his own rusty voice. "Believed, hell. They took a thirty-eight slug out of the guy he shot." Bales switched voices again. " 'Los Angeles informs us that it is particularly important to apprehend this subject alive. He is wanted for questioning.' " Bales snorted. "Ever arrest anyone who wasn't wanted for questioning about something?" Bales chuckled. "Like how many beers he had before he started driving."

Chee grunted. He eased the carryall around a place where the soil was cut away from a ridge of stone. The rearview mirror assured him again that Sharkey's pickup was still behind him.

"I don't see how we can compromise," Mary Landon had said. "I just don't see how we can work it out." And he'd said, "Sure, Mary. Sure we can." But she was right. How could you compromise it? Either he stayed with the Navajo Police or he took a job off the reservation. Either he stayed Navajo or he turned white. Either they raised their children in Albuquerque, or Albany, or some other white city as white children or they raised them on the Colorado Plateau as Dinee. Halfway was worse than either way. Chee had seen enough of that among displaced Navajos in the border towns to know. There was no compromise solution.

"You know what we heard?" the deputy said. "We heard that this business was tied up with an FBI agent getting killed out in L.A. We heard that Gorman and Lerner, the guy he shot at the laundry, was both working for some outfit on the Coast. Some outfit that stole cars. Big operation. And some big shots got indicted. And an FBI agent got knocked off. And that's why the Feds are so hot to talk to this Gorman."

"Um," Chee said. He steered the carryall cautiously around a juniper, but not cautiously enough. The left front wheel dropped into a hole the parking lights hadn't revealed. The jarring jolt shook the deputy's hat down over his eyes.

"The car the dead guy was driving," the deputy said. "It was rented there at the Farmington airport. They tell you that?"

"No," Chee said. As a matter of fact, they hadn't told him anything much—which was exactly what Chee had learned to expect when he was running errands for the Federals. "Got a little job for you," Captain Largo said. "We need to find that fellow in the parking lot." It had seemed an odd thing to say, since the Shiprock agency of the Navajo Tribal Police, along with every other cop along the Arizona–New Mexico border, had all been looking for that fellow. But Chee had also come to expect Largo to say odd things. Largo had then explained himself by handing Chee a folder. It included a copy of the photograph of Albert Gorman that the FBI had provided, a rap sheet showing several arrests and one conviction for larceny of motor vehicles, and some biographical statistics. There were no blank spaces on the forms used by the Los Angeles Police Department for the sort of information Chee needed: Gorman's mother's name and her clan, which Albert Gorman had been "born to," and the clan of Gorman's father, which Albert had been "born for." Unless Albert Gorman had forgotten how to be a Navajo in Los Angeles or, as sometimes happened off the reservation, had never learned the Navajo Way, the homes of these clansmen would be the place to look for Albert Gorman. Largo knew that.

"What I want you to do is drop everything else you're fooling around with. Just come up with this guy," Largo had said. "He didn't pass the roadblocks at Teec Nos Pos, and we had a car there fifteen minutes after the shooting, so he didn't go west. And he didn't get to the roadblock at Sheep Springs, so he didn't get through us going south. So unless he turned east to Burnham, and that road doesn't go anyplace, he must have gone up into the Chuskas."

Chee had agreed to that, mentally changing the "must have" into a "most likely."

Largo pushed himself out of his chair and walked to the wall map, a bulky man with a barrel chest and thin hips—the top-heavy wedge shape so common among western Navajos. He waved a finger around a portion of the map encompassing the Shiprock massif, the Carrizo and Lukachukai mountains, the north end of the Chuskas, and the country between them. "Narrows it down to this little area," Largo said. "See how quick you can find him."

The little area was about the size of Connecticut, but its population wouldn't be more than a few hundred. And the few hundred would be people who would unfailingly notice and remember anything unusual. If Gorman had driven his green sedan into the country south of Teec Nos Pos, or west of Littlewater, it would have been seen and talked about and remembered—the subject of speculation. It was simply a matter of driving and driving and driving, and talking and talking and talking, for however many days it took to track it down. "How quick I find him depends on how lucky I get," Chee said.

"Get lucky, then," Largo said. "And when you find him, just call in. Don't try to arrest him. Don't go anywhere near him. Don't do nothing to spook him. Just get on the radio and get word to us, and we tell the Agency." Largo was leaning against the map, staring at Chee, expression neutral at best. "Understand what I'm saying? Don't screw it up. It's an FBI case. It is not, repeat not, a case for the Navajo Tribal Police. It's an Agency case. It is not our affair. It is not the affair of Officer Jim Chee. Got it?"

"Sure," Chee said.

"Chee finds. Chee calls in. Chee leaves it at that. Chee does not do any freelance screwing around," Largo said.

"Right," Chee said.

"I mean it," Largo said. "I don't know much about it, but from what I hear, this guy is tied up somehow or other with some big case in Los Angeles. And an FBI agent got killed." Largo paused long enough to allow Chee to consider what that meant. "That means that when the FBI says they want to talk to this guy, they *really* want to talk to him. You just find him."

And so Chee had found him and now, having found him, was guiding in the FBI to finish the job, with Deputy Bales along to properly represent the San Juan County Sheriff's Department.

Deputy Bales stifled a yawn. "Yeah," he said. "The dead guy came in on a chartered plane. Or anyway, the people at the airport said a private plane flew in, and he got out of it and rented the car. A hood out of Los Angeles. With a long rap sheet."

"Um," Chee said. He'd heard about the plane and the rented car and the police record. The homicide was exotic enough to be fuel for gossip. The FBI told nobody anything. But the Farmington Police told the New Mexico State Police, who told the Sheriff's Office, who told the Navajo cops, who told the Bureau of Indian Affairs law and order people, who told the Arizona Highway Patrol. In the small, dull world of law enforcement, anything unusual is a precious commodity, worth weeks of conversation.

"I wonder if he really is wounded," the deputy said.

"Pretty sure about that," Chee said. "Old Joseph Joe is supposed to have seen him hanging on the car door, looking hurt. And when I looked in the car, there was blood on the front seat."

"Been wondering about that," the deputy said. "How'd you find it?"

"Just took time," Chee said. "You know how it is. Just keep asking until you ask the right person."

It had taken three days to find the right person, a boy getting off the bus from the Toadlena school. He'd seen the green sedan going by on the road that led from Two Gray Hills southward toward Owl Springs. Chee had stopped at the Two Gray Hills Trading Post and got a fix on who lived down that road and how to find their places. Then another hard afternoon of driving on doubtful trails. "Found it about dark yesterday," he added.

Bales had tilted his hat far back on his head. "And Sharkey decides to wait and catch him about daylight, when he's sleeping. Or when we hope he's sleeping. Course we don't even know he's there."

"No," Chee said. But he had no doubt at all that Albert Gorman was there. This terrible road led to the Begay hogan and nowhere else. And from his abandoned car, Gorman's tracks led toward the Begay place. They were the uncertain, wavering tracks of a man either drunk or badly hurt. And finally, there was what he'd learned at the trading post at Two Gray Hills on his way back. The trader wasn't there, but the woman handling the cash register had told him that, yes, Old Man Begay had a visitor.

"Hosteen Begay came in three–four days ago and asked what medicine to buy for somebody who hurt himself and had a lot of pain," she'd said. She'd sold him a bottle of aspirin and a stamp for an envelope he'd wanted mailed.

For several hundred yards the dim parking lights had been picking up the black gloss of spilled crankcase oil. Now they reflected from a green Plymouth sedan, blocking the trail. Chee parked his truck behind it, cut the lights and the engine, and climbed out.

Sharkey had the window of his pickup down. He was leaning out, looking at Chee.

"About three quarters of a mile up the track here," Chee said, pointing.

It was then he noticed for the first time that fog was forming. A trace of it drifted like gray smoke through the beam of Sharkey's lights just as he turned them off, and then the smell of fog was in Chee's nostrils and the dampness on his face.

3

IN THE HIGH, dry mountains of the Colorado Plateau, fog is out of its element. It forms as part of a climatic accident, produced when a cold front crosses a mountain range and collides with warmer air on the opposite slope. And it survives no longer than a fish out of water. By dawn, when the four of them reached the place of Hosteen Begay, the fog had already lost its character as a solid blinding cloud. Now it survived only in pockets, as patches and fragments. Chee stood at the edge of one such fragment, exactly where Sharkey had told him to stand—on the slope west of the meadow where Begay had built his hogan. His role was to make sure that if Gorman tried to escape he would not escape in that direction. Chee rested a hip against a boulder. He waited and watched. At the moment, he watched Deputy Bales, who stood beside a ponderosa pine, right hand against the tree trunk and his left holding a long-barreled revolver, its muzzle pointing at the ground. The bottom of the tree trunk and Bales's lower legs were obscured by the mist, making—in the dim light—man and tree seem somehow detached from solid earth. Over the meadow, the fog was almost solid, frayed only here and there by the very beginning of a cold dawn breeze. Chee glanced at his watch. In eleven minutes it would be sunrise.

The hogan was a little below where Chee and the deputy waited. Through the ebbing mist, Chee could make out its conical roof, which seemed to be formed of slabs sliced from ponderosa logs in their first trip past the blade at the sawmill. The mist eddied and obscured this and eddied again. The short tin smoke pipe jutting from the center of the roof cone seemed to be blocked, closed by something pressed up into it from inside the hogan. Chee stared, straining his vision. He could think of just one reason to block a hogan's smoke hole.

Chee clicked his tongue, producing a nondescript sound just loud enough to catch the deputy's attention. Then he motioned his intention to move. Bales looked surprised. He tapped the face of his wristwatch, reminding Chee of the few minutes left. Just at sunrise, Sharkey and his man would be at the hogan's east-facing door. If Hosteen Begay emerged to bless the new day in the traditional fashion, they would pull him out of harm's way, rush into the hogan, and overpower Gorman. If he didn't appear, they'd rush in anyway. That was the plan. Chee had a feeling now that it would be an exercise in futility.

He moved along the slope away from Bales toward the north side of the hogan. From what Chee had learned of Hosteen Begay at Two Gray Hills he was an old-fashioned man, a traditional man, a man who knew the Navajo Way and followed it. He would have built this hogan as Changing Woman taught—with a single doorway facing the direction of dawn, the direction of all beginnings. North was the direction of darkness, the direction of evil. It was through the north wall of a hogan that a corpse must be removed in the sad event of death striking someone inside. Then the smoke hole would be plugged, the entrance boarded, and the place abandoned—with the corpse hole left open to warn the People that this had become a death hogan. The body could be removed, but never the malicious *chindi* of the dead person. The ghost infection was permanent.

Chee had circled about a hundred yards, keeping out of sight. Now he was almost due north of the place. Through the thinning mist he could see the dark hole where the logs of the wall had been chopped away. Someone had indeed died inside the hogan of Hosteen Begay and left his ghost behind.

4

"THE THING TO DO is find the body—if there is one," Sharkey said. "You take care of that, Chee. We'll see what we can find around here."

Sharkey was standing at the hogan doorway, a small, hard-looking man of maybe forty-five with blond hair, short-cropped and curly.

"Here's some more old bandage." Bales's voice came from behind Sharkey, inside the hogan. "Dried blood on this one, too."

"What else are you finding?" Chee asked. "Any bedroll?"

"See if you can find where they put the body," Sharkey said, his voice impatient.

"Sure," Chee said. He already had an idea where the body might be. From the description they had of Gorman he wouldn't be particularly heavy. But Begay was an old man, and carrying a full-sized corpse wouldn't be easy. Probably he'd have dragged it on the blankets that had been its bed. And the best convenient burial site was obvious. A line of cliffs towered over Begay's little meadow to the northwest, their base littered with giant sandstone boulders tumbled out of their walls. It was the ideal place to put a body where it would be safe from predators. Chee headed for the talus slope.

Sharkey's agent was climbing out of the arroyo that ran behind the hogan. He nodded at Chee. "Nothing in the corral or the sheep pens," he said. "And the manure looks old."

Chee nodded back, wishing he could remember the man's

name and wondering what "old" meant when he defined animal droppings. Yesterday or last year? But he wasn't particularly interested in any of this. It was Sharkey's business, and none of his own. Gorman might be a Navajo by blood but he was a white man by conditioning, by behavior. Let the whites bury the whites, or however that quotation went. He needed to get back to Shiprock, back to his own work and his own problems. What was he going to do about Mary Landon?

Chee followed the only relatively easy pathway into the boulders, noticing very quickly that he'd guessed right. Something heavy had been dragged here, leaving a trail of broken weeds and disturbed dust. Then Chee noticed, just up the talus slope ahead of him, the raw scar where rocks had been dislodged—pried and pushed to cause gravity to produce a rockslide. The easy way to cover a body. Then he saw blue denim.

The body had been placed atop a slab of stone that had tumbled out of the cliff eons earlier. The corpse was out of reach of coyotes there, and the stones pushed down atop it had made it safe from birds. The denim that had caught Chee's eye was the bottom of a trouser leg. He walked around the burial, inspecting it. He could see nothing of the head and little of the body, just the sole of the right shoe and, through a gap between stones, a bit of the shoulder of a blue shirt.

Something was bothering Chee, something a touch out of harmony with things as they should be. What? He climbed the slope and inspected the burial site from above. Just an unnatural-looking slide of rocks. He looked beyond it, inspecting the place of Hosteen Begay. The sun was up now, high enough above the horizon to be warm on his face. Below, the hogan was still in shadow. A neat place, well made, with a well-made brush arbor beside it, and a fairly new Montgomery Ward storage shed, and a welded pipe rack for the oil drums in which Hosteen Begay kept his water for cooking and drinking, and a shed in which he kept feed for his livestock. A good place. Beyond it, through a fringe of ponderosas, the morning sun had lit the rolling gray velvet of the San Juan basin. Sheep country—buffalo grass, grama, sage, chamiza, and snakeweed—punctuated by the soaring black gothic spires of Shiprock and, beyond Shiprock, 50 miles away, the smudge that marked the smokestacks of the Four Corners power plant.

Chee drank in the view, letting the grandeur of immense space lift his spirits. But something still nudged at his consciousness. Something didn't fit. In this great harmony, something was discordant.

Chee looked down at the hogan again, studying it. Bales was beside the brush arbor. The two FBI agents were out of sight—perhaps inside the death hogan, where their ignorance protected them from the malice of Gorman's *chindi.* A perfect site. It had everything. Firewood. Summer grass. Spring water for livestock in the arroyo behind the hogan. Beauty in the site and in the view. And the isolation, the sense of space, which the Pueblo Indians and whites called loneliness but the Navajos treasured. True, winters would be snowed in here, and bitter cold. The place must be well over 8,000 feet. But the hogan had been built for winter. It must have been terribly hard for the old man to abandon it. And why had he?

It was this question, Chee realized, that had been bothering him. Why hadn't the old man done what the Dinee had done for a hundred generations when they saw death approaching? Why hadn't he moved the dying Gorman out of the hogan, out under the eye of Father Sun, into the pure open air? Why hadn't he made this kinsman a death bed under the arbor, where no walls would have penned in his *chindi* when death released it, where the ghost could have lost itself in the vastness of the sky? Gorman must have died a slow, gradual death brought on by lost blood, internal damage, and infection. Death would have been nothing strange to the old man. The Navajos were not a culture that hides its people away in hospitals at their dying time. One grew up with the death of one's old people, attending death, respecting it. Begay must have seen this death coming for hours, heard it in Gorman's lungs, seen it in his eyes. Why hadn't he moved the man outside in the fashion of the People? Why had he allowed this valued homeplace to be eternally infected with ghost sickness?

Sharkey appeared in the hogan doorway and stood staring up toward Chee. Chee stared back, unseen among the boulders. Bales and the other agent were invisible now. What was the man's name? It came to him suddenly: Witry. Another thought suddenly occurred to Chee. Could the body under the rocks be Begay's? Could it be that Gorman had killed the old man? It didn't seem likely. But Chee found that his bleak mood had changed. Suddenly he was interested in this affair.

He stepped out where Sharkey could see him. "Up here!" he shouted.

Removing the rocks was quick work.

"I left the photographs in the truck," Sharkey said. "But he fits Gorman's description."

The body obviously couldn't be Hosteen Begay. Far too young. Mid-thirties, Chee guessed. It lay on the stone, face up, legs extended, arms by the sides. A plastic bread sack, its top twisted shut, was beside the right hand.

"Here's what killed him," Bales said. "Hit him right in the side. Probably tore him all up, and the bleeding wouldn't stop."

Sharkey was looking at Chee. "I guess there's no way to get a vehicle in here," he said. "I guess we'll have to carry him out to the pickup."

"We could bring a horse in," Chee said. "Haul him out that way."

Sharkey picked up the sack and opened it. "Looks like a jar of water. And cornmeal," he said. "That make sense?"

"Yes," Chee said. "That's customary."

Sharkey poured the contents of the sack carefully out on the rock, leaving Gorman's persona to make its four-day journey into the underground world of the dead with neither food nor water. "And here's his billfold. Cigaret lighter. Car keys. Comb. Guess it was the stuff he had in his pockets." Sharkey fished through the various compartments of the wallet, laying the odds and ends he extracted on the boulder beside Gorman's knee and then sorting through them. The driver's license was first. Sharkey held it in his left hand, tilted Gorman's face toward him with the right, and made the comparison of face to photograph.

"Albert A. Gorman," Sharkey read. "The late Albert A. Gorman. Eleven thousand seven hundred thirteen La Monica Street, Hollywood, Cal." He counted quickly through the money, which seemed to be mostly hundred-dollar bills, and whistled through his teeth. "Twenty-seven hundred and forty-odd," he said. "So crime paid fairly well."

"Hey," Witry said. "His shoes are on the wrong feet."

Sharkey stopped sorting and looked at Gorman's feet. He was wearing brown low-cut jogging shoes—canvas tops, rubber soles. The shoes had been reversed, right shoe on left foot.

"No," Chee said. "That's right."

Sharkey stared at him quizzically.

"I mean," said Chee, "that's the way it's done. In the traditional way, when you prepare a corpse for burial you reverse the moccasins. Switch 'em." Chee felt his face flushing under Sharkey's gaze. "So the ghost can't follow the man after death."

Silence. Sharkey resumed his examination of the artifacts from Gorman's billfold.

Chee looked at Gorman's head. There was dirt on his forehead, and his hair was dusty from the rockfall that had buried it. But it was more than dusty. It was tangled and greasy—the hair of a man who had lain for days dying.

"Lots of money," Sharkey said. "VISA, Mastercard, California driver's license. California hunting license. Membership card in Olympic Health Club. Mug shots of two women. Coupon to get two Burger Chefs for the price of one. Social Security card. That's it."

Sharkey felt in the pockets of Gorman's jacket, unbuttoned it and checked his shirt pockets, turned the pockets of his trousers inside out. There was absolutely nothing in Gorman's pockets.

Walking back to the carryall, Chee decided he had a second puzzle to add to the question of why Hosteen Begay had not saved his hogan from the ghost. Another piece of carelessness. Begay had in some ways prepared his relative well. Albert A. Gorman had gone through the dark hole that leads into the underworld with plenty of money he could no longer spend. No ghost could follow his confusing footprints. He had been left with the symbolic food and water for the journey. But he would arrive unpurified. His dirty hair should have been washed clean in yucca suds, combed, and braided. Boiling yucca roots takes time. Had something hurried Hosteen Begay?

5

THE BEGINNING OF WINTER bulged down out of Canada, dusted the Colorado Plateau with snow, and retreated. Sun burned away the snow. The last late Canada geese appeared along the San Juan, lingered a day, and fled south. Winter appeared again, dry cold now. It hung over the Utah mountains and sent outriders of wind fanning across the canyon country. At the Shiprock subagency office of the Navajo Tribal Police the wind shrieked and howled, buffeting the walls and rattling the windows, distracting Jim Chee from what Captain Largo was saying and from his own thoughts about Mary Landon. The Monday morning meeting had lasted longer than usual, but now it was ending. The patrolmen, shift commanders, dispatchers, and jailers had filed out. Chee and Taylor Natonabah had been signaled to stay behind. Chee lounged in his folding chair in the corner of the room. His eyes were on Largo, explaining something to Natonabah, but his mind was remembering the evening he had met Mary Landon: Mary watching him in the crowd at the Crownpoint rug auction, Mary sitting across from him at the Crownpoint Café, her blue eyes on his as he told her about his family—his sisters, his mother, his uncle who was teaching him the Mountain Way and the Shooting Way and other curing rituals of the Navajo Way, preparing him to be a *yataalii,* one of the shaman medicine men who kept the People in harmony with their universe. The genuine interest on Mary's face. And Mary, finally, when he had given her a chance to talk, telling him of her fifth-graders at Crownpoint elementary, of the difference between the Pueblo Indian children she'd taught the year before at the Laguna-Acoma school and these Navajo youngsters, and of her family in Wisconsin. He'd known, he thought now, even on that first meeting, that this white woman was the woman he wanted to share his life with.

A fresh blast of wind rattled sand against the windows and seeped through some crack somewhere to move icy air around Chee's ankles. His memory skipped ahead to the weekend he'd taken Mary back on the plateau to his mother's summer hogan south of Kayenta. When he'd asked his mother later what she'd thought of Mary, his mother had said, "Will she be a Navajo?" And he had said, "Yes, she will be." Now he knew he had been wrong. Or probably wrong. Mary Landon would not be a Navajo. How could he change that? Or, if he couldn't change it, could Jim Chee stop being a Navajo?

Now Natonabah was leaving, zipping up his fur-lined jacket, his face flushed, his mouth grim. Clearly the captain had, in his low-key way, expressed disapproval. Chee quit thinking about Mary Landon and reexamined his conscience. He'd already done that automatically when Largo had signaled him to stay behind and had thought of no violations of Largo's rules and regulations. But now Captain Largo's large round face considered him, even blander and milder than usual. Often that meant trouble. What had he done?

"You all caught up on your work?"

Chee sat up straight. "No, sir," he said.

"You catch that Yazzie who's bootlegging all that wine?"

"No, sir."

"Found that kid did the cutting on the Ute Reservation?"

"Not yet." It was going to be worse than he'd expected. He'd only had the Ute stabbing added to his case list Friday.

Largo was peering down into the file folder in which he kept Chee's reports. It was a bulky file, but Largo apparently decided to shorten the ordeal a little. He flipped rapidly through it, then closed it and turned it face down on his desk. "All this still-unfinished business then?" he asked. "You got plenty to keep your mind occupied?"

"Yes, sir," Chee said. "Plenty of work to do."

"I got the impression that you had time on your hands," Largo said. "Looking for something to keep you occupied."

Chee waited. Largo waited. Ah, well, Chee thought, might as well get it over with. "How's that, sir?" he asked.

"You pulled the file on the Gorman business," Largo said. His expression asked why.

"Just curious," Chee said. Now he would get a lecture on respecting jurisdictions, on minding his own business.

"You find anything interesting in there?"

The question surprised him. "Not much in there at all," he said.

"No reason for there to be," Largo said. "It's not our case. What were you looking for?"

"Nothing specific. I wondered who Gorman was. And who was the man who came after him. The one Gorman shot at the laundry. What Gorman was doing in Shiprock. How Begay fit in. Things like that."

Largo made a tent of his fingers above the desk top and spent a moment examining it. "Why were you curious?" he asked, without taking his eyes off his fingers. "Fight in a parking lot. The survivor runs to his kinsman to hide out and heal. Everything looks normal. What's bothering you?"

Chee shrugged.

Largo studied him. "You know," he said, "or anyway you heard from me, that an FBI agent got killed back in California in this one. The Agency is always touchy. This time they're going to be extra touchy."

"I was just curious," Chee said. "No harm done."

"I want you to tell me what made you curious."

"It wasn't much," Chee said. He told Largo about the way Gorman's corpse had been prepared, with its hair unwashed, and of wondering why Begay had not moved Gorman outside before the moment of death.

Largo listened. "You tell Sharkey about this?"

"He wasn't interested," Chee said.

Largo grinned.

"Maybe no reason to be," Chee admitted. "I don't know much about Begay. Lots of Navajos don't know enough about the Navajo way of getting a corpse ready. Lots of 'em wouldn't care."

"Younger ones, maybe," Largo said. "Or city ones. Begay isn't young. Or city. What do you know about him?"

"They call him Hosteen, so I guess the people up there respect him. That's about it."

"I know a little more than that," Largo said. "Begay is Tazhii Dinee. In fact, I'm told his aunt is the *ahnii* of that clan. He's lived up there above Two Gray Hills longer than anybody can remember. Has a grazing permit. Runs sheep. Keeps to himself. Some talk that he's a witch."

Largo recited it all in a flat, uninflected voice, putting no more emphasis on the last sentence than the first.

"There's some talk that just about everybody is a witch," Chee said. "I've heard you were. And me."

"He seems to have a good reputation," Largo said. "People up there seem to like him. Say he's honest. Takes care of his relatives." That was the ultimate compliment for a Navajo. The worst insult was to say he acted like he didn't have any relatives. In Navajo country, families come first.

Chee wanted to ask Largo why he had learned so much about an old man who kept to himself high in the Chuska Mountains. As Largo had said, the Gorman shooting was an FBI case—white-man business completely outside the jurisdiction of the Navajo Tribal Police. Instead of asking, he waited. He'd worked for Largo two years, first at the Tuba City subagency and now here at Shiprock. Largo would tell him exactly what Largo wanted him to know and all at Largo's own pace. Chee knew very little about the Tazhii Dinee—only that the Turkey People were one of the smallest of the sixty or so Navajo clans. If Begay's aunt was the clan's *ahnii,* its matriarch/judge/fountain-of-wisdom, then his was a most respected family and he would certainly know enough of the Navajo Way to properly prepare a kinsman for burial.

"Gorman was the son of Begay's youngest sister," Largo said. "The Bureau of Indian Affairs relocated a bunch of that clan in Los Angeles in the nineteen forties and fifties. In fact, Begay seems to have been among the few of that outfit that didn't go. I think one of his daughters also stayed. Lived over around Borrego Pass. Dead now. And a few Tazhii Dinee are supposed to have moved over to the Cañoncito Reservation. But the clan doesn't amount to much any more."

Largo walked to the window and stood, back to Chee, inspecting the weather in the parking lot.

"We've got a girl missing from St. Catherine Indian School," Largo said. "Probably a runaway. Probably nothing much." The captain exercised the storyteller's pause-for-effect. "She's the granddaughter of Hosteen Begay. Told a friend she was worried about him. The nuns at St. Catherine called the police there at Santa Fe because they said she wasn't the type that runs away. Whatever type that is." Largo paused again, still looking at something or other in the parking lot. "Attended her morning classes on the fourteenth. Didn't show up for classes after lunch."

Chee didn't comment. The bloody business in the parking lot had happened the night of the eleventh. On the twelfth Old Man Begay had walked into the Two Gray Hills Trading Post, bought his futile bottle of aspirin, and mailed a letter. How long would it take a letter to get from Two Gray Hills to Santa Fe? Two days?

Largo walked back to his desk, found a package of cigarets in the drawer, and lit one. "The other thing," he said through the cloud of blue smoke, "is the FBI is unusually uptight about this one. Very grim. So I did some asking around. It turns out one of their old-timers got killed a couple of months ago, like I told you. He was on something that ties in with this business." Largo turned away from his parking lot inspection to gaze at Chee. "You been a cop long enough to know how it is when a cop gets killed?"

"I've heard," Chee said.

"Well, anyway, they *never* want us interfering in their jurisdiction. So think how sore they'd get if it happened when they've got an agent dead. And nobody to hang it on."

"Yeah," Chee said.

"Unfortunately," Largo said, "you're the logical one to handle this missing St. Catherine girl."

Chee let that pass. What Largo meant was that he had a reputation for being nosy. He couldn't deny it.

"You want me to be careful," Chee said.

"I want you to turn on the brain," Largo said. "See if you can pick up the girl. If you run into anything that bears on what happened to Gorman, then you back off. Tell me. I tell Sharkey. Everybody's happy."

"Yes, sir," Chee said.

Largo stood by the window, looking at him. "I really mean it," he said. "No screwing around."

"Yes, sir," Chee said.

6

THE GIRL'S NAME was Sosi. Margaret Billy Sosi. Age seventeen. Daughter of Franklin Sosi, no known address, and Emma Begay Sosi (deceased) of Borrego Pass. The form listed Ashie Begay, grandfather, care of Two Gray Hills Trading Post, as the "person to be notified in event of emergency." The form was a photocopy of an admissions sheet used at the Santa Fe boarding school, and there was nothing on it, or on the attached Navajo Tribal Police missing persons report form, that told Chee anything he didn't already know. He slipped the two sheets back into their folders and turned to the copies he made from the Gorman homicide report.

The wind, blowing from due north now, gusted around his pickup truck and rattled particles of parking lot debris against its door. Chee did not consciously dislike the wind. It was part of the totality of day and place, and to dislike it would be contrary to his Navajo nature. But it made him uneasy. He read quickly through the Gorman file, covering first the chronology of what had happened at the laundry and then turning to the investigating officer's transcription of his interview with Joseph Joe, looking for the oddity that had bothered him when he had first gone through the report.

"Subject Joe said Gorman had called him to the car and engaged him briefly in conversation. Joe said that as he walked away from the Gorman vehicle, the rented vehicle driven by Lerner came into the lot. . . ."

Engaged him briefly in conversation. About what? Why

had Gorman driven from Los Angeles to be shot at a laundromat? It seemed to Chee that an answer to the first question might offer some clue to the answer of the second. It certainly seemed a logical question—something he would have asked Old Man Joe. Why hadn't it been asked? Chee glanced at the name of the investigating officer. It was Sharkey. Sharkey seemed smart.

Chee read through the rest of the report. Lerner had chartered a plane at a Pasadena airport, flown to Farmington, and rented an Avis car. Judging from the time elapsed, he had driven directly and rapidly to Shiprock. Looking for Gorman, obviously. How had he found him at the laundry? That could have been easy enough if he knew the car Gorman was driving. He would have been looking for it, and the highway in from Farmington passed directly by the lot where Gorman was parked. That left the question of why? The data in the report on Gorman himself made him seem trivial enough—simply a car thief. Lerner, from the report and what gossip Chee had heard, was a minor Los Angeles hoodlum. The chartered plane seemed grotesquely glossy and expensive for an incident involving such unimportant people.

Chee put the report back in its folder and looked quickly through the papers he'd picked up from his in-basket. Nothing much. A Please Return Call slip showing that "Eddie" had called about "Blue Door." Eddie pumped gas at night at the Chevron station beside the San Juan bridge. His mother was an alcoholic, Eddie did not like bootleggers, and the Blue Door Bar at the reservation boundary outside Farmington was a haunt for those who hauled beer, wine, and whiskey into the reservation's outback. Eddie meant well, but unfortunately his tips never seemed to lead anywhere.

The next memo informed all officers of the theft of a pinto mare from the Two Gray Hills Trading Post; of a pickup order on a man named Nez who had beaten his brother-in-law with a hammer at the family sheep camp above Mexican Water, and of the confirmation of identification of a middle-aged woman found dead beside the Shiprock–Gallup highway. Cause of death was also confirmed. She'd been run over by a vehicle while sprawled, unconscious from alcohol, on the pavement.

Chee took a second look at the identification. He didn't know the name, but he knew the woman, and a score like her, and their husbands and their sons. He had arrested them, and manhandled them into his patrol car, and cleaned up after them, and eased their bodies onto stretchers and into ambulances. In the milder seasons, they drank themselves to death in front of trucks on U.S. 666 or Navajo Route 1. Now, with the icy wind beginning to blow, they would drink themselves to death in frozen ditches.

That wind buffeted his truck, stirring a cold draft around his face. Chee turned on the ignition and started his engine. Where was Mary Landon at this moment? Teaching her fifth-graders at Crownpoint. Chee remembered the afternoon he had stood on the walk outside the windows of her classroom and watched her—a silent pantomime through the glass. Mary Landon talking. Mary Landon laughing. Mary Landon coaxing, approving, explaining. Until one of her students had seen him standing there and looked at him, and he had fled in embarrassment.

He turned his mind away from that and rolled the pickup out of the lot. He would see Eddie about the Blue Door later. The stolen pinto mare and the angry brother-in-law and the rest of it could wait. Now the job was to find Margaret Billy Sosi, aged seventeen, granddaughter of Ashie Begay, clanswoman of a dead man whom people called Albert Gorman, who seemed to have been running, but not running fast enough or far enough. And thus the first step to finding Margaret Billy Sosi was finding Hosteen Joseph Joe and asking him the question Sharkey hadn't asked, which was what Albert Gorman had said to him at the Shiprock Economy Wash-O-Mat.

7

FINDING JOSEPH JOE proved simple enough. In cultures where cleanliness is valued and water is scarce, laundries are magnets—social as well as service centers. Chee took for granted that the people at the Shiprock Economy Wash-O-Mat would know their customers. He was correct. The middle-aged woman who managed the place provided Joseph Joe's full family genealogy and directions to his winter place. Chee rolled his patrol car southward across the San Juan bridge with the north wind chasing him, then west toward Arizona, and then south again across the dry slopes of snakeweed and buffalo grass toward the towering black spire of basalt that gave the town of Shiprock its name. It was the landmark of Chee's childhood—jutting on the eastern horizon from his mother's place south of Kayenta, and a great black thumb stuck into the northern sky during the endless lonely winters he spent at the Two Gray Hills Boarding School. It was there he'd learned that the Rock with Wings of his uncle's legends had, eons ago, boiled and bubbled as molten lava in the throat of an immense cinder cone. The volcano had died, millions of years had passed, abrasive weather—like today's bitter wind—had worn away cinders and ash and left only tough black filling. In today's bleak autumn light, it thrust into the sky like a surreal gothic cathedral, soaring a thousand feet above the blowing grass and providing—even at five miles' distance—a ludicrously oversized backdrop for Joseph Joe's plank and tarpaper house.

"I already told the white policeman about it," Hosteen Joe told Chee. Joe poured coffee into a plastic Thermos bottle cap and into a white cup with RE-ELECT MCDONALD FOR TRIBAL PROGRESS printed around it, handed Chee the political cup, took a sip from the other, and began telling it all again.

Chee listened. The wind seeped through cracks, rustling the Farmington *Times* Joe was using as a tablecloth and stirring the spare clothing that hung on a wire strung across a corner of the room. Through the only south window, Chee could see the tall cliffs of Shiprock, now obscured by blowing dust, now black against the dust-stained sky. Joseph Joe finished his account, sipped his coffee, waited for Chee's reaction.

Chee took a courtesy sip. He drank a lot of coffee. ("Too much coffee, Jim," Mary would say. "Someday I will reform you into a sipper of tea. When I get you, I'm going to make sure you last a long time.") He enjoyed coffee, respected its aroma, its flavor. This was awful coffee: old, stale, bitter. But Chee sipped it. Partly courtesy, partly to cover his surprise at what Joseph Joe had told him.

"I want to make sure I have everything right," Chee said. "The man in the car, the man who drove up first, said he wanted to find somebody he called Leroy Gorman?"

"Leroy Gorman," Joe said. "I remember that because I thought about whether I had ever known anybody by that name. Lots of Navajos call themselves Gorman, but I never knew one they called Leroy Gorman."

"The man you were talking to, his name was Gorman too. Did the white policeman tell you that?"

"No," Joe said. He smiled. "White men never tell me much. They ask questions. Maybe they were brothers."

"Probably the same family, anyway," Chee said. "But it sounds like this white policeman didn't ask you enough questions. I wonder why he didn't ask you about what Gorman said to you."

"He asked," Joseph Joe said. "I told him."

"You told him about Gorman asking you where to find Leroy Gorman."

"Sure," Joseph Joe said. "Told him the same thing I told you."

"Did you tell the policeman about the picture Gorman showed you?"

"Sure. He asked me a bunch of questions about it. Wrote it down in his tablet."

"That picture," Chee said. "A house trailer? Not a mobile home? Not one of those things that has a motor and a steering wheel itself, but something you pull behind a car?"

"Sure," Joseph Joe said. He laughed, his wrinkled face multiplying its creases with amusement. "Used to have a son-in-law lived in one. No room for nothing."

"Two things," Chee said. "I want you to remember everything you told the white policeman about the picture—everything in it. And then I want you to see if you can remember anything you didn't tell him. Was it just a picture of a trailer? Was it with a bunch of other trailers? Hitched behind a car? One man in the picture, standing there?"

Joseph Joe thought. "It was a color picture," he said. "A Polaroid." He walked to a tin trunk against the wall, opened the lid, extracted a photo album with a black cardboard cover. "Like this one," he said, showing Chee a Polaroid photo of Joseph Joe standing beside his front door with a middle-aged woman. "Same size as this," he said. "Had the trailer in the middle, and a tree sort of over it, and just dirt in front."

"Just one man in it?"

"Standing by the door. Looking at you."

"What kind of tree?"

Joe thought. "Cottonwood. I think cottonwood."

"What color leaves?"

"Yellow."

"What color trailer?"

"It was aluminum," Joe said. "You've seen 'em. Round on both ends. Round shape. Big things." Joe indicated the bigness with his hands and laughed again. "Maybe if my son-in-law had one that big, he'd still be my son-in-law."

"And the picture," Chee said. "You said he took it out of his wallet. Did he put it back in again?"

"Sure," Joe said. "Not in those little pockets where you

keep your license and things. Too big for that. He put it in with the money. In the money place."

"You tell the white policeman that?"

"Sure," Joe said. "He was like you. He asked a lot of questions about the picture."

"Now," Chee said. "Did you think of anything you didn't tell him?"

"No," Joseph Joe said. "But I can think of some things I haven't told you."

"Tell me," Chee said.

"About the writing," Joe said. "On the back side it had an address written, and something else, but I couldn't see what it was. I don't read. But I could see it was something short. Just two or three words."

Chee thought about it on the way back. Why had Sharkey said nothing of the picture in his report, or of Albert Gorman trying to find Leroy Gorman? Had that part been deleted before the Navajo Tribal Police received their version? What kind of a game was the Agency playing? Or was it Sharkey's game, and not the FBI's?

"The FBI wants you," Mary said. "You impressed them at the Academy. They accepted you when you applied. They'd accept you again if you applied again. And they'd keep you close to the reservation. You'd be more valuable to them here. Why would they move you someplace else?" And he'd said something about not to count on it. Something about in Washington an Indian was an Indian, and they'd be as likely to have him working with the Seminoles in Florida, just like they have a Seminole over in Flagstaff working with the Navajos. And Mary had said nothing at all, just changed the subject. As Chee changed it now, forcing his memory away from the soreness.

He remembered Sharkey standing beside Gorman's body, Gorman's wallet in his hand, piling its contents on the boulder. No photograph of a trailer. Had Sharkey palmed it? Hidden it away? Chee's memory was excellent, the recall of a People without a written memory, who keep their culture alive in their minds, who train their children to memorize details of sand paintings and curing ceremonials. He used it now, recreating the scene, what Sharkey had said and done, Sharkey looking into the money compartment of the wallet, removing the money, looking again, inspecting flaps and compartments: Sharkey seeking a Polaroid photograph that wasn't there.

8

THE LIGHT WAS turning red. The sun had dipped beneath the western horizon, and the clouds in the west—dazzling yellow a few moments earlier—were now reflecting scarlet. Soon it would be too dark to see. Then Chee would confront his decision. He would either walk back to his pickup truck, go home, and write off this idea as a waste of time or he would search the one place he hadn't searched. That meant taking out his flashlight and stepping through the hole into darkness. At one level of his intellect it seemed a trivial thing. He would crouch, step over the broken siding, and find himself standing erect inside the abandoned death hogan of Hosteen Begay. To the Jim Chee who was an alumnus of the University of New Mexico, a subscriber to *Esquire* and *Newsweek,* an officer of the Navajo Tribal Police, lover of Mary Landon, holder of a Farmington Public Library card, student of anthropology and sociology, "with distinction" graduate of the FBI Academy, holder of Social Security card 441-28-7272, it was a logical step to take. He had repeated the long, bumpy drive into the Chuskas, made the final two-mile trudge from his pickup to this place, to see what he could find at this hogan. How could his logical mind justify not searching it?

But "Jim Chee" was only what his uncle would call his "white man name." His real name, his secret name, his war name, was Long Thinker, given him by Hosteen Frank Sam Nakai, the elder brother of his mother and one of the most respected singers among Four Corners Navajos. Since he had gone to Albuquerque to study at the University of New Mexico, he did not often think of himself as Long Thinker. But he did now. He stood on the talus slope above where he had found the Gorman corpse looking down at the Begay hogan as a Navajo would look at it. The east-facing door was boarded shut. (He had resealed it before he'd left, repairing the damage done by Sharkey.) The smoke hole was plugged. The *chindi,* which had left the body of Gorman at the moment of Gorman's death, was trapped inside—a summation of all in the dead man's life that was evil and out of harmony with the Navajo Way.

Everything in Long Thinker's training conditioned him to avoid *chindis.* "If you have to be out at night, go quietly," his mother had taught him. "The *chindis* wander in the darkness." And his uncle: "Never speak the name of the dead. Their *chindi* thinks you are calling it." He had come to terms with these ghosts in high school and reduced them to rational terms at the university, converting them into something like the dietary taboos of Jews and Moslems, the demons of Christians. But from this talus slope, in the dying light, in the dead stillness of this autumn evening, the rationality of the university was canceled.

And there was another side to all this. "You did it," Mary Landon would say. "When you stepped through that corpse hole, you proved that you can be a Navajo on an emotional plane but an assimilated man intellectually." And he would say, "No, Mary, you simply don't understand," and she would say . . .

He turned away from that and considered what he'd learned. Almost nothing. He'd driven straight from the place of Joseph Joe and started his work here with a meticulous examination of the hogan yard. He'd learned that Hosteen Begay used his sweat bath more than most, that he kept goats as well as sheep, and that he owned two horses (one newly shod). Recent additions to Begay's garbage dump included an empty lard can, an empty Shurfine flour sack, and tin cans that had held peaches, creamed corn, and pork and beans. The garbage told him that Begay dipped snuff (an addiction unusual among Navajos), that he did not use beer, wine, or whiskey, and (judging from the discarded Dr. Scholl's footpads) that he suffered from bunions. None of that was helpful.

Nor had he found anything helpful in the second stage of his hunt, an equally careful sweep up and down the arroyo behind the hogan and around the wooded slopes above and below Begay's little meadow. He simply confirmed what he'd learned on his original inspection. Begay had, as would be expected of any prudent shepherd, taken his flocks to downhill pastures weeks ago, before early winter storms could trap them. And when he'd abandoned this place, he'd ridden the newly shod horse and led the other, heavily loaded. He'd headed downhill, probably for some shortcut he knew to reach the road to Two Gray Hills. Maybe, Chee thought, he could follow those tracks far enough to get some hint of his destination. But that seemed wildly unlikely. Time, wind, and the dry season made tracking doubtful, and even if he could track, his work would also certainly simply lead him to the road to the trading post.

Today's wind had been the sort any tracker hates—dry and abrasive, blasting sand against the face and erasing signs. But it had died away in late afternoon, and now the total calm of an autumn high-pressure area had settled over the high country. From his place on the talus slope Chee could see, across Begay's empty homestead, a hundred miles to the southeast all the way to the dark blue bump on the horizon that was Mount Taylor, Mary Landon's favorite mountain. (Now Mary would be finished with her school day, finished with her supper, out for her evening walk—sitting someplace, probably, looking at it from much closer quarters. Chee could see her vividly, her eyes, the line of her cheek, her mouth. . . .)

Old Man Begay had taken time to clean out his hogan and pack his stuff on his horses. Why hadn't he taken the time to collect the few yucca roots required to make the suds to wash his kinsman's hair? What had hurried him? Had it been fear? An urgent need to attend some duty? Chee stared down at the homestead, trying to visualize the old man smashing with his ax at the broken wall where the corpse hole was formed, destroying what must have been important to him for much of his life.

Then he heard the sound.

It came to him on the still, cold air, distant but distinct. It was the sound of a horse. A whinny. The sound came from the arroyo—from the spring or from Begay's corral just beyond it. Chee had been there two hours earlier and had spent thirty minutes establishing from tracks and manure that no animal had been there for days. Nor was this the season for open range grazing this high in the mountains. Livestock had been taken, long since, to lower pastures and even strays would have moved downhill, out of the intense morning cold. Chee felt excitement growing. Ashie Begay had come home to collect something he'd forgotten.

The horse was exactly where Chee expected it to be—at the spring. It was an elderly pinto mare, roan and white, fitting the description of the one stolen from Two Gray Hills. It wore a makeshift rope halter on its ugly hammer head. Another bit of rope secured it to a willow. Hardly likely that Hosteen Begay, who owned horses of his own, would have taken it. Who had? And where was he?

The night breeze was beginning now as it often did with twilight on the east slope of mountains. Nothing like the morning's dry gusts, but enough to ruffle the mare's ragged mane and replace the dead silence with a thousand little wind sounds among the ponderosas. Under cover of these whispers, Chee moved along the arroyo rim, looking for the horse thief.

He checked up the arroyo. Down the arroyo. Along the ponderosa timber covering the slopes. He stared back at the talus slope, where he had been when he'd heard the horse. But no one could have gotten there without Chee seeing him. There was only the death hogan and the holding pen for goats and the brush arbor, none of which seemed plausible. The thief must have tied his horse and then climbed directly up the slope across the arroyo. But why?

Just behind him, Chee heard a cough.

He spun, fumbling for his pistol. No one. Where had the sound come from?

He heard it again. A cough. A sniffling. The sound came from inside Hosteen Begay's hogan.

Chee stared at the corpse hole, a black gap broken through the north wall. He had cocked his pistol without knowing he'd done it. It was incredible. People do not go into a death hogan. People do not step through the hole into darkness. White men, yes. As Sharkey had done. And Deputy Sheriff Bales. As Chee himself, who had come to terms with the ghosts of his people, might do if the reason was powerful enough. But certainly most Navajos would not. So the horse thief was a white. A white with a cold and a runny nose.

Chee moved quietly to his left, away from the field of vision of anyone who might be looking through the hole. Then he moved silently to the wall and along it. He stood beside the hole, back pressed to the planking. Pistol raised. Listening.

Something moved. Something sniffled. Moved again. Chee breathed as lightly as he could. And waited. He heard sounds and long silences. The sun was below the horizon now, and the light had shifted far down the range of colors to the darkest red. Over the ridge to the west he could see Venus, bright against the dark sky. Soon it would be night.

There was the sound of feet on earth, of cloth scraping, and a form emerged through the hole. First a stocking cap, black. Then the shoulders of a navy pea coat, then a boot and a leg—a form crouching to make its way through the low hole.

"Hold it," Chee said. "Don't move."

A startled yell. The figure jumped through the hole, stumbled. Chee grabbed.

He realized almost instantly he had caught a child. The arm he gripped through the cloth of the coat was small, thin. The struggle was only momentary, the product of panic quickly controlled. A girl, Chee saw. A Navajo. But when she spoke, it was in English.

"Turn me loose," she said, in a breathless, frightened voice. "I've got to go now."

Chee found he was shaking. The girl had handled this startling encounter better than he had. "Need to know some things first," Chee said. "I'm a policeman."

"I've got to go," she said. She pulled tentatively against his grip and relaxed, waiting.

"Your horse," Chee said. "You took her last night from over at Two Gray Hills."

"Borrowed it," the girl said. "I've got to go now and take her back."

"What are you doing here?" Chee asked. "In the hogan?"

"It's my hogan," she said. "I live here."

"It is the hogan of Hosteen Ashie Begay," Chee said. "Or it was. Now it is a *chindi* hogan. Didn't you notice that?"

It was a foolish question. After all, he'd just caught her coming out of the corpse hole. She didn't bother to answer. She said nothing at all, simply standing slumped and motionless.

"It was stupid going in there," Chee said. "What were you doing?"

"He was my grandfather," the girl said. For the first time she lapsed into Navajo, using the noun that means the father of my mother. "I was just sitting in there. Remembering things." It took her a moment to say it because now tears were streaming down her cheeks. "My grandfather would leave no *chindi* behind him. He was a holy man. There was nothing in him bad that would make a *chindi.*"

"It wasn't your grandfather who died in there," Chee said. "It was a man named Albert Gorman. A nephew of Ashie Begay." Chee paused a moment, trying to sort out the Begay family. "An uncle of yours, I think."

The girl's face had been as forlorn as a child's face can be. Now it was radiant. "Grandfather's alive? He's really alive? Where is he?"

"I don't know," Chee said. "Gone to live with some relatives, I guess. We came up here last week to get Gorman, and we found Gorman had died. And that." Chee pointed at the corpse hole. "Hosteen Begay buried Gorman out there, and packed up his horses, and sealed up his hogan, and went away."

The girl looked thoughtful.

"Where would he go?" Chee asked. The girl would be Margaret Sosi. No question about that. Two birds with one stone. One stolen pinto mare and the horse thief, plus one missing St. Catherine's student. "Hosteen Begay is your mother's father. Would he . . . ?" He remembered then that the mother of Margaret Billy Sosi was dead.

"No," Margaret said.

"Somebody else then?"

"Almost everybody went to California. A long time ago. My mother's sisters. My great-grandmother. Some people live over on the Cañoncito Reservation, but . . ." Her voice trailed off, became suddenly suspicious. "Why do you want to find him?"

"I want to ask him two questions," Chee said. "This is a good hogan here, solid and warm, in a place of beauty. Good firewood. Good water for the cattle. Enough grass. Hosteen Begay must have seen that his nephew was dying. Why didn't he do as the People have always done and move him out into the air so the *chindi* could go free?"

"Yes," Margaret Sosi said. "I'm surprised he didn't do that. He loved this place."

"I have heard Hosteen Begay lived the Navajo Way," Chee said.

"Oh, yes," Margaret said. "My grandfather always walked in beauty."

"He would have known how to take care of a corpse then? How to get it ready for its journey?"

The girl nodded. "He taught me about that. About putting a little food and water with the body. And things it needs for four days."

"And what you do so the *chindi* will not follow it?"

"Oh, yes," she said. "After you make the yucca suds and wash the hair, you reverse the shoes." She pantomimed the act of switching. "So the *chindi* will be confused by the footprints." As she finished the sentence her voice trailed off, and she glanced at the corpse hole, the irregular broken doorway into the darkness of the hogan. She looked, and Chee felt her shiver under his hand. Seventeen, by the record, he thought, but she looks about fifteen.

"I wouldn't have gone in there if I had known it wasn't Grandfather." She looked up at Chee. "What do I have to do? What can you do when you've been where you catch the ghost sickness? How do I get rid of the *chindi?*"

"You're supposed to take a sweat bath," Chee said. "And as soon as you can you have a sing. Tell your family about it. They'll call in a Listener, or a Hand Trembler, to make sure you have the right ceremonial. Usually it would be part of the Night Way, or the Mountaintop Way. Then your family will hire a singer, and . . ." It was occurring to Chee that Margaret Sosi didn't have much family to depend on for such familial duties. "Is there somebody who can do that for you?"

"My grandfather would do it," she said.

"Anyone else? Until we find him?"

"I guess just about everybody went to Los Angeles," she said. "A long time ago."

"Look, Margaret," Chee said. "Don't worry about it. Let me tell you about *chindi.* Do you know much about religion?"

"I go to a Catholic school. We study religion."

"A lot of religions have rules about what not to do, what not to eat, things like that. The Koran tells the Moslems not to eat pigs. When the wise men were writing that, a lot of diseases were spread by eating pork. It was smart to avoid it. Same with some of the Jewish rules about foods. Most religions, like us Navajos, have rules against incest. You don't have intercourse within your own family. If you do, inbreeding makes bad stock. And with us, Changing Woman and Black God taught us to stay away from where people have died. That's wise too. Avoids spreading smallpox, bubonic plague fleas, things like that."

Even in the twilight, Chee could see Margaret's face was skeptical.

"So the ghost is just disease germs," she said.

"Not exactly," Chee said. "There's more to it than that. Now we know about germs, so when we violate the taboo about a death hogan we know how to deal with any germs we might catch. But we also know we've violated our religion, broken one of the rules the People live by. So we feel guilty and uneasy. We no longer have *hozro.* We no longer live in beauty. We're out of harmony. So we need to do what Changing Woman taught us to do to be restored in the Navajo Way."

Margaret's expression was slightly less skeptical. "Did you go in there?"

"No," Chee said. "I didn't."

"Are you going to?"

"Only if I have to," Chee said. "I hope I don't have to." The answer surprised him. He had avoided the hogan, and the decision, all afternoon. Suddenly he understood why. It had something to do, a great deal to do, with Mary Landon—with remaining one of the Dinee or with stepping through into the white man's world.

"I would break the taboo because it is my job," he said. "But maybe it won't be necessary. You stay right here. I've got a lot of questions I need to ask you."

The hole had been made by chopping the logs forming part of the lower wall of the hogan away from the frame that held them. Chee aimed his flashlight through the hole. In the center, directly under the smoke hole, five partly burned logs lay on the hearth, their charred ends pointing neatly inward. Just beside the hearth, Begay's cooking stove stood, a heavy cast-iron affair that he must have taken apart to haul in. Nothing else had been left behind. A clutter of cardboard boxes lay near the boarded east entrance with a red Folger's coffee can standing near them. Except for that, the packed earthen floor was bare. Chee swung the flash around, examining the walls. Wooden crating had been fashioned into shelving on both sides of the east entrance and a wire was strung along the south wall, about chest high. Chee guessed Begay had hung blankets across it, screening off about a third of the hogan's floor space for privacy. He let the beam of the flashlight drift along the logs, looking for anything that might have been left in the crevices. He saw nothing.

He switched the flash back to the cardboard cartons. Obviously Sharkey and Bales had examined them. Must have. No reason for him to go inside. What would he do if he went in? Run his fingers between the logs. Poke into cracks. Looking for what? There was no reason to go inside. No reason to step through the hole into the darkness. What would he tell Margaret Sosi to make her believe that?

As soon as he turned away from the hole, into the redder darkness of the dying twilight, he realized he wouldn't have to answer that question. Margaret Sosi was gone.

"Margaret!" he shouted. He exhaled through his teeth, a snorting sound expressing anger and disgust. Of course she was gone. Why wouldn't she be? Gone with the important questions left unanswered. Unasked, in fact, because he, in his shrewdness, had left them for the last, until the girl had time to come to trust him. The obvious questions.

Why did you run away from school, run to your grandfather's hogan, steal a horse in your hurry to get here? Why did you tell your friend at St. Catherine you were worried about your grandfather? What did you expect to find here? What did you hear? How did you hear it?

Chee stared out into the darkness, seeing nothing but the shape of trees outlined against the night sky. She couldn't be far, but he would never find her. She would simply sit down and wait, silently, while he floundered around. He could walk within six feet of her and not see her unless she betrayed herself with panic. With Margaret Sosi, he thought, there was no chance of that whimper of fear, that panicky movement that would betray concealment. She was young and thin, but Chee had seen enough to respect her nerve. He remembered the quick control of fear when he'd grabbed her. The quick tug to test his grip. Margaret Sosi would not lose her courage.

And tonight, she'd need it. The air against his cheek was already icy. In the thin, dry air here, 9,000 feet above sea level, the temperature would drop another 30 degrees before sunrise.

Chee cupped his hands and shouted toward the mountain slope. "Margaret. Come back. I won't arrest you."

He listened, waiting for the echo to subside, and heard nothing.

"Margaret. I'll take you wherever you want to go."

Listened again. Nothing.

"I'm leaving the horse. Take it back where you got it. Find a warm place."

Again, silence.

On his way back to the pickup, Chee detoured down into the arroyo and jammed his lunch sack between the willow limbs where the mare's halter was tied. One of his two bologna sandwiches was left in it, and an orange. The mare snorted and rubbed against his shoulder, wanting company as much as food.

9

JIM CHEE WAS about two thirds of the way through his account of what he had seen and heard at the places of Hosteen Joe and Hosteen Begay when Captain Largo raised his large brown hand, palm out, signaling a halt. Largo picked up the telephone, got the switchboard.

"Call Santa Fe. St. Catherine Indian School. Get me that sister I talked to earlier. The principal. Tell her I need to talk to that friend of the Sosi girl. Need some more information from her. See if you can get me that girl on the telephone. Ring me back when you get her. Okay?"

Then he turned back to Chee and heard the rest of it without comment or question. His black eyes watched Chee without expression, drifting away now and then to study his thumbnail, then back to study Chee.

"First piece of advice I need from you," he said when Chee had finished, "is what to tell Sharkey when he finds out the Navajo Tribal Police have been questioning one of his witnesses in a federal murder case."

"You mean Joseph?"

"Of course, Joseph," Largo said, shifting his eyes from thumbnail to Chee. "I don't have any trouble explaining why you went to Begay's hogan. You went there looking for a runaway girl, and Sharkey has to swallow that one because you're lucky, as usual. She was there."

"Tell him I talked to Joseph for the same reason," Chee suggested.

"Doesn't work."

"I guess not," Chee admitted. "Change the subject then. Ask him why the Agency left that stuff out of the report they sent you. Ask him why no mention was made of Gorman coming to Shiprock looking for somebody else named Gorman. Ask him why the picture of the trailer . . ." Chee didn't finish the sentence. Largo's expression said he wasn't liking this suggestion.

"What am I going to tell Sharkey?" he repeated. "Are you going to give me an explanation, or do I have to tell him that one of our men violated department regulations and the direct and specific orders of his commanding officer and is therefore being suspended without pay to teach him some better manners?"

"Tell him the *girl* disappeared right after all this happened, and she's Hosteen Begay's granddaughter and we think—"

The telephone interrupted him. Largo picked it up. "Good," he said. "What's her name again?" He listened, then pushed the selector button.

"Miss Pino? This is Captain Largo of the Navajo Tribal Police in Shiprock. Could you give us a little more information to help us find Margaret Sosi? . . . What? . . . No, no, we think she's all right. What we need is a clearer idea of just why she left when she did."

Largo listened.

"A letter?" he said. "When? . . . Did she say anything about what her grandfather said in it? . . . Uh-huh. I see. Did she mention the name? . . . Sure. I can understand that. Would you remember it if you heard it? Was it Gorman? . . . You're sure. How about the first name. . . . Her uncle? . . . Okay. Go over it again, would you please? Everything you remember she said."

Largo listened, jotting notes now and then on his pad.

"Well, thank you very much, Miss Pino. This is very helpful. . . . No, we think she's safe enough. We just want to find her." Largo looked at Chee with no expression whatever and added, "Again.

"One other thing. Did she say when she planned to come back? . . . Okay. Well, thanks again."

Largo replaced the receiver, gently.

"You are one lucky Navajo," he said, "which is almost as good as being smart."

Chee said nothing.

"It turns out I can tell Sharkey that Margaret Sosi got a letter from her grandfather mailed the day after the shooting, and in this letter he told her about some danger. Warned her to stay away from Shiprock and not to go around Gorman."

"Danger?"

"That's all she told the Pino girl. Or all the Pino girl could remember her saying about it. She said Margaret told her her grandfather must be very upset, because writing a letter was very hard for him to do. She said she was worried about him and she was going to see about him."

"That was the letter he mailed from Two Gray Hills," Chee said.

"Probably," Largo said. "Been nice if you'd have asked her some things like that. Something practical. You know, Sharkey's going to be curious about that. He's going to say, 'Now, your policeman had this girl in his custody. But he didn't ask her why she came to the hogan. Or find out about the letter. Or find out that her grandfather warned her about something dangerous. Or anything useful.' And Sharkey is going to say, 'What do your officers chat about in cases like this? I mean, how do they keep the conversation going until they let the suspect walk away?' What do I tell Sharkey about that?"

"Tell him we talked about ghosts," Chee said.

"Ghosts. Sharkey will enjoy that."

"I heard you asking the Pino girl if Margaret Sosi mentioned a first name for Gorman," said Chee, changing the subject. "You thinking the same thing I am?"

"I'm thinking we don't know for sure which Gorman she was supposed to stay away from. The one who had already been shot or the one that one was looking for."

"The occupant of the aluminum house trailer," Chee said.

"Maybe," Gorman said. He scratched his nose. "Or maybe he was just having his picture taken." He got up, stretched, walked to the window, and scrutinized the parking lot. "Put it together," he said, finally, "and what have you got? Albert Gorman, a car thief, drives from L.A. to Shiprock, looking for Leroy Gorman. A minor hoodlum rents himself an expensive plane ride and comes after Albert. They shoot each other. Gorman goes to his uncle's place, gets there in the night, tells the old man what happened. Next day Uncle Begay goes out to the trading post and mails a letter to Margaret Sosi. Tells her something or other is dangerous and to stay away from Shiprock and to stay away from Gorman. Which Gorman? I'd guess it wouldn't be the Gorman with the bullet in him. Old as Begay was, he's seen enough hurt people to know when one's bad hurt. He'd have known Albert wasn't dangerous to anybody. The warning would be about Leroy. Stay away from Leroy."

"Yes," Chee said. "Probably, anyway."

Largo abandoned the parking lot and sat again behind his desk. He regained his interest in his thumbnail, holding the heel of his hand on the desk top, thumb rampant, flexing slowly when he inspected it. "I am going to call Sharkey," he said. "I think we better find that Sosi girl." He glanced from thumb to Chee. "Again," he added.

"Yes," Chee said. "I think so."

"And Leroy Gorman," Largo said. "You think Sharkey has that photograph? Of the trailer?"

"No." Chee described Sharkey's search of Albert Gorman's wallet.

"So either Gorman got rid of the photograph or somebody else took it out of his wallet. Old Man Begay, maybe. Or Joseph Joe didn't know what the hell he was talking about."

While he was saying that, Largo was picking up his telephone. He told the operator to call the FBI in Farmington and get Sharkey for him. "You sure Joe told Sharkey about the photograph, about Albert Gorman looking for Leroy Gorman?"

"I'm sure."

"That son of a bitch," Largo said. He didn't mean Joe.

Sharkey was in.

"This is Largo," Largo said. "We have a teenage girl missing, which looks like it's tied in with this Gorman shooting of yours. Name's Margaret Billy Sosi. You heard anything we should know about?"

Largo listened.

"She's a student at St. Catherine Indian School in Santa Fe. Granddaughter of Ashie Begay. She got a letter he mailed the day after the shooting. Her granddaddy told her something about staying away from Shiprock and not to go around Gorman because it was dangerous."

Largo listened.

"I don't know why," he said, and listened again. "Well, it was worth a call anyway," he said. "She cut out from school after she got the letter and went up to the Begay place. We were puzzled about why old Ashie Begay would think Gorman was dangerous when he had a bullet in him—dying right there in the hogan, you know. Could there be another Gorman the old man was talking about?"

Largo listened very briefly.

"We can't ask her because"—he glanced at Chee—"she got away and disappeared again. What? Granddaughter. Margaret Sosi is Ashie Begay's granddaughter. You guys got anything that would point us to looking for another Gorman around here? A dangerous one?"

Largo listened again. He covered the mouthpiece with his palm, looked at Chee, said, "Lying son of a bitch," and listened some more.

"Well," he said, "we went out and talked to Joseph Joe to see if Albert Gorman had said anything to him, and he told us that Albert was looking for a guy named Leroy Gorman." Largo winked at Chee. "I guess Joe forgot to tell you about that. And Joe said Gorman showed him a photograph of an aluminum house trailer, which was where this Leroy Gorman was supposed to be living. You know anything—"

Largo looked slightly surprised. "All right," he said. "We'll keep in touch."

He hung up, looking suspiciously at the telephone and then at Chee.

"Sharkey tells me that Joe didn't say anything to them about Albert Gorman looking for anybody, or about a picture, and that there was no picture on Gorman's body."

"Interesting," Chee said.

"Wonder what's going on," Largo said. "I don't think Sharkey's lying just to keep in practice."

"No," Chee said. He was thinking that he would start hunting the aluminum house trailer.

"I think we better see if we can find that house trailer," Largo said.

10

FINDING AN ALUMINUM TRAILER in Shiprock, New Mexico, required only persistence. The town is the most populous of the hundreds of dots that mark populated places on the vastness of the Navajo Big Reservation. Even so, it counts less than 3,000 permanent residents. Knowing the trailer was parked under a cottonwood tree simplified the search. On the arid Colorado Plateau, cottonwoods grow only along streams, or beside springs, or in places where the runoff from snowmelt augments their water supply. In and around Shiprock, natural cottonwood habitat was limited to the San Juan river bottom and a few places along Salt Creek Wash and Little Parajito Arroyo. Chee checked the San Juan first, working upstream from the old U.S. 666 highway bridge and then downstream. He found hundreds of cottonwoods, and scores of places where a trailer might be parked, and dozens of trailers of all descriptions, including aluminum. Just before noon, he found an aluminum trailer parked under a cottonwood. It had taken a little less than two hours.

It was parked perhaps a mile below the bridge, near the end of a dirt track which led behind the Navajo Northern District Health Clinic, went past a pump station of the Shiprock town water system, and finally petered out on a low bluff overlooking the San Juan River. Chee parked just off the track and inspected his discovery.

The glossy metal reflected a pattern of sun and shadow in streaks caused by the bare branches above. Nothing on the ground indicated occupancy—neither litter nor the boxes, barrels, broken furniture, cots, or other effluvia of life that those who occupy trailers or hogans or other crowded spaces tend to leave outside to make room inside. There was nothing on the ground except a yellow mat of fallen cottonwood leaves.

Chee was instantly aware of this departure from the normal, as he always was of any deviation from the harmony of the expected. He noticed other peculiarities too. The trailer looked new, or almost new. Its glossy skin was clean and polished. Trailers that housed Shiprock Navajos and those who lived among them would more typically have the look of second-, third-, and fourth-hand models, wearing the dents, scrapes, and rust marks of hard wear and poor maintenance. Second, Chee noticed the trailer was tied to two black wires, telephone and electric power. The powerline was no surprise, but telephones were relatively rare on the reservation. The Navajo telephone book, which covered more territory than all the New England States and included Hopi country as well as Navajo, was small enough to fold neatly into one's hip pocket, and nearly all the numbers in it were for some sort of government or tribal office or a business. Residential telephones were unusual enough to draw Chee's attention.

He took off his uniform jacket and hat and put on his nylon windbreaker. As he walked toward the trailer he became aware that the telephone was ringing. The sound was faint at first, muffled by distance and whatever insulation the walls of such trailers held, then louder as he came nearer. It rang as if it had always been ringing, as if it would ring on through the noon hour, and into the evening, and forever. Chee stopped at the retractable metal step below the trailer door, hesitated, then tapped on the metal. The telephone's ring coincided with the knock. He waited, knocked again into the silence, listened. No response. He tried the knob. Locked.

Chee walked away from the trailer and stood beside the cottonwood's trunk, thinking. Below, on a path leading down to the riverbank and along it, a man was walking. He was whistling, coming up the path toward Chee. He wore neatly fitted denims, a long-sleeved shirt of blue flannel, a denim vest, and a black felt hat with a feather jutting from its band.

When the path tilted upward so that Chee could see his face, he recorded a man on the young side of middle age, clean-shaven, slender, distinctly Navajo in bone, with a narrow, intelligent face. He walked with an easy grace, swinging the heavy stalk of a horseweed like a cane. He walked now through a tunnel of sunlit yellow where the willows and alders arching over the path had not yet lost all their foliage, still not seeing Chee. But suddenly, he heard the persistent summons of the telephone bell.

He dropped the stick and sprinted for the trailer, hesitating when he noticed Chee, then regaining stride.

"Got to catch the phone," he said as he ran past. He had his key out when he reached the door, unlocked it deftly, scrambled inside. Chee stood at the steps by the open door, waiting.

"Hello," the man said, and waited. "Hello. Hello." He waited again, then whistled into the speaker. "Anybody home?" He waited, then whistled again, waited again, watching Chee. Whoever had dialed his number had apparently put down the phone and left it to ring. "Hello," the man repeated. "Anybody there?" This time he seemed to receive an answer.

"Yes, this is Grayson. . . . Well, I wasn't far. Just went for a walk down the river." Then he listened. Nodded. Glanced at Chee, his expression curious. "Yes," he said. "I will." He leaned his hip against the trailer's cooking stove and reached into a drawer to extract a note pad and pen. "Give it to me again." He wrote something. "All right. I will."

He hung up and turned to face Chee.

Chee spoke in Navajo, introducing himself as born to the Slow Talking Clan, born for the Bitter Water People, naming his mother and his deceased father. "I am looking for a man they call Leroy Gorman," he concluded.

"I don't understand Navajo," the man said.

Chee repeated it, clan memberships and all, in English.

"Gorman," the man said. "I don't know him."

"I heard he lived here. In this trailer."

The man frowned. "Just me here," he said.

Chee was conscious that the man hadn't identified himself. He smiled. "You're not Leroy Gorman then," Chee said. "Is that a safe bet?"

"Name's Grayson," the man said. He stuck out his hand and Chee shook it. A hard, warm grip.

"Wonder how I got the wrong information," Chee said. "This is the place." He gestured at road, tree, river, and trailer. "Supposed to be an aluminum airflow trailer like this. Strange."

Grayson was studying Chee. Behind his smile his face was stiff with tension, the eyes watchful.

"Who is he, this Gorman? Who told you he lived here?"

"I don't really know him," Chee said. "I was just supposed to deliver a message."

"A message?" The man stared at Chee, waiting.

"Yeah. To Leroy Gorman."

The man waited, leaning in the doorway. Past him Chee could see dishes beside the sink, but except for that the interior of the trailer was utterly neat. The man was a Navajo, Chee was sure of that from his appearance. Since he didn't speak the language, or pretended not to, and since he didn't follow Navajo courtesy, he might be a Los Angeles Navajo. But he said he wasn't Leroy Gorman.

"You're the second person to show up today looking for this Gorman guy," he said. He laughed, nervously. "Maybe Gorman himself will show up next. You want to leave that message with me so I can pass it along if he does?"

"Who was the first one?"

"A girl," Grayson said. "Cute little skinny girl. Late teens."

"She tell you her name?"

"She did. I can't think of it."

"How about Margaret? Margaret Sosi."

"Yeah," Grayson said. "I think so."

"How little? How was she dressed?"

"About so," Grayson said, indicating shoulder height with a gesture of his hand. "Thin. Wearing a blue coat like in the navy."

"What did she want?"

"Seemed to think I was this Gorman. And when she understood I wasn't, she wanted to ask me about her grandfather. Had he been here. Things like that. Don't remember his name. She wanted to find this Gorman because he was supposed to know something about where her grandfather was." Grayson shrugged. "Something like that. Didn't make much sense."

Chee put his foot on the step, shifted his weight. He wanted the man to invite him inside, to extend the conversation. Who was Grayson? What was he doing here?

"Maybe I could leave that message," he said. "You got a place I could write it down?"

Grayson hesitated a heartbeat. "Come on in," he said.

He provided a sheet from his note pad and a ballpoint pen. Chee sat on the built-in couch beside the table and printed, in a large, slow hand:

LEROY GORMAN—
ALBERT GOT KILLED. GET IN TOUCH WITH CHEE AT

He hesitated. The tribal police switchboard operator responded to calls with "Navajo Tribal Police." Chee imagined Grayson hearing that and hanging up, his curiosity satisfied. He wrote in the number of the Shiprock Economy Wash-O-Mat and added:

LEAVE MESSAGE.

Chee didn't look up while he printed. He wanted Grayson to be reading the message—and he was sure that he had. He folded the paper, and refolded it, and wrote on the final fold:

FOR LEROY GORMAN, PRIVATE.

He handed it to Grayson.

"Appreciate it," Chee said. "If he does show up."

Grayson didn't look at the note. His face was tense. "Sure," he said. "But it ain't likely. Never heard of him until that girl showed up."

"Did she say where she was going when she left?"

Grayson shook his head. "Just said something about going off to find some old woman somewhere. Didn't mean much to me."

It didn't mean much to Jim Chee either, except that finding Margaret Sosi probably wouldn't be easy.

11

FINDING MARGARET SOSI, Chee thought, would take a lot more time and hard work than finding an aluminum trailer under a cottonwood tree. Maybe she'd gone to Los Angeles. Maybe she hadn't. Chee remembered himself at seventeen. Easy enough to talk about Los Angeles, and to dream about it, but for a child of the reservation it represented a journey into a fearful unknown—a visit to a strange planet. He could never have managed it by himself. He doubted if Margaret Sosi would have taken that long and lonely leap into God-knew-what. More likely she was hunting Old Man Begay on the Big Reservation. Maybe she was tracking down members of their clan who'd moved to the Cañoncito. That was exactly what Chee would begin doing. Unfortunately, members of the Turkey Clan seemed to be scarce.

But Chee's route back to his office led past the intersection of U.S. 666 and Navajo Route 1. The 7-Eleven store there served as depot for both Greyhound and Continental Trailways. It would only take a minute to check, and Chee took it. A middle-aged Navajo named Ozzie Pete managed both the store and bus ticket sales. No. No tickets had been sold to Los Angeles for weeks. Maybe months. For the past several days he was dead sure he had sold no tickets at all to a skinny teenage girl in a navy pea coat.

From his office, Chee called south to the trading posts at Newcomb and Sheep Springs. Same questions. Same answers. He called Two Gray Hills. The mare was back in the corral, neither better nor worse for its abduction, but no one had seen anyone who looked like Margaret Sosi. So much for that.

Chee tilted his chair back against the wall and crossed his boots on his wastebasket. What now? He had no idea how to start looking for Turkey Clan people. It could only be purely random. Driving around, stopping at trading posts, chapter houses, watering points, every place where people collected, to ask questions and leave word. Sooner or later someone would either be Turkey Clan or know someone who was. And since the Turkey Clan was virtually extinct it would more likely be later rather than sooner before he made connections. Chee did not feel lucky. He dreaded the job. But the only alternative to starting it was to see if he could think of an alternative.

He thought.

What had Margaret done when she slipped away from him at the hogan? Taken the mare back to Two Gray Hills, obviously. Before that she had, perhaps, taken time to take a sweat bath. Hosteen Begay's sweat bath was handy and in plain view from where she'd tied the mare. Perhaps she had made sure Chee was gone, built a fire, heated the stones, poured spring water over them, and cleansed herself in the healing steam to rub away Gorman's ghost. Chee himself had taken a steam bath in his trailer home—putting his frying pan, superheated on the stove, on the floor of his shower and pouring boiling water from his teakettle onto the hot metal to create an explosion of steam. He'd felt limp, very clean, and generally better when he'd finished his rubdown. The same would have been true of Margaret. Say she'd taken the bath, ridden the mare down to U.S. 666 and turned it loose to find its way back to Two Gray Hills, and then caught an early-morning ride back into Shiprock. Then she'd gone to Grayson's trailer looking for Leroy Gorman. How the devil had she found it? Perhaps Hosteen Begay had told her where it was when he wrote her, warning her away from Gorman. More proof that Margaret Sosi didn't scare easily. Not when her grandfather was involved. Chee thought some more. Perhaps this explained what had happened to the Polaroid photograph. Perhaps Hosteen Begay had taken it from the dying Albert Gorman and mailed it to Margaret. Whatever was on that photograph had brought Albert Gorman racing to Los Angeles to find Leroy Gorman. Would Hosteen Begay use it to keep Margaret away? The Margaret Sosi who didn't scare?

Chee sighed, took his feet down, and reached for the telephone. Maybe she *had* gone to L.A., scary as it seemed to him. Anyway, until he knew for sure, he had a reason not to start hunting elsewhere.

By midafternoon Chee knew everything about bus schedules from Shiprock southward toward Gallup and westward through Teec Nos Pos, including who drove which bus and where they lived. He knew that one Greyhound driver didn't remember having a skinny Navajo girl in a pea coat as a passenger yesterday, and another Greyhound driver was still out on his run and incommunicado. The very first Continental Trailways driver he reached made all this beside the point.

"Yeah," he said. "She flagged me down north of the Newcomb Trading Post. She wanted a ticket to Los Angeles, but she didn't have enough money."

"How much did she have?"

"She had enough to get to Kingman, right there on the California border, and forty cents left over."

"Describe her to me," Chee said.

The driver described Margaret Billy Sosi. "Nice-looking kid," he concluded, "but she looked like she needed some fattening up and her face washed. Looked wore out. What are you fellas after her for?"

"Trying to keep her from getting hurt," Chee said.

Chee called the station at Kingman. The L.A.-bound bus from points east had arrived on schedule and departed, also on schedule, about fifteen minutes ago. Had anyone noticed a small, thin, tired Navajo girl with black eyes and black hair getting off? She was wearing a navy pea coat and her face needed washing. No one had noticed.

Chee called the Kingman police station, identified himself, and asked for the watch commander. He got a Lieutenant Monroney and described Margaret Sosi for what seemed to be the eleventh time. "I guess she'd be hitchhiking," Chee said. "She's trying to get to Los Angeles."

"And the bus got in when, quarter hour ago? And she's seventeen?"

"Seventeen but looks fifteen. Small."

"Pretty girl?"

"I guess so," Chee said. "Yeah. Kind of thin but she looks okay. Would have needed to have her face washed, though."

"We'll look for her," Monroney said. "And I'll call the California Highway patrol across the line and give them the word. But don't count on anything. A boy, he'd still be out there thumbing. Girl, pretty girl, that age—she'd be picked up. Long gone. But we'll look. Give me your number. We find her, we'll call. Just want her held for runaway, that it? No crime?"

"No crime," Chee said. "But there's a homicide in the background. Just keep her safe."

But maybe it was already too late for that.

12

THE "ELEVEN THOUSAND seven hundred thirteen La Monica Street" address Sharkey had read from Albert Gorman's driver's license translated into a single-story U-shaped building of faded pale-green stucco. Chee parked his pickup behind an aging Chevy Nova with an off-color fender and looked the place over. The building seemed to house ten or twelve small apartments, with the one on the left end of the U wearing a small sign that said MANAGER. Attached to that, a cardboard placard proclaimed VACANCY.

Chee walked up the narrow pathway to the porch in front of the manager's apartment. Beside the door, opposite the vacancy sign, another sign listed apartment occupants. Chee found no Albert Gorman, but the name slot beside number 6 was empty. He cut across the weedy bermuda grass to the entrance porch of number 6, rang the bell, and waited. Nothing. A mailbox was mounted beside the door, its lid closed. Chee rang the bell again, listened to the buzz it produced inside the apartment, and, while he listened, pushed open the lid of the mailbox.

Two envelopes were in it. Chee moved his body to shield what he was doing from the direction of the manager's office and extracted the envelopes. One was addressed to OCCUPANT and the other to Albert Gorman. It seemed to be a telephone bill, postmarked two days earlier. Chee dropped both envelopes back into the box, rang the bell again, then tried the door. Locked. Again he shielded the action with his body because he was aware that someone was watching him. A woman, he thought, but he'd only had a momentary glimpse of the form standing behind the partly pulled curtain of the office window.

Chee turned from the door and recrossed the weedy lawn. He rang the office manager's doorbell, waited, rang it again, waited again. He glanced at his watch. What could the woman be doing? He rang the bell again, watched the second hand of his watch sweep around a full minute, and then another. The woman did not intend to come to the door. Why not? She had an apartment to rent. He rang the bell again, waited another minute, then turned and started toward his truck.

He heard the door open behind him.

"Yes?"

Chee turned. She held the door halfway open. She was as tall as Chee, gaunt, and gray—a bony, exotic face which showed Negro blood and perhaps Chinese.

"My name's Jim Chee," Chee said. "I'm looking for a man named Albert Gorman. In apartment six, I think."

"That's right," the woman said. "Apartment six is Gorman."

"He's not in," Chee said. "Do you have any idea where I could find him?"

"I think he'll be back in a little while," the woman said. "You wait. There's a chair there on his porch." She gestured across the lawn. "Just make yourself comfortable."

The accent was marked. Spanish? Probably, but not the sort of Mexican Spanish Chee heard around the reservation. Filipino, perhaps. Chee had heard there were lots of Filipinos in Los Angeles.

"Do you know when he'll be back? Actually, I'm trying to find some of his relatives. Do you—"

"I don't know anything," the woman said. "But he'll be right back. He said if anyone came looking for him to just have them wait. It wouldn't be long."

"I'm a policeman," Chee said, extracting his credentials and showing her. "I'm trying to locate a girl. About seventeen. Small. Thin. Dark. An Indian girl. Wearing a navy pea coat. Has she been here?"

The woman shook her head, expression skeptical and disapproving.

"It would have been early this morning," Chee said. "Or maybe late last night."

"I haven't seen her."

"Does Albert Gorman have any other address you know about? Where he works? Any relatives I could check with?"

"I don't know," the woman said. "You wait. You ask him all that."

"I have a friend looking for an apartment," Chee said. "Could I look at the one you have vacant?"

"Not ready yet. Not cleaned up. Tenant still has his stuff in it. You wait." And with that she closed the door.

"All right," Chee said. "I will wait."

He sat in the chair on the porch of number 6 and waited for whatever his visit here had triggered to start happening. He made no effort to calculate what that might be. The woman, obviously, had called someone when she saw him on Gorman's porch. Apparently she had been told to keep him there, and so she had stalled. He would stay partly because he was curious and partly because there was no other choice. If he drew a blank here, he knew of no promising alternatives. This address was his only link to the Turkey Clan and Margaret Sosi. Unfortunately, the chair was metal and uncomfortable.

He got up, stretched, sauntered across the grass, fingers stuck in the back pockets of his jeans, sending the woman who was surely watching from behind the curtain the signal of a man killing time. He walked down to the street and looked up and down it. Across from him, a neon sign over the entrance of a decaying brick building read KOREAN GOSPEL CHURCH. Its windows were sealed with warped plywood. Next door was a once-white bungalow with a wheelless flatbed truck squatting on blocks before its open garage door. Once-identical frame houses stretched down the block, given variety now by age, remodeling projects, and assorted efforts to make them more livable. The line terminated in a low concrete block building on the corner which, judging from the sign painted on its wall, was a place where used clothing was bought and sold. In general, it was a little worse than the street Chee had lived on as a student in Albuquerque and a little better than the average housing in Shiprock.

Gorman's side of La Monica Street was of a similar affluence but mostly two-story instead of one. Below his U-shaped apartment house were two more, both larger and both badly needing painting. Up the street, the remainder of the block was filled by a tan stucco building surrounded by lawn and a chain-link fence. Chee ambled along the fence, examining the establishment.

On the side porch, five people sat in a row, watching him. They sat in wheelchairs, strapped in. Old people, three women and two men. Chee raised a hand, signaling greetings. No reaction. Each wore a blue bathrobe: four white heads and one bald one. Another woman sat in a wheelchair on a concrete walk that ran just inside the fence. She, too, was old, with thin white hair, a happy smile, and pale blue vacant eyes.

"Hello," Chee said.

"He's going to come today," the woman said. "He's coming."

"Good," Chee said.

"He's going to come today," the woman repeated. She laughed.

"I know it," Chee said. "He'll be glad to see you."

She laughed again, looking happily at Chee through the fence. "Got shore leave," she said. "He's coming."

"Wonderful," Chee said. "Tell him hello for me."

The woman lost interest in him. She backed her wheelchair down the walk, humming.

Chee strolled along the fence, looking at the five who lined the porch. This was a side of white culture he'd never seen before. He'd read about it, but it had seemed too unreal to make an impression—this business of penning up the old. The fence was about six feet high, with the topmost foot tilted inward. Hard for an old woman to climb that, Chee thought. Impossible if she was tied in a wheelchair. Los Angeles seemed safe from these particular old people.

He turned the corner and walked past the front of the place. SILVER THREADS REST HOME, a sign on the front lawn said. Here there were flowers—beds of marigolds, petunias, zinnias, and blossoms of the mild coastal climate that Chee could not identify. Banks of flowers flourishing safe from the old people.

Silver Threads occupied the entire end of the block. Chee circled it, glancing at his watch, killing time. He turned into the alley separating the rest home from Gorman's apartment complex and walked down it toward Gorman's porch. He'd used up almost ten minutes.

A man, bent and skinny, was standing inside the fence watching him approach with bright blue, interested eyes. He was standing in a waist-high aluminum walking frame, its four legs planted in the grass.

"Hello," Chee said.

"You Indian?" the man asked. He had trouble with "Indian," stopping mid-word, closing his eyes, exhaling breath, trying again until he pronounced it.

"Yes," Chee said. "I'm Navajo."

"Indian lives there," the man said. He removed a hand from the walker and gestured toward Gorman's apartment.

"Do you know him?" Chee asked.

The old man struggled for words, shook his head, sighed. "Nice," he said finally. "Talks."

Chee smiled. "His name is Albert Gorman. That the one?"

The man was frowning angrily. "Don't smile," he said. "Nobody talks to me but that . . ." His face twisted with a terrible effort, but he couldn't manage the rest of it. "Him," he said finally and looked down at his hands, defeated.

"It's a good thing to be friendly," Chee said. "Too many people never have time to talk."

"He's not home," the man said. Chee could see he wanted to say something else, and waited while his fierce will struggled with his stroke-blighted mind, making it work. "Gone," he said.

"Yes," Chee said. "He has an uncle who lives on the Navajo Reservation. In New Mexico. He went back there to visit him." Chee felt a twinge of guilt when he said it, as he always did when he was being deceptive. But why tell the old man his friend was dead?

The old man's expression changed. He smiled. "Kin?"

"No," Chee said. "But we're both Navajos, so we're kin in a way."

"He's in bad trouble," the man said, clearly and plainly. Whatever short circuit of nerve tissue impeded his speech, it seemed to come and go.

Chee hesitated, thinking like a policeman. But what was required here was not the formula in the police manual.

"Yes, he is. I don't understand it, but when he left here someone went after him. Very bad trouble."

The old man nodded, wisely. He tried to speak, failed.

"Did he tell you about it?"

The man shook his head in the negative. Thought. Canceled the denial with a shrug. "Some," he said.

A little round woman in a tight, white uniform was approaching across the lawn. "Mr. Berger," she said, "time for us to start or we'll miss our lunch."

"Shit," Mr. Berger said. He grimaced, picked up the walking frame carefully, and pivoted.

"Don't talk dirty," the round woman said. "If we were in a wheelchair like we should be, I could push you." She glanced at Chee, found him uninteresting. "That would save us time."

"Shit," Mr. Berger said again. He moved the walking frame up the lawn, stumbling along inside it. The round woman walked behind, silent and relentless.

Only the angle of the morning sun had changed on the porch of Gorman's apartment. Chee sat in the metal chair beside the door and thought of Mr. Berger. Then he thought about Grayson: who he might be, and what Grayson was doing in Shiprock, and how he might be connected with this odd business. He tried to guess what might have caused Albert Gorman's confusion about who lived in the aluminum trailer—if in fact it was confusion. And try as he did to avoid it, he thought about Mary Landon. He wanted to talk to her. Immediately. To get up and go to a telephone, and have her called out of her classroom at Crownpoint, and hear her voice: "Jim? Is everything all right?" And he would say . . . he would say, "Mary, you win." No, he wouldn't say it that way. He'd say, "Mary, you're right. I'm going to send in the application for the FBI job. And when I hang up this telephone, I'm going to walk right to my truck and drive directly, without stopping, to Crownpoint, and that will take me about twelve hours if I don't get stopped by the highway patrol for speeding, and when I get there, you have your bags packed, and tell the principal to get a substitute teacher, and . . ."

A white Ford sedan pulled up behind his pickup truck. Two men in it. The one on the passenger side got out and hurried up the walk to the manager's office. He was a short man, middle-aged, with a stocky, disciplined body and a round pink face. He wore gray pants and a seersucker coat. The door of the office opened before he reached it. The conversation there was brief. The short man looked over at Chee, saw him, and came directly across the grass toward him. At the Ford, the driver's door opened and a much larger man emerged. He stood for a moment watching. Then he, too, came sauntering toward the Gorman apartment.

The short man was talking before he reached the porch.

"Lady says you're looking for Albert Gorman. That right?"

"More or less," Chee said.

"That your truck?"

"Yes."

"You from Arizona?"

"No," Chee said. He had bought the license plates when he was stationed at Tuba City, before his transfer to Shiprock.

"Where you from?"

"New Mexico."

The bigger man arrived. Much bigger. Six-foot-four or so, Chee guessed, and broad. Much younger too. Maybe thirty-five. He looked tough. While he waited on the porch, Chee had decided he might expect FBI agents to arrive. These men were not FBI agents.

"You're a long way from home," Shortman said.

"Nine hundred miles," Chee agreed. "You fellows know where I can find this Albert Gorman? Or any of his family? Or his friends?"

"What's your connection with Gorman?" Shortman asked.

"Don't know him," Chee said. "What's your interest?"

Under Shortman's coat, Chee could see just the edge of a brown leather strap, which might be part of a harness holding a shoulder holster. Chee couldn't think of anything else it might be. Shortman wasn't interested in answering Chee's question. He reached under his jacket and extracted a leather folder from the inside pocket. "Los Angeles Police Department," he said, letting the folder flop open to display a badge and photograph. "Let's see some identification."

Chee fished out his wallet, opened it to show his own badge, and handed it to Shortman.

"Navajo Tribal Police," Shortman read. He eyed Chee curiously. "Long way from home," he said again.

"Nine hundred miles," Chee repeated. "And now can you tell me anything about this Gorman? We have a girl—" He stopped. The big man was engulfed in laughter. Chee and Shortman waited.

"Mister," the big man said, "Shaw here can tell you everything about Albert Gorman. Shaw is the world champion expert on everything about Gorman. Gorman is part of Shaw's hobby."

Chee held out his hand to the short man. "My name is Chee," he said.

"Willie Shaw," the short man said, shaking hands. "This is Detective Wells. You have time for a talk? Cup of coffee?"

Wells shook Chee's hand with the soft, gentle grip he'd learned to expect from huge people. "Good thing Shaw is retiring," he said. "Police work is starting to interfere with the hobby."

"Mr. Chee here will give me a ride, I'll bet," Shaw said. "We'll go to that Vip's down on Sunset." He said it to Wells, but Wells was already walking back to the Ford. "Now," Shaw said, "I want you to start off by telling me what got the Navajo Police interested in Albert Gorman."

Chee kept the explanation simple—just the oddity of Gorman's unfinished burial preparations, the question of where Hosteen Begay had gone, the problem of finding Margaret Sosi and learning from her what Begay had said in his letter. He had finished it by the time they slid into a booth in the coffee shop. Shaw stirred sweetener into his coffee. It was time for questions.

"The way I got it, Lerner just drove up to Gorman in the parking lot and shot him. Gorman shot back and drove off. Lerner dead in the lot. The Feds find Gorman dead of his gunshot wound later, at his uncle's house. That's it?"

"Not quite," Chee said. He filled in the details.

"And Albert had stopped in the lot to talk to an old man there?"

"Yes," Chee said. "To ask directions." Apparently Shaw had seen the FBI report. Why would he have seen it?

Wells had driven into the Vip's lot and come in and spotted them.

"Scoot over," he said, and sat beside Shaw.

"What did they talk about?" Shaw asked. "Gorman and the old man?"

It was exactly the right question, Chee thought. Shaw impressed him.

"What's your interest in Gorman?" Chee asked, keeping his voice very friendly. "I mean, as a Los Angeles Police Department detective?"

"In fact, as an arson squad detective," Wells said. "It's a good question. One of these days, the captain is going to ask it. He's going to say, Sergeant Shaw, how come everybody is burning down Los Angeles and you're chasing around after car thieves?"

Shaw ignored him. "I'd like to find out exactly why Gorman went to New Mexico," he said. "That would be interesting."

"You going to tell me what I need to know about this end? Help me find the Sosi girl?"

"Of course," Shaw said. "But I need to know what's behind the Navajos sending a man a thousand miles outside his jurisdiction. It's got to be better than a runaway teenager."

"They didn't send me," Chee said. "I'm taking vacation time. Sort of on my own. Makes it simpler."

Wells snorted. "Lordy," he said. "Spare me from this. Two of them in the same booth. The vigilantes ride again."

"My friend here," said Shaw, tilting his round, red face toward Wells, "thinks police should just stick to their assignments."

"Like arson," said Wells. "Right now we're supposed to be over on Culver looking into a warehouse fire, which is every bit as much fun as a New Mexico homicide and which the taxpayers are paying us for."

"You're on your own then?" Shaw said. "Nothing official. A personal interest?"

"Not exactly," Chee said. "The department wants to find the girl, and Old Man Begay. They're more or less missing. And me doing it on time off makes it less complicated." Chee could see Shaw understood the implications of that.

"Yeah," Shaw said. "It's an FBI case." Some of the caution had left his face, and there was a touch of friendliness there now. And something else. Excitement?

"You were going to tell me what Gorman talked about in the parking lot," Shaw said.

Chee told him.

"Albert was looking for Leroy?" Shaw frowned. "Had a picture of a house trailer?" He extracted a leather-covered notebook from a pocket of his coat, put on his bifocals, and read.

"Joseph Joe," he muttered. "I wonder why he didn't tell the Feds about that."

"He did," Chee said.

Shaw stared at him.

"He told the FBI everything I've told you."

Shaw digested that. "Ah," he said. "So."

"If that interests you," Chee said, "you might like to know that when the FBI emptied out Albert Gorman's pockets, the photograph Gorman had shown Joe wasn't there."

"Stranger and stranger," Shaw said. "What happened to it?"

"Two obvious possibilities. Gorman threw it away after he got shot. Or Old Man Begay took it."

Shaw was reading his notebook. "I suspect you thought of a third possibility," he said, without looking up.

"That the FBI agent palmed it?"

Shaw glanced up from his notebook, a look that mixed appraisal and approval.

"I'm almost certain that didn't happen. I found the body. I was watching. He didn't have a chance."

"Could you find that trailer? Albert thought it was in Shiprock. Isn't that a small place?"

"We found it. The man living in it said his name was Grayson. Said he didn't know any Leroy Gorman."

"Do you know who Leroy Gorman is?" Shaw asked.

"That's one of the things you were going to tell me."

"Let me see that identification again."

Chee dug out his ID folder and handed it to Shaw. Shaw studied it, memorizing the information, Chee guessed. "I'll make a telephone call," he said. "Back in a minute."

Chee sipped his coffee. Through the window came the sound of traffic, the clamor of an ambulance hurrying somewhere. Wells slid his cup back and forth across his saucer, pushing it with a finger.

"He's a good man, Shaw," he said. "Great record. But he's going to screw himself up with this. Mess around until he gets into trouble."

"Why? Why's he so interested?"

"His friend got killed," Shaw said. "Died, actually." He drained the cup and signaled a waitress for a refill. "However it was, Shaw thinks they killed him, and they're getting away with it. It drives him crazy."

"He's not happy with the investigation?"

"There isn't any," Wells said. He waited for the waitress to finish pouring. "The man had a coronary. Natural causes. No sign of foul play."

"Oh."

Wells's face was moody. "I've been his partner for four years, and I can tell you he's a dandy. Three commendations. Smart as they get. But he can't seem to turn loose of this Upchurch business."

"Upchurch. Was he the FBI agent?"

Wells stared at him.

"I heard the FBI lost a man on this case," Chee explained. "And they seem to be acting funny."

"They're going to be acting even funnier when they find out Shaw—" He stopped. Shaw slid back into the booth.

"Albert Gorman was a car thief," Shaw began without preamble. "He and Leroy. They're brothers, and they both stole cars for a living. Worked for an outfit called McNair Factoring. Old outfit down on the Santa Monica docks. Imports coffee beans, cocoa, raw rubber, stuff like that—mostly from South America, I think, but some from Asia and Africa too. Exports whatever is going out—including stolen cars. It's sort of a specialty. Mostly expensive stuff. Ferraris, Mercedes, Caddies. So forth. Mostly to Argentina and Colombia, but now and then to Manila and wherever they had orders. That's the way they worked. Gorman and the others were on commission. They'd get orders for specific models. Say a Mercedes Four-fifty SL. And a delivery dated when the right ship was at the wharf. They'd spot the car, wait until the date, then nail it and drive it right onto the dock. Have it on the ship before the owner missed it. Pretty slick."

Shaw paused to see if Chee agreed. Chee nodded.

"Then an FBI agent got into this. His name was . . . Kenneth . . ." Shaw's voice choked. The muscle along his upper jaw tensed. Wells, who had been watching him, looked quickly away to study the traffic passing on this seedy end of Sunset Boulevard. Chee thought of the Navajo custom of not speaking the name of the dead. For Shaw, the name had certainly called back the ghost.

Shaw swallowed. "His name was Kenneth Upchurch." He stopped again. "Sorry," he said to Chee. "He was a good friend. Anyway, Upchurch worked up a case on the McNair operation. A good one."

Shaw had control again now. A man who had made a thousand reports was making another one, and he made it clearly and concisely. When Upchurch had gone to the grand jury he found his witnesses slipping away. A first mate fell overboard. A ship's captain remained behind in Argentina. A thief lost his memory. Another changed his mind. Upchurch got some indictments, but the top people got away clean.

"Went scot-free," Wells said sourly. "A pun. The clan McNair went scot-free. Ha ha." He didn't smile and neither did Shaw. A bad old joke.

"That was nine years ago," Shaw continued. "After a while McNair Factoring went back into the car business, and Upchurch got wind of it, and the word was they were tying it in now with Colombia cocaine trade. He told me that what went wrong the first time was that everybody knew about it. This time he was going to make a case by himself. Keep it totally quiet. Just work on it by himself; you know, take his time. Nail a witness here and there and keep 'em in the bag until he was ready. Tell nobody except whoever he had to work with in the U.S. District Attorney's office, and maybe somebody in Customs if he had to. So that's the way he did it. Worked for years. Anyway, this time he had everything cold. He was really tickled, Ken was." Shaw's red face was happy, remembering it. "He had witnesses nailed down to tie in the top people, old George McNair himself, and a guy named Robert Beno, who sort of ran the stealing end, and one of McNair's sons—everybody big."

Shaw gestured with both hands, a smoothing motion. "Like silk. Seven indictments. The whole shebang." Shaw grinned at the recollection. "That was on a Tuesday. Complete surprise. Got 'em all except Beno, mugged and fingerprinted and booked in and bonded out on Wednesday. Kenneth, he made some of the arrests himself—McNair, it was, and his boy—and then he made sure he got his witnesses tucked in safe. He had 'em in the Witness Protection Program, and as soon as they got through talking to the grand jury, he'd take 'em himself and tuck 'em back in. Not taking any chances this time. By that weekend he was all finished with it."

Shaw stopped, staring straight ahead. He took a deep breath and let it out.

"That weekend, Saturday night, we was going to celebrate. My wife and Kenneth and Molly. Had reservations. Saturday he was driving down the Santa Monica Freeway. Don't know where he was going, but he was just about at Culver City, and he lost control of the car and hit a van and another car and went over an off ramp."

There was another dragging moment of silence.

"Killed him," Shaw said.

Wells stirred, started to say something, shrugged instead.

"How?" Chee asked. "In the crash?"

"Autopsy showed he had a coronary," Shaw said, glancing at Wells. "Death by natural causes."

"Nice timing," Chee said.

"Sure, it makes you suspicious," Wells interjected. "It made the FBI suspicious too. One of their own had just closed a big case. They got right on it, heavy. I know for sure they had the autopsy rechecked. Had their own doctor in on it. They didn't find anything but a guy driving down the freeway having a heart attack."

"The FBI," Shaw said. "Lawyers and certified public accountants."

"LAPD Homicide helped them," Wells said. "You know that. You know those guys as well as I do. Better. They don't miss much when they're interested, and they didn't find a damn thing either."

"Well," Shaw said, "you know and I know that McNair killed him. Just killed him to get even. Had money enough to do it so it wouldn't show. Induced the heart attack."

Wells looked angry. Obviously it was something they had covered before. Often. "Nothing wrong with the brakes. No sign of drugs in the body. No skin punctures. No poison darts fired from airplanes. No canisters of poison gas. Nothing in the blood."

"The car was all torn up," Shaw said. "So was the body."

"They're used to that," Wells said. "The pathologists—"

"We won't argue about it," Shaw said. "Kenneth is dead. He was as good a friend as a man ever had. I don't want somebody getting away with killing him, casual as swatting a fly."

"What's the motive?" Chee asked.

Shaw and Wells both looked at him, surprised.

"Like I said, getting even," Shaw said. "For starters. And it got him out of the way before the trial."

"But the D.A.'s office would handle that, wouldn't it? Was he an important witness?"

"I guess not," Shaw conceded. "But the case was his baby. He'd be in the background, making sure nothing went wrong, making sure the witnesses were okay, that the prosecutor knew what the hell he was doing. That sort of thing."

"Witnesses all safe?"

"Sure. Far as I know, and I think I would have heard. But it's the Witness Protection Program. All secret, secret, secret."

"Albert Gorman wasn't safe," Chee said.

"Albert wasn't a witness," Shaw said. "Kenneth couldn't turn him. Couldn't get anything on him. Leroy, now, he's a witness. Ken got him cold, in a stolen Mercedes with his hot-wire kit and keys. And he even had written himself a note about the model and when to deliver it to what dock. Two previous convictions."

"So now Leroy's a protected witness?" Chee said.

"I'd guess yes," Shaw said. "Wouldn't you? I know he hadn't been in town since before the grand jury. If I was guessing, I'd guess maybe they assigned him the name of Grayson and hid him in a trailer on the Navajo Reservation."

"So why shoot Albert?" Chee asked. But he was already guessing the answer.

"I don't think they planned to do it. I think they were watching him to see if he'd lead 'em to Leroy, and they followed him to Shiprock. Sent Lerner. Lerner was supposed to follow Al or get him to tell where Leroy was hiding. Something went wrong. Boom."

"Makes sense," said Chee. "The FBI report didn't say much about Lerner. Who was he?"

"We have a folder on him," Shaw said. "Long-time hood. Used to work in one of the longshoremen's rackets, extortion, collecting for the sharks. Then he was bodyguard for somebody in Vegas, and for a long time he worked for McNair."

"Sort of a hit man?" Chee asked. He was uneasy with the expression. It wasn't a term in the working vocabulary of the Tribal Police.

"Not really," Shaw said. "Their regular muscle, from what Upchurch told me, was a freelancer. A guy named Vaggan."

"Wonder why he didn't go," Chee said. "Looks like it would have been important to them."

Shaw shrugged. "No telling. Maybe it cost too much. Vaggan is supposed to be expensive."

"But good," Wells said. "But good."

13

VAGGAN RARELY wasted time. Now, while he waited for 3 A.M. and time to begin Operation Leonard, he listened to Wagner on his tape deck and reread *The Navajo.* He sat in the swivel chair in the rear of his van, light-tight curtains drawn over its windows, and absorbed the chapter about Navajo curing ceremonials. The page he read was illuminated by a clip-on battery-powered light that Vaggan had ordered from *Survive* magazine at a cost of $16.95 plus COD charges. He kept the light in the glove box of the van for just such occasions, the long waits in dark places where he had business to do and where he didn't want to be noticed. The light was advertised for reading in poorly lit motels, on aircraft, and so forth, and it made turning pages awkward. But its light focused narrowly on the page and nowhere else. If anyone was snooping around Vaggan's van they'd see nothing reflecting on his windshield.

It wasn't likely that anyone would be outside. The Santa Ana had started blowing early in the afternoon. It was blowing harder now, and Vaggan had picked this place carefully—the screened off-street parking apron outside the four-car garage of a massive, colonial-style mansion on Vanderhoff Drive. The owners of the mansion were elderly, their only live-in servant a middle-aged woman. The light went off early, and the parking area offered Vaggan an unobtrusive place to wait, out of sight of the Beverly Hills police patrol. The patrol prowled the streets at night looking for those, like Vaggan, who had no legitimate after-hours business here among the richest of the rich.

In addition, it was near enough to Jay Leonard's home to make it convenient for Vaggan to scout his grounds. He had done that at 11 P.M., and again a little after midnight, and twice since midnight. And it was far enough from Leonard's to reduce the risk of being noticed in the event someone else was watching. Vaggan had considered that possibility—as he considered all possibilities when he took on a job—but it didn't seem to be happening. Leonard seemed to be content to base his safety on a triple line of defense. He had a rent-a-cop staying in his home with him, he'd installed a fancy new burglar alarm, and he'd rented two guard dogs.

Vaggan found the thought of the dogs intruding into his concentration. The paragraph he'd just read concerned the taboo violations which could be counteracted by the Enemy Way ceremonial, a subject that interested him mildly. But the thought of the dogs excited him. He had inspected them (and they had inspected him) on each of his scouting trips. Dobermans. A male and a female. The dog man at Security Systems, Inc., had assured him that the dogs were trained not to bark, but Vaggan had wanted to check that out. Even with the Santa Ana blowing, even with the whine and howl of the wind covering just about every sound, Vaggan didn't want the animals raising a clamor. Leonard was a drinker, and a coke snorter, and Leonard might be out of it. But he would be nervous. So might the rent-a-cop.

"You can ask Jay Leonard," the dog man said. "He's had 'em better'n a week now and they ain't barked for him. If they'd been bothering his neighbors, I don't think he'd have recommended us to you."

"Maybe they haven't had any reason to be barking," Vaggan said. "But what if somebody walks along the fence there with a dog on a leash, or a cat, or if somebody wants to come through the gate. What if a cat gets in the yard?"

"No barking," the man said. "One kind of watchdog, you teach him to bark when somebody shows up. Encourage it when they're pups. Another kind of guard dog, attack dog, you don't want barking. You teach 'em right away they bark they get punished for it. Before long, nothing makes 'em bark. We can rent you a pair like that."

Vaggan had reserved two dogs for December, long after he'd be finished with Leonard. He used a name and address he'd picked out of the Beverly Hills telephone book and paid a $50 deposit to make sure the man would know the deal was made and wouldn't be calling Leonard about the barking business. Leonard was into the Man for $120,000, not counting interest and Vaggan's collection fee. And Vaggan's collection fee—usually 15 percent—was going to be a lot fatter this time.

"Publicity," the Man had said. "That's what we need. You know what that silly little bastard said to me? What Leonard said? He said don't give him any of that crap about breaking kneecaps. Them days is past, he said. He said take him to court. Did I know you couldn't collect a gambling debt in court?"

Vaggan had just listened. The Man was very, very angry.

"I said I'd turn it over to my collection, and he said screw my collection. He said try to get tough with him and I'd end up in the pen."

"So you want a kneecap broken?"

"Something or other," the Man said. "Whatever is appropriate. But I want people to know about it. Too many deadbeats saying sue me. Let's get some publicity out of Leonard. Cut down on the bad debts."

"Whether or not we get the money?"

"I don't mean kill him," the Man said. "Kill him, I'm out a hunnert and twenty grand and interest. He ain't gonna name me in his will."

Vaggan didn't respond to that. He sat easily in the telephone booth, receiver to his ear, and watched a woman trying to back a Cadillac into a space at the shopping center across the street. He let the silence tick away. Better to let the Man start the next phase of the negotiations.

"Vaggan," he said at last. "There'd be a bonus for the publicity."

"I can see that," Vaggan said. "What you're asking me to do is sort of challenge the cops to do something about it. Roughing up Leonard is one thing. Roughing him up so it's public is like daring 'em to catch me. And if I do it right, I'm putting myself out of the collection business. All you have to do is mention Jay Leonard and they hand you a cashier's check."

"What's fair?" the Man asked.

"I'd say all of it," Vaggan said. "You lose the Leonard money but you make the point with everybody else. All of it, if I really do it right. I mean, make the TV news shows, and the *Times.* Get a big splash."

They argued for a while, haggling, each man objecting. But they settled on a price. Several prices, actually, depending on the nature of the publicity and on Leonard paying up promptly. Even the lowest one was enough to pay for putting in the reinforced concrete storage house that Vaggan was going to build into the hillside next to his place. It made the lost $50 dog deposit seem reasonable.

Vaggan glanced at his watch. Twelve minutes now. He put down the book. The wind gusted against the van, shaking it on its springs and battering it with a barrage of twigs and whatever the dry Santa Ana gale picked up from the lush lawns of Beverly Hills. The sound of *Götterdammerung* muttered from the speakers—turned low in the interest of safety but, at this thunderous point in the opera, loud enough to be heard over the storm. The passage always moved Vaggan. The Twilight of the Gods, the end of the decayed old order, the cleansing. Blood, death, fire, chaos, honor, and new beginnings. "Nietzsche for thought, Wagner for music," his father would say. "Most of the rest of it is for niggers." His father . . .

He turned his thoughts instantly from that, glanced at the watch again. He would leave a little early. He slipped off his shoes, pulled the chest-high waders from their box, and slipped his legs into them, the splint on his left forefinger making the action clumsy. Vaggan hated the splint for reminding him of his moment of carelessness. But the finger had healed quickly, and he'd soon be done with the bandage. Meanwhile, he'd not think about it. "Think about your strength," the Commander had said. "Forget weaknesses." The waders were heavy with the equipment he had stuffed in their pouch. He pulled the rubber over his hips and adjusted the suspenders. Even in the waders he was graceful. Vaggan exercised. He ran. He lifted weights. He weighed 228 pounds, and every ounce of it was conditioned to do its job.

Vaggan picked up the canvas airline bag he used to carry

his bulkier equipment, locked the van behind him, and walked slowly up the sidewalk, getting accustomed to the clumsy waders. At the corner, the view opened before him. The lights of Los Angeles, bright even at 3 A.M., spread below. Vaggan thought of a luminescent southern sea, and then of the phosphorescence of decay. An apt thought. He shuffled along on the waders' felt soles, keeping silent, keeping in the shadows, looking at the glow of sleeping Los Angeles. The glow of a rotting civilization. One day soon it would be sterilized, burned clean. Very soon. The article he'd clipped from *Survival* estimated fourteen Soviet warheads targeted on the Greater Los Angeles area, including LAX, the port at Long Beach, and the city center, and the attendant military installations and industrial areas. Hydrogen bombs. They would clean the valley. When it was over, and safe again, he could climb these hills at night and look down into clean, quiet darkness.

The dogs heard him coming or perhaps—despite the wind—smelled his scent. They were waiting for him at the fence. He examined them while he extracted his wire cutter and his pipe wrench from the wader pouch. The dogs stared back, ears forward, tense and expectant. The smaller one, the female, whined, and whined again, and made a quick move toward the wire, drawing her lips back in a snarl. The Santa Ana had blown clouds and smog out to sea, as it always did, and there was enough late moon to reflect from white, waiting teeth. Vaggan pulled on his heavy leather gauntlets and snipped the first wire. The dogs wouldn't bark. He was sure of that now.

He had made sure on his second visit to the fence, taking along the cardboard box with the cat in it. The cat was a big Siamese tom which Vaggan had adopted at the Animal Shelter in Culver City—paying $28 to cover the cost of license, shots, and neutering. The dogs had charged the fence, standing tense, and the cat had smelled them. He had scratched and struggled inside the box so frantically that Vaggan had to put it on the ground and hold the lid down with one hand while he cut the cord holding it. Then he had thrown the box over the fence.

The cat had emerged in midair. It landed running and lasted a minute or so. Vaggan had wanted to learn if the dogs' training to silence would hold even during the excitement of an attack. It had. They had killed the cat with no more sound than their breathing. He had also learned something useful about how they worked. The female was the leader. She struck, and then the big male went in for the kill. Instinct, probably. It hardly seemed to Vaggan that it was something animals could be taught.

Vaggan's sentiments, oddly for him, had been with the cat. For the cat was the foredoomed loser in this affair, and Vaggan had no regard for losing, or for those who did it. Vaggan, however, admired cats, respected their self-sufficient independence. He identified with that. Often, in fact, he thought of himself as a cat. In the world that would come after the missiles and the radiation he would live as a predator, as would everyone who survived more than a week or so. Cats were first-rate predators, requiring no pack to hunt, and Vaggan found them worthy of his study.

Vaggan had started clipping wires at the bottom of the fence, wanting to be standing erect when he had cut enough to make it possible for the dogs to attack. But the dogs made no move. They waited, skittish and eager, aware that Vaggan was the enemy, wanting the wire out of the way for what was inevitable.

He clipped the last wire, holding the severed fence between him and the Dobermans. He dropped the clippers, fished his buck knife from the waders' pocket, and opened it. He held the blade upward, like a saber in his left hand, dropped the fence, and snatched up the pipe wrench in his right. The dogs stood, waiting. He studied them a moment, then stepped through the fence onto the lawn.

The male wheeled to Vaggan's left, whining eagerly, and the female took two or three steps directly backward. Then she lunged, fangs bared—a black shape catapulting at his chest. Had there been a single dog, Vaggan would have met the charge directly, to give the blow of the pipe wrench its full, killing force. But the male dog would also be coming. Vaggan wheeled to the right as he struck, taking some of the force out of the swing but putting the female's body between him and the charging male. The wrench slammed into the Doberman's skull in front of the ear, breaking jawbone, skull, and vertebrae. But the force of her lunge knocked Vaggan against the fence just as the male struck. It fastened, snarling, on the rubber leg of his waders, its weight pulling and tearing at him, jerking him off balance. Vaggan hit it across the lower back with the wrench, heard something break, and hit it again across the chest. The dog fell away from him and lay on its side on the lawn, struggled to get to its front feet, tried to crawl away from him. Vaggan walked after it and killed it with the wrench. The female, he saw, was already dead.

Vaggan knelt beside the male dog's body, eyes on Leonard's house, listening. No lights came on. The Santa Ana had faded a little for the moment, as if it were listening with him. Then it howled again, bending the eucalyptus trees that shaded the swimming pool and battering the shrubbery behind him. Vaggan walked back to the hole in the fence and looked through it, up and down the moonlit street. The wind moved everything, but he could see no sign of human life.

He dragged the male dog back to the shrubbery and hung it, head dangling, in the thick limbs. He extracted a rubber ice pack from his airline bag, unscrewed its oversized cap, and cut the Doberman's throat with the buck knife. He'd bought the ice bag at a medical supply store, choosing it because of its mouth, wide enough for ice cubes or to catch a flow of blood in the dark. He collected a pint or so from the dog's severed artery and then replaced the cap. Next he took out two plastic garbage bags and unfolded them on the grass. He decapitated both dogs and amputated the left foreleg of the male. He stuffed the bodies in one bag and the heads and foreleg in the other. That done, he stripped off his heavy gauntlets, blood-soaked now, replacing them with a pair of thin rubber surgical gloves.

He stepped out of the waders. The male dog's teeth had torn through the heavy rubber at the knee, leaving multiple rips. He checked the leg of his coveralls. It, too, was torn but his skin hadn't been punctured. He put the gauntlets, wrench, and buck knife back in the airline bag. He took out his shoes, and slipped them on, and extracted a roll of adhesive tape, a small .32 caliber pistol, four pairs of nylon restraint handcuffs, a pressure spray can of foam insulation, and, finally, a pair of plier clamps and two cattle ear tags he'd purchased at a veterinarian supply store in Encino. He arranged this assortment in his pockets and stacked the waders and the bag containing the bodies under the shrubbery. If the situation allowed he would retrieve them. If not, it wouldn't matter because he'd left no fingerprints or any way of tracing anything. But having the dogs' bodies missing would add another touch of the macabre, and Vaggan was going to make it macabre to the maximum—macabre enough to make page one of the L.A. *Times* and the lead item on tomorrow's newscasts.

He walked quietly across the lawn, carrying his burden. Dogs out of the way, the next step was the burglar alarm.

Vaggan knew a lot about the alarm. The second time he'd scouted the house, he'd noticed a BURGLARS BEWARE sticker the alarm company had pasted on the side-entrance window. He'd examined the sticker through his binoculars, looked up the company's name in the phone book, and spent an afternoon as a potential customer, learning how the system worked. Jay Leonard was big in Los Angeles, a television talk show host people were proud to have as a customer. As he had with the dog trainer, Vaggan implied that Leonard was a friend. He mentioned that Leonard was well pleased with his alarm system and had suggested he get one like it. The salesman had shown him the model and explained how it worked, and Vaggan had bought one, saying he'd install it himself.

He found the control box about where the salesman had said it should be put, mounted on an inside wall of the open carport near both a power source and a telephone line. It was equipped with an anti-tamper device that set off the alarm inside the house and flashed a signal to the Beverly Hills police if the power was cut off. Vaggan fished the aerosol can from his jacket pocket, shook it vigorously, and inserted the nozzle into the heat/moisture vent on the side of the metal box. He depressed the button and listened to the hiss of the foam insulation gushing in. The label specified a drying time of thirty minutes but, when Vaggan had checked it, it had been solid in eighteen minutes—solid and expanded to congeal all the alarm's relay switches and circuits into useless immobility. But he waited the full thirty minutes to be safe, leaning against the carport wall, coming down from the high he'd experienced in dealing with the dogs.

There was no reason to think about what he'd do next. That was carefully planned. Instead he thought about the Navajo Project. The message from his answering service had said simply, Call Mac. That meant call McNair, which in turn meant that something must have come unglued again. Not surprising. In Vaggan's experience, jobs that started sloppily tended to continue to screw up. But it was no skin off his ass. He didn't even know what the operation involved. Something, he guessed, to do with getting rid of witnesses. McNair was under indictment, with some of his people. McNair was fairly big, and certainly very senior, in the West Coast car-stealing business, and fairly big in cocaine too, from what Vaggan had heard. And he had Koreans, and Indians, and Filipinos, and Mexicans, and such people doing his stealing. In Vaggan's estimation, that was asking for trouble, since such people were poor stock. Some of them would surely screw up and get caught and talk. Had talked, already, to the grand jury, from what he'd heard, and would be ready to nail McNair in court. Which is what you should expect when you deal with such people. Losers. All of them, except maybe the Navajos.

Something about the Navajos appealed to Vaggan. Since he'd gotten into this business, he'd been reading about them. They, too, were survivors. It was because, he was sure, of their philosophy of staying in harmony with conditions, being in tune with whatever was coming down. That made sense. He did it himself. The people who refused to believe the missiles were coming and tried to turn it off by denying it, they would die. He'd gotten in harmony with that inevitable truth, accepted it, prepared for it. He would survive. And he'd gotten in harmony with this Santa Ana wind. It didn't bother him. In fact, he'd made it a part of his cover, like the quills on a porcupine. He listened to the wind, battering and shaking things, and smiled slightly. He glanced at his watch and pushed the tip of his little finger against the foam insulation in the vent. It was stiff. Time for the final phase. Time for the rent-a-cop.

Vaggan used his glass cutter on the window, removing a pane and reaching inside to unfasten the lock and then closing it behind him quickly, as soon as he had himself and his supplies inside, to shut out the wind sound. He stood listening, giving his eyes time to adjust to this deeper darkness. He'd made no sound himself. Vaggan could be quiet as the cats he admired. But opening the window would have changed the sound level of the storm for anyone awake inside. If that had alerted anyone it was better to know it now. So he waited, stock still, using up a full five minutes.

To his right a click, a low hum. The thermostat turning on the refrigerator motor. Vaggan smelled something astringent—a cleanser, perhaps—and coffee, and dust. Behind the purr of the refrigerator, the sound of distant music. Perhaps a radio playing, or a tape. In a bedroom somewhere. Then the sound of the Santa Ana rose again, pounding against the windows, rattling limbs across the roof, screeching at the corners. It subsided. The music was replaced by a male voice, inaudibly low, and then became music again. Vaggan strained to hear. It was "Daniel," the Elton John tune. Vaggan folded his handkerchief over the lens of his penlight, pointed it at the floor, and turned it on. His eyes had adjusted now, and the glow was adequate—illuminating a modern kitchen and reflecting into an expansive living area beyond.

Vaggan crept through the open archway, his crepe soles moving from the sibilance of the kitchen tile to the total silence of a thick gold carpet. He stopped and listened again, light off. The music was a bit louder now, coming from the hallway that led from the living area into what must be a bedroom wing. He removed the handkerchief, dropped it back into his pocket, and turned on the flash. A second hallway to the left led into what seemed to be some sort of atrium-greenhouse and beyond that into darkness. Vaggan moved down the carpeted hall of the bedroom wing. He stopped at the first door, listening with an ear pressed to a wooden panel. Hearing nothing, he turned off the flash, tried the knob, turned it slowly, eased the door open. He smelled deodorant, an air freshener, soap, bathroom aromas. A flick of the flash confirmed it. Guest bathroom. Vaggan closed the door and moved to the next one. Silence again, knob turning easily, door easing open. Vaggan aimed the flash at the floor, flicked it on. The reflected light showed him an empty bed, a neat, unused bedroom. He backed out, pausing to examine the door's locking mechanism under the light. A typical bedroom lock. In the hallway again, he noticed the music was loud enough now to make out an occasional word.

"Daniel," the voices sang, "my brother . . ."

Vaggan pressed an ear against the next door. Heard nothing. The knob wouldn't turn. He tried it again to confirm it was locked, then extracted a credit card from his wallet and knelt. The lock was new, and the tongue slid back easily without a sound. Vaggan stood and pulled the door open a half inch. He replaced the credit card, fished a section of nylon stocking from his pocket, and spent a moment adjusting the holes he'd cut into it over his eyes. He inhaled, feeling the same exhilaration he'd felt facing the dogs at the fence. Adrenaline. Strength. Power. Vaggan took the .32 from his pocket, held it briefly in his palm, then returned it to the pocket. He eased the door open and looked into a room lit by moonlight reflecting through translucent drapes.

The rent-a-cop had hung his clothing across a chair beside the bed, with his belt and holster dangling from the chairback. Easy to reach, Vaggan thought, when the guard heard the dogs or heard the alarm. A careful man. He extracted a revolver from the holster, dropped it in the pocket of his jacket. The cop was sleeping in shorts and undershirt, on his side, face to the wall, breathing lightly.

Vaggan switched on the flash and shined it on the man. He was young, maybe thirty, with curly black hair and a mustache. He slept on, snoring lightly. Vaggan extracted his .32, leaned forward, touched him.

The man jerked, stiffened.

"No sound," Vaggan said. He moved the light back so it illuminated the pistol. "No reason in the world for you to get hurt. They don't pay you enough for that."

The guard rolled on his back, eyes wide, staring at the gun barrel. The light reflected from dilated pupils.

"What?" the guard said. He said it in a whisper, back pressed against the mattress. "Who . . . ?"

"You and I have no problem," Vaggan said. "But I've got to talk to Leonard, so I got to tie you up."

"What?" the guard said again.

"You make any trouble, I kill you," Vaggan said. "Noise or trouble and you're dead. Otherwise, no harm done. You just stay tied up for a while. Okay? I'll look in now and then, and if you've tried to get loose, then I have to kill you. You understand that? Do you?"

"Yes," the guard said. He stared at the pistol, and into the light that illuminated it, and above the light, looking for the source of Vaggan's voice.

"On your stomach, now," Vaggan whispered. "Wrists behind you."

Vaggan fished two sets of nylon handcuffs from the jacket. He secured the guard's wrists behind him, then pulled him down the bed by his ankles. He cuffed the ankles together, one foot on each side of the metal bedpost.

The man was shaking, and his skin was wet with perspiration under Vaggan's hand. Vaggan grimaced and wiped his palm against the sheet. This one would never survive, and should never survive. When the missiles came, he would be one of the creeping, crawling multitude of weaklings purged from the living.

"Lift your face," Vaggan whispered. He taped the guard's mouth, winding the adhesive around and around, in quick movements. "My business will take an hour," Vaggan said. "I can tolerate no sound from this room for one hour. If I hear you moving in here, I will simply step inside and kill you. Like this." He pressed the muzzle of the pistol against the skin above the guard's ear. "One shot."

The guard breathed noisily through his nostrils, shuddering. He closed his eyes and turned his face away from the pistol. Vaggan felt an overwhelming sense of repugnance. He wiped his palm against his trouser leg.

Back in the hallway he used up another full minute listening. He could hear the guard breathing, almost gasping, through the door behind him and, from the door at the end of the hall, music. Elton John had been replaced by a feminine voice singing of betrayal and loneliness. He moved to the door and pressed his ear against it. He could hear only the song. He tried the knob. Locked. He extracted the credit card, slid it through the slit, pressed back the tongue, and eased the door a half inch open. His heart was beating hard now, his breathing quick, the sound of blood in his ears. He made sure the pistol was cocked. Then he opened the door.

This room was also lit by moonlight. It shone directly on thin, translucent drapes pulled across a wall of glass—making the drapes luminescent and illuminating a pale carpet and a huge bed. On it two people slept. Jay Leonard lay on his back, right hand dangling, left arm across his face, legs spread. He wore a pajama top, unbuttoned. The other person was a woman, much younger—a brunette curled on her side away from Leonard, the filtered moonlight giving the smooth, bare skin of her buttocks the look of ivory. Vaggan smelled perfume, human sweat, the inevitable dust of the Santa Ana, and the sweet smell of marijuana. The music ended and became the muted voice of the disc jockey, talking about dog food. The radio tuner was built into the headboard of the bed, its dial a bright yellow slit in the dimness. Vaggan wondered how anyone could sleep with a radio on.

In his pocket, he touched the sharp interlocking serrations forming the teeth of the ear tags and found the plier-clamp that would crimp them together. Outside, the Santa Ana rose again, screaming in the moonlight. Vaggan glanced at his watch. 3:18. He'd planned for 3:20, and he waited for 3:20.

"Leonard," Vaggan said. "Wake up. I've come to get the money."

When Vaggan got back to his van it was a little after 4 A.M. He stored the plastic garbage bag with the bodies of the dogs in the back, put away his other gear, and then let the van roll quietly back down the street before starting the engine. He ticked off all he'd done, making sure that nothing had been overlooked. After finishing with Leonard, he'd taken the dog's leg and used it and the ice bag of blood to make a crazy pattern of paw prints across the living room carpet and down the hall to Leonard's bedroom. He'd put the dogs' heads, side by side, on the mantel and poured the remainder of the blood over them. He'd called the hospital emergency room to tell them Jay Leonard, the TV talk show host, was on his way and would need attention. Finally he called the city desk of the *Times* and the night shift of the newsrooms of the three network TV stations. At each place someone was waiting for a call "about three forty-five" just as Vaggan had told them to be.

"I'm the man who called earlier," Vaggan said. "The celebrity I told you about who was going to get hurt tonight is Jay Leonard. He's on his way right now to the emergency room, just like I told you he would be. His girlfriend is driving him. He's got cattle ear tags clamped through both ears, and he'll need a little surgery to get them removed. If you sent a crew there, like I suggested, you should get some good stuff."

And then he told them the motive of this affair—a matter of not paying one's gambling debts. Leonard had been a fellow who didn't believe kneecaps still got broken, but Leonard knew better now, and Leonard was paying up in full, with interest.

Finally, Vaggan added, Leonard had left his house open and the lights on, and if they hurried and got there before the Beverly Hills police got the word, they would find something interesting.

14

CHEE EMERGED from sleep abruptly, as was his way, aware first of the alien sheet against his chin, the alien smells, the alien darkness. Then he clicked into place. Los Angeles. A room in Motel 6, West Hollywood. He looked at his watch. Not quite five thirty. The sound of the wind, which had troubled his sleep throughout the night, had diminished now. Chee yawned and stretched. No reason to get up. He had come with a single lead to finding Begay and Margaret Billy Sosi, the Gorman address. That had led nowhere. Beyond that he had nothing but the chance of picking up some trace of the Gorman family or the Turkey Clan. He and Shaw had tried the Los Angeles County Native America Center with no luck at all. The woman who seemed to be in charge was an Eastern Indian, a Seminole, Chee guessed, or Cherokee, or Choctaw, or something like that. Certainly not a Navajo, or any of the southwestern tribes whose facial characteristics were familiar to Chee.

Nor was she particularly helpful. The notion of clans seemed strange to her, and the addresses of the three Navajos she finally managed to come up with had been dead ends. One was a middle-aged woman of the Standing Rock People, born for the Salt Cedars, another was a younger woman, a Many Goats and Streams Come Together Navajo, and the third, incredible as it seemed to Chee, was a young man who seemed to have no knowledge of his clan relationships. The project had taken hour after hour of fighting traffic on the freeways through the endless sprawl of Los Angeles, hunting through the evening darkness and into the night and getting nothing from it but a list of names of other Navajos who might know somebody in the diminished circle of Ashie Begay's diminished clan. Probably, Chee knew, they wouldn't.

Chee got up and took a shower with the water on low to avoid disturbing his motel neighbors. The shorts and socks he'd rinsed the night before were still damp, reminding him that even with the dry Santa Ana blowing all night there was a lot more humidity on the coast than in the high country. He sat in the clammy shorts, pulling on clinging wet socks, noticing that the light wind he had awakened to had faded into a calm. That meant the Pacific low-pressure area into which the wind had been blowing had moved inland. It would be a day of good weather, he thought, and the thought reminded him of how impressed Mary Landon had been (or pretended to be—it didn't really matter) with his grasp of weather patterns.

"Just like the stereotype," she'd said, smiling at him. "Noble Savage Understands the Elements."

"Just like common sense," Chee had told her. "Farmers and ranchers and people who work outside, like surveying crews and tribal cops, pay attention to the weather news. We watch Bill Eisenhood on Channel Four, and he tells us what the jet stream is doing and shows us the hundred-and-fifty-millibar map."

But he didn't want to think about Mary Landon. He opened the blinds and looked out into the gray dawn light. Still air. Street empty except for a black man in blue coveralls standing at a bus stop. The world of Mary Landon. A row of signs proclaiming what could be had for money stretching up the decrepit infinity of the West Hollywood street. Chee remembered what he'd seen on Sunset Boulevard last night on his Navajo hunt with Shaw. The whores waiting on the corners, huddling against the wind. Chee had seen whores before. Gallup had them, and Albuquerque's Central Avenue swarmed with them in State Fair season. But many of these were simply children. He commented on that to Shaw, surprised. Shaw had merely grunted. "Started a few years ago," he said. "Maybe as early as the late sixties. We don't try to buck it any more." This, too, was part of Mary Landon's world. Not that the Dinee had no prostitution. It went all the way back to the story of their origins in the underworld. The woman's sexuality was recognized as having monetary value in their marriage traditions. A man who had intercourse with a woman outside of wedlock was expected to pay the woman's family, and to fail to do so was akin to theft. But not children. Never children. And never anything as dismal as he'd seen last night on Sunset.

The black man at the bus stop put his hand in his rear pocket and scratched his rump. Watching, Chee became aware that his own rump was itching. He scratched, and made himself aware of his hypocrisy.

All alike under the skin, he thought, in every important way, despite my Navajo superiority. We want to eat, to sleep, to copulate and reproduce our genes, to be warm and dry and safe against tomorrow. Those are the important things, so what's my hang-up?

"What's your hang-up, Jim Chee?" Mary Landon had asked him. She had been sitting against the passenger door of his pickup, as far from him as the horizon. "What gives you the right to be so superior?" All of her was in darkness except for the little moonlight falling on her knees through the windshield.

And he had said something about not being superior, but merely making a comparison. Having a telephone is good. So is having space to move around in, and relatives around you. "But schools," she'd said. "We want our children to get good educations." And he'd said, "What's so wrong with the one where you're teaching?" and she'd said, "You know what's wrong," and he'd said . . .

Chee went for breakfast to a Denny's down the street, putting Mary Landon out of his mind by escaping into the problem presented by Margaret Sosi. This puzzle, while it defied solution, improved his appetite. He ordered beef stew.

The waitress looked tired. "You just getting off work?" she asked, jotting the order on her pad.

"Just going to work," Chee said.

She looked at him. "Beef stew for breakfast?"

Mexican, Chee thought, but from what Shaw had said she probably wasn't. Not in this part of Los Angeles. She must be a Filipino. “It’s what you get used to,” Chee said. “I didn’t grow up on bacon and eggs. Or pancakes.”

The woman’s indifference vanished. “Burritos,” she said. “Refritos folded in a blue corn tortilla.” Smiling.

“Fried bread and mutton,” Chee said, returning the grin. “Down with the Anglos and their Eggs McMuffin.” And so much for Shaw’s generalizations about his home territory. The only people Chee had ever known who would willingly eat refried beans wrapped in a tortilla were Mexicans. Chee doubted if Filipinos would share any such culinary aberration.

He ate his stew, which had very little meat in it. Maybe this woman was the only Spanish speaker in West Hollywood who wasn’t from the Philippines, but Chee doubted it. Even if she was, she represented the flaw in generalizing about people. On the Big Reservation, where people were scarce and scattered, one tended to know people as individuals and there was no reason to lump them into categories. Shaw had a different problem with swarming masses in his jurisdiction. People in West Hollywood were Koreans or Filipinos, or some other category that could be labeled.

Just like people in old folks’ homes were senile. Policemen wouldn’t bother questioning senile people. Chee hurried through his stew.

The legend on the door of the Silver Threads Rest Home declared that visiting hours were from 2 to 4 P.M. Chee glanced at his watch. It was not yet 8 A.M. He didn’t bother to ring the bell. He walked back to the sidewalk and began strolling along the chain-link fence. On his third circuit, four old people had appeared on the east-facing porch, sitting in their mute and motionless row in their immobile wheelchairs. While Chee strolled, a red-faced boy wearing a white smock backed through the doorway with a fifth wheelchair in tow. It held a frail woman wearing thick-lensed glasses. Mr. Berger and his aluminum walking frame had not appeared. Chee continued his circumnavigation, turning up the alley and confirming that residents of the nursing home had a fine view of the apartments where the late Albert Gorman had lived—from the porch or from the lawn. On the next circuit, Berger appeared.

As Chee rounded the corner that brought him past the east

porch, the old man was shuffling his way toward the fence, moving the walker, leaning on it, then bringing his legs along. Chee stopped at the fence at the point for which Berger was aiming. He waited, turning his back to the fence and to the old man's struggle. Behind him he could hear Berger's panting breath.

"Sons a bitches," the man was saying. Describing, Chee guessed, either the nursing home staff or his own recalcitrant legs. Chee heard Berger place the walker beside the fence and sigh and grunt as he dragged his legs under him. Only then did he turn.

"Good to see you, Mr. Berger," Chee said. "I was hoping I wouldn't have to wait for visiting hours."

"Coming to see . . ." The surprise was in the tone before Berger's tongue balked at the rest of it. His face twisted with the struggle, turning slightly red.

"I wanted to talk to you some more about Gorman," Chee said. "I remember you asked me if he was in trouble, and as a matter of fact he was in very deep trouble, so I thought maybe you had some idea of what was going on." Chee was careful not to phrase it as more than an implied question.

Mr. Berger opened his mouth slightly. Made a wry expression.

"He might have been in worse trouble than he knew. Somebody followed him from here to Shiprock. In New Mexico. On the Navajo Reservation. They shot each other, Gorman and this guy. Gorman killed the man. And then Gorman died himself."

Berger looked down at his hands, gripping the metal frame of the walker. He shook his head.

"We don't know why anyone would have wanted to kill Gorman," Chee said. "Doesn't seem to be any reason for it. Did Gorman tell you anything that would help?"

Berger's white head rose. He looked at Chee, drew a deep and careful breath, closed his eyes, concentrated.

"Man came," he said.

Chee waited.

Berger struggled, gave up. "Shit," Berger said.

"Would it help if I fill in the gaps? I'm going to guess at

some of it. And if I'm wrong you shake your head and I'll stop. Or I'll try another guess."

Berger nodded.

"A man came to see Gorman, here at the apartment."

Berger nodded.

"The day before Gorman left for New Mexico?"

Berger took his hands from the walker, held them about a foot apart, moved them together.

"Less than that," Chee said. "The night before Gorman left."

Berger nodded.

"You saw him?"

Berger nodded. He pointed to Gorman's apartment. Then indicated height and breadth.

"A big man," Chee said. "Very big?"

Berger agreed.

"How old?"

Berger struggled with that. Chee held up his hands, flashed ten fingers, another ten, stopped. Berger signaled thirty, hesitated, added ten.

"Maybe forty," Chee said. "Another Navajo?"

Berger canceled that, pointing to his own hair.

"White," Chee said. "Blond?"

Berger nodded.

"A big blond man came here just before Gorman left for New Mexico," Chee said. Lerner, he was thinking, was neither big nor blond. "Had you seen him before?"

Berger had.

"Often?"

Berger held up two fingers.

"They talked?" Chee had begun wondering where this was taking him. What could Berger know that would be useful?

Berger had taken his hands from the walker. His fingers, twisted and trembling, became two men standing slightly apart. Wagging fingers indicated one man talking, then the other man talking. Then the two hands moved together, parallel, to Berger's left. He stopped them. His lips struggled with an impossible word. "Car," he said.

"They walked together to a car after talking. The blond man's car?"

Berger nodded, pleased. His hands resumed their walk, stopped. Suddenly the right hand attacked the left, snatched it, bent it. Berger looked at Chee, awaiting the question.

Chee frowned. "The blond man attacked Gorman?"

Berger denied it.

"Gorman attacked the blond man?"

Berger agreed. He struggled for words, excited.

Chee bit back a question. "Interesting," he said, smiling at Berger, giving him time. He had an idea. He tapped Berger's right hand. "This is Blond," he said, "and the left hand is Gorman. Okay?"

Berger grasped his right hand with his left, began to enact a struggle. Then he stopped, thinking. He grasped an imaginary doorknob, opened the imaginary door, watching to see if Chee was with him.

"One of them opened the car door? The blond?"

Berger agreed. He held his left hand with his right, released it, then pantomimed, fiercely, the slamming of the door. He clutched the injured finger, squirming and grimacing in mock pain.

"Gorman slammed the door on the blond man's finger," Chee said. Berger nodded. He was a dignified man, and all this play-acting was embarrassing for him. "That would suggest that Gorman wasn't going to the car willingly. Right? You were standing about here, watching?" Chee laughed. "And wondering what the hell was going on, I'll bet."

"Exactly," Berger said, clearly and distinctly. "Then Gorman ran." He motioned past the fence, up the alley, a gesture that caused Gorman to vanish.

"And the blond man?"

"Sat," Berger said. "Just a min . . ." He couldn't finish the word.

"And then I guess he drove away."

Berger nodded.

"You have any idea about all this?"

Berger nodded affirmatively. They looked at each other, stymied.

"Any luck writing?" Chee asked.

Berger held up his hands. They trembled. Berger controlled them. They trembled again.

"Well," Chee said, "we'll figure out a way."

"He came," Berger said, pointing to the gravel where Chee was standing. "Talked."

"Gorman. About the trouble he was in."

Berger tried to speak. Tried again. Hit the walker fiercely with a palsied fist. "Shit," he said.

"What did Gorman do for a living?"

"Stole cars," Berger said.

That surprised Chee. Why would Gorman tell Berger that? But why not? A new dimension of Albert Gorman opened. One lonely man meeting another beside a fence. Berger's potential importance in this affair clicked upward. Frail, bony, pale, he leaned on the walker frame, trying to form another word, his blue eyes intense with the concentration.

Chee waited. The woman whose son was coming to see her had posted her wheelchair down the fence. Now she rolled it across the parched, hard-packed lawn toward them. She noticed Chee watching her and turned the wheelchair abruptly into the fence. "He's coming," she said to no one in particular.

"Gorman stole cars," Chee said. "And the man he stole them for—the man who paid him—got indicted by the federal grand jury. Maybe the reason he went to New Mexico, and the reason somebody followed to shoot him, was because he was going to be a witness against his boss. Maybe the boss . . ."

But Berger was denying that, shaking his head.

"You don't think so?"

Berger didn't. Emphatically.

"He talked to you about that, then?"

Berger agreed. Waved that subject off. Tried to form a word. "Not go," he managed finally. His mouth worked to say more, but couldn't. "Shit," he said.

"Not go?" Chee repeated. He didn't understand that.

Berger was still trying to find words. He couldn't. He shrugged, slumped, looked ashamed.

"He showed him a picture." The words came from the woman in the wheelchair. She was looking out through the fence, and Chee didn't realize that the statement had anything to do with Berger until he saw the old man was nodding eagerly.

"Gorman showed Mr. Berger a picture?" he asked.

"That Indian showed that fella you're talking to there a picture," the woman said. She pointed at Berger. "Like a postcard."

"Ah," Chee said. The photograph again. Why was it so important? It didn't surprise him to see the woman's senility fall away. It would come again just as quickly. Chee had grown up surrounded by the old of his family, learning from them, watching them grow wise, and ill, and die. This end of the human existence had no more mystery for him than its beginning.

"Picture," Berger said. "His brother."

"Was it a picture of an aluminum trailer with a man standing by it?"

It was.

"And Gorman said it was from his brother?"

Berger nodded again.

"I don't know what you meant when you said 'Not go.' I'm confused because we know Gorman went. Was it that Gorman had decided not to go and then changed his mind?"

Berger denied it, emphatically. He recast his palsied hands in the roles of Gorman and the blond man. The hand representing Gorman dipped its fingertip affirmatively. The hand representing the blond man shook its fingertip negatively.

"I see," Chee said. "Gorman wanted to go. The blond man said not to." He glanced at Berger, who was agreeing. "So Gorman was going, the blond man tried to stop him, they fought, and Gorman went. Good a guess as any?"

Berger shrugged, unhappy with that interpretation. He pointed to the dial of his watch.

"Time?" Chee was puzzled.

Berger tapped the dial, pointing to where the hour hand was. Then he moved his finger around the dial, counterclockwise.

"Earlier?" Chee asked.

Berger nodded.

"You mean this happened earlier? This business about Gorman wanting to go and the blond man telling him not to?"

Berger was nodding vigorously.

"Before the fight? Before the evening Gorman hurt Blond Man's hand? A day before? Two days?"

Berger was nodding through all this. Two days before was correct. "And Gorman told you about that?"

"Right," Berger said.

"Do you know why Gorman wanted to go?"

"Worried," Berger said. He tried to say more, failed, shrugged it off.

The red-faced young man Chee had noticed earlier was slouching across the lawn toward them, whistling between his teeth. The woman spun her wheelchair and hurried it down the fence away from him. "Mean old bitch," the young man said, and hurried after her.

"Do you know what was written on the postcard? The one with the picture on it?"

Berger didn't.

"The woman said it was like a postcard," Chee said. "Was it?"

Berger looked puzzled.

"Did it have a stamp on it?"

Berger thought, closed his eyes, frowning. Then he shrugged.

"She was a very observant woman," Chee said. "I wonder if either one of you happened to see a Navajo girl show up at Gorman's apartment yesterday. Little. Skinny teenager, wearing a navy pea coat. You see her?"

Berger hadn't. He looked after the woman, wheeling furiously across the grass with the red-faced man hurrying after her. "Smart," he said. "Sometimes."

"I had an aunt like that," Chee said. "Actually my mother's aunt. When she could remember she was very, very smart. Yesterday our friend couldn't remember anything."

"Excited," Berger said. He tried to explain. Failed. Stopped. Stared down at his feet. When he looked up again, he was excited. And he had a plan.

"War," he said. He held up two fingers.

Chee thought about that. "World War Two," he guessed.

"Son," Berger said. He tried to go on and failed.

"In the war," Chee said.

Berger nodded. "Navy."

"He was killed," Chee guessed.

Berger shook that off. "Big shot." he said. "Rich." That exhausted Berger's supply of words. His mouth twisted. His face turned pink. He pounded at the walker.

The red-faced young man had caught the woman's wheelchair and was pushing her toward the porch. She sat, eyes closed, face blank. So her son was rich and important, Chee thought. What was Berger trying to tell him with that? Her son had been in the navy forty years ago, now he was rich and important, and that was related to something causing her to be excited yesterday.

"Hey!" Chee shouted, suddenly understanding. "Yesterday. Yesterday morning she saw a sailor, is that it?"

Berger nodded, delighted at the breakthrough.

"Maybe she saw a sailor," Chee told Berger. "Maybe she saw Margaret Sosi in her pea jacket. What's that woman's name?"

Berger got it out the first try. "Ellis."

"Mrs. Ellis," Chee shouted. "Did you see a sailor yesterday? At the apartments?"

"I saw him," Mrs. Ellis said.

"He looked like your son. In a blue pea coat?"

"I don't have a son," Mrs. Ellis said.

15

THE MAN MCNAIR called Henry brought Vaggan his water in a crystal glass. Vaggan had said, "No ice, please," but the man named Henry hadn't listened, or hadn't cared. Henry's expression had suggested that he found bringing Vaggan a glass of water distasteful. He was a plump, soft man, with a soft voice and shrewd eyes that he allowed to give him an expression of haughty contempt. Vaggan placed the glass on the coffee table, aware of the two ice cubes floating in it but not looking at it.

"You're a day late," McNair said. "I called you yesterday morning, and I said there was a hurry for this." McNair opened a black onyx box on his desk, extracted a cigaret, and tapped it against his thumbnail. "I don't like people who work for me to be late."

Vaggan was feeling fine. He'd gotten home from the Leonard business before dawn, showered, done his relaxing exercises, and slept for six hours. Then he'd exercised again, weighed, and had a breakfast of wheat germ, alfalfa sprouts, and cheese while he watched the noon TV news. The NBC channel had led with Leonard being rushed through the emergency room doors and propelled away with one bloody ear visible. He switched quickly to ABC-TV and caught the tag end of his own voice, recorded from his final telephone call, explaining about the welshed debt. The Man could hardly ask more. Perfect. He'd switched off the set then and called the McNair number. He'd told the man who answered—probably Henry—to tell McNair he'd be there at 2 P.M.

It was an easy hour's drive. He killed the remaining time reading through his new copies of *Survival* and *Soldier of Fortune.* He clipped out an article on common medicinal herbs of the Pacific Coast and circled an advertisement of Freedom Arsenal offering an FN-LAR assault rifle for $1,795. He'd looked at an FN in a Pasadena sporting goods store—the same model built by Fabrique National in Belgium for NATO paratroops. He'd been impressed, but the price there had been $2,300, plus California sales tax. With the Leonard money, he could afford either price, but most of that money would have to go to the contractor to finish the concrete work on his storage bunker, and he also wanted to install a solar generator and add to his stock of ammunition. However, there'd be more money coming in from McNair. Vaggan felt fine.

He left at 1 P.M., giving himself a bit more time than he needed to drive into the Flinthills district, where the McNair family had bought itself a hill and built itself an estate and raised its offspring. And now he sat in the McNair office, or study, or library, or whatever such rooms were called in such houses, and here across the desk was McNair himself. McNair interested him. Very few men did.

"I am never late," Vaggan said. "Maybe Henry didn't tell you." He glanced over his shoulder at Henry, who was standing stiffly beside the doorway. "Henry," he said. "Come here."

Henry hesitated, looking past Vaggan at McNair. But he came.

"Here," Vaggan said. He extracted the two ice cubes from the glass and held them out to Henry. "You can have these," he said. "I said no ice."

Henry's face flushed. He took the cubes and stalked out of the room.

Vaggan took out his handkerchief and dried his fingers.

"Hard to get reliable help," he said to McNair.

McNair had understood the subtlety of the point Vaggan was making, appreciating how the threat had been made without ever being spoken. He made a wry face and nodded.

"Henry," he called.

Henry reappeared at the door.

"Bring Mr. Vaggan a glass of water, please."

"Yes, sir," Henry said.

"So what needs doing?" Vaggan said.

"More Navajo business," McNair said. He had a heavy, rawboned face, pale and marked with the liver marks common with lightly pigmented people when they age. His eyes were an odd color, something near green, sunken under heavy, bristling gray brows. His expression was sour. "More trouble from the Gorman screw-up," he added. "A young woman named"—McNair looked down at a note pad on his desk—"named Margaret Sosi came to Los Angeles from Shiprock. She had a photograph of Leroy Gorman, and she came to Albert's place in West Hollywood looking for him. I want you to find her."

"Just find her," Vaggan said.

McNair grinned, more or less, showing white, even teeth. Henry had not had even teeth. It seemed to Vaggan that it was one of the few remaining signs left in America of social position versus family poverty. Rich people could afford orthodontists.

"I don't get involved with what happens after you find her. Just make sure she doesn't make any trouble." He lit the cigaret with a silver lighter extracted from the end of the onyx box. "Absolutely sure. I do not want her talking to anybody."

He exhaled a cloud of smoke.

"And I want that picture. I want it brought to me, personally. I want an end to it."

Vaggan said nothing. A map of Scotland printed on something that looked like parchment dominated the wall behind McNair. Its borders were decorated by patches of plaid which Vaggan presumed were the tartans of the Scottish clans. A bagpipe and a heavy belt holding a scabbarded sword hung beside it. A claymore, Vaggan thought. Wasn't that the Scottish name for it? Down the wall were photographs. People in kilts. People in fox-hunting coats. A photograph of Queen Elizabeth II, an autograph scrawled across the bottom.

"Here's her description," McNair said. He held out a sheet of typing paper.

"I hope you have a little more than that," Vaggan said. "If you want her found this year."

"I have an address."

"Addresses help," Vaggan said.

"If she's still there," McNair said. "It was yesterday morning when I called you."

"Maybe we'll be lucky," Vaggan said. "Anyway, it's a place to pick up the trail."

McNair was holding the typing paper, folded, between his fingers, tapping the edge of the fold against the desk, looking at Vaggan.

"How'll you do it?"

"What? Find her?"

"Kill her."

Henry had replaced the water with another crystal glass and disappeared. No ice cubes. Vaggan sipped, looking over the rim of the glass at McNair. He was thinking of tape recordings, but he could think of nothing McNair could gain by taping this conversation. Still, it was an odd question. Vaggan answered with a shrug and put down the glass. McNair interested him more and more. But the job was suddenly less appealing. Such things should be strictly business. No pleasure mixed in.

"I would have thought you'd have a favorite method," McNair said. His expression was bland, but the greenish eyes in their deep sockets were avid.

It should be purely business, Vaggan thought. Otherwise things get too complicated. Hard to calculate, which made them needlessly risky. Did he need this job? Did he still want to work for McNair?

"If I did your work, I'd have a favorite method," McNair repeated.

Vaggan shrugged again, took another sip of the tepid tap water. Outside, the McNair lawn sloped away toward the Pacific. The grass was like green velvet.

"I can't see how you're going to get off," Vaggan said. "From what the story in the L.A. *Times* had to say, you're indicted on eleven counts, witnesses tying you into the business personally, everything neat and tidy the way it sounded. Why don't you jump bail, cash in a little of this"—he gestured around him at the room—"and make a run for it?" He sipped again. "Actually, there wouldn't have to be any actual running. Just transfer some cash to wherever and get some papers and fly away. Easy. No worry. No risk."

Vaggan had been studying McNair's face. It registered irritation, then distaste. About what Vaggan had expected.

"I'm not guilty," McNair said.

"Not until the jury convicts you," Vaggan said. "Then you are, and the judge raises the bail way up there, and it's all going to be a lot tougher and more expensive."

"I have never been convicted of anything," McNair said. "No McNair has ever been in prison. Never will be." He got up and stood by the window, his hand resting on a form Vaggan presumed was a sculpture cast in steel. "Besides, if you walk away from it, you can't take this along."

He seemed to mean the sculpture and what he saw from the window. Or perhaps it meant the bagpipe and being a McNair. Vaggan could appreciate this. One of the rulers. The hard men. An interesting man, Vaggan thought. He'd be dealing with the McNairs after the missiles, the tough ones. He understood the old man better again. The avidity he'd seen was as much like greed as it was cruelty. Cruelty bothered him because it seemed beside the point, a waste of emotions that seemed strange to him. But Vaggan could understand greed perfectly.

"I have a feeling you're balking," McNair said, still looking out the window. "Why else all this impertinence? All these questions? Will you take care of it for me?"

"All right," Vaggan said. He got up and took the paper from the old man's fingers, unfolded it, and read. The address was on a street he'd never heard of. He'd get it located on his map, and wait for dark, and get it over with.

16

JIM CHEE, who had always considered himself an excellent driver, drove now uneasily. The mixture of precise timing, skill, and confidence in their immortality that Los Angeles drivers brought to their freeway system moved Chee back and forth from anxious admiration to stoic resignation. But his luck had held so far, it should hold for another afternoon. He rolled his pickup truck through the endless sprawl of the city and the satellite towns that make Los Angeles County a wilderness of people. For a while he managed to keep track of just where he was in relation to where he had been, noticing direction shifts and remembering when he switched from one freeway to another. But soon it overwhelmed him. He concentrated solely on the freeway map, which Shaw had marked for him, and on not missing his turns. The land had risen a little now out of the flatness of the city basin, and there were traces of desert visible in vacant lots, which became vacant blocks, which became entire vacant hillsides, eroded and dotted with cactus and the dry, prickly brush common to land where it rarely rains. The poor side of the city. Chee examined it curiously. He no longer had a sense of where he was in relation to his motel. But there, low on the southwestern horizon, hung the sun. And eastward over those dry ridges lay the desert. And behind him, somewhere beyond the thickening smog of the city, was the cold, blue Pacific. It was enough to know.

And now just ahead of him was the exit sign Shaw had told him to watch for. He angled the truck cautiously across the freeway lanes and down the exit ramp and rolled to a stop on the parking ramp of a Savemor service station. Here tumbleweeds grew through the broken asphalt. A paunchy, middle-aged man in bib overalls leaned against the cashier's booth, eyeing him placidly. Chee spread his Los Angeles street map across the steering wheel, making sure he was in the right place. The sign said Jaripa Street, which seemed correct. Now the job was to locate Jacaranda, which intersected somewhere and led to the address that Shaw had pried, finally, from Gorman's landlady. Watching Shaw work had been impressive.

Chee recalled the interview. Two interviews, to be correct, although the first one had been brief. He had rung her doorbell, and rung, and rung until finally she had appeared, staring at him wordlessly past the barely opened door. She had reinspected his Navajo Tribal Police credentials, still with no sign they impressed her. No, she'd said, she hadn't seen anyone like Margaret Billy Sosi. And then Chee had told her that a witness had seen the girl here.

"They lied," the woman had said, and closed the door firmly in Chee's face.

It had taken almost an hour for the dispatcher at LAPD to locate Shaw, and maybe twenty minutes later Shaw had arrived—driving up alone in an unmarked white sedan. The second interview had gone much better.

They'd done this one inside, in the woman's cluttered office-sitting room, and Chee had learned something from the way Shaw had handled it.

"This man hasn't got any business here," Shaw had said, pointing a thumb at Chee. "He's an Indian policeman. Couldn't arrest anybody in L.A. I don't care what you told him. You could tell him to go to hell. But now I'm here."

Shaw fished out his identification and held it in front of the woman's face. "You and I've done business before, Mrs. Day," he said. "You called me when this guy showed up asking about Gorman, just like I told you to. I appreciate that. Now I need to find this girl, Margaret Sosi. She was here yesterday. What'd she say to you?"

Chee was trying to read Mrs. Day's expression. It was closed. Hostile. Was it fearful? Call it tense, he thought.

"Trashy people are always showing up here, ringing my doorbell." She glanced at Chee. "You can't expect me to remember them."

"I can," Shaw said. "I do expect it." He stared at her, face hard. "We're going to find the girl, and I'm going to ask her if she talked to you."

Mrs. Day said nothing.

"If she did, then I'm going to get the fire marshal's boys interested in this place of yours. Wiring. Exits. Trash removal. You familiar with the fire code for rental property?"

Mrs. Day looked stubborn.

"When we find this girl, if she's got her throat cut, like maybe she will have from what we know now, and you haven't helped us, then that makes you an accessory to murder. I don't guess we could prove it, but we can get you downtown, and book you in, and then you have to deal with the bonding company, and get a lawyer hired, and show up for the grand jury, and—"

"She was looking for Gorman," Mrs. Day said.

"We know that," Shaw said. "What did she say about him?"

"Nothing much. I told her Gorman wasn't here."

"What else—" Shaw began, but the telephone cut him off.

Mrs. Day looked at Shaw. On the wall behind her, the telephone rang again.

Shaw nodded.

Mrs. Day said hello into the mouthpiece, listened, said no, said I'll call you back. "Just a sec," she said. She reached behind her and wrote a number on a calendar mounted to the wall beside the phone. "I don't know. Maybe fifteen minutes," she said, and hung up.

"What else did she say?" Shaw continued.

"She was trying to find some old man. I don't remember his name. Her grandfather. Wanted to know if the old man had come here looking for Gorman."

"Had he?" Shaw asked.

"I never seen him if he did. Then she wanted to know if I had any other address for Gorman, and I gave her what I had and she went away."

"What did you give her?"

"Next of kin," Mrs. Day said. "I make my renters fill out a little card for me." She took a metal box from the desk, fingered through it, and handed Shaw a file card. "Gives them the idea that if they steal everything you got a way at getting back at 'em."

Shaw copied information into his notebook.

"Jacaranda Street? That right?"

Mrs. Day nodded.

"Never heard of it," Shaw said. "And the name's Bentwoman Tsossie? Could that be right?"

"What he said," Mrs. Day said. "Who knows about Indians?"

Shaw returned the card. Chee was looking at the calendar pad beside the telephone. It was divided into the thirty-one days of October, and Mrs. Day had written the telephone number of whoever had just called her in the October 23 space—which was today. October 22 was blank, as were many of the days. Others bore terse notations, accompanied by numbers. In the October 3 square, the word Gorman was written, with a number under it. A line ran from Gorman to another number in the margin. Chee recognized the second number. It was on a card in his billfold—the number of Shaw's telephone. Whose phone would the first number ring?

Now, as he sat in his pickup amid the tumbleweeds beside this rundown service station, the significance of all this began to take shape in Jim Chee's mind. The date was wrong. Too early. Days too early.

There was a pay phone booth at the sidewalk adjoining the station. Chee opened the truck door, swung his legs out, and stopped to think it through again. Mrs. Day had written Gorman's name in the October 3 box, at least a week before Shaw had recruited her as a watcher. Then she had written the number of Shaw's arson office number in the margin and linked it to Gorman's name with a line. But someone had contacted her a week before that and arranged for her to call a number relative to Gorman. Had she been watching him for someone else before she had watched his apartment for Shaw? What was the number? Chee recalled the number, as he'd expected to recall it, without feeling particularly proud of the feat. Chee had been taught to remember when he emerged from infancy, and it was a skill his training as a *yataalii* had honed. He climbed out of the truck.

Chee called the arson number, hoping only to extract Shaw's home number. But the detective answered.

"It don't mean a thing to me," Shaw said. "It's a downtown telephone, judging from the prefix. Have you tried it?"

"No. I thought I'd ask you. It's after five so nobody is going to be there."

"Who knows?" Shaw said. "We'll just give a try. I'm going to put you on hold a minute and call it." The telephone clicked.

Chee waited. Through the dirty window of the telephone booth, he could see a row of rundown residences scattered down a street that was mostly weedy vacant lots. From across the hills, smoke rose white and gray. A brush fire, Chee guessed. Shaw had called this "poor boy territory," the habitat of losers, of transients and bums and other marginal people. He'd warned Chee not to expect the streets to match the street maps.

"I wish I could get off and go along," Shaw had said. "It's a good place to get lost, if you want to get lost. Or to lose something if you got something you don't want nobody to find. Including bodies. Every once in a while we get one reported from out there. They just turn up. Dumped behind the brush. Or somebody notices a foot sticking out after a mudslide, or old bones in a rotten sleeping bag."

The telephone clicked again. "Turned out to be an answering service," Shaw said. "And of course nobody knew anything about anything except the boss and he wasn't in. Sort of establishment you have to go down and show a badge to find out something. I'm going to put you on hold again and call the landlady."

The telephone booth smelled dusty. Chee pushed open the door to admit the outside air and got with that the aroma of warm asphalt. There was also the smell of smoke, the perfumed smoke of the desert burning that drifted down from the fire over the ridge. Through that, faintly and only now and then, he could detect an acrid chemical taint—the bad breath of the city. Last night's Santa Ana wind had blown the Los Angeles smog far out over the Pacific. But that was many hours ago. The city had exhaled again. Through the window of the cashier's cage, the service station attendant was watching Chee, openly curious. Chee thought about Mary Landon. About now she'd be in her little Crownpoint teacherage preparing her supper. He saw her, as he had often seen her from his favorite chair in that tiny living-dining room, working at the drainboard, hair pulled to the top of her head, slender, intent, talking as she did whatever she was doing to the vegetable she was working on.

Chee closed his eyes, rested his head against the cool metal of the telephone box, and re-created the scene and his feeling for it. Anticipation. A good meal. But not that, really. Anticipation of a good meal in good company. Mary across from him, checking his response to whatever she had given him, caring whether he liked it, her knee against his knee. Her—

Click. "You still there?" Shaw asked and went on without waiting. "Day said that some fellow had called her on the phone and told her that if she was willing to keep an eye on Gorman's apartment and let him know anything interesting, he was going to mail her a hundred bucks, and there would be another hundred anytime she called with anything interesting."

"Like what?"

"Like any visitors. Like Gorman packing up, moving out. Anything unusual."

"Did she make any calls?"

"She said just one. The day Gorman left for Shiprock."

"You believe her?"

"No," Shaw said. "But it might be true. Far as we know, nothing else happened."

"That's true," Chee agreed.

"Call me if you locate the girl," Shaw said. He gave Chee his home telephone number.

The service station attendant, with considerable gesturing, showed Chee that if he drove directly north on Jaripa he would inevitably drive right past its junction with Jacaranda.

"Map's screwed up," he said. "Jacaranda runs up into the hills about a mile from here. Access to some jackleg housing development, but the city never put in the utilities so the whole thing went down the tube. You bought in there, you got burned."

"I'm trying to find some people at thirteen thousand two hundred and seventy-one Jacaranda," Chee said. "That sound like it would be back in there?"

"God knows," the attendant said. "They got all sorts of street names and numbers back in there. Just no house to put 'em on."

"But some people do live back there," Chee said. "That right?"

"There's some," the man said. "Beats sleeping under a bridge. But if you're sleeping under a bridge, at least somebody didn't sell it to you." He laughed and glanced at Chee to see if he enjoyed the humor.

But Chee was thinking something else. He was thinking that whoever had paid Mrs. Day to keep track of Albert Gorman almost certainly knew all about this address.

17

CHEE FOUND 13271 Jacaranda Street just as the setting sun was converting the yellow-gray smog along the western horizon into oddly beautiful layers, pink-gray alternated with pale rose, making a milder, more pastel display than the garish sunsets of the high desert country. He had enjoyed the hunt. The scenery was different: desert, but low-altitude desert, and without the bitter winters of the Big Reservation it produced a different kind of vegetation. He had decided fairly early that he wouldn't find the Jacaranda address, that it was simply a number Gorman had pulled from the air to satisfy Mrs. Day's requirement. Tomorrow morning he would get up early, drive back to Shiprock, and put out feelers at St. Catherine and Two Gray Hills and here and there, to make sure he'd know if and when Margaret Sosi returned to home country. And he'd drive over to Crownpoint and talk to Mary Landon. And, having time to think about it, Mary Landon would have decided that raising their children Dinee and among the Dinee was, after all, what she really wanted to do. Or maybe not. Probably not. Almost certainly not. And what then? What would he do?

Meanwhile Chee drove. The junction of Jacaranda Street was marked by a huge billboard that rose from a fieldstone base and was topped by the legend J C R ND EST TES in raised wooden letters, once red. Even expecting it, it took Chee a moment to recognize JACARANDA ESTATES with the A's stolen. And to wonder who had such a specialized need for letter A's. Below the defaced name the billboard featured a map. The great green blob in the middle was labeled Golf Course, and a dim blue oblong near the center of the green was marked Trout Lake. Other landmarks included Shopping Center, Post Office, School and Country Club. Nothing on the map seemed to bear any relationship to the reality of lonely desert foothills around him, but Chee studied the network of streets it displayed. Jacaranda meandered east-southeast to a main artery. He felt encouraged.

The encouragement was brief. Jacaranda's asphalt surface, already cracked and weedy, gave way to gravel within a quarter mile, and the gravel that replaced it was soon replaced in turn by graded dirt, replaced by a rutted track from which streets led, streets which were nothing more than a few passes made by a bulldozer years ago. Chee passed street signs (Jelso, Jane, Jenkins, Jardin, Jellico), warped plywood boards mounted on two-by-fours with their paint weathered almost beyond the point of legibility. Jane Street had offered a half dozen dilapidated mobile homes clustered near a rusty water tank. On Jenkins he passed a concrete foundation, on Jellico an abandoned frame house from which doors and window frames had been looted. But mostly there was only emptiness. Judy, July, Jerri, and Jennifer streets offered nothing but creosote brush, sandstone, and cacti. Beyond Jennifer, the erosion of an arroyo had erased Jacaranda.

Chee detoured, and detoured again, and rediscovered Jacaranda—worse than ever. And finally, over a ridge, there were homes again—a dented aluminum mobile home on a foundation of cinder blocks and, beyond it, a frame shanty partly covered with roofing shingles, and beyond that a charred jumble of partly burned boards. In front of the mobile home, three old cars and a school bus were parked. A middle-aged man, shirtless, a blue bandanna tied around his head, had the front wheel off the bus and seemed to be replacing a brake lining. Chee stopped, rolled down his window.

"Thirteen two seventy-one Jaracanda," he shouted. "You know where it is?"

The man looked up from his work, squinted, wiped sweat from his eyebrow.

"That them Indians?" he asked. "That old woman and all?" He had a high-pitched, whining voice.

"Sounds right," Chee said. "Name's Tsossie, or something like that."

"I don't know about that," the man said. "But their place is over that ridge yonder." He gestured down the track.

Over the ridge was a house. It was a patchwork affair, apparently built by a series of owners with diminishing ambitions, money, and hope. The front section was made of neat red bricks. A subsequent builder had tried to finish it with cinder-block walls and an addition to the pitched roof, using asphalt shingles that didn't quite match the original. To this a lean-to of planks had been added, with a roof of corrugated sheet metal. The lean-to jutted from the side, and behind it was the framework skeleton of another room, roofless, floorless, and open to the wind. Judging from the collection of dead weeds the framework had accumulated, this project must have been abandoned years ago.

Beyond this house, the rusted corpses of three vehicles stood in a neat row—a delivery van, a pickup truck too cannibalized for easy identification, and a red Dodge sedan with its hood and engine missing. Beside the house, an old Chevy sedan was parked, the window of its driver's-side door held together with tape.

Chee parked on the side of the track in front of the house, tapped twice on the horn, and waited.

Almost five minutes passed. The front door opened just a little and a face peered out. A woman. Chee got out and walked slowly toward the house.

The woman at the door was old, with a round, plump face framed with graying hair. She was obviously a Navajo, and Chee introduced himself in their language—telling her his mother's clan and his father's clan and naming various aunts and uncles—both maternal and paternal—old enough or prominent enough in affairs ceremonial or political that this old woman might have heard of them.

She listened, nodded when he was finished, and motioned him inside.

"I am born to the Turkey Clan," she said. "My mother is Bentwoman Tsossie of the Turkey Clan and my father was Jefferson Tom of the Salt Dinee." She spoke in a rusty old-person's voice, giving Chee the rest of her clan genealogy, mentioning relatives and clan connections, a litany of names of her extended family and its ancestors. Chee recognized a few of them: a woman who had served long before he was born on the Tribal Council, a singer of the Mountain Way Chant whom his own father had sometimes mentioned, and a man who had been, long, long ago, a tribal judge. When she had finished all the formalities and offered him a bottle of cold Pepsi-Cola, Chee accepted it, and sipped from it, and allowed the proper amount of time to pass, and then put the bottle on the floor beside his chair.

"My grandmother," he said, "I come here from Shiprock in the hope that I can find a woman of your clan. She calls herself Margaret Billy Sosi." Chee paused. "I hope you can help me find her."

"The girl isn't here," Bentwoman's Daughter said. "Why do you wish to see her?"

"I work for the Dinee," Chee said. "I am a member of the Navajo Tribal Police. We hope to find a man of the Turkey Clan who is called Hosteen Ashie Begay. He is the grandfather of Margaret Billy Sosi. She is hunting for him too." Chee paused, noticing the expression on the old woman's face. It was skeptical. He would not look to her like a Navajo Tribal Policeman—out of uniform, in a travel-rumpled plaid shirt and blue jeans. Chee had the usual Navajo's propensity for personal cleanliness, plus a little more. But his only packing for this journey had been to stick his toothbrush holder in his shirt pocket and a spare pair of socks and shorts in the glove box of his pickup. Now he looked like he'd spent two nights in jail. He extracted from his hip pocket and displayed his police credentials.

The expression of Bentwoman's Daughter did not change. Perhaps, Chee thought belatedly, her skepticism was not of Chee, the rumpled stranger, but of Chee, the Navajo Policeman. The relationship between the Dinee and their police force was no more universally serene than in any other society.

"You should talk to Bentwoman," the old woman said.

Chee said nothing. Bentwoman? When he'd seen the age of Bentwoman's Daughter, he'd presumed that Bentwoman would be dead. Chee was not good at guessing ages, particularly of women. But she must be eighty. Perhaps older.

Bentwoman's Daughter was waiting, her wrinkled hands folded motionless in the folds of her voluminous skirt.

"If she will talk to me," Chee said. "Yes. That would be good."

"I will see," said Bentwoman's Daughter. She raised herself painfully from her chair and hobbled past the heavy blanket that hung over the doorway leading to the rear of the house.

Chee examined the room. The blanket was a black-and-gray design popular among weavers of the Coyote Canyon area and looked very old. The only furniture was the worn overstuffed sofa where the old woman had put him, a rocking chair, and a plastic-topped dinette table. A calendar hung on the wall opposite him—a color print of the gold of autumn cottonwoods in Canyon de Chelly issued by a Flagstaff funeral home. The calendar page was August, and seven years old. Two cases of Pepsi-Cola bottles were stacked against the wall and, beside them, three five-gallon jerricans that Chee guessed held water. A kerosene lamp, its glass chimney smudged with soot, stood on the table. Obviously, such amenities as water, gaslines, electricity, and telephone service had not yet been provided by whoever had sold this addition.

Chee heard the voice of Bentwoman's Daughter, loud and patient, explaining the visitor to someone who apparently was deaf, saying that he wanted to see "Ashie Begay's granddaughter." So she's been here, Chee thought. Almost certainly, she's been here. And then the blanket curtain pushed aside and a wheelchair emerged.

The woman in the chair was blind. Chee saw that instantly. Her eyes were open, aimed past him at the front door, but they had the clouded look of the glaucoma that takes such a heavy toll among the old of his people. Blind, and partially deaf, and immensely old. Her hair was a cloud of fluffy white, and her face, toothless, had collapsed upon itself into a mass of wrinkles. This was Bentwoman.

Chee stood and introduced himself again, talking slowly and very loud, and making sure he followed all of the traditional courtesies his mother had taught him. With that out of the way, he paused a moment for a response. None came.

"Do I speak clearly enough, my grandmother?" he asked.

The old woman nodded, a barely perceptible motion.

"I will tell you then why I have come here," Chee said. He started at the beginning, with going to the hogan of Ashie Begay, and what he found there, and of meeting Margaret Billy Sosi there later, and what Margaret had told him, and what he had forgotten to ask her. Finally he was finished.

Bentwoman was motionless. She's gone to sleep, Chee thought. This is going to take time. Bentwoman's Daughter stood behind the chair, holding its handles. She sighed.

"The girl must go home," Bentwoman said in Navajo. Her voice was slow and faint. "There is nothing for her here but trouble. She must go back to her family and live among them. She must live in Dinetah."

"I will take her back to her people," Chee said. "Can you help me find her?"

"Stay here," Bentwoman said. "She will come."

Chee glanced at Bentwoman's Daughter, inquiring.

"She took the bus," Bentwoman's Daughter said. "She went into the city when the sun came up. She said she would be back before it gets dark."

"It's getting dark now," Chee said. He was conscious of how elusive Margaret Sosi had been. Something was making him uneasy. The number written on Mrs. Day's calendar hung in his mind.

"Has anyone else been here looking for the girl?" Chee said. "Asking about her?"

Bentwoman's Daughter shook her head.

"When do you think she'll be back?"

"The bus comes every hour," Bentwoman said. "It stops down there where the map is. Every hour until midnight."

"About when does it stop?"

"Twenty minutes after the hour," Bentwoman's Daughter said. "When it's on time."

Chee glanced at his watch. It was 5:35. Two and a half miles to the bus stop, he guessed. She might be home in fifteen or twenty minutes. If she walked fast. If the bus was on time. If—

Bentwoman made a noise in her throat. "She should go

home to her family," Bentwoman said. "She wants to find Ashie Begay, my grandson. Ashie Begay is dead."

It was an unequivocal statement. A fact stated without emotion.

Bentwoman's Daughter sighed again. She looked at Chee. "He was my nephew," she explained.

"Ashie Begay is dead?" Chee asked.

"He is dead," Bentwoman said.

"Did Margaret Sosi tell you this?"

"The girl thinks he is still alive," Bentwoman said. "I told her, but she believes what she wants to believe. The young sometimes do that."

Chee opened his mouth. Closed it. How should he frame the question?

"When I was young, I too believed what I wanted to believe. But you learn," the old woman said.

"Grandmother," Chee said. "How did you learn that Ashie Begay is dead?"

"From what you told me," Bentwoman said. "And from what the girl told me."

"I thought he might be alive," Chee said. "The girl is sure he is alive."

Bentwoman's eyes were closed now. She was asleep, Chee thought. Or dead. If she was breathing under those layers of blankets and shawls, Chee could see no trace of it. But apparently Bentwoman was simply mustering her strength for what she had to tell him.

"Ashie Begay has Tewa blood in him," Bentwoman said. "His grandmother was from Jemez. The Salt Clan went out toward the morning sun, beyond the Turquoise Mountain, to get some sheep one winter, and they came back with some children from Jemez. Some of them they sold back for corn and horses, but Ashie Begay's grandmother became the wife of one of the men in the Salt Clan and bore the child who was Ashie Begay's mother. So Ashie Begay has the blood in him of the People Who Call the Clouds. Tewa blood, and Salt Clan blood, and his father married into the Turkey Clan, and his mother's lineage was Standing Rock on her father's side. And all that has to be considered when you understand why I know Ashie Begay is dead."

Bentwoman paused, to catch her breath—which was laboring by now—or perhaps to allow Chee to comment. Chee had no comment to make. He didn't understand why Ashie Begay had to be dead. None of this had helped.

Bentwoman inhaled a labored breath, stirring her layers of coverings. She began explaining Ashie Begay's lineage in terms of the character of ancestors. Bentwoman's Daughter stood patiently behind the wheelchair, thinking her thoughts. Chee glanced at his watch. If the bus was on time, if Margaret Sosi had been on it, if she had walked rapidly, she should be within half a mile of here by now.

"So you see," Bentwoman was saying, "Ashie Begay, my grandson, has my blood in him too. All this blood combines, and it makes a certain kind of man. It makes the kind of man who would not have allowed the Gorman boy to die in his hogan. He would have been prudent. The Tewas are prudent. The Salt Clan is a prudent clan. He would have taken the Gorman boy out of the hogan so he could die in the safe, clean air. So the hogan would not be ruined by the *chindi.*"

It had taken Bentwoman a long time to say all of this, with many pauses. Now she was silent, breathing heavily.

"But the hogan was broken," Chee said. "The smoke hole was closed. The north wall was broken open. Everything in it was gone."

"Was everything gone?" Bentwoman asked. "Nothing was left?"

"Nothing but trash," Chee said.

"Did you look?" Bentwoman asked.

"It was a *chindi* hogan," Chee said. "I did not go inside."

Bentwoman breathed. She coughed. She exhaled a long breath. She turned her blind eyes toward Chee, as if she could see him. "So only a *belacani* looked?"

"Yes," Chee said. "A white policeman." He knew what Bentwoman was suggesting.

She sat for a long time, her eyes closed again. Chee was aware of the changing light outside the window. The sky turning red with sunset. Darkness gathering. Margaret Sosi would be walking through that darkness. He remembered the telephone number on Mrs. Day's calendar. He wanted urgently to go and meet Margaret. He would ask her immediately what was said on that postcard. He would take no more chances.

"If Ashie Begay is alive," Bentwoman said, "one day I will hear it. Someone in the family will know and the word will come to me. If he is dead, it would not matter. But it matters because this child believes he is alive, and she will always look for him." Bentwoman paused again, catching her breath, turning her face toward Chee again. "She should be looking for other things. Not for a dead man."

"Yes," Chee said. "Grandmother, you are right."

"You think Ashie Begay is alive?"

"I don't know," Chee said. "Maybe not."

"If someone killed him, would it have been one of the People? Or would it have been a *belacani?"*

"A white man," Chee said. "I think it would have been a white man."

"Then a white man buried Albert Gorman. And a white man broke the hogan?"

"Yes," Chee said. "If Ashie Begay is dead, that must have been what happened."

"I don't think a *belacani* would know how to do it right," Bentwoman said.

"No," Chee said. He was thinking of Albert Gorman's unwashed hair.

"Somebody should find out for sure," Bentwoman said. "They should do that so this child can know her grandfather is dead. So this child can finally rest."

"Yes," Chee said. And who else would there be to do that but Jim Chee. And doing it meant going into the ghost hogan, climbing through the black hole in the north wall. It meant stepping through the doorway into darkness.

Bentwoman was facing him, awaiting his answer. Chee swallowed. "Grandmother," he said, "I will go and do what I can do."

18

CHEE DROVE SLOWLY through a darkening landscape under a glowing copper-colored sky. He was something of a connoisseur of sunsets, a collector of memories of gaudy cloudscapes and glowing western horizons that the Colorado Plateau produces in remarkable season-changing variety. But Chee had never seen a sunset like this one—with the slanting evening light filtering through an atmosphere of oceanside humidity and chemical fumes. It gave a golden tint to objects that should be gray or tan or even blue; and made the cool evening seem warmer than it was, and caused Jim Chee to feel somehow that he was in a strange land, and that the bird call he was hearing from somewhere to his right was not produced by a bird at all but by something unknown, and that when he topped the ridge he would not look down upon the billboards proclaiming the entrance to Jacaranda Estates but upon God knows what.

At the top of the ridge, Chee pulled his pickup off the track and turned off the engine. A small figure was walking up the slope toward him. He took his binoculars from the glove box and focused them on the walker. It was Margaret Billy Sosi, as he'd guessed, looking tired. Down the slope far below a car moved along the asphalt, its lights on. Through his open window he could hear the muted roar of freeway traffic somewhere beyond the next hill. Another vehicle, driving with its parking lights, slowed to a stop past the Jacaranda entrance billboard, backed, and turned onto the development road. Chee watched it a moment, then switched back to the girl. She'd left her pea jacket somewhere and was wearing jeans and a white shirt. She was even smaller than he'd remembered. And thinner. Would she be willing to come back to the reservation with him? Maybe not. Bentwoman would help if he needed help. But first he would get the answers to the questions he had failed to ask at Begay's hogan. He would get the answer to that mean little puzzle.

The vehicle coming up the dirt track was a van, dark brown or maybe dark green. Its lights came on, illuminating the girl with backlighting. She moved off the track. The van drew even with her and stopped. The driver leaned out the window, talking to Margaret. Then the door opened, and the man stepped out. A big man, blond, maybe six-two or -three and bulky. He towered over Margaret, showing her something in his hand. Through the binoculars, the object seemed to be a wallet. Chee sucked in his breath. The big man's other hand, dangling stiffly by his side, was marked by something white. One finger was bandaged.

Chee put down the binoculars, remembering Mr. Berger's pantomimed account of the blond man who had come for Albert Gorman and had his finger slammed in the car door. He also thought of his own pistol, locked in a drawer beside his bed in Shiprock. He turned on the ignition and started the pickup rolling down the hill.

19

VAGGAN HAD NOTICED the pickup truck parked on the ridge almost the moment he'd turned on the cracked asphalt at the entrance of Jacaranda Street. It registered in his attention merely as a nuisance. If it was occupied, the occupant would be a witness. That would affect, necessarily, the way Vaggan conducted his business. The immediate business was determining if the female figure trudging up the hill in the direction of the pickup truck was Margaret Billy Sosi, as Vaggan suspected. If it was, it was good luck. Much better to pick her up here than at whatever residence he'd find at that address McNair had given him. Here it should be simple enough to get the woman in the van and to do it without arousing any alarm. Thus Vaggan had been conscious of the pickup, but only as a minor irritant. Now, suddenly, the truck engine had started and it was rolling down the hill toward him.

Vaggan had stopped the van so that when he leaned out of its driver-side window he was just behind the woman. He had said "Miss Sosi" in a clear, emphatic voice. She had stopped and turned, and stood staring at him doubtfully.

"I'm Officer Davis, Los Angeles County Sheriff's Office," Vaggan had said, holding out the leather folder of credentials he used when the situation called for him to be police. "I need to talk to you."

"What about?" Margaret Sosi had asked. "Is it about my grandfather?"

"Yes," Vaggan had said, and, sure now that she'd stand

there and wait for him, he opened the van door and stepped toward her. "It's about your grandfather. I need to take you to him."

Vaggan had held out the identification folder again and, as she looked at it, taken her forearm in his hand. It was a skinny arm—a bone—and Vaggan's confidence that this girl would be no problem at all was reinforced. The girl made no attempt to pull away.

"Where is he?" she asked, looking into Vaggan's eyes. "Is he all right?"

"At the hospital," Vaggan said. "Come along." It was then that Vaggan heard the truck, its motor racing suddenly, bumping erratically down the hill. It ran off the rutted track, bumping across a hummock of cactus, and then jolted back onto the road, rolling directly for them.

"Crazy son of a bitch!" Vaggan shouted. He jumped toward the van door, then jumped back. There wouldn't be time to move it. He pulled the girl away from it.

"What's wrong with him?" she said.

Vaggan didn't respond. He'd reached under his jacket, extracted his pistol, cocked it, and held it against his back.

The pickup engine died as suddenly as it had started. It ran off the road again and slid to a stop, the door opening while it was still rolling. A man was leaning out the door, and as he leaned his hat fell off.

"Ya-tah-hey!" the man shouted. He half fell out the door, straightened himself, and retrieved his hat. *"Ya-tah-hey!"* he shouted again.

"I think he's drunk," the woman said.

"Yes," Vaggan said. Some of the tension left him. The man reset his hat, a worn felt cowboy job, and said something to Vaggan. The man was smiling broadly, and the words were Navajo. He stopped, laughed, and repeated them.

"What'd he say?" Vaggan asked. He kept his eyes on the drunk. The man was youngish, early thirties, Vaggan guessed, and slightly stooped. His shirttail was out on one side and one of the legs of his jeans was caught in the top of a dusty boot. A streak of spittle had run down from the corner of his mouth.

The woman said nothing for a moment. She was staring at

Vaggan, her expression strange. Then she said, "He said he's having trouble with his truck. It won't drive straight. He wants you to help him with it."

"Tell him to screw off," Vaggan said. He slipped the pistol back under his belt, suddenly aware he had a headache. He hadn't gotten his sleep out. Last night had been exciting. It would take him hours to unwind.

Vaggan had studied his Greater Los Angeles street map after he left McNair. Jacaranda Street was nowhere on it. It had taken, finally, a call to the Los Angeles County Road Maintenance Department to pin down its location. Vaggan's policy was to arrive at a scene where he expected to engage in any sort of action just at dusk—when it was still light enough to see, if you knew what you were looking for, but dim enough so that witnesses would be doubtful about what they'd witnessed. Under some circumstances he would have made a preliminary trip to the site, looked it over, learned the ground. This time he located the street, but when he realized its isolation he stayed away and waited for evening. He wanted no one in Jacaranda Street remembering that they'd seen the van twice, the first time in clear daylight.

Vaggan had tuned in the all-news station, carried the radio outside, and put it on the concrete retaining wall beside his second cup of coffee. Like everything Vaggan owned which required power, the radio was battery-operated. In the future as Vaggan anticipated it, the radio battery would have to last only about three weeks after THE DAY. Broadcasting would be restored within hours after the bombs—and the devastating electrical surge of the nuclear explosions—had erased civilization's grid of electrical power. The emergency generators would take over, and the frequencies would be babbling with panic: civil defense orders and, mostly, cries for help. Vaggan estimated that phase would last several weeks and then die away, and there would be no more use for his radio receiver. For that brief but important period, Vaggan kept four silicon radio batteries in a little box in his freezer. More than enough.

The local news led with an account of Vaggan's operation. Vaggan sipped his coffee and listened.

"Police report a bizarre crime in Beverly Hills—with TV

talk show host Jay Leonard maimed by an intruder who broke into his palatial home and drove staples through his ears.

"Police say the intruder called local newspapers and television stations after the attack to tell them that Leonard was being taken to the emergency room at Beverly Hills General. Leonard was reported in good condition at the hospital but was not available for comment. Here's what Detective Lieutenant Allen Bizett of the LAPD had to say."

Bizett said very little, reporting in a gravelly voice that Leonard said he didn't know the motive of the attack, that he had received an anonymous telephone threat, and that he had hired a guard to protect him. Bizett said the guard had been overcome by the intruder, who had also killed two guard dogs. He described the suspect as a "large Caucasian male."

With that subject exhausted, the announcer skipped to the continued hunt for an armed robber who had killed a customer and wounded a clerk in a convenience store robbery the day before, and from that to the record-breaking traffic snarl on the San Diego Freeway caused by a two-truck accident. The item had been brief, but it had been enough, and it would be bigger for both the afternoon papers and the evening TV shows. They'd have the dogs' head business, with the bodies missing, and more of the odd stuff he'd worked in, and his telephone calls, and that would give them the motive. Enough to earn him his bonus, but he'd never had any doubt of earning that.

He finished the coffee, considered having another cup, rejected the idea. Coffee was his only deviation from his father's rule. He'd slipped into the habit his first year at West Point and rationalized its use as a stimulant his nervous system needed. Even so, even now, twenty years since the Commander had last spoken to him, he drank with a sense of uneasiness he'd never quite defined. "Weakness," the Commander had said, sitting across the breakfast table. "People make being a child an excuse for it. But it's no excuse. In Sparta they started their males at the age of eight. Took 'em away from the women. Enduring the pain. Enduring the cold. Enduring hunger. Weeding out the weakness. We encourage weakness." Vaggan could see it clearly. His father in his perfect whites, his bristling blond hair, his trim mustache, his row of ribbons. His blue eyes staring at Vaggan, proud of Vaggan, teaching Vaggan to be strong. The thought led Vaggan, as it almost always did, into ground he didn't want to enter: to West Point, and being caught, and to Roser, Cadet Captain Roser. Vaggan considered it again—just a glance at the memory for something that might have been overlooked. No. Nothing changed. The decision was correct: to kill Roser quickly, before he could make any report. The tactic had been proper. The blow with the softball bat should have been both lethal and untraceable. But somehow Roser hadn't died. Expulsion hadn't really mattered. The Point had been a disappointment, with its endless homilies about the old, dead verities which were no longer verities—if they ever were. But the report had gone to the Commander. And the Commander had sent the telegram.

I HAVE BURIED YOU BESIDE THE WOMAN.

Vaggan hadn't known the woman. She had borne him. She must have given him the genes that accounted for his size, because the Commander was a small man. But even his earliest memories did not include her. The Commander had never mentioned her. Asking the Commander was unthinkable.

The newscaster was talking about Berlin, a subject that always caught Vaggan's attention. The Commander had believed it would begin over Berlin and Vaggan never doubted it. But this item was inconsequential—a vote of confidence in the Bundestag. And so was the rest of the newscast. The avalanche would not begin today. And so he had finished his coffee, and made a quick check of his hillside and the redoubt he was building into it, and—when the time was right—had left to find Jacaranda Drive, and now he was facing this drunken Indian who was grinning at him foolishly and ignoring his order to leave.

"Beat it," Vaggan repeated. "Or you're spending the night in the tank."

The Indian said something in Navajo and laughed. He walked around Vaggan's van, opened the passenger side door, and climbed in.

"Son of a bitch," Vaggan snarled. He would have to deal

with the Indian the hard way, apparently, which would take time and maybe even attract attention. But with any luck he could pull him out by the feet, whack him, and be done with it and gone with the girl with no problems. It was almost dark, and that would help. He rushed around the van, jerking the pistol from under his belt.

He saw what was coming far too late to avoid it. A split-second awareness of the Indian launched out of the van door, the flashlight swinging, and then the burst of pain. He had time only for reflex action. His reflexes were fine, but they only flinched him away from the full force of the blow. The flashlight—four D batteries in a heavy Bakelite tube—smashed against his upper jaw, staggered him away from the door, slammed him into the side of the van. The shock of the blow blinded him for a moment, caused him to lose awareness. Then he was on the ground, the Indian atop him. Vaggan reacted with explosive violence before the Indian could hit him again. He grabbed the man's elbow, jerked, twisted his body. The blow missed.

After that it was no contest. Vaggan weighed himself every morning just before he began his routine of pre-breakfast exercises. That morning he had weighed 225 pounds—three pounds off the weight he considered his standard. All of it was bone, muscle, and gristle, conditioned and disciplined by a regimen the Commander had started him on before he could remember. In fact, his very first memory of this part of his life was the time he had cried. He had been doing leg lifts, the Commander standing over him, the Commander's voice chanting, "Again, again, again, again . . ." and the pain of the straining muscles had come through the haze of his fatigue and started his tear ducts flowing. He hadn't been able to control it, and the Commander had noticed, and it had been an experience of searing shame. "It doesn't help you if it doesn't hurt you," the Commander always said. The pain of that experience had taught him to control his tears. Vaggan had never cried again.

Now he made no sound at all. The Indian was quick. The Indian was strong for his size. The Indian definitely was not drunk. That illusion had vanished from Vaggan's mind with the pain of the blow. But the Indian was younger than Vaggan, and fifty pounds lighter, and without Vaggan's skills at this sort of business. It took only a matter of seconds—a brief flurry of struggle—and the Indian was pinned under him. Vaggan could feel the flashlight against his knee. He'd dropped his pistol somewhere, so he'd use the light. He slammed the heel of his hand against the side of the Indian's head, twice, stunning the man. Then he snatched the light, raised it and struck.

"Drop it," the voice said.

Margaret Billy Sosi was standing just behind him, his pistol held in both hands, pointed at his head. Vaggan let the flashlight drop on the Indian's chest.

"Get off of him," the girl ordered instantly. Vaggan was studying her. Would she shoot him? Probably not. He could get the gun from her, but it would take a little time. Vaggan rose. He touched a fingertip to the cheekbone where the blow of the flashlight had broken the skin. "He hit me," Vaggan said. He held out his hand. "Here," he said. "Give me the pistol before you shoot somebody."

The girl took two steps backward, keeping the pistol aimed at his stomach. "He told me who you are," she said. "You're no policeman."

"Yes I am," Vaggan said. "And if you—"

"Pick him up," she said, not taking her eyes off Vaggan's face. "Put him in your truck. We've got to get him to a hospital."

"First," Vaggan said, "I've got to have my gun back." He took a step toward her.

"I'll kill you," she said.

"No you won't," Vaggan said. He laughed and took another step toward her, hand reaching.

The shot burned past his face and struck the side of the van with a thumping sound almost as loud as the muzzle blast.

Vaggan stopped, hands held open, chest high.

"The next one hits you," the girl said. "Put him in your truck."

Vaggan stopped, and slid one arm under the Indian's shoulders and the other under his knees, and lifted him gently into the passenger's side seat. The girl slid in behind him, the pistol held carefully, and they drove away.

20

CHEE HAD BEEN AWAKE perhaps forty-five minutes when he heard the voice of Shaw loud in the corridor. He'd had plenty of time to attract a nurse's aide. The girl had been willing to make a call to Shaw's office and leave word about where Chee was and to tell Shaw the hospital he was in. But Chee hadn't felt up to explaining exactly why he was in it, or how. The why was clear enough. His head was bandaged, and under the protection he could feel a great sore knot over his left eye, and a throbbing pain about at the hinge point of his jaw on the opposite side, and a persistent internal ache. Aside from that, his left hip hurt—the burning sensation of a bruised abrasion—and his nose was swollen. When he had tried to remember exactly how each of these misfortunes had occurred he found, at first, a total alarming blank. But then he recalled that injured persons, especially those suffering head injuries, often go through a brief period of amnesia. A doctor at Flagstaff had explained it to him in typical medical fashion once. "We don't understand it, but we know it doesn't last long." And gradually the details became willing to be remembered if he tried. But he didn't try much, because the headache was spectacular. Obviously the big blond man had clobbered him. That was enough to know for the moment.

Earlier, when he had first awakened, Chee had tried to get up. That mistake had touched off explosive pain behind his forehead and waves of nausea—enough to convince him that he was in no shape to do anything even if he could remember what he should be doing. So he had sent word to Shaw, and now Shaw was beside his bed, looking down at him, eyes curious.

"You found her," Shaw said. "What'd you find out?"

"What?" Chee asked. Everything seemed sort of foggy.

"The Sosi girl. The one who brought you here," Shaw said. "Who was the man with her? What'd she tell you?"

Chee began framing questions. It made his head hurt. "Just tell me about it," he said. "This end of it. How did I get here?"

Shaw pulled back the curtain screening off the adjoining bed, confirming it was empty. He sat. "From what I can find out so far, a vehicle arrived at the emergency entrance a little after eight last night." Shaw paused, extracted a notebook from his coat pocket, and checked it. "Eight ten, you were admitted. Admitted by a girl, late teens. Thin. Dark. Probably Indian or Oriental. Large blond man driving the vehicle. He drove away while the girl was admitting you. The girl signed the admission papers as Margaret Billy Sosi." Shaw restored the notebook to his pocket. "What'd you find out?" he asked. "And how're you feeling?"

"Wonderful," Chee said. "And nothing."

He told Shaw what had happened, up to the point of hitting the blond man with the flashlight. After that it was misty.

Shaw had listened without a word, face blank, eyes on Chee's eyes.

"Describe the van," he said.

Chee described it.

"You saw the gun. No doubt about it?"

"None. And he had an arsenal in the back of the van. I just had time for a glance, but he had a rack of weapons. Automatic rifles, maybe two different kinds, shotgun, long-barreled sniper rifle with a telescopic sight, other stuff."

"Well," Shaw said. "That's interesting."

"And a metal cabinet. God knows what was in that."

"And the girl thought he was a policeman?"

Chee nodded. And wished he hadn't. His head throbbed.

Shaw took a huge breath, exhaled it. "Well, hell," he said. "You got any notions?"

"I've got a headache," Chee said.

"I'll make a phone call," Shaw said, getting up. "Get somebody to that Jacaranda address and see if we can pick up Sosi." He glanced back from the doorway. "Too bad you didn't hit him harder."

Chee didn't comment on that. Through the general haziness, he was becoming aware of what the girl had done. She'd gotten the big man to bring him to the hospital. How the hell had she managed that? He had given up looking for an answer when Shaw returned.

"Okay," he said. "They'll find her."

"I doubt it."

"Whatever," Shaw said. He stared down, peered at Chee. Made a quizzical face. "What's going on here? Have you figured it out?"

"No," Chee said.

"I know the man in the van," Shaw said. "Eric Vaggan. That guy I told you about who works for McNair. Or he has, now and then. And for other people, I guess. Sort of an enforcer."

Chee didn't say anything. He was wishing Shaw would go away.

"The girl has something to do with the McNair business," Shaw said. "No other reason for any of this. Why else would Vaggan be out there looking for her?" He waited for Chee to tell him.

"Why don't you pick up this guy? Ask him?" Chee said.

"We don't know him all that well," Shaw said. "Don't have a file on him to amount to anything. No address. Just some stuff off some telephone taps from the other end of the call. Things like that. Witnesses describing a guy who looks like that, and so forth. Nothing concrete. You said he was taking her in?"

"She said he said he was a cop."

"Had to be a reason for it. What could it be?"

Chee closed his eyes. It didn't help much.

"What we need to do," Shaw said slowly, "is go see Farmer about this."

"Farmer?"

"The Assistant U.S.D.A. The man handling the McNair

case. Maybe it fits something he knows. When can you get out of here?"

"I don't know," Chee said.

"I'll handle it, then," Shaw said. "I'll do it right now."

It was late afternoon when Shaw called. A nurse's aide had brought Chee his lunch, and a doctor had come in and removed the bandage and inspected him, and said something about not trying to knock down walls with his head. This had caused the nurse attending to chuckle. Chee had asked when he could check out, and the doctor had said he was suffering from concussion and should stay another day to see how things went. They seemed to be going well, physically. He felt better after the meal; his vision was no longer blurred, and the headache had become both intermittent and tolerable. When the woman came up from the business office to talk to him about who was going to pay for all this, he found his memory had regained full Chee-like efficiency. He rattled off the name of his Tribal Police Medical Insurance company, the amount of the deductible, and even the eight digits of his account number. By the time the telephone beside his bed rang, the only thing bothering him much was the scraped bruise on his hip.

Shaw hadn't had much luck.

"Typical," he said. "Farmer's long gone. He quit the Justice Department and went to work with some law firm up in San Francisco. The man who has the case now apparently hasn't even read the file on it."

The noise Chee made must have sounded incredulous.

"What's the hurry?" Shaw said, sounding a little bitter. "McNair doesn't come to trial for a couple of months, and then there'll probably be an extension. So I sit there in his office cooling my heels while he reads through the file, and then he looks up and says, 'Okay, now, what was it you want?' Like I was asking him some damn favor."

Chee made a sympathetic sound.

"So I tell him all about the business with Margaret Sosi, and so forth, and he listens politely and gets rid of me."

"Did you tell him about the Leroy Gorman angle, and Grayson, and the trailer?"

"I mentioned it," Shaw said. "Yes."

"What'd he say?"

"He opened the file again, and looked through it, and then he changed the subject."

"What'd ya think?"

"Well," Shaw said, slowly, "I think that Grayson showed up in his file as one of his protected witnesses. Namely, Leroy Gorman."

"Yeah," Chee said. "I don't see how it could be any other way."

"Wasted time," Shaw said. "Wasted time. We could already guess that." There was silence on the telephone while Shaw considered this. He sighed. "Ah, well," he said. "I don't guess that lawyer was as dumb as he acted. At least he's alerted now that they're after Gorman. Either he'll move him someplace safer or watch him."

Chee didn't comment on that. He hadn't had enough experience with Assistant U.S. District Attorneys to judge.

"What I think I'll do now is try to get a line on this Vaggan. I'd like to find out where he lives and pick him up on something. I'll get you to sign a complaint. Pick him up and see if I can learn something. What are you going to do?"

"I guess I'm going to keep trying to find Margaret Sosi. Unless you found her?"

"No," Shaw said. "She'd got back to that place on Jacaranda and got her stuff and took off. At least that's what the old woman out there said. And she wasn't around." Shaw paused. "Where you going to look for her now?"

Chee's head was aching again.

"It takes too long to explain," he said.

21

HE CALLED MARY LANDON that afternoon and told her what had happened to him, and that he'd come home as soon as they'd let him out of the hospital, which would probably be tomorrow. And when he'd finished the conversation he felt much better. Mary had been suitably upset: alarmed at first, then angry that he'd let it happen, then concerned. She'd take time off from school and come right out. No, he'd told her. By the time she got to Los Angeles, he'd probably be on his way back to Shiprock. She'd come anyway. Don't, he told her. Far too much hassle and there'd be nothing she could do. And then they'd talked of other things, never allowing the talk to drift anywhere near the central core of their problem. It was like their old warm, happy times, and when the nurse came in and Chee said he had to hang up, Mary Landon said, "I love you Jim," and Chee, conscious of the nurse watching him and listening, said, "I love you, Mary."

He really did. More important, he sometimes thought, he liked her, too. Admired her. Enjoyed her company, her voice, her laugh, the way she touched him, the way she understood him. He was right, this decision he was making. And he'd made it without even being conscious of it. He would be wrong to lose her. Having made his decision, he set about confirming it—thinking of all the things that were wrong with his job, with the reservation, with the Navajo culture. Making comparisons: This hospital room and the cold discomfort of his grandmother's hogan; the security of life with a regular paycheck and the sheep rancher's endless nervewracking dependence on rain that wouldn't fall, comparing the comforts of white society with the unemployment and poverty of the People. Perversely, these thoughts led him to the Silver Threads, and Mr. Berger, and the woman whose son was coming to see her, and to the old women who lived on Jacaranda Street, Bentwoman Tsossie and Bentwoman's Daughter.

In fact, it was three days before he could get out of the hospital. The next day the headache returned, fierce and persistent. That provoked another round of X-rays and a renewed verdict that he was suffering from concussion. Mary called in the afternoon and had to be persuaded again not to drop everything and visit him. The following day he felt fine, but the doctors weren't finished with some test or other. Shaw dropped in and reported he had nothing to report. Vaggan had proved surprisingly invisible. He was suspected of being involved in a bizarre assault case involving one of Southern California's television personalities; the description fit and it seemed to involve a welshed bet, which was the sort of work Vaggan did. But there was no hard proof. A witness hadn't gotten a look at him, and the victim and his girlfriend reported he was wearing a stocking mask. He dropped a copy of the Los Angeles *Times* on Chee's bed so he could read about it. Shaw looked tired and defeated.

Driving home the next day, Chee felt the same way. He also felt depressed, nervous, frustrated, irritated, and generally miles from that condition for which the Navajo word is *hozro.* It means a sort of blend of being in harmony with one's environment, at peace with one's circumstances, content with the day, devoid of anger, and free from anxieties. Chee thought of his neglected studies to become a *yataalii,* a shaman whose work it would be to restore his fellow Navajos to *hozro.* Physician, heal thyself, he thought. He drove eastward on Interstate 40 faster than he should, glum and disgruntled. Mary Landon hung in his mind—a problem he had solved but which refused to stay solved. And when he turned away from that, it was to the frustration of the postcard, which seemed to have come from no one to Albert Gorman, and on to Ashie Begay, and then to disappear—unless Margaret Sosi had it.

Chee stopped at a Flagstaff motel. The weathercast at the close of the ten o'clock news was on, the map showing a high-pressure area centered over northern Utah that promised to hold winter at bay for at least another day. Chee fell into bed, tired but not sleepy, and found himself reviewing it again.

Simple enough on the Los Angeles end. A car-theft operation broken, some indicted, some persuaded to be witnesses. One was Leroy Gorman. That much seemed sure. Leroy Gorman tucked away under the Witness Protection Program under the name of Grayson, and denying he was Gorman because the Federals had told him to deny it. If Shaw's information was correct, Albert Gorman had refused to cooperate. Upchurch had nothing to scare him with. But something—apparently that photograph/postcard of the trailer—had caused Albert to decide to come to Shiprock to find his brother. He'd been pursued. Why? Presumably because his employers wanted him to lead them to Leroy so that Leroy could be eliminated as a witness. Albert Gorman had resisted. Albert Gorman had been shot.

Chee lay listening to the truck traffic rumble on the Interstate, thinking of that. One odd hole in the Los Angeles end. Albert Gorman hadn't been followed to Shiprock. They'd known he was going there. Lerner had flown directly to Farmington and driven directly to Shiprock. And if what Berger had told him was true, Vaggan had come to Gorman's apartment to keep him from going to Shiprock. So much for that. So much for the reasonable, logical explanation. But at least he knew now why Lerner had gone to do the dirty work instead of Vaggan. Vaggan was having a splint put on a finger broken when Albert slammed the car door on it. Fat lot that helped.

Chee groaned, punched the pillow into better shape, rolled over. Nothing fit. Tomorrow morning he'd call Captain Largo, and tell him he'd be back in Shiprock by midafternoon, and see if Largo had learned anything while Chee was wasting his time in California. And he would complain about his headache and ask for a week of sick leave. He had some work he wanted to do.

22

FROM FLAGSTAFF, near the western edge of the Navajo Big Reservation, to Shiprock, near its northern border, is about 230 miles if you take the most direct route through Tuba City. Chee took that route, checking out of his motel before sunrise and stopping briefly at Gray Mountain to call Largo.

First he dealt with official business. He was going to apply for a week of sick leave to let his head heal. Would it be approved? All right, Largo said, sounding neutral.

He'd told Largo in a call from the hospital the basics about what had happened to him and what he'd learned. Now he told him a little more, including what Shaw had learned, or failed to learn, in his visit to the U.S.D.A.'s office. "Shaw doesn't have any doubt that this Grayson is really Leroy Gorman," Chee said. "Neither do I. But it would be a good thing to confirm it. Is there a way you could do that? Find out for sure he's a protected witness?"

"He is," Largo said.

"You checked?"

"I checked," Largo said. "Grayson is Leroy Gorman. Or I should say Leroy Gorman is Grayson and will be until they haul him back to Los Angeles and have him testify. Then he'll be Leroy Gorman again."

Chee wanted to ask Largo how he'd found out. Obviously the FBI would not tell Largo or anyone else anything about this supersecret witness business. It was a long-time sore point with the local law that the Federals moved all sorts of known felons into their jurisdiction under false identities with no warning to anybody. The Justice Department said it was essential to the safety of witnesses. Local law saw the insult built into it—another statement from the Federals that locals couldn't be trusted. So how had Largo checked? The first possibility that occurred to Chee was a visit to the local telephone office to find out who ordered the telephone line connected to the trailer.

"Is Sharkey paying Grayson's telephone bill?" Chee asked.

Largo chuckled. "He is. And the bill for hauling that trailer in there from Farmington—the hauling company sent that right to the FBI. But when I told Sharkey what we know about all this, you'd have thought he couldn't imagine why I thought he'd be interested."

"Well," Chee said. "I'll see you next week."

"When you come back to work," Largo said. "I want you to make one more try to find that Sosi girl. And this time handcuff her to your steering wheel or something to get her to hold still long enough to find out about that postcard. You think you can do that?"

Chee said he could try, and he asked the captain to switch him to the dispatcher.

"Dispatcher?" Largo said.

"Yeah," Chee said. "If I haven't had any mail, I'll skip coming in."

Largo switched the call.

Chee didn't have any mail. He hadn't expected to. Then he arranged to have a horse saddled and a horse trailer ready for him for the afternoon. Captain Largo could have arranged that, but Captain Largo would have wanted to know why he wanted the horse.

Outside the Gray Mountain store, Chee stretched, yawned, and sucked in a huge lungful of air. It was cold here, frost still rimming the roadside weeds, and the snow-capped shape of the San Francisco Peaks twenty miles to the south looked close enough to touch in the clear, high-altitude air. The winter storm being held at bay by the Utah high in last night's weather cast was still hung up somewhere over the horizon. The only clouds this morning were high-altitude cirrus so thin that the blue showed through them. Beautiful to Chee. He was back in

Dine' Bike'yah, back Between the Sacred Mountains, and he felt easy again—at home in a remembered landscape. He stood beside his pickup, postponing for a moment the four or five hours he still had to spend driving, and studied the mountain. It was something Frank Sam Nakai had instructed him to do. "Memorize places," his uncle had told him. "Settle your eyes on a place and learn it. See it under the snow, and when first grass is growing, and as the rain falls on it. Feel it and smell it, walk on it, touch the stones, and it will be with you forever. When you are far away, you can call it back. When you need it, it is there, in your mind."

This was one of those places for Chee—this desert sloping away to the hills that rose to become Dook'o'oosli'id, Evening Twilight Mountain, the Mountain of the West, the mountain built by First Man as the place where the holy Abalone Shell Boy would live, guarded by the Black Wind *yei.* He had memorized this place when he worked out of the Tuba City agency. He leaned his elbows against the roof of his pickup and memorized it again, with rags of fog drifting away from the snowy peaks and the morning sun making slanting shadows across the foothills. "Touch it with your mind," Frank Sam Nakai had told him. "Inhale the air that moves across it. Listen to the sounds it makes." The sounds this place was making this morning were the sounds of crows, hundreds of them, moving out of the trees around the trading post back toward wherever this flock spent its winter days.

Chee climbed back into the truck and rolled it onto U.S. 89 North. He wanted to get where he had to go a long time before dark.

He got there about midafternoon, driving steadily and fast despite a quickening north wind, which told him the storm was finally bulging down out of Utah. He made a quick stop at his trailer in Shiprock to strap on his pistol, get his heavy coat, and collect a loaf of bread and what was left of a package of bologna. He picked up the horse and trailer at the tribal barns and ate on the long bumpy drive back into the Chuskas, trailed now by a cold north wind. He parked where Albert Gorman had abandoned his ruined Plymouth, unloaded the horse, and rode the rest of the way to the Begay hogan. The sky was clouding now, a high gray overcast moving down from the northwest. Chee tied the horse in the shelter of Begay's empty corral and quickly scouted the hogan yard. If anyone had been here since he'd left the place, they'd left no sign. Then he walked around the hogan to its broken north wall.

The wind was gusty now, whipping dust around his feet and making sibilant noises in the corpse hole. Chee squatted and peered inside. In the gray light of the stormy afternoon, he could see just what he'd seen by the light of his flash when he'd been here before: the rusty iron stove, the stove pipe connecting it to the smoke hole, odds and ends of trash. The wind hooted through the hole and sent a scrap of paper scuttling across the hard-packed earthen floor. The wind eddied around the collar of his padded coat, touching his neck with cold. Chee shivered and pulled the collar tight. By Navajo tradition, Albert Gorman now would have completed his journey to the underworld, would have vanished into the dark unknown which the metaphysics of the People had never tried to explain or explore. But his *chindi* would be here, an unhappy, discordant, malevolent evil—whatever in Gorman had been out of harmony—trapped forever inside the hogan when Gorman had died.

Chee took a deep breath and stepped through the hole.

He was instantly aware that it was warmer inside, and of the smell of dust and of something sharper. He paused a moment, trying to identify the aroma. Old grease, old ashes, old sweat—the smell of human occupation. Chee opened the stove door. Nothing in the oven. He opened the fire box. The ashes had already been stirred, probably by Sharkey. He picked up the scrap of paper the wind had moved. A torn bit of old envelope with nothing written on it. He found the place at the west side of the hogan where Begay had habitually laid his sheepskins for sleeping. He took out his knife and dug into the packed earth, looking for he knew not what. He found nothing at all, and paused, squatting on his heels, thinking.

Jim Chee was aware of the sound of the wind outside, whispering around the corpse hole and at the blocked smoke hole over his head. He was very much aware of the ghost of

Albert Gorman in the air around him, and suddenly he was aware, clearly and surely, of the nature of the Gorman *chindi.* Like Gorman—of course like Gorman since it was Gorman—it was Los Angeles, and the little girl whores he'd seen along Sunset Boulevard, and the impersonal precision of the herds on the freeways, and the chemical gray air, and Albert Gorman's landlady, and the pink-faced aide at the Silver Threads. And now it was Jim Chee's ghost because Jim Chee had chosen it—stepped through the corpse hole into the darkness freely and willingly, having decided to do so rationally. Having chosen Los Angeles over Shiprock, and Mary Landon over the loneliness and poverty and beauty of *hozro.* Chee squatted on his heels, and looked around him, and tried to think of what he should be looking for. Instead, he remembered the song from the hogan blessing ceremonial.

This hogan will be a blessed hogan.
It will become a hogan of dawn,
Dawn Boy will live in beauty in it,
It will be a hogan of white corn,
It will be a hogan of soft goods,
It will be a hogan of crystal water,
It will be a hogan dusted with pollen,
It will be a hogan of long-life happiness,
It will be a hogan with beauty above it,
It will be a hogan with beauty all around it.

The words of Talking God came back to Chee. They would have been sung here, when Begay's family had gathered to help him bless this hogan a long time ago. Chee got to his feet, took out his knife again, and walked to the east wall. Here, under the end of the base log just atop the foundation stones, the singer hired by Ashie Begay to conduct his hogan ceremonial would have placed a choice piece of Begay's turquoise.

Chee chipped away with the knife tip at the dried adobe plaster, dislodged a chunk of it, and crumbled it in his fingers. The turquoise was there, a polished oval of clear blue gemstone. Chee wiped it on his shirt, inspected it, and put it back under the log. He walked to the west wall, dug under the end of the foundation log, and extracted a white seashell. The abalone shell symbolized the great *yei* Abalone Boy, just as the turquoise represented the Turquoise Boy spirit. But what had finding them told him? Nothing, Chee thought, that he hadn't believed he knew—that Begay was orthodox, that this hogan had been properly blessed, that Begay, in abandoning his home, had left these ritual jewels behind. Would that be orthodox? Probably, Chee thought. Unless Begay had thought to remove them before Albert Gorman died they wouldn't be removed at all—just as no wood from this hogan would ever be used again, not even for a fire. But removing them before Gorman died would have been prudent, and Begay must have seen the death coming, and Bentwoman had described her son as a prudent man. What would a prudent man salvage from his hogan if he saw death approaching it? What had Bentwoman expected him to find in here?

Of course! Chee walked around the stove to the east-facing entrance. He felt along the log lintel above the door, running his fingers through the accumulated dust. Nothing. He tried to the right of the door. There, his fingers probing into the space over the log encountered something.

Chee held it in his left hand, a small brown pouch of dusty doeskin tied at the top with a leather thong. His fingers squeezed it, feeling exactly what he expected to feel. The pouch contained four soft objects. Chee untied the thong and dumped into his palm four smaller pouches, also of doeskin. He held Ashie Begay's Four Mountains Bundle.

The instant he saw it, he knew that Ashie Begay was dead.

Chee stepped through the corpse hole into snow. The wind now was carrying small, light flakes, which blew across the yard of Ashie Begay's hogan as dry as dust. He climbed down to the corral, the Four Mountains Bundle tucked in his coat pocket, to where he had tied his horse—thinking about what he'd found. The bundle represented weeks of work, a pilgrimage to each of the four sacred mountains to collect from each the herbs and minerals prescribed by the Holy People. Chee had collected his own the summer of his junior year at the University of New Mexico. Mount Taylor and the San Francisco Peaks had been easy enough, thanks to access roads to

Forest Service fire lookouts on both of their summits. But Blanca Peak in the Sangre de Cristos and Hesperus Peak in the Las Platas had been a different matter. Begay would have gone through that ordeal in harder times, before roads led into the high country. Or he might have inherited it from his family. Either way, he would never have left it behind in a death hogan. It would have been his most treasured belonging, an heirloom beyond price.

So what had happened at Ashie Begay's hogan?

Chee had brought the horse because he intended, no matter what he might find in the hogan, to make a general search of Ashie Begay's home territory. Now that search took on new purpose. The horse stomped and whinnied as he approached, cold and ready to move. Chee untied it, dusted the snow off its haunches, and swung into the saddle. What had happened at this hogan? Could Begay have gone away, returned to find Gorman dead, and forgot the sacred pouch when he abandoned the hogan? That was inconceivable. So what had happened?

Had someone else come after Albert Gorman after Lerner had failed to stop him, and found him at Ashie Begay's hogan, and killed them both, and then taken the time for Gorman's ceremonial burial, emptying the hogan and hiding Begay's body? Chee considered that. Possibly. In fact, something like that must have happened. But what would be the motive? He could think of none that made sense.

Chee circled the hogan yard and then rode east on a sheep trail leading down the arroyo rim. He rode slowly, looking for anything that might deviate in any way from normal. After more than a mile of finding absolutely nothing, he trotted the horse back to the hogan yard. It was snowing more heavily now and the temperature was dropping sharply. The second trail he tried led up past the talus slope, past the place where Gorman's body had been left, and followed under the cliff west of the hogan. It took him into the wind, making the horse reluctant and visibility difficult. He pulled his hatbrim down and rode with head bowed to keep the snowflakes out of his eyes—plodding along studying the ground, knowing what he was looking for without letting the thought take any exact shape in his mind. The snow was sticking, accumulating fast. Soon it would cover everything and make his search futile. He should have done this long ago. Should have used his head. Should have attended his instinctive knowledge that Hosteen Ashie Begay would not have abandoned this place to a ghost, would not have left his nephew half prepared for the journey to the underworld. There was this trail to check out, and at least two more, and there wouldn't be time to do it all before the snow covered everything.

There almost wasn't time.

Chee saw the horse without realizing he was seeing anything more than a round boulder coated with snow. But there was something a little wrong with the color where the snow hadn't stuck, a redness that was off-key for the gray granite of this landscape. He pulled up on the reins, and wiped the snowflakes out of his eyebrows, and stared. Then he climbed down out of the saddle. He saw the second horse only when he'd walked down into the trail-side gully to inspect the first one.

Whoever had shot them had led them both far enough down from the trail so that, if they had both fallen as he must have intended, they would have been out of sight. But the one Chee had seen apparently hadn't cooperated. It was a big bay gelding, and the bullet fired into its forehead apparently had touched off a frantic struggle. It had lunged uphill, two or three bounding reflex jumps judging from the dislodged stones, before its brain turned off in death.

Hosteen Begay's belongings were dumped out of sight farther down the wash, behind a screen of piñons. Chee sorted through them quickly, identifying bedding, clothing, boxes of cooking utensils, and two sacks of food. Begay's furniture was also here. A kitchen chair, a cot, a light chest of drawers, enough other odds and ends of living to convince Chee that even with two horses hauling, it must have taken more than one trip to move it all here. He stood beside the cache and looked around. This was what he'd expected, had expected since his mind had time to calculate what finding the Four Mountains Bundle had meant. He'd expected it, but it still left him sick. And there was one more thing to be found.

He found Ashie Begay a bit farther down the wash, his body dumped as unceremoniously as the furniture. Begay had been shot in the head, just like his horses.

23

IT TOOK CHEE THREE HOURS to get his pickup out of the Chuskas. Twice it involved digging through drifts, and twice he had to unload the horse and lead it up slopes where the truck lacked the traction to pull the load. By the time he reached the graded road leading to the Toadlena boarding school he was weary to the bone, with another thirteen miles through the snow to Highway 666 and thirty more to Shiprock. The snow blew steadily from the north-northwest, and he drove northward alternately through a narrow white tunnel formed by his headlights reflecting off the driven flakes and brief blinding oblivions of ground blizzards. His radio told him that Navajo Route 1 was closed from Shiprock south to Kayenta, and Navajo Route 3 was closed from Two Story to Keams Canyon, and that U.S. 666 was closed from Mancos Creek, Colorado, to Gallup, New Mexico. That helped explain why Chee's pickup truck had the highway to itself. He drove about twenty-five miles an hour, slowing as well as he could when he sensed the ground blizzards coming, his fingers sensitive to traction under his wheels and his shoulder muscles aching with fatigue. He'd covered the body of Hosteen Ashie Begay with Begay's bedroll, thinking that he, like Gorman, had had to make his journey into the underworld with his hair unwashed—without even the imperfect preparations Gorman's corpse had received. But the man who killed him had at least sent along with Begay the spirits of his horses. Had he known that sacrifice of the owner's horse had been an ancient Navajo custom? Possibly. But Chee had no illusions that this was why the horses had been killed. They were killed for the same reason Begay was killed, and his hogan emptied, and Gorman's corpse prepared for burial—a great deal of trouble to make it seem that nothing unusual had happened at Begay's hogan. But why? Why? Why?

There seemed to Chee to be little enough mystery about who the killer was. It was Vaggan, or some surrogate Vaggan—one of those who, in white society, did such things for pay. But it was probably the man Shaw had identified as Vaggan. This seemed to be his job, whatever its purpose. And it would have been easy enough to learn about Navajo burial customs. They would be covered in any of a half-dozen books available in the Los Angeles library. Anyone who could read could have learned enough to fake what had happened at the Begay hogan. Who had done it didn't matter—Vaggan or someone like him. The question was why.

Chee was finding he couldn't make his mind work very well. The headache had returned. Fatigue, probably, and eyestrain induced from staring into the reflecting snow. He put Begay's body out of his consciousness and thought only about driving. And finally there to his right was the sign indicating the entrance road to the Shiprock landing strip, and he could feel the highway sloping downward into the San Juan river bottom, and Shiprock was just ahead.

He turned the horse into the shelter of the tribal barn, and left the horse trailer in the lot, and drove into the village. Across the bridge he hesitated a moment. A left turn at the junction would take him to his trailer home, to hot coffee, food, his bed. To a telephone to report to Captain Largo what he had found. To deal again with the question of why. The postcard would come up again. Inevitably. It lay at the center of all of this. Had, apparently, triggered it. What had been written on that postcard? Chee turned right, downriver toward the place where the aluminum trailer was parked under a cottonwood tree.

It looked different, somehow, in this storm. Before temperatures had dropped, snow had crusted on the cold aluminum and collected more snow, and cost the trailer its machine-made look. It loomed in Chee's headlights now as a great white shape, tied to the earth by a drift, as natural as a snow-caked boulder and looking as if it had stood below its tree forever. Light glowed from the small windows. Grayson, or somebody, was home. Chee honked the pickup's horn and waited a moment before it occurred to him that Grayson was a city man who wouldn't be aware of this rural custom of giving warning before invading privacy. He turned up his coat collar and stepped out into the blowing snow.

If Grayson had heard his horn, there was no evidence of it. Chee rapped his knuckles against the aluminum door panel, waited, and rapped again. The wind worked under the bottom of his coat and around the collar and up his pants legs, as cold as death. It reminded Chee of the corpse of Hosteen Ashie Begay lying frozen under the old man's bedroll. And then the voice of Grayson, through the door.

"Who is it?"

"It's Chee," Chee shouted. "Navajo Police."

"What do you want?"

"We found your uncle's body," Chee said. "Ashie Begay. I need to talk to you."

Silence. The cold gripped Chee's ankles, numbed his cheeks. Then Grayson's voice shouted, "Come on in."

The door opened. It opened outward, as trailer doors open to conserve inside space, no more than six inches, and then the wind pushed it shut again. Chee stood a moment, looking at it, wondering what Grayson was doing and finally understanding. Grayson was playing it safe, as a protected witness might be expected to do. He opened the door and stepped in.

Grayson was sitting behind the table, his back against the wall, examining Chee. Chee shut the door and stood against it, enjoying the warmth and letting Grayson see his hands were empty.

"You found whose body?" Grayson said. "Where? What happened?"

Grayson's hands were out of sight beneath the table. Would he have a weapon? Would a protected witness be allowed to have a gun? Perhaps even be encouraged to keep one? Why not?

"Not far from his hogan," Chee said. "Somebody had shot him."

Grayson's face registered a kind of dismay. He looked a little older than Chee had remembered, a little more tired. Maybe it was the artificial light. More likely it was Chee's mood. The corner of his mouth pulled back in the beginning of one of those wry clicks of sympathy or surprise or sorrow, but Grayson stopped it. He brought his hands out from under the table, rubbed his face with the right one. The left one lay on the table, limp and empty. "Why would anyone want to kill that old man?" Grayson said.

"Your uncle," Chee said.

Grayson stared at him.

"We know who you are," Chee said. "It saves time if we get that out of the way. You're Leroy Gorman. You're in the Department of Justice Witness Protection Program under the name of Grayson. You're living here under the Grayson name until it's time to go back to Los Angeles to testify in federal court."

The man who was Leroy Gorman, older brother of Albert Gorman, nephew of Ashie Begay, stared at Chee, his expression blank. And bleak. And Chee thought, What is his real name? His war name? The name his maternal uncle would have given him, privately and secretly when he was a child, the name he would have been whispered through the mask at the Yeibichi ceremonial where he changed from boy to man? The name that would label his real identity, that no one would know except those closest to him, what was that? This Los Angeles Navajo doesn't have a war name, Chee thought, because he doesn't have a family. He isn't Dinee. He felt pity for Leroy Gorman. Part of it was fatigue, and part of it was pity for himself.

"So much for the goddam promises," Leroy Gorman said. "Nobody knows but one guy in the Prosecutor's office and your FBI guardian angel. That's what they tell you. Nobody else. Not the local fuzz. Not nobody, so there's no way it can leak." He rapped his hand sharply on the Formica tabletop. "Who'd they tell? They have something about it on TV? Front page of the *Times?* On the radio?"

"They didn't tell anybody as far as I know," Chee said. "The postcard you wrote gave you away. The one you sent to your brother."

"I didn't write any postcard," Gorman said.

"Let me see your camera," Chee said.

"Camera?" Gorman looked surprised. He stood, opened the overhead cabinet behind him, and extracted a camera from its contents. It was a Polaroid model with a flash attachment. Chee inspected it. It was equipped with an automatic timer.

"Not exactly a postcard," Chee said. "You set this thing up, and took a picture of yourself and this trailer house, and sent it to your brother. Whatever you wrote on it, it caused him to come running out here to Shiprock looking for you. And when Old Man Begay saw it, something on it, or something Albert told him, caused him to send it along to his granddaughter to tell her to stay away."

Gorman was looking at him, thinking. He shook his head.

"What did you write on it?" Chee asked.

"Nothing, really," Gorman said. "I don't remember, exactly. I just figured Al would be worried about me. Just wrote a little note. Like wish you were here."

"Did you say where 'here' was?"

"Hell, no," Gorman said.

"Just a little note," Chee said. "Then what do you think it was that brought your brother running?"

Gorman thought. He clicked his tongue. "Maybe," he said, "maybe he heard something I need to know about."

"Like what?" Chee said.

"I dunno," Gorman said. "Maybe he heard they were looking for me. Maybe he heard they knew where to find me."

That had a plausible sound. Albert had heard Leroy's hiding place had leaked. When Leroy's card arrived, he'd seen the Shiprock postmark and had hurried here to warn his brother and hadn't quite made it. And then someone had been sent to make sure that Albert Gorman didn't survive his gunshot wound. How had Albert Gorman really died? The coroner had said gunshot wound, which was obvious and what they'd expected, and what they'd have looked for. But if they were looking for something else, what would they have found? That Albert Gorman had been suffocated, or something like that, which didn't show but would hurry the death from the gunshot wound along? Or had whoever had come to the hogan found him already dead and killed Ashie Begay because of what Albert might have told him? It didn't really matter. Chee's head ached, his eyes burned. He was thinking maybe Albert Gorman died outside the hogan after all. Maybe he hadn't stepped through the corpse hole into a *chindi* hogan. Maybe he wasn't contaminated with ghost sickness. But that didn't matter either. The ghost sickness came when he made the step—out of *hozro* and into the darkness. Out of being a Navajo, into being a white man. For Chee, that was where the sickness lay.

"Any idea who killed him," Leroy Gorman asked, "or why?"

"No," Chee said. "Do you?"

Gorman was slumped back in his chair, his hands on the table in front of him, looking over them at nothing. He sighed, and the wind outside picked up enough to remind them both of the storm. "Could be just meanness," Gorman said. He sighed again. "Did you find that girl?"

"Not exactly," Chee said.

"I don't guess she'll be coming here," Gorman said. "Didn't you say her grandfather told her to stay away? Something dangerous?"

"Yeah," Chee said. "But it didn't stop her the first time."

"What did he tell her?" Gorman was still looking past his hands, his eyes on the door. The wind pressed against it, letting in the cold. "She know I'm a car thief?"

"I don't know what he told her," Chee said. "I intend to find out."

"She's kinfolk of mine," Gorman said. "I don't have many. Not much family. Just Al and me. Dad run off and our mother was sickly and we never got to know nobody. She my niece, isn't she? Begay's granddaughter. That'd be by my mother's sister. I knew she had one out here somewhere. I remember she mentioned that. Wonder if that aunt of mine would still be alive. Wonder where that little girl went."

Chee didn't comment. He wanted a cup of coffee badly. And food, and sleep. He tried to think of what else he could ask this man, what he could possibly learn that would keep this from being just another in a long line of dead ends. He could think of nothing.

"I'd like to get acquainted with her," Leroy Gorman said.

"Meet her family. I didn't make much of a white man. Maybe when I get through with all this I could make some sort of Navajo. You know where I could find the Sosi family?"

Chee shook his head. He got up and thanked Leroy Gorman for his time and went through the aluminum door into the driving snow, leaving Gorman sitting there looking at his hands, his face full of thought.

24

HE CALLED LARGO from his trailer while the coffee perked and told the captain what he had found at Begay's hogan. It took Largo something like a micromillisecond to get over his sleepiness and then he was full of questions, not all of which Chee could answer. Finally that part of it was over, and it was a little after 2 A.M. and Chee was full of hot coffee, and two sandwiches, and in bed, and asleep almost before he could appreciate the sound of the winter outside.

He awoke with the sun on his face. The storm had moved fast, as early winter storms tend to move in the Mountain West, and had left in its wake a cold, bright stillness. Chee took his time. He warmed himself some leftover mutton stew for his breakfast and ate it with corn tortillas and refried beans. He ate slowly and a lot, because he had a lot to do and a long way to go, and whether or not he had another hot meal this day would depend on road conditions. He put on his thermal underwear, his wool socks, the boots he used for mud. He made sure that his tire chains were in the box behind the seat in his pickup, that his shovel, his hand winch, and his tow chain were in their proper places. He stopped at the gas station beside the San Juan bridge and topped off his gas tank and made sure the auxiliary tank was also full. And then he drove westward out of Shiprock to find Frank Sam Nakai. Nakai was his teacher, his friend since earliest boyhood, and, most important of all in the Navajo scheme of things, the brother of his mother—his key clan uncle.

The first seventy miles, through Teec Nos Pos, Red Mesa, Mexican Water, and Dennehotso, was easy enough going over the snow-packed asphalt of Route 504. Beyond Dennehotso, reaching the winter hogan of Frank Sam Nakai involved turning southward off the highway on a dirt road that wandered across Greasewood Flats, dipped across the usually dry Tyende Creek Canyon, and then climbed Carson Mesa. Five miles down this doubtful route, Chee decided it wasn't going to work. The air was still cold but the hot sun was turning the snow pack into mush. He had put his chains on before he left the highway, but even with them, the truck slipped and slid. As the day wore on it would get steadily worse until sundown froze it all again. He made it back to the highway and made the hundred-mile circle back through Mexican Water and southward to Round Rock and Many Farms and Chinle, and then the long, slippery way to the south side of Black Mesa past the Cottonwood Day School and through Blue Gap, to an old road which led to Tah Chee Wash. It was as bad as the road south from Dennehotso but, from where the passable stretch ended near Blue Gap, much shorter. Chee drove down it in second, at a cautious ten miles an hour. He'd drive as far as the melting snow would allow, walk in the remaining miles, and walk out again when the cold darkness turned the snow into ice and the mud into frozen iron.

The walking part turned out to be a little less than ten miles—a hard four hours in the soft snow. It gave Chee time to think, to sort it all out again. It resolved itself into a single central puzzle. Why had someone gone to so much trouble to conceal the murder of Ashie Begay? Chee could understand why Gorman might have been followed to the Begay hogan. That simply continued the effort to find Leroy Gorman. McNair, somehow, seemed to have learned that Leroy was in Shiprock, learned that Albert was going there, decided that Albert's arrival would scare the FBI into moving Leroy before his exact location could be pinned down, and sent someone to catch Albert and learn from Albert where Leroy could be found. Albert had resisted, been wounded, fled. Albert had been tracked down at Begay's place by someone (probably Vaggan) seeking an answer to the same question. Vaggan had either found Albert dead, or dying, or had killed him, and had killed

Ashie Begay to eliminate a witness to the crime.

That was all plausible enough. It left questions, true. How had Vaggan found Albert Gorman so quickly at the Begay hogan? Probably because the McNair people knew enough about Albert's connections on the reservation to make an educated guess. After all, one of those involved was a Navajo: Beno. Robert Beno, Upchurch had said. High enough in the organization to warrant grand jury action, and the only one who managed to run. Another relative, perhaps. Another member of the Turkey Clan. Someone who could guess the only place Albert Gorman could find refuge. Or maybe it was simpler than that. Albert surely had intended to visit his uncle when he came to the reservation—to Chee's Navajo mind such a visit by a nephew was certain and inevitable—and he had told Mrs. Day, who had passed the information along. Anyway, that didn't seem to matter. What mattered was why all the trouble to make the crime at Begay's hogan invisible.

Chee plodded along through ankle-deep snow, examining possibilities. Because Vaggan didn't want the law to know he was looking for Leroy and was within a hundred miles of finding him? That looked good for a moment, but the shooting in the parking lot had already alerted the FBI. What other motive could there be? Chee could think of none and skipped over to another question. If the McNair people knew, or even suspected, that Leroy was hidden away in Shiprock, why weren't they looking for him? Largo had said there was no sign at all of that. No strangers asking around. Largo had put the word out, at the gas stations, and trading posts, and convenience stores, the post office, the laundry, everywhere. It was an old and simple and absolutely efficient system, and Chee had no doubt that if anyone—anyone at all—had shown up in Shiprock, or anywhere near Shiprock, asking questions, Largo would have known it within fifteen minutes. And unless McNair knew about the aluminum trailer and had some idea of where it was parked, Leroy Gorman couldn't be found without questions—hundreds of them. Chee had hunted enough people on the reservation to know how many weary hours of questions. And if McNair did know about the aluminum trailer and the cottonwood tree, Leroy would have been found with no questions at all. And Leroy would be just as dead as Albert.

And so the thinking went, leading around in the same circle back to the picture of the aluminum trailer mailed as a postcard with something, apparently, written on its back that had brought Albert running and started all this. Something, even though Leroy didn't remember writing such a stirring message—or claimed he didn't remember it. What would Leroy have written that he'd refuse to admit? Chee would know, he hoped, when he found Margaret Billy Sosi again—for the third time—and pinned her down long enough to extract from her either the card itself or her exact and detailed memory of what was written on it, and what her grandfather had told her about why Gorman (which Gorman?) was dangerous to be around. And just about when Chee was thinking this, he smelled smoke.

It was the smell of burning piñon, the sweet, perfumed smell of hot resin. Then a blue wisp of the smoke against the junipers on the next hillside, and the place of Frank Sam Nakai was in view. It was an octagonal log hogan, a rectangular frame house covered with black tarpaper, a flatbed truck, a green pickup, a corral with a sheep pen built beyond it, the tin building where Nakai kept his cattle feed, and, off against the hillside, the square plank building where the mother of Frank Sam Nakai's late wife lived with Frank Sam Nakai's daughter. The smoke was coming from stovepipes in both houses, making wisps of blue as separate as the suppers the occupants were cooking. Chee's uncle and his uncle's mother-in-law were following the instructions of Changing Woman, who had taught that when men look upon the mothers of the women they marry it may cause blindness and other more serious problems. To Jim Chee it seemed perfectly natural.

It also seemed natural to Chee that Frank Sam Nakai was absolutely delighted to see him. Nakai had been shoveling snow into barrels, where the sun would convert it into drinking water, when he saw Chee approaching. His shout of welcome brought Chee's aunt out of the house. His aunt by white man's reckoning was Mrs. Frank Sam Nakai. Her Navajo friends, neighbors, and clansmen called her Blue Woman in honor of her spectacular turquoise jewelry. But to Chee she was and always had been and would be Little Mother, and in honor of his visit she opened cans of peaches and candied yams to augment the spicy mutton tacos she served him for his supper. Only when all that was finished, and the utensils cleared from the table, and news of all the family covered, did Chee bring up what had brought him here.

"My father," he said to Frank Sam Nakai, "how many *yataalii* are left who know how to cure someone of the ghost sickness?"

Behind him, where she was sitting beside the stove, Chee heard Little Mother draw in her breath. His uncle digested the question.

"There are two ways it can be done," he said finally. "There is the nine-day sing and the five-day. I think not many know the nine-day anymore. Maybe only an old man who lives up by Navajo Mountain. Up in Utah. You could find somebody to do the five-day cure a little easier. There was a man who knew it, I remember, when we were teaching young people to be *yataalii* at the Navajo Community College. I remember he said he learned it from his uncle, and his uncle lived over on the Moenkopi Plateau, over there by Dinnebito Wash. So that would be two. But the uncle was old even then. Maybe he is dead by now."

"How could I find this man? The younger one?"

"Tomorrow we will go to Ganado. To the college. They kept a list there of everybody who knew the sings, and where they lived." His uncle's face was asking the question that his courtesy would never allow him to put in words. Who suffered from ghost sickness? Was the victim Jim Chee?

"I'm trying to find a girl of the Turkey Clan who people call Margaret Billy Sosi," Chee said. "She was in a *chindi* hogan, and I think she will be having a sing." He heard a sigh from Little Mother, a sound of relief. He didn't want to tell these two that he, too, was infected. He didn't want to tell his uncle what he had done. He didn't want to tell him that he was going to get a job with the FBI, and leave the People, and give up his idea of being a *yataalii* like his uncle. He didn't want to see the sadness in that good man's face.

▼ ▼ ▼

They'd had coffee and bread and had three horses saddled before it was time for his uncle to take a pinch of pollen and a pinch of meal and go out to bless the rising sun with the prayer to Dawn Boy. Little Mother rode with them to lead their horses back, and everything went very rapidly. The drive back over the now-frigid snow was like driving over ground glass, squeaking and crunching under Chee's tires. They were on the good road past Blue Gap in thirty minutes. Before noon, they were in the library at Navajo Community College, working their way through the roster of men and women who are shamans of the Navajos.

Chee hadn't known it existed. He should have known, he thought. It would be useful to any policeman. And even while he was thinking that, another part of his consciousness was shocked and dismayed. So few names. And so many of them listed as knowing only the Blessing Way, or the Enemy Way, or the Yeibichi, the Night Chant, or the more common and popular curing rituals. He glanced at Frank Sam Nakai, who was running his finger slowly down the page. His uncle had told him that the Holy People had taught the Dinee at least sixty such rituals, and that many of them were lost in those grim years when the People had been herded into captivity at Fort Sumner. And he could see by this that more were being lost. He looked down the list to see how many singers knew the Stalking Way, which he had been trying to learn. He saw only the name of his uncle and one other man.

"Just two know the Ghostway," his uncle said. "That fellow I told you about and his old uncle, way over there west of Hopi country. Just two."

"It would probably be the younger man," Chee said. "The Turkey Clan seems to be eastern Navajos—mostly on this side of the Chuskas."

"You can see why we need you," Frank Sam Nakai said. "Everybody is forgetting everything. There won't be anybody left to cure anybody. Nobody to keep us being Navajos."

"Yeah," Chee said. "That's the way it looks." He'd have to tell Frank Sam Nakai soon. Very soon. But today he just couldn't do it.

The fellow who knew the Ghostway (and the Blessing Way

and Mountaintop Way) was on the book as Leo Littleben, Junior. And he lived not way the hell a thousand miles down a dirt track on the other side of the reservation but at Two Story, just twenty-five miles down the highway toward Window Rock. And—rarity of rarities on the reservation—he was listed in the Navajo-Hopi telephone book.

"I think my luck's changing," Chee said.

Somebody answered the telephone at the Littleben residence. A woman.

"He's not here," she said.

"When do you expect him back?" Chee asked.

"I don't know. Three–four more days, I think."

"Anyplace I can reach him?"

"He's doing a sing."

"Do you know where?"

"Way over there on the Cañoncito Reservation."

His luck hadn't changed much, Chee thought. Cañoncito was as far as you could get from Ganado and still be in Navajo country. It was a fragment of reservation separated from the Big Reservation by miles of private land and by the Acoma and Laguna Indian reservations. It was practically in Albuquerque. In fact, it was outside Dine' Bike'yah, on the wrong side of the Turquoise Mountain. Some strictly orthodox medicine men would refuse to hold a sing there.

"Do you know who it's for?" Chee said. "Who hired him?"

"For some woman named Sosi, I think it is."

"A Ghostway?"

"A Ghostway," the woman agreed. "He's doing the five-day sing. Be back in another three–four days."

So Chee's luck had changed, after all.

25

IT WAS ALMOST DARK when Chee turned off Exit 131 from Interstate 40 and took the worn asphalt that led northward. For the first miles the road ran between fences bearing the No Trespassing signs of the Laguna Indian Pueblo—grass country grazed by Herefords. But the land rose, became rockier. More cactus now, and more juniper and chamiza and saltbush, and then a fading sign:

WELCOME TO THE CAÑONCITO RESERVATION
HOME OF THE CAÑONCITO BAND OF NAVAJOS
POPULATION 1600

Leroy Gorman would have no trouble getting this far, Chee thought, not if he could read road signs well enough to navigate the Los Angeles freeways. Chee had called him from the college, using his Tribal Police identification number to wring Grayson's unlisted number from the information operator's supervisor.

"You said you wanted to meet some kinfolks," Chee said. "You want to enough to drive a couple of hundred miles?"

"What else have I got to do?" Gorman said. "Where do I go?"

"South to Gallup. Then take Interstate 40 east through Grants, and after you pass Laguna start looking for the Cañoncito Reservation interchange. Get off there and head into the reservation and look for the police station. I'll leave a map or something for you there to tell you where to go."

"You found the girl? They're having a curing thing for her?"

"Exactly," Chee said. "And the more of her relatives are there, the better it works."

Five miles beyond the entrance sign, a green steel prefabricated building, a shed, a mobile home, a parked semi-trailer, and a Phillips 66 gasoline sign marked the site of a trading post. Chee stopped. Anyone know the Sosi family? No Sosi family at Cañoncito. Anyone know where a sing was being held? Everybody did. It was way back on Mesa Gigante, at the place of Hosteen Jimmie Yellow. Easy to find it. How about the police station, where was that? Just down the road, three–four miles, before you get to the chapter house. Can't miss it.

It would, in fact, have been hard to miss—a small frame building not fifty feet from the road wearing a sign that read simply POLICE STATION. It was manned, as Chee recalled the situation, not by the Navajo Tribal Police but by the Law and Order Division of the Bureau of Indian Affairs, a part-time patrolman who also worked the east side of Laguna territory. On this particular afternoon it was manned by a young woman wearing bifocals.

Chee showed her his identification. "I'm trying to find a sing they're having at Jimmie Yellow's place," Chee said. "You know how to get there?"

"Sure," the woman said. "Up on Mesa Gigante." She extracted a piece of typing paper from the desk, wrote *North* at the top of it and *East* on the right-hand side, and drew a tiny square near the bottom and labeled it *Cops.* Then she drew a line past the square northward. "This is Route Fifty-seven. Stay on it past"—she drew a cluster of tiny squares west of the line—"the chapter house and the Baptist Church off here, and then you angle westward on Road Seventy forty-five. There's a sign." The map took precise shape under her pen, with unwanted turns identified and blocked off with X's, and landmarks such as windmills, watertanks, and an abandoned coal mine properly indicated.

"Finally it winds around up here, under this cliff, and then you're on top of the mesa. Only road up there so you don't have any choice. There's an old burned-out truck there right at the rim, and about a mile before you get to Yellow's place, you pass the ruins of an old hogan on the left. And you can see Yellow's place from the road."

"And I can't miss it," Chee said, grinning.

"I don't think so. It's the second turnoff, and the first one is to the old torn-down hogan." She looked up at him over her glasses, somberly. "Somebody died there, so nobody uses that track anymore. And after the turnoff to Yellow's place, that's all of them for miles because Jimmie Yellow's people are about the only ones up there any more."

Chee told her about Gorman driving down from Shiprock, instructed to stop here for directions. Would that be any problem? It wouldn't be. But as Chee drove away, he was nagged by a feeling that something would be a problem, that he was forgetting something, or overlooking something, or making some sort of mistake.

Jimmie Yellow's place, even more than Ashie Begay's, seemed to have been selected more for the view than for convenience. It was perched near the rim of the mesa, looking down into the great empty breaks that fell away to the Rio Puerco. To the west, across the Laguna Reservation, the snowy ridges of Turquoise Mountain reflected the light of the rising moon. To the east, the humped ridge of the Sandia Mountains rose against the horizon, their base lit by the glowing lights of Albuquerque. To the north, another line of white marked the snowcap on the Sangre de Cristo Mountains, and the bright smudge of yellow light below them was Santa Fe, one hundred miles away. A spectacular view, but no water, and only a scattered stand of juniper to provide firewood, and the snakeweed around Chee's boots indicated what too many sheep a long time ago had done to the grazing on the mesa top.

Still, the view was impressive, and normally Jim Chee would have enjoyed it and added it to his internal file of beautiful places memorized. Not tonight. Tonight, when Chee allowed himself to think of it, he looked at the mountains with a sense of loss. He had no illusions about where his career in the FBI would take him. They would identify him as an Indian, he was sure enough of that. And that would mean he'd be used in some apparently appropriate way. But they wouldn't send him home to work among people who were family, his kinsmen and clansmen. Too much risk of conflict of interest in that. He'd work in Washington, probably, at a desk coordinating the Agency's work with the Bureau of Indian Affairs. Or he'd be sent north to be a cop among the Cheyennes, or south to deal with federal crime on Seminole land in Florida. Aside from that dismal thought, Chee was not enjoying the view because he was not in the mood to enjoy anything. He had found Margaret Billy Sosi for the third time, and extracted from her the last missing piece of the puzzle, and it told him absolutely nothing.

He took Ashie Begay's Four Mountain Bundle from his coat pocket and tossed it in his hand. From behind him, the sound of a pot drum drifted on the cold, still air, and with it the sound of Littleben's voice, rising and falling in the chant which told how the Hero Twins had decided that Old Man Death must be spared and not eliminated in their campaign to cleanse Dinetah of its monsters. The same faint breeze which carried the sound brought the perfume of woodsmoke from the fire in the hogan, reminding Chee that it was warm in there, and that the cold out here at this slab of sandstone on which he was sitting was seeping into his bones. But he didn't want to be inside, sitting with his back to the hogan wall, watching Littleben build the last of the great sand paintings of this ceremonial, sharing the music and the poetry and the goodwill of these people. He wanted to be out here in the cold, trying to think, going over it all again.

He'd done his talking to Margaret Sosi when Littleben finished the segment that recounted how Monster Slayer and Born for Water had returned to the Earth Surface World with the weapons they had stolen from their father, the Sun. Littleben had come out of the hogan, wiping perspiration from his forehead, under the red headband, and looking curiously around him as people do who've been indoors too long. Then the others who were sharing in the blessing of the ceremony came out, and with them was Margaret Sosi, her face covered with the blackening that made her invisible to ghosts. Margaret Sosi seemed exhausted and thin, but the eyes that looked out through the layer of soot were alive and excited. Margaret Sosi is being cured, Chee thought. Someday, perhaps, he could be.

Margaret Sosi was delighted to see him. She asked him about his head and told him he shouldn't be out of the hospital.

"I want to thank you for getting me there," Chee said. "How in the world did you do it?"

"When you hit him, he dropped his gun. I just picked it up and told him to take us to the hospital."

"As easy as that?"

Margaret Sosi shivered. "I was scared," she said. "I was scared to death."

"Before anything like that happens again," Chee said, "I need to ask you some questions. Did Hosteen Begay send you a postcard he'd gotten from Albert Gorman? A picture—"

"Yes," Margaret said.

"I'd like to see it."

"Sure," Margaret said. "But it's in my room. At St. Catherine. We went back there before we came here for the sing."

Of course, Chee thought. It wouldn't be here. He would never, ever actually see that postcard. Never.

"What did it say on it?"

Margaret Sosi frowned. "It just said, 'Don't trust nobody.' That's all. There was Mr. Gorman's name, and an address in Los Angeles, and that 'Don't trust nobody.' That's all there was. And at the bottom 'Leroy.' "

Chee didn't know what to say, so he said, "No return address?"

"No," Margaret said, "and not even a stamp. The postman had put that 'Postage Due' stamp on it."

"Well," Chee said. "Hell."

"Have you found my grandfather yet?"

Chee knew the question would be coming. He had prepared himself for it. He had decided that the best thing for all concerned was simply to tell Margaret that her grandfather was dead. Straight out. Get it over with. He drew a deep breath. "Margaret," he said. "Uh, well . . ."

"He's dead, isn't he," Margaret Billy Sosi said. "I guess I knew it all along and just couldn't face it. I knew he would never abandon his hogan like that. Not and just go away with no word to anyone."

"Yes," Chee said. "He's dead."

Tears were streaking the soot on her face, a line of wetness that reflected the cold moonlight, but her voice didn't change. "Of course he was," she said. "Of course. He was killed, wasn't he? I guess I really knew it."

"And I don't think it was really a ghost hogan you were in," Chee added. "I think Gorman died outside. It was just made to look like Hosteen Begay had buried him, and broke the hogan wall, and abandoned it. So nobody would be looking around for him."

"But why?"

"I don't know," Chee said. "I don't know why." But he knew there must be a reason. Had to be. If he could just be smart enough to figure it out. And that brought him back to the picture.

"Was the address on that picture . . ." he began, but Margaret Sosi was talking.

"It doesn't matter now," she said. "Whether it was a ghost hogan or not. In just a few hours I'll be cured of that. Mr. Littleben will finish just when the sun comes up. And I feel cured already."

Chee did not feel cured. The ghost sickness clung to him as heavy as a rain-soaked saddle blanket. He felt dizzy with it. Sick.

"The address on that picture," he continued. "Was it the same place you went when you went to Los Angeles?"

"Yes. That's how I knew to go there. I wanted to find the family, and that woman there told me what bus to catch to get to the place of Bentwoman and Bentwoman's Daughter."

"And all it said on the picture was 'Don't trust anybody'?"

" 'Don't trust nobody,' " Margaret corrected. "That was all, and 'Leroy' down at the bottom."

That was exactly all he had learned. He told Margaret Sosi that when this was over he would drive her back to Santa Fe and pick up the picture card. But even as he said it, his instinct told him that even if he held the card in his hand it would tell him nothing he didn't already know. The final piece of the puzzle found; the puzzle unresolved.

They had eaten then, about thirty altogether, from two pots of mutton stew and a basket of fry bread. They ate bakery-made oatmeal cookies for dessert, and drank Pepsi-Cola and coffee. Hosteen Littleben came over and agreed to purify the Begay Four Mountains Bundle, a rite that involved rinsing it with some of the emetic made for the patient to drink when the ceremonial ended.

"Frank Sam, he tells me you're going to be a *yataalii.* Said you already know most of the Blessing Way and you're learning some of the others. That's a good thing." Hosteen Littleben was short and fat, and when he walked he tilted a little because of a stiff leg. His two pigtails were black, but his mustache was almost gray and his face was a map of deep-cut lines. If Frank Sam Nakai was right, if Hosteen Littleben was the youngest medicine man left who knew the Ghostway, then the People would be losing another piece of their inheritance from the Holy People.

"Yes," Chee said. "Learning the songs is a good thing." Was a good thing, he thought. The verb is "was."

And then it was time for the final segment of the Ghostway chant. The very last glow of twilight was gone, the moon climbing, the mesa dark, and the lights of Albuquerque glowing against Sandia Mountain forty miles (and a world) away. Hosteen Littleben would twice cover the earthen floor of the hogan with the ceremonial's elaborate dry paintings, illustrating episodes in the mythic adventures by which the Holy People resolved the problem caused by death's disruptive residue. Margaret Sosi would sit surrounded by this abstract imagery, and by the love and care of this ragtag remnant of the Turkey Clan, and be returned to beauty and *hozro,* cleansed of the ghost. Chee didn't follow the participants back into the hogan. To do that properly, one's mind must be right—free of wrong thoughts, anger, and disappointment and all things negative. Chee stayed out in the cold, his mind full of wrong thoughts.

Leroy Gorman arrived a little later, parking a white Chevy among the cluster of vehicles in the yard of the Yellow place. Chee watched him walk up the slope to the hogan, the moonlight reflecting from the crown of his Stetson and the blue and white plaid of his mackinaw.

"Hell of a place to find," he said. "The police station was closed, but they had your map pinned there on the door. But even with a map, I've been all over the landscape. Taking the wrong turns. How do they make a living out here?"

"They don't make much of one," Chee said.

Gorman was staring at the hogan, from which the sound of Littleben's chant was issuing again, and then back down the slope at the shabby cluster of shacks and outbuildings that housed the families of the Yellow outfit. He shook his head. "My kinfolks," he said.

"What did you mean when you wrote 'Don't trust nobody' on that picture?"

Gorman was staring at the hogan again. For a moment, the question didn't seem to register. "What?" he said.

"The picture you mailed to Albert, back in Los Angeles. Why did you write that on it?"

"I didn't," Leroy Gorman said. "I don't know what the hell you're talking about."

"You said you'd written to your brother back in L.A. Just good wishes. That sort of stuff. We find this card. It's addressed to Albert, and it says 'Don't trust nobody.' "

"Not me," Leroy Gorman said.

Chee studied him, trying to see his face in the moon shadow under the broad felt brim. He could see only the glint of reflection from the lens of his glasses.

"I wrote right after I got to Shiprock. I sent Albert a letter and I told him I was all right. And I asked him to call somebody for me and tell 'em I'd be away for a while, and not to worry."

"Who?"

Leroy Gorman didn't say anything for a while. Then he shrugged. "Friend of mine. A woman." He shrugged again. "Didn't want her worried and all pissed off. Had her phone number but I wasn't sure of her address, so I sent Al the number and asked him to tell her."

"So how did Albert get this photograph of you standing there by your trailer, with the note on the back?"

"Part of that's easy," Leroy said. "I sent him the photograph. Put it in the letter. But I didn't write nothing on it."

"You mailed him the Polaroid photo then?"

"Yeah. Set the camera over on the hood of my car, and set the timer and stood over by the trailer while it took the picture. But I didn't write on the back of it. I think if you do that it spoils the picture. The ink works through."

Chee digested that. The final piece dropped into the puzzle and created a new puzzle. Who had written *Don't Trust Nobody* on the back of that damned photograph? And when? And how had they gotten it. And why? Why? Why?

"Somebody sent it," Chee said. "In the mail. It had a 'Postage Due' thing stamped on it. And somebody signed it 'Leroy.' "

"Said 'Don't trust anybody'? Nothing else?"

"Right," Chee said.

"Who could it have been?" Gorman asked. He pushed his hat brim back, and the moonlight lit his lined face and reflected from his glasses. "And why?"

Those were exactly the questions in Chee's mind.

They hung in his mind, unanswered. He and Gorman had poked at the questions for a while, adding nothing to their understanding. And Chee had explained to Gorman that it wouldn't be proper for Gorman, a stranger, to enter the hogan at this stage of the ceremony. If he'd arrived an hour earlier, he could have met his niece and his other kinsmen at their supper. Now he would have to wait until dawn, when the ritual ended. Gorman wandered over to the fire, where spectators who weren't joining in the hogan ceremonial were visiting. Chee heard him introducing himself and, a little later, the sound of laughter. Leroy Gorman had found at least the fringes of his family.

Chee went back to his pickup and turned on the engine. No place left to look now. He'd drive Margaret Sosi to Santa Fe, get the picture and look at it, and see what had already been described to him. That would be the end of that. There were no loose ends, nothing. Just a sequence of murderous incidents which seemed to violate reason. They certainly violated Frank Sam Nakai's basic rules for the universe—which had become Jim Chee's rules. Everything is connected. Cause and effect is the universal rule. Nothing happens without motive or without effect. The wing of the corn beetle affects the direction of the wind, the way the sand drifts, the way the light reflects into the eye of man beholding his reality. All is part of totality, and in this totality man finds his *hozro,* his way of walking in harmony, with beauty all around him.

"Don't trust nobody," Chee said aloud. He turned on the heater, confirmed that the engine was still too cold to help, and switched it off again. People were sleeping in the cars and trucks around Yellow's house, and in bedrolls on the ground, waiting for dawn, when Margaret Sosi would emerge from the hogan with the soot washed from her face. She would drink the bitter emetic Hosteen Littleben would have prepared for her, vomit up the last traces of her ghost sickness, and be happily returned to the beauty of her way.

Chee's mind wouldn't leave it alone. Why the warning against trust? he thought. Who wasn't to be trusted? Should he take the advice himself? Just who was he trusting in this affair?

There was Shaw. The cop motivated by love for a friend and desire for justice. Was that credible? Chee thought about Shaw for a while and came up with nothing helpful. There was Sharkey. Chee could think of no reason not to trust what he'd learned from the FBI agent—which was nothing much. There was even Upchurch. Had he done something untrustworthy before he died? Who else was Chee depending on? Leroy Gorman. He'd learned nothing much from Leroy, except for Leroy's denial that he'd written the warning on the picture. Chee considered that a moment. Did he trust Gorman? Of course not, no more than he trusted Albert Gorman's landlady. He simply trusted them to behave in the way they were conditioned to behave. Just as you trusted the mailman to deliver mail. Chee remembered Albert Gorman's mailbox, shielding it with his body so Gorman's landlady couldn't see that he was checking its contents. Abruptly a whole new line of thought opened. The letter Leroy Gorman had mailed would have been delivered to that mailbox, visible to Mrs. Day—the landlady who was being paid to keep McNair informed. But the picture, mailed as a postcard with an address, but no stamp and no return address, would have been delivered just a little differently. The mailman would have tapped at the door and collected the postage due. Mrs. Day would have had no chance to intercept that. Was that important? Chee could see how it might be. He considered.

"Ah," he said. If he was thinking correctly, the McNair people would have known Leroy Gorman was hidden at Shiprock very soon after he got there. Mrs. Day would have seen the letter Leroy Gorman had mailed in Albert's mailbox, and noted the return address, and made her $100 call. And in such a small community they could have found a stranger. Not quickly, perhaps, because Albert obviously had the photograph and they didn't. But they could have found him. Apparently they didn't try. Why not?

Chee sighed. What about the card? Leroy Gorman said he'd mailed the Polaroid photograph in an envelope and hadn't written the warning on it. But the photograph had "Postage Due" stamped on it, and an address. What explained that? Two photographs? Hardly possible with a Polaroid print. Albert Gorman had told old man Berger he received the photograph from his brother, that he was worried. The "Wish you were here" note Leroy said he'd written would hardly provoke worry. The "Don't trust nobody" message would.

Chee closed his eyes, shutting out the moonlight and the sound of Mr. Littleben's chanting as best he could to better reproduce the scene on the Silver Threads lawn. There was Mr. Berger, using his hands to tell the story of the blond man coming, of Albert Gorman slamming the door on the blond man's hand. Gorman had told Berger that he wasn't supposed to go to Shiprock, but he was going anyway. Berger believed the blond man had come to prevent that. That hadn't made sense to Chee then, and it made no sense now. If they hadn't found Leroy, they would have wanted Al to go find him for them. What if they had found him. Would it matter then? Perhaps.

Abruptly Chee sat bolt upright, eyes open. It would matter a lot if the man Albert Gorman found when he found the trailer was not his brother. What if the McNair people had found Leroy in his trailer, and removed him, and replaced him? But that couldn't possibly work. Chee did a quick scan of his memory for reasons it couldn't work.

There were none. Upchurch, who would have recognized

the switch instantly, was dead. Farmer, the only man in the U.S.D.A.'s office Upchurch had trusted with his witnesses, was far away working for a private law firm in San Francisco. Who did that leave who would know Leroy Gorman? Sharkey? Not likely. Sharkey would know he had one under his wing, would be in telephone contact, would be alert. But he would also stay away to avoid drawing any attention to the man.

Looking back on it, Chee could never say exactly when enlightenment came. First he finally really understood how the postcard had originated. Leroy Gorman must have realized he had been found. They must have sent Vaggan to dispose of him. Perhaps he'd seen Vaggan first. He would have known instantly that the Witness Protection Program had failed. He had been trying to talk his brother into cooperating with the Feds. Now he knew that was a fatal mistake. He'd be desperate to warn his brother. He'd managed to jot the address and the warning on the only thing he had with him that would drop through the mailbox slot—the Polaroid print. "Don't trust nobody" included the FBI, the McNair bunch, and everyone else.

After that breakthrough, the rest of it became clear and simple. The death of Upchurch must have triggered it, and it didn't matter whether Shaw was right, or the coroner. Probably the death had been natural. What mattered was that McNair knew of it quickly, and recognized the chance it offered. Upchurch's secrecy had been the downfall of Clan McNair, but now it presented McNair a way out, a witness switch. It made what had happened at the Begay hogan totally logical. Everything had to be done to avoid raising any question, drawing any attention to the man in the aluminum trailer at Shiprock. Once again Frank Sam Nakai's immutable law of cause and motivation was confirmed.

About then, Jim Chee began thinking of who the man he'd been calling Leroy Gorman might really be, and the implication of what this man was doing. And he realized that if things went as planned he might not leave Mesa Gigante alive.

And neither would Margaret Billy Sosi.

26

CHEE UNLOCKED the glove box, fumbled among the maps, tools, and papers in it, and pulled out his pistol. It was a short-barreled .38 caliber revolver, and Chee looked at it without pleasure. Nothing against this particular pistol; it was just that Chee had no fondness for any of them and wasn't particularly good at using them. Keeping up his marksmanship certification, a condition of employment, was an annual chore. While he always managed to pass, there was never any margin to spare. Now, however, the heft of the pistol was reassuring in his hand. He examined it, made sure it was loaded, and cocked and uncocked it. Then he dropped it into the side pocket of his coat. That out of the way, it was time to make a plan. That involved trying to figure out what was likely to happen here.

The key to it all was simple: Leroy Gorman was not Leroy Gorman. He might be Beno, or whatever his name was—the Navajo Shaw said the grand jury had indicted and who had never been picked up. That made sense. Shaw had said finding him was tough because he had no arrest record, which meant no pictures or fingerprints, and no useful information. Thus nobody was going to recognize him. And when the time came for McNair to go to trial, a Navajo identified as Leroy Gorman would be placed on the witness stand, and how would they work it then? Chee guessed he knew. When the D.A. examined him, he'd recite his testimony in a halting, uncertain way, raising doubt in the jury. Then, under cross examination, he'd say that he'd been coached in what to say by Upchurch; that Upchurch had given him all this information, and assured him it was true, and warned him that if he didn't recite in court he'd be sent to prison as a thief. He would say that he actually knew none of it; he was simply passing along what the FBI agent had told him. And that, of course, would taint everything any other prosecution witness said, and raise at least a reasonable doubt, and McNair would go home free.

The genuine Leroy Gorman was undoubtedly dead. Carefully dead. They would never want his body found.

Chee reconsidered. Sharkey? No problem. Leroy's warning had been mailed almost immediately after he was put in place. There was almost no chance that Sharkey would have seen him. So Leroy Gorman was not Gorman. Chee found himself thinking of the man as Grayson once again. What to do about Grayson?

Chee climbed out of his pickup and looked toward the hogan. The chanting of Littleben was silent now. Chee imagined him on his knees, building the final sand painting. With the exception of two men and a very fat woman talking beside the fire, those waiting for dawn to bring the ceremony's end were waiting in the relative warmth of their cars. Chee stared at Gorman's Chevy, trying to see if the man was in it. He couldn't tell. He put his hand on the pistol in his coat pocket, took two steps toward Gorman's car. Then he stopped. The entire theory suddenly was nonsense—the product of being hit on the head and too many hours without sleep. He imagined himself arresting Gorman.

"What's the charge?"

"I think you're impersonating a federal witness."

"That's a crime?"

"Well, it might be."

And he imagined himself standing in front of Largo's desk, Largo looking at him, wordless, sad, stricken with the latest Chee stupidity. And Sharkey, maybe, at the back of the room, too furious to be coherent.

Chee walked back to his pickup truck and leaned against it, trying to think. If Gorman was a plant working for McNair, what would he have done when Chee called him and told him the Sosi girl was found, and invited him to come and meet her?

He wouldn't have come. Of course not, because Margaret Sosi would have seen Leroy Gorman's picture and would recognize he wasn't Leroy Gorman, and that would screw everything up. He came, so of course he was the genuine Leroy Gorman.

Chee thought some more. His theory, wrong as it was, made everything click into place. Everything. It explained what had happened at the Begay hogan. Nothing else explained that. So the man was an imposter and he'd come anyway.

But of course! Grayson had to come. Here Chee would meet Sosi, see the photograph, know Grayson wasn't Leroy Gorman, and everything would collapse around him. So he'd come, late enough so that Margaret Sosi wouldn't see him in any decent light. And so far, for that matter, she hadn't seen him at all. He'd come because it was a last chance to get the picture back before it did any serious harm, and to eliminate Sosi, who'd seen the picture.

Chee had a second chilling thought. Whoever he was, he wouldn't have come alone if he could help it. He would have called Los Angeles and had Vaggan sent to help. How long would that take? A chartered plane, a rented car. Chee tried to calculate. Plenty of time to fly to Albuquerque and then drive. An even worse thought occurred to him. Vaggan hadn't waited around Los Angeles all the time Chee was mending in the hospital there. More likely he'd have confirmed, somehow, that the Sosi girl had left and he'd have driven directly to the reservation to look for her. That would have made getting here simple indeed. He might have driven out with Gorman. Chee doubted that. He'd have brought his own vehicle. And where would he have left it?

Chee had a possible answer for that. He trotted down Mr. Yellow's entrance track to the road that had brought him up Mesa Gigante. And then he walked, keeping well away from it. The ruined hogan the girl in the police station had described to him was about a mile away, near the rim of the mesa. Chee approached it cautiously, keeping behind the cover of junipers when he could, keeping low when there was no cover. Where the track forked off from the road toward the ruin, Chee stopped, knelt, and studied the ground. Tire tracks. The moonlight was dim now, slanting from near the western horizon, but the tracks were plain enough. Made today. Made only hours ago, with neither wind nor time to soften them. Still on his knees, Chee started toward the hogan, out of sight just over a fold of land. No Cañoncito Navajo would drive in there at night and brave a ghost. The hogan had been marked on the map he'd left for the man who wasn't Leroy Gorman. The man must have left the map for Vaggan, and Vaggan—obviously, from what had happened at the Begay place—had taken the trouble to educate himself about Navajo attitudes about ghosts and ghost hogans.

Chee moved cautiously down the track, keeping behind the junipers. He didn't have to go far. After less than fifty yards he had enough visibility over the hillock to see the top of what remained of the hogan's wall. And over the wall, the top of a dark van. Chee stared at it, remembering the last time he had seen it—and what he had seen in the frantic moment he had been inside it, remembering the locked gun rack behind the driver's seat and what it had held. He'd seen an automatic shotgun, something that had looked like an M16 automatic rifle, and at least two smaller automatic weapons—an arsenal.

It occurred to Chee, fairly early in his walk back to the Yellow place, that if things went bad here—as they seemed likely to—it was purely because of Jim Chee's stupidity. He had found Margaret Sosi for them, and then he had called them down on her. Two other things also seemed apparent. Vaggan would do nothing overt here, at this sing, because he was smart enough to know how long it would take him to drive from here to any place he could lose himself. Empty, roadless country made troubles for law enforcement, but it also had advantages, and one of them was that roadblocks are extremely efficient. If you have a wheeled vehicle, there's no place to go with it. If you don't, hiding is easy enough, but there's no water. So Vaggan would wait. Follow them away from here, probably. Pass them on the highway, perhaps, and finish it all with a burst of fire from that automatic rifle. Or at least follow Margaret Sosi. Chee, until he saw the photograph, would be harmless. And he'd told the substitute Gorman that the picture was in Santa Fe.

Finally it occurred to him that he had one advantage. He knew Grayson was the enemy. He knew Vaggan was out there waiting. What he didn't know, not yet, was how to use that advantage. He moved rapidly through the snakeweed and cactus, back toward Yellow's hogan. On the eastern horizon now he could make out the ragged outline of the Sandias and the Manzano Mountains, backlighted by the first glimmer of dawn. He had very little time to decide.

The fire had been rebuilt with a fresh supply of logs and was sending sparks high above the hogan when Chee returned. Everybody was up, waiting for the final act of the drama that would free Margaret Sosi from the ghost that rode her and return her to the ways of beauty. Chee searched through the crowd, looking for Grayson. He spotted him at the edge of the cluster just as the sound of Littleben's chanting stopped. It was a moment too early. Chee ducked back into the crowd, away from Gorman's vision.

The door of the hogan opened out, and Littleben emerged, trailed by Margaret Sosi. He held a small clay pot in his right hand and a pair of prayer sticks, elaborately painted and feathered, in the other. He held the feathered *pahos* high, their shafts crossed in an X. *"Now our daughter will drink this brew,"* he chanted.

> *Now our daughter, she being daughter of Black*
> *God,*
> *Now our daughter, she being daughter of Talking*
> *God,*
> *Now our daughter, she being Blue Flint Girl,*
> *Now our daughter, she being White Shell Girl,*
> *Now our daughter will drink away the evil,*
> *Now our daughter will return to hozro,*
> *Now our daughter will walk again in the male*
> *rain falling,*
> *Now our daughter will walk with the dark mist*
> *around her,*
> *Now our daughter will go with beauty above her.*
> *Now our daughter . . .*

Chee had lost sight of Grayson again. He turned away from the poetry of the chant to look for him. When the time was right, he wanted to know exactly where he could find the man. He wanted Grayson close. And Grayson was close. He had simply moved a little nearer the hogan. But he was still keeping himself where Margaret Sosi couldn't see him—or so it seemed to Chee. It also seemed to Chee that Margaret Sosi would hardly notice him. She had drunk the steaming emetic now and was staring at the east. She was supposed to vomit just as the red first rim of the sun was visible on the horizon. It was apparent from the strained look on her face that her inclination was to vomit instantly. But there, suddenly, was the rim of the sun. It was time to use his one advantage.

Chee hurried through the onlookers to Grayson and grabbed him by the elbow.

"Leroy," he said. "Trouble."

"What?" Grayson looked startled.

"Vaggan is here," Chee said. "Big blond man who's a killer for McNair. He's got his van parked out there."

"Vaggan?" Gorman said. "My God."

"He must be waiting until this is over. Until the crowd breaks up. Or he's waiting for you to leave and he'll follow you."

"Yeah," Grayson said. He looked suitably nervous.

"There's another way out of here," Chee said. "On past this place, the road winds down the other side of the mesa. It's bad but it's passable."

Around them the spectators were laughing and clapping. Margaret Sosi had gotten rid of her evil and was returned to *hozro.* Her relatives crowded around her.

"Just turn left where Yellow's drive comes off the road and keep driving. I'll get Margaret and follow you."

"Left," Gorman said. "Okay."

He ran for his car. Chee hurried through the crowd to Margaret Sosi. She was talking to an old woman, with Littleben standing beside her.

"Come on," Chee said. "Vaggan is here. We've got to run."

Margaret Sosi looked puzzled. With the ghost blacking washed away, she also looked pale. "Vaggan?"

"The big man back in L.A. Remember? The one who pretended to be a cop. The one who hit me."

"Oh," Margaret Sosi said. She hurried along with him. "Good-by. Good-by. And thank you."

Grayson's Chevy was roaring down the track away from the Yellow place. Chee started his pickup, backed it around in a flurry of dust, and roared down the track. At the bottom of the arroyo, he slid the pickup to a stop, shifted into low gear, and edged it carefully up the wash, banging and slamming over the rocks and scraping through the thickets of mountain mahogany and chamiza that flourished in the stream bottom. When he was far enough from the track to be out of sight he turned off the engine. Margaret Sosi was looking at him, the question on her face.

He had time enough to explain it all to her, because now there was nothing to do but wait. . . .

"And so," Chee concluded, "I told the guy who's pretending to be Gorman that I'd spotted Vaggan, and I told him to make a run for it on a road down the other side of the mesa, and I told him you and I would follow. He drove right off, but where he'll go is to tell Vaggan we've seen him, and that we're running."

"But when he goes after us—" Margaret Sosi began.

"We give him time to do that, and then we run ourselves."

"But why didn't we just go down the other side?"

"The road doesn't go anywhere. That's what they told me at the police station. It wanders around a little up here and turns into wagon tracks. But there's no other way down off the mesa; just back the way we came. The only way down is right past where Vaggan is parked."

"Oh," Margaret Sosi said. "Okay."

They sat in silence.

"How long do we wait?"

Exactly the question in Chee's mind. Chee had counted four of the seven vehicles that had been parked at the Yellow place passing on the track behind them. Now track and road were silent. The other three, he guessed, must be staying for breakfast and a visit. He had to allow enough time for Gorman to reach the old hogan, and give Vaggan the word, and for them to drive back past Yellow's turnoff. More than that was time wasted—because it probably would not take Vaggan long to realize the road was playing out into nothing. But less than that would be fatal. Chee had no illusions about the outcome of any shooting match between his pistol and Vaggan's automatic weapon.

He squeezed his eyes shut, trying to estimate time elapsed and match it with Vaggan's actions.

"About now, I think." He started the engine again and bumped the pickup backward down the arroyo floor. At the intersection, nothing was in sight on the road in either direction. He had allowed a little more time than necessary, which meant pursuit would be a little quicker than it might have been. He roared down the rutted dirt. Dawn was bright enough now to make headlights needless, but still dim enough to make it hard to see the uneven road surface. He skidded the pickup around the sharp turn where the road dipped suddenly over the mesa rim, braked again where it made another hairpin bend around a great upthrust of sandstone and slate, then jerked the wheel sharply to the right to bend it around the wall of stone.

Just behind the wall, the big brown van was parked, blocking the way. Vaggan was standing behind it, the automatic rifle aimed at Chee's windshield. Chee stood on the brakes, sending the truck into a sidewise skid that stopped it parallel to the van. He shifted frantically into reverse, spinning the rear wheels in the roadside sand. Grayson was standing beside the road, not fifteen feet away, a pistol pointed at Chee.

"Kill the engine," Vaggan shouted. "Or I kill you now."

Chee killed the engine.

"Stick your hands out the window where I can see them," Vaggan ordered.

Chee put his hands out the window.

"Now reach down, outside the door where I can see the hand, and open the door, and get out, and keep your hands where I can see them. Your hand gets out of my sight and I kill you right then."

Chee opened the door and stepped out on the ground. He was conscious of the weight of the .38 in the right-hand pocket of his coat. How long would it take him to reach it and shoot Vaggan? Far, far, far too long.

"I'm going to handcuff you and put you in the van here

with me," Vaggan said. He was walking toward Chee, the automatic rifle aimed at Chee's midsection. "And then you and the girl and all of us will go someplace where it's quieter and we can talk this all over. Where's your pistol?"

"No pistol," Chee said. "I'm off duty. It's back at my place in Shiprock."

"I'm not stupid," Vaggan said. "If I was stupid I'd be off chasing down that road where you told Beno you'd be. Lay down on your face. On the ground. Hands and feet spread. Beno, come here and get his gun. Probably a shoulder holster or under his belt."

Chee stood, trying to think of something useful.

"Down," Vaggan said. He speared Chee in the chest with the rifle barrel.

Chee dropped to his knees gasping. He knew exactly what was coming. Vaggan would take them to some more isolated spot, where the gunshots would not bring someone immediately to check. Then he would kill them. Just two shots, Chee guessed. One each. The less shots, the less chance of arousing curiosity.

"Down," Vaggan ordered, jabbing Chee in the back with the rifle. Chee dropped to his belly.

"There it is," Vaggan said. "In his coat pock- . . ."

The sound of the gunshot drowned out the rest of it. Vaggan had shot him, but he felt nothing except the pain where Vaggan's rifle barrel had stuck him. For a crazy split second Chee's mind searched for the point of impact, for the feeling that the bullet must be causing. He saw, past the clump of snakeweed in which his cheek was pressed, the motion of Vaggan falling, falling sideways, arms thrown out.

"Don't," someone screamed. "Don't."

In another fragment of that moment, Chee realized he had not been shot. The voice was Grayson's, and as he scrambled up from the dirt, his mind was making the automatic correction from Grayson to Beno. He staggered to his feet, trying to tear the pistol out of his coat pocket, trying to cock it. But he didn't need the pistol.

Margaret Sosi was leaning out of the driver's side of the pickup, a huge revolver gripped in both hands. The revolver was aimed at Beno. Vaggan was sprawled on his side, face turned toward the earth, one leg slowly bending toward his chest, his rifle in the dirt beside him.

"Don't," Beno screamed again. "Don't shoot." Beno held his arms stretched high over his head.

Chee finally got his own pistol untangled from the jacket pocket. Beno had no weapon now. He'd dropped his pistol beside Vaggan's leg. Chee picked it up. He heard a metallic rapping sound. Margaret Sosi was shaking, the barrel of her pistol rattling against the metal of the pickup window. Where had she gotten the gun? And then he remembered. It must be the same pistol Vaggan had dropped when Chee had hit him with the flashlight back in Los Angeles. She'd kept it. That was the sensible sort of thing Margaret Billy Sosi could be expected to do. And she had shot Vaggan with his own gun.

27

WHEN CHEE GOT BACK to Shiprock, the letter was in his mailbox. He saw immediately that the handwriting on the envelope was Mary Landon's and that it was thick enough to contain two or three sheets of paper. A long letter. He put it in his jacket pocket along with what seemed to be a solicitation from an insurance company.

Back in his trailer, he put the letter on the table. He hung up his jacket and his hat, locked his pistol in the drawer, and poured a pot of water into his Mr. Coffee machine. He stripped and took a hot shower. That left him feeling clean and a little more relaxed. But he was tired. Absolutely, utterly tired, and it was that, probably, that was causing his head to ache. He sat beside the table in his bathrobe and looked at the letter. In a moment, he would open it. Was there anything else he needed to do first—any loose ends? He could think of none. The helicopter ambulance had come from the University of New Mexico Medical Center and its attendants had inspected Vaggan, their faces grim. And then they had flown away with him. The New Mexico State Policemen had come to the Cañoncito Police Station with two FBI agents Chee had never met. They had taken Beno off Chee's hands. Margaret Sosi had eaten breakfast with him in the Albuquerque bus station, and had made a telephone call, and had shortly thereafter been picked up by a middle-aged woman who Chee gathered was the mother of a schoolmate from Isleta Pueblo. The woman had not seemed to approve of Chee and had fussed over Margaret and taken her away to get some sleep. And then he'd checked into a motel intending to sleep a little himself. But he was too tense to sleep. So he'd made the 200-mile drive back to Shiprock, and called Captain Largo to tell him what had happened, and picked up his mail and come home.

No loose ends. Nothing. All finished. He pushed the envelope with his finger, turning it around so that he could read his name, right side up, in Mary Landon's bold, reckless handwriting.

Then he opened it.

My darling Jim,

Why am I writing you a letter? Because I want to make sure I manage to say just what I want to say so that you understand it. Maybe that will help me understand it, too.

What I have to say is that I have a friend named Theresa McGill who when she was in college fell in love with a man who was just finishing with the seminary—learning to be a Catholic priest. She loved him, maybe not as much as I love you, but she loved him a lot. And they got married, which meant, of course, he didn't go through with being ordained a priest. He got a job teaching, and they had a daughter, and I thought for a long time that she was happy. But last summer she told me how it really was. She'd notice him being very quiet. Maybe just looking out the window or sitting out in the backyard alone. Or taking long walks by himself. And one Saturday afternoon she followed him, and she saw him go into a church. An empty church. No services. No one there. But he stayed inside for an hour. Theresa told me that she has been living with that. She loves her husband, and she knows she deprived him of something that was terribly important to him. And always will be important.

Well, that's what I'm trying to say. I don't want that to happen to us, so I want to tell you that I've changed my mind. I won't marry you on my terms—

that we get off the reservation and raise our family somewhere else. Maybe I will marry you on your terms—that we live here among your people. If you still want to. But I've got to have time to think about it. So I'm going home—back to Wisconsin. I'm going to talk to my family, and walk around in the snow, and go ice skating, and see what happens to my mind. But I'm not going to change my mind about one thing—I'm not going to force my Jim Chee to be a white man. . . .

Chee put the letter on the tabletop beside the envelope and tried to examine himself for a reaction. He was tired, and suddenly sleepy as well. He was not surprised, particularly. This letter was exactly in character for Mary. Exactly. He should have known it. Perhaps he did. Otherwise, why the lack of surprise? And what else did he feel? A sort of blank numbness, as if all this concerned someone else. That was fatigue too, he guessed. Tomorrow the numbness would be gone. And tomorrow he'd decide what to do. Call Mary, probably. But what would he say to her? He couldn't seem to think what it would be. He found himself thinking, instead, of Leo Littleben, Junior, and wondering if Littleben really was going to be the last man alive to know the Ghostway ceremony.

He got up, already stiff, poured himself a cup of coffee, and leaned against the sink while he sipped it. When he finished it, he would go to bed and sleep until spring. And when he awoke, whenever that was, he would think about Mary Landon's letter and what he should do about it. He would also get in touch with Frank Sam Nakai and ask his uncle to arrange for Hosteen Littleben to sing a Ghostway cure for him. And then, he thought, he would talk to Littleben. Feel him out about what he would charge Chee to teach him the ritual. It would be a good thing for a younger man to know it.

And thinking that, Chee fell across his bed with his bathrobe still on and went, almost instantly, to sleep.

ABOUT THE AUTHOR

TONY HILLERMAN writes with the expertise of one who knows the desert. Among his many honors, he has won the Silver Spur Award for best novel set in the West, the Navajo Tribe's Special Friend Award, and a Public Service Award from the U.S. Department of the Interior. He is a past president of the Mystery Writers of America, and has received their Edgar and Grandmaster Awards. He has also won France's Grand Prix de la Littérature Policière, and his novel *Skinwalkers* was voted best mystery of 1987—the "Anthony"—at the 1988 Bouchercon. Hillerman's other novels include *Coyote Waits*, *Talking God*, *A Thief of Time*, *The Fly on the Wall* and the Joe Leaphorn mysteries, *The Blessing Way*, *Dance Hall of the Dead*, and *Listening Woman*. Hillerman lives with his wife, Marie, in Albuquerque, New Mexico.